RUMO

Walter Moers was born in 1957 and is a writer, cartoonist, painter and sculptor. He is the creator of the comic strips *The Little Asshole* and *Adolf* and the author of the cult bestseller *The 13½ Lives of Captain Bluebear* and *A Wild Ride Through the Night*. He lives in Hamburg.

ALSO BY WALTER MOERS

The 13½ Lives of Captain Bluebear
A Wild Ride Through the Night

Walter Moers

RUMO

& His Miraculous Adventures

A NOVEL IN TWO BOOKS
ILLUSTRATED BY THE AUTHOR

TRANSLATED BY
John Brownjohn

VINTAGE BOOKS
London

Acknowledgements
My thanks to Wolfgang Ferchl, Oliver Schmitt, Rainer Wieland and, of course, Elvira, without whose selfless assistance none of the Zamonia books could have been written.

Published by Vintage 2005

4 6 8 10 9 7 5 3

First published in Great Britain in 2004 by
Secker & Warburg

Vintage
Random House, 20 Vauxhall Bridge Road,
London SW1V 2SA

www.randomhouse.co.uk/vintage

Addresses for companies within The Random House Group Limited can be found at:
www.randomhouse.co.uk/offices.htm

The Random House Group Limited Reg. No. 954009

A CIP catalogue record for this book
is available from the British Library

The publication of this work was supported by a grant from the Goethe-Institut

ISBN 9780099472223 (from Jan 2007)
ISBN 0099472228

The Random House Group Limited makes every effort to ensure that the papers used in its books are made from trees that have been legally sourced from well-managed and credibly certified forests. Our paper procurement policy can be found at: www.randomhouse.co.uk/paper.htm

Printed and bound in Great Britain by
William Clowes Ltd, Beccles, Suffolk

RUMO
RALA

Imagine a chest of drawers!

Yes, a big chest with lots of drawers
containing all the marvels and mysteries of Zamonia
arranged in alphabetical order.
A chest of drawers floating in absolute darkness.

Can you imagine that?

Good, now watch: one of those drawers is opening!
The one bearing the letter R.
R for Rumo.

And now look inside - deep inside,
before it shuts again.

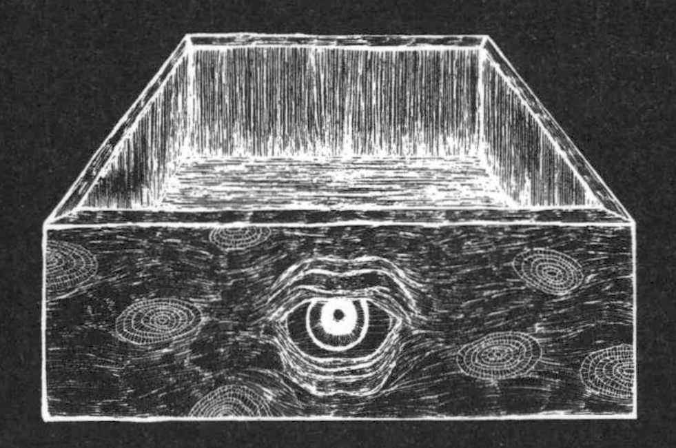

Book One

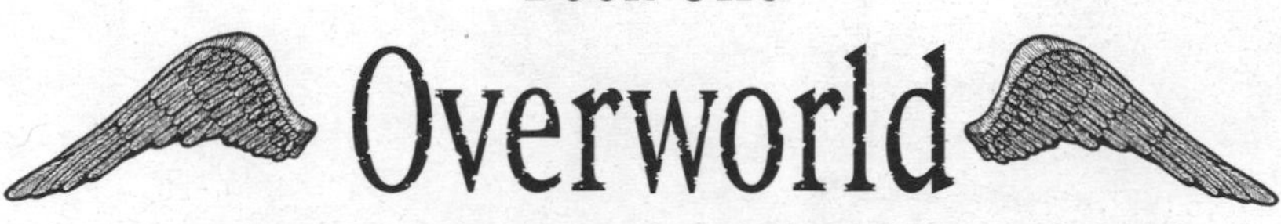

Overworld

Book Two

Netherworld

Book One
Overworld

I. The Silver Thread

was good at fighting.

At the beginning of his story, however, he still had no inkling of this, nor did he know that he was a Wolperting and would one day become Zamonia's most illustrious hero. He had no name, nor did he have the faintest recollection of his parents. He didn't know where he came from or where he would go. All he knew was that the farmyard where he grew up was his kingdom.

King of the farmyard

For Rumo, each day began when the farmer's entire family, seven Hackonian dwarfs, formed a doting circle around the sleeping puppy's basket and woke him with a melodious Hackonian song. Then they showered him with caresses. They tickled him behind the ears, rocked him in their arms, stroked his fur and kissed his tiny horns - marks of affection which he acknowledged with a pleasurable grunt. Wherever Rumo tottered on his four clumsy little legs, he instantly became the centre of attention. All his activities were applauded. He was even fondled and tickled for tripping over his own paws. The Hackonians set aside the freshest milk for him, barbecued him the most succulent sausages, reserved him the coolest place in the shade and the warmest place beside the stove. They went around on tiptoe when he was having his afternoon rest and regaled him with apple pie and whipped cream when he yawningly awoke. There were always volunteers ready to romp with Rumo or allow him to bite them with his toothless gums. And at night, when he had tired himself out with play, they groomed his fur with a soft brush and sang him to sleep. Yes, Rumo was the uncrowned king of the farmyard.

There were many other animals on the farm. The dairy cows, horses and pigs were all much bigger and stronger and more useful than Rumo, but none enjoyed the same popularity. The only creature that failed to acknowledge his supremacy was a black, long-necked goose twice his size, which hissed malevolently whenever he ventured too close, so he gave her as wide a berth as possible.

Pains in the mouth

One morning Rumo was awakened in his basket, not by the Hackonians' melodious singing but by a sharp pain. There was a strange sensation in his mouth. The interior normally felt like a wet, slimy cave in which his tongue glided over soft, smooth, rounded shapes, but it had now acquired a new and alarming feature. In his upper jaw, just inside the upper lip, the gum had gone taut and something sharp seemed to be growing beneath it. This was the source of the throbbing pain Rumo found so disagreeable. He decided to invite due sympathy and caresses by informing a wider public of his condition.

But there was no one around. He would have to toil across to the barn, where the Hackonians were usually engaged at this hour – for reasons Rumo found unfathomable – in tossing hay around with pitchforks. Experience had taught him that the route to the barn was fraught with difficulty. Through the kitchen, across the veranda with its menacing splinters, down the steps, across the muddy farmyard, past the stupid goose, round the drinking trough, which was always surrounded by pig dung – it was a wearisome trip, and Rumo preferred to undertake it in the arms of one of the farmer's children. If only he didn't have to go down on all fours and trip over his own paws in the process! How lovely it would be if he could walk on two legs like the Hackonians!

Rumo climbed out of his basket, planted his hind legs on the floor and straightened up with a groan. He swayed first to the right, then to the left, and finally stood straight as an arrow. Hey, it was easy!

He set off, striding along like a grown-up Hackonian. He was filled with pride, a novel and inspiring sensation. Without stumbling once, he plodded all the way across the kitchen, pushed open the door, which was ajar, and even managed to descend the four veranda steps. Then he marched off across the farmyard. The morning sun warmed his fur, the air felt cool and refreshing. Rumo drew a deep breath, put his forepaws

W. MOERS

on his hips and walked past the black goose, which he now matched in height. She backed away, staring at him in astonishment, and started to hiss something nasty, but she was too flabbergasted to get it out. Rumo didn't spare the bird a glance; he simply strode on, feeling bigger and more pleased with himself than ever before.

Rumo paused to enjoy the warmth of the sunlight on his fur. He blinked in the dazzling glare and shut his eyes, and there it was again, the world he saw whenever he did this. It was a world of smells that floated and flickered before his inner eye in hundreds of different colours: thin, fluttering wisps of red, yellow, green and blue light. The green light was given off by the luxuriant rosemary bush growing right beside him, the yellow by the delicious lemon cakes being baked in the kitchen, the red by the smoke of the smouldering compost heap, the blue by the cool morning breeze, which was laden with the tangy scent of the nearby ocean. And there were many, many more colours, some of them dirty and ugly like the brown of the dung in which the pig was wallowing. What really astonished Rumo, however, was a colour he had never smelt before. High above all these terrestrial scents floated a silver ribbon. It was thin and delicate - no more than a thread, in fact - but he could clearly see it with his inner eye.

Rumo was overcome by a strangely restless feeling, a vague and

unprecedented yearning to leave everything behind and set off into the blue on his own. He involuntarily drew a deep breath and shivered, so strong and splendid was the feeling that arose within him. Deep in his childish little heart Rumo sensed that, if he used this silver thread of scent as a guide and followed it to its source, happiness would await him there.

But first he must go into the barn and make a fuss. He opened his eyes and strode on. When he was standing in front of the big red curtains that kept the sunlight from parching the straw in the barn and setting it ablaze, he came to a halt. A strange new sensation had prompted him to interrupt his triumphal progress: his knees went weak and he had to fight off an urge to go down on all fours again. The blood shot to his head, his forepaws trembled and sweat broke out on his forehead.

Rumo didn't realise that the curtains marked a new chapter in his life and that he was about to slough off his animal heritage. He didn't know, either, that if he walked into the barn on his hind legs he would be regarded quite differently, because a Wolperting walking upright was treated with considerably more respect than a wild Wolperting. All he did sense was that his entry into the barn would be an event of importance. Bewildered and intimidated by his own audacity, he felt his little heart beat wildly: Rumo was suffering from stage fright.

He did what every actor does when afflicted by this form of nervous tension: he peeked through the curtains to check out the audience. Cautiously thrusting his head through the crack, he peered into the barn's interior.

One-eyed giants

It was dark inside and his sun-dazzled eyes took a moment to adapt themselves to the new conditions. All he made out at first were the shadowy shapes of wooden beams and bales of straw interspersed with shafts of sunlight slanting down through the barn windows. He blinked a couple of times, then saw that something wholly unexpected was going on in there. The Hackonians were *not* engaged in filling sacks with straw. On the contrary, they themselves were being stuffed into sacks by some huge, one-eyed creatures with horns and shaggy black fur.

Rumo didn't worry too much at first. He was used to mysterious things happening daily in the grown-up world. Only a few days ago a Camedary had been led into the farmyard. What a commotion! Everyone had scattered in different directions like hens before a thunderstorm and the Camedary had bleated for hours like a mad thing. Now it was tethered there, placidly munching the fodder in its nosebag, and had become a boring everyday sight. The giants didn't perturb Rumo either – Hackonian farmers kept animals just as hideous. For instance, the sight of an Ornian Swamp Hog was bearable only if one knew how delicious it tasted when stripped of its warty hide and roasted on a spit. But there was something about the horned giants that differentiated them from Marsh Hogs: the evil glint in their eyes. Rumo couldn't interpret it because he lacked experience. He didn't even know what evil was, so he parted the curtains and strode into the barn. His stage fright had evaporated, to be replaced by icy composure. For the first time ever, Rumo became aware of his ability to remain almost preternaturally calm in a tense situation. He took a step forward and announced his presence in the usual Wolpertingian manner: he gave two self-important sniffs.

No one took a scrap of notice, he had to admit. The giants continued to stuff the Hackonians into sacks, the Hackonians continued to wail and whimper. Rumo felt hurt. They were ignoring him – him, who could walk on his hind legs. Him, whose mouth was sore.

Suddenly he knew what to do: he would speak. He had learnt to walk straight off, so why shouldn't he speak as well? He decided to attract attention by uttering two sentences.

First: 'I can walk!'

Second: 'My mouth hurts!'

That would make everyone take notice – that would make them shower him with congratulations and expressions of sympathy. He opened his mouth, drew a deep breath and uttered his two sentences.

'Aa ha waa!'

'Ma ma haa!'

The words hadn't come out quite as he'd intended, but they'd emerged from his lips and sounded impressive. What was more, they worked. The shaggy black giants stopped stuffing Hackonians into sacks and the Hackonians stopped wailing and whimpering. Every eye turned in Rumo's direction.

All of a sudden his legs went trembly and his backside felt as heavy as lead. He struggled to retain his balance for a moment, then toppled over backwards into the dust. Rumo had chalked up a new experience: he'd made the first big blunder of his life. One of the giants stalked over to him, grabbed him by the ears and thrust him into a sack.

The story of the Demonocles

Demonocles were a vicious type of one-eyed giant found only on Roaming Rock. It was regarded as scientifically inaccurate to classify these monsters as members of the Zamonian pirate fraternity, since pirates only sail the seas in ships, strictly speaking, and do at least obey the rules of navigation. Demonocles, on the other hand, sailed the seas on a natural phenomenon, the legendary Roaming Rock, a buoyant amalgam of oxygen and minerals the size of a city block, and obeyed no rules except the laws of nature. They drifted around at random on their hollow rock, spreading panic and terror wherever the tides happened to wash them ashore.

If asked what fate he hoped to avoid at all costs, the average Zamonian tended to reply: *Being captured by the Demonocles*. There were captains who scuttled their own ships merely because they had sighted Roaming Rock on the horizon. They preferred to drown themselves and their crews rather than fall prey to these monsters. No coastal region was safe from them and few of Zamonia's seaside towns had not been raided by them in the course of the centuries.

Roaming Rock was originally a huge mass of lava vomited into the ocean by a subterranean volcano many thousands of years ago. There it cooled and rose to the surface because of the oxygen trapped inside it. From sea level it resembled a group of steeply jutting rocky islands, but it was really a composite structure, like an iceberg whose jagged extremities are visible while most of it is underwater. We do not know how and when the Demonocles settled on their floating island, but accounts in town archives of raids by vandals of Demonoclean origin suggest that it must have been several centuries ago. Presumably, one of their raiding parties sighted the great rock stranded off the coast of Zamonia, climbed aboard it and was unexpectedly swept out to sea when the tide turned.

It seems that the Demonocles abandoned themselves to their fate and made no attempt to influence the direction taken by their floating island. They were too uninventive to equip their bizarre vessel with sails, rudders or anchors, so it was left to the tides and ocean currents to determine which ill-starred stretch of coast they landed on. If washed up somewhere by a favourable current, the Demonocles immediately went ashore, raiding towns and villages, and taking prisoners until the waves bore them and their floating island away again.

Broadly speaking, such was the not particularly heart-warming story of the Demonocles and this time they had been stranded on the coast of Hackonia.

Rumo still had no forebodings, even when he was put into the sack. All grown-ups looked like giants to him, and he was used to them picking him up and carrying him around for unfathomable reasons. The sack seemed merely a new variation of an old game.

But his toothache was really bothering him. Persistent pain was something that conflicted with his cosy picture of the world. He had occasionally had to endure pain, but never for long: a tumble on the nose, a splinter from the veranda in his paw. Far from subsiding, however, this new pain was steadily becoming more intense. Worse still, another place in his mouth had started to hurt in the same way. Even so, he lay there quietly and scarcely moved.

The Demoncles' diet

For some days, now, the Demonocles left behind on Roaming Rock had noticed how the rising waves were tugging at their floating home. Only another few hours and they would be back on the high seas once more. Nervously, they scanned the cliffs surrounding the muddy tongue of land on which they were stranded. Nearly all the other raiders had returned from their forays, but a dozen were still missing.

A spine-chilling sound, almost like a cry, pierced the mist that floated between the sea and the mainland. It was the note of a seashell horn, which sounded to the Demonocles' ears like music. The dozen stragglers were returning at last.

The one-eyed vandals appeared on the clifftop, triumphantly holding aloft the bulging sacks in which their prey were still – they registered this with satisfaction – struggling and kicking violently.

What is the worst thing one living creature can do to another? Those brave enough to pursue that question to its logical conclusion might answer it as follows: Eating a fellow creature *alive*. It was quite all right to kill an Ornian Marsh Hog as quickly and painlessly as possible, strip off its hideous, warty hide, stuff it with rosemary and roast it on a spit; on that point all Zamonians - except the vegetarians among them - were agreed. But to cut the beating heart out of a live pig and devour it raw was quite beyond the pale - indeed, there were laws against it. Of course, not everyone obeyed those laws - werewolves, for example, and one or two other less sensitive life forms. However, no one could more blatantly have contravened the general agreement not to eat things alive than the Demonocles. Those one-eyed demons enjoyed their food only if what they devoured *was still moving*.

When on the high seas they ate live fish. If they captured a ship they wolfed its entire contents alive: captain, crew, passengers - even the last rat, cockroach and weevil in its hold. If they became stranded somewhere they ate the local inhabitants. It mattered little what form of prey they ate - Demonocles weren't choosy. They would even have devoured a Spiderwitch provided it was still twitching nicely. Liveliness was the main criterion by which the one-eyed giants judged the quality of their fare.

They had developed some ingenious ways of keeping their victims alive for as long as possible while gobbling them up. They saved vital organs such as the heart, brain and lungs till last, but eventually devoured those too, together with toenails, bones, scales, claws, eyelashes and tentacles. The Demonocles thought it particularly important to keep any sound-producing organs and innards intact to the end: the tongue, larynx and vocal cords were regarded as special delicacies to be reserved for the culmination of a meal. Screams, groans or whimpers took the place of a pinch of salt, a hint of garlic, or the scent of a bay leaf. The Demonocles were gourmets of the ear as well as the eye.

They divided their food into three grades. The lowest of these, acceptable only in an emergency, comprised creatures that were alive but barely moved and couldn't make sounds, for instance mussels, oysters, snails and jellyfish. In the medium grade were creatures which, although unable to scream, could twitch or wriggle: fish of all kinds, octopuses, lobsters, crabs and marine spiders. The highest category included creatures capable of speaking, screaming, yelling, screeching, crowing, twittering, bleating, or making noises of some other kind. The Demonocles didn't care what their victims were - Norselanders or Hackonians, Gargylls or Wolpertings, coastal dwarfs, seagulls or chimpanzees - as long as they made a frightful din while being eaten.

If the Hackonians had only known how effectively they were whetting the Demonocles' appetite by moaning and struggling inside their sacks, they would all have kept as quiet as Rumo, who was still wondering when this curious grown-up game would come to an end.

The giants' larder

What surprised Rumo most, when he was finally released from his stuffy prison, was that he was no longer in the farmyard. He noticed to his astonishment that the ground beneath him kept rocking to and fro. However, he was quickly reassured to find that his family were all there too. Although the ground was unsteady, uneven and slippery, he managed to stand up on his hind legs, but he couldn't grasp why everyone failed to notice this feat and congratulate him on it. Even his family were ignoring him, and their behaviour was very odd in general. Their usually amiable faces had turned into tragic masks and some of them had water trickling from their eyes. Rumo wondered where his basket was. Surely they hadn't left his basket behind? No, that was impossible. He was sick of this game. He wanted something nice to eat, a Hackonian lullaby and a little nap.

The Hackonians took a different view of the situation. They had heard the rumours about Roaming Rock, and some of them had had grandparents or other relations abducted by the Demonocles. They knew what awaited them unless some miracle occurred.

To the Demonocles, on the other hand, the situation was neither mysterious nor tragic but simply satisfactory: they had just restocked their larder after a successful raid ashore. Now they were heading out to sea again, bound for a life of glorious freedom on the ocean waves.

Rumo and the Hackonians were herded into a big cave in the heart of Roaming Rock – in the Demonocles' opinion the finest place on their island. This was where they stored their food, where they went first thing each morning to get their breakfast and last thing at night to get their supper. Many of them even visited the cave in the small hours, half asleep but eager for an unwholesome little midnight snack.

Embedded in the walls of the vast cave were iron rings to which the Hackonians were secured with chains round their necks, wrists or ankles. Basins hewn out of the rocky floor teemed with plump fish and octopuses. Wild animals – lynxes, bears and lions – were imprisoned in cages. Domesticated animals such as hens, pigs, horses or cows roamed around freely behind the sliding wooden grille with which the Demonocles shut off the mouth of the cave. Lobsters and crayfish crawled over and under each other in stone tubs and earthenware jars filled with sea water, which also contained oysters. The one thing Roaming Rock wasn't short of was live food.

A sleepless night

Like most of the other inmates of the cave, Rumo didn't sleep a wink that night. What with the incessant motion, the puddles of sea water sloshing to and fro, and the sobs and whimpers, grunts and cackles, whinnies and roars of his fellow captives, he had never before had to endure such uncomfortable conditions. The Demonocles hadn't troubled to chain him up because they obviously rated him a harmless domesticated animal. What he found most shocking of all was that the Hackonians hardly spared him a glance when he tried to snuggle up to them. Chained to the wall, they wept continuously.

Feeling hurt, Rumo went looking for affection elsewhere in the cave, but the same depressing atmosphere prevailed everywhere. Nobody wanted to play with him; everyone was self-absorbed; sobs and cries of despair filled the air.

Rumo eventually took refuge in a niche with a narrow entrance. Originally formed in the volcanic rock by a fat round air bubble, it afforded some protection from the sea water splashing around. He curled up and shut his eyes, but that only seemed to aggravate his seasickness, so he opened them again and simply lay there, as dejected and frightened as everyone else.

It was the longest and worst night of Rumo's life to date. Every now and then a Demonocle would visit the cave for something to eat: a hen, a lobster, a pig, or a Hackonian. The hens cackled, the pigs squealed, the Hackonians screamed – sleep was impossible under such circumstances.

The noise became really deafening when one Demonocle felt peckish for a lion. Rumo had never seen a lion before, but he sensed that the golden-maned creature in the biggest cage of all was a proud and dangerous beast. When the hungry Demonocle unbolted its cage the beast emitted a sound that made the other prisoners' blood run cold: a low growl that seemed to emanate from a natural disaster, not a living creature. Although anyone with any sense would have put as much distance as possible between himself and that sound, the Demonocle entered the cage without hesitation. The growl gave way to a roar that shook the walls of the cave. The Demonocle's hand shot out and grabbed the lion by the neck. Winding its tail round his other wrist, he slung the huge cat over his shoulder like a sack of coals and plodded out.

Rumo curled up again. What kept him awake, apart from the incessant din, was his sore mouth. The gum had swelled up in two new places and this perturbed him almost more than the goings-on in the cave. From one day to the next the world had become a hostile place – even his own body was turning against him. He whimpered for a bit and a few tears trickled down his nose. It was dawn by the time he fell into a brief, troubled sleep filled with wild and sinister dreams.

Breakfast time

The first thing Rumo noticed when he awoke was that the ground wasn't swaying as much. His fur was sodden with water dripping from the roof. He badly needed a pee, so he relieved himself outside his niche. Then he went on a tour of inspection to see if the situation had taken a turn for the better. Perhaps someone would play with him at last.

To begin with it seemed unlikely. It was breakfast time, and grumpy, grunting Demonocles were stomping around the cave in search of ingredients for their first meal of the day. Most of them favoured pork for breakfast, so the squeals were ear-splitting. One Demonocle had decided on some octopus. He fished a huge, eight-armed specimen out of a pool and promptly got into a tangle, much to his companions' amusement. The octopus wound its tentacles round the one-eyed giant's body, neck and ankles, its suckers taking hold with a sound like someone smacking his lips. The Demonocle started to sway, lost his balance and crashed to the ground. His companions threw back their heads and emitted gurgling noises - their way of laughing, Rumo gathered. The fallen giant struggled to his feet, grabbed one of the tentacles and summarily tore it off. The octopus relaxed its grip, but it was too late for conciliatory gestures. The Demonocle gripped three more tentacles in both hands and swung the octopus round his head like a hammer thrower, then smashed it against the wall of the cave. It burst like a barrel of ink, spraying black liquid over everyone unlucky enough to be within range. Despite himself, Rumo vomited.

When the Demonocles left their larder at last, Rumo tottered over to a puddle on trembling legs and rinsed out his mouth. He was so frightened that he had gone back to walking on all fours - it seemed safer. The water was lukewarm and brackish, and tasted of fish. Rumo was just about to throw up again when he noticed a welcome development: one of the sore places in his mouth had stopped hurting, and something smooth and pointed had emerged there. He explored it with his tongue. It felt strange but somehow nice. Although the other places still hurt, they didn't worry him as much, now that one of them had undergone such a pleasant transformation.

He, too, was hungry. He found a trough full of gooey mush and ate some, reluctantly at first, then more and more greedily as he noticed that the hollow sensation in his tummy was subsiding. Then he crawled back into his little niche for a closer inspection of his first tooth, exploring it with his tongue again and again. He felt as if he had been given a present.

Cries of mortal agony drifted in from outside. The Demonocles were taking time over their breakfast and some of them were clearly eating it in the immediate vicinity of their larder. The Hackonians clung to each other, weeping and wailing even more loudly than before. Rumo noticed that the head of the family was missing, but that didn't surprise him. The farmer had often disappeared for days on end, only to return when he was least expected.

Rumo went on another tour of the cave, sniffing the air as he went. He was finding it hard to get used to the smells given off by the sea, which were so utterly different from those of the farmyard. Everything there had smelt of soil, herbs and life, whereas here the only scents were of rotting fish and death. He gave the cages containing wild animals a wide berth. Incredible how big and powerful many of them were! There was a red gorilla, a wild dog with two heads, another lion with only one eye, a huge polar bear with bloodstained fur. These beasts filled Rumo with a mixture of fear and wonder.

The murky pools

But what he found really sinister were some deep, dark pools in a side chamber of the cave: eight circular basins, nearly all of which were filled with murky water. Kept in them with other sea creatures were giant squid, and the colour of the water came from the clouds of inky black fluid they excreted like a smokescreen when alarmed. Slimy tentacles, pointed horns, black dorsal fins and glowing eyes on stalks broke the surface by turns, and issuing from one of the pools was a plaintive, sing-song cry. During the night Rumo had seen an inquisitive goat venture too close to the edge of one such basin. Without warning, a yellow tentacle equipped with fat suckers had emerged from the black, soupy water, wrapped itself round the animal's neck at lightning speed and, with a low gurgle, dragged it into the depths before it could even bleat. Since then, Rumo had maintained a respectful distance from the pools.

Three of the artificial basins appeared to contain creatures which the Demonocles kept as iron rations for consumption when times were hard. Even they seemed to find them scary, because they kept well clear of the pools in question. They contained no squid, so the water in them was clearer. To his astonishment, Rumo sighted some small but awe-inspiring denizens of a dark world inhabited by creatures with heavily armoured scales and rows of fearsome teeth. They had grim faces with pugnaciously jutting lower jaws, and their eyes glowed and rolled wildly in their sockets as if they weren't entirely sane. Many of them had long antennae tipped with glowing balls like miniature lanterns. Rumo saw a puffer fish as transparent as glass, with a red heart pulsating inside it. He also spotted a long, thin oceanic worm that continually changed colour as it wove its way along below the surface. He kept returning for another look at these fascinating prodigies of the deep and studied their mysterious modes of behaviour, because they were the only things in the cave that helped him, for a moment or two at least, to forget his depressing surroundings.

Most mysterious of all, however, was the furthermost basin, which was situated a little apart from the others at the back of the cave. Its water was dark-green, unlike that of the blue-black pools, but just as cloudy. It struck Rumo that none of the Demonocles went near it and that the free-range animals also kept their distance - mainly, no doubt, because of the foul stench it gave off.

Rumo would dearly have liked to know what sort of creature the oily surface concealed. For the most part, however, all that protruded from the murky soup was a big grey dorsal fin or a broad back that might have belonged to a whale or a fat sea cow. The baleful eye that sometimes lurked beneath the surface resembled that of a marine predator.

What particularly attracted Rumo to the furthermost basin were some faint vibrations he had picked up during the night, while trying to sleep. In his mind's eye they had assumed the form of some concentric red ripples in the pool from which the dorsal fin occasionally protruded. The little Wolperting couldn't interpret these mental images, but he felt that they were trying to tell him something - indeed, it was almost as if he could sense that this mysterious subaquatic creature wanted to get in touch with him. On the other hand, perhaps it was simply trying to lure him close enough to catch him. Rumo had refrained from obeying its signals and remained in hiding all night.

However, he felt braver now that everyone was awake and activity reigned throughout the cave. For a while he prowled around near the pool, but not so near that some slimy, sucker-studded tentacle could seize the opportunity to drag him into its murky depths. He gambolled around it on all fours. The eye beneath the surface revolved, observing his every movement, and when he had made two circuits the dorsal fin rose slowly out of the water. It rotated on the spot like the iron pointer of a sundial, following him as he made his third circuit.

This went on for quite a while. Sometimes the fin sank below the surface, sometimes it resurfaced. Rumo sauntered off and returned, sauntered off and returned, but he never took his eyes off the pool. Two creatures with no idea what to make of each other were engaged in covert mutual observation.

A small party of Demonocles entered the cave in search of a second helping of breakfast. Rumo always hid in his niche when the one-eyed giants visited their larder, so he scampered back there - only to find that it was already occupied by the black goose, the same bird that had given him such a hard time back on the farm.

With a roar, the leading Demonocle shooed away some hens while the others looked around enquiringly. One of them grinned when he caught sight of Rumo and came stomping towards the little Wolperting. Rumo growled at the goose, hoping to scare her away, but she stuck out her tongue and gave a menacing hiss. The Demonocle stopped short, distracted by a litter of piglets.

Rumo remembered the trick he'd tried before. He made himself as tall as the goose by rising on his hind legs. Then he growled again, louder and more menacingly than before, and bared his gums to display his solitary tooth. The bird did not hiss back this time, but waddled silently out of the niche so that Rumo could sneak inside. The Demonocle caught sight of the goose standing there at a loss. He licked his lips, reached her in three strides and seized her by the neck. 'Quaaa–' was the last Rumo heard of her.

The mysterious eye

A measure of peace and quiet returned once the giant had disappeared clutching the goose and a handful of piglets, so Rumo ventured out of his hiding place. As if magnetically attracted to it, he approached the evil-smelling pool with the mysterious eye in its depths. He prowled around in its vicinity for a while, waiting for the creature to emerge in its entirety for once, but all that happened was a familiar sequence of events: the fin emerged and submerged, the eye appeared below the surface, a few bubbles rose sluggishly and burst with a pop.

At length Rumo ventured a little closer, this time flat on his belly. He crawled nearer, inch by inch, until he was only a couple of feet from the edge. The unknown creature had submerged completely. Neither the fin nor the eye could be seen, just more fat green bubbles that burst with a pop and gave off a noxious stench.

Lying there undaunted, Rumo shut his eyes and strained his senses. Oh yes, the red vibrations were immensely strong! They seemed to pulsate in time to the beating of a mighty heart, slowly, steadily and reassuringly.

Unseen by Rumo, the water silently parted and a massive grey form emerged from the dark-green depths. It was a creature with the head and teeth of a big shark and the body of an abnormally bloated maggot.

'Hello,' the creature said in a sepulchral voice.

Rumo's eyes snapped open. Horrified, he jumped back three or four feet and stood there on all fours, barking as viciously as a Wolperting whelp can. The creature made no move to leave the pool, still less attack him. Waving around on either side of its maggotlike body were seven pairs of puny little arms.

'Come here,' the creature purred amiably. 'I won't hurt you.'

Although Rumo didn't understand a word, the creature's gentle, sonorous voice inspired confidence. He kept his distance, but he stopped barking and merely growled.

'Come here,' the creature repeated. 'Come on, I'm your friend.'

'Graa ra graaha,' Rumo replied. He didn't know what it meant, but he felt bound to make some response.

'You can speak? Better and better! You're a Wolperting, did you know that?'

'Waapaawaa,' said Rumo.

'Wolperting,' the creature said again, pointing to him with several of its numerous fingers.

'Walpaataa,' said Rumo.

'You learn fast.' The creature laughed so hard that water slopped over the edge of the pool. 'Say "Smyke",' it said coaxingly.

Rumo hesitated.

'Go on, say "Smyke"!'

'Maiee?'

'Smyke! Say "Smyke"!'

'Smaiee,' said Rumo.

'Excellent.' The creature gave another laugh. 'Smyke, Volzotan Smyke. That's my name.'

Volzotan Smyke's story

Volzotan Smyke was a Shark Grub. As such, he was quite capable of leaving the water and living on land, but while on Roaming Rock he thought it wiser to convey the impression that he was a sea creature pure and simple. At least five hundred years old, according to his own rough estimate, he had heard many things about the Demonocles in the course of his life to date, one of them being that they found land animals more to their taste than sea creatures.

When the Demonocles captured the pirate ship on which Volzotan Smyke happened to be a passenger, he had promptly thrown himself into a tank filled with drinking water and, with great histrionic panache, impersonated an obese and unappetising sea creature. Although the Demonocles were taken in by his act, they transported him back to their cave and stored him in one of the pools for consumption in an emergency. They devoured all the pirates within a month, but Smyke miraculously survived.

However, he was feeling rather unwell in his watery element. True, he could breathe underwater if he chose, but that was just an embarrassing legacy inherited from his aquatic ancestors, whom he despised. He would have preferred to disavow that part of his family tree, but in his present predicament he clung to it desperately, because his ancestors were – so to speak – saving his life every day. Smyke had been living in this pool on Roaming Rock for two and a half years – by far the longest period any creature had ever spent in the Demonocles' larder. This had given him time to study their habits – or, at least, those they indulged in when visiting the cave. He had been compelled to listen to their gruesome singing, the discordant din made by their seashell horns and their totally unrhythmical drumming. Smyke estimated that these performances occurred every six months at particular phases of the moon and went on for days, so he could tell when their next festivity – or orgy – was due. This knowledge was vitally important, because the Demonocles' gluttony on such occasions could spell the premature end of every living creature in the cave. Smyke had had to witness the disappearance of several captured ships' crews in quick succession. Indeed, one or two prisoners had been eaten alive before his very eyes. When these festivities were at their height, it was not uncommon for a drunken Demonocle to come storming into the cave, tear a shrieking victim to pieces and devour him in the presence of his horrified fellow captives. At such times blood seemed to affect the Demonocles in much the same way as high-proof liquor.

While these atrocities were in progress, Volzotan Smyke dived as deep as he could and excreted a substance from his sebaceous glands that dyed the pool dark-green, transforming it into a malodorous soup so unappetising that even the Demonocles found it repulsive. He hated doing this, because it reminded him of another, still more unpleasant branch of his family tree, at the lower end of which came the primeval Sulphur Grub, a creature whose offensive smell was all that had enabled it to survive in a world full of voracious dinosaurs. Smyke could hardly endure the stench himself, but in this case the end really did justify the means.

So as not to become demented under these conditions, Smyke had created a fantasy world of his own. He regarded his sojourn on Roaming

Rock as an ordeal imposed on him by fate and designed to toughen him for his further journey through life. He was like a sword being tempered in the furnace – that was his favourite image of himself, little though it accorded with his physical appearance. Nothing in the world was more terrible than the constant fear of being eaten alive. Equally, and of this he was just as convinced, nothing could better steel one to resist terrors of all kinds. If he survived Roaming Rock, he kept telling himself, death would have lost its sting.

Smyke's memories were another powerful aid in his fight for survival on Roaming Rock. It was only in captivity that he had learnt to appreciate moments of happiness experienced in the past. In the corridors of his brain he had constructed a chamber to be visited whenever his hopes had been dashed yet again, when his fear was at its greatest and his despair overpowering. This was the *Chamber of Memories*.

Major and minor incidents in his life hung on its walls like oil paintings, frozen in time and waiting for him to reactivate them. These mental images would have meant nothing to anyone else. They could be a view across a gloomy bay or a little hillside inn at dusk, a battlefield in turmoil, a chessboard bearing an exceptionally complicated arrangement of pieces, or a leg of roast pork with a knife about to carve it.

When Smyke stood in front of one of these pictures and devoted his attention to it, it seemed to come to life, expand and literally suck him in. He then experienced some pleasurable memory as if for the first time. Such was the solitary skill he had developed at the bottom of his pool. It was neither thinking nor dreaming but a mental activity that lay midway between the two – one he immodestly termed *smyking*. It was the art not of remembering, but of *reliving* a remembrance.

Smyke used to reactivate these memories as required. Some of them were big and dramatic, others small, simple and intimate. If afflicted with hunger and a yearning for something more varied to eat than the seaweed and plankton the Demonocles tossed into his pool, Smyke would summon up the image of a little inn at dusk. There, over a hundred years ago, he had enjoyed one of his life's most satisfying gastronomic experiences. He had dined outside on the terrace, which afforded a panoramic view of a bay that glowed orange at night, thanks to the phosphorescent jellyfish that congregated there at that season of the year. Smyke started with the *Whole Baked Truffle Encased in Pâté de Foie Gras*, went on to the *Slaked Jellyfish on a Bed of Algae* followed by a *Venus's-Shell Risotto* and *Ginger Salad in a Cream Dressing Scented with Lemon Grass*, and rounded off the meal with some *Five-Year-Old Grailsundian Blue* and a bottle of *Cataclysmian Port*. Although this was a rather trivial memory, Smyke revived it more often than any of the others.

Only one mental image in his Chamber of Memories - an exceptionally large one - was permanently covered up. Smyke always hurried past this picture, which was draped in a black cloth, but he couldn't delete it from his mind.

Other memories were preserved in urns. The walls of the chamber were lined with little pillars bearing urns of various colours. If Smyke opened one of these vessels a smell would issue from it: *The scent of fresh snow. The dusty odour of an ancient book. Rain falling on a city street in springtime. The smoke from a campfire. A wine cork straight from the bottle. Oven-warm bread. A cup of coffee.*

Each of these smells set off a chain reaction of memories in which Smyke could lose himself for hours. If only for a while, they made him forget his fear and despair - until the blare of a seashell horn or the rattle of the grille over the mouth of the cave jolted him back to reality.

And now, into this harsh reality had stumbled a Wolperting puppy that still walked on all fours, hadn't yet learnt to speak and was seasick from time to time. Smyke knew that this little creature personified the reason why he had constructed his Chamber of Memories. It embodied the hope that had kept him going in the depths of his stinking pool, the one remaining desire he still cherished in this dreadful world: to escape from Roaming Rock. This personification of his desire required a name, Volzotan Smyke decided. He didn't take long to think of one. There was a Zamonian card game, a particular favourite of his, in which the most important card, and the one that gave the game its name, was known as the *rumo*. If you played a rumo you were challenging fate and risking everything - absolutely everything. On the other hand you could score a resounding victory. And that was how Rumo got his name.

Words and pictures

'Rumo!' said Rumo.

'That's right!' Smyke exclaimed. 'You Rumo, me Smyke.'

'You Rumo, me Smyke,' Rumo repeated eagerly.

'No, no.' Smyke chuckled. '*You* Rumo, *me* Smyke.'

'*You* Rumo, *me* Smyke!' Rumo said defiantly, slapping his chest with his forepaw.

Smyke taught Rumo to speak. Or rather, Rumo could already speak. All he needed were the right words, and those he learnt simply by sitting beside the pool and listening to the Shark Grub. At first it seemed to him that the creature was emitting a hotchpotch of hisses, croaks and noises that made no sense, but he soon noticed that many of these sounds conjured up mental images, while others generated emotions like fear or bewilderment or gaiety. Still others filled his head with geometrical shapes and abstract patterns.

The little Wolperting soaked up these strange sounds like a sponge. Certain of Smyke's utterances made heavenly music ring out in Rumo's ears and suffused his whole body with an unaccountable feeling of happiness. Sometimes he pictured things he couldn't put a name to: a big, dark city in which many fires were burning, or a mountain range agleam with snow, or a desert valley shimmering with intense heat. Then again, he would fall into a trance, dreaming with his eyes wide open and his heart beating wildly. He could still see Smyke swimming in the pool and gesticulating with his fourteen arms, but a stream of events, sensations and presentiments flowed through his body. He felt as if the words were penetrating his brain in a thousand places and exploding there, and the images they conjured up formed themselves into confused, incoherent scenes that followed and obliterated each other in quick succession. It was as if an immense wealth of age-old experience had been slumbering within him. Now it had awakened and sprung potently to life. No, Smyke didn't teach

Rumo to speak, he merely roused the words inside him from their sleep.

'Yes! Yes!' Rumo kept exclaiming. 'Go on, go on!'

Words, images, sensations – Rumo couldn't get enough of them.

Smyke's favourite topic was fighting. He himself was no fighter, that was obvious, but his knowledge of the theoretical aspects of the subject was second to none. He had made a meticulous study of all forms of fighting: sporting contests, pitched battles in the field, duels to the death with sabres, boxing matches with padded gloves, rapid-fire shoot-outs with crossbows, the Marsh Dwellers' ancient art of cudgel-fighting, the Bluddums' appallingly sanguinary affrays with ball and chain. Smyke had witnessed duels in which adversaries daubed with pitch set each other ablaze with flaming torches. Armed with a magnifying glass, he had spent days watching the incredibly bloody battles waged by rival ants' nests. He could tell of contests that brought you out in a sweat at the sight and sound of opponents breaking each other's bones. Rumo was so enthralled by Smyke's anecdotes that he sometimes sat beside the pool like a spectator at a prizefight, punching the air with his little paws clenched.

Smyke had refereed the Fangfangs' professional boxing matches. He had also been a military adviser during the Norselanders' guerrilla wars, an officially licensed second at duels between Florinthian aristocrats, and a timekeeper at the Wolpertings' chess tournaments in Betaville. Other professional capacities in which he had served included cockfight organiser, treasurer of the Zamonian Vermiluct (an annual wrestling match between Ornian Strangleworms), cheerleader at the Midgardian Dwarf Joust and croupier at Fort Una, the city where gambling went on round the clock. No, Smyke was no fighter; he was a gambler, which was why he studied contests and contestants, and analysed victories and defeats of all kinds. Anyone who knew how contests functioned could bet on their outcome. That was Smyke's ruling passion, his *raison d'être*: steadily improving his ability *to know who would win*.

'I once watched a fight between two Hydroscorpions,' he remarked one day, out of the blue, and Rumo pricked up his ears. *Hydroscorpions*, he thought, and something small with lots of legs went scuttling through his head.

'Hydroscorpions are tiny but highly venomous creatures with seven extremely mobile tails, each of which is tipped with a poisonous sting,' Smyke went on.

Rumo shuddered.

'Would you like to hear how the fight turned out?'

'Yes, please!' Rumo said eagerly.

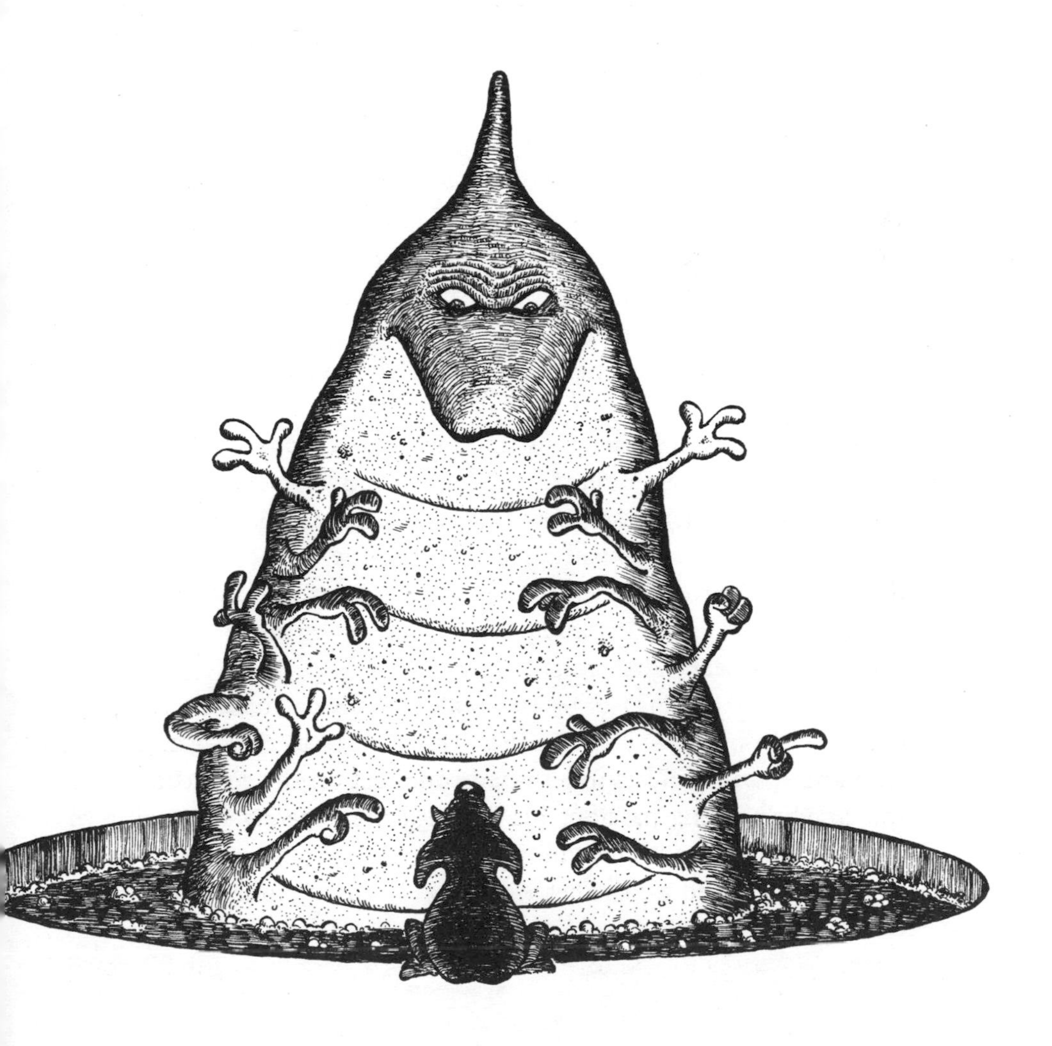

'It was in a desert and I happened to be at a loose end, so I watched those two venomous creatures and made a bet with myself. I bet on the smaller, more agile scorpion. At first they merely danced around each other in the sand – a stiff, decorous dance, like that of two courtiers in olden times. Then, all at once, it happened: the larger scorpion feinted, lashed out, killed the smaller one in an instant and devoured it. Crash, bang, wallop – all over! I'd lost my bet with myself and won it at the same time.'

Rumo knitted his brow and thought hard.

'But the most surprising thing of all happened after that. Having devoured its opponent, the victorious scorpion stung itself in the head, went into convulsions and died in agony.'

'Ooh . . .' said Rumo.

'Later I had this explained to me by someone who knew all about Hydroscorpions. He explained that they were male and female.'

'Male and female?'

'Yes, they were a couple,' said Smyke, as if this concluded his story with a satisfactory moral. 'They were in love, you see?'

'No,' said Rumo, 'I don't.'

'Neither do I.' Smyke sighed. On that note he submerged.

Rumo lay awake for a long time that night, trying to read some meaning into the words 'male' and 'female'. He failed, and besides, new teeth were about to emerge at three different points in his mouth. On the other hand, four more had already done so. He enjoyed running his tongue over them, delighting in their smooth sides, and sharp points and cutting edges. His mouth would soon be as full of such teeth as that of the big white bear in its cage.

Then he fell asleep after all. He dreamt he was an immense, muscular, menacing bear with snow-white fur and silver teeth. He rose on his hind legs and emitted a fearsome roar, and swarms of shadowy figures fled from him in terror. The little Wolperting laughed in his sleep.

By now, Rumo was moving around the cave with somewhat more self-confidence. There were five rules which Smyke had impressed on him and which he strictly observed:

Smyke's five rules

Rule No. 1: Keep away from cages containing wild animals!
Rule No. 2: Keep away from pools containing creatures with tentacles!
Rule No. 3: Never try to climb over the sliding grille!
Rule No. 4: Hide in your niche when Demonocles appear!
Rule No. 5: If you fail to make it to your niche, keep as still as you can when Demonocles are around!

Rumo enjoyed more freedom than any other prisoner in the cave. He wasn't locked up, tethered or chained, and he didn't have to hide underwater. He could help himself to any of the food or water troughs - apart from those of the wild animals. He could explore every nook and cranny, and was the only free-range inmate of the cave with a sleeping place hidden from the Demonocles' gaze. He also enjoyed the privilege, when fear threatened to overwhelm him, of being able to call on Volzotan Smyke for a story. Particularly when the Demonocles made a racket with their conch-horns and drums - an increasingly frequent occurrence of late - Rumo used to sneak off to Smyke for something to take his mind off the alarming din.

'Tell me a story!' he commanded on such occasions.

Smyke enjoyed telling Rumo stories because, figuratively speaking, they transported him as far from Roaming Rock as they did the little Wolperting.

'Would you like to hear the story of the battle of Lindworm Castle?' asked Smyke.

'A battle?' Rumo exclaimed. 'Yes, please!'

Smyke inhaled so deeply, he might have been intending to recount the story in a single breath.

The story of Lindworm Castle

'The story of Lindworm Castle is the oldest story in Zamonia - possibly the oldest story in the world,' he began. 'Are you ready to listen to Zamonia's longest and oldest story, my boy?'

Rumo nodded.

'It's billions of years old.' Smyke waved his fourteen arms dramatically.

'Billions?' Rumo wasn't expressing surprise, just imitating the word.

'Yes, billions! A billion is a thousand million and a million years are a thousand thousand – but you'll learn all that soon enough. What matters is, a billion years ago a very small animal appeared in the ocean: the world's first living creature.'

'Out there in the water?'

'Yes, out there in the ocean.'

'What kind of animal?'

Smyke racked his brains. The youngster was starting to ask some disconcerting questions. What kind of creature? Something beginning with . . . It was on the tip of his tongue. But anyway, was 'animal' the correct term for the creature he was thinking of? Smyke was shocked at himself. After all, he'd once done a three-week course on Zamonian palaeontology at the night school in Florinth. That was . . . Good heavens, that was a hundred and fifty years ago already!

'What kind of animal?'

Smyke couldn't remember. Hadn't the first living creatures been cells? Cells that divided and . . . Or didn't cells count as living creatures? Didn't two cells have to combine in order to produce a living creature? Which then divided, or something like that? He really must brush up his knowledge of palaeontology. And biology. And science in general.

'That's immaterial. What matters is, the animal was very small and it, er, divided into two.'

'Divided into two?'

'Yes, *divided into two*! What are you, a parrot?'

'A parrot?'

Smyke became aware that it was quite some time since he had told a long, coherent story. He had definitely gone back too far.

'Anyway, the animal divided into two and formed other animals. Those animals developed jaws, grew scales and teeth—'

'Teeth!' cried Rumo, proudly baring his little stumps, but Smyke ignored the interruption.

'They grew bigger and bigger, and then they went ashore. They were the dinosaurs.' That's one way out, thought Smyke. Short and painless.

'Dinosaurs?'

For the first time ever, Rumo was rather getting on the Shark Grub's nerves. Until now his questions had always amused Smyke and provoked him into giving detailed explanations, but today his patience was being sorely tried. The drumming had started again some days ago. He was the only one who realised that terrible events lay in store – events that could seal the fate of every living creature in the cave – and this knowledge was preying on his mind. The story of Lindworm Castle had been meant to distract himself as well, and now Rumo kept interrupting.

'Yes, dinosaurs. Or dragons. Or lindworms, if you like. Big, powerful lizards. Some of them – the herbivores – were merely big. Others were vicious, predatory carnivores. They had huge claws and teeth, were encased in scales and gristle, and could be up to a hundred feet long. The dinosaurs were enormous monsters.'

'Oh,' said Rumo.

Now I've captured his attention, thought Smyke. *Monsters always do the trick . . .*

'So these monsters, these dinosaurs, went ashore all over the world. The one place where they remained in the water was Loch Loch, the big volcanic lake between the end of Demon Range and the Dullsgard Plateau. Unlike the oceans, which were cooling, Loch Loch retained its warmth because of the volcano that heated it from below. It also had large underwater caves in which the monsters could dwell in safety. The dinosaurs of Loch Loch thought: Why should we traipse around outside when it's so nice and warm in here? So they remained in the lake while the other dinosaurs conquered terra firma. Then came the great catastrophe!'

'Catastrophe?' What a great big word, thought Rumo. It seemed to portend something bad.

'Yes, some huge meteorites came crashing down from outer space. A gigantic dust cloud enshrouded the whole of Zamonia for millions of years and the dinosaurs died out – all except the ones in Loch Loch. They went on living in their underwater caves, mated with the surviving dinosaurs of other breeds and developed bigger brains. It was only then that they went ashore.'

Rumo opened his mouth to ask what 'mate' meant, but Smyke went on quickly, 'So there they were, standing around on dry land and wondering what to do next. It was cold and draughty, and winter was on the way, but right beside Loch Loch stood a mountain riddled with caves and tunnels. It was warm and windproof inside, like a huge tiled stove, because it had been heated for thousands of years by the waters of the lake. So the dinosaurs crawled inside. That's to say, the ones that could squeeze through the openings did so. The others, the really big ones, had to remain outside and were frozen to death.'

'Frozen,' Rumo repeated in a whisper, shivering.

'The mountain was swarming with blind marmots. They were easy to catch and didn't taste too bad, so the dinosaurs survived their first winter on dry land. To begin with they ate the marmots raw, but one day a shaft of lightning ignited some straw and they discovered fire. They learnt how to cook. From then on their menu included barbecued marmot kebabs and marmot soup, or marmots encased in clay and baked in glowing charcoal until they were done. All soft and juicy inside, and on the outside . . .'

Smyke broke off. A distant blare of seashell horns came drifting into the cave and the drums resumed their nerve-racking, thunderous din. Smyke cleared his throat.

'The dinosaurs hollowed out the mountain some more and made it habitable. Because the winters were so cold and they were used to living in warm water they started to wear clothes. Marmot-skin cloaks at first, but then they stole some sheep from the neighbouring farms, invented spinning wheels and looms, and wove garments of wool. They also learnt how to smelt iron from the ore of which the mountain was composed. In short, they were clearly skilled at handicrafts and became steadily more intelligent and civilised. The local inhabitants had no idea they were dinosaurs, because dinosaurs had long been extinct, so they mistook them for dragons or lindworms, and believed them capable of breathing fire and devouring damsels. Anyway, they treated them with great respect and christened their mountain *Lindworm Castle*.'

Rumo carefully memorised the name.

'The Lindworms, as the dinosaurs now called themselves, maintained distant but friendly relations with the people round about. Once they had rid them of their superstitious prejudices as regards the devouring of damsels, they carried on a modest trade in manufactured goods and foodstuffs but never allowed them inside their stronghold. They fortified the entrances and carved staircases, doors and windows, tunnels and caverns out of the rock. The whole mountain was

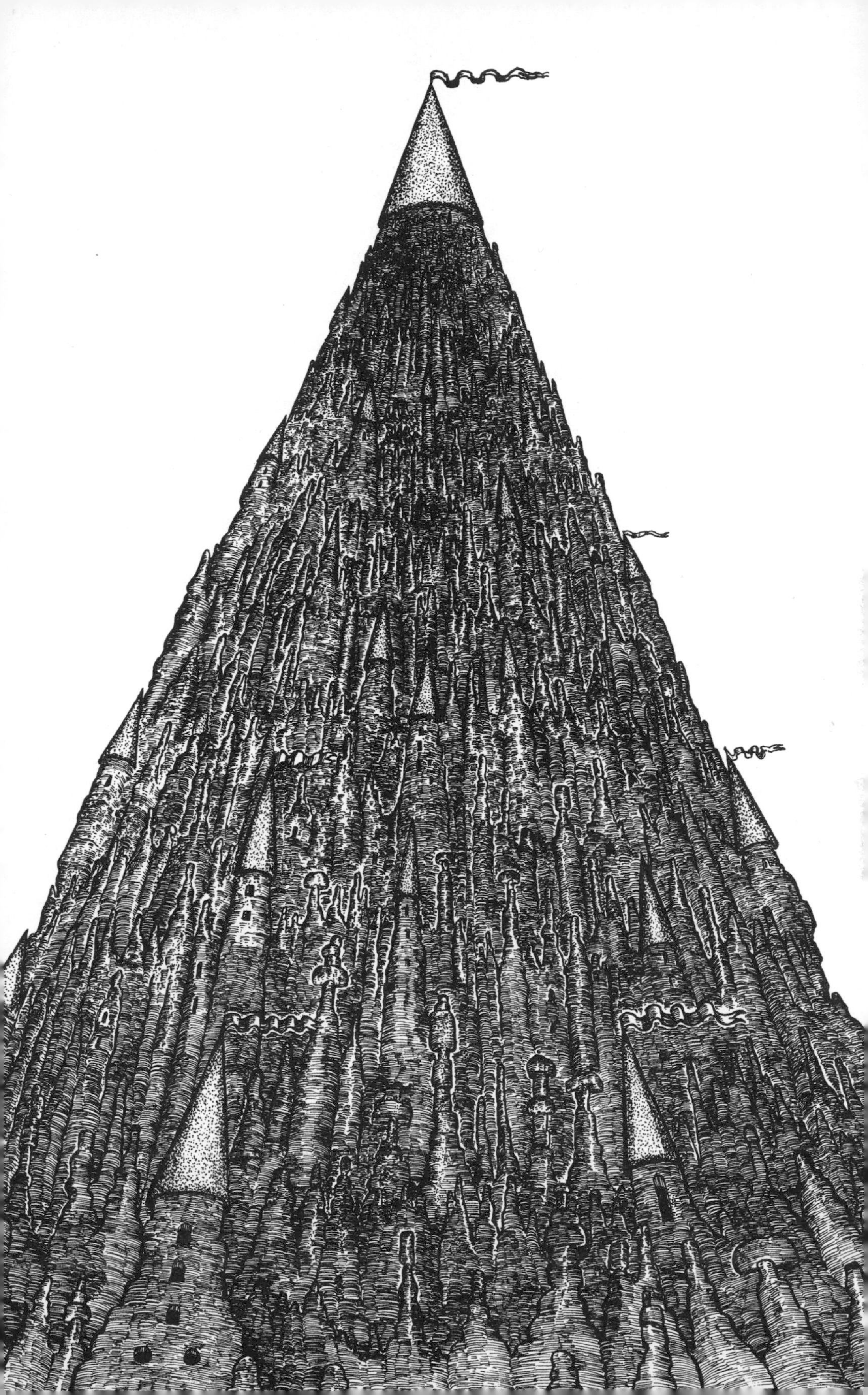

transformed into a big, well-defended fortress. As the Lindworms' mental powers steadily developed, so their savage, dinosaurian instincts withered away. Having hitherto communicated in a mixture of grunts and sign language, they learnt Zamonian from the farmers and traders with whom they came into contact. Later, they began to record their words and thoughts in writing. Language was one of their principal pleasures. They took to speaking in rhyme, wore long robes and elaborate jewellery. They . . . Well, they became *artists*, you understand? Artists and poets!'

Rumo stared at Smyke uncomprehendingly.

'No, you don't understand – no normal living creature could, but never mind. They liked to regard themselves as something special. Because they could write poetry, they thought their sweat smelt like perfume. They . . .'

The little Wolperting yawned.

'In other words the Lindworms became *soft* – get it? They lost their natural instincts. They wore flashy clothes and weird, made-to-measure

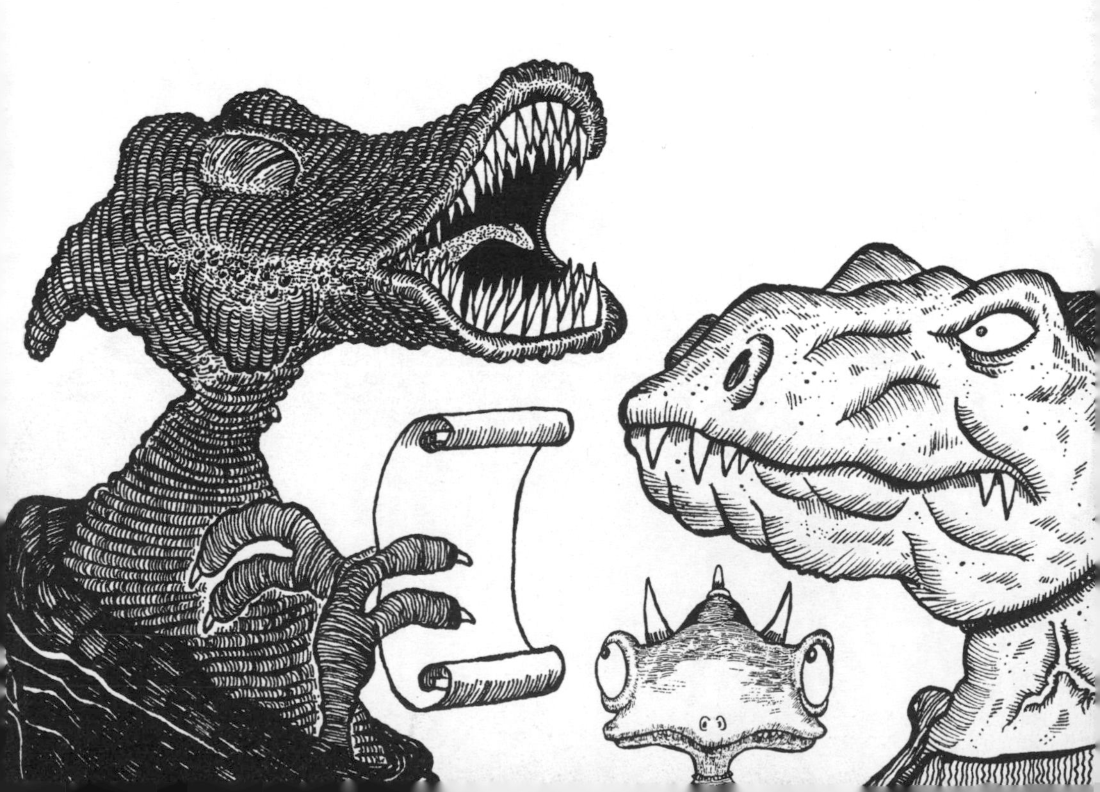

helmets designed to protect them from the fragments of rock that sometimes broke off. They paraded around in jewellery fashioned from their mountain's deposits of iron ore and crystal. No wonder the local inhabitants started to gossip. Before long it was rumoured that the occupants of Lindworm Castle were a bunch of effeminate lizards knee-deep in gold and diamonds – easy meat for anyone courageous enough to storm their stronghold. One thing led to another, until one day a besieging army suddenly appeared at the foot of Lindworm Castle.'

Rumo sat up with a start. Some fighting at last!

'It was a rabble of ill-organised Yetis – some two hundred of them, perhaps. They kicked up a din, hammered on the locked gates and yelled insults at the Lindworms – who tipped a few buckets of pitch over them and that was that. The pitch-smeared Yetis withdrew. They only attacked unfortified villages after that.'

Rumo subsided.

'But then came the *Darkmen*.'

Rumo sat up again. More fighting!

'The Darkmen were twice as numerous as the Yetis and better armed. They came equipped with scaling ladders and battering rams, and they were a fearsome-looking crew, having daubed themselves with pitch from head to foot – hence their name. There would have been little point in tipping more pitch over them, so the Lindworms used molten lead instead. That put paid to the second siege as well. The Darkmen didn't go anywhere after that.'

Smyke grinned.

'But that was when it really started! Rumours of the treasures in Lindworm Castle became ever more fanciful and exaggerated. If the Lindworms defended themselves so stoutly, it was said, they must have something to hide. There were stories of caverns filled with gold coins and precious stones; of mines in which rubies the size of a fist could be chipped from the walls with a hammer; of the so-called Lindworm Diamond, which was reputed to be as big as a house; of a secret tunnel to the centre of the earth, which the scientists of those days believed to consist of molten gold. And those were only the commonest theories about the Lindworms' treasures. Every wayfarer, every adventurer, every

fairground charlatan had a version of his own, and before long half the population of Zamonia was fantasising about them. Every mercenary eager to line his pockets put the capture of Lindworm Castle at the very top of his list. As you can imagine, it was besieged again and again by armies of Bluddums, Werewolves, Demonic Warriors and every kind of loathsome riff-raff to be found in Zamonia. But the Lindworms had only to boil up some tar or lead and tip it over them, and the besiegers got the worst of it. Indeed, plain boiling water did the trick in many cases.'

Smyke reeled off a whole series of attackers – *Mad Prince Oggnagogg and his Cadaverous Cannibals, The Stone Giants, The Horrendous Horde, The Venomous Vampires, the Implacable Impalers, The Sinister Slayers, The Diabolical Death's-Heads* – all of whom had been deluged with tar or lead or water or all three. It was the same every time.

Rumo's eyelids drooped.

'And then,' Smyke said abruptly in a low voice, 'came *The Copper Killers.*'

Rumo didn't know why, but there was something about the way Smyke laid stress on those words that made him prick up his ears.

The Copper Killers . . .

The words seemed to have been slumbering deep inside him, and now they came to life. They sounded ominous. Rumo was suddenly wide awake.

Someone rattled the grille over the mouth of the cave and grunted malevolently. Smyke and Rumo gave a start and their fellow prisoners milled around in alarm. Then the Demonocles walked off, laughing, and silence fell.

'That's the Demonoclean sense of humour for you,' said Smyke.

'Go on!' Rumo insisted.

'Ah yes, the Copper Killers. Where besiegers were concerned, they really did represent an improvement in quality, because they were said to be a cross between living creatures and machines. That made them considerably tougher and harder to wound, let alone kill, than ordinary troops. The Copper Killers were products of the legendary Battle of Nurn Forest.'

'Ah, a battle!' Rumo whispered.

Smyke grinned and leant forward.

'You mean you'd like to hear the story of the Battle of Nurn Forest before I go on with the siege of Lindworm Castle? Are you sure?'

Rumo nodded.

'A wise decision, because one story can't be understood without the other. But I must warn you!' Smyke raised several of his arms in an admonitory fashion. 'It's a terrible, bloodthirsty tale – probably the craziest episode in the history of Zamonia! Do you really want to hear it?'

The faint flush that had appeared on Smyke's face was a mark of excitement. He was into his stride. His troubles seemed temporarily forgotten and the words flowed from his lips in a steady stream.

'Yes, yes!' Rumo exclaimed. 'Go on!'

'Very well, my boy. The Battle of Nurn Forest was one of the worst bloodbaths in the annals of Zamonia. It was fought between two armies made up of every conceivable type of creature found on the mainland: Demons, Bluddums, Bearwolves – the whole caboodle. The actual reason for the battle is lost in the mists of time. We only know that when it was over, neither side could regret having started it because all involved were dead.'

The battle of Lindworm Castle

'All dead?' Rumo said disappointedly. Was the battle over already?

'Well, not all of them were really and truly dead. Many of the warriors had been butchered, but a lot of them were still alive – maimed and cut to ribbons, but more or less alive.'

Smyke sighed hoarsely. He sounded like one of those warriors breathing his last on the battlefield.

'Try to picture the scene: the gloomy depths of Nurn Forest wreathed in swaths of mist. Strewn across the blood-sodden grass were swords, pieces of armour, helmets, spears, breastplates, mailed gauntlets, greaves, clubs, battered shields, crossbows, balls and chains, knives, axes, halberds, splintered glass daggers, iron whips, knuckledusters – the participants in the Battle of Nurn Forest were the best-equipped warriors of their day, so it's said. Then there were all the dead and maimed, the severed arms and legs and heads and ears and noses and fingers and lips and eyebrows and whatever else a blade can hack off. The branches of the surrounding trees were thick with ravens and crows lured to the scene by the moans of the dying, the scent of blood. Their avid croaking and cawing filled the air, interspersed with cries of pain, vile oaths and death rattles. The birds hopped impatiently from foot to foot, pecking one another as they competed for the best places. Soon, very soon, when the last of the warriors had expired, Nurn Forest would witness its next bloodbath: the banquet of the scavenging carrion eaters.'

Rumo didn't stir. Smyke raised one hand as though listening.

'But suddenly, growing louder and louder as it neared the battlefield from a westerly direction, came the sound of voices, the rustle of footsteps on dry leaves, the squeak of wagon wheels, the jingle of harness. Was it another army?'

Rumo pricked his ears as if trying to hear the distant commotion.

'Yes, my boy, pay attention, because now comes the craziest part of the story. Approaching the forest from the west was no army, but a delegation of *Grailsundian master surgeons* on their way to an appendix conference.'

'Surgeons?'

'Yes indeed, medical experts trained to carry out operations of the most complex kind. Reattaching severed limbs, sewing up wounds, lancing veins, carrying out blood transfusions and amputations, trepanations and transplants.'

Rumo's head was spinning with unfamiliar words.

'But that isn't the craziest part of the story – oh no, my boy, for approaching from the east was a party of *itinerant watchmakers* bound for the pocket-watch fair at Wimbleton. These people specialised in constructing and repairing clocks and other intricate mechanisms. They were craftsmen with the steadiest hands, keenest sight and strongest nerves in all Zamonia.'

Rumo didn't altogether understand, but he nodded.

'But not even *that* is the craziest part of the story! For approaching from the south were over a hundred *armourers and locksmiths* on their way to Florinth, where some power-hungry prince had commissioned them to build a monstrous war machine. They were craftsmen adept at screwing and welding iron components together, constructing flintlocks and fragmentation bombs, forging metal, sharpening blades and alloying gold, silver and copper – craftsmen of war, in other words.'

'War,' said Rumo, savouring the word.

'Well, that would be enough crazy coincidences for an averagely crazy story, but the Battle of Nurn Forest involved *the most improbable set of coincidences in the history of Zamonia.* For entering the forest, this time from the north, came a delegation of *alchemists.*'

'Al . . . alki . . .'

'Alchemists! Alchemists belonged to a professional class . . . well, let's call them scientists with artistic leanings or artists with scientific aspirations, take your pick. Very erudite men, in any case. They may have been physicians or quacks or charlatans, who are we to judge at this distance in time? In those days it was possible to master the rudiments of all the sciences. The alchemists believed so, at least, and they tried to amalgamate the sciences – to interweave them so as to develop cures for diseases, or formulas for the manufacture of precious metals, or elixirs of life. They sought to discover the philosophers' stone, or perpetual motion, or the fountain of eternal youth, or ointments that would render you invulnerable or invisible. Or cheeses for use as ice skates.'

Rumo's ears were buzzing now, but not only with the thunderous roar of the waves that broke against Roaming Rock. The unfamiliar words Smyke kept spouting had combined to form a tidal wave that went foaming through the convolutions of his little brain, washing away any clear-cut ideas it contained.

'And so,' Smyke went on implacably, 'we now have alchemists, surgeons, mechanics and weaponsmiths – four very different professional groups that would not, under normal circumstances, have had anything to do with each other. After all, why should they have? And they met up in Nurn Forest of all places, on a battlefield littered with mortally wounded warriors, in a blood-soaked clearing strewn with limbs and weapons and bits of metal and battered armour.'

Rumo fidgeted impatiently. 'Well?' he said.

'What followed was an unprecedented occurrence in the history of Zamonia. These very different experts decided to pool their skills, their tools, their knowledge and equipment, and render first aid. The smiths erected their smelting furnaces and bellows, the surgeons sterilised their instruments, the mechanics polished their magnifying glasses and set up their microscopes, the alchemists heated mysterious liquids in glass retorts and stirred herbal extracts in huge cauldrons. Now, where swords had clashed and death cries had rung out only a few hours before, molten metal bubbled, whetstones sang, furnaces roared, bellows wheezed and smiths' hammers beat time. Severed limbs, discarded weapons and pieces of armour were gathered together in a big heap and carefully sorted. Separate piles were made of arms, legs, heads, helmets, knees, knee-guards and so forth. Wounds were sterilised, painkillers administered, bones splinted and one or two mercy killings performed. The experts exchanged requests and suggestions, limbs and organs, in a courteous and businesslike manner. They sometimes held brief but constructive discussions, and always decided on the simplest solution, the most logical course to adopt. Thin copper tubes were attached to arteries, muscles repaired with wires, sinews with leather thongs, nerve fibres with silk thread. An iron axe became a forearm, a watchmaker's glass an eye, a hammer a foot. Why not replace a broken spine with the pendulum from a grandfather clock, an ear with an ear trumpet, a tongue with a bell clapper?'

Rumo instinctively fingered his tongue.

'If an alchemist urgently needed some molten silver, a surgeon a microscopically small scalpel, or a locksmith a fully functional cardiac valve made of iron, the relevant experts promptly set to work to fulfil their requests. Knuckledusters were converted into teeth, watch movements into brains, sponges and gauze filters into livers and kidneys, bellows into lungs, electrified wires into nerves, vials of mercury into

blood. Herbal extracts took the place of bodily fluids, visored helmets deputised for skulls and mailed gauntlets fitted with intricate clockwork became hands. A nose missing? Screw in a spigot instead! A finger off? Substitute a clasp-knife! A heart cut out? Insert a steam pump! No surgeon had ever replaced an artery with copper tubing, no alchemist had ever assisted a watchmaker, and no locksmith had ever worked with pincers and cotton swabs. Only an incredible set of coincidences had facilitated this explosion of creative energy, this unique interaction of science, art and handicrafts, experience, ingenuity and precision engineering, that ultimately gave birth to the army of the Copper Killers.'

Smyke drew a deep breath.

'When the final hammer blows died away, the furnaces went out, and all the alchemists' potions were used up, a brand-new, spick-and-span army stood arrayed in that clearing in Nurn Forest. Because it was the fashion in those days to embellish armour and weapons with decorative designs in copper, and because that reddish metal glinted and gleamed so brightly, the creators of the bionic soldiers christened them the Copper Killers.'

'Ah,' said Rumo.

'But the army simply stood there. It stood there quite motionless, like a gigantic war memorial. The watchmakers murmured, the surgeons whispered together, the locksmiths swore. At length one of the alchemists, Zoltep Zaan by name, stepped forward and spoke: "This army will never move unless it's ordered to. Soldiers are like that – they need a commander." Zaan pointed to the remaining pile of armour, limbs and weapons – leftovers for which no use had been found.

"Let's manufacture a commander out of those," Zaan went on. "Let's make a general for the Copper Killers, and in place of a heart, brain and soul I'll insert a nugget of zamonium."

'Zam what?' asked Rumo.

'Zamonium, the rarest element in Zamonia! In addition to being able to think, it's reputed to be insane. I told you this was the craziest story of all.'

Rumo did his best to memorise the word 'zamonium', but it eluded him like a slippery fish.

'The surgeons, alchemists and armourers spent the rest of the night fitting the remaining bits and pieces together. They were so keen to use up the last little screw, the smallest spring and tiniest cogwheel, that their bionic man grew steadily bigger and more intricate.

'The crowning moment came when Zoltep Zaan added the nugget of zamonium to the last of the Copper Killers. He made a big thing out of this operation, which he performed under a blanket so that no one could see exactly where he inserted it. When the warrior was complete, the experts stepped back and inspected their latest creation. It was twice as tall as the rest and looked even more terrifying. The creature raised its head, opened its mouth, which was lined with razor-sharp blades, and spoke in a metallic voice punctuated – as if by hiccups – by the ticking of a clockwork mechanism inside it. "We have been [tick] created [tock] to kill! We are [tick] the Copper [tock] Killers!" Then it smote its breast with its fist. The other warriors did likewise, again and again, until the whole of Nurn Forest rang with the sound and all the birds flew off, squawking in alarm. "We are the Copper Killers! We are the Copper Killers!" they chanted.

'Their leader raised his hand in a soothing gesture and they all fell silent. "I," he proclaimed, "am [tick] the greatest [tock] of all [tick] Copper Killers [tock]. Call me General Ticktock!"

"General Ticktock! General Ticktock!" the Copper Killers shouted, beating time on their shields.

'Now they all waited for General Ticktock to issue his first order. The gigantic Copper Killer levelled his finger at the surgeons and watchmakers, alchemists and craftsmen to whom he owed his existence.

'"Those [tick] men there," he cried, "created us [tock]. They created us [tick] to kill [tock]. We mustn't [tick] disappoint them! [tock] Let's kill them! [tick] Let's kill them [tock] good and proper!"'

Rumo gasped. What a devil he was, this General Ticktock!

It hadn't escaped Smyke that Rumo was finding the story quite harrowing enough, so he decided to spare him the details of the ensuing butchery.

'It was a frightful massacre, but it lasted only a few minutes. The men were slaughtered like cattle. Only a few of the weaponsmiths, watchmakers, surgeons and alchemists managed to escape and spread word of what had happened in Nurn Forest. Zoltep Zaan, the inventor of General Ticktock, was among them.'

Smyke drew another deep breath.

'Well, that was the story of the Battle of Nurn Forest. But the story of the Copper Killers has only just begun.'

'Go on!' Rumo said coaxingly.

Smyke sighed. 'Do you realise that this is the third story in succession and we still haven't finished the story we began with?'

'Never mind! Go on!'

Smyke inclined his head in a submissive little gesture.

'Very well. This army of invulnerable, invincible fighting machines roamed Zamonia for years on end, spreading universal fear and trepidation. The Copper Killers captured every town they besieged, slaughtered every living creature within its walls and ended by razing it to the ground. They didn't murder and pillage in order to survive, for they weren't really alive any more. They didn't steal in order to eat and drink, for they were immune to hunger and thirst. They simply killed for killing's sake. The Copper Killers were like fate – like a natural disaster that occurred without warning, suddenly and for no reason, with the merciless fury of war itself. Their victims heard a distant ticking, a distant clatter and there they were. And, sure enough, there came a day when these copper devils, under the command of General Ticktock, appeared outside Lindworm Castle.'

'Wow!' said Rumo.

'Exactly! That's more or less what the Lindworms must have said when they saw the Copper Killers march up to their gates. The air was filled with metallic, mechanical, electrical noises: the creak of hinges, the wheezing of bellows, the crackle of alchemical batteries, the ticking of the mechanisms that served the Copper Killers as organs, sinews or muscles. It sounded as if an army of clocks had deployed outside Lindworm Castle. Bells chimed and alarms rang and the army came to a halt. All that could now be heard was the thousandfold whirring of clockwork devices and the rhythmical pounding of pistons.'

Smyke bent over and blew his nose into the pool.

'The warriors' polished copper accoutrements glittered in the sunlight,' he went on, 'and their black pennants fluttered in the wind. They conveyed an impression of absolute invincibility.'

'Pitch!' cried Rumo. 'Boiling water, molten lead!'

Smyke grinned. 'Although the Lindworms were impressed, they were very far from being intimidated. They had become accustomed to the sight of fearsome-looking warriors marching up to their stronghold armed to the teeth and they were just as accustomed to seeing them withdraw, demoralised and defeated. So they leant nonchalantly over their battlements and called down, "Push off! Beat it, you tinpot twerps! You're only wasting your time here. Others have tried what you have in mind and they all beat a hasty retreat – if they could still walk.

As for us, we're still here, as you can see. So take your warlike toys and push off. Go raid a few defenceless villages in your usual style." So saying, they chucked some flowerpots at the Copper Killers and laughed.

'For a while the army stood quite still. The Lindworms were just wondering whether flowerpots would be sufficient to put these creatures out of action when a terrible clatter filled the air. It sounded as if a huge machine had been set in motion. Metal clanked against metal, hinges creaked, and the Copper Killers' ranks parted to reveal a fearsome-looking warrior twice the size of the rest. He marched up to the foot of Lindworm Castle and spoke in a metallic voice: "I [tick] am General Ticktock. We [tock] are the Copper Killers. You [tick] are conquerable. We [tock] are invincible. You [tick] are mortal. We [tock] are immortal." '

Smyke threw up his fourteen arms. 'At that, pandemonium broke out. The Copper Killers hammered on their shields with their swords, clubs and axes, and fanatical cries issued from their iron throats.'

Rumo shuffled excitedly to and fro.

'The Lindworms, who had heard many such impudent speeches from besiegers in the past, were not overly impressed by General Ticktock's threats. They blew raspberries and showered the Copper Killers with pebbles that noisily rebounded off their armour. Thoroughly amused by the way the metallic creatures simply stood there without moving, the Lindworms proceeded to boil some pitch. The besiegers continued to stand there – excellent targets, as the pitch boilers appreciatively noted. Having positioned their buckets far more accurately than in the case of moving targets, they yelled defiance and deluged the attackers with pitch.'

'Ha ha!' said Rumo, smirking.

'But the Copper Killers didn't budge an inch. They simply stood there with the molten pitch congealing on their armour. At a signal from General Ticktock they all proceeded to shake themselves, and the solidified pitch simply cracked and fell off. Then they began to burnish one another with metal polish.'

'Molten lead!' cried Rumo.

'Well, the Lindworms weren't at a loss for long: buckets of molten lead were already bubbling away. They tipped generous helpings of it over the Copper Killers and waited for the usual cries of agony to ring out. But the Copper Killers just stood there, let the lead cool and peeled it off their armour. They were quite unscathed. General Ticktock signalled to them to storm the main gate.

Rumo was breathing heavily.

'The Lindworms assembled in the market place. They had poured away all their pitch and their lead, and boiling water would have been useless under the circumstances. That appeared to have exhausted their methods of defence, because fighting wasn't one of them. No Lindworm had ever taken up arms. Literature was their forte, not warfare! The mayor of Lindworm Castle, a many-horned black lizard of the Styracosaurian family, stepped forward and spoke in a voice trembling with agitation.

'"*This*", he said gravely, "*is the Unwelcome Moment!*"

'"*The Unwelcome Moment!*" repeated the inhabitants of Lindworm Castle, for they were now performing a well-rehearsed ritual.

'"*We all hoped it would never occur*," said the mayor, "*but we hoped in vain.*"

'"*We hoped in vain*," chanted the Lindworms.

'"*Inhabitants of Lindworm Castle!*" boomed the mayor and his voice carried to the Copper Killers waiting below. "*We're on the brink of the abyss. What shall we do?*"

The music of the stars

"*We shall dance to the music of the stars!*" chorused the Lindworms.'

Rumo looked at Smyke, but the Shark Grub seemed to be lost in another world – far, far away from Roaming Rock.

'Well,' he went on, 'it was broad daylight. There wasn't a star to be seen in the sky, nor could any music be heard, far less the music of the spheres. But that wasn't the point. "Brink of the abyss" and "music of the stars" were metaphorical phrases devised many years before by some Lindworm poets who wanted to lend the ritual a solemn, sophisticated character. Well, the metaphors weren't all that sophisticated – they were rather banal, in fact, but they served their purpose: they put the Lindworms in a belligerent frame of mind appropriate to the gravity of their predicament.'

Rumo opened his mouth to ask what 'music of the spheres' and 'metaphorical' meant, but Smyke steadfastly continued his account.

'Then the Lindworms proceeded to dance. Some of them seized musical instruments – tambourines, flutes and guitars – and struck up a lively tune that went straight to the legs. This, too, was part of the ritual. The melody and rhythm were strictly preordained, and every inhabitant of Lindworm Castle had been drilled in the dance steps at school, the essential thing being to stamp as hard as possible.

'The Copper Killers, listening far below, were puzzled. "They're making music," one of General Ticktock's aides whispered to him.

'It wasn't the music that alarmed General Ticktock, it was the rhythmical stamping that was giving him food for thought.

'Why? Because the walls shook when a dinosaur danced. When several dinosaurs danced they produced an earthquake. And when all the dinosaurs in Lindworm Castle danced at once the world itself began to crumble.'

Rumo gasped.

'Quite suddenly the sky seemed to fall in. A chunk of rock the size of a house came hurtling down and struck the ground not far from General Ticktock and his aides – not without burying twenty Copper Killers beneath it.

'"They're throwing stones!" cried one of the general's aides.

'"They're throwing boulders!" cried another.

'"They're throwing mountains!" cried a third. There was a "whoosh!" as if a flock of birds were swooping down on him, and a boulder hammered him ten feet into the ground.

'"Damnation [tick]!" cried General Ticktock. "Withdraw at once [tock]!" And he turned about and clanked off.

'The Copper Killers were completely flummoxed by this order. They had never retreated before, always advanced. Had they misheard? Instead of promptly obeying the general's word of command as usual, they marked time for a few seconds. It was that moment of indecision which sealed the fate of the majority. There was another even louder, even more ominous rumble as if the bowels of the earth were in turmoil. Then they saw, descending on them from Lindworm Castle, a huge grey avalanche of rock. It engulfed the Copper Killers like a curtain and relentlessly crushed them into scrap iron.'

Smyke emitted a weary sigh.

'Two thirds of the Copper Killers' army was destroyed within seconds and buried beneath many feet of debris. The remainder, including General Ticktock, managed to escape. He went straight to hell, so it's said.'

Rumo gasped. The villain had got away. That wasn't right.

'Well,' said Smyke, 'that was the story of the Copper Killers, but it wasn't the last time Lindworm Castle was besieged, not by a long chalk.'

Rumo was flabbergasted. Would another army – an even more fearsome army than that of the Copper Killers – come marching along? He prepared himself to hear the worst.

'No, that was only the last *military* siege of Lindworm Castle. After the way they'd dealt with the Copper Killers, not even the boldest mercenaries in Zamonia would have dreamt of attacking them again. On the contrary, for a long time life in Lindworm Castle was very, very uneventful. Nobody ventured near the place and the inhabitants began to get bored. Indeed, they even began to yearn for the old warlike days.'

The drums had started up again outside on Roaming Rock, far enough away to be muffled by the thunder of the surf.

The Smarmies' stratagem

'Then along came the Smarmies, and with them the first *peaceful* siege of Lindworm Castle.'

Rumo pricked up his ears. A peaceful siege? Was that possible? Still, anything seemed possible on this night of wondrous stories.

'Yes,' Smyke went on, 'the Smarmies came in peace. A motley bunch of vagabonds from all parts of Zamonia, they dressed in clothes of many colours. The Lindworms' poems and other writings, which had now been circulating for decades, had clearly gained a lot of admirers. What was more, accounts of the sieges they underwent had earned them a heroic reputation. The Lindworms had never picked a fight with anyone, they had merely defended themselves. And, heedless of these incessant threats, they had bravely continued to turn out literary works. No wonder they were idolised.

'The Smarmies pitched their tents around Lindworm Castle, tossed bouquets and eulogies over the battlements, proclaimed that the Lindworms were geniuses, read aloud from their writings and held poetry festivals in their honour. The Lindworms leant over the battlements and watched this spectacle – sceptically at first, being experienced in the ways of besiegers. However, the Smarmies' motives seemed irreproachable. Around the castle they set up small print shops devoted exclusively to publishing the Lindworms' writings, as well as glowing reviews of the same. The Lindworms threw down handwritten poems, which were ceremoniously read aloud and guarded like precious relics.

'After a few weeks' mutual observation and cautious contacts, the Lindworms conferred in the market place and resolved to send some delegates to check on the situation. Five Lindworms made their first exit from the castle for a long time. Having received a rousing ovation from the Smarmies, who strewed flowers and laurel leaves in their path, they were escorted into the tent of the Smarmies' leader – a rather portly individual, so it's said.

'"Dear Lindworms," he said, "let's forget all that nonsense about the treasure hidden in your castle. It's just a fairy tale designed to appeal to demented Yetis. The treasure you *really* possess is of far greater value."

'The Lindworms stared at each other in surprise. The Smarmy's tone conveyed less respect than they were accustomed to.

'"This," he said, picking up a sheaf of their poems, "is the true treasure of Lindworm Castle."

'The Lindworms were flattered, but they wondered what he was getting at.

'"Cards on the table, gentlemen. I'm a publisher. I publish books and I make money out of them. A lot of money."

'The Lindworms winced at the note that had suddenly come into his voice.

"Heroism, martyrdom – those are what win literary prizes. What you write about isn't so important. *Celebrity* – that's the magic word."

'The Lindworms were still at a loss for words.

'"Yes, celebrity and popularity, that's what constitutes your treasure. A whole castle full of heroes who write poems – what better authors could a publisher wish for? My dear Lindworms, your poems coupled with my printing machines and the Smarmies' word-of-mouth – that's better than a licence to mint money. I would ask you to think it over carefully."

'The Lindworms were furious. The Smarmies had duped them, wounded their literary self-esteem and made them an insulting offer. Fuming, they left the tent and returned to the castle to inform their fellow dinosaurs of what had happened.

'The other Lindworms were just as infuriated. One or two ultra-radical artistic souls advocated tipping molten lead over the Smarmies. An argument broke out and one of the dinosaurs ventured to predict what would happen if they drove the Smarmies away: they would withdraw, leaving Lindworm Castle to stew in its own juice. No one would besiege it any more, not even with peaceful intent. They would read their poems aloud to each other until they dropped, and one day in the not far distant future the Lindworms would become extinct, like their stupid ancestors. They would sink into oblivion. That was one possibility.

'The other was that they come to terms with the Smarmies. The result? Fame, money, literary prizes, immortality. Weren't those the true objectives of any writer?

'No, cried another Lindworm. Truth and beauty - those were the virtues, the grand aspirations a writer should cultivate, nothing else. He was shouted down.

'The previous speaker took the floor again. He spoke very loudly and deliberately: *They, the inhabitants of Lindworm Castle, were on the brink of an abyss. Would it not be appropriate for them to dance to the music of the stars?*

'He had put his finger on the salient point: "the abyss" was artistic anonymity; "the music of the stars" was public acclaim.

'"I want to make my mark!" shouted one Lindworm.

'"I want some good reviews!" shouted another.

'A babble of voices filled the market place. Everyone talked at once. "This is a commercial sell-out!" cried one very elderly Lindworm, but that was the last critical comment to be heard. It was decided to invite the Smarmies to a big reception in the market place. For the first time ever, and only for their most devoted admirers, the Lindworms would throw open their castle gates. It was the beginning of a golden future.'

Rumo was growing impatient. He wondered when Smyke would get down to business again.

'The great day soon came. A long ceremonial procession of Smarmies wound its way up into the castle, scattering flowers and laudatory leaflets as it went. There was music, singing and red wine for all. When the Smarmies reached the market place, their portly leader waddled forward. Beckoning the mayor to his side, he made an announcement: "This is the dawn of a new era. It will be an era devoid of Lindworms."

'The Lindworms looked startled.

'"It will be an era in which the dissemination of Lindworm literature is prohibited on pain of death – an era in which being a Lindworm carries the death penalty."

'The mayor stared at him in horror. Was this a joke? How dared the fellow profane this solemn occasion in such an unseemly fashion? Then the Smarmies' leader reached under his robe, drew out a dagger and held it to the mayor's throat.

'"Seriously, folks!" he cried. "It's up to you. If you want to survive, you must answer a few simple questions. Where's your diamond the size of a house? Where's your lake filled with emeralds? Where's your tunnel to the centre of the earth?"'

Rumo gave a start. Had the Smarmies come armed?

'Several Lindworms cried out in alarm as the Smarmies tore off their colourful robes. Swords, daggers and suits of armour came to light beneath them.

'"Yes, that's how it is! No more soft soap!" the leader said with a laugh. He released the mayor and left the dirty work to his soldiers.'

Rumo gasped. The Smarmies were even worse than the Copper Killers! Even he had been taken in by them.

'Yes,' said Smyke, 'the Smarmies were really ex-soldiers who had all taken part in some of the sieges of Lindworm Castle. Their bodies were covered with burns, their faces glowed with hatred. Not long ago some of them had met up in a disreputable Grailsundian tavern and talked themselves into a rage. The innkeeper was the Smarmies' corpulent commander, and it was he who had devised the cunning plan to mobilise all the soldiers wounded while besieging Lindworm Castle and capture the stronghold by devious means. And the plan had really worked!'

Rumo growled. What a low-down, dirty trick!

'On one side were the heavily armed, battle-hardened, vengeful, bloodthirsty soldiers; on the other the effete, poetry-writing, unarmed Lindworms – bereft of their boiling pitch and molten lead. The final battle for Lindworm Castle seemed to be developing into a very unequal contest.'

Rumo nodded gravely. It would be no battle, just an even more frightful massacre than the one the Copper Killers had perpetrated on their creators.

'But then . . .' – something in Smyke's tone made Rumo prick up his ears again – 'a remarkable thing happened. It came as a surprise to the soldiers, but even more so to the Lindworms themselves. For a few moments absolute silence reigned in the market place. Even the soldiers froze as if sensing imminent disaster. Then a change came over the Lindworms' appearance, their manner, their eyes and faces. Their whimpers of fear gave way to terrifying, predatory snarls; they bared their carefully hidden fangs, their jaws opened wide like bear traps, slaver overflowed their chops, and their throats emitted sounds that would have sent a troop of red gorillas clambering up the nearest tree in double-quick time. Some of them tore off their silken robes and displayed their mighty packets of muscle. Yes, the slumbering instincts of the Lindworms' huge carnivorous ancestors had been awakened by this immediate threat. In an instant' – Smyke snapped his fingers – 'the effeminate dwellers in an ivory tower had turned into ravening primeval lizards.'

Rumo clenched his little fists and punched the air in excitement. There was going to be a fight after all!

'It was only now that the real battle for Lindworm Castle began – a bloodbath compared to which the Battle of Nurn Forest must have been a minor skirmish. The Lindworms possessed no weapons; they *were* their own weapons – perfectly constructed fighting machines more deadly even than the Copper Killers and equipped with dragons' armoured scales instead of iron shields, razor-sharp fangs instead of daggers, gigantic claws instead of sabres.

'But don't imagine that the soldiers dropped their weapons in alarm. They were dumbfounded by the sight of the Lindworms' gaping jaws, not having expected to encounter any resistance, but they were the most experienced warriors in Zamonia, veterans whose mettle had been tested in countless battles, countless ordeals by fire. They had dealt with dangers quite different from those presented by a bunch of wild beasts. Besides, they were armed to the teeth and dinosaurs were not invulnerable.

'The carnage was appalling. Unprecedented scenes unfolded in the alleyways of Lindworm Castle. It was men versus primeval beasts, sabres versus fangs, swords versus claws. The dinosaurs roared, the soldiers bellowed, blades buried themselves in saurian bodies, heads were ripped

off by saurian teeth, blood spurted, fragments of flesh flew in all directions, spears pierced the great lizards' scaly armour, dragonlike tails sliced bodies in half at a single stroke. The battle raged all day, and there was no one anywhere on the castle rock who remained unstained with blood, whether his own or that of his foes.

'Half the inhabitants of Lindworm Castle lost their lives that day, but the only one of the Smarmies to survive, so it's said, was their leader. Nobody knows his name and nobody knows how he escaped the slaughter. When nightfall came, anyone wishing to traverse the castle's alleyways had to step over mounds of corpses. The blood was ankle-deep. It flowed into the sewers and down the mountainside, staining the entire castle blood-red.'

Rumo was breathing heavily. It had been more of a fight than he'd expected.

'And that, my boy,' Smyke concluded, 'was the story of the sieges of Lindworm Castle. There are many lessons to be drawn from it. Pick one when you get a chance.'

And he rolled his eyes and slowly submerged.

Growing pains

Rumo had acquired twenty-five new teeth in the eight weeks he'd spent as a prisoner on Roaming Rock. Many were broad, short and blunt, others long with needle-sharp points or flat and thin with cutting edges as keen as a knife. The pain inflicted by Rumo's sprouting teeth had become an unpredictable visitor that kept moving around his mouth. Sometimes it lodged at the back of the upper jaw, sometimes at the front of the lower jaw, sometimes in the left cheek, sometimes in the right, and sometimes in three or four places at once. Rumo's efforts to ignore it were aided by the rewards this agony brought in its train. Whenever a place stopped hurting it meant that nature had presented him with a new work of art.

Besides, he had learnt how to use these new tools of his. There was a piece of driftwood lying in the corner of his niche and he chewed it as often as he could. After only a few days it looked as if it had been attacked by termites.

Rumo noticed other changes in his body. His funny little forepaws were developing into slender hands composed of three fingers and a thumb armed with sharp, graceful claws. The most fascinating thing was that he could now grasp objects with them. This gave him a wonderfully pleasurable sensation, as if he had been presented with additional power over things. The muscles in his hind legs were swelling and his fur was becoming smoother. Everything about him seemed to be growing tauter, more supple, bigger and stronger. His coat was losing its pinkish shade and turning white as snow. He didn't look as cute, but this was offset by his increasingly handsome appearance. His snub nose was developing into a thin, elegant muzzle, his baby fat into symmetrical rows of stomach muscles and his forelegs were becoming athletic, muscular arms. His shoulders were growing broader while his waist remained slim, his big saucer eyes were narrowing into mysterious, predatory slits. Rumo was growing up, an abnormally rapid process in the case of a Wolperting.

'I can actually see you growing,' Smyke told him. 'You walk across the cave and you're a head taller when you reach the other side.'

Rumo gave a sheepish laugh. He had been unable to squeeze into his niche for several days. Like all the rest, he now had to remain in the cave when the Demonocles came visiting, and they couldn't fail to notice him in the end. Their mouths watered at the sight of such an interesting beast. Lions and red gorillas were considered great delicacies, and it delighted them to watch their muscles and sinews twitch as they skinned them alive. But this creature – this horned dog with dark eyes and silky white fur – was unlike any animal they had ever kept on Roaming Rock before. It promised to be even more delicious than all the big game they had ever torn to pieces. The Demonocles treated Rumo as if he were maturing in their cave like an exceptionally precious bottle of vintage wine.

Rumo thought his hour had struck whenever the one-eyed monsters came to gawp at him, which they continually did. Smyke had urged him to walk on all fours and he did so whenever Demonocles were present, but that could not disguise his attractions. The cave was sometimes visited by Demonocles who thrust him into a corner, grunting and smacking their lips – their way, it seemed, of discussing his physical development. They pinched his legs and stomach muscles, sniffed his fur, plucked out hairs and examined them. The saliva gushed from their stinking mouths as they rejoiced in his lightning reflexes, and he could tell that it was all they could do not to sink their fangs into him on the spot. Every time they departed without dragging him away he felt he had been born anew.

Rumo's physical development was matched by his linguistic progress. He was now capable of conversing fluently with Smyke. Although his own use of words was still on a par with that of a traveller who has been studying a foreign language for only a few weeks, he could understand nearly everything.

The Wolpertings

'What's happening to me?' Rumo asked Smyke one night. The waves were breaking against Roaming Rock with exceptional violence, filling its interior with a thunderous, awe-inspiring roar. 'Why am I growing so fast?'

'Because you're a Wolperting,' Smyke replied.

Rumo put his head on one side, as he always did when an answer dissatisfied him.

Smyke sighed. 'Oh well,' he said, 'I think it's about time you learnt something about yourself and your breed. I don't know all that much, but . . .'

'Go on!' Rumo commanded.

Smyke drew a deep breath. 'There's a saying about Wolpertings that probably conveys more about them than any other. It's: *You might as well tangle with a Wolperting.*' Smyke grinned. 'The Zamonians often use that phrase when they want to dissuade someone from doing something incredibly stupid, something that could be lethal or is doomed to failure. Wolpertings have inherited the characteristics of wolves and deer. That makes them strong, wild, skittish, nimble and dangerous. They have instincts and reflexes possessed by no other living creature in Zamonia and their sensory organs have developed in a unique way. They can see with their noses and ears if need be. They're so fast and agile that their movements sometimes convey a magical impression.'

Rumo pricked up his ears. Although Smyke was using rather high-flown language, he gathered that he was trying to explain that Wolpertings were very special creatures. Why had he withheld this gratifying information for so long?

'Wolpertings fall into two categories: the wild ones, who never learn to speak and spend their lives on all fours, and the civilised ones, who sooner or later stand up on their hind legs and start to speak. When Wolperting whelps reach the age at which they develop their first fangs it becomes apparent which they are, wild or civilised. You clearly belong to the second category.'

The words that had slumbered inside Rumo, the peculiar mixture of thoughts and sensations that had arisen within him . . . He was beginning to understand them now.

'Intellectually, wild Wolpertings are more or less on a par with wolves and live mainly in the forests and steppes of Zamonia. Many of them can even be tamed and spend their lives on farms, where they act as well-tended watchdogs.'

Smyke gave Rumo a long look before he went on. Yes, he had decided to tell him the truth, even if he couldn't grasp it yet.

'You're an orphan, Rumo. It's one of the ruthless traditions of your breed that Wolperting parents, both wild and civilised, abandon their newborn whelps in the wilderness soon after birth. If they develop into wild Wolpertings they've already found their natural habitat. If they're capable of speech they have to find their way to civilisation unaided.'

Rumo was feeling overtaxed. Words like *orphan*, *ruthless*, *habitat* and *civilisation* meant nothing to him. 'So where am *I* going?' he asked.

Smyke laughed. 'You're going nowhere. You're on Roaming Rock.'

Rumo cocked his head again.

'Listen,' said Smyke, lowering his voice. 'If I told you of a plan to escape from this cave and release the others, what would you think of it?'

'It would be good,' said Rumo.

'What if I said you're the most important part of this plan?'

'I'd be proud,' said Rumo.

'And what if I said you'd have to risk your life in order to carry it out?'

'I'd be even prouder.'

'Good. I'll give the plan some more thought and tell you about it when the time is ripe,' said Smyke, holding out one of his little hands. Rumo shook it. It was moist and sticky, but he felt very honoured all the same.

Smyke taught Rumo something new about fighting every day. Tricks and technique were seldom mentioned. Smyke enjoyed lecturing on the theoretical aspects of combat, and there were times when Rumo didn't understand a word. One day, for instance, Smyke told him, 'It's trite but true to say that thinking too much while you're fighting is a positive disadvantage. Don't get me wrong: a good fighter mustn't be a brainless idiot. He must simply have the strength to decide to act rather than think at the crucial moment. No, what am I saying? Strength doesn't come into it. The opposite is true. The decision mustn't be an effort. It must be like relieving yourself.'

Rumo gave a puzzled growl and knitted his brow.

'When you pass water you're releasing something pent up inside you, right? It's like being set free – it's easy, satisfying and positively enjoyable: you simply let go. If you wanted to you could pass water all day long, wherever you happen to be, but you don't. Instead of making a mess you hold it in until it hurts. Then you let it flow and it's a relief, am I right? Well, that's just the way you should fight: as if you were peeing.'

Rumo was bewildered. Smyke had been rhapsodising about heroic battles and victories the whole time, and now he was talking about passing water. Wolpertings urinated often, like any Zamonian life form whose veins contained the blood of primeval dogs, but he couldn't fathom what his fat friend was getting at.

'Think about it!' said Smyke.

Rumo recalled Smyke's remarks later on, when he was relieving himself in a dark corner of the cave, but he still didn't understand. What had peeing to do with fighting?

Rumo dreams of vengeance

By now, nearly all the Hackonians who had raised Rumo were gone. The Demonocles had dragged them out of the cave one by one and none had ever returned. Rumo lamented their disappearance because by this time he knew what had happened to them. In addition to teeth and muscles, he was developing an unpleasant feeling as regards the Demonocles. It was a hopeless, helpless, desperate emotion – a wish to make the Demonocles pay for what they had done to his dead friends. In other words he thirsted for revenge. He knew at the same time that he was powerless against the Demonocles, being so small and weak by comparison. He was growing, yes, and growing fast, but even if he developed into the strongest and most dangerous Wolperting of all time, what could one solitary creature do against hundreds of Demonocles? He couldn't expect any assistance from the surviving Hackonian dwarfs, nor from Smyke, that ungainly tub of lard. Even if the strongest creatures in the cave, the wild beasts, joined forces with him, they wouldn't stand a chance against the one-eyed giants.

What on earth could Smyke's plan be?

Giant-repellent

The prisoners in the cave had resigned themselves to their fate as time went by. They'd grasped that it was pointless to spend the whole day weeping and wailing. Not even fear lasts for ever; sooner or later everlasting danger transforms it into apathy. Although the Hackonians' hearts still missed a beat whenever a Demonocle entered the cave, they had devised ways of making themselves look as inconspicuous, unattractive and unappetising as possible. Many of them had smeared themselves with slime from Smyke's pool, which Rumo, being free to move around, gladly distributed among them. Word had spread that movement whetted the Demonocles' appetite, so they kept as still as possible or pretended to be asleep whenever one of them inspected the cave.

This had no real effect on the one-eyed monsters' voracious habits, because they had ways and means of making their prey twitch if they thought it necessary. The only place they steered well clear of was Smyke's pool, the source of the evil-smelling slime.

Rumo was proud of being the only one in the cave with a potent antidote to fear: he could go to see Volzotan Smyke and be transported into another world. Words were so incredibly powerful! Although many still meant nothing to him and were simply meaningless sounds, others had barely escaped Smyke's lips when they became transformed into marvellous images that filled Rumo's head and drove his fear away. Sometimes, when Smyke was telling an especially interesting story, image succeeded image until the flood of impressions transported Rumo far away into other, better times. Smyke had an answer to every question, sometimes satisfying, sometimes productive of even greater bewilderment, but even bewilderment was preferable to frozen despair.

Netherworld

One evening, when some Demonocles had behaved even more barbarously than usual and torn a piglet to pieces before Rumo's eyes, his feeling of impotence threatened to turn into uncontrollable panic. Dark questions took shape in his head. Unable to answer them himself, he went to see Smyke.

'What's new, Rumo?' asked Smyke. He propped his head on the edge of the pool like a lazy seal while the rest of his body remained hidden in the slime.

Rumo sighed. 'I was wondering if there's any place more frightful than this one.'

Smyke had to think harder than usual before something occurred to him.

'They say there is,' he replied.

'Worse than here? What's it called?'

'Netherworld,' said Smyke.

'Netherworld . . .' Rumo repeated. It sounded sinister.

'I don't know if it's an actual place or just a word. Perhaps it's just a tall tale. I've often heard soldiers speak of it around their campfires. They say there's another world beneath this one and it's filled with evil, vicious creatures. Everyone has his own idea of the place, but I've never met anyone who has actually been there.'

'Maybe it's because no one who goes to evil places ever comes back.'

'You're in a grim mood today, my boy. How about a riddle?'

'All right,' said Rumo. 'Ask me one.'

Smyke had taken to setting Rumo simple problems. It sharpened the youngster's wits and dispelled his gloomy thoughts.

'What can penetrate a wall but isn't a nail?' asked Smyke.

'No idea,' said Rumo.

'I know, but I want you to work it out.'

And he sank back into his pool, because he couldn't have endured any more questions that evening.

One afternoon the grille slid back with a crash and four Demonocles charged in, bellowing. Rumo had an uneasy feeling as the giants strode across the cave. They came straight for him, grabbed him by the arms and threw him into the empty cage from which they'd taken the lion. Then they locked the door of the cage and strode out. Rumo's free-ranging days were over. He shook the bars and growled at the departing giants. The cage was cramped, which meant he would have to relieve himself where he slept. He too was now at the Demonocles' mercy. He shook the bars again, but they were immovable and not even his teeth could bite through metal. How would Smyke explain his plan now? He couldn't visit the pool any more and the Shark Grub had never left his slimy basin. Rumo had no idea if he was capable of doing so.

Smyke had dived to the bottom of his pool, where not even his dorsal fin showed above the surface. The big fat bubbles that rose from the depths burst with a revolting sound, pervading the cave with a noisome stench of sulphur.

Smyke was pondering. One aspect of his escape plan had still to be worked out. For this he needed certain information. He couldn't quite put his finger on it, but he knew that he could refresh his powers of recall in the Chamber of Memories. Having excreted some extra big bubbles of slime, he set off through the convolutions of his brain in the slow, leisurely way that came naturally to him.

Then he entered the Chamber of Memories. Ignoring the draped picture as usual, he resolutely made for one he hadn't looked at for a long time. It was a picture of a table: one of the red felt gaming tables to be found in all Fort Una's gambling dens. The felt was littered with coloured wooden gaming chips, and as he looked at them he also heard the hum of voices, the whirr of roulette wheels and the rattle of dice – all the sounds that had once filled his days and nights. And then he was sitting at the table, *his* gaming table, which he ran in his capacity as an officially certified croupier and dealer. He wanted to remember one particular night – the night the mad professor had come to his table.

The professor with seven brains

'Excuse me,' said the peculiar little gnome, 'but would you permit me to have a bit of a flutter?'

Being a croupier accustomed to people with far coarser manners, Smyke was amused by his courteous tone.

'Of course,' he replied. 'How about a hand of rumo?'

'Whatever you suggest,' said the gnome and he took his place at the table. He was obviously a Nocturnomath, a Zamonian life form with several brains. Smyke had never seen one before, but the grotesque excrescences on the goggle-eyed, humpbacked creature's head matched other people's descriptions of the breed.

'May I introduce myself? Nightingale's the name - Professor Abdullah Nightingale.'

Smyke inclined his head. 'Smyke - Volzotan Smyke. For a start, then, a hand of rumo.' He dealt the cards.

The professor won every game they played: rumo, Midgardian rummy, Florinthian poker, Catch the Troll and, finally, rumo again. Before three hours were up a small fortune in coloured chips was piled high in front of him. He was clearly using a system based on the number seven - that much Smyke had gathered.

Nightingale placed his bets in stacks of seven chips on numbers divisible by seven, and he also played his cards according to a system somehow based on seven. He not only drew attention to this each time but explained his intricate calculations, which entailed the addition, multiplication and division of figures up to seven digits long, until Smyke's brain was in turmoil. The Nocturnomath won again and again. He wasn't there to make money, he declared, but to test a mathematical system.

The sweat that was streaming down Smyke's face had nothing to do with the torrid atmosphere of the gambling den; it was the cold sweat of mortal fear. The table was surrounded by curious spectators, among them the owners of the saloon, two Vulpheads named Henko and Hasso van Drill. One-eyed twins and former highwaymen, Henko and Hasso had amassed their starting capital by strangling well-heeled travellers in the neighbourhood of Devil's Gulch. It was their hard-earned money that was passing into the professor's possession.

Although Fort Una's gambling dens did not cheat their patrons outright, they were run on semi-criminal lines. This meant that the ultimate winners were the owners of the gambling dens, not their customers. To ensure that the system ran smoothly, the owners employed people like Smyke, professional card-sharks who could beat the average player without cheating. They sometimes let the gamblers win and even paid out substantial sums, but the house always made a decent profit by the end of the night. And now this professor was overturning the whole concept of Fort Una. He was winning every game without exception. That wasn't just a run of luck; it was a breach of Fort Una's unwritten law: *Everyone loses in the end.*

Smyke was powerless to prevent Nightingale from multiplying his winnings every time. If he went on this way the house would be bankrupt after a few more games. The Vulpheads gave Smyke a look that conveyed some idea of the treatment he could expect in the alley behind the saloon if he failed to end the professor's lucky streak in a very short time.

'How about another hand?' the professor asked brightly as he arranged his chips in stacks of seven. 'I'm developing quite a taste for gambling.'

'As you wish,' Smyke said in a choking voice. 'With us, the customer is king.'

'You ought to do something about that excessive perspiration of yours,' the professor said, glancing at the film of sweat on Smyke's brow. 'Salt tablets work wonders sometimes.'

Smyke dealt the cards with an agonised smile. The professor mumbled some figures, staked his entire winnings on a single hand, played his cards in accordance with his absurd system of sevens – and won again.

'My goodness.' He chuckled as he raked in his winnings. 'What am I to do with all this money? I shall probably invest it in darkness research, or possibly construct an oracular chest of drawers. The possibilities are limitless! Another hand?'

He won four more games, which almost cleaned out the Vulpheads. Smyke's heart was pounding, his head spinning. He yearned to wring the mad professor's scraggy, vulturine neck, but the Vulphead brothers would save him the trouble. Another mysterious accident in a lawless town: a fatal fall down the back steps of a gambling den sustained by an absent-minded, intoxicated professor whose clothes reeked of brandy. No one would give a damn. A doctor bribed by the Vulpheads would

make out the death certificate ('Accidental death, self-induced. Evidence of alcohol abuse.') and there would be one more nameless grave in the desert behind Fort Una.

In despair, Smyke longed to inform the Nocturnomath that he was gambling with his own life as well as the dealer's. The spectators and the Vulphead brothers pressed closer, listening expectantly to the polite conversation in progress between the dealer and the gambler.

'**I know**,' said a voice in Smyke's head.

'That's great!' he thought. 'I'm so scared I've lost my wits. I'm starting to hear voices.'

'**You're only hearing one voice and it's mine. It's me, Nightingale**,' said the voice. '**Don't give yourself away**.'

Smyke tensed, staring across the table. The professor appeared to be engrossed in his hand.

'**Listen: I possess the gift of telepathy. No big deal for a Nocturnomath - we all have it. And now to your problem. I may seem a trifle unsophisticated, but I'm not tired of life. I've no intention of letting two notorious villains stab me to death in a dark alley, or something similar, for the sake of filthy lucre. However, I'd like to finish testing my system,**

savour my triumph to the full and leave these crooks to sweat a little longer. Shall we play another hand of rumo?'

Either it really was the professor's voice he was hearing, or he'd gone mad after all – Smyke wasn't sure. The Nocturnomath hadn't favoured him with a single glance throughout his speech; in fact, he been joking with the gamblers and crooks standing around them. Mechanically, Smyke dealt the cards.

'What, another hand?' the professor said loudly. 'I was going to call it a night, actually, but never mind. One more, then. All or nothing as before?'

The Vulphead brothers scowled and felt in their pockets to satisfy themselves that their Florinthian glass daggers were there.

'All or nothing!' the professor cried gaily. Everyone held their breath.

'Er, *777,777,777.77* divided by *7,777,777.777* divided by *77* comes to, er, er . . .' the professor muttered to himself, moving his cards around with maddening deliberation. Smyke's rivulets of perspiration had combined to form an oily film that covered his entire body. He glistened like a waxed apple.

'Professor?' he called desperately in his head. 'Professor? Surely you don't intend to win *again*? That would be suicide. Suicide and murder, if you include me!'

But there was no reply.

'Let's see,' muttered the Nocturnomath. 'The square root of *777,777,777,777.7* divided by the product of *77,777,777.777* times *777* to the power of, er, 7, makes, er . . .' The rest was unintelligible. The professor laid his cards down one by one. He had won yet again.

'Professor?!' If Smyke's thoughts had been audible; that would have been an anguished cry.

Nightingale looked at him expressionlessly. 'Where can I cash in my chips?' he asked. 'I hope you'll provide me with some sacks to carry my winnings in.'

'Of course,' one of the Vulpheads said coolly. 'We'll settle up with you in our office, that's the best plan. Over a couple of drinks on the house.'

Smyke's head was spinning. He could already see himself lying sprawled in the alley, choking on his own blood.

'Another hand?' he cried desperately.

If anything had sealed his fate it was those words. The Vulpheads might otherwise have let him off with a few broken arms and a tongue-lashing, but now he had focused everyone's attention on the professor once more – just when the brothers had almost persuaded him to accompany them to their office. That was tantamount to a self-imposed death sentence.

'Another hand of rumo?' said the professor. 'Double or quits?'

Smyke nodded.

Nightingale grinned. 'Why not?'

Smyke shuffled the cards again and dealt. Nightingale began to mumble figures to himself, and it was all the Vulpheads could do not to murder the professor and their croupier in front of everyone.

'7,777,777.7 multiplied by 7 is, er . . .' Nightingale glanced at the Vulpheads to see whether they were sweating too. They were.

Smyke made another half-hearted attempt at mental communication. 'Professor?' he telepathised. 'Professor Nightingale?'

No response. Nightingale was tapping his cards, lost in thought.

'7,777,777.7 multiplied by 7 to the power of 7 minus the square root of 777 makes, er . . .'

'Professor!' Smyke yelled in his head. 'Are you there?'

Nothing. Not a sound, not a flicker of emotion on Nightingale's face. So he really had succumbed to a hallucination engendered by his own panic.

'777,777,777.777 multiplied by 77 divided by the sum of 7,777 plus 777,777 times 777 divided by 6 . . .' burbled the professor.

Smyke gave a start. Divided by *six*? It was the first time Nightingale's calculations had included any number apart from seven.

The Nocturnomath laid his cards down with an amiable smile. The spectators bent over the table. A groan ran round the saloon. The professor had lost.

'**Yes?**' said Nightingale's voice in Smyke's head. '**You called me?**'

Smyke didn't reply, he was too busy raking in the professor's chips and exchanging looks of relief with the Vulphead brothers, who could now let go of their glass daggers.

'That was an interesting experience,' the professor told Smyke in his normal voice as the crowd dispersed. 'Easy come, easy go! It seems that the mathematical system capable of defeating chance has yet to be devised. At all events, mine will be consigned to the *Chamber of Unperfected Patents*. Self-criticism is the mother of invention.'

Smyke stared at him. 'But you could have gone on winning for ever, you know that perfectly well.'

Nightingale rose and laid his hand on Smyke's shoulder. 'There's only one thing that goes on for ever, and that's darkness.'

At that moment something happened: the reason why Smyke had entered the Chamber of Memories and seen the picture of the gaming table. When the professor's hand touched his shoulder a tidal wave of information surged through Smyke's brain so swiftly and unexpectedly that it jolted his head and almost sent him toppling over backwards, complete with his chair.

Through that brief physical contact the absent-minded Nocturnomath had deliberately or inadvertently collated the ideas that were racing through his various brains and transmitted them to Smyke by means of his telepathic ability to infect others with intellectual bacteria – for Nightingale a quite commonplace process, for Smyke a memorable experience. Briefly summarised, those ideas related to seismographic oscillations in the Gloomberg Mountains; astronomical vortex physics (black holes, nebular motion, solar-system rotation); chemical communication between South Zamonian insects, reptiles and orchids (olfactory transmission of information, exchanges of fluid between garter snakes, pollen vibration by nectar-producing Venus flytraps and the haptic ability of Zamonian honey bees to communicate with Zamonian flora); geodetic anomalies in the Demerara Desert and their influence on Zamonian travelogues; the connection between the alpenhorn music of Demon Range and the prevalence of avalanches in the same region; and the repercussions of nocturnomathic philosophysics on the pseudo-scientific writings of Hildegard Mythmaker. They also related to the Zebraskan glorification of obstinacy; to deposits of sea salt in algal dimensions; to the telepathic perception of multicerebral life forms when massively bombarded with scintillas and irradiated with will-o'-the-wisps; to the densification of darkness in the cerebral convolutions of persons artificially dispirited by being subjected to brass band music and low barometric pressure; and – the real reason why Smyke had activated this memory in the first place – to *the abnormal structure of Demonocles' tongues and its effects on their sense of balance.*

Smyke had found the memory that would help him to perfect his escape plan.

Rumo's special diet

Rumo grew at an even more breakneck pace in the next few weeks. He discovered some change in his body almost daily, whether it was a powerful muscle, a fully developed claw, an enlarged bone, or a brand-new tooth.

The Demonocles' interest in him had steadily intensified since he'd been in the cage. He had previously been allotted the same fare as all the others: the scraps of fish and bone the Demonocles tossed into the cave, the indeterminate mush they tipped into troughs for the vegetarians among their captives, and the pools they continually replenished with rainwater. The Demonocles were not particularly intelligent, but they were not so stupid as to let their prisoners starve. In any case the food they gave them – millet, raw vegetables, gnawed bones and the like – was worthless to themselves from the culinary aspect because it could neither kick nor scream.

Ever since his confinement in the cage, however, Rumo had enjoyed a diet that was the envy of the other inmates of the cave. The one-eyed monsters brought him buckets of cool rainwater, freshly caught fish, lobsters, crabs and crayfish, plucked seabirds and seal meat. Although he felt rather embarrassed, Rumo wolfed the lot. He had recently developed an insatiable appetite and could have gone on eating without a break. It was as if his body converted every meal into bigger muscles, additional teeth, or a centimetre's growth. He devoured slabs of whale blubber, half sharks and once, even, an octopus tentacle almost as big as himself. The Demonocles, who rejoiced at his appetite, laughed and prodded him with sticks to test his reflexes, and the bigger and stronger he grew the more their eyes shone with undisguised voracity.

A group of eight Demonocles regularly visited the cave to check on Rumo's progress. They were the floating island's chieftains, the strongest and most ferocious of all their kind. Rumo had been watching them for some time. They evidently possessed privileges that ranked them above the rest of the one-eyed giants. They were entitled to pick out the finest titbits and possessed cages of their own in which they kept and fattened wild beasts that no one else could touch. They had lately taken to visiting Rumo several times a day and tossing live fish through the bars. He wolfed them without a qualm - in fact, he devoured them ravenously. The masters of the island registered this with an evil grin, delighted by the wild dog's willingness to eat live food like themselves. They proceeded to discuss something in their raucous language - something that highly excited them, to judge by the way their voices trembled with greed and saliva oozed from the corners of their mouths. Finally, they thumped one another on the chest until the cave rang. Among the Demonocles, not that Rumo knew it, this was a sign of pleasurable anticipation.

The giants' pecking order

The Demonocles of the island spent most of the time vegetating. They either hammered away at the rocks with primitive stone tools or lay around in the sun, staring at the sea or the clouds, which they believed to be flying mountains on which they would dwell when they died. The remainder of the time they devoted to sleeping or eating.

There was no kind of government on Roaming Rock, the Demonocles weren't advanced enough for that. Mentally, they were on a par with cave men who had just discovered fire but didn't really know what to do with it. All the man-made objects on the island - the cages, chains and clubs - were the proceeds of forays ashore. It was one of the island's greatest intellectual feats to have grasped how a looted padlock and key worked. The Demonocles believed that the sun was the eye of a one-eyed giant who held a bowl of water in which floated Roaming Rock and a few other islands. That was their conception of the universe.

The island witnessed occasional stirrings of something akin to social life, for instance when two Demonocles had chosen the same place in the sun or the same live prey for supper. They usually got down to business right away. It wasn't pleasant to watch two Demonocles fighting. Tactics didn't come into it. All that mattered were strength and brutality coupled with stamina and an ability to soak up an exceptional amount of punishment. The giants fought without even considering the possibility of ducking or taking evasive action. They simply smote each other in the face until one of them fell dead, because a Demonocle remained on his feet for as long as he possibly could. That was how the group of eight chieftains had fought their way to the top in the course of time: by having tougher chins and being able to dish out more punishment than the average Demonocle. They were the rulers of the island, but their administrative activities were confined to evicting other Demonocles from the best places in the sun or snatching the choicest titbits from under their noses. They also led raiding parties ashore and claimed the best items of plunder for themselves. Their notions of rulership and authority were no more well-defined than that.

Smyke's forebodings

Meantime, Smyke remained at the bottom of the pool and continued to excrete his vile-smelling slime. The giants' drumming, which had grown louder by the day, was audible even down there as a series of rhythmical vibrations. If Smyke's prognosis was correct, the Demonocles would soon be in a feeding frenzy. The cave's stocks of food had dwindled in recent months and they were becoming less choosy. Smyke's chances of survival improved with every drop of stinking slime he produced.

But his current problem was of a different nature. He had to overcome a fear that had steadily grown in the course of his sojourn on Roaming Rock and was now almost paralysing him: the fear of emerging from his pool. In order to tell Rumo his plan he would have to leave the protective slime and make his way over to the cage. The very thought of it made him feel sick. It was fear that weighed Smyke down like a ten-ton anchor.

That night Rumo had a dream. His dreams had become more and more vivid and terrifying since he'd been in the cage, and most of them concerned the Demonocles. They often showed the one-eyed giants entering the cave en masse for a final bloodbath, and Rumo had to watch them – powerless because he was either chained up, imprisoned in the cage, or simply unable to move – until they eventually fell on him too.

But this dream was different. He was free, he was on dry land, and he was trotting across a field of tall grass beneath a cloudless sky. High in the air above him hovered the Silver Thread whose presence he had first sensed back on the farm. And he was gripped by an indefinable emotion, a feeling of unbridled anticipation. He couldn't tell what it portended, but he sensed that it was the finest thing life would ever have to offer him. Not that he knew it, Rumo was dreaming of love.

Feeding time

Next morning Rumo was roused by someone kicking the bars of his cage – not an unusual form of awakening. A doltish-looking Demonocle was standing outside with a dead seal in one great paw and a cudgel in the other. He thrust the seal through the bars and tested Rumo's reflexes by prodding him with the cudgel. He wasn't one of the chieftains, so he performed this chore sullenly and unenthusiastically, well aware that he wouldn't get a share of such a prize delicacy. Rumo growled, the Demonocle turned away and resolved to console himself by devouring a plump Marsh Hog, so he plodded off towards the pigsty. A second Demonocle entered the cave, yawning, and strode resolutely towards the pigsty – clearly, he also felt peckish for some squealing piglets. The island gave a lurch just as they got there, throwing them off balance, and they collided.

They snarled angrily at each other. The first Demonocle raised his cudgel, but a fist crashed into his face. Before he could recover from the blow a second punch caught him full on the jaw. He tottered backwards, stumbled and fell flat on his back. His opponent, who was on him in a flash, punched him unmercifully, again and again, until he lay still. Then, grunting with exertion, he dragged him out of the cave.

Smyke had been covertly watching this brief but barbarous contest from his pool. He wondered whether the Demonocles were cannibals who ate their dead. They were certainly voracious enough to render this a possibility. Most of the one-eyed giants had a very low tolerance threshold and were capable of flying into a rage at the drop of a hat. This was the moment Smyke had yearned for most ardently and feared most intensely. An opening had presented itself, and unless he seized it the chance would be gone for ever. The time to act had come.

Smyke leaves his pool

Rumo stared in surprise at Smyke's pool. Strange sounds – revolting gurgles and squelching noises – were issuing from it, and the water was sloshing and splashing in all directions. Panting, cursing and groaning, Smyke emerged from the ooze, hauled himself over the edge of the pool and crawled across the cave. He made straight for Rumo's cage, leaving an oily trail of olive-green slime behind him. This remarkable spectacle was watched in silence by all the other inmates of the giants' larder.

Rumo stood up and poked his nose through the bars. Smyke was panting hard by the time he reached the cage.

'Listen carefully . . . I don't have much time . . . If the Demonocles catch me out here . . .' Smyke looked at Rumo and drew a deep breath. 'I'm scared.'

Rumo nodded.

'But I've got a plan I'd like to tell you about.'

'All right.'

Smyke outlined his plan. It was outrageous. It was totally insane. It sounded like a grisly fairy tale, a bloodthirsty dream of revenge – and it had absolutely no prospect of success. 'Well,' he said, 'what do you think?'

'I'll try it,' Rumo replied.

'Great. Now listen: I've taught you all I know about fighting, but practical experience of fighting is another matter. That you'll have to gain by yourself. I'm sure it'll come quite naturally. Simply let it flow, like—'

'I know,' Rumo cut in. 'You'd better get back into the pool now. It's too dangerous.'

'One more thing! It's the most important point of all – the whole key to my plan!' Smyke clung to the bars and Rumo pricked up his ears. 'There's something you should know about Demonocles' tongues, my boy . . .'

Blood lust

Rumo had now been imprisoned in the cage for so long that he'd abandoned his attempts to escape unaided. He no longer rattled the bars or chewed the padlock. When not eating or sleeping, he simply sat there in idleness. The most he ever did was pace restlessly to and fro, to and fro, in the confined space. His mouth had stopped hurting some days ago and his ravenous hunger had also subsided. He contented himself with smaller helpings, and became more and more choosy as regards the food the Demonocles tossed him through the bars.

In recent days the motion of Roaming Rock had steadily increased in violence, as had the thunder of the waves that broke against it. The floating island seemed to be labouring through heavy seas. Chaos reigned in the cave. The surviving Hackonians hung limp in their chains, their helpless bodies striking the walls like bell clappers. The piglets started biting each other, and the few remaining wild animals roared and rampaged in their cages. The stinking water in Smyke's pool slopped over the edge and flooded the cave.

The Demonocles appeared to have reached the climax of their festivities. The sound of their instruments, their shouts and singing, filled the tunnels and caverns of Roaming Rock. Worst of all, they visited the cave three times more often than usual.

Rumo was clinging to the bars of his cage and, for the umpteenth time, going over the various phases of Smyke's plan – there were only two – when three Demonocles came blundering into the cave. They were dead drunk, to judge by the blood with which they were smeared from head to foot.

For a while they staggered aimlessly to and fro, sniffing the contents of their larder. One of them slipped on Smyke's slime and measured his length on the floor of the cave, much to his companions' amusement. Stung by their raucous laughter, the angry giant crawled over to the pool and thrust his arm into it, doubtless intending to punish Smyke by devouring him. Rumo clung to the bars of his cage, transfixed.

The Demonocle fished for his prey in the ooze, cursing, but Smyke was not to be caught so easily and kept slipping through his fingers. Suddenly there was a terrible crash. A huge wave must have struck Roaming Rock, because the floor of the cave gave a violent lurch and inundated the giant with slime. The other two burst into a terrible roar of laughter. Really infuriated now, the dripping Demonocle bent over the pool and punched downwards in the hope of connecting with Smyke's submerged form. One of the other Demonocles remembered why he had come and seized a Hackonian. He simply wrenched the dwarf away from the wall without removing his chains, tearing off one of his spindly arms. The Hackonian screamed like a stuck pig, kicking and struggling with his little legs and one remaining arm. This attracted the attention of the third Demonocle, who strode up and grabbed one of the unfortunate victim's legs. Thoroughly incensed by this, the other giant gave a menacing roar and tugged at his supper. His competitor hung on to the leg and hauled on it in a frenzy, ripping the Hackonian in half. This enraged the Demonocles even more because their lifeless quarry, being past screaming and struggling, was worthless to them. The dwarf had made a terrible escape from an even more terrible fate. The disappointed giants hurled hoarse reproaches at each other while their companion continued to fish for Smyke.

Rumo's blood began to boil and red lights danced before his eyes. He shook the bars of his cage, growling and barking like one of his wild ancestors. The Demonocles looked over at the furious Wolperting, puzzled at first, then amused, then with gluttony written all over their hideous faces. Saliva oozed from the corners of their mouths and their eyes shone with greed, but they dared not break the taboo and lay hands on their chieftains' property. They tossed the remains of the Hackonian heedlessly aside and stood there swaying, seemingly hypnotised by the sight of the frantic Wolperting.

Rumo redoubled his efforts. He rampaged wildly back and forth, charged the door of the cage with his shoulder and rattled the bars until the hinges creaked. His behaviour was infectious. The other imprisoned wild animals roared and snarled in imitation of Rumo's attempts to escape.

All this din and commotion sent the Demonocles into a feeding frenzy. They lumbered over to Rumo's cage and kicked and shook the bars like maniacs. They had no key, but they were determined to break open his prison by main force. Using every ounce of their strength, they tried to wrench the door off its hinges. Rumo lay flat on the floor of the cage and gave a low growl. All he could see was iron bars and straining bodies. His view of the cave was blotted out by furry black bodies and faces contorted with greed. The cage was built entirely of iron, but it was only a matter of time before the hinges gave way under the combined onslaught of three mountains of muscle. There was a sudden thud and one of the frenzied Demonocles stopped short, staring at Rumo glassy-eyed. Then he collapsed, restoring Rumo's view of the cave. Eight more Demonocles were standing there, one of them with a lump of rock in his hand. It was the rulers of the island.

There followed a short, extremely one-sided fight in which the two surviving drunks came off worst. A flurry of punches on the jaw left them breathing their last on the ground.

Rumo realised that this wasn't a normal tour of inspection. The moment of truth had come. He didn't make a sound and lay quite still when the giants opened the cage, seized him and dragged him outside. He was behaving just as Smyke had instructed.

The chieftains were surprised and rather disappointed by his lack of resistance. They punched him in the ribs and tweaked his ears as they carried him along the torchlit tunnels, but he moved as little as possible. Cold rain lashed his face when they manhandled him into the open air. The keen sea breeze was a relief after the fug and stench of the cave and he drew it deep into his lungs. The sky was obscured by inky blue clouds, flashes of lightning and flying spray. It was Rumo's first glimpse of the exterior of Roaming Rock, whose jagged peaks protruded from the sea like the towers of a city sinking beneath the waves. Ablaze in the mouths of many caves were the fires beside which the Demonocles warmed themselves and played their diabolical music.

The banqueting table

Rumo was carried out on to a rocky plateau with a rough-hewn circular slab in the middle. Stained dark-red with the blood of countless meals, this was the chieftains' banqueting table. Several Demonocles were seated on the boulders nearby, beating drums or blowing seashell horns as they watched the ritual unfold with avid, envious eyes. The chieftains laid Rumo down on his back on the slab. Four of them held his legs while a fifth positioned himself behind his head. The latter raised his arms to the sky and bellowed at the clouds. The Demonocles interpreted the answering peal of thunder as a sign of divine approval: their banquet could commence. The one-eyed monster behind Rumo's head bent over him, opened his jaws and prepared to sink his yellow fangs in fresh, live meat.

Rumo's nostrils were assailed by the metallic smell of cold blood mingled with a frightful stench: the kind of mouth odour that results from decades of dental neglect. The giant was convinced that his victim would start to struggle and scream as soon as the first sinews and nerve fibres were ripped from his body.

Rumo uses his teeth

But Rumo opened his jaws too. For the first time ever, he bared his full armoury of teeth – an array of weapons such as only a Wolperting possessed: eighty-eight incisors, canines, bicuspids and molars, all brand-new, snow-white and as flawless as freshly glazed china.

They shimmered faintly in the semi-darkness, because a Wolperting's teeth contain a small proportion of phosphorus. The long fangs and tiny abraders were arranged in one, two or three rows. The eye-teeth were shaped like fish-hooks, the molars looked as if they'd been scattered with sparkling diamond dust, the incisors were as sharp as cut-throat razors. There were also other kinds of teeth, thin as needles and almost invisible, that occupied the spaces between the bigger ones.

This mouthful of biting implements seemed to have been designed by an expert weaponsmith, for woe betide anyone who ended up between a Wolperting's jaws! The Demonocles uttered envious grunts and ran their tongues experimentally over their own neglected tusks. The four who were holding Rumo instinctively tightened their grip. The dog could show off his fangs as much as he liked; he was harmless as long as they held him down, and each of the one-eyed monsters was far superior to Rumo in physical strength. Meanwhile, the Demonocles on the nearby pinnacles of rock were working themselves into a frenzy, dancing, yelling, drumming and blowing agonisingly discordant fanfares on their seashell horns. For a second or two a dazzling shaft of lightning lit up the plateau as bright as day, instantly followed by an ear-splitting tattoo on the impatient sky god's celestial drum.

The Demonocles blinked, momentarily dazzled by the glare, and almost imperceptibly relaxed their grip. Rumo decided that the time had come to fight back. He did something that was anatomically impossible under the circumstances: he turned his head, seemed to stretch his neck to twice its normal length, and bit the wrist of the giant who was holding his right forepaw. It happened so swiftly that no one saw a thing. The Wolperting's immaculate teeth were stained with blood, the giant released Rumo's foreleg with a yell and held his arm in the air. Blood spurted from a dozen tiny puncture wounds.

With his free paw Rumo reached into the Demonocle's mouth, which was still open in astonishment. Gripping the tongue, he twisted it vigorously, first one way, then the other. There was a crack like a rotten branch snapping. Rumo had done the worst thing anyone could do to a Demonocle: he had broken the giant's tongue.

After Smyke had crawled over to Rumo's cage and confided his plan, he also acquainted him with what Professor Nightingale knew about the anatomical structure of Demonocles' tongues. Briefly summarised, this was that while normal tongues are supported only by muscles and sinews, a Demonocle's tongue contained an intricate and complicated system of bone and gristle not unlike a miniature spinal column. This osseous system was essential because the giants' tongues were heavier and more complex than that of other living creatures, being equipped with considerably more nerve cells and taste buds. Nightingale had also discovered that this unique part of their anatomy was connected to the spine and controlled their sense of balance. If you snapped a Demonocle's tongue, therefore, you not only caused him terrible pain but turned him into a totally defenceless being.

Demonocles' tongues

The injured chieftain put his hand over his mouth and uttered a pitiful groan. He reeled backwards, tripped over his own feet and tumbled over the stone parapet into the sea. That was *Phase 1* of Smyke's plan: *Snap the tongue of the first Demonocle that tries to bite you!*

Phases 1 and 2

That was done, but *Phase 2* was a considerably harder proposition: *Kill as many Demonocles as possible!*

The startled chieftains had let go of Rumo. They clapped their hands protectively over their mouths and cowered away. A broken tongue! How could one living creature do anything so cruel to another?

Rumo rolled over and crouched down on all fours on the blood-encrusted slab. He took aim at one of the Demonocles, narrowing his eyes, and flexed his hind legs slightly. What came next happened so fast that all the one-eyed giants saw was another white streak of lightning. As though shot from a catapult, the Wolperting somersaulted over the Demonocle and landed just behind him. As he flew through the air there was a sound like a tree being torn up by the roots. To everyone's astonishment the Demonocle was standing there without a head.

A scream rang out from high above. Everyone except Rumo looked up at the sky. What the giants saw was their companion's head soaring through the air in a wide arc. It uttered a final, long-drawn-out wail, then splashed into the sea.

While two of the flabbergasted Demonocles were still craning their necks, Rumo ripped out their larynxes with his claws. They clutched their gaping, bleeding throats in horror. The decapitated giant rotated on his own axis several times as if seeking his missing head. He staggered forward for a few steps, then plunged over the edge of the cliff and joined his head in the sea. Rumo had taken only a few moments to neutralise four of the eight strongest Demonocles on Roaming Rock.

He rose on his hind legs. Although still half the size of his opponents, he suddenly looked like a colossus. The four remaining chieftains stood rooted to the spot. They had thought themselves the strongest creatures in the world, invincible demigods who represented a threat only to one another, and now they were confronted by a creature – a creature considerably smaller and less muscular than themselves – that had neutralised four of their number including the strongest of them all. The two giants whose throats Rumo had torn out had fallen to the ground and were writhing around in a pool of blood. The Demonocles who had witnessed the whole incident from the rocks nearby uttered a confused babble of cries and made for the nearest caves.

One of the four remaining chieftains came to life at last. He gave Rumo one last, terrified look, turned tail and dashed through a rocky gateway into the island's interior. The other three stood watching this unprecedented spectacle: for the first time ever one of their number had been put to flight by another living creature. They stared at each other in utter bewilderment, then lumbered after him.

For a while Rumo continued to stand there in the rain, inhaling the fresh sea air. The drums and seashell horns had fallen silent. He threw back his head and opened his jaws to let the downpour rinse his bloodstained teeth. Then he went down on all fours and bounded towards the cleft in the rocks through which the Demonocles had disappeared.

Smyke was listening. The music had ceased abruptly – to him an unmistakable sign that the young Wolperting had carried out *Phase 1* of his plan. His predominant emotion was one of pleasure, although he briefly regretted having been unable to witness such a unique spectacle – a choice form of combat technique devised by himself! Slowly, he made his way to the surface. The pool had spilt half its contents, so the edge was at least five feet above him – an almost insurmountable obstacle for a sluggish and bloated Shark Grub. Plastering his flabby body to the stone side, he clung there by suction and proceeded to worm his way upwards. He inched up the side of the basin like a monstrous slug, accompanied by glutinous sounds, then rolled over the edge and looked around, panting. The island was rocking less violently and the other captives were preserving an expectant silence. Smyke listened again. Screams should soon be heard.

A Demonocle chieftain bites the dust

The first chieftain to take flight was standing in a dark tunnel, nursing his bleeding wrist. He wondered what he had done wrong. He had never harmed anyone, so why was he being punished?

He had always endeavoured to lead a simple, god-fearing, Demonoclean existence. He awoke in the morning, had breakfast (a squealing pig, a screaming dwarf, a thrashing octopus, or whatever else came to hand), spent the rest of the morning dozing on a rock in the sunshine, had lunch, treated himself to another little nap, had supper and then retired to a cave, where the waves rocked him to sleep. He and his companions sometimes went whaling: they stood on the island's rocky pinnacles and harpooned any of the giant creatures unlucky enough to stray within range. When the island ran aground they went ashore to forage for supplies. He could still hear the screams of the prey they'd amassed on their last raid. The Demonocles had laughed and sung, and he himself had blown the seashell horn. What wonderful, carefree days those had been!

A big tear oozed from the giant's single eye. Now he was standing here in the dark with a pounding heart, hiding from an evil spirit.

He had given some other Demonocles a frightful beating, of course, and had even sent a few of them straight to the Sun-God in the Flying Mountains above the sea, but he was fully entitled to do so. He was one of the chieftains, after all.

The giant suddenly remembered his friend Okk. True, he had hurt him terribly - and how! - but why had Okk usurped his favourite place in the sun? He had punched his friend in the face until his lower jaw flew off, then stamped on his head until his eye oozed out, but the obstinate fellow should simply have made room for him, at least when he lost his lower jaw. But no, Okk always had to act tough.

Could it be Okk's ghost that was stalking him through the tunnels with bloodthirsty vengeance in mind? It would be just like him - he'd always been inclined to bear a grudge - but how had a weakling like Okk developed such mysterious powers? Did one acquire them in the Flying Mountains? And why had he taken on the shape of a white dog? On the other hand, if it really was Okk he might be able to finish him off after all, ghost or no ghost.

Never had a Demonocle's head been awhirl with as many thoughts and questions all at once. Why was his heart beating so fast? What was this unpleasant, irresistible sensation that made his knees tremble and brought him out in a sweat? Was that his own shadow creeping along the wall? Was it Okk? What was that he could feel on his neck? A hand? A row of teeth?

A spinal cord snapped in the darkness and the giant's lifeless body collapsed. Rumo leapt off his back. If his soul really was winging its way to the Flying Mountains it would run into a terrible thunderstorm.

The evil spirit

It was dark inside Roaming Rock. The frantic Demonocles had omitted to illuminate the interior in the usual way, so isolated torches provided the only light. They groped their way along in the darkness, strangers in their own home. In the few places where fires dispelled the gloom they clustered round and talked with bated breath of the ghost that haunted Roaming Rock and was even now creeping along the tunnels, intent on killing them all. Many claimed that it could make itself invisible and turn up in several places at once. It possessed magical powers, declared someone, and it could even fly as well. Others surmised that it had come from the Flying Mountains, a vengeful deity born of the thunderstorm, because they had paid insufficient homage to the Sun God.

But most of the one-eyed giants roamed around on their own, totally disorientated. They kept blundering into each other in the dark. When two of them collided there was a terrible scrap which only one survived. Quite a few Demonocles died by their own hand that night and many others plunged wildly into the sea, where sharks attracted by the blood of the injured were ready and waiting.

Rumo's inner eye

To his own surprise, Rumo needed no light – he could see with his nose. To him the darkness was filled with undulating colours and thin streaks of scent. He could smell where beads of sweat were trickling and hearts pulsating with terror – he could smell the fear and desperation. It was child's play for him to locate a perspiring Demonocle. The fleeing giants left behind broad yellow streaks that offended his nostrils. He had only to follow such a carpet of smells and, sure enough, it would lead him to a Demonocle quaking in the darkness, never guessing what lay in store for him. Rumo could smell his pounding heart – he could see it throbbing with his inner eye. A furious growl, a scream cut short, and another giant slumped lifeless to the ground. Then Rumo would pick up the next scent.

But it wasn't always that easy. Although frightened, the Demonocles were no cowards and desperation lent them twice their normal strength. Sometimes, when Rumo failed to put an opponent out of action with his first bite, a fight ensued. Then he had to contend with a rampaging mountain of muscle who punched holes in the darkness with mighty fists, forcing him to duck and evade the blows. In such cases Rumo relied on his speed. He either severed the giant's hamstrings with his teeth or sprang straight at his throat.

If the Demonocles had a torch and were present in strength, he avoided a direct confrontation. He would snarl at them, displaying his bloodstained teeth, and disappear into the darkness to attack some lone giant wandering nearby. Before long the tunnels were strewn with dead, dying and badly injured Demonocles. Their cries reverberated around the entire system of tunnels and filled the hearts of the survivors with dread. For the first time the one-eyed monsters learnt the meaning of mortal fear, the terrible emotion their prisoners were compelled to experience daily, the persistent fear of being killed at any moment by creatures far superior to them in strength.

Rumo continued to prowl through the darkness. He soon had a better knowledge than any dim-witted Demonocle of the network of tunnels with which the floating island was riddled. His inner eye visualised it like a three-dimensional blueprint criss-crossed and illuminated by coloured threads, undulating wisps of scent, pulsations of fear. He worked his way tirelessly and systematically through the labyrinth, sometimes killing his victims, sometimes only mauling them. The cries of the ones he only maimed and put out of action bore witness to his triumphs. Now and then he would pause at an intersection, go down on all fours, and utter a ghostly howl that was audible all over Roaming Rock.

Rumo decided that it was time to release the prisoners in the cave, though he knew they wouldn't be much help. A Hackonian dwarf couldn't have brought himself to hit a Demonocle with a buttercup. This had nothing to do with cowardice. Hackonians were brave and steadfast individuals under normal circumstances, but they simply couldn't do a person harm. Rumo wanted to reassure them that their troubles were over.

The Hackonians flinched when he entered the cave. His white fur was completely sodden with blood. He stood there in the flickering torchlight like the statue of a vengeful god come to life. Inserting the shaft of an extinguished torch through the iron ring that attached the main chain to the wall, he levered it out with a jerk. Then he made his way over to Smyke.

'Nice work,' said Smyke.

'Dirty work,' Rumo retorted. 'Harder than I thought, too.' And he disappeared into the labyrinth once more.

The determined dozen

Rumo was back in the world of smells. The green glow that enveloped everything was the scent of the salt sea rising and falling beneath his feet. The fine red threads that drifted along the tunnels were the scent of spilt blood.

Silently he followed the yellow streak a Demonocle had left in his wake. A second streak joined it, followed by more and more until twelve were all leading in the same direction. A dozen giants had teamed up and barricaded themselves in a cave. Emboldened by their superior numbers, they would stop at nothing – Rumo realised that. He could smell their sweat and hear their hearts beating wildly.

They had illuminated their refuge with several torches whose light penetrated the mouth of the tunnel that led to it. Rumo paused just short of the cave and drew a deep breath. He had never tackled a dozen Demonocles at once – *no one* had ever done that – but after all, he had disposed of the eight strongest giants on the island and they hadn't been as demoralised as these. He decided to extinguish the torches as quickly as possible and attack under cover of darkness. Going down on all fours, he darted between the Demonocles' legs and into the cave as nimbly as a lizard. The next moment a torch hit him plumb on the nose. Without knowing it, he had come up against the giant with the best reflexes of all – one who had spent years training himself to stun passing sharks with a club. As soon as he saw Rumo come flitting in he lashed out like lightning and landed the blow of a lifetime.

Rumo's world of smells exploded into a shower of multicoloured sparks. The torch had singed his muzzle and blinded him at the same time. His eyes were showered with glowing fragments of pitch that stung them like pinpricks and imprinted his vision with pulsating red flecks. The startled giants formed a circle round him as he crawled across the floor of the cave, trying to rub the burning specks out of his eyes. They hadn't thought it would be so easy. They had been prepared for a costly life-or-death struggle, a costly battle with a god of death, a flying ghost. And now, one blow and it was all over. They vented their relief by laughing sheepishly and slapping the lucky torch wielder on the back. They said nothing, but the looks they exchanged spoke volumes: they were going to devour the Wolperting alive – here and now.

Roaming Rock runs aground

Volzotan Smyke was listening again, this time with the greatest misgivings. The screaming had stopped. Although he could still hear the odd groan, there were no more cries of terror or surprise. It would be only too understandable if Rumo's strength was beginning to give out and his reflexes were flagging. Smyke knew perfectly well that his plan hadn't really been a plan at all, just a gamble, and years of experience had taught him that when you staked everything on a single card, your chances of winning were as great as your chances of losing. Curiously enough, though, you lost more often than you won.

At that moment there was a mighty jolt and everyone was hurled across the cave. The Hackonians uttered cries of alarm, the animals bellowed and bleated. Bulky though he was, Smyke sailed through the air and crashed into a stalagmite protruding from the floor of the cave. With a groan he rolled off into a big puddle formed by water that had spilt from one of the basins, and wriggling around him were squat black fish with fearsome-looking teeth. He sat up. All was still. No more jolts, no pitching or tossing. He looked round. The water in the pools was motionless now - even the chains had stopped rattling against the walls. That could mean only one thing: Roaming Rock had run aground.

The world of sounds

'Sound!' Rumo thought suddenly. *That* was the answer to Smyke's riddle! *What can penetrate a wall but isn't a nail?* Sound, of course.

Rumo's hearing had always been good. Once, back on the farm, he had heard a rose rustle as its petals unfolded. He could hear the wing-beats of a butterfly and the sound of insects burrowing in the soil, but he'd never paid much attention to that sense as long as he could see and smell. Now he was almost blind and his nose was so badly scorched that all he could detect with it were the wildly rotating colours of pain. Now, as the Demonocles closed in with the intention of devouring him, Rumo explored another world: the world of sounds.

Anyone with average hearing could have heard the giants laughing and their feet scuffing the rocky floor, likewise the crackle of torches and the sound of the one that had blinded Rumo being replaced in its holder. But Rumo could hear much, much more. He could hear the Demonocles' joints creaking and their hoarse breathing, and the rhythmical thud of their heartbeats. He could hear the electrical crackle of their fur when they brushed together and the rustle occasioned even by the slowest of their movements. His ears conjured up a mental image of the entire cave, but colourless this time. It was silhouetted in nebulous shades of grey and lacked the fine detail his senses of sight and smell would have conveyed, but he could tell accurately where a Demonocle was standing and what he was doing. He could also hear the location of the three torches. That was all he needed to know.

Suddenly there was a violent jolt. Rumo slithered across the floor and the giants went crashing into the walls. For a moment they were as startled as the chieftains had been by the thunderbolt on the rocky plateau, and Rumo decided to exploit this distraction as before.

Heedless of his smarting eyes and nose, he sprang up and made straight for the crackling sound of a torch. Before the Demonocles could react he had snatched it from its holder. The nearest giant recovered his wits and made a move in Rumo's direction – the creaking of his knee joints was clearly audible. He raised his weapon, a short iron chain composed of massive links that jangled in Rumo's ears. He also made the mistake of blinking his only eye. To Rumo it sounded like a lizard closing and opening its gooey mouth. He thrust the torch straight at that juicy sound, and a bestial scream, accompanied by a noise like frying fat, told him that he had hit the target fair and square. The torch stuck fast in the blinded Demonocle's eye socket and went out with a hiss, but his blood-curdling screams went on and on. His companions seemed paralysed by this cold-blooded act. Their ferocious determination and voracity evaporated in a flash – the flying ghost had come to life again! Rumo, who had already snatched the second torch from its holder, located the screams and doused it in the sightless giant's gaping mouth.

This spectacle was too much for the others. They milled around in panic, blocking their own escape route by all trying to squeeze through the narrow exit simultaneously.

Rumo took the last torch from the wall and thrust it into their confused, jostling mass of bodies. One of them caught fire. The sparks from his fur set two more ablaze and within a few seconds they were all burning fiercely. A couple of them managed to squeeze through the gap and ran screaming along the tunnels like torches on legs. The others rolled around on the floor of the cave, desperately trying to put out the flames. Rumo paid them no more heed. He leapt over their burning bodies and out of the cave.

The escape

The screams had started again. They were issuing from many throats and they sounded even more desperate than before, so Rumo was still alive and busy completing *Phase 2* of the plan. Smyke decided that it was time to organise an exodus from the cave.

'Listen, folks,' he called. 'It looks as if the island has run aground. I advise you all to leave this accursed cave as fast as possible and make your way down to the water's edge. Don't be afraid of the Demonocles, they've got enough on their plates. When you get outside, simply dive into the sea and swim for it. Land can't be far away. Better to be eaten by sharks than by those one-eyed monsters.'

The terrified Hackonians hadn't stirred since the island ran aground. Now they pulled themselves together and made for the exit.

'Incidentally,' Smyke called after them before they disappeared down the tunnels, 'your saviour's name is Rumo. You ought to make a note of it.' Then he, too, made for the exit.

Rumo tottered along Roaming Rock's subterranean passages. The shower of sparks in front of his eyes had subsided – all he occasionally saw were red and white specks – but he still wasn't capable of smelling anything. His warlike exertions had taken their toll: he was tired, injured and unsteady on his legs. He heard an unidentifiable crackling sound, possibly from a discarded torch, to judge by the shadows dancing along the walls of a side tunnel. Rounding the bend, he caught sight of three Demonocles. Armed with clubs and stone axes, they were standing mutely over the smouldering corpse of one of their number. The surprise factor was equally great on both sides. The giants would probably have found Rumo easy meat in his present state, but he merely growled and bared his bloodstained teeth, and they turned and ran off. He staggered after them in the direction of the cool breeze that was wafting along the tunnel towards him.

Will-o'-the-Wisp Bay

Rumo emerged on to the rocky plateau and looked at the sea. The storm had abated and the horizon was illuminated by the first rays of the rising sun. To the west, a thick blanket of inky-blue clouds still hung low over the water, but the rain had stopped. A few hundred yards away Rumo could see land, bare sandstone cliffs and little beaches. Several Demonocles and Hackonians were swimming ashore. Swarms of luminous insects were dancing above the sea, their busy hum filling the air.

Some more dwarfs emerged from the cave behind Rumo. Having respectfully squeezed past him, they jumped off the rocks and into the sea. Someone had released the red gorilla, which suddenly appeared beside the bloodstained Wolperting. After giving him a long look, it too jumped into the sea. Rumo was left on his own.

He looked down at the water, and the sight of the choppy waves turned his legs to jelly. The dry land was near and the water couldn't be very deep. There were no sharks in sight – they were probably feasting far out to sea – but they weren't the reason for his deep-seated fear.

'You can't swim, can you?'

Rumo knew who had spoken without turning round. Volzotan Smyke came crawling out of the tunnel behind him.

'No,' said Rumo, 'I can't.'

'No Wolperting can,' said Smyke. 'No need to be ashamed, it's hereditary. You're lucky I'm still here. Climb on my back.'

Rumo did so. The Shark Grub's body felt soft but firm beneath him as he clung to its plump curves. Smyke slithered down the almost vertical rock face like a raindrop trickling down a window-pane. Rumo hung on even tighter and dug his heels into Smyke's yielding blubber.

'It rather embarrasses me to be able to do this, but it's something I've inherited from my disgusting marine ancestors,' said Smyke, whose body was making hideous squelching noises as it slid down the rock. He glided smoothly into the sea and Rumo involuntarily drew up his legs as the sea water wetted his feet.

'As soon as we're ashore I shall seek out the most decadent company I can find,' said Smyke. 'I intend to live in the lap of luxury and sophistication. I yearn for sofas and sedan chairs, gilded columns and marble floors. Nature I want to see only in the form of well-tended gardens or oil paintings. I never want to set eyes on the sea again. Or, if I do, only from afar – from the terrace of my summer palace, as I gaze at it with distaste through my telescope.'

The insects dancing overhead glowed with crystalline colours of every shade. It looked as if it were raining diamonds – the very air seemed to be on fire. 'Springtime,' said Smyke. 'Those are will-o'-the-wisps on their mating flight. The miracle of love, my boy! We appear to have landed in Will-o'-the-Wisp Bay; it's the only place where so many of those creatures are to be found. You've another reason to be thankful: we've run aground on the shores of Hackonia. You're back home, so to speak.'

Like a bloated swan, Smyke glided through the gentle swell past panting Hackonians and frantic, doggy-paddling Demonocles. Swimming among them was the red gorilla, which was propelling itself leisurely along on its back with sweeping movements of its arms. The sun had almost risen and the will-o'-the-wisps humbly extinguished themselves. They formed a long, humming, flying carpet and headed off, as if attracted by magnetism, towards the dazzling orb on the horizon.

The first Demonocles had reached land and were running wildly along the shore. Many were already scaling the sandstone cliffs.

'I can't guarantee those pea-brained monsters have learnt their lesson,' said Smyke, 'but I'm sure they'll treat other life forms with greater respect in the future. All the same, I wouldn't like to bet on it. Ah, land at last!'

He splashed another few yards through the surf and stopped. 'You can get off now. It's only knee-deep here.'

Rumo slid off his back and promptly began to wash. The bloodstained water ran down him in discoloured streams, reddening the sea at his feet. One by one, the last Hackonians waded ashore and plodded past him in silence with their heads bowed, a bedraggled procession of dwarfs.

When his fur was white at last, he too went ashore.

Ashore at last

Smyke crawled across the beach, grunting with delight as his plump body dug a circular furrow in the sand. He let the grains trickle through his little fingers. 'Land!' he cried. 'Terra firma! I still can't take it in.'

Rumo raised his head and sniffed the air. His nose was still dripping and it would be some time before it regained its sensitivity, but it was functioning, albeit to a very limited extent. He shut his eyes.

The wisps of scent were paler and more tenuous than usual. Everything seemed to be covered with a thin film, but he could smell the sea, the moist sand, the nearby fields of grass. And up there, fluttering high above the other wisps, wasn't that the Silver Thread? Yes, there it was again. It was very much thinner than before, but he could definitely see it – it was no dream. His inner eye had lost sight of it for a while, that was all.

Smyke's voice broke in on his thoughts. 'What do you intend to do now? Are you going back to the Hackonians?'

Rumo opened his eyes and looked at the departing dwarfs, who were going home to their looted and devastated farmsteads.

'No,' he said, 'I'm going that way.' He pointed in the direction of the fluttering Silver Thread.

'Good,' said Smyke. 'I'll accompany you for a while, if you've no objection.' He looked Rumo up and down. 'The first thing we must do is get you something to wear.'

Rumo looked down at himself. The morning sun was beginning to dry his fur.

'To wear?' he repeated. 'Why?'

Volzotan Smyke bared his teeth in a grin. 'We'll soon be entering civilisation. You're a grown-up now, my son.'

II.
The Non-Existent Teenies

Smyke and Rumo took advantage of the daylight and remained on the move all day. Sunlight, the open sky, an unobstructed view, the countryside, clouds – it took them a while to get used to these obvious things, and although they were back on dry land the ground still seemed to sway around like a floating island. Smyke bombarded Rumo with umpteen questions as they made their way across the sand dunes. He propelled himself along like a caterpillar, with the upper part of his body erect and the lower part advancing in a series of rhythmical undulations. To Rumo's surprise they made good progress, although Smyke needed to rest considerably more often than a Wolperting.

Most of Smyke's questions concerned Rumo's battles in the labyrinth on Roaming Rock. How had the Demonocles fought? What methods, what instinctive tactics, had Rumo employed? As for Rumo's account of the episode in which he'd been temporarily blinded, Smyke insisted on hearing it again and again.

By evening they had reached a spot where the flat coastal plain gave way to sparsely wooded hills. There were also some bushes and shrubs from which a few berries and nuts could be picked, and they even found a tree laden with sour little apples. Rumo didn't care what he ate. After what had happened on Roaming Rock he preferred to feel hungry rather than full up. It was almost as if he'd eaten enough for a lifetime in the Demonocle chieftains' cage. The mere act of eating would always remind him of those bestial one-eyed giants, and he disliked the feeling of repletion and the lethargy that accompanied it. Sleeping and eating would never be among his favourite occupations. He preferred to be alert and hungry.

Smyke, on the other hand, indulged in culinary fantasies as soon as they lay down to sleep in a small copse. In him the fresh apples had aroused an almost uncontrollable craving for some decent food. He had suppressed this while on Roaming Rock, but now they were back on dry land, and to Smyke dry land meant lush pastures in which sleek cows munched the juicy grass that augmented their fat reserves and filled their udders with rich milk from which one could ladle delicious cream for use in the most sumptuous gateaux . . . and so on and so forth. Smyke's powers of imagination were almost inexhaustible. Eventually, in the midst of describing a dish in which stuffed mouse bladders played a central role, he quietly went to sleep.

Rumo, too, enjoyed a really good night's sleep for the first time for ages. He dreamt that the Silver Thread was floating above fields of golden-yellow wheat. It had a voice this time, but the voice didn't speak; it hummed a strange and enchanting melody.

Civilisation

The district Rumo and Smyke explored the next morning was threaded with numerous rivers and streams. Rumo would have found it quite impossible to wade through anything deeper than a waist-deep stream, so Smyke's ability to swim more than compensated for the many rests they had to take for his sake.

The water had transformed the whole area into a paradise. The berry-laden bushes, rhubarb plants, apple trees and flowers that grew everywhere attracted creatures of all kinds. Bees hummed, birds darted after insects, and the place abounded in rabbits, partridges, deer, ducks and pigeons. Rumo could easily have killed one of the deer or rabbits, which showed little fear, but – much to Smyke's vociferous regret – his memories of the Demonocles would have made that seem like sacrilege.

After half a day's march the countryside became flatter and more monotonous, the rivers rarer, the tracks more frequent and well-trodden. Here and there, isolated farms could be seen on the hilltops, and the scenery was dominated by fields of grain and fenced-in pastureland instead of woods and wild meadows.

'Can you smell that?' asked Smyke.

Of course Rumo could smell it, even with his dripping nose. For some time now the air had been filled with the unmistakable aroma of roast pork. Rumo had tried to ignore it, because it was mingled with several other rather unpleasant smells. He could detect tobacco smoke and sweat. And horse dung.

'Somebody's doing some serious cooking somewhere,' Smyke said in a tremulous voice.

'Three of them. Over there behind the hill.' Rumo pointed in the direction from which he was receiving this information. Smyke put on speed.

In a dip beyond the hill, at the intersection of two tracks, stood a gloomy building rather inexpertly knocked together out of rough-hewn timber. The beams were crooked, the windows triangular, the gables absurdly askew. Smyke could now smell it too, that blend of cold ashes, burnt fat and stale beer. Only one type of building smelt that way.

'An inn,' he gasped, licking his lips. Tethered beside a drinking trough outside the building were two farm horses with black coats and white manes.

'There are some Bluddums in there,' Smyke whispered. 'At least two of them. Only Bluddums ride plough horses without saddles. That makes at least three including the innkeeper.'

Rumo nodded. 'Three of them. All unwashed.'

Smyke thought for a moment.

'Listen,' he said at length, 'I've a favour to ask – one that probably won't appeal to you.'

Rumo pricked up his ears.

'When we go inside I'd like you to walk on all fours.'

'Why?'

'It's a combat tactic I call the *surprise element*. You're bound to find it useful.'

'Hm.' Rumo recalled how he'd entered the twelve Demonocles' cave on all fours. That hadn't been such a good idea.

'Don't say a word when we get inside – not a word, understand? I'll do the talking. At some point I'll leave the room for a minute or two. All you have to do then is listen carefully to what's said. There are two possibilities: it'll be either something good or something bad. If it's bad, give me a sign when I come back. Paw the ground with your right foreleg. The rest will come by itself.'

Rumo nodded and went down on all fours.

The Glass Man Tavern

There's a story attached to every building. The story can be more exciting or less, depending on who lives there. If a house is occupied by a Hackonian farmer the probability is that he keeps his garden well weeded and pays his taxes regularly, so the story of his house will be relatively uneventful. If the occupants are werewolves, on the other hand, they spend the day in sealed coffins in the coal cellar, and at night, when the coffins creak open, scenes of unparalleled horror unfold. Thus, Zamonian buildings are associated with all kinds of stories. This one is the story of *The Glass Man Tavern*.

Kromek Toomah was a second-class Bluddum, which meant that he was regarded as badly off, even for a Bluddum. At some stage – nobody knew exactly when, because no self-respecting historian would ever have wasted time on the history of their breed – the Bluddums had established a fairly simple class system designed to distinguish between *not too badly off* and *very badly off* Bluddums. However, it soon turned out that the borderline between moderate and abject poverty was fluid and hard to define, so this class system lapsed into oblivion as time went by. All that needs to be said here is that if the yardstick of the old class system had been applied to Kromek Toomah it would have been necessary to invent a third class.

Of all the inhabitants of Zamonia endowed with the power of speech, the Bluddum was regarded as the life form with the least well-developed social instincts. Most Bluddums pursued occupations in which oafishness and insensitivity were not only tolerated but indispensable. They became bouncers or mortuary attendants, infantrymen or fairground boxers, slaughtermen or executioners. Anyone lacking the qualifications even for those jobs opened an inn like Kromek Toomah.

Kromek hadn't always been an innkeeper. He had embarked on a comparatively respectable career by Bluddum standards, having joined the private army of Hussein Banana, the Ornian princeling, at the age of ten. A veteran of twenty-five years' service, he had taken part in all of Hussein's frontier wars, losing four toes, one eye and two fingers in the process. His body bore 114 large scars and countless smaller ones. He was also deaf in one ear, having fired too many cannon, and suffered from occasional spasms in the spine where a poisoned arrow had struck him.

None of this would ever have induced Kromek to change his occupation. No, fate and the economic situation were responsible. One day Prince Hussein had paraded his troops and announced, 'Men, I'm bankrupt! Sorry not to have any more welcome news to impart, but my treasury is empty. Those confounded flame-throwers, which persisted in firing backwards, cost a fortune to develop, and our attack on Florinth has not been crowned with the success its strategic brilliance deserved. In short, men: You're dismissed!'

Kromek would never have believed, even in his wildest dreams, that a prince could go bankrupt. He had envisioned himself as a military instructor at the age of 180 and a retired war veteran at 250, yet here he was, unemployed at 35. Together with the other Bluddums he lynched the prince and carried his head around on a spear for an hour or two. This didn't get them their jobs back, however, so they split up and roamed Zamonia alone or in groups.

Kromek set off into the blue with a fellow veteran named Tok Tekko. For some years they scraped a living as highwaymen and paid duellists. Then Tok was so badly mauled by savage forest werewolves that Kromek had to bury him alive, that being the only way of preventing people mauled by werewolves from turning into werewolves themselves. Thereafter Kromek trudged on alone, waylaying any travellers unfortunate enough to cross his path and stealing their money and provisions. One day, having penetrated ever deeper into south-west Zamonia, he came to a crossroads and wondered aloud which direction to take. Then he heard a voice.

'Kromek Toomah,' said the voice.

'Huh?' said Kromek.

'Snrt fints. Mmfi dratbla.'

Kromek Toomah scratched his head. He hadn't understood a word apart from his name, and no wonder. The fact of the matter was, he was in the process of going insane. Not that he realised it, of course, he was suffering from a hereditary mental disorder quite commonly found in Bluddums. This condition, which caused metabolic disturbances in the brain, had chosen to attack him at that particular moment. A relatively predictable disease with fairly typical symptoms, it made its victims hear voices and commands or music from other planets. Having rotated on the spot for several days, barking madly, they would sometimes return to normal for months on end. What had happened at the crossroads that day was that the disease was trying to formulate its first commands. Kromek stood there for the next three days, barking like a dog, rotating on the spot and endeavouring to make sense of the unintelligible gibberish in his head. Then, all of a sudden, the voice became crystal clear and said, 'I command you to build an inn here.'

'Who are you?' asked Kromek.

'I am, er, *The Glass Man,*' said the voice.

As far as Kromek Toomah was concerned, that was reason enough for him to build an inn – a thoroughly favourable outcome to the disease, because many of its victims received far stranger orders, some of them bloodthirsty in the extreme. In Kromek's case his sick brain had laid the foundations of a comparatively healthy business, because inns were always in demand, especially in such outposts of civilisation.

Zorda and Zorilla

By his standards, Kromek Toomah was in a fairly stable mental state when Smyke and Rumo approached his inn – Rumo growling and walking on all fours, as instructed. Having had his last attack three weeks earlier, the innkeeper could look forward to two or three months' normality. He had recently acquired some regular customers in the shape of two Bluddums named Zorda and Zorilla, who had found him after his last seizure. To his horror, Kromek had discovered that some shameless bandits had taken advantage of his helpless, deranged condition and looted his storeroom in the interim. That was why Zorda and Zorilla dropped in every day, just to see that all was well. They had quickly become a permanent feature of *The Glass Man*, eating and drinking a great deal, and playing cards all the time. They insisted on putting everything on the slate, so their bill was mounting steadily.

Zorda and Zorilla were in an irritable mood, unlike Kromek, but they took care not to show it. On their first visit to *The Glass Man* a few weeks earlier, Kromek had been standing behind the counter, barking. To begin with they had merely found this amusing. Then, when they helped themselves to the wine barrel without being asked to pay, it had dawned on them that the innkeeper was completely incapacitated. They sat down, drank his wine, ate his roast pork and waited. After a couple of hours Kromek started to rotate on his own axis, still barking. They watched him all night, egging him on and getting disgustingly drunk. When they awoke next morning Kromek was still behind the counter, whimpering now. They proceeded to ransack his storeroom and bear off its contents to their lair. Kromek recovered his wits just as they returned to the inn to complete the job, so they put on an act and blathered something about some bandits who had taken to their heels at the sight of them. Kromek thanked them effusively, and Zorda and Zorilla now visited *The Glass Man* every day, waiting for him to start barking again.

But Kromek's mental condition remained stable. He carefully noted every drop of wine and morsel of food they consumed, and made a corresponding mark on his slate. Zorda was now toying with the idea of settling matters in the time-honoured fashion and braining Kromek with a wine jug. That was how he had solved most of the problems in his life. The only trouble was, the innkeeper was a tough nut, a war veteran and still in good shape, so the outcome of such a course of action was anything but predictable.

Two new customers

'An exceedingly good day to you, gentlemen.' Smyke's melodious bass voice jolted Zorda out of his violent daydream. 'I trust I'm permitted to enter?'

Smyke and Rumo surveyed their surroundings. Although primitively furnished, *The Glass Man* fulfilled the basic requirements of the innkeeper's trade. There was a makeshift bar nailed together, some rickety chairs and tables that had clearly been improvised out of tree stumps, and two broached barrels, one of beer and the other of wine. A half-charred Ornian Marsh Hog was sizzling on a spit over the open fire. Smyke had often dreamt of such a spectacle in his pool on Roaming Rock.

The startled Bluddums turned to stare at the door. Zorilla instinctively reached for his ball and chain, which was lying under the table, and Kromek gave such a start that he knocked a glass off the counter. Customers were rare enough in this wilderness, and the taproom of *The Glass Man* had certainly never been patronised by such a strange pair. Zorda and Zorilla had never seen a Wolperting before, let alone a Shark Grub. Kromek, on the other hand, had seen a Shark Grub on at least one occasion, because Prince Hussein Banana had temporarily employed one as his minister of war. This specimen bore a strong resemblance to the war minister, but then Shark Grubs probably all looked alike. As for Rumo, Kromek surmised that he was a wild mongrel.

Smyke undulated over to the bar while Rumo remained near the door.

'I trust you'll permit us to warm ourselves beside the fire for a few minutes,' said Smyke.

Kromek gave a reluctant grunt. 'Something to drink?'

'I fear not, alas. My dog and I are on a strict diet for, er, health reasons.' Smyke's gaze lingered on the wine barrel. His mouth watered as all the memories garnered by his taste buds and the gustatory nerves in his gums transmitted themselves from his brain to his salivary glands. Memories of vintage Grailsundian Burgundy. Of the velvety aftertaste of Ornian Rosé. Of chilled Florinthian Chardonnay quaffed at the height of summer. Of tannin, and delicate acidity, and the hint of oak imparted by ageing in the wood. Of ruby-red Midgardian Port, which caressed the tongue like silk. It was three years since Smyke had drunk a glass of wine, smoked a phogar, or eaten roast meat.

'All right, but make it quick,' growled Kromek Toomah, bringing Smyke down to earth with a bump. 'This is an inn, not a waiting room.'

Smyke wobbled over to the fire and inhaled the scent of roast pork. Big blisters were swelling and subsiding beneath the joint's blackened skin. Now and then one would burst and deflate with a faint whistle, and blobs of mingled fat and meat juice would fall into the fire, where they hissed and turned into steam. As soon as one of these appetising little clouds rose to Smyke's nostrils, his four stomachs began to bubble like a marsh in hot weather. Sewage gas forced its way through his intestines, which squeaked like a litter of mice, and sheer culinary excitement made him let off a mighty fart.

Kromek Toomah was afraid his peculiar customer would fall on the roast pork like a ravening wolf, so he made sure his crossbow was in its proper place beneath the counter. One false move and he would nail that fat maggot to the wall.

Meanwhile Rumo continued to stand waiting just inside the door. He registered the prevailing tension with all his senses. He could smell the cold sweat of fear, hear hearts racing. No one in the room - himself included - was behaving naturally. To him, everything *smelt wrong*, and that had nothing to do with his scorched nose. Smyke was doing his utmost to sound amiable, but even his voice was trembling with duplicity. With an effort he transferred his gaze from the roast pork to the two Bluddums.

'May one ask what card game you're playing?'

'Rumo,' said Zorda.

Smyke chuckled. 'Ah, rumo, my favourite game.'

Rumo itched to say something, but he obeyed the rules and limited himself to a low growl.

'You should keep that mutt on a lead,' Zorilla said ungraciously.

'He won't bite you.'

'Funny, that's what all dog owners say,' said Zorilla, and Zorda gave an evil chuckle.

'Listen,' Smyke said gravely, 'I won't try to fool you. How could I? I'm not wearing any clothes and I don't have any luggage with me, so it's obvious I don't have a bean.'

The two Bluddums gave a grunt of disappointment.

'But I'd like to play a hand with you. I've a suggestion to make. You see that wonderful Wolperting? He's one of the wild specimens, and I'm sure you know how much in demand they are as watchdogs, especially with the farmers around here. A Wolperting has fetched a thousand pyras at auction before now.'

The Bluddums looked dubious. Then they noticed the horns on Rumo's head.

'That's a . . . a Wolperting?'

'One thousand pyras. That's for a normal Wolperting, but this one is something else. Wolpertings are very stubborn creatures – they can't really be tamed, as I'm sure you know – but this one obeys to order. Watch this.' Smyke looked at Rumo. 'Sit! Go on, sit!'

Rumo went on standing there and flattened his ears, looking offended. The Bluddums laughed.

'Sit!' Smyke repeated in a thunderous voice. He gave Rumo a piercing look. Rumo reluctantly accepted the challenge in Smyke's gaze and sat down on his haunches with a growl.

'You see!' Smyke said triumphantly. 'A trained specimen – a genuine rarity. A creature without a will of its own. An obedient tool in the hands of its owner. But be careful! In the wrong hands a Wolperting can be

misused – it can become a dangerous living weapon! You'd have to promise me only to use him for peaceful purposes.'

The Bluddums leant across the table looking interested.

'What good is it to *me* if the beast obeys *you?*' Zorda demanded. 'I might win him, but it wouldn't mean he'd do what I say.' For a Bluddum, this was an extremely intelligent objection.

'He'll, er, obey anyone I entrust with authority over him,' Smyke replied. He waved one of his little arms in Zorda's direction. 'There, now you're in charge of him. Give him an order.'

'What, me?'

'Yes, go on. Any order you like.'

Zorda thought hard, then started to grin. He turned to Rumo.

'All right, roll in the dirt!'

Rumo couldn't believe his ears. He cocked his head and narrowed his eyes.

'Like hell he'll obey anyone! He didn't even understand what I said.'

Zorda and Zorilla laughed. Smyke gave Rumo another look – a look of entreaty this time, not of insistence. Rumo gathered that learning this new combat technique required self-control and, worse still, a readiness to humiliate himself. That came harder to him than fighting ten Demonocles.

'Tell him again,' said Smyke. 'He understood you all right – he's a bit slow on the uptake, that's all.'

'Go on, you stupid mutt, roll in the dirt!' yelled the Bluddum.

Rumo lay down on his side and rolled to and fro on the dusty taproom floor. Wood shavings and bits of fluff became lodged in his fur.

'That's more like it,' said Zorilla.

Smyke sat down at the table.

'In that case, gentlemen, if you've no objection . . .'

Zorda tossed him the pack of cards.

'You deal. We'll allow you a hundred pyras' credit on the dog. If you lose them he's ours. Minimum stake ten pyras.'

'That seems fair enough,' said Smyke, shuffling the pack.

'What, rumo? Rumo again?' snapped Zorilla, throwing down his cards. 'This fat slob has all the luck! I ask you, six rumos on the trot!'

Rumo foils the double crossbow

Barely an hour had gone by and Smyke was the richest person in *The Glass Man*. He had bet his entire stake six times and won every game. Zorda and Zorilla were cleaned out – they'd been playing on Kromek Toomah's credit for the last two hands.

Smyke decided that it was time to carry out the test he'd planned. He rose and turned to Kromek. 'Where can one, er . . .?'

Kromek laughed. 'Outside. Find yourself a tree.'

Smyke undulated to the door, throwing Rumo a conspiratorial glance as he went. Rumo continued to do what he'd been doing the whole time: he lay on the filthy taproom floor and pretended to be asleep.

'What are we going to do?' asked Zorilla. 'He's cleaned us out completely.'

'We could hit him on the head with the wine jug,' Zorda suggested. 'In the usual way.'

Zorilla agreed. 'All right, we'll play another hand. Afterwards, get up and refill the jug. When you come back, sneak up behind him and smash it over his head.'

'He's a maggot. You can't tell where a maggot's head begins and ends.'

'It was your idea! You must hit him hard enough, that's all. If he's still budging after that, I'll finish him off with my ball and chain.'

'But the jug goes on your bill,' Kromek growled from behind the counter. He had overheard every word.

'We'll sell the Wolperting, or whatever it's called, and split the proceeds three ways,' said Zorda. Privately, he thought, *'As for you, you barking idiot, you'll be the next to get a jug on the head. Then we'll burn your lousy joint to the ground.'*

'We'll drag that fat slob into the woods. The werewolves will do the rest.' Zorilla said this in an undertone, because the front steps were already creaking under Smyke's weight.

Rumo pretended to be stirring restlessly in his sleep. He whimpered faintly and scratched the floor with his right forepaw.

Just as Smyke was oozing past Zorda, he did something Rumo would never have believed him capable of. Quick as a flash, he drove his head into the back of the Bluddum's neck and Zorda crashed forward on to the table top. His head collided with a dice cup and catapulted it into the air. Zorilla reacted quickly. He jumped up, brandishing the ball and chain he'd concealed beneath the table. Kromek took cover behind the counter, the dice cup went skittering across the floor and shed its contents: a double six.

Rumo added to the general confusion by rising on his hind legs. 'Drop that!' he commanded Zorilla.

Zorilla was impressed. His chin sagged, giving Rumo a good view of the ruined teeth in his lower jaw, but he didn't drop his weapon. He raised it in both hands and began to whirl it round his head. The iron ball whistled ominously as it rotated. Zorilla backed away from the table, but Rumo darted beneath it and between the Bluddum's legs before he'd grasped that the Wolperting wasn't there any longer. He reared up behind Zorilla, gripped his wrist and wrenched it downwards. The chain wound itself round the Bluddum's neck, the ball circled him three times, getting closer and closer, and hit him on the head. Stunned by his own weapon, Zorilla crashed to the taproom floor, sending up a little cloud of dust.

The innkeeper came out from behind the counter holding a double crossbow. He pointed it at Rumo and cried, 'Get out, the two of you, and be quick about it!'

'You've forgotten to cock the thing,' said Smyke.

Kromek stopped short. Feverishly, he proceeded to fiddle with the cocking mechanism.

A mechanical weapon was a novel challenge for Rumo. Smyke had told him a lot about the various kinds of crossbows, the way they worked and the speed at which their bolts travelled. This one was a Grailsundian double arbalest with two bows of eight-layered birchwood, reindeer-gut strings, a wrought-iron stock, and a trigger mechanism such as only officially certified watchmakers were permitted to manufacture. The bolts were made of compressed reeds twisted like ropes and armed with notched bronze tips. This lent them the requisite spin in flight and enabled them to penetrate solid brick.

Click! went the crossbow. Kromek aimed it at Rumo again.

'Get out of here, both of you!' he yelled.

'What would you say to a little wager, *Kromek Toomah?*' asked Smyke.

'What! How come you know my name?' Startled, Kromek lowered his crossbow for an instant.

Smyke reeled off his details. 'Sergeant Kromek Toomah, weight three hundred and fifty pounds, height eight foot three inches, forty-seven decorations for gallantry in the face of the enemy, artilleryman, hard of hearing. I raised your pay three times, had you forgotten?'

Kromek looked bewildered. Could this really be the ex-minister of war?

'When we were encamped outside Florinth,' Smyke went on, and his voice took on a crisp note, 'Prince Hussein proposed to send the Fourth Division - of which Sergeant Kromek Toomah was also a member - to attack the palisades, although everyone knew the Florinthians were waiting for them with boiling pitch - we could smell it from our camp. I persuaded the prince to break off the siege, don't you remember?'

Smyke had been saving this appeal to Kromek's emotions until now. He had recognised the Bluddum immediately. Kromek was somewhat older and heavier, but his face still wore the moronic expression typical of a born warrior faithful unto death. Smyke gave a mocking smile and extended two of his little arms as if about to embrace him.

'Surely you remember your old minister of war?'

Yes, Kromek remembered him. At the time he'd thought him a lily-livered coward. He'd been itching to brave a shower of boiling tar for his prince's sake - he would sooner have died than turn tail. The retreat from Florinth had been the worst humiliation he'd ever suffered.

'You cowardly swine! We could have trounced those Florinthian bastards with ease.'

Smyke's little excursion into the past didn't seem to be having the desired effect. 'All right, let's forget about the old days. We need some food, water and clothing - and, let's say, a hundred pyras to see us on our way. I bet you can't kill my Wolperting with that crossbow of yours.'

Kromek thought hard.

'What do I get in return?'

'Your life will be spared.'

'No, I mean, what do I get if I win the bet?'

'You can't win.'

'You're crazy, both of you! Get out of here!' The Bluddum was looking rather disconcerted again.

'Go on, Kromek Toomah, shoot him!' Smyke said sharply.

Rumo was disconcerted too. Was Smyke subjecting him to another test? He'd never seen how a mechanical weapon worked. Up to now the fastest thing he'd ever had to avoid was a Demonocle's fist.

Kromek mechanically did as he was told. The twin triggers clicked twice, releasing the gut bowstrings and loosing off both bolts simultaneously. A whirring noise filled the air. As if guided by invisible wires, the projectiles came spinning towards the Wolperting. He could see particles of dust spiralling along in their wake.

The whirring noise expanded in Rumo's ears, slowing and deepening until it became a low, resonant hum. He knew what this portended. It was the moment of supreme danger, when his physical and mental processes speeded up in an almost miraculous way. He had first experienced this phenomenon on the plateau on Roaming Rock, when he ripped off the Demonocle's head. All at once he had ample time to debate how to react. There were three possibilities. He could simply bend his head aside, which would probably make the most nonchalant impression. Or he could crouch down and let the bolts fly over him – that would look athletic. Or he could bend from the waist, paws on hips, and make a thoroughly daredevil impression. He simply couldn't decide.

He was still pondering the problem when a fly went buzzing across the bolts' flight path. It just missed the one on the left but was sucked into its slipstream. This was bad luck on the insect, Rumo sympathetically noted, because it lost both its wings to the spinning feathers and fell to the floor, badly injured, instead of dying a swift and merciful death.

The bolts were now only inches away – Rumo could already make out the weaponsmith's trademark on their copper tips. At that moment he heard a movement behind him. It was Zorda, who had recovered his senses and was drawing a knife from the sheath strapped to his leg beneath his trousers. The Bluddum was doing his utmost not to make a noise – he lay quite still with his head on the table top and was extracting the blade from its sheath with great deliberation – but to Rumo's ears it sounded like an executioner's axe being whetted on a grindstone.

Under these circumstances Rumo decided on a fourth method of evasion. Casually propping one fist on his hip, he inclined the upper part of his body a little to one side to avoid both crossbow bolts. At the same time he raised his other paw and brushed the feathers of one of them – only gently, but hard enough to change its direction considerably. The other bolt he intended to pluck out of the air. Just as he reached for it he was struck by a painful realisation: he might as well have planted his paw on a red-hot stove. The friction occasioned by the braking process scorched his palm and the shaft's tiny reed fibres tore away shreds of skin, but he didn't let go; he tightened his grip and brought the spinning bolt to a standstill. Meanwhile the second bolt sped on, transfixed the table top on which Zorda's head was resting and nailed the hand holding the haft of the dagger to his leg. Too shocked to utter a sound, the Bluddum passed out once more. Rumo clenched his teeth and stood there gripping the arrow with a thin trickle of blood seeping between his fingers.

Smyke gave a low, admiring whistle.

And Kromek Toomah started barking again.

Rumo and Smyke left the taproom and made their way outside. Smyke tossed a half-gnawed pork chop over his shoulder and filled his lungs with tobacco smoke. Although there hadn't been any phogars in the inn, just a box of cheap South Zamonian cheroots, they were quite good enough to satisfy him after years of abstinence. His eyelids were heavy with wine, but his heart was lighter than it had been for a long time. Having drained a jug of Kromek Toomah's red wine without drawing breath, he was feeling liberated – free at last from the memories and fears that had haunted him ever since Roaming Rock. He was truly back in civilisation.

'I'm quicker than other creatures,' said Rumo. He was still marvelling at his own achievement.

'Much quicker,' said Smyke, blowing a smoke ring. 'You're a Wolperting.'

Rumo tugged at his new clothes. He was wearing Zorilla's scuffed leather pants, which ended just below his knees, and a Troll-fur waistcoat taken from Kromek Toomah. Both garments reeked of Bluddum.

'Do I really have to wear these?' he asked Smyke.

Smyke was weighing a purse in one of his predatory little hands. He shook it, listening entranced to its jingling contents.

'Yes,' he said, 'you do.'

'One thing struck me as odd,' said Rumo as they left *The Glass Man Tavern* and set off in an easterly direction.

'Really? What?'

'That card game had the same name as me.'

'Yes.' Smyke grinned. 'Funny, isn't it?'

The Nocturnomath

That night they camped in a small wood that struck them as safe – at least, Rumo picked up no alarming signals. They lit a fire, which meant that Rumo, under Smyke's instructions, gathered some dry grass, bark and twigs, and knocked two specially selected stones together until sparks flew from them and ignited the kindling.

'That's something else I've taught you,' said Smyke. He was lounging on a soft bed of maple leaves and sampling a skin of red wine appropriated from *The Glass Man*. Rumo had sniffed it and declined with thanks, so Smyke had it all to himself. 'You're clever with your hands. People of my age are past making fires. In the larger cities, public braziers tended by Glimmerdwarfs glow on every street corner. You pay them a copper for a blazing torch and take it home with you. That's the way it ought to be.'

A swarm of Elf Wasps circled the fire, Crackchafers buzzed round Smyke's head, menacing with their tiny pincers, and Will-o'-the-Wisps darted giggling through the rising smoke. Springtime in Zamonia had unleashed hordes of insects. Death-defying Dust Moths plunged into the flames and exploded with a hiss. Smyke grimaced with distaste.

'That's what I dislike most about the great outdoors: it belongs to the insects. Well, they're welcome to it. Insects can have the countryside as long as we can have the cities. We steer clear of the great outdoors and insects steer clear of the cities – that would be a fair division. What business has a spider in a bedroom? As much as we have in this confounded wood.'

Rumo was busy blowing the fire as instructed by Smyke. It fascinated him to see how fast the flames took hold.

'In the civilised world we kill insects when we come across them,' Smyke went on plaintively. 'Insects do the same to us, but in a more subtle way. In this district there are said to be Mummy Ticks whose bite doesn't simply kill you, it makes you *un*dead, can you imagine that? No bigger than a grain of sand, they lurk in trees for years and land on your head if you're unwise enough to sit down beneath them. Then they burrow into your brain and lay their eggs there. You don't even notice it, but when the eggs hatch your head goes mouldy inside and you turn into a walking corpse that lives on moths.'

Rumo looked up at the leafy canopy overhead and ruffled his fur.

Smyke's gaze brightened when he looked back at the flames. He was thinking of big-city fires, of skyscrapers as high as the Gloomberg Mountains, of streets lined with busy shops, of inns and taverns. He knew of a bar in Grailsund where . . . A branch exploded in the fire and brought him down to earth again.

'I wish we had a little Swamp Hog we could roast.' He sighed. 'I know an excellent recipe for Swamp Hog in which caraway seeds play a sensational part. Did you know that caraway seeds go perfectly with resinous cheese?'

Rumo wished Smyke would give his monologues a rest, if only for a moment. He had scented something and he wanted to monitor the wood without being distracted by the Shark Grub's chatter. He shut his eyes and concentrated hard. The results gleaned by his nose and ears were contradictory and confusing. He could smell a living creature hidden in the undergrowth some twenty paces away. Its heartbeat, which he could hear, was slow and regular, from which he deduced that no attack was to be feared – unless the creature was so self-assured that not even the imminence of combat made its pulses race. But he could also hear another four organs at work: an incessant crunching, crackling sound. Rumo had never encountered anyone whose insides produced such noises.

'Tomorrow we'll go hunting,' Smyke ordained. 'It's time you got over your aversion – it's against your nature. I'll teach you how to hunt. We may even find a Swamp Hog, the ground is marshy enough for–'

'There's something over there in the undergrowth,' Rumo whispered. 'Some creature or creatures. I can hear puzzling noises.'

'Puzzling noises?' Smyke lowered his voice too. 'What sort of noises?'

'Crunches and crackles. They could be bodily organs functioning, but I've never heard anything like them before. There seem to be four of them.'

'Kackertratts have several livers, I believe,' whispered Smyke, 'but they only operate in packs.' He deplored his lack of general knowledge, because he was far from sure of either assertion.

Two lights shone through the undergrowth. They were circular, yellowish and not particularly bright, but they appeared so suddenly that Rumo reared up into his attack stance and Smyke reached for a thin branch. Then the lights began to move towards them. The bushes parted, and out of the undergrowth stepped a wizened little creature with a disproportionately large head on its shoulders. The lights turned out to be its big, round, luminous eyes, and the movements of this peculiar apparition were so clumsy and ill coordinated that Rumo instinctively relaxed.

'I trust I didn't startle you, gentlemen,' the nocturnal visitor said in a high-pitched, nasal, almost arrogant voice. 'But I saw the fire and since I was passing through a relatively uninhabited district where campfires are conspicuous by reason of their statistical rarity, my curiosity was aroused and I took the liberty of coming closer. I myself would never have dared to light a fire in this part of the world, given its scientifically proven incidence of Werewolves and Lunawraiths. But a little defensive community like yours can afford to do so, eh?'

'A Nocturnomath,' thought Smyke.

'Yes, you're right, I'm a Nocturnomath – in other words, gentlemen, harmless. I'm dangerous only on the mental plane, so you'd better not cross swords with me when it comes to intellectual matters, ha ha! Permit me to introduce myself. My name is Kolibri, Professor Ostafan Kolibri.'

Smyke was impressed by the fearless way this frail little gnome had walked up to him and Rumo. He was evidently a mind-reader and bore a faint resemblance to the professor from whom Smyke had acquired his knowledge of Demonocles' tongues in Fort Una. He had the same glowing eyes, the same puny body, the same outsize head. But something about him was different.

'You're welcome,' said Smyke. *'We should be glad to share our campfire with any well-disposed wayfarer.'*

The Atlantean Hiker's Code laid it down that this was the traditional sentence to be recited on such occasions. Originally formulated by some Natifftoffian politicians whose hobby was hiking, it signalised courtesy and hospitality. But it also conveyed a veiled threat, being a clear intimation that the hosts would defend themselves vigorously if attacked by their guest or guests. There was no legal obligation to use this flowery phrase, but it was widely recognised and taught in many Zamonian schools. The correct response to it ran: *'I thank you for your offer of hospitality and promise not to take undue advantage of it.'*

'I thank you for your offer of hospitality and promise not to take undue advantage of it,' Ostafan Kolibri replied and added, 'I feel I should mention that I'm in possession of some Midgardian biltong sausages which, in return for your hospitality, I should be happy to share with you, campfire-owning gentlemen. Would that be convenient?'

The Nocturnomaths' trademark was a certain linguistic eccentricity believed by many scientists to be a form of disease stemming from the immense output of words generated by their multiple brains. Kolibri held up a cloth bag from which he extracted a long, thin sausage.

'It would indeed be convenient!' Smyke exclaimed. Delightedly, he beckoned their nocturnal visitor closer.

Although Rumo had abandoned his hostile stance, he remained alert and eyed Kolibri suspiciously.

Once the newcomer's contribution had been silently consumed beside the crackling campfire (Smyke got the biggest share, the Nocturnomath ate very little and Rumo abstained altogether), Smyke endeavoured to strike up a civilised conversation.

'May one enquire where your travels are taking you?' he asked.

'I'm on my way to Murkholm.'

Smyke stared at Kolibri in astonishment.

'Murkholm,' Kolibri went on, 'lies north of Florinth on the coast of West Zam–'

'I know,' Smyke broke in. 'I was only wondering. I mean, are you going there *voluntarily?*'

The Nocturnomath laughed. 'I'm familiar with the old saying about Murkholm. *If you go to Murkholm . . .*'

'*. . . don't bring any murk home!*' Smyke amplified. They both laughed politely. Rumo stared uncomprehendingly at the fire.

'I've only heard the usual rumours,' Smyke went on. 'How the city is eternally blanketed in fog, how people keep disappearing there – that sort of thing.'

'My own state of knowledge is little better. I'm going there to conduct some scientific experiments. I may be able to substitute proven facts for some of the wilder stories and theories about the place.'

'Stories? What stories?'

'Are you really interested?'

'Stories always interest me.'

'Are you acquainted with the legend of Netherworld?'

'Netherworld?' Smyke said enquiringly.

Rumo pricked up his ears too.

'The world beneath the world. The Kingdom of Evil, et cetera.' Kolibri waggled his bony fingers in the air.

'I've heard the odd rumour,' said Smyke. Superstitious nonsense – barrack-room gossip.'

'Shall I?' asked Kolibri.

'Please do!' Smyke replied.

Murkholm

The professor threw a dry log on the fire. 'For many centuries now, things have been happening in Zamonia for which there's no satisfactory explanation. Whenever they do, folk start muttering about Netherworld. Where do Demerara Dragons hail from? Netherworld! Where did the inhabitants of Nairland disappear to? Netherworld! Where did the Nurns come from? Netherworld! Where did General Ticktock and his Copper Killers escape to? Netherworld!'

Rumo stiffened. Did this dwarf know about General Ticktock?

'So what's the answer?' asked Smyke. 'Is there a genuine connection?'

'That's the question! People have always had a tendency to divide everything into two categories: above and below, light and dark, good and evil. Scientists, on the other hand, strive to illuminate and define the areas between them. Massed in Netherworld, so it's said, are the forces that thrust Zamonia to the surface – the scum that will one day rise and take over the whole continent. Theoretically, Netherworld is a gigantic cave system running beneath Zamonia, a world of darkness filled with dangerous and demonic life forms. There are many legends concerning Netherworld, one of them being that Murkholm is the secret entrance to it.'

'Ha ha,' said Smyke.

'Yes, ha ha,' said the professor. 'An incorrigible old wives' tale. On the other hand what about all the people who keep disappearing in the neighbourhood of Murkholm? What about the inhabitants' strange behaviour? Last but not least, what about the scientifically unaccountable behaviour of the fog over the city, which never disperses?'

'You arouse my curiosity,' said Smyke.

'Let's stick to the facts as we know them,' said Kolibri. 'Not far north of Florinth on the west coast of Zamonia stands the city of Murkholm, which owes its name to the ultra-stable pall of fog that hovers over it. Some especially simple souls believe this fog to be a living creature, and you'd be surprised how many far more preposterous little myths surround that part of the world. But, as so often, those myths contain a microscopic grain of truth. If that grain of truth exists in Murkholm I shall find it, preserve it, dissect it, measure it, and draw my scientific conclusions. I specialise in microscopic life forms.'

'What method do you use?' asked Smyke. 'As a scientist, do you favour some kind of, er, *tactical* approach?'

'Well, my first step will be to go to Murkholm in person. I've already sent my equipment on ahead and rented a lighthouse there. The Murkholmers are more helpful than is generally believed – a few polite letters did the trick. That in itself was almost enough to disprove all those myths. People often go there on holiday, after all, so it can't be as bad as all that.'

'You've got guts,' Smyke said admiringly.

'Pah! If no one had ever shed light on darkness we would still be sitting in caves, convinced that clouds are flying mountains.'

'What will you do when you get to Murkholm?'

'Investigate the fog, of course. I shall take an auracardiogram of it.'

'A what?'

'Please don't ask me to explain, I wouldn't want to spoil our evening, but I'll tell you this much: I intend to examine the fog's microscopic heart. All secrets can be fathomed in miniature.'

'Aha,' said Smyke.

Professor Nightingale

'Believe me, even I, with my four brains, hardly understand how an auracardiograph works. For that one needs seven brains like its inventor, Professor Nightingale.'

'You know him?'

'He was my doctoral supervisor. I studied under him when he was still teaching at Atlantis University. You know him too?'

'"Know" would be an exaggeration. I met him once.'

'Zamonia is a big place, but Nightingale is everywhere!' The Nocturnomath laughed. 'No matter where I go, Nightingale has been there before me. He's like a disembodied spirit, everywhere and nowhere at once. Where did you come across him?'

'At Fort Una.'

'The gambler's heaven!' Kolibri chuckled. 'The old fox!'

'He was there for scientific reasons, if I understood him correctly. Any idea where he is now?'

'I know nothing definite, as usual. Nightingale tends to keep his activities under wraps. Is he here or is he there? Is he vibrating his way through a mountain or walking on water in H_20-densifying aquashoes? I heard he was planning to found an elite academy in the Gloomberg Mountains. Others say he's invented a machine for deep-freezing tornadoes. Still others claim he lost his mind and jumped off Mount Apex. According to the latest rumour he's travelling with a fairground attraction – trying it out on the rural population of Zamonia. But as I say, I know nothing definite. He's probably sitting in the dark again, meditating on darkness research.'

'Are you also into darkness research?'

'No. Or rather, no longer. In my youth I assisted Professor Nightingale and acquired some knowledge of the subject, but in the end, because I didn't want to spend my entire life in the Gloomberg Mountains, I had to liberate myself from him. The best way to sever one's ties with a role model is to proceed in the opposite direction. You see, the main difference between my scientific methodology and Nightingale's is one of perspective. His gaze is focused on the very big: the universal. I concentrate on the very small: the microcosmic.'

'I envy you Nocturnomaths your brains,' Smyke said with a sigh. 'I've forgotten nearly everything I learnt at school. I'd have to swot for twenty years to get back all the stuff that's trickled through my sieve of a memory.'

Knowledge is night

'Would you like a mental refill?' Kolibri asked. There was a curiously expectant note in his voice.

'Would I!' said Smyke. 'If only it were that easy!'

'It is! At least, it is where the primitive basic knowledge whose loss you deplore is concerned. Elementary Zamonian mathematics, history, creaturology – is that the sort of stuff you mean? That's easy to transmit. It can be done *that* fast.' Kolibri snapped his fingers.

Smyke remembered the ideas that had flooded his brain when Professor Nightingale laid a hand on his shoulder at Fort Una.

'Yes, it's something along those lines,' said Kolibri, as if it went without saying that he'd read Smyke's thoughts. 'But that was just a random thought transmission – scientifically worthless.'

'It certainly helped *me*,' Smyke replied with a smile, involuntarily remembering the Demonocles' tongues.

'No,' said Kolibri, 'I'm talking about restoring the whole of the knowledge you acquired at school in a few seconds – and expanding it a little as well.'

'You're joking.'

'Nocturnomaths don't joke about the transmission of knowledge.'

'Could you be a little more explicit?'

'Well, I possess several brains. Four, to be exact. That makes me a Nocturnomath Grade Four. Nocturnomaths of the fourth grade and upwards are capable of transmitting knowledge bacterially.'

'Could you really do that?'

'Yes, but only if you want. Not everyone does. And I must warn you: even though it's a very rapid process, completely painless and not injurious to one's health, it has immense repercussions. It will expand your consciousness and change your life, and there's no guarantee it will do so for the better. Knowledge can be dangerous. *Knowledge is night.*' Kolibri giggled.

'I'll chance it,' Smyke rejoined.

'But the knowledge I can impart is limited. I can only transmit what I myself, with my limited cerebral capacity, have learnt. Compare Nightingale. He has seven brains, I have only four.'

'All the same,' said Smyke. He now knew what differentiated Kolibri from Nightingale. He lacked the excrescences on his head that contained additional brains.

'I can think as much as I like and learn as much as I'm able, but I'll never be as brilliant as Nightingale. Have you heard of the Grailsundian Prizefighters' Guild?'

'Yes, certainly. I've trained a few boxers myself.'

'Then you'll know they're divided into various classes. Some fighters have two arms, others three, four or five. There are some very talented boxers with three arms, but they'll never be contenders for the five-armed title.'

'You're too modest.'

'It's just that I don't want you to be disappointed by the knowledge I impart. The other limitation is that you'll only get the knowledge that happens to be passing through my brains at the time. It could be utterly irrelevant, useless stuff - mental baggage unneeded on your journey through life.'

'I'll chance it, as I say. How much does this business cost?'

The Nocturnomath raised his head and shot Smyke a glance of blazing indignation.

'I apologise,' Smyke mumbled. 'I'm a life form that's accustomed to thinking in commercial terms.'

Kolibri subsided quickly. 'You're champing at the bit, I can see, and I'm bound to say it would really give me pleasure to infect you a little. It's a long time since I've done that. I'm not betraying any professional secrets when I say that passing on a mental infection sends us Nocturnomaths into a state of rapture verging on euphoria. A triumphant feeling of elation devoid of remorse.'

'Shall we get on with it?' Smyke asked impatiently.

'One moment! Some minor preparations are essential. First I must inform your companion that he'll be responsible for our safety in the immediate future. We're utterly helpless while the infection is taking hold. We fall into a kind of trance and could be devoured alive without noticing it. So, if danger threatens –'

'– I can't think of a better bodyguard than Rumo,' said Smyke.

'Does he have any combat experience?'

Smyke grinned. 'Does he! As soon as this business is over I'll tell you an interesting story about Rumo's combat experience.'

'Oh, good! I adore exciting stories.' The Nocturnomath clapped his hands. 'Let's begin, then. What treatment would you like? Light, medium, or the full programme?'

'If a job is worth doing, it's worth doing well.'

'Fine. "Light" means we wouldn't even have to touch. "Medium" requires moderate physical contact. If you want the full programme, you must stick your finger in my ear.'

'What?!'

'You must insert one of your fingers in this aperture.' Kolibri indicated a small hole beneath his temple. 'That's a Nocturnomath's ear. It won't work unless you do.'

'I understand.' Smyke hesitated, but only for a moment. He looked at Rumo. 'Rumo, keep your eyes and ears open.'

Rumo gave a sullen nod.

'This is a dangerous part of the world,' Kolibri told him. 'And please don't try to separate us, no matter what happens. If contact between us were severed we might have to spend the rest of our lives in a state of mental derangement.'

'Really?' Smyke stopped short.

'Well, do you want to do it or not?'

'All right,' said Smyke. 'Rumo, you heard what the professor said, so look out!'

Rumo nodded again.

As though preparing to dive, Smyke drew a deep breath and stuck his finger in the Nocturnomath's ear. It felt as if he had dipped it in a jar of lukewarm jam.

'Enjoy your flight,' Kolibri said with a smile. 'And don't be surprised if you run into Professor Nightingale in there.'

'Nightingale? What do you . . .'

Smyke was dazzled by a white flash, then everything went black. 'I'm passing out,' he thought, but the next instant it was light again. He was soaring high in the air, and stretched out below him was something that resembled the street map of a vast city.

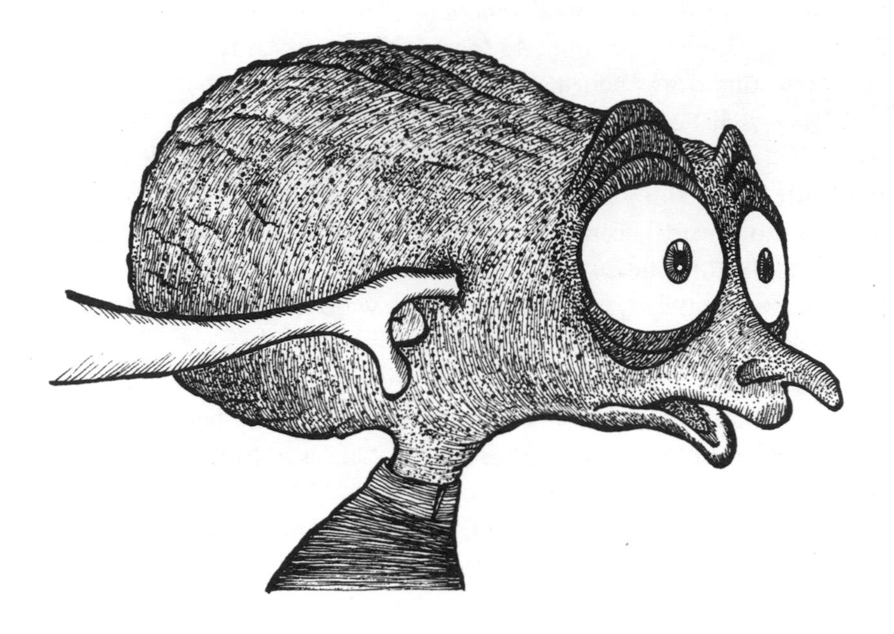

'I can fly,' he thought. 'Great! Is that Atlantis down there?'

'No,' replied the voice of Professor Ostafan Kolibri. It came from above, from below, from all directions, like the voice of an invisible god. 'No, you can't fly. It's just your mind's way of coming to terms with your present location: the interior of a Nocturnomath's brain. That isn't Atlantis down there either, it's Ostafan, my native city. Actually, it's only a city district: North Ostafan. There's North Ostafan, South Ostafan, West Ostafan and East Ostafan. Each district represents one of my four brains. Let us descend.'

Rumo gave a start. Smyke was squealing like a stuck pig, loud and long, as if falling into a bottomless pit, but he kept his finger in Kolibri's ear, so Rumo did nothing. Smyke and the Nocturnomath were standing motionless. The Shark Grub's mouth was wide open, his tongue jerking back and forth like a bell clapper.

This was a strange night, but Rumo had known stranger ones in his time. He tossed another log on the fire.

Smyke was in free fall. He wasn't flying any longer, he was plunging towards the city like a stone. It wouldn't be long before he was dashed to pieces.

North Ostafan

'Eeeeeeeeee!' he cried.

'Don't make such a fuss!' Kolibri called from overhead. 'You aren't really falling, it's only an illusion. If you scream in here you'll be screaming out there as well, and that could attract unwelcome visitors to our campfire.'

Smyke stopped screaming. 'It's an illusion,' he muttered, 'just an illusion. In reality I'm standing beside a Nocturnomath with my finger in his ear. This isn't happening at all. An illusion.'

'That's right,' said Kolibri. 'We're flying - or rather, *illusioning* our way - along the main street, Ostafan Avenue.'

Smyke levelled out into a horizontal glide along North Ostafan's widest thoroughfare. He noticed only now that there wasn't any city or street at all. What he had mistaken for buildings were geometrical bodies of every conceivable shape, colour and size: hemispheres, parallelepipeds, pyramids, trapezoids, cubes, cones, octahedra, and . . . layer cakes. And none of them had any doors or windows.

'Layer cakes?' Smyke said wonderingly.

Seated on his tree stump, Rumo was mistrustfully watching the remarkable spectacle of Smyke, dramatically illuminated by the flickering campfire, with his finger stuck in Kolibri's ear. At least he'd stopped screaming. Rumo listened: all was still. He cocked his head and sniffed the cool evening breeze: nothing. Just small creatures asleep beneath the trees, slow and steady heartbeats, deep and regular breathing, drowsy and contented snuffles. No danger. Tomorrow, Rumo decided, he would force the pace. They were going far too slowly. Smyke had no objective, so he didn't mind how little progress they made. It was different for Rumo. He had an objective: the end of the Silver Thread.

Layer cake

'Layer cakes?' he heard Smyke mutter.

'The buildings resembling layer cakes are information silos,' Kolibri explained. 'They contain preserved knowledge arranged in layers according to subject, rather like libraries. Would you like to see inside one?'

'Of course,' said Smyke. He had already banked to the right and was making for a point halfway up a circular orange-coloured building. It seemed to be hundreds of feet high, with floors that steadily diminished in size the higher they went. There were no doors or windows or other openings. He raced towards it at the speed of a cannon ball.

'Aaaaaaah!' he yelled.

Rumo gave a jump. Smyke had started yelling again. A gust of wind blew across the clearing and wafted his long-drawn-out cry of fear into the depths of the wood.

Rumo was becoming inured to the idea that this would be a pretty long night as well as a strange one. He hadn't a clue what the two of them were doing in Ostafan Kolibri's world of ideas, but it seemed they wouldn't emerge for some time. He would gladly have gone to sleep and dreamt of the Silver Thread, but he was responsible for their safety. How on earth could anyone stick his finger in the ear of such an oddball? It served Smyke right if what was happening to him was unpleasant enough to make him yell.

Brain music

'Aaaaaaah!' Smyke was still yelling as he hit the wall, but he wasn't smashed to pieces. There was a squelching sound and he went straight through it.

'It's like diving without getting wet,' he thought. For a second or two he was engulfed by a pulsating orange glow. His ears crackled loudly, there was another squelch, and he found himself hovering inside the information silo. He was in the midst of a beam of light, with luminous bubbles in every shade of orange floating above and below him. He hung there for an instant, motionless, then plunged into the depths like a puppet whose strings have been severed.

'Aaaaaaah!' he yelled again.

'Quiet, please!' snapped Kolibri, who seemed to be with him in the silo. 'Pull yourself together. This is like a library. A place for introspection.'

Smyke's dive ended abruptly and he fell silent. 'It's only an illusion,' he muttered, 'only . . . an . . . illusion.' He was hovering in space, and revolving around him was a wall with numerous circular openings. He could hear faint singing accompanied by a rhythmical 'boom-boom-boom'.

'Strange,' he thought. 'Somehow, that music sounds intelligent.'

'It's brain music,' Kolibri explained. 'The song of the synapses. That's what thought processes sound like.'

'But where am I?' asked Smyke. 'What kind of knowledge is stored here?'

'Hm, you might find it rather boring. Early Zamonian history, creaturology.'

'Creaturology?' Kolibri had whetted Smyke's thirst for knowledge.

'The study of all life forms. Shark Grubs, for instance. Would you like to learn something about Shark Grubs?'

'No thanks,' said Smyke. 'I already know too much about them.'

'Norselanders? Junglies? Fangfangs? Yetis? Moomies? Turnip-heads? Take your pick. We also have information about the most disagreeable life forms: Werewolves, Nurns, Demonocles, Luna-wraiths, Vrahoks.'

'I know all I need to know about Demonocles,' said Smyke, 'but what are Vrahoks?'

'Ah, I can only offer you rumours about them. Nothing scientifically definite.'

'Lunawraiths, then. Are those the things you mentioned just now, beside the campfire? I'd never heard of them before.'

'A rare species. Unpleasant individuals.' Kolibri's voice sounded as if he were shivering. 'You really want to know something about Lunawraiths?'

Rumo was growing impatient. The two of them were still standing there almost motionless, like an absurd monument to the advisability of keeping one's ears clean. From to time they burbled semi-intelligibly to themselves. They might have been two sleepwalkers trying to converse.

'Unplsnt indvdls,' Kolibri was muttering. 'You rly wnt to know smthng abt Lnwrths?'

Rumo hadn't the faintest idea what this meant, nor did he want to know. His dearest wish was to get some sleep so as to be able to cover plenty of ground the next day. He tossed a couple of dry logs on to the fire, which was dying down, and watched the sparks twinkle like stars as they soared into the night sky.

The infochamber

Smyke turned horizontally on his own axis, sped towards one of the rotating apertures and slipped through it. He was now in a cool grotto whose translucent walls shed an amber glow.

'You're now in an infochamber - something unique to a Nocturnomath's brain. We can store substantial quantities of knowledge for a lifetime without forgetting even a tiny particle of it. The information is perfectly preserved.'

'Is this your doctoral thesis on Lunawraiths?'

'My doctoral thesis?' Kolibri laughed. 'No, that would require a building to itself. This is just a brief, off-the-cuff lecture I had to deliver as a student. The professors gave you a subject and you had to rattle off any relevant details that came into your head. It's a little information picked up from encyclopedias, that's all.'

A gong sounded. Kolibri proceeded to hold forth, but his voice seemed considerably younger than before.

Lunawraiths

'Describing a Lunawraith is no easy matter. The creatures are colourless – those who have seen them speak of black, chimpanzee-like figures with short legs and long arms. They make no sound and emit no smell. Lunawraiths are also said to be faceless and in certain parts of Zamonia they are known as *Fridgimakers*. Many scientists assign Lunawraiths to the vampire family because they practise a procedure similar to bloodsucking. They attack sleepers and, in a still unexplained manner, suck the life force out of their ears until their victims are frozen stiff or dead - hence their nickname. Far more common during the Zamonian Middle Ages than they are today, Lunawraiths were then regarded as a thorough pest. They gave rise to the invention of lockable shutters and so-called vampire grilles. Lunawraiths cannot open doors or windows, they prefer to operate in the open air or enter by way of doors or windows that have been left unsecured. Thus shutters and grilles have dramatically reduced their population over the centuries. Today their sphere of activity is restricted to wooded areas and lonely places where travellers are compelled to spend the night in the open. In other respects Lunawraiths are the least well-researched life forms in Zamonia - in fact, many scientists doubt that they should be classified as life forms at all.'

Another gong. Smyke spun round, shot through the hole and floated back into the grotto.

'Good heavens!' he exclaimed. 'You mean those creatures are prowling around outside in the wood?'

'You told me your young companion was an excellent sentry.' Kolibri's voice, which was once more coming from overhead, sounded older and more mature. 'Lunawraiths are bigger cowards than hyenas. They only attack sleeping people.'

'That's good,' said Smyke. 'Rumo isn't fond of sleeping.'

Rumo sat down on the ground, propped his back against a tree trunk and watched the grotesque pair, who were now only dimly illuminated by the dying campfire. The clearing was becoming suffused with darkness that seemed to flow from the trees and bathe every detail in dark-grey. He didn't feel like feeding the fire any longer. The other two could do that when they emerged - very soon, he hoped - from their trance.

He consulted his ears and nose. Nothing. No ominous sounds or scents, no lurking dangers. He stretched, yawned, and slid a little further down the tree trunk. The ground beneath him still seemed to be swaying, a distant reminder of Roaming Rock, but this time the sensation was soothing. He shut his eyes, just for a moment. He wouldn't go to sleep, only shut his eyes for a few seconds in these peaceful surroundings. Scarcely had he done so when he saw the Silver Thread. He couldn't open his eyes again right away, it was far too beautiful.

The construction site

Volzotan Smyke glided along the deserted streets of North Ostafan. The geometrical structures that flanked them glowed in the most fantastic colours, and he was relishing this artistic spectacle, which came very close to his ideal conception of a big city, the only missing feature being a few good hostelries. He was starting to enjoy this mode of travel, and the more he enjoyed it the more control he gained over his aerial movements. It was all a question of will-power, he gathered.

His eye was caught by a large structure in the distance that differed from all the other buildings in its bizarre outlines. Towering over everything in its vicinity, it resembled a palace designed by an architect who had gone mad while work was in progress. With its crooked towers and shapeless annexes, its domes erected on top of domes, its bulges and protrusions, it was less a building than a monstrous construction site.

'Heavens alive,' Smyke exclaimed, 'what's that?'

Kolibri gave an embarrassed little cough from overhead.

'Is that another information silo? Why does it look so odd?'

'No, it's not a silo.'

'What is it, then?'

'Nothing.'

'What do you mean, nothing?'

'Nothing of importance.'

'So why is it the most conspicuous building in the city?'

'I'd rather not talk about it.'

'Come on, professor, out with it.'

'It's, er, a doctoral thesis.'

Smyke laughed. 'That's a relief. I thought it was some frightful disease.'

'So is a doctoral thesis, in a way.'

'I'm going to take a closer look,' said Smyke, and he headed straight for the curious excrescence.

'Out of the question!' cried Kolibri. 'It's still incomplete! It's one of my unfinished doctoral dissertations - work in progress, nothing more.'

'Never mind!' Smyke flew lower.

'Please don't! Let's look at a few thought balloons instead.'

Undeterred, Smyke continued to make for the building. He was pleased to note that Kolibri seemed unable to influence his movements if he didn't want him to.

'This is embarrassing,' the professor exclaimed with a note of entreaty in his voice.

'Oh, go on!' Smyke chuckled. His growing command of illusory flight was making him cocky. 'Whee!' he cried. He looped the loop twice, went into a vertical dive, and plunged into the dark shell of the bizarre structure.

'Please don't!' Kolibri wailed again, but Smyke had already vanished into his thesis.

'Whee!' cried Smyke, and his exultant cry went echoing through the gloomy wood.

'Whoo!' replied a distant owl.

Smyke and Kolibri were still standing there transfixed. The fire was just a mound of embers and all that lit the clearing was a faint yellowish glow.

'Please don't!' muttered Kolibri.

Rumo was still seated with his back against the tree. His chin had sunk on to his chest, a thin thread of saliva was issuing from the corner of his mouth, and he was snoring. Rumo was fast asleep. He was dreaming of love.

Kolibri's doctoral dissertation

Smyke continued his dive. It was so dark, he might have been diving into a vat of ink. He could hear hundreds and thousands of voices talking simultaneously. He barely understood a word, but it sounded as if they were reciting scientific formulae and theorems. All at once he could see again and the voices ceased abruptly. He was floating in the midst of a vast, dimly illuminated dome. He looked around him. The floor was invisible from this height, because the lower reaches of the building were wrapped in a kind of dense grey mist. Half-finished walls projected from the gloom, spiral staircases ended in space, towers were devoid of windows. Either the architect had gone mad or his client had run out of money.

'This is embarrassing,' Kolibri repeated sheepishly. 'I can't have people seeing my work in progress. It all looks so unfinished.'

'Nonsense!' said Smyke. 'This is the most interesting ruin I've ever seen.'

'It's an edifice of ideas.' Kolibri sighed. 'My everlasting construction site. Half-baked theories, ideological debris. I doubt if I shall ever complete this thesis in my lifetime.'

A swarm of grey snakes came wriggling through the air and flew past Smyke with a whispering sound. They didn't seem genuinely tangible, and he got the impression that they were composed of tiny black particles. He stared after them in surprise.

'Footnotes,' Kolibri explained. 'They're a nuisance, but indispensable to any thesis. One needs vast numbers of them.'

He whistled and the grey swarm came to a halt. One of the snakes flew past Smyke at close range, and he now saw that the black particles were characters and numerals.

He read,

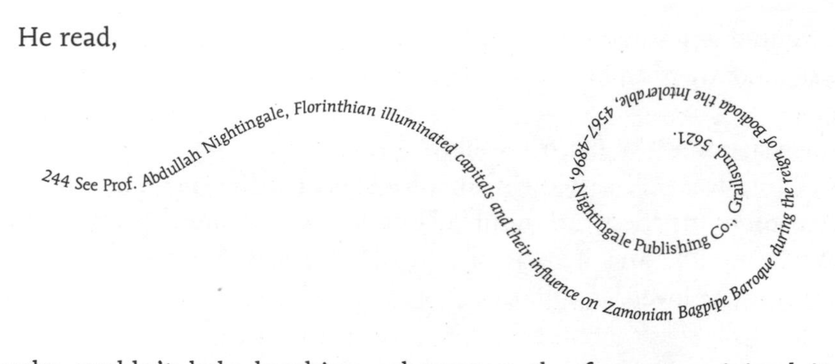

Smyke couldn't help laughing, whereupon the footnote rejoined its companions in a huff. They milled around together, whispering. Then the whole swarm giggled and vanished into the gloom.

There was a rumble as if truckloads of stone were being unloaded and a dark tower sprouted from the grey mist like a spear of asparagus. No sooner was it up than a second tower sprouted beside it, but only half as tall.

'You see?' exclaimed the professor. 'I can't stop working on it even now. Those are two new ideas that support my main contention.'

'What's the subject of your thesis?' Smyke enquired.

'The Influence of the Non-Existent Teenies on Zamonian micromechanics,' Kolibri replied crisply.

'Aha,' said Smyke, 'that sounds exciting.'

Kolibri sighed. 'No, it doesn't. It sounds utterly quirky and hopelessly abstruse. But thanks all the same.'

'You're being too modest again.'

'I am, I grant you. Believe me, my chosen subject may well harbour the solutions to our greatest problems.'

'Problems like what?'

'Well, dying, for example. Death.'

Smyke guffawed. 'Don't tell me you're an alchemist in disguise!'

'I'm a scientist, not a charlatan,' Kolibri said in a firm, businesslike tone. 'I don't blend unappetising bodily fluids together or subject dead bullfrogs to electric currents. I make measurements. Extremely accurate, microscopic measurements.'

'Measurements of what?'

'Of what indeed? Actually, I measure something that has long been extinct. I measure the Non-Existent Teenies.'

Nightingale reappears

An indistinct murmur issued from one of the passages leading off the dome and Smyke – who could hardly believe his eyes – saw Professor Nightingale coming towards him out of the gloom, burbling unintelligibly to himself. The professor was not only four times as big as in real life but transparent. Ignoring Smyke, he floated straight past and disappeared into the mist that enshrouded the dome. Smyke rubbed his eyes.

'Was that really Nightingale?' he asked uncertainly.

'No. Yes. No. Well, in a manner of speaking. It was the embodiment of one of Nightingale's doctoral theses: *The Use of Bipolar Lenses in Multiple Classifications*. I badly need it for my theoretical superstructure.'

'*That* was another doctoral thesis? Why does it look like a living creature?'

'Doctoral theses can appear in many forms,' Kolibri replied. 'It all depends on their quality. All of Nightingale's theses resemble him. That's because of his potent personality, his style. They're quite unmistakable.'

'But why did he look so hostile?'

'The thesis is rather annoyed because so far it hasn't melded with the basic theory underlying my own work. It's still looking for an interface to lock on to. I told you to be prepared to run into Professor Nightingale in here, didn't I?'

'Now I understand.'

'Every doctoral thesis is composed largely of others,' Kolibri explained. 'A new thesis is always an orgiastic agglomeration of old theses that, er, fertilise each other so as to give birth to something new and unprecedented.'

'I'm finding it thoroughly instructive to have scientific processes explained to me in such a graphic way,' said Smyke. 'But there's one thing you must tell me: Who or what are these Non-Existent Teenies?'

'Well, to be honest, that's the kind of specialised knowledge that would only burden your brain unnecessarily. What about something more useful? A little practical mathematics? A course in elementary biology?'

'You raised the subject, now you must follow it through. I insist on a thorough explanation.'

Kolibri sighed, but it was the sigh of a diva who deigns to give an encore after endless ovations.

'Very well,' he said. 'On your own head be it.'

Smyke's surroundings began to revolve. The stairways, towers and walls became distorted, the entire dome was in motion. Feeling dizzy, Smyke shut his eyes for a moment. When he opened them again it was all over. He was in a kind of lecture hall, seated on something that felt like a cold stone slab, and in front of him was a platform with a lectern on it. Professor Kolibri was leaning on the lectern, smiling at him.

'Professor Kolibri?' said Smyke. 'Is that you?'

'Of course not,' the apparition replied. 'I'm an illusion, like everything else in here. I'm really standing in a clearing with your finger in my ear. These surroundings are merely illustrative. Surely this is nicer than having to float around in space listening to my disembodied voice?'

Smyke looked at Kolibri more closely. He seemed to be slightly transparent, like a ghost.

'Am I an illusion too?' he asked.

'No,' said Kolibri, 'you're real. Our physical contact has generated a three-dimensional telepathic projection in my brain that really does possess a body. A very small body, but still. I myself cannot materialise inside my own brain, unfortunately, but you can.'

'Aha,' Smyke said uncomprehendingly.

'Very well,' said Kolibri, 'let's start the lesson.'

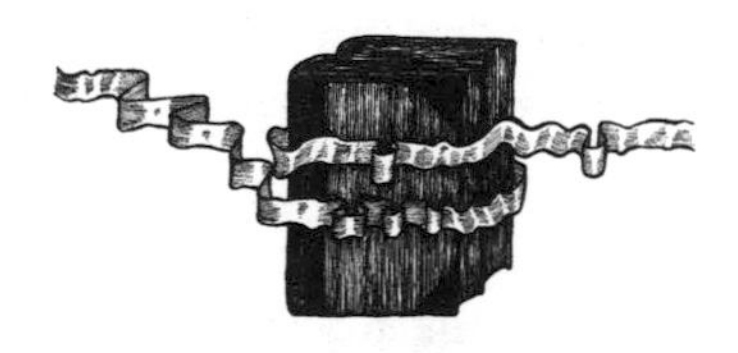

The ostascope or kolibriscope

'I've already told you of my, well, let's say, obsessive interest in microscopy.' Ostafan Kolibri opened the lid of the lectern and removed a curious object. It was a pair of spectacles consisting of numerous superimposed lenses of steadily diminishing size. He put this contraption on his nose and stared at Smyke. It made him look like a mechanical insect from another planet.

'With the aid of ultra-small lenses, I succeeded in inventing some wearable microscopic spectacles, which I have now developed into in my personal, optometrical masterpiece: the *ostascope* or *kolibriscope*, whichever you prefer. How does it suit me?'

'Excellently!' lied Smyke.

'While darknessologists and astronomers were striving to develop bigger and bigger lenses for bigger and bigger telescopes, I hit upon the idea of producing smaller and smaller lenses for smaller and smaller microscopes. There was a limit to this process, of course, because the lens-making instruments became too small for hands to manipulate them, so I had some dwarfs trained as lens grinders under my supervision. Although this reduced the size of my lenses by two thirds, they were very far from small enough for me. I eventually sought a solution to this problem in nature - and found it. On the beaches of Florinth's Diamond Coast there are grains of sand whose cores are miniature lenses of extreme precision and delicacy. They occupy the exact centre of the grains like little hearts of glass. How to extract them from their surrounding shell, that was the problem. I solved it with the aid of an Aeolian sandblaster, which works on the principle . . .' Kolibri broke off. 'But I'm digressing.'

'What can you do with these, er, spectacles?'

'The ostascope enables me to examine the structure of objects - of every solid material including stone. But I can also see things in the air that would otherwise remain invisible to us. Did you know that colours consist of colours? Of considerably more delicate and indescribably beautiful shades compared to which the colours of the visible world are tasteless, vulgar, dingy and - how can I put it? - positively *colourless*?'

'No,' said Smyke, 'I didn't know that.'

'Were you aware that one can see emotions? Rage? Fear? Love? Hatred? That one can see perfumes? Have you any idea how incredibly beautiful the scent of a rose looks? How repulsive the stench of a cesspit? Can you imagine the shapes that sound can assume? If you only knew how immensely fascinating good music looks - unlike bad music, which looks utterly hideous! But don't imagine that the microcosm doesn't have its dark sides too, far from it. Everything is far smaller, varied and complex, that's all.' Kolibri removed his spectacles.

'I became thoroughly dependent on my invention, I'm bound to admit. I conducted ostascopic experiments wherever I was, day and night. I left no stone, no leaf or grain of sand unturned. And then, one especially fine day, I made it: *the discovery of a lifetime.*'

Kolibri's voice reverberated around the lecture hall. Apparently oblivious of why he was there, he seemed to be engrossed in pleasant memories.

'Come on, professor, don't keep me in suspense!'

Kolibri clicked his tongue. 'Well, it happened at the foot of an ancient oak tree. I'd begun to turn over every leaf, every grain of soil, with a pair of miniature pincers and examine them through the ostascope. I shall never forget that moment. I picked up an ancient oak leaf with my pincers and beneath it lay . . .' Kolibri stopped short.

'Well?' Smyke cried impatiently. 'What was underneath it?'

'Beneath that leaf lay a city.'

'A city?' said Smyke. 'An anthill, you mean?'

'No, I mean a *real city*. A big city, to be exact. A metropolis that had clearly been built by highly intelligent beings, with umpteen buildings and a maze of streets, lanes and alleyways. With towers and palaces, tenements and skyscrapers, shops and factories. In all, it was about the size of a walnut and overgrown with grass.'

'Incredible.'

'Quite so. I was completely taken aback. I rubbed my eyes, checked my pulse, pinched myself, polished a lens or two and looked again. And again. But there was no doubt: I had discovered a tiny, microscopically small civilisation, an archaeological find of diminutive size but incalculable importance. It was the smallest but, at the same time, the biggest ruin in the history of Zamonian archaeology!'

The professor briefly shut his eyes and massaged his eyelids before continuing.

'I began by submitting the city to a preliminary microscopic examination. There were buildings, as I have said: dwelling houses, civic buildings, factories – everything that belongs in an average city, but in an architectural style unfamiliar to me. The buildings had walls, roofs, windows and doors, but they were all – if you'll pardon my scientifically imprecise terminology – *odd* in some way. There weren't any really bizarre buildings. One simply got the impression that those who built them were unacquainted with our own structural conventions. The staircases had circular treads, for example, and the doors and windows – if that's what they were – took the form of extremely tall, thin slits. And there were no signs of life – no signs of death either. No cemeteries. No minute skeletons or other testimony to the inhabitants' former existence. In view of their microscopic size and non-existent presence, I christened the builders of this city *The Non-Existent Teenies*.'

'I'm beginning to understand now,' said Smyke.

'First I took my find to a safe place. Having carefully dug away the soil around the city, I transported it to my laboratory with my fingertips and submitted it to months-long microscopic examination. I mounted three ostascopes on a stand, one behind the other, so that I could explore every corner of the city. I had no instruments small enough to enable me to touch anything inside it. I could only observe it, but from every conceivable angle.'

The Non-Existent Teenies

Kolibri sighed.

'One day I discovered what appeared to have been a magnificent public building – a museum, perhaps, or a university. You can imagine the excitement that overcame me when I saw that, as luck would have it, the roof over the whole of the upper floor had fallen in: I could look inside with my ostascope! And the building really was something in the nature of a museum: a building full of artefacts, the products of a vanished civilisation! My surprise – and disappointment – was all the greater when I was forced to conclude that the Non-Existent Teenies seemed not to have had any art in our sense of the word. I looked in vain for any paintings, sculptures or books. What I had at first mistaken for objets d'art were machines. My theory is that the Non-Existent Teenies grew out of art many thousands of years ago, or that their arts had developed into something that must have been considerably more important to them, namely, science.'

Kolibri inserted a brief pause for effect.

'I'm convinced that the Non-Existent Teenies attained a degree of civilisation that still, I hope, lies before us. They welded together the arts and sciences, which we so studiously keep separate, and thereby took a giant leap forward. Imagine scientific disciplines being pursued with the concentrated creativity of artistic genius, or arts being based on highly complex scientific calculations! Biology, literature, mathematics, painting, music, astronomy, sculpture, physics – imagine all those disciplines amalgamated into a single . . . well, whatever one cares to call such a super-discipline. I still haven't devised a name for it.'

'Scart?' hazarded Smyke. 'Or artience?'

Kolibri ignored his interjection.

'What mainly differentiated the exhibits in this museum from works of art was that they all seemed to have had some practical function. They all looked *as if one could do something with them.* Except that I didn't know what.'

Kolibri was becoming more and more agitated. He flapped his hands and rolled his big, glowing eyes.

'I was close to despair, believe me. The technology of a tiny, vanished civilisation within arm's reach, but my fingers were too big to touch it.' He regarded his spindly fingers with contempt. 'So my only alternative was to investigate all those micromachines theoretically. I proceeded to measure and compute them optically. With the aid of these data and some detective work on the part of my four brains, I managed, little by little, to determine their functions. If only I'd possessed Professor Nightingale's *seven* brains!'

He clasped his head in a gesture of despair.

'Assisted by my calculations in the field of hypothetical mechanics,' he went on, 'I discovered that one of the contraptions was a machine for milking slipper animalcules. Another could put influenza viruses into a trance. Another was a bacteria mill for grinding bacteria to dust. But that was only small stuff. The really interesting machines could do things of which we can only dream today.'

'What, for instance?'

'You'd never believe me. Think of the things modern science is furthest from achieving – those machines could accomplish them.'

Smyke sighed. 'I wish I could see those things.'

'Really? I can show you some.'

'Pictures of them, you mean?'

'No, in reality.'

Kolibri's figure started to flicker gently. His silhouette became distorted. He grew mistier than before, then completely transparent, until all that remained of him was something that resembled a phantom. Finally he became airborne.

'Follow me,' he commanded impatiently. His voice, too, had acquired a tremulous, ghostly quality. 'We can't hang around here for ever. Think of your poor friend in the clearing.'

The lecture hall folded up like a huge fan. Smyke's seat and the floor beneath him dissolved into thin air, and he was once more hovering inside the monstrous building that was Kolibri's doctoral thesis.

'This way!' called Kolibri's ghost, darting off down one of the gloomy corridors.

The ideosprites

Smyke hurried after him and they sped through a seemingly endless maze of passages. The professor kept turning abruptly left and right, ascending and descending flights of stairs. At length some little coloured specks of light came flying towards them. Softly humming and buzzing, flashing and sparkling, the initially isolated specks multiplied in number until Smyke felt as if he were in the midst of a blizzard of luminous, multicoloured snowflakes.

'Those are Nocturnomathic ideosprites,' Kolibri explained. 'Don't worry, there's nothing supernatural about them, we simply call them that. They're embodiments of the thirst for knowledge in my brains. What corpuscles are to the circulation of the blood, ideosprites are to one's circulation of ideas. They're inquisitive little things, more ambitious than ants and busier than bees. They want to know everything and never get tired.'

Kolibri chuckled and disappeared down a side turning. Smyke suddenly wondered what would happen if he lost touch with the professor and went astray in this labyrinth. Was it possible that he might get lost in a Nocturnomathic doctoral thesis? Might he and Kolibri continue to stand in the clearing in a trance until they starved to death and turned into skeletons? But there was always Rumo, it occurred to him. Rumo would sooner or later extract his finger from the professor's ear, but then they might both go insane . . .

Before he could pursue this thought any further he caught up with the Nocturnomath, who had paused beside an illuminated aperture in the wall of the passage. Smyke slowed to a hover.

'What I am about to show you,' Kolibri announced in a voice tremulous with excitement, 'are my gems of Teenyological research.'

The passage was teeming with ideosprites. Hundreds of the humming creatures were flitting in and out of the opening in the wall.

A submarine, a spaceship and a time machine

Kolibri glided forward into the dazzling glow and Smyke followed. They were now in a chamber that seemed to consist entirely of light: floor, walls and ceiling were all a luminous white. Red, green, yellow and blue ideosprites flew in all directions like startled butterflies, filling the chamber with an electrical hum.

'There they are, my prize specimens!' said Kolibri, his voice vibrant with pride. Hovering in the middle of the chamber, seemingly supported by the brilliant light itself, were three machines. 'According to my calculations they're the Non-Existent Teenies' most highly developed micro-machines,' the professor went on. 'Or the most complex, at least. Their private lives must be immensely complicated.'

'What can they do?' asked Smyke.

'Well,' Kolibri replied, 'they all have one function in common: you can go places in them.'

'You mean they're vehicles?'

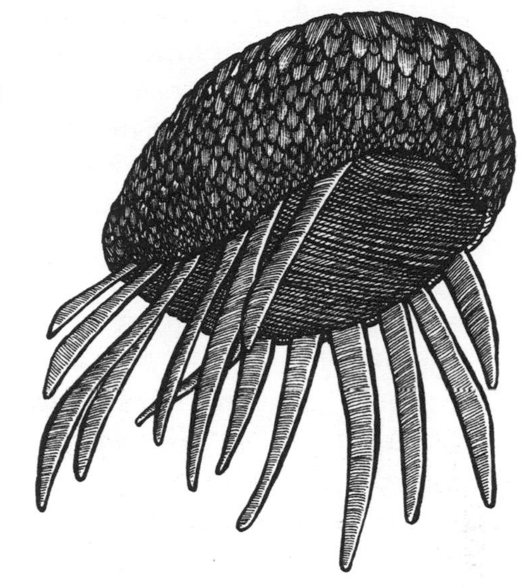

'Yes, if you like to put it that way, although they aren't vehicles in the traditional sense – that would be too primitive. My measurements suggest that the one in the centre was designed to travel through viscous fluid. The one on the left can move in conditions of zero gravity and the third seems capable of propelling itself through the fourth dimension.'

'You mean . . .?'

'Yes indeed. They're a submarine, a spaceship and a time machine.'

Rumo was dreaming of the Silver Thread. Shimmering high overhead beneath some fluffy, snow-white clouds, it was making wonderful, unearthly music. The strains filled him with a sensation of warmth. Waves of well-being surged through his body as he recalled that, where the thread ended, happiness awaited him. He smiled in his sleep.

But what was that? The clouds had suddenly darkened. They turned greyer and greyer, and Rumo was buffeted by a cold wind from above. A gust tore the Silver Thread and blew it away, and the beautiful music was replaced by an ugly sound. Big fat raindrops detached themselves from the clouds and fell to earth, chilling Rumo to the bone wherever they landed on him. He opened his eyes to find that he was surrounded by five dark, shadowy forms with long arms and short legs. They were bending over and probing him with their fingers. How had they managed to get so close without his hearing them? Or scenting them? Why couldn't he smell anything even now? Why weren't they making any noise? He tried to discern their faces, but they were faceless! Was he still dreaming? Why were they so cold to the touch?

Wide awake now, Rumo had already worked out a way of putting them to flight. He turned his head to the right, intending to bite the nearest figure in the throat.

But he might as well have tried to bite an icy wind. His teeth closed on nothing, jarring his jaws, and the figures moved imperturbably closer.

He felt colder and colder.

Professor Kolibri glided over to the machine in the centre, shooed away some inquisitive ideosprites with his hand and said, 'This one is the submarine.'

'You mean it can travel underwater?' asked Smyke.

'No, under *skin*. That's what comes of using inexact terminology – I should really have called it a *subcutaneous* submarine. I infer from its streamlined shape that it was designed to propel itself through liquids considerably more viscous than H_2O. Blood is thicker than water, *n'est-ce pas*? This machine was built to travel along veins and arteries.'

'Good heavens! What for?'

'For medical reasons, I surmise. My measurements lead me to assume that it contains some extremely sophisticated instruments capable of being extended and used to carry out microscopic operations inside the bloodstream.'

'Incredible!'

'Quite so.' Kolibri glided over to the next machine. 'And in this, or so I conjecture, one can fly through space. The surface alloy is capable of withstanding the heat of a solar flare without damage. As for the engine, it may well be powerful enough to enable one to exceed the speed of light.'

'You mean that contraption may be faster than light?'

'No, it may be *smaller* than light.'

'I don't understand.'

'Neither do I, to be honest.' Kolibri gave a despairing laugh. 'I'm still working it out – using inconceivably small figures. The Non-Existent Teenies may have used such machines to leave our planet.' He glided over to the third machine. 'And this, unless my observations, theoretical deliberations and Nocturnomathic speculations have deceived me, is a time machine.'

'Really?'

'It's possible that the Non-Existent Teenies disappeared into time, not space – into another, more desirable age or a smaller dimension that suited them better.'

'But these machines don't look like illusions,' said Smyke. 'Don't be offended, professor, but everything inside your brain – yourself included – makes a rather artificial impression. These machines don't. They look so real. So . . . genuine.'

'That's probably because they are.'

'Meaning what?'

'These three machines *are* genuine – they're *real*. They're inside my brain, yes, but not in the form of Nocturnomathic memories or stored information. They're originals. I implanted them.'

'How did you manage that?'

Kolibri groaned. 'Oh dear, do you really want to know? It's not a very pleasant story. All right, I'll be brief. First, I decided to take the whole city in which the museum was situated and pickle it in formaldehyde to preserve it from further oxygenous decay. I was then able to syphon off individual objects – like the micromachines – through a length of gut which I'd removed from the liver of a dwarf microbe . . . But that's irrelevant here. Simply believe me when I say that I succeeded in extracting these three machines from the city of the Non-Existent Teenies.'

Smyke nodded submissively.

'The rest was easy. I drew them off into a syringe filled with a solution of brine, stuck the needle into my head and injected them into one of my brains – straight into this doctoral thesis. The task of transporting the machines into this chamber was undertaken by my inquisitive little friends.' The professor waved a hand in the direction of some humming ideosprites.

'You actually injected these machines into your head?'

'I told you it wasn't a story for the squeamish. But it was an entirely safe procedure. I specialised in trepanning when I studied Nocturnomathic medicine. Give me a can opener and a rubber tube and I'll drain your cerebral fluid in five minutes.'

'No thanks.' Smyke waved the suggestion aside. He inspected the machines more closely. He found them even more fascinating now he knew they were real.

'May I touch them?'

'You may even try them out,' Kolibri said with a sudden tremor in his voice.

'Try them out? Try the Non-Existent Teenies' machines? Me?'

'Of course. Since you're here . . .'

Smyke gave a start. There was an expectant note in the Nocturnomath's voice. He gave a little cough and his ghostly figure undulated gently.

Suddenly it dawned on Smyke. He wasn't there because the nice professor wanted to do him a favour or infect him with knowledge free of charge. *He was there because Kolibri wanted him there.* He stared at the Nocturnomath.

'What is it?' Kolibri demanded innocently. 'Why are you looking at me like that?'

'The way you steered me straight into the right brain! The way you made me "accidentally" stumble on your thesis! What a convincing act you put on! Come off it, professor!'

Kolibri gave another little cough.

'I'm here because you need a stooge – someone to try out your machines, right?'

'You've got the perfect build for subcutaneous travel,' Kolibri admitted. 'I spotted that as soon as I saw you.'

'Ahaaa!' Smyke cried triumphantly. 'I knew it! You want me to play the guinea pig!'

'I wouldn't put it that way,' Kolibri protested. 'I'd prefer to call it a historic opportunity. You can make history.'

'Oh yes? What if I press the wrong button? What if the time machine whisks me back to the Zamonian Ice Age or the spaceship transports me to the nearest galaxy, eh? What then?'

'These machines don't work as simply as that. There are no buttons of any kind. In order to perform such complex functions you have to do a bit more than throw a switch. But I can't compel you. All right, forget it. In that case you'll play no part in what may well be the most important discovery in the history of Zamonian scientific research. Someone else will do it instead.'

Smyke grinned.

'Come on, professor, can't you do better than that? You really think you need only appeal to my ambition to embroil me in a suicide mission?'

'Quite apart from the fact that I've no wish to try out the time machine or the spaceship myself,' said Kolibri, 'what would it avail me if the time machine transported you out of my brain and into another dimension? I would only know that it worked, but the machine itself would be gone. And what if you got the spaceship working and flew off? The most I'd be left with is a hole in my skull.' Kolibri felt his head. 'No, all I want is for you to get into the subcutaneous submarine and operate its hidden instruments. Here in this chamber. You won't even need to submerge.'

'So why don't you do it yourself?'

'I already told you: I'm not present here in the flesh. I can't touch or move anything. Only you can do that.'

'What about your luminous little assistants?'

'Ideosprites are just brainless organisms. It was all they could do to haul the machines in here. This extremely complex conveyance must be manned by an intelligent being. To operate it one needs hands. One needs eyes. One needs a voice. You possess all those requirements. It was fate that brought you to me, don't you understand?'

Kolibri fixed Smyke with an imploring gaze.

'And what do I get out of helping you?'

'What do the people of Zamonia get – that's the question you should be asking. I suspect that this machine is capable of conquering death itself.'

Smyke drew a deep breath. 'That's impossible. It would be a miracle.'

'You're right. There aren't any miracles, only scientific advances, but many scientific advances verge on the miraculous.'

'How could such a microscopically small gadget prevail over death?'

'That's easy. It could start a dead heart beating again.'

'Impossible.'

'Get in and follow my instructions and I'll show you.'

'What makes you so sure?'

'My computations, my carefully constructed theories, years of quadruple brainwork. But as I said, either you do it or you don't. The chances are fifty-fifty, eh?' Kolibri tried to sound indifferent.

Now he's got me, thought Smyke and he smiled. Wittingly or unwittingly, Kolibri had put his finger on Smyke's weak spot: his love of gambling. Red or black, heads or tails, stick or twist, win or lose.

'All right,' said Smyke, 'the subcutaneous submarine. I'm game. What do I have to do?'

'I knew it!' Kolibri cried in relief. 'You're a man of science, a pioneer! You've got an inquiring mind!'

'Enough of that,' Smyke said dismissively. 'Just tell me what to do. How do I get inside there?'

Kolibri clapped his hands and the ideosprites formed a big, humming, slowly revolving circle above the submarine. 'Take up your position beside it. Yes, there. Stop! And now touch it. Anywhere will do.'

Smyke leant forwards and hesitantly brushed the surface of the machine. It felt as smooth, hard and as robust as armour plate. There was a faint hiss like air being released somewhere and a circular opening appeared on the left-hand side of the craft. It looked as if it was just the same width as Smyke. Pulsating red light was issuing from the interior.

Kolibri laughed. 'You see? The machine is highly intelligent – it's adapting itself to your physical dimensions. It's accepting you! Crawl inside!'

Smyke drew a deep breath and squeezed through the aperture.

Rumo wondered why he was being so slow. He was in extreme danger,

but he couldn't speed up his reactions the way he'd done in *The Glass Man Tavern*. On the contrary, he was getting slower and slower. Even thinking had become a supreme effort. Although he could feel nothing but the cold they gave off, the shadowy forms that were wrapped round him possessed a strength that seemed to increase the weaker he himself became. He couldn't even have risen to his feet, so much of his own strength had already been drained by this bizarre wrestling match. He was squandering his energy. This wasn't a fight, it was drudgery – drudgery that would sooner or later send him to sleep from sheer exhaustion. Was that what the shadowy figures wanted?

The subcutaneous submarine

Smyke was now inside the submarine, whose hull was made of no material he recognised. It was dark-red, looked soft and organic, and emitted a subdued glow. There were no levers, steering wheels or instruments to be seen, just this oval red chamber, which resembled a coffin tailor-made to fit his body.

'Is there a membrane in front of you?' Kolibri's voice sounded rather muffled now that Smyke had closed the door behind him. He took a closer look. Yes, there in the red wall was a circular patch of slightly porous appearance. That might be the membrane.

'What makes you think there's a membrane here?' asked Smyke.

'My calculations. Isn't there one?' Kolibri's voice was trembling with curiosity.

'What do *you* think?'

'I think there is one, of course. Don't keep me on tenterhooks!'

'But there isn't,' called Smyke. He couldn't help grinning.

'What, no membrane? Really not?'

'Yes, there is. I was only joking.'

'Don't make me nervous!' Kolibri bellowed. 'Just do as you're told!'

'Yes, yes, no need to shout.'

'Put your head down close to it and purr.'

'What?'

'You must purr. Into the membrane.'

'What for?'

'Purring starts the engine acoustically. It's fitted with a contentment servo-mechanism.'

'A what?'

'You heard me. It's important for the boat to feel good. Trust me.'

'I'm not a cat. I can't purr.'

'Try!'

'No.'

'Go on!'

'Bzzzzzz . . .' went Smyke, feeling thoroughly ridiculous. Nothing happened. Acoustic servo-mechanism! A machine with emotions! What utter nonsense!

'That wasn't purring, it was buzzing,' the professor said testily. 'What do you think you are, a bumblebee?'

'Prrrrrr! Prrrrrr!' went Smyke.

'That's better! Keep purring!'

'Prrrrrrrrrrrr!'

Smyke's purring was joined by a multitudinous hum that seemed to emanate from the blood-red hull. Just in front of him a large section of wall steadily paled until it became transparent. Smyke could now see outside. It was like looking through a pink window-pane.

'I can see, professor!' he said.

'Translucent material!' gasped Kolibri. 'Incredible!'

'Can you see me too?' asked Smyke.

'No. Go on purring.'

Smyke was starting to feel euphoric. Something in the bowels of the boat began to throb like a slow heartbeat, and the sound mingled with his purring.

Outside, Kolibri was excitedly circling the machine. 'That's the engine!' he cried. 'It's started up!'

'I hope this thing isn't getting under way!' Smyke called, panic-stricken.

'Don't stop purring!' commanded the professor.

'Prrrrrr . . .' went Smyke. 'Prrrrrrrrrrrrr . . .'

Rumo was still trying to fight, but there was no one prepared to fight him. The faceless shadows besetting him on all sides were intangible. All he ever caught hold of was a fistful of cold, slippery nothingness. The shadows were above, beside and below him. They had formed a shell that enclosed him so tightly, it was like being buried alive. The air was running out, he noticed. He felt his body losing all its strength and flexibility, becoming slower and weaker. He lashed out desperately, still determined to escape from this entanglement of cold and darkness, but his onslaughts had no effect. He might have been fighting a squid with a thousand tentacles.

Something soft and cold closed over his right ear and clung there like a limpet. Was it a mouth? There, another had attached itself to his left ear! There was a slurping sound in his auditory canals, so loud that it hurt, and an icy chill pervaded the space between his temples. He felt as if the shadows were trying to suck the brain out of his skull.

Smyke and Kolibri were still standing rooted to the spot beside this dramatic spectacle. Smyke was purring like a contented cat beside the fire.

The ideosprites humming round Kolibri were growing more and more agitated.

The Non-Existent Teenies' tools

'We shall now try to activate the instruments!' cried the professor. 'Are you ready?'

'I'm ready,' said Smyke. 'Ready for anything.'

'Then please extend your six upper arms and touch the hull on either side of you.'

Smyke complied. He touched the boat's inner hull with three pairs of hands. It felt warm and yielding. Wherever his fingers touched an orange light came on. The rhythm of the engine accelerated.

'Very good!' called Kolibri. 'Now tickle it!'

'Huh?'

'Tickle the hull. Anywhere will do.'

'You must be joking!'

'That's the haptic part of the contentment servo-mechanism. Go on!' With a sigh, Smyke did as he was told. He proceeded to tickle the soft, warm surface with the fingers of his right hand. The orange glow intensified and a violent shudder ran through the hull.

'Perfect!' cried Kolibri. 'It's working!'

Looking through his pink window, Smyke saw an oval aperture take shape in the bow of the vessel. The noises inside the hull increased in volume and the opening disgorged a bizarre instrument suspended from a serpentine metallic arm.

'I knew it!' Kolibri exclaimed triumphantly. 'That's an *amalorican grappling hook*!'

'Well, well,' said Smyke.

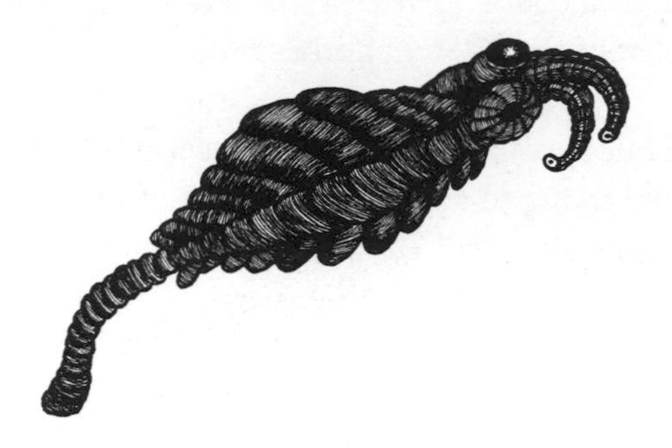

'Tickle it somewhere else, go on!'

Smyke obeyed and a second oval slit appeared in the bow immediately beside the first.

Another outlandish instrument emerged. 'Yes, yes!' Kolibri said exultantly. 'My calculations were correct. That's a *hallucinogenic key*!' Kolibri strove to keep calm.

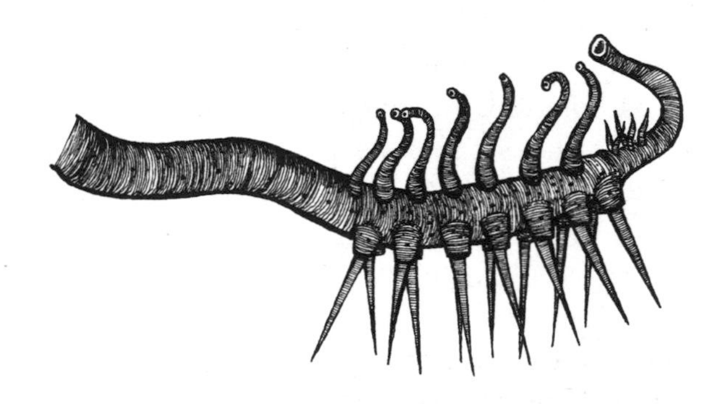

'Go on tickling! Tickle one place after another!'

Smyke did so. Another opening appeared and a third instrument emerged.

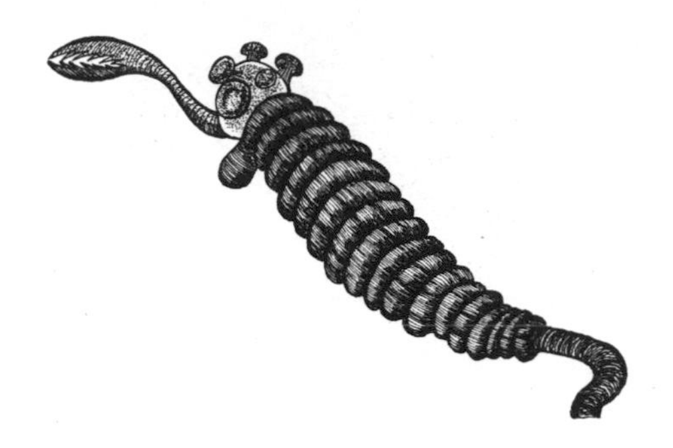

'Yes! Yes! A *scorpionic forceps*! I knew it!' The professor was completely beside himself with excitement.

Smyke proceeded to activate the machine without Kolibri's say-so. A fourth instrument emerged and was greeted with equal enthusiasm.

'A *multipedalian prehensor*! Yes, yes, that's a multipedalian prehensor, no doubt about it!

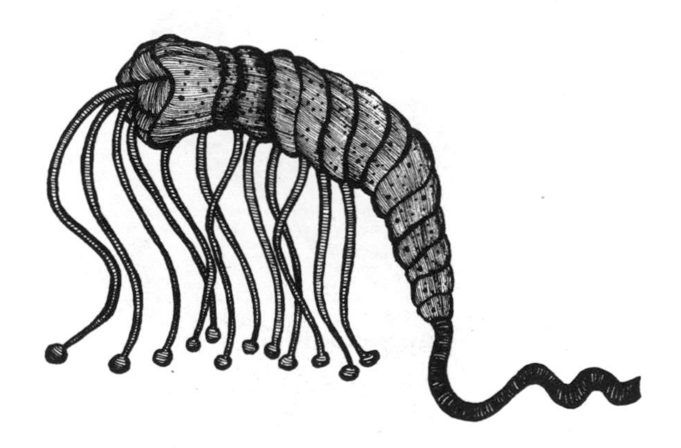

'Go on tickling!' commanded the professor.

'Aye-aye, sir!' croaked Smyke, eager to know more. He himself was now in the throes of a scientific frenzy.

A fifth instrument appeared.

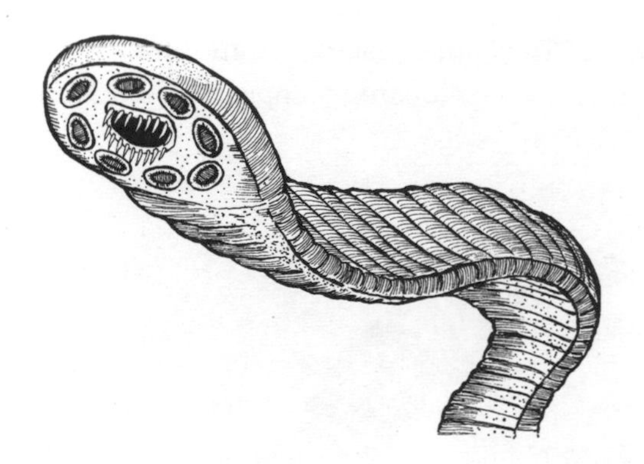

Kolibri uttered a squawk. 'A *denticulated screwdriver*! That nearly completes the set!'

Smyke tickled the hull again and a sixth instrument emerged from its opening.

Kolibri had to bite his fist to stifle a hysterical scream. 'An *odontoid extractor*!' he moaned. 'The finest sight I ever saw!'

'Shall I go on tickling?' Smyke inquired from the interior of the machine.

'It all fits!' the professor cried triumphantly. 'Everything is just as my calculations predicted!'

The ideosprites were circling the submarine in a multicoloured festoon, humming excitedly.

'You can come out now,' called Kolibri. 'That was all I wanted to know.'

Smyke squeezed through the opening and rejoined the professor, who was examining the various instruments in high spirits.

'What now?' asked Smyke. He was also feeling exhilarated. 'What do we do with these things? Operate on the heart of some dead creature? Conquer death? I'm game for anything.'

'We don't have the requisite patient, unfortunately.' Kolibri laughed. 'However, I've seen all I need to know for the moment.'

'And that's it? Is that all?' Smyke made no attempt to conceal his disappointment.

'Is that *all*?' said Kolibri, looking grave. 'Don't you realise what you've just done?'

'I still don't understand how you hope to conquer death with such tiny instruments,' said Smyke.

Kolibri shrugged. 'I can't explain it either. All I can tell you is it isn't a question of how *big* an impulse you need to start a dead heart beating again, but how *small*. There are six microscopically small points in the centre of every heart – ultra-fine nerve endings and immensely sensitive miniature arteries and muscles unknown to traditional medicine because they're so infinitely small – visible only through an ostascope. If these are stimulated with an amalorican grappling hook, a hallucinogenic key, a scorpionic forceps, a multipedalian prehensor, a denticulated screwdriver and an odontoid extractor, all at the same time, the heart will start beating again, however long it's been dead. Understand?'

'No,' said Smyke.

'Ah well, maybe we'll see it happen one day.' At a signal from the professor, the ideosprites began to circle the submarine and its array of instruments more feverishly still. 'Shall I show you the infodiscs now?'

Smyke nodded. 'Please do. Glad to have been of help. Perhaps you'll give me a mention in your doctoral thesis, or something.'

'You'll get a footnote all to yourself,' Kolibri promised.

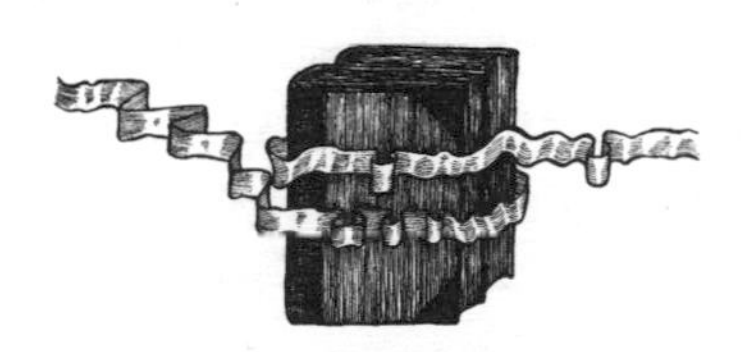

Rumo's powers of resistance were steadily weakening. The slurping noise in his ears persisted, and he now realised that the shadows weren't feeding on his brain, they were draining away his energy, his will-power, his very life.

He redoubled his efforts, and his assailants were so surprised that they stopped slurping for a moment. Was that why he could suddenly feel something in his left paw? Something that was not merely cold and slippery but seemed to have a solid core? He gripped it with all his might. 'That's odd,' he thought, 'it feels like a Demonocle's tongue.'

The colours of knowledge

Smyke found himself at the foot of a skyscraper composed of circular transparent discs floating one above another. Each disc was the size of a fairground roundabout in diameter and each was a different colour. Superimposed but separated by several feet of thin air, they towered high into the sky above North Ostafan.

'How do I get in there?' Smyke asked. 'What do I have to do?'

'Dive in,' Kolibri's disembodied voice called from nowhere in particular. 'Simply dive through the discs from above.'

'From above?'

Before he knew it Smyke had shot to the top of the tower like a rocket. He didn't yell; he was past being alarmed by anything that happened inside Kolibri's brain. Once at the top, he glided slowly towards the centre of the uppermost disc. He looked down. Together, the superimposed discs produced a colour he'd never seen before.

'It's called *intellimagenta*,' said Kolibri. 'The colour of knowledge. Are you ready?'

'Yes, I'm r—' Smyke just managed to say. Then he was in free fall. The first disc he dived through was pale-blue.

'Blue: astronomy!' Kolibri's voice intoned solemnly.

Betelgeuze. Elevation. Geoid. Gravitational constant. Ellipse. Parallactic orbit. Solar volume. Heliocentric latitude. Emission spectrum. Entropy. Lunar eclipse. Orion. Pleiades. Quite suddenly, these had ceased to be meaningless words and become subjects on which Smyke could have lectured extempore for hours. He felt the blue light permeate his brain and infuse it with astronomical knowledge. *Andromeda. Sirius. Light years. Radiation belt. Triton. Arcturus. Antares. Vega. Sinope. Ecliptic coordinates.*

Smyke's brain absorbed these and hundreds more astronomical terms within a second. Then it was over. He was falling through a colourless gap towards a luminous green disk.

'Green: biology!' called Kolibri.

Blue algae. Interferon. Isogamy. Morphosis. Tanning agents. Lower Zamonian leaf mould. Self-detonating bacteria. Anthozoa. Mimicry. Secretion. Ventricle. Kackertrattian metabolism. Ciliates. Wind pollination. Hornless unicorns. Scintillogenesis . . .

Another gap. Heavens, what a speed! Smyke was now falling towards a red disc.

'Red: history!' *The Norselandian laws of succession. The Demonoclean War. The genealogical table of the Atlantean mayoral dynasty. The Grailsundian Constitution. The Hundred-Year Peace. The Coal Age. Government policy towards druidical hybrids in the reign of King Bodioda the Intolerable. The ratification of the Pooph Plan. The Twelve Stone Kings. The revolt of the Porcelain Princesses. The Sewer-Dragon Crisis. The Yellow Peril. The expulsion of the Five Hundred Generals. The Demonic Amnesty.*

'Yellow: physics!' *Frequency modulation. Hydrostatic paradox. Genffatic gaseous density. Polarisable molecules. Cucumbrian angular velocity. Nightingalian postulates. The Gryphonian Constant. Hackonian interference tubes. Repercussive density. Telepathic wave frequencies. The Lemurian intolerator. Zones of silence. Counteractive effects. The Palaeo-Zamonian law of falling bodies . . .* And so it went on. Subject followed subject in quick succession. Violet: mathematics. Turquoise: philosophy. Carmine: Zamonian grammar. Orange: medicine. Smyke fell through a hundred infodiscs in as many seconds and they filled his brain until nothing more would go in. He plummeted through the last few storeys without being able to absorb the knowledge stored there.

When he reached the ground floor at last, his fall ceased abruptly. For an instant he hovered a hand's breadth above the ground, then landed as slowly and gently as a feather.

Dazedly, he tried to sort out his impressions. His head ached like mad.

'Don't worry,' the professor called from above. 'It won't last long, that nasty feeling of intellectual repletion between the synapses. The information hasn't settled yet.'

Smyke belched.

'I suggest you simply remove your finger from my ear,' said Kolibri. 'We'll see each other back in the clearing. Our joyride is over.'

Cold shadows

Smyke looked around. He was back in the clearing once more. The fire was nearly out and his eyes took some time to get used to the semi-darkness. Rumo was seated on a big tree root, panting hard. In the ashes around the fire lay five dark forms. They looked rather like monkeys. Like dead black monkeys.

'What are those?' asked Smyke.

'Lunawraiths,' said Kolibri, who had bent over one of the figures and was prodding it with an inquisitive finger.

'Lunawraiths? Are they dead?'

'They're cold, at least,' said the Nocturnomath. 'As cold as moonlight.'

'They're dead all right,' said Rumo.

'How did you manage it?' Kolibri asked eagerly. 'Until now it was always thought that the only way of killing such creatures was to deprive them of food and starve them to death.'

'They've got tails with spines,' said Rumo. 'Snap them and they're done for.'

'Interesting,' muttered the professor.

'I owe you my life again,' said Smyke. 'We both do.'

Rumo brushed this aside. 'Can we get some sleep now?'

'You do that. The professor and I will keep watch.'

Kolibri nodded and turned to Smyke. 'You promised to tell me an exciting story about our youthful saviour's fighting abilities.'

'I will,' said Smyke, 'but don't be surprised if my story features Professor Nightingale and some interesting information about Demonocles' tongues.'

'Oh, Professor Nightingale pops up everywhere - one has to be prepared for that,' Kolibri replied. 'As for Demonocles' tongues, the more one knows about them the better.'

Parting of the ways

Rumo felt thoroughly refreshed when he awoke the next morning. He had fallen at once into a swoonlike sleep from which not even his companions' interminable talk and laughter could rouse him.

Smyke and Professor Kolibri bade each other a verbose and protracted farewell while Rumo stood there pawing the ground. The night's conversation seemed to have sealed their friendship. They clearly found it hard to say goodbye, but they eventually tore themselves away. Kolibri headed north-west, repeatedly turning to give the other two a wave, whereas Smyke and Rumo set off in the opposite direction. Smyke waved back until the professor was out of sight.

They hardly spoke during the next few hours. Smyke, who seemed engrossed in his own thoughts, was striving to master the turmoil in his head. He felt as if someone had not only renovated his brain but added a few extra storeys, and he revelled in all the novel and exciting ideas and items of information that were now stacked there.

Meanwhile, Rumo gathered nuts and berries. He checked occasionally to ensure that they were still following the Silver Thread, relieved that Smyke was preoccupied with himself for once. The countryside became more and more sparsely wooded, and they eventually found themselves in a hilly region consisting almost entirely of grassland. They were followed throughout the afternoon by a huge black dog, but it was too timid to go near them. It disappeared at dusk, but they could hear it howling half the night.

In the days that followed they traversed an endless prairie inhabited by vast numbers of grasshoppers. The insects almost drove them mad with their chirping, especially at night. In the midst of one of these green expanses Rumo and Smyke came to a ghost town built of plaited grass. In one of the houses they found two skeletons seated facing one another across a table, each with a discharged crossbow in its hand and a crossbow bolt in its skull. Prairie bandits, Smyke surmised.

After a week, when Smyke had more or less marshalled his thoughts, he tried to arouse Rumo's interest in the beauties of Florinthian ultralogic, invertebrate biology and druidical mathematics, but with little success. Rumo's sole concern was to make as much progress as possible. Smyke, who knew the reason for his haste, felt sentimentally regretful that it would also be the reason for their imminent and inevitable parting of the ways.

Forest Pirates, a Werewolf, a Minotaur and a Stranglesnake

It would be an understatement to say that Smyke's and Rumo's further progress through South Zamonia was uneventful, because they encountered no less than four different hazards: a five-strong band of Forest Pirates, a rabid Werewolf, a mummified Minocentaur and a Nocturnal Stranglesnake.

Compared with previous events, however, these encounters followed a rather unspectacular course, even though Rumo left the Forest Pirates with several nasty compound fractures, buried the Werewolf alive (head downwards, of course), converted the Minocentaur to vegetarianism and strangled the Nocturnal Stranglesnake in the middle of the night.

The travellers also had a number of peaceful encounters: for instance, with a party of Druids in search of the legendary Wandering Egg, which was reputed to meditate; with an impudent ferryman who attempted to charge them so exorbitant a fare for ferrying them across Loch Loch that it amounted to criminal extortion (he eventually took them free of charge); and with vast numbers of harmless sheep and cattle, and the equally peaceable shepherds and cowherds who populated the broad, tranquil grasslands of southern Hackonia.

When Rumo and Smyke had already penetrated deep into south-west Zamonia, Smyke was unusually silent at breakfast one morning. He sighed over every mouthful and was wearing a morose expression, which Rumo could only attribute to their meagre meal. They were sitting in the midst of a wide expanse of grassland grazed bare by sheep, gnawing some raw turnips.

'Listen, Rumo,' Smyke said suddenly. 'The time has come.'

Rumo cocked his head.

'The time for what?'

'For us to go our separate ways.'

'What! Why should we do that?'

'For various reasons. In the first place it's time, that's all. The longer I stay with you the further out of my way I go. I want to return to civilisation. I want to see big cities and meet new people. Instead of that I'm following you ever further into this godforsaken wilderness.'

Rumo couldn't think of a suitable rejoinder.

'And another thing,' Smyke went on. 'I'm not blaming anyone because I honestly don't know whose fault it is, but danger seems to have dogged us ever since we met. Hadn't that occurred to you?'

'There have been a few excitements lately,' Rumo admitted.

'Which may be all right from your point of view, my boy. You're young – you take it all in your stride – but I hanker after a little peace and quiet. We should each go our own way from now on.'

'I'm going my own way.'

'I know, and that's the last and most important reason. That's why *I'm* going to change direction. You're bound for Wolperting, and I've no business there.'

'You know where I'm going?'

'Of course. All intelligent Wolpertings go to Wolperting sooner or later.'

'Why not come with me?'

'You'll see why not when you get there.'

'But where will *you* go?'

'I'll head north-west, more or less, and make for some big city. Florinth, maybe.'

Rumo nodded.

'All right, my boy, let's not overdo our farewells. We've had some really grand times together. Perhaps we'll meet again.'

'I'm sure we will.'

'Don't be too sure, Zamonia is an immense continent. Let me give you some advice to take on your way. If anyone asks who you are, say *I'm Rumo the Wolperting*. That'll impress them, even if they've never seen a Wolperting before.'

'All right,' said Rumo, getting to his feet.

'How about a last riddle?' asked Smyke.

Rumo shrugged. 'Why not?'

'Then listen: *What grows shorter and shorter the longer it gets?*'

'No idea.'

'I'm counting on you to answer that question if we meet again.'

Their actual leave-taking was considerably less dramatic than one would have expected in the case of two friends who had been through so much together. It was mainly owing to Rumo's natural reserve that they limited themselves to a handshake and then went their separate ways.

The source of the Silver Thread

Rumo had but a single aim: to follow the Silver Thread to its source. He was interested neither in the countryside nor in its inhabitants. Without Smyke in tow he could at last ignore the world as he thought fit. He jogged along for hours on end, allowing himself very few breathers. If he stopped to eat at all it was only to munch some raw vegetables or freshly picked fruit. He avoided inns and villages, and at night he would make for a small wood in which to curl up and grab a few hours' sleep.

Sometimes he was afraid the Silver Thread might suddenly snap or disappear. Then he would shut his eyes and breathe a sigh of relief, because the thread was still there, becoming stronger and brighter with every day, every week that went by.

When he awoke one morning Rumo saw that the Silver Thread had been joined by others – by scents like those he remembered from his days back on the farm: woodsmoke and fresh bread, cattle and oats, dung and hay. But there were still other scents that resembled his own. Those he found very puzzling.

At dusk that day Rumo reached the summit of a vine-covered hill from which he could look far out over the undulating landscape. In the midst of it, traversed by a river and enclosed by a massive wall, stood a city. He shut his eyes and breathed in deeply through his nose. The Silver Thread and all the other coloured threads led straight down from the sky and lost themselves in the maze of buildings and streets. This could only be the city of which Smyke had spoken. It could only be Wolperting.

Rumo had reached his destination.

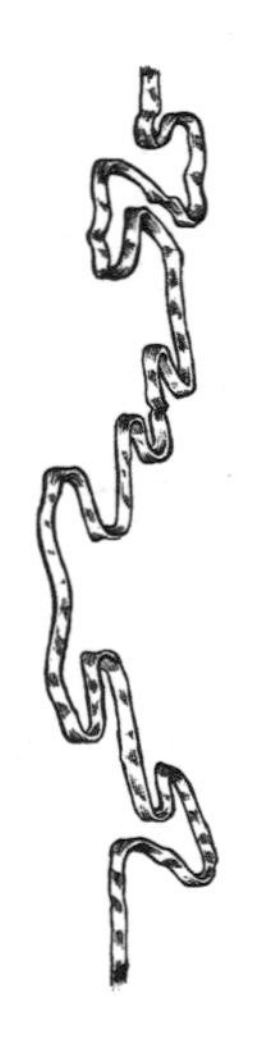

III.
Wolperting

Wolperting – if cities could speak – would probably have greeted a passing traveller as follows:

'Hello, stranger! Are you a Wolperting? No? Then get lost! Yes, push off, vamoose! Don't even dream of entering this city! Are your intentions peaceful? Very well, walk round me once, take a look at my excellent fortifications and then move on. Tell everyone what an impregnable and uninviting, well-guarded and dangerous impression Wolperting made on you. Thanks and goodbye for evermore!

But if your intentions are hostile, stranger, you'd be wiser to cut the heart out of your ribs right away, because that would be a merciful death compared to what awaits you if you attack me. Do you see my fortified towers? Do you see the Wolperting aiming his double crossbow at your head through that loophole? No, of course you don't, he's far too well concealed. Besides, soon you won't see anything at all because a pair of arrows will have transfixed your eyes. But you can see my big black gates, can't you? No, you fool, that's not wood, that's solid Zamonian cast iron, so you may as well pack up your battering ram. And you see those thin tubes protruding from my walls? If, by some improbable chance, you manage to cross the moat under a hail of arrows, my elaborate sprinkler system will shower you with a natural secretion obtained from Ornian Etchworms – even a single drop could eat its way right through you from your skull to the soles of your feet. You'd be lucky if an arrow cut short those few seconds of agony, but I never waste arrows on principle! But don't let that deter you from attacking me, stranger! I can hardly wait for you to sample my catapults and poisoned spears, my arbalests and cauldrons of boiling pitch, my burning arrows and throwing axes. Or my walls themselves. They look quite normal, don't they? It should be child's play to scale them in view of the big gaps between them, don't you think? Yes, but when you're about halfway up they'll begin to move and you'll say to yourself, Hey, what's going on? But by then it'll be too late for questions, because many of the blocks of stone will have slid forwards and many backwards. Then they'll start to revolve, and it'll dawn on you that you've ended up in the biggest mincing machine in Zamonian military history. You can still jump, of course – it's only a fifty-foot drop to the pointed iron stakes that have just emerged from the ground beneath. So come on, stranger! Come and meet your end!'

But cities cannot speak, so nothing was said to Rumo as he approached the city gates. He crossed the bridge over the moat and paused in front of the massive portcullis protecting the city's western entrance. He was so determined to get inside that he would, if necessary, have attacked it with his bare paws.

'Who goes there?' the gatekeeper called from above. Rumo couldn't see him, but he could hear which loophole he was hiding behind.

'I'm Rumo the Wolperting,' he called back, loud and clear. He debated how long it would take him to scale the wall, squeeze through the loophole, put the gatekeeper out of action, climb down the other side and lose himself in the bustling streets beyond. At a rough estimate, thirty or forty heartbeats.

'You're a Wolperting? In that case come in!' the gatekeeper called cheerfully. He operated some well-oiled machinery that almost silently raised the portcullis far enough for Rumo to slip beneath it. Then the grille descended again.

Rumo's 'municipal friend'

Rumo was inside the city. A Wolperting emerged from the tower that must have housed the gate machinery. At least a head shorter than Rumo, he was wearing grey leather trousers, a cowhide waistcoat and a pair of black buckskin boots. He shook hands with the newcomer and said affably, 'Welcome to Wolperting.'

Having briefly eyed him up and down, Rumo nodded and walked on. The gatekeeper hurried after him.

'Hey!' he called. 'Not so fast, my friend. You can't just waltz in like this. Rules are rules.'

'I'm no friend of yours,' Rumo growled pugnaciously. Smyke had coached him for combat, not for social chit-chat.

'Aren't you? Suit yourself, but I'm a friend of *yours*, whether you like it or not. I'm Urs, your municipal friend.'

Rumo strode on with Urs at his heels. He could see Wolpertings on all sides. Dozens of them were walking the streets and there had to be many more elsewhere – their scent was overpowering.

'All new arrivals are assigned a municipal friend, it's the law,' said Urs. 'It helps them to overcome their initial feeling of strangeness. If you weren't a Wolperting I'd be your municipal *enemy*. Anyone who *isn't* a Wolperting and manages to get this far is assigned a municipal enemy. If you weren't a Wolperting we wouldn't be having this friendly chat. I'd have wrung your neck and catapulted you into the moat. But in the first place you wouldn't have got inside and secondly you're a Wolperting. So I'm your friend, understand? What was your name again?'

Rumo came to a halt. He shut his eyes and looked for the Silver Thread, but all he could see was a tangle of coloured strands. The smell of his own kind was too overpowering for him to pick out an individual scent.

'Hey, what's your name?' Urs demanded. 'I didn't get it the first time.'

Rumo opened his eyes. 'My name is Rumo,' he replied.

'Rumo? No kidding? You're really called Rumo?' Urs grinned. 'Did anyone ever tell you it's the name of a card game?'

'Yes, they did,' said Rumo. 'I'm here because I'm looking for something.'

'I know,' said Urs. 'You're looking for the Silver Thread.'

Rumo was taken aback. 'How did you know?'

Urs grinned again. 'We all are, aren't we?'

'You mean you're also looking for the Silver Thread?'

'Yes. No. That's to say, all in good time. Come on, simmer down. You're at home now.'

Rumo did his best to relax. This Wolperting meant him well, he could sense it.

'I can sleep here, you mean?'

'Better than that. You can stay here – in fact, you can live here. But as I said, all in good time. First you must call on the mayor. That's the way things are done around here. Come on, I'll take you to him.'

Hoth

'Who built this place?' Rumo asked Urs as they made their way through the narrow streets.

'Nobody built Wolperting. Somebody must have, I mean, but no one knows who. It's like this: several hundred years ago a Wolperting named Hoth visited this area and found the city as it is today, complete with walls, houses and streets. The gates were open, but there wasn't a living soul inside. Legend has it that the moment Hoth approached the city a pigeon and a bee tried to fly through the open gates. The pigeon was transfixed by a hail of automatically fired arrows and the bee by a poisoned needle. Hoth thought for a bit, then walked through the gateway holding a shield over his head – he was brave but no fool. Nothing happened, so he concluded that the place belonged to him.'

'I see.'

'Well, that's the legend, but it all happened a good while ago, so who can tell for sure? All this Hoth worship gets on my nerves a bit, to be honest. Hoth here, Hoth there, Hoth Street, Hoth High School, Hoth Bakery, the Grand Hoth Jubilee? Hoth, Hoth, Hoth! What would Hoth himself have thought? I mean, he breezed into the city – what was so great about that? If *I'd* passed by a hundred years ago, everything here would be called Urs. Can you imagine it? We'd now be walking along Urs Street, not Hoth Avenue.' Urs sighed.

'You talk a lot,' said Rumo.

Urs ignored this remark. 'Who cares? Anyway, I think it's great that the city's defences still function as well as they did in the legend. I mean, we may not have any needles and arrows capable of shooting down bees and pigeons, but we can take good care of ourselves, get it? I wouldn't like to be the person that tried to invade our fine city.'

'I understand.'

'All right, let's obey the rules. I'll take you first to the mayor and then to your new lodgings.'

The 'other' Wolpertings

The further into the city they progressed, the more the streets were thronged with Rumo's distant relations. All were short-horned dogs that walked on their hind legs. Some had menacing jaws like bull terriers or massive rib cages like Rottweilers, others displayed the slanting eyes of a Nordic husky or the pendulous jowls of a boxer. Rumo saw wolves and greyhounds, dachshunds and Alsatians. Many even bore a resemblance to foxes. There were also some that resembled Rumo himself and others that looked like Urs, but they all emitted the same reassuring scent. Rumo's nose told him that they were his own kind.

'Bowls you over, doesn't it?' said Urs. 'The scent, I mean. It makes you feel at home right away. Safe and snug. We're all the best of friends here.'

But there was another distinction Rumo found thoroughly perplexing. There were Wolpertings and Wolpertings - for the moment, he couldn't put it any better than that. Some Wolpertings smelt like himself: wild, canine and unthreatening. Others smelt wild, canine and - what, exactly? They smelt nice. Very nice, in fact. Much better than the first category. They smelt . . . more interesting. In other respects they differed from their own kind only in the most discreet way. Their clothes were identical - leather trousers, waistcoats, jerkins or fur jackets, linen shirts - but somehow they fitted them better. Their eyes were different - bigger, more lustrous, more mysterious. Above all, their movements were more graceful. Although their characteristics appealed to Rumo, something about these *other* Wolpertings made him feel rather nervous of them. What could it be?

Urs gave him a sidelong look.

'Well, how do you like our girls?'

'Girls?'

'Yes, our girls. What do you think of them?'

'What are girls?'

'You're kidding!'

'What are girls?' Rumo asked again.

'Oh boy, you really are wet behind the ears, aren't you? You honestly don't know what girls are?'

Smyke had never said anything about girls. Rumo was beginning to dislike the subject.

'You're in luck, my friend, I'm Wolperting's leading expert on girls – in fact, I'm *the* authority on them. I can teach you all you need to know, but more of that later.' Urs chuckled in a way Rumo didn't like.

Girls . . . He made a note of the word. It sounded nice.

Rumo noticed something else. Many of the Wolpertings – the overwhelming majority, in fact – were armed. They wore hatchets in their belts or crossbows strapped to their backs, but mostly they carried cut-and-thrust weapons such as daggers, swords and sabres. Others strolled around armed only with books or loaves of bread, and many carried little square boards with checkered patterns. It was a city filled with mysteries.

They came to a river flanked on either side by walls. It was fast-flowing and looked deep and dangerous.

'That's the Wolper,' Urs explained. 'As you can see, our river is enclosed by walls. There's a reason for that.'

'Wolpertings can't swim,' said Rumo.

'Aha, so you know that. You don't know what girls are, but you know you can't swim. Ever been near any water?'

Rumo nodded.

'Several citizens get drowned every year and always in the summer. Although it's against their natural instincts, they simply want to know what swimming's like. We can do plenty of things, but there are two we're no good at: flying and swimming.'

They walked on through the narrow streets, Urs in the lead with Rumo, peering around and nervously sniffing the air, at his heels. Smyke would have liked the city if he'd been allowed to enter it. There were plenty of those taverns he was always raving about. Wolpertings sat at wooden tables outside them, eating and drinking or poring over their checkered boards. There were shops, cobblestones, brick buildings, milling crowds, noise, music and smells of all kinds. And those *other* Wolpertings, many of whom glanced at Rumo in an enigmatic way.

Rounding a corner, they were abruptly confronted by a scene that thoroughly surprised Rumo. Two Wolpertings lay sprawled on the

cobbles, locked together in an unmistakable effort to throttle each other. A group of young Wolpertings had gathered round, but none of them made any attempt to separate the adversaries. On the contrary, they were egging them on.

'What's going on?' asked Rumo.

'Unarmed combat training,' Urs said dismissively. He halted outside a building distinguished from the rest by its size and ornate façade.

'This is City Hall. I'll take you up to the mayor's office. Wipe your feet and mind how you answer his questions. He's got no sense of humour at all.'

Jowly of Gloomberg

'What's your name?' The mayor was seated behind a plain wooden desk, studying some papers. To judge by the bags under his eyes and his melancholy gaze, there was a St Bernard among his ancestors. His fur displayed innumerable folds and bulges, and there was a notch in the centre of his massive cranium that suggested he'd been hit with an axe in the far-distant past.

'Rumo.'

The mayor looked up for the first time.

'Trying to make a fool of me, are you? Didn't they tell you I've no sense of humour? I asked your name.'

'My name is Rumo.'

The mayor pushed the papers aside and eyed him sympathetically. 'Like the card game?'

Rumo shrugged his shoulders.

'And your surname?' asked the mayor.

Rumo had no idea what a surname was.

'You'll be assigned one in due course. So your name is Rumo, poor boy. Never mind, pleased to meet you. My name is Jowly of Gloomberg. You may call me Your Honour.'

Rumo nodded.

'What are you good at?'

Rumo thought for a moment. 'Fighting,' he said.

The mayor gave a mirthless laugh. 'So is everyone else in this place. You might just as well say "I'm good at cocking my hind leg." All Wolpertings are. I meant, what are you good at *apart* from fighting?'

Rumo pondered this question for quite a while, but nothing occurred to him.

'Do you have a trade?'

Rumo racked his brains. Was picking up scents a trade?

'Are you a blacksmith? A carpenter? A compositor? A cook?'

Rumo shook his head.

'What about this?' The mayor pointed to his mouth. 'Are you good at speaking?'

Another shake of the head.

'So you can't do anything at all.'

Rumo had an urge to tell him about his prowess on Roaming Rock, but that would have sounded conceited.

The mayor cleared his throat as though about to deliver an official speech. 'No Wolperting can do absolutely nothing. I'd go so far as to say that *all Wolpertings are capable of doing something exceptionally well* – it's just that they have to discover what it is. Many find out very early on, many very late in life and many never at all. That's their bad luck, but even they had a talent for something. They never discovered what it was, that's all. Such is my philosophy – not a particularly sophisticated one, but then, I'm not a particularly good philosopher. I'm just a particularly good mayor.'

Rumo was shuffling impatiently from foot to foot.

'Wolpertings can do more than fight. It's simply that the word has still to get around. We're working on this – we're going to see to it that Wolpertings become sought after as something other than bouncers and bodyguards. Some day we'll be renowned for our intellectual abilities as well. We're excellent chess players.'

Rumo was becoming uneasy. The interview was lasting longer than he'd hoped. What was chess? He wanted to fight, not play games.

'What do you intend to do with your life, my boy?'

Rumo didn't understand the question.

'What's your aim in life?'

'I'm looking for the Silver Thread.'

The mayor cast his eyes up to heaven. 'So are we all, youngster, but there are a few other things in life. For instance, er . . .' He stared hard at the table top as if it bore a written record of the meaning of existence. 'Oh well, you'll cotton on sooner or later, eh?' He laughed woodenly. 'Right, let's get the formalities over.'

He opened a drawer and took out a sheet of paper.

'Once you've signed this form you'll be a citizen of Wolperting. That will entitle you to free board and lodging. You'll also have the right to attend school and use our library without charge. Your civic duties will be as follows . . .'

Rumo switched off, as he always did when someone lectured him on a subject other than fighting. The words congealed into a monotonous, meaningless series of syllables.

'Sign here.'

'Huh?'

'Your name. Sign here.'

'I can't write.'

'I guessed as much. Most new arrivals can't. In that case you'll have to bleed.'

'What?'

'Anyone who can't write has to bleed. Here!' The mayor handed Rumo a big pin. 'Prick yourself. The thumb bleeds best.'

'Just a minute,' thought Rumo, *'what am I doing here?'* Hadn't something just been said about duties? It would be wrong to commit himself to something that imposed duties on him. He'd only just escaped from captivity. He wanted to explore Zamonia and sample a life of freedom. He wasn't even sure he wanted to stay in Wolperting. There were lots of Wolpertings here, granted, but Smyke had said there were some in every big city. Besides, he wasn't so dead set on the company of his own kind. It suited his nature better to pursue a loner's existence. He wanted to find out about the Silver Thread; then he would move on.

The mayor grunted impatiently. 'So you need convincing?'

Rumo wasn't sure. No, he thought, I'd sooner move on.

'There are two reasons for staying here, fighting for one.'

Rumo pricked his ears. 'What about it?'

Combat techniques

'We'll teach you it at our school. *Real* fighting, I mean, not these stupid scuffles any Wolperting is good at. It would be foolish of us not to promote and cultivate that aptitude. We have the finest instructors in hand-to-hand combat. There are courses in shadow-boxing, wrestling, kick-boxing, night fighting, axe wielding, ball and chain, crossbowmanship, archery, Far Eastern aerial combat, blind knife throwing, fighting with three weapons at once. Et cetera, et cetera.'

'You teach fighting with weapons?'

'Reluctantly, yes, but it's necessary sometimes. On this dangerous continent it would be naive to suppose that we can get by with our fists alone, especially when we're Wolpertings and every highwayman thinks he has to test his mettle on us. The fencing master at our school is no less a person than Ushan DeLucca!' The mayor's voice took on a dramatic note. 'Ushan DeLucca is the finest exponent of the épée in all Zamonia!

And of the rapier! And of the foil! And of the sabre! He'd beat all comers with the truffleplane too, if he had to. He's the finest fighter with anything that has a blade.'

Rumo was suddenly galvanised.

'If I went to this school, would he teach me swordsmanship?' Smyke had told him a great deal about that dangerous form of combat.

'Among other things. You'd also learn reading, writing, arithmetic, chess, the heroic sagas, and a little Zamonian literature. Dental care too, of course. But fighting has pride of place at our school. The weekly curriculum includes thirty hours of self-defence alone.'

Rumo picked up the pin.

'One moment!' said the mayor. 'I still haven't told you the second reason.'

Rumo pricked up his ears.

'The second reason is, you'll only find your Silver Thread here in Wolperting.'

Resolutely, Rumo pricked his thumb and anointed the form with a few drops of blood.

'Those two reasons are enough to convince any Wolperting,' the mayor said with a grin. 'It would save me a lot of time if all you young shavers could read. I'd write everything down on a slate and hang it above my desk. Then I could dispense with all this palaver.'

No. 12 Hoth Street

Rumo's lodgings were at no. 12 Hoth Street, the little half-timbered house he shared with Urs and three other young Wolpertings: Tobby, Axel and Obert, triplets of collie extraction, who gave him a warm welcome. His own room was small but fully furnished: his first bed, his first chair, his first table, his first fireplace. Rumo looked out of his first window. Wolpertings of both categories, the *some* and the *others*, were strolling past below, chatting and laughing together. He stretched out on the bed and wondered if he had made the right decision. Still wondering, he fell asleep surrounded by the reassuring noises and smells of a civilised environment that didn't contain a single natural enemy. The last time Rumo had slept as long and as soundly was in his little basket at the farm.

Coffee and clothes, rights and duties

The next morning Urs came to escort Rumo to school. He knocked on his door laden with a bundle of clothes, some bread and a pot of coffee. They breakfasted at Rumo's table.

'What's this?' asked Rumo as he sipped the hot beverage.

'It's coffee.'

'Coffee,' Rumo repeated. He liked the drink. It made you feel alert, not sleepy or full up.

'Oh, by the way, before anyone else mentions it, your things reek of Bluddum.'

'I know.'

'It isn't a very popular smell in this place. Better put on something else before we go to school. I've brought you a few things of Axel's. He's about your size.'

Rumo was only too pleased not to smell of Bluddum any more. The garments – trousers, waistcoat and boots – were of black buckskin and fitted him as perfectly as Urs had predicted.

On the way to school his 'municipal friend' tried to explain as briefly as possible how life in Wolperting was organised. The community functioned thanks to a complex system of rights and duties in which money and laws played little part. The only law was: 'Those who fail to fulfil their duties forfeit their rights and must leave the city.' The system was supervised by the mayor and a few dozen city councillors, all of them respectable old Wolpertings to whom derelictions of duty could be reported and who then acted accordingly. Civic duties included school attendance, sweeping the streets, shovelling snow in winter, weeding the municipal vegetable gardens, working on the communal farms, chopping firewood for the sick and feeble, kneading dough for the municipal bakeries and medical duty at the hospital. The city's inhabitants were assigned these tasks in accordance with an annual rota worked out by the mayor's office. Another duty was to defend Wolperting to the death if some enemy took advantage of the city's hospitality to launch an attack from outside – not that this had ever happened to date. In return, citizens were entitled to free board and lodging, free schooling, and free use of Wolperting's public library and sports and medical facilities. They also had the right to attend the big fair held annually just outside the city gates and were provided with pocket money for this purpose. The municipal exchequer derived an abundant income from the sale of agricultural products to other cities in the region. You could go to a bakery and collect your daily bread ration free of charge, but you got some funny looks if you tried it twice the same day. Try it a third time and the baker would hurl his shovel at your head.

Urs explained all this to Rumo as they walked to school. Rumo thought it sounded like a fair bargain. It entailed hard work and a disciplined way of life, but after all, he would be taught to fight with lethal weapons. For that he would have handled the whole of Wolperting's refuse collection by himself.

'That's the fire station.'

Urs was pointing out various places of interest as they passed them.

'That's the municipal butcher's. The finest black puddings in Zamonia, my friend.'

'That's the theatre.'

'The theatre?'

'Yes. Culture and all that. Know what I mean?'

'No,' said Rumo.

'And that's a public convenience.'

Rumo stared at it uncomprehendingly.

'You can have a quiet pee there. Into a bucket. It stops everyone peeing in the street.'

'Why shouldn't they?'

'Hey, a good thing you asked. It's prohibited here. This is a civilised city, not the jungle, understand? We Wolpertings are as fond of peeing as our ancestors, but we pee into buckets that get emptied. Think what it would be like if everyone relieved themselves in the street! Think of the mess! Better get that straight if you want to remain a citizen of this place!'

Public convenience, Rumo memorised.

'That's the Black Dome over there.'

They were crossing a square with an impressive building in the middle

– the biggest Rumo had ever seen. It was a vast hemisphere that looked as if it had been carved out of a single chunk of black rock.

'What's inside?'

'No idea. Nobody knows. There's no entrance, not even a window. No one ever goes in or comes out. We call it the Black Dome because it's a dome and it's black. That's all we know about it. People have attempted to make a hole in the thing. They broke a few pickaxes and that was that. It may be a monument erected by the former inhabitants, or something of the kind. Look, there's another public convenience.'

'Another?'

'Our city has more of them than anywhere else in Zamonia. And here we are at the school.'

School

The school was the biggest building in Wolperting, bigger even than the Black Dome, and situated at its highest point. Its granite walls and towers were reminiscent of a fortress, an impression accentuated by the fact that it was built on a rock. It was cool and dark in the labyrinthine passages along which Urs conducted Rumo. They were filled with young Wolpertings who strolled around or stood together in groups, talking and laughing. Rumo never guessed that the moment when he entered the classroom with Urs would transform his life completely. Had he decided to turn his back on Wolperting instead of going to school, his existence would have followed a different course. A less adventurous and dangerous one, perhaps, but also less happy, for awaiting him in this classroom was the object of his long-standing dreams. It contained the thing that had spurred him on – the thing whose true nature was still unknown to him: this classroom contained his Silver Thread.

Rumo began surveying the form as a whole. He saw twelve young Wolpertings gazing at him intently from behind their battered, scribbled-on desks. Next he saw the teacher, a thickset, rough-haired Wolperting wearing a monocle and a chalk-smeared sweater, who was standing in front of a blackboard covered with unintelligible signs. Finally, he saw *her.*

Rala.

Rala

He didn't know, of course, that her name was Rala – he didn't even know she was a girl, still less what girls actually were, but despite his embarrassing state of ignorance he instinctively sensed that she was the reason for his long trek to Wolperting. He shut his eyes for a moment, then he saw it. Stronger and brighter than ever before, the Silver Thread was flowing back and forth between him and her.

Rumo opened his eyes again. He reeled sideways and had to cling to the doorpost, or he would have fallen flat on his back, the way he had when he first encountered the Demonocles.

The other pupils tittered, the teacher looked perplexed. Urs swung round. 'Come on,' he hissed, 'don't run out on me now!'

Rumo tottered forward and bumped into him, triggering another outburst of hilarity.

'Great entrance,' whispered Urs. He turned to the teacher and raised his voice. 'This is a new boy, sir, officially registered as such by the mayor. I'm his municipal friend. Address: no. 12 Hoth Street. Pardon the interruption.'

Then he went out, but not before muttering 'Pull yourself together!' to Rumo as he passed him. The door slammed and Rumo was alone with a dozen strangers, half of whom were *different.*

'What's your name?' asked the teacher.

Here we go again, thought Rumo. 'Rumo,' he said.

'Like the card game?'

Rumo sighed. 'Yes, sir.'

Smirks all round.

'Rumo what?'

Huh?

'Your surname?'

My surname? The mayor had mentioned that. Rumo remained tongue-tied. He was starting to sweat. The others giggled. He had never expected to find himself in such an unpleasant situation in peaceful surroundings populated by his own kind.

'We all have surnames here,' the teacher explained. 'For example, my forename is Harra. I come from the Midgard area, so my full name is Harra of Midgard.'

The other pupils were whispering together.

Rumo debated feverishly. Where did he come from? Hackonia? He couldn't be sure, and besides, Hackonia was a stupid surname. Where

else had he been? Roaming Rock? Great! 'Rumo of Roaming Rock' would send everyone into fits of laughter.

Impatient murmurs were coming from the back of the class.

Where did he come from?

'Hurry up!' someone called.

He had a flash of inspiration. If there was one thing he could be sure of about his origins, it was that. 'My full name', he said, 'is Rumo of Zamonia.'

The startled silence that descended on the classroom was broken by a young Wolperting with terrierlike features. 'Why not Emperor of Florinth while you're at it?' he demanded. 'Or Ruler of the Universe?'

Laughter.

'That's enough, Rolv!' snapped Harra of Midgard. 'Well, why not? Rumo of Zamonia . . . It's a nice name.'

Rolv gave Rumo an impudent grin. The laughter subsided.

'You can sit at the back, Rumo. Follow the lesson as best you can. We're just doing the heroic sagas. I'll explain everything later.' The teacher indicated a vacant place at the back of the class.

Still feeling bemused, Rumo sat down.

The others turned to eye him curiously, whispering together. How was it possible for him to feel so helpless and uneasy in surroundings devoid of any natural enemies or dangers? It would all have been far simpler outside the city gates – more hazardous but simpler. Inside it was safe but complicated. The rules. The duties. The questions. The surnames. The *other* Wolpertings . . .

He itched to dash out into the wilderness, howling, and beat up a few Bluddums.

Rumo tried to concentrate on the lesson. Harra of Midgard was striding up and down in front of the class, holding forth in a gruff but soothing voice. Now and then he took a piece of chalk and scrawled some indecipherable marks on the blackboard. As far as Rumo could gather, the lesson was about heroes.

The first proven hero in Zamonian history, Harra of Midgard recounted, was an anonymous, thumb-sized Zamazon whose heroic deed had consisted in climbing aboard a leaf during a hurricane and crashing into the side of a volcano. The volcano had preserved the shattered remains of the Zamazon in a stream of lava, so the palaeontologists who subsequently discovered their imprint were able to describe him in considerable detail. The Zamazon had fulfilled the minimum requirement demanded of a hero in those primeval days: a futile display of suicidal daring.

The heroic sagas

In more civilised times a more specific objective was required to transform a mundane action into a heroic act. A quest for some mysterious object rendered mysterious by its sheer mysteriousness, for example, was enough to justify any lethally foolish venture. The warrior knights who had been torn to pieces by Werewolves or crushed to death by rockfalls while seeking *The Accursed Towel* or *The Three Square Balls* – all were heroes. Even their names were on record: Looni Botkin, Minko Morella, Thelonius Zilch and Knoth Fryggenbart. In their day dying for some indeterminate reason was one of the fundamental characteristics of heroism.

At about the same time – Harra of Midgard stressed that this theory was scientifically uncorroborated – there was said to have been an island off the coast of Zamonia, since submerged, on which heroes were systematically bred.

Legend had it that death was prohibited on this island, the name of which was Hypnos. There were no burials or coffins, no graves or graveyards, no wreaths or urns, no tears or lamentations. Even the word 'death' did not officially exist. People did die, of course, whether in accidents or of heart attacks, in which case the authorities were left with a corpse on their hands. However, the body would be promptly removed by the so-called *Darkmen of Hypnos*, who ferried it far out to sea and weighted it down with heavy stones. If someone fell seriously ill, the doctors would bend over him with grave expressions, smother him with a pillow and have him carted away by the Darkmen. Those who enquired after the patient were informed that he was convalescing abroad and would not be back for some time. If they persisted in asking after him the Darkmen came and disposed of *them* on the high seas.

The point was that none of the heroes reared on the island was permitted to know that death existed. Only a hero ignorant of death could be completely fearless. The selected candidates were transported to the island in infancy, suckled and cherished by wet-nurses, educated by sage tutors and trained in every form of combat. Everything conceivable was done to ensure that they led a life of happiness and fulfilment – until they were sent into battle. They sang as they took the field, not because they were courageous but because they had no notion of what fear was. They weren't exceptionally skilful warriors for that very reason. They were reckless, they declined to wear armour, and they considered it unmanly to take cover. Attack was deemed acceptable, defence cowardly. As a result, they died in droves.

The next generation of heroes pursued different ideals. In early medieval Zamonia a particularly cautious form of heroism was cultivated. Its practitioners attached great importance to meticulous planning and elaborate security measures. They took account of weather conditions, their own current form and astrological predictions, and would sooner defer some heroic deed than plunge recklessly into the fray. One contemporary example was Peregrine the Procrastinator, who repeatedly postponed a duel with his arch-enemy, the cruel Baron of Baysville, until the latter developed a peptic ulcer that rendered him chronically unfit for combat. Another was Simeon the Circumspect, who did not perform any heroic deeds at all. Instead, he wrote a number of successful but appallingly tedious books on *how* to perform them – or rather, on the elaborate and protracted preparations they necessitated.

The heroes of the next period, Harra of Midgard went on, had ceased to be brainless midgets, romantic nincompoops or dithering vacillators. Genuine heroes (or heroines) who fought for just causes, exalted aims or the love of their nearest and dearest, they included Violetta Valentina, who freed her fiancé from the dungeons of mad Prince Oggnagogg; Hiram the Hooligan, who single-handedly put down the Midgardian Turnipheads' rebellion with a golden axe; and Damon of Dullsgard, who threw himself into the jaws of the Sewer Dragon after swallowing enough sewer-dragon venom to kill a whole army of the beasts. These were historically proven heroes of flesh and blood, not dubious legends or products of mythological conjecture.

In very recent times, or during the last two hundred years, the heroic spectrum had widened yet again. A hero didn't necessarily have to be dead, nor was it essential for his heroic deeds to be performed on the field of battle. They could also involve art, music, literature, medicine, or some branch of science.

Hildegard Mythmaker, that titan among Zamonian novelists, Professor Abdullah Nightingale, the brilliant scientist and inventor, Colophonius Regenschein, the legendary book hunter who disappeared into the catacombs of Betaville, and Utta Raptrap, the originator of silent music - *those* were the new heroes! The representatives of modern heroism no longer had to wield bloodstained axes; a pen dipped in ink or a conductor's baton would also suffice in case of doubt.

With this bold assertion Harra of Midgard brought the lesson to a close. Rumo's own idea of heroism, shaped by Volzotan Smyke's anecdotes, was altogether different. He couldn't, with the best will in the world, conceive of a hero who wielded a violin bow instead of a sword.

Not that he noticed it, Rumo's feeling of helplessness and strangeness had subsided. By the time the lesson ended, in fact, he had even grown used to sitting on a chair. A bell rang. He gave a start as if roused from some vivid dream. So that was what lessons were like. They enabled you to dream with your eyes open.

Vasko, Balla and Olek

Recreation time. Rumo left the classroom with his head awhirl with all the school rules Harra had explained to him. Exercise books and pencils were to be collected from the administration block; he would be given special tuition in reading, writing and arithmetic; chess and combat techniques were so-called 'extras'; the timetables were displayed in such and such a place; the heroic sagas were an optional subject; there were no exams or homework. Rumo trailed after the other pupils as they streamed out into the big playground. In the middle was a tent where hot coffee, cocoa and chicken soup were dispensed and apples distributed.

Rumo was far too excited to feel hungry. He roamed restlessly around the playground. Little groups of chattering, laughing pupils were standing everywhere, most of them divided into Wolpertings of *this* category and *that*. Now and then they engaged in mock battles, chasing one another and exchanging volleys of apples.

In one group of *different* Wolpertings Rumo spotted Rala. Quickly turning away because he could feel the blood rush to his head, he lurched backwards in search of a tree to hide behind – and tripped. He nearly fell over but recovered his balance just in time. Then he saw that he'd tripped over a foot.

'Oh, sorry,' Rolv said with a grin, withdrawing it. 'My mistake.' He was standing with his back against the tree, flanked by three Wolpertings who weren't in Rumo's form. Rolv tossed a shiny green apple into the air and caught it. Then he indicated each of his companions in turn.

'Allow me to make the introductions: Vasko of the Red Forest; Balla of Betaville; Olek of the Dunes.'

The trio inclined their heads. Vasko had white fur and menacing, narrow green eyes like the ice dogs of the north, Balla was a terrier like Rolv but with brown fur, and Olek was of Alsatian stock.

'And this is Rumo of Zamonia,' said Rolv. 'The new boy with the grand name.' He turned to Rumo. 'Whither away so fast, Your Majesty?' He grinned. 'Urgent government business?'

Rumo felt the blood rush to his head again.

Rolv's gang obediently guffawed at their leader's witticism. Rumo tried feverishly to think of some nonchalant retort, but nothing occurred to him, so he said, 'We can fight if you like.'

'Huh!' Vasko and Olek said simultaneously.

Balla stepped aside, Rolv lowered his voice until it was almost inaudible.

'You're quick off the mark. *Can* you fight? How good are your reflexes, Rumo of Zamonia?'

Rumo was surprised by the speed at which the apple came hurtling towards him – faster even than the bolts from Kromek Toomah's crossbow. Rolv seemed hardly to move despite the immense strength he must have exerted, but Rumo still had time to plot the apple's trajectory and coordinate his reactions. He waited until it had nearly reached him, averted his head a fraction to let it sail past – then, quick as a flash, sank his teeth in it. He grinned at Rolv with the apple in his mouth, then threw back his head and tossed it into the air. One gulp and it disappeared down his throat. He licked his lips.

'Phew!' Olek exclaimed. 'He's fast!'

Rolv blinked nervously. The new boy certainly was fast, but he took care to conceal his astonishment. Still in a low, calm voice, he said, 'Sure, that's how wild boar piglets react in the bush. They bolt their food quicker than the eye can see.'

'That's enough,' thought Rumo. *'He's positively asking for it.'*

He now felt almost sorry for Rolv. What came next would happen so fast that they would all believe he was a magician. He didn't intend to hurt the bully too much, just humiliate him by dumping him on his backside before he knew what had hit him. He lunged at lightning speed.

When Rolv saw his opponent coming for him the White Fire blazed up briefly in his mind's eye. Having learnt not to let it get the better of him, however, he promptly suppressed it.

Rolv's story

Rolv's wild parents had abandoned him and his twin sister in the Great Forest, where they were captured by a hunter. The latter had sold them to someone who called himself a farmer but wasn't one. The Bluddum who acquired the puppies for two bottles of home-distilled hooch was really a bandit who dealt in watered-down spirits and disguised his activities by keeping a wretched farm that boasted only three animals: an emaciated pig, an emaciated cow and an emaciated sheep. Rolv was to be his watchdog. Niddugg by name, the Bluddum knew nothing about Wolpertings – he was so drunk he barely noticed their little horns – and mistook the pair for wild dogs of some kind. To instil some respect in his new watchdog he resorted to a drastic expedient: he chained Rolv up and made him watch while he slowly and deliberately beat his sister to death. Then he dragged her body into the forest as a sacrifice to the deity he believed in: the Wild Bear God.

Niddugg put Rolv on a strict diet (too much food only made an animal dozy and inattentive), kept him shut up in a slatted wooden cage that let in the rain and, sometimes, snow (great aids to remaining alert), and gave him a daily thrashing with his leather belt. Invariably blind drunk, he used to beat the puppy until one of them passed out.

When Rolv reached adolescence, Niddugg was at first surprised and then pleased by the thought of owning such a fast-growing beast, which seemed to become a little more dangerous every day. He was also rather perturbed, however, so he chained Rolv up in the barn. The advantage of this was that Rolv was protected from the elements, the disadvantage that Niddugg now came to beat him in any kind of weather.

Rolv tested his growing teeth on the wooden beam to which his chain was attached. He bit and gnawed and chewed away without a thought of escape, so he was very surprised one day when the staple came away from the gnawed beam and fell into the straw. He still had a chain round his neck, but he was free.

Rolv had never yet harmed a living creature; until now he had merely resigned himself to his fate. His undernourished body was covered with cuts and scars. He even had a notch in his ear where Niddugg's belt buckle had dealt him a particularly painful blow, inflicting a wound that bled and suppurated for weeks. Rolv was in two minds. He could have run off into the forest, but he didn't. He could have slunk into the house and attacked Niddugg from behind, but he didn't do that either. He simply lay down in the barn and awaited the usual course of events. At dusk the barn door burst open and Niddugg blundered in with the belt in his fist.

That was when Rolv first saw the White Fire. A dazzling white sheet of flame blazed up before his eyes and he genuinely thought the barn had caught fire. Then the blaze subsided and all was still. Niddugg had disappeared. Rolv thought at first that he'd run back into the farmhouse or off into the surrounding woods, but then he saw that Niddugg was still in the barn. One of the bandit's arms was lying on the ground, the bales of hay and wooden walls were spattered with his blood, and his head had been stuck on a fence post. His legs and his other arm lay scattered around. Looking down at himself, Rolv saw that he was smothered in blood. He and Niddugg had passed through the White Fire together. Rolv had often seen the White Fire since then, and always when he was feeling seriously threatened. It was only in Wolperting that he'd learnt to control the dangerous forces it unleashed – as, for instance, when Rumo charged at him.

Rumo sprang at Rolv like lightning, but the operation was carefully planned. He knew precisely what would happen: Rolv's movements would appear to slow down. He would dart past his opponent, trip him up and send him sprawling on his bottom by driving an elbow into his ribs. Rolv and his pals would be transfixed – shocked by the speed of his attack.

Ushan DeLucca

But something else happened. Something Rumo found almost as disconcerting as what had happened when he entered the classroom: Rolv's movements didn't become slower.

They speeded up.

Yes, Rolv moved just as swiftly as he did. He stepped aside and Rumo blundered forward into thin air. Before he knew it Rolv had seized him by the throat from behind and thrown him to the ground.

Rumo had never yet encountered a living creature as quick as himself. The Demonocles had been stronger than him, the Bluddums better armed, the Stranglesnakes more agile. His main asset was speed. Rumo now learnt to his cost that this was *every* Wolperting's main asset. What had been sensational outside the gates of the city was taken for granted in the schoolyard.

The result was that Rolv didn't end up on his bottom and the two of them went rolling across the ground.

What looked like a confused tangle of growling, snarling Wolpertings was really a precise sequence of combat tactics. Rolv countered Rumo's every kick and hold with one of his own, and every attack Rolv launched met with an appropriate response. Although they instinctively refrained from using their teeth, there was clearly more at stake than in an ordinary playground scrap. A knot of spectators gathered round the antagonists. They had seldom seen such a serious fight so doggedly contested by both parties.

Suddenly Rumo felt his neck seized by a powerful paw that didn't belong to Rolv. Abruptly hauled to his feet, he saw his opponent, as grimy and breathless as himself, standing there likewise gripped by the neck. Then he looked up into the saddest Wolpertingian face he'd ever seen. The paws and the face belonged to Ushan DeLucca, the school's legendary fencing master, who was on duty that day. He released the pair and stood looking down at them.

'What *is* all this uncivilised conduct?' he demanded quietly. 'You're behaving like mongrels, the two of you.'

The thing that first struck one about Ushan DeLucca was his curiously melancholy cast of feature. His entire face seemed abnormally subject to the force of gravity, which exerted a downwards pull on the corners of his mouth, the furrows in his brow and the bags under his eyes. He spoke in a low, deliberate voice. 'And who might you be?'

'Rumo. Rumo of Zamonia.'

'A new boy, eh? Rumo of Zamonia? Sounds like the professional name of a megalomaniac card-sharp.'

Rolv laughed.

'You ought to know better, Rolv. You've been here long enough to know I don't tolerate fighting outside class.'

'He started it,' said Rolv.

'I'm sure you found a way to make him do so.' DeLucca pointed to the school building. 'Clean yourselves up and keep out of each other's way in future. If I catch you fighting again you'll clean the school toilets for a week.'

Rolv and Rumo slouched off in different directions, doubly humiliated by their failure to win and the teacher's dressing-down. The other pupils stared at Rumo as he patted the dust off his fur and slunk inside.

Dental hygiene, maths and chess

The lessons after break seemed interminable. Tasso of Florinth, a Dalmatian with a perfect set of teeth, lectured them on dental hygiene and demonstrated how to clean the narrow gaps between their teeth with silken thread. He stressed the importance of dental care in general and for Wolpertings in particular.

'The teeth,' he kept repeating, 'are a Wolperting's most important tool. Looking after them is our prime duty. Our direst foes are not large wild beasts but tiny little creatures that make themselves at home in the gaps between our teeth. We have to wage a daily battle against them!' Then he drew a cross section of a typical Wolperting's tooth on the blackboard and explained how the diminutive creatures insinuated themselves between gum and tooth and did their diabolical work there.

Rumo had no difficulty in following the lesson as long as he didn't look in Rolv's direction. That wasn't so easy – recent events had left him too worked up – but his agitation gave way to mounting boredom as the hours went by. Next, Tasso of Florinth took the class for mathematics, a subject to which Rumo developed an instant aversion. He was not asked to take an active part in this lesson because the others were at a more advanced stage, so he was put to learning elementary maths with a group of beginners, but he had to sit there quietly while the teacher reeled off a soporific series of figures. Tasso also wrote some incomprehensible equations on the blackboard. With the aid of those, he grandly asserted, one could calculate the dimensions of the entire universe – something Rumo had absolutely no wish to do.

He would not have believed it possible, but the next double period was even more of an ordeal: Harra of Midgard taught them chess. The apparent object of this board game played with wooden pieces was to bore your opponent to death. Rumo's classmates spent the whole time sitting mutely over the checkered boards he'd seen so often. Someone would very occasionally move a piece across the board, then relapse into brooding silence. Meanwhile, the teacher unashamedly dozed. The only form of diversion occurred when someone said 'Check!' or 'Checkmate!'.

Rumo wasn't made to play, so he had plenty of time to reflect that there seemed to be some subjects he approved of (heroic sagas, dental hygiene), some that left him cold (chess) and some he didn't like at all (mathematics). His first day at school hadn't featured a single subject that aroused his enthusiasm.

Wolpertingesses

Rumo emerged from school that afternoon to find Urs waiting outside with a paper bag full of pastries.

'Well,' he asked with his mouth full, 'how did it go?' He proffered the bag.

Rumo shook his head. 'No thanks. Fine. I had my first fight.'

'Well done. Who with?'

'Someone called Rolv.'

'Rolv, of all people? Congratulations, you picked on the best fighter in Wolperting. Was it bad?'

'It was a draw.'

'A draw? Against Rolv?' Urs whistled admiringly.

'I was hoping to do better.'

They walked on in silence for a while, Urs cramming one pastry after another into his mouth. 'And in other respects? How was school?'

Rumo pulled a face. 'Well . . .'

'Nearly everyone feels like that. Only idiots take to school the first day, but you get used to it.'

'I certainly won't. What gets me most of all is the *other* Wolpertings.'

'The other Wolpertings? What do you mean?'

Unobtrusively, with the tip of his nose, Rumo indicated the opposite side of the street, where Rala was standing in the midst of a group of giggling classmates.

'Them? The girls, you mean?'

'*Those* are girls?'

'Sure they are. The one with the long hair is Rala. A regular knockout.'

'Rala,' murmured Rumo.

Urs looked at him pityingly. 'I can't believe it. You honestly don't know what girls are?'

Rumo didn't know why, but he found the question embarrassing.

'They aren't Wolpertings, strictly speaking. They're Wolperting*esses*.'

'Esses?'

'Well, I'll be . . .' said Urs. 'You really don't have a clue, do you?' He laid a paw on Rumo's shoulder and looked deep into his eyes. He lowered his voice. 'My poor friend,' he said, 'I think it's high time I told you a bit about girls . . .'

The miracle of life

Rumo lay on his bed fully dressed, listlessly munching a pastry and reviewing the events of the last few hours. It had been quite a day! His view of the world had been shaken to its foundations more than once. What Urs had told him on the way home was liable to give him a sleepless night.

It was incredible! There really were two different kinds of Wolpertings: boys and girls. And that was far from all. Just to complete his bewilderment, Urs had told him that there were two kinds of almost every Zamonian life form: two kinds of Hackonians, two kinds of Bluddums, two kinds of this, two kinds of that. Then he'd told him about the *miracle of life.* Bees somehow did something with flowers and the result was two different kinds of butterflies – or something like that. Girls were very important. They had a scent that drove boys mad: the Silver Thread that lured them to Wolperting. Every girl could emit that scent and every boy wanted to follow it to its source, and nobody knew why this was so.

Urs also spoke of baby Wolpertings that came from somewhere and were then abandoned in forests, but he either couldn't or wouldn't explain that either.

Rala. Girls. Rolv. The heroic sagas. Nasty little creatures lurking between your teeth. Chess. Arithmetic. The miracle of life . . . It was definitely too much for Rumo – far too much for one day. He tossed and turned for hours, got up, paced to and fro, lay down again and listened to the voices in the street. Rala, he thought.

Rala.

Rala.

Rala . . .

Wolpertingian general knowledge with Harra of Midgard

When Rumo awoke the next morning it took him a moment to remember where he was. After dreaming wildly for three hours of Rala and the little creatures that lived in his mouth, he had slept until roused by the sounds drifting in through the open window. The whole house was already pervaded by an aroma of freshly brewed coffee. There was a knock, Rumo opened the door, and Urs was standing outside with a coffee pot.

After breakfast they walked a little way across town before going their separate ways. Urs had to report for work at the communal sausage factory on the western outskirts of Wolperting. Rumo made his way to school alone. He even found – right away – the room where exercise books and pencils were given out. He was also issued with a leather satchel, some books covered with indecipherable words, a toothbrush, a long piece of silk thread, a small pot of dentifrice and an apple. Then he went off to his classroom. Outside the door he hesitated, but only for a moment. He would enter the room, look the other pupils in the eye and take his place. He would sit there and learn things till his backside was sore, if need be. Why? Because he now had a motive for enduring it all. That motive was a girl and she even had a name: Rala.

Rumo opened the door, forged a path through his noisy classmates – and found his seat already taken. Rolv was sitting there. He seemed to have been waiting for him.

'That's my place,' said Rumo.

'If it's yours,' drawled Rolv, 'take it.'

The hubbub died away. All eyes turned in their direction.

Very deliberately Rumo deposited his satchel on the floor. Surprise tactics wouldn't work with Rolv, he knew that now. This time it would be a genuine, possibly protracted trial of strength that would go on until one of them gave up.

'That's my place,' Rumo repeated quietly. 'Please get up.'

Rolv looked at him without flinching. He spat on the floor.

'*That's* your place,' he said, indicating the little blob of spittle at Rumo's feet. 'Sit down, why don't you?'

Rumo was impressed by Rolv's imperturbability. His opponent was clearly at a disadvantage. From where he stood, Rumo could have pounced on him with ease.

'Get up, Rolv,' said a high-pitched voice. 'Sit down in your own place and leave Rumo alone!'

Rumo looked round. Rala was standing behind him with a pencil in her long fingers. Her expression was grave. Rolv grinned and got up with ostentatious deliberation, but he didn't argue. He went back to his place and sat down.

Just then Harra of Midgard entered the classroom. Rumo and the other pupils sat down too. How had Rala succeeded, with a word or two, in doing what he had failed to achieve with all his strength? What was this power she had over Rolv?

'Wolpertingian general knowledge,' Harra announced. He took a sponge and wiped the previous day's lesson off the blackboard, which was actually a sheet of dark-green slate. Then, having rather inexpertly drawn a dog's head adorned with two small horns, he turned to face the class. Rumo noticed some dried yolk of egg on his knitted waistcoat.

'Have you ever wondered about the origin of those little horns on your heads?' asked Harra.

A few of the pupils instinctively felt their horns. Murmurs and puzzled laughter filled the classroom.

'Does any of you have a deer in the family? Or a springbok? Anyone here with a red deer among his ancestors?'

They all tittered.

'You may laugh, but have you ever seen a dog with horns or a deer with fangs? Why do we Wolpertings carry the genes of so many different life forms? Of predators *and* their prey? Of wild carnivores and harmless ruminants? Have you never asked yourself that question?'

Silence.

'Then I'll tell you a story. It won't provide an exhaustive answer to the question, I'm afraid, but it may shed a little light on your darkness. But I should warn you that it's a horror story. Is anyone here such a sensitive soul that he'd prefer to leave the classroom? Rolv? Rumo?'

Prince Sangfroid and Princess Daintyhoof

Everyone tittered except Rolv and Rumo. Word of their scrap in the playground had evidently gone the rounds of the staff room.

'The story is set in the Great Forest, which, as you know, is still a blank space on the map of Zamonia. It's largely unexplored and guards its secrets well, so I can't vouch for the scientific accuracy of this version of events.'

The pupils exchanged amused whispers and settled down to listen. Harra's stories were clearly very popular. Rumo also listened closely.

'When groans of despair assail your ears at dusk,' Harra of Midgard began in theatrical tones, 'when shadowy forms grimace malevolently behind your back and swaths of mist loom up like menacing figures – you know that the Great Forest must be close at hand. Walk on, shivering, for the space of two toad-croaks and one owl-hoot, and you will find yourself on its outskirts, confronted by a dark, forbidding wall of trees whose dead branches form an entanglement high overhead. No one ever penetrates its depths, for everyone knows that they harbour *The Hundred-Fingered Moomy, The Ever-Ravenous Omnivore, The Faceless Man, The Wicked Wolf,* and *The Spiderwitch.* Thus the sinister forest remained untrodden for many a long year . . .'

Harra perched on the windowsill and surveyed the class.

'One day, however, a young roe deer named Princess Daintyhoof appeared on the scene. She was no stranger to evil life forms, having originally been a human child whom a perfidious Hazelwitch had transformed into a deer and abandoned on the edge of the Great Forest.'

The girls sighed, the boys grinned. It wouldn't be long before this deer got into serious difficulties.

'Princess Daintyhoof knew nothing of *The Hundred-Fingered Moomy, The Ever-Ravenous Omnivore, The Faceless Man, The Wicked Wolf* or *The Spiderwitch,* so she unsuspectingly ventured into the gloomy forest. It wasn't long before the forest began to spin a web of dusky shadows around her, because night was falling, so Princess Daintyhoof was relieved to see a dim light shining through the darkness. Having trotted closer, she discovered that the light came from a little cottage in a clearing.'

Harra got up off the windowsill and went over to the first row of desks. Resting his paws on one of them, he stared fixedly at the class.

'Little cottages in clearings in the Great Forest are bound to house ill-intentioned creatures, aren't they?' The pupils nodded as though mesmerised.

'But Princess Daintyhoof was naturally unaware of that, the innocent little thing, so she timidly knocked on the door.'

Harra turned and gently tapped one wing of the blackboard, then cautiously folded it back. The hinges creaked like those of a door slowly opening.

'The person who opened the door was *not* the most loathsome creature the princess had ever seen, or anything like that. No, it was a nice old granny who kindly invited her in. The old lady expressed pleasure at this unexpected visit and offered her guest some delicious stew from a pot simmering on the stove. Princess Daintyhoof declined with thanks because she'd been a vegetarian ever since her transformation, but she gladly accepted a place beside the fire. No problem, said the granny, she could whip up some tasty nut cutlets in no time and she set to work at the stove right away. Daintyhoof warmed herself at the fire, stretched out her weary limbs and watched the soothing flicker of the flames while listening to the old woman's sing-song voice. She nearly fell asleep.'

Harra's voice had sunk to a whisper.

'Nearly, but not quite!' he bellowed suddenly and everyone gave a start.

'Then, all at once – bang! – the door flew open and a nocturnal storm blew into the house, a violent whirlwind that spun once across the room like a dervish and out again, and when it subsided Princess Daintyhoof was alone. All that remained where the old woman had been standing was a welter of blood, half of it on the floor and half splashed over the stove, and strewn around it were a hundred severed fingers, still twitching, armed with long, vicious-looking nails. And in the saucepan on the stove was a severed head.'

'I get it,' Rolv said grimly.

Harra glanced at him suspiciously. 'For the old woman at the stove wasn't a hospitable old granny at all, but *The Hundred-Fingered Moomy*.'

A murmur ran round the classroom.

'The next day,' Harra went on, 'when Princess Daintyhoof continued on her way through the forest she encountered a very, very thin man seated on a rock beneath an oak tree.' He had lowered his voice again, and his tone was calm and businesslike.

'"I'm an ascetic," said the thin man, "which means that I eat almost nothing – just a pebble and a pinch of sand every few weeks, to keep my digestive organs occupied. By so doing I hope to attain a state of spiritual enlightenment that far transcends the norm. Would you care to fast with me, pretty child?"

'Princess Daintyhoof didn't understand a word, but she had no objection to taking a brief rest, so she stretched out on the grass at the thin man's feet. He proceeded to recite his formulas for fasting – words like tinkling bells, sentences like murmuring streams. Daintyhoof found them so soothing, she almost dozed off.'

Some of the pupils felt their eyelids begin to droop.

'Almost, but not quite!' Harra shouted. 'Because at that moment a wind sprang up. It came roaring through the trees, enveloping Princess Daintyhoof in a cloud of swirling autumn leaves, and when it subsided the thin man and the oak had become one: he was stone dead, wound round the big tree like a rope with every bone in his body broken. When Daintyhoof went behind the tree for a closer look at this grisly spectacle, she came upon a mound of neatly gnawed skulls belonging to all kinds of forest creatures, from foxes to squirrels. There were also many deers' skulls, for the thin man hadn't been on a starvation diet at all: he was *The Ever-Ravenous Omnivore* and he'd very nearly devoured Princess Daintyhoof.'

Harra paused for effect.

'And so,' he went on, 'she continued on her way through the forest until darkness fell once more. Having lost faith in little cottages and big oak trees, she sought shelter in some undergrowth. The night wind whispered in the trees and her heart was heavy, as heavy as her eyelids. And that was how she nearly fell asleep for the third time.' Harra fell silent.

'Nearly, but not quite!' he thundered again, so loudly that Rumo almost fell off his chair. 'Because something was breathing in her ear. Sitting up with a start, she saw a shadowy figure bending over her. It was as cold as ice, she could sense that, and when the moon came out from behind the clouds she saw it was a man without a face. She was very weak by this time – too weak to get to her feet, because he'd been draining the life force from her body. But suddenly a fierce gale blew through the forest and the Faceless Man broke off. He bellowed with fury as the gale

tore him away from Princess Daintyhoof and whirled him through the air in a cloud of dancing leaves. When the wind dropped he was lying motionless on the forest floor in a strangely contorted position, as if his spine had been broken.'

'I get it,' Rumo whispered and Harra of Midgard gave him, too, a suspicious glance.

Then he counted on his fingers: '*The Hundred-Fingered Moomy* – dead. *The Ever-Ravenous Omnivore* – dead. *The Faceless Man* – dead. How many of the Great Forest's evil creatures does that leave?'

'The Wicked Wolf and The Spiderwitch,' half the class cried in unison.

'Correct, and one of them was now standing beside the corpse of the Faceless Man, looking at Princess Daintyhoof: a big black wolf that could walk on its hind legs.'

'Ooh!' said the class.

Harra put his paws on his hips and adopted a nonchalant pose.

'"Hello," said the Wicked Wolf.

'"Hello," Princess Daintyhoof said timidly. "What do you want?"

'"I want to eat you," said the wolf.

'Princess Daintyhoof wept bitterly at this, whereupon the wolf went down on all fours and came over to her. "Hey," he said, "don't cry, only joking, have a sense of humour! I've no intention of eating you." It transpired from the ensuing conversation that he wasn't a wolf at all, but a human being under a spell. Prince Sangfroid by name, he had fallen in love with Princess Daintyhoof as soon as she entered the Great Forest and had followed her every step of the way so as to shield her from its dangers. He was the wind that had disposed of *The Hundred-Fingered Moomy*, *The Ever-Ravenous Omnivore* and *The Faceless Man*. And, as luck would have it, he had been put under a spell by the very same witch that had transformed Princess Daintyhoof. That sort of thing forms a bond, so she returned his love. Well, to cut a long story short, they went off into the darkest part of the Great Forest and there, er, the miracle of love took place.'

Rumo and the other boys pricked up their ears.

'Ahem! Not long afterwards,' Harra went on quickly, 'Princess Daintyhoof gave birth to a son that was neither a deer nor a wolf, but a wolf cub with two little horns. And that, according to legend, is how the first Wolperting came into being.'

Harra clasped his hands together and assumed a sorrowful expression.

'And because this is a Zamonian legend, and Zamonian legends must always end in disaster, here's its tragic conclusion. One day, Princess Daintyhoof and Prince Sangfroid got caught in the evil Spiderwitch's web and were, well, sucked dry before their little son's very eyes. All they left behind was a lonely orphan.'

Harra gave a final 'Ahem!' and fell silent.

Some of the girls were sobbing. The boys grinned and nudged each other to show how hard-boiled they were.

'Well, that was a legend,' said Harra, 'but like most legends it contains a germ of truth. For instance, *The Faceless Man* is probably a mythical forerunner of the creatures we call Lunawraiths. As for *The Spiderwitch*—'

'What was that about the miracle of love?' Rumo broke in. He was more surprised than anyone that he had dared to ask the question out loud.

Harra stared at Rumo. The whole class stared at him too. Rumo stared at Harra.

'Er . . .' said Harra.

Someone dropped a pencil. The school bell rang.

'Ah, there's the bell!' cried Harra. 'Well, that's it for today. Time for break! Off you go! Hurry, hurry, hurry!'

Harra of Midgard had never ended a lesson so abruptly. Rala turned and gave Rumo a long, enigmatic look. Harra bustled out of the classroom and the others streamed after him.

Rumo sensed that he'd made another blunder, but he had no idea what it was. He didn't feel like the playground and decided to stay put until the next lesson.

'What's the next lesson?' he asked a boy who was just leaving.

'Fencing,' he was told. 'Fencing with Ushan DeLucca.'

Rumo was electrified. Fencing! Fighting with lethal weapons at last! But he didn't have any weapons. Were they issued with them before the lesson?

Oga of Dullsgard

'Rumo of Zamonia?' A plump little schoolmistress with the face of a bulldog was standing in the doorway. 'Is that you?'

Rumo stood up.

'Come with me!' she barked.

'My name is Oga of Dullsgard,' she went on as she towed Rumo along the corridor. 'You share your name with a card game, did you realise that?'

'Yes,' said Rumo. 'Where are we going?'

'I shall be teaching you to read and write.'

'But I've got fencing next.'

'The others have. You've got reading.'

She conducted him along the corridor and down into the basement of the school building, past discarded classroom furniture and stacks of yellowing, dog-eared school books. Their trek ended in a small, ill-lit room where three other pupils were waiting. Rumo sat down with a sigh. One thing was certain: there was no escaping from this cellar, not even visually, because it had no windows through which to gaze. It was dimly illuminated by some big, flickering candles.

The teacher spent the next few seemingly interminable hours holding up cards that depicted simple objects and creatures - a teapot, a wheel, a cat, a duck, a hat, a mouse - and writing the relevant words on a blackboard for the class to copy in their exercise books. This she did with relentless persistence, picture after picture and word after word for hour after hour, over and over again, until Rumo and his fellow prisoners could have written the words in their sleep.

Oga concluded the lesson by informing her pupils that they would not be permitted to undergo any combat training until they had mastered at least the rudiments of reading and writing. She stifled their protests by stating that this was the rule, and she made no secret of the fact that it had been instituted to encourage them to learn the Zamonian alphabet all the quicker.

'A donkey,' she said, 'trots faster if you dangle a carrot in front of its nose.'

When Rumo emerged from school that afternoon it took him some time to become accustomed to the dazzling glare of the setting sun. Urs was waiting for him with a string of fresh sausages round his neck.

'Been down in the dungeon, have you?' He grinned. 'They teach reading and writing in that gloomy hole to persuade you to learn quicker. It really works. You're so anxious to get out of there as soon as

possible, you beaver away like mad. I learnt to read and write in six weeks flat.'

'Six weeks! You call that quick?'

'If you flunk the exam it could take twelve. Like a sausage?'

The dungeon

Rumo spent most of the time in isolation for the next few weeks, cooped up in the 'dungeon' with Oga of Dullsgard and his three fellow victims. Now and then he was permitted to attend a lesson on dental hygiene or listen to a lecture on Wolpertingian general knowledge, but whenever his classmates trooped off en masse to fencing lessons he was shut up in the cellar, being forced to memorise the signs for soap, ball, tree, or oven.

The words they learnt to spell became longer every day, and soon they could dispense with pictures on cards. Rumo found it interesting that you could capture objects on a sheet of paper by writing down the letters that spelt them. Pretending you were hunting them made learning easier. He sat there, imprisoned in a gloomy dungeon, but in his imagination he was out on the sunlit prairie, spearing wild words with his pencil.

What really irked him was being separated from Rala while Ushan DeLucca might well be teaching her and Rolv and the others how to slice an opponent in half with a sabre.

The evenings he spent laboriously copying out the Zamonian alphabet at home in his room, because he had vowed to pass the exam at the first attempt and embark on combat training as soon as possible. At night he dreamt of letters and Rala.

Civic duties

Although Rumo regarded the school building as a battleground characterised by spiteful enemies (Rolv), imponderable dangers (Rala), interminable torments (chess), humiliating captivity (the cellar) and cruel persecution (mathematics), the rest of Wolperting was a place where he could give free rein to his inclinations and aptitudes. He scored some notable triumphs where his civic duties were concerned, largely because of his manual dexterity. Hand Rumo a mason's trowel and he would erect a stout brick wall within hours. Give him a shovel and he would single-handedly excavate the foundations of an entire building. To his own surprise he found he could do almost anything at the first attempt – as long as it involved physical or manual labour. It took him only a few weeks to master the rudiments of the potter's craft; a blacksmith taught him to fashion wrought iron and shoe horses; he could make bricks and dig wells. He welcomed any form of physical exercise in the belief that it would hone his body and reflexes in preparation for combat training. Every activity improved his stamina and exercised a different set of muscles and sinews. His paws were strengthened by working at the potter's wheel, his legs by running errands, his arms by laying bricks, his shoulders by hammering horseshoes, his back by shovelling earth. Labouring at a hot stove inured him to pain and fishing in the fast-flowing waters of the Wolper speeded his reactions.

Ornt El Okro's workshop

One afternoon, when Rumo walked into a cabinetmaker's workshop to deliver a baulk of timber for Zaruso the timber merchant, he was overwhelmed by a multitude of sensory impressions. Most Wolpertings would have found them uninteresting or even unpleasant, but to Rumo's ears the scream of the foot-operated circular saw was like music. As for the smell of wood glue and varnish, it seemed as delicious to his nose as the aroma of a Sunday joint. He surveyed his surroundings, sniffing delightedly. Reflected by the wood dust in the air, the sunlight slanting down through the workshop's little windows seemed to bathe every tool in a magical glow. Standing in the middle of the room were two big black benches strewn with wood shavings. On them lay various planes, a gouge, some keyhole saws and a mitre box. Each bench had a massive vice bolted to it.

Rumo unloaded the baulk of timber and went over to one of the benches. Ignoring the cabinetmaker, who was mechanically cutting up a plank on the pedal-operated sawbench, he took an offcut from the floor, clamped it between two pegs and proceeded to plane it.

Ornt El Okro, the cabinetmaker, removed his foot from the pedal and turned to look. A young Wolperting was standing at one of his benches, planing away at an offcut. This was not only odd, it was outrageous! He alone was entitled to train apprentice cabinetmakers and he alone decided who those apprentices should be. And if someone was an apprentice of his, he alone decided what that someone should do.

Ornt suspected that his neighbours had sent this young stranger to his workshop as a practical joke. He went to the door and peered out, but there was no one in sight. When he turned back again the impudent youngster had gone over to his lathe and was turning a chair leg.

Instead of giving Rumo a piece of his mind and throwing him out of the workshop right away, as he had intended to, Ornt leant against a beam and watched him. He had never seen anyone turn a chair leg so fast. Rumo removed the leg from the lathe, weighed it experimentally in his paws, laid it aside and started to turn another.

Ornt lit his pipe.

After producing four chair legs – in the time it would have taken Ornt himself to complete one – Rumo took a largish slab of wood from a shelf and proceeded to fashion a seat in the same incredibly swift, craftsmanlike manner. Next, he constructed the back of the chair from three turned spindles and one spoke-shaved crosspiece. Having briefly sniffed twenty pots of glue, he unerringly selected the one Ornt himself would have chosen. He drilled three holes in the seat and crosspiece, glued the spindles into them, secured them with screws and smoothed the edges with sandpaper.

Rumo deposited the chair in the middle of the workshop and sat down on it. It emitted a last little groan as the screws, timber and glue adapted themselves to their new environment. Not until then did Rumo look at Ornt El Okro – vaguely, as if awaking from a pleasant dream.

'I'd like to be a cabinetmaker,' he said.

'You already are one,' said Ornt.

As soon as the four prisoners in the dungeon could read whole sentences, spell the words of which they were composed and write them down, their instruction in reading and writing was reduced to two hours a day and they were permitted to attend ordinary lessons more often.

Rumo enjoyed being back in Rala's immediate vicinity, and his ability to read and write lent lessons a different character. He was not only capable of deciphering what teachers wrote on the blackboard but could even jot down the occasional note.

However, it riled him to see the increasingly blatant way in which Rolv sought Rala's company. What was more, Rala didn't object! Rolv was forever dancing attendance on her during break. He shamelessly showed off in front of her, scuffling with his classmates, and once he even gave her an apple – which, to Rumo's horror, she actually accepted. He himself would never have taken such a liberty; in fact, he still hadn't exchanged a word with her. The most audacious thing he'd done in this respect was to write their names side by side on a slip of paper, but he'd torn it into little pieces immediately afterwards.

Heroes

Although he still wasn't permitted to take part in combat training, Rumo now went to school as a matter of course because he'd grasped that he couldn't have one thing without the other. Chess lessons he found a torment, being the diametrical opposite of what came naturally to him. Whenever an opponent had manoeuvred him into a hopeless position during a lesson – something that happened all the time – he yearned to pick up the board and hit him over the head with it. However, it was one of the fundamental rules of chess that you didn't do such a thing.

Worse still, Rala was the school's leading exponent of the game. She was every bit a match for the teachers and could play several classmates at once - sometimes as many as ten of them. Worst of all, the only person who seemed more or less a match for her was Rolv! She fought endless duels with him, sometimes winning, sometimes losing. Rumo envied Rolv all the time he spent so close to her.

Mathematics was little better. It wasn't that Rumo *couldn't* do maths; he didn't *want* to. Everything within him balked at adding, subtracting or dividing abstract figures. Words he liked - he could fill them with images or sensations and they helped him in everyday life - whereas numbers only confused him. Maths was like trying to clasp smoke with your paws or munch a scent. Maths was for bores, for budding accountants and bank managers. Sure enough, the biggest bores in his class were the best at figures. Even during break they would stand there cracking the mathematical brain-teasers they'd begged the teacher to set them. Rumo spent maths lessons gazing out of the window and hoping that the teacher wouldn't summon him to the blackboard. This the teacher eventually ceased to do because Rumo seemed such a hopeless case that time spent on him was time wasted.

The heroic sagas, on the other hand, were a subject after Rumo's own heart. He happily memorised the heroes' and heroines' resounding names and deeds: Kondor the Bold, who had strangled the three child-eating bears of Paw Island; Dogmo the Doughty who, at the age of 190, had repaired a breach in the Muchwater Dam by plugging it with his own body; or Andromeda Crystal, who became a frozen memorial to her own self-sacrifice by pouring water over herself during a blizzard on the shores of Shivering Sound, thereby forming a windbreak that shielded her children from the icy wind.

However, his lessons on the heroic sagas made Rumo painfully aware of something: heroes were always of another species. The occupants of Lindworm Castle, who had repelled the Darkmen, the Diabolical Death's Heads and the Copper Killers; the Princesses of Grailsund, who had defended their city against the Mistwitches; or Okin the Mighty, who - singing as he did so, be it noted - plunged to his death complete with the bridge over Wotan's Cleft to prevent the Vampire Army from crossing it – almost every Zamonian life form had its heroes. But not the Wolpertings. No Wolperting had ever been a hero. Not a single, solitary one!

Not even Hoth. True, he enjoyed universal popularity, but all he'd done was enter a deserted city. That didn't make him a hero. Wolperting had never been besieged. The city had never sustained a catastrophic natural disaster, never been ravaged by fire or attacked by an army of demons on which its inhabitants could have tested their capacity for heroism. It was as if danger steered clear of the city, deterred by the Wolpertings' reputation and warlike appearance. Rumo felt sure he had the makings of a hero. His prowess on Roaming Rock was certainly cut from the cloth of which lessons on the heroic sagas were tailored, but there was no one around to sing his praises. Smyke was far away. Some of the Hackonians might possibly be recounting his heroic deeds to their children, but there was no guarantee that they were even pronouncing his name correctly. For all anyone knew or cared, they might be calling him Moru or Urmo. No, there were no two ways about it: Rumo had had his chance to be a hero – and he'd blown it. As for encountering perilous adventures within these city walls, he had as much prospect of that as of beating Rala at chess.

The Black Dome

Harra of Midgard's lessons on Wolpertingian general knowledge were a peculiar mishmash of biology, history and etiquette, of rules, facts and legends, of practical information and absurd speculation – a kind of stew made up of scraps from every branch of knowledge that had failed to qualify as a subject in its own right. They might be devoted to the olfactory perception of danger, or the system of civic duties, or the hygienic importance of Wolperting's public conveniences, or the dangers of trying to swim – Harra's pupils never knew what awaited them in one of his general knowledge lessons. This time his subject was the Black Dome.

'The Black Dome,' he pontificated, 'was here before we existed, is here with us now, and will still be here long after we have ceased to exist.'

He left the form to chew on this enigma for a few moments before continuing.

'There's a theory that the dome is really a sphere composed of some non-Zamonian metal from outer space. Indeed, there are some who believe that it's a meteor half buried in the ground, and that the city was erected around it a long time ago. What supports this theory is that no one has ever discovered what material it consists of.'

He wrote '(1) Meteor Theory' on the blackboard.

'Another theory is that the unknown builders of Wolperting constructed the Black Dome last of all, using some material that no longer exists. Stupidly, they built the dome from the outside in and forgot to leave a door, thereby entombing themselves and dying a miserable death from lack of oxygen. If this theory is correct, there's a building in the middle of our city full of skeletons.'

He wrote '(2) Tomb Theory' on the blackboard.

'A third theory claims that the dome neither fell from the sky nor was artificially constructed, but is an organic growth: a stone plant, a metal mushroom, possibly a boil emanating from the centre of the earth. If the last alternative is correct I wouldn't like to be here when the boil bursts.'

Everyone laughed and Harra wrote '(3) Boil Theory' on the blackboard.

'What all these theories really imply – and I could quote you several dozen more – is that there's no rational explanation for the Black Dome's existence. My own very personal theory is this: whether it existed before Wolperting was built or was erected by the builders of the city themselves, the Black Dome seems to me to be a sculpture symbolic of the *Great Unknown* – a gigantic question mark designed to remind us all that, for as long as we live, *one* task will never be completed. The one performed in here.'

Harra tapped his skull with his knuckles.

'I know it won't appeal to you, the notion of a never-ending task, but you must reconcile yourselves to the idea that brainwork and the thirst for knowledge, the desire to solve riddles, will never cease.'

Rumo was reminded of Smyke's riddle: *What grows shorter and shorter the longer it gets?* He still hadn't found the answer.

The ambush

Rumo was rather proud of his newly acquired knowledge of the alphabet. Lately, when walking home from school with Urs in the evening, he'd taken to reading out every sign they passed.

'Well? How was it in the dungeon?'

'Municipal Bakery.'

'Care for a frankfurter?'

'Hoth Boulevard.'

'I think I'm going to give up the sausage factory and start work at the bakery. I'm getting sick of sausages.'

'Zaruso & Sons, Timber Merchants.'

'Maybe I should get a job in the communal kitchen.'

'No fly-tipping!'

'Or a restaurant of my own – that would be best. I've already got a whole folder full of recipes. All invented by me.'

'Clean your teeth five times a day!'

'What Wolperting needs is some Florinthian cuisine. Our local nosh is so utterly unrefined.'

'Leatherwear of all kinds.'

'I'd screw chessboards to the tables. Then the customers could go on playing during their meals and wouldn't have to stop eating.'

'Fire Station! Keep Clear!'

'You could be my partner. I'll cook, you wash up and eject the drunks. We'll go fifty-fifty. If the joint does well we'll open a whole chain of restaurants: "Chez Urs and Rumo".'

'Hoth Avenue.'

'Or "Chez Rumo and Urs", if you prefer. Florinthian cuisine – *that's* the gap in the market. Light and sophisticated is the coming trend.'

'Danger! Fast-flowing river, bathing prohibited!'

'Hey, have you been listening to a word I say?'

'Municipal Laundry.'

'How's the spelling going? Making progress?'

They took the usual short cut via Laundry Lane, the alleyway running behind the municipal laundry, an area Wolpertings tended to shun because the detergents' acrid fumes offended their keen sense of smell. Rumo and Urs were holding their noses as usual, so they failed to detect what awaited them round the next bend. There, standing amid some big baskets brimming with dirty laundry and looking studiously offhand, were Rolv and his gang: Vasko of the Red Forest, Balla of Betaville and Olek of the Dunes.

'An ambush!' Urs hissed.

The foursome sauntered into the middle of the alley, barring their path.

'What do you want?' Urs demanded.

'Nothing to do with you,' said Vasko, 'so stay out of this.'

'We'll see about that,' Urs replied quietly. Rumo was surprised by his menacing tone of voice.

'Cool it, Urs,' said Balla. 'We aren't involved either. This is just between Rolv and Rumo.'

Rolv grinned. 'And this time there's no Rala around to let you off the hook. If you want to get past you'll have to go through me.'

'Hold this,' said Rumo. He handed Urs his satchel. Vasko, Balla and Olek retired to the pavement while Rolv performed some limbering-up exercises.

'All right, get cracking!' cried Olek. 'Wolpertingian street-fighting rules apply: no weapons, no teeth. Everything else goes. The fight lasts till one of you gives up. Time!'

The battle of Laundry Lane

Had there existed a secret history of Wolperting, a chronicle of all the memorable events that had occurred in the city's backyards and gloomy alleyways, cellars and ruins, it would undoubtedly have included several chapters devoted to the Black Dome. There would have been one section that solved the mystery of the notch in the mayor's head and another that explained how Hoth contrived to populate a deserted city with nothing but Wolpertings. There would also have been an account of the wooden-sword fight waged some fifty years earlier by the Reds and the Blacks, two rival gangs of schoolboys, and a detailed description of the three-day duel with raw eggs which Ornt El Okro, then in his youth, had fought with Hacho of the Wolves. As for the fight between Rumo and Rolv, it would have gone down in the city's secret annals as *The Battle of Laundry Lane.* Unfortunately, however, no such history existed.

To call their fight a battle was justified if only because all who witnessed it gained the impression that the combatants numbered a dozen, not just two. The strength, stamina and endurance displayed by both parties would have sufficed to put an army of Werewolves to flight. This clash amid the acrid fumes of Laundry Lane seemed less between two creatures of flesh and blood than between two elemental forces or evil spirits endowed with supernatural powers.

It might have been fair to give Rolv a one-point handicap during the preliminaries, not only because of his friends' yells of encouragement but because he had mastered various tactics of which Rumo still knew nothing. Rolv hit hard and often, and he was shrewd enough not to neglect his own guard. He was immensely skilled at ducking and weaving, so most of Rumo's punches missed their mark.

But Rumo did not make the mistake of losing his temper. He took Rolv's punches and absorbed them without flinching, and it wasn't long before he had the measure of his well-trained opponent. He became accustomed to his speed and his tricks, had gauged his strength and its limits. Rumo was a good scrapper by nature and this scrap was teaching him a great deal.

Increasingly thwarted by Rumo's more effective guard, Rolv was not only landing fewer punches but sustaining some painful blows himself. It was as if the two of them had swapped roles. Rumo was returning each of Rolv's attacks with interest, imitating his movements perfectly, appropriating his technique. Now it was Rolv's turn to suppress his mounting fury. One punch connected so unerringly with his left eye that it swelled up within seconds. His friends' shouts of encouragement were definitely growing fainter, whereas Urs's were steadily increasing in volume.

Rolv sensed that a change of tactics was indicated, so he tried to embroil Rumo in a wrestling match on the ground, never suspecting that his opponent was better equipped in that respect. Here, where swift reflexes counted for more than technique, Rumo enjoyed an advantage from the start. His lightning holds were harder to break, his limbs more supple, his strength and stamina greater. They rolled around in the dirt, growling and snarling, knocking over laundry baskets and tumbling down the cellar steps, but Rolv always ended up in a headlock or flat on his back, with Rumo sitting on his chest and bombarding him with punches.

Rolv realised that he was bound to acquire another black eye sooner or later, so he broke off the wrestling match and switched to a form of fighting at which he was the best in the school: kick-boxing. Scrambling to his feet, he adopted the basic kick-boxing position: legs slightly bent, shoulders back, both fists at eye level.

'Now I'm going to finish you,' he announced.

'I'm waiting,' Rumo retorted.

'Now you're for it!'

'I'm still waiting.'

'I'm going to make you eat dirt!'

'I'm still waiting.'

They were both breathing heavily and their fur was sodden with sweat. They circled each other for a while, recouping their energies as they continued their dialogue in the same vein.

'Now I'm going to show you the difference between a civilised Wolperting and a wild one,' Rolv said menacingly. 'I'll show you what you can learn in school if you pay attention.'

Rumo got ready for another furious exchange of punches, only to encounter a sudden flurry of kicks. Rolv used his fists only in order to retain his balance while lashing out with his feet. He launched these attacks in a variety of ways: standing, leaning backwards, lying on the ground, leaping, rotating his body, scything the air with his leg. The kicks landed with the force of a battering ram. Laundry Lane resounded to a series of dull thuds as they bit into Rumo's body. Urs winced as his friend was knocked about like a lifeless straw doll. Blow followed blow in such quick succession that he had no chance to protect himself adequately.

Rolv ran through his entire repertoire. He kicked Rumo in the back, in the stomach, on the shins - he kicked him wherever he chose and as hard as he could, but one thing he failed to do: he couldn't put his opponent down for good. Rumo struggled to his feet every time, puffing and blowing but always with his wits about him. Urs wished he would abandon the fight and spare himself further punishment.

Rolv resorted to his fists again. Rumo was subjected to a volley of punches from all directions: left, right, above, below. He had also sustained a black eye by now, and had almost ceased to fight back. He was merely endeavouring to stay on his feet and protect his head while Rolv belaboured his body like a punchbag.

Vasko, Balla and Olek were urging their friend on again, and their cries redoubled the speed of his onslaughts. Simply unable to watch any more, Urs averted his gaze for the first time - and missed the best punch of the entire fight: a perfect uppercut from Rumo that landed smack on Rolv's chin. Rolv took three unsteady steps backwards, fought to clear his head for several seconds, and just stood there with his knees buckling.

Now they were both in dire straits. Rolv had expended all his energy and escaped defeat by a hair's breadth; Rumo had conserved his strength but taken innumerable punishing blows to the body. Ponderously, they went for each other again.

Darkness had fallen by now. The laundry was shut and everyone who worked there had gathered in the lane to watch the spectacle. Torches had been kindled and their light sent Rolv's and Rumo's huge shadows dancing across the whitewashed walls. Utterly exhausted, they relapsed into a war of words - a contest in which neither displayed much talent or imagination.

'I'll get you!'

'Come on, then!'

'Don't worry, I will!'

'All right, I'm waiting!'

'Yellow-belly!'

'Yellow-belly yourself!'

'Chicken!'

'Chicken yourself!'

'Scaredy-cat!'

'Scaredy-cat yourself!'

Urs had grown tired of watching. He toyed with the idea of knocking them out with a coal shovel, so peace would at last be restored and they could all go home. Before long, however, no such measure seemed necessary because Rolv and Rumo had tripped over their own feet. They circled one another at a crawl, each trying for a necklock. The other spectators' enthusiasm had also waned and some were already leaving the scene, yawning.

Rumo finally succeeded in getting a stranglehold on Rolv just as Rolv got him in a scissors hold. They remained in this position, motionless, for quite some time. Urs, Balla, Vasko and Olek eventually went over, intending to separate the pair before they could do each other any more damage. But Rumo and Rolv weren't fighting any longer: they had fallen asleep in each other's arms.

The outcome of the fight seemed clear, so most of the spectators had dispersed by now. The Battle of Laundry Lane was over. Balla and Olek carried Rolv home while Vasko helped Urs to put Rumo, who was snoring loudly, to bed.

The examination

When Rumo woke up the next morning he couldn't at first account for all his aches and pains. He thought he was seriously ill until Urs came in with some coffee and refreshed his memory.

'Who won?' Rumo asked.

'That remains to be seen. You really must get up and go to school. If you fail to show, everyone will interpret it as a victory for Rolv.'

'I don't think I can.'

'I'll help you. First have some coffee.'

Rumo hobbled to school leaning on Urs. Outside the gates they met Rolv, who was being carried rather than supported by Vasko and Balla. They made it to their places in class and slept through the first two periods, both of which were devoted to chess. The legend of the Battle of Laundry Lane was already spreading like wildfire, complete with a few preliminary exaggerations.

Next, Rumo dragged himself off to a lesson in the cellar. Although he could scarcely keep his eyes open, Oga of Dullsgard's curiously solemn and silent manner wasn't lost on him. Without a word she handed out some blank sheets of paper and pencils – and they all suddenly grasped that the crucial examination was imminent. None of them had been expecting it, and it couldn't have come at a worse time for Rumo in particular. He could scarcely remember his own name.

The schoolmistress dictated a short text consisting of simple sentences: *The cat drinks milk. The bird lays an egg. The chicken crosses the road. The Werewolf sleeps in the forest.*

Rumo and his classmates wrote them down, panting and groaning as if engaged in some strenuous physical activity. Then Oga of Dullsgard collected their papers and sat down at her desk to correct them in silence. Her pen scratched away, lacerating their nerves, as the minutes crawled by. Rumo wondered if he'd spelt *Werewolf* correctly. Should it have been *Wearwolf?*

At long last Oga handed back the sheets of paper without a word, her grim expression seeming to imply that the whole class had failed miserably.

'Well,' she said as though accusing them of some inexpiable sin, 'you've all passed the examination, but don't go thinking you can now read and write. You have, however, acquired a tool that will enable you to decipher every word you come across. It's in your heads. Look after that tool – look after it as carefully as you clean your teeth! The best way of doing that is to read. Read as much as you can! Read street signs and menus, read the notices outside City Hall, read trashy paperbacks for all I care, but read! Read, or you'll be done for!'

Oga focused her dread gaze on each pupil in turn.

'From tomorrow you'll be allowed to take part in combat training. To those of you who may regard this as an honour or a pleasure I would say this: It's neither one nor the other. Many of you will yearn for the days when you learnt to spell one-syllable words under my supervision, but by then it'll be too late.'

Combat instruction

Rumo was allowed to take part in combat training the very next day, but that, too, could not have come at a worse time. Although he ached in every limb and could only see properly with one eye, he struggled gamely through the first few lessons - indeed, he would probably have attended class decapitated, with his severed head beneath his arm. After a week the bruises he'd acquired in the Battle of Laundry Lane began to fade, to be replaced by new ones sustained in training.

Kick-boxing, boxing, wrestling, aerial combat, fighting on all fours, biting - those were the unarmed combat disciplines. The ones that involved fighting with weapons were nocturnal fencing, axe wielding, ball and chain, crossbowmanship, archery and blind knife-throwing. Most of the pupils soon discovered what suited them and what didn't. In Rumo's own opinion he had a natural aptitude for *every* discipline. You had to master the rudiments of unarmed combat before embarking on weapons training. Physical control was the prime requirement. If you couldn't master your own body you couldn't master a weapon.

Rumo was surprised at all he had still to learn: holds, punches, kicks, leaps, defensive and disengagement techniques, tactics and teamwork. He had never applied himself to the fundamentals of movement or engaged in stamina-enhancing and limbering-up exercises. He was now taught how to flex his sinews, warm up his muscles, and run for hours without becoming winded. Training often took place outside the school. On their long endurance runs Rumo and his classmates became familiar not only with the forests, hills and fields around Wolperting, but also with the streets and steps, bridges and squares of Wolperting itself, and especially with the Great Wall, on which one could run right round the city. Training took place wherever conditions for a particular discipline were ideal. It was commonplace for pupils to be catapulted into the air in Hoth Square to teach them aerial combat. Citizens who crossed one of the bridges and found themselves in the midst of a mass riot had no need to alert the mayor's office – it was just a collective limbering-up exercise. Battle-cries rent the air as youthful trainees sprinted along the alleyways of the inner city, loudly urged on by their instructors. The atmosphere of Wolperting as a whole was coloured by combat training.

Rumo learnt to treat his own body like an extremely intricate, sensitive machine requiring careful maintenance. The functions of the bones, muscles, nerves and sensory organs were explained during lessons devoted to theory. Stances, holds, kicks, blows, leaps and defensive measures were drummed into the pupils' heads. They had to memorise them with the aid of diagrams and learn their often bizarre names by heart: the *Double Mitten*, the *Serpentine Stranglehold*, the *Narcotic Sledgehammer*, the *Lethal Butterfly Punch*, the *Cockerel Kick*, the *Twin-Fingered Thrust with Elbow Follow-Up*.

One discipline to which everyone attached great importance was that of biting. Wolpertings regarded biting as the noblest and most natural form of combat, just as teeth were nature's most precious gift. A fundamental distinction was drawn between bites intended to warn, grip, restrain, crush, tear, lacerate, and kill. Biting was one of Rumo's favourite subjects.

He noticed that far from all Wolpertings took the same interest in combat training as he did. Those who were descended from more peaceable and easygoing canine breeds – the ones with pug faces or floppy ears – used to stand aside with their chessboards under their arms and pour scorn on those who enjoyed clobbering each other.

But there were plenty of pupils who distinguished themselves like him, displayed above-average ambition and did their utmost to come top of the class in one or more subjects. Rala, for instance, was an excellent archer. Rolv had a talent for knife-throwing that would have earned him a job in any circus. Balla excelled at aerial combat, Vasko was very proficient with the crossbow, and Olek's forte was the sling, a weapon few Wolpertings rated highly.

Rumo was particularly good at Four-Legged Combat, a technique that had been developed at the school itself. In this discipline Wolpertings were taught how to return to their roots – how to use their arms like legs and their legs like arms. Rumo learnt that there was nothing magical about scaling the wall of a building; it was merely a question of practice.

Rumo and Rolv often came up against each other in training, but from now on with mutual respect. Although the Battle of Laundry Lane had not made friends of them, their burning desire to defeat one another in combat seemed to have evaporated, so they avoided one another by tacit agreement. If they competed at all, it was only in accumulating as much knowledge as possible of as many subjects as possible.

A challenge

'Who'd like to take me on?'

Ushan DeLucca's words died away. It was Rumo's first lesson with the legendary swordsman. He was surprised to note that the pupils on the benches around him had lowered their gaze. They were all trying to avoid the teacher's eye.

'What's the matter? Are you Wolpertings or sheep? Born fighters or born cowards?' DeLucca strutted up and down in front of the benches, noisily slashing the air with his rapier.

'Ssst, ssst, ssst!' went the rapier.

'So you're sheep, are you? Look at me – look me in the eye, you yellow-bellies!' Ushan DeLucca was in one of his grim moods, everyone in the class could tell. Everyone except Rumo.

'How can I teach you anything if you're too scared to fight?'

'*I'll* fight you!' cried Rumo, jumping up. He was itching to cross blades with Ushan DeLucca. He'd been issued with his very first weapon – a rapier – when the lesson began. The hilt felt as warm in his paw as if it had just come from the smithy.

Ushan DeLucca gave a gentle, understanding smile, every inch the fatherly friend and teacher. 'So you'd like to fight me, Rumo of Zamonia? You're thirsting for armed combat, eh? Excellent. You aren't like these cowards here – you're a youngster after my own heart! Come here, my son!'

Rumo stepped forward. His classmates ventured to look up again.

DeLucca had settled on his victim.

Ushan DeLucca discovered that he was the best swordsman in Zamonia when his life had hit rock bottom. It happened around midnight, in a dark side street in the seediest district of Baysville. Almost blind drunk, he had been robbing a helpless farmer with six confederates.

Ushan DeLucca's story

Ushan's wild parents had abandoned him in the woods near the town. One day, while rummaging in a municipal rubbish dump for something fit to eat, he fell into the clutches of a dog catcher. The latter shut him up in a big wooden cage with a couple of dozen lice-infested mongrels and taught him some painful and humiliating lessons on the subject of 'might is right' – until Ushan entered the fast-growing phase and became ruler of the roost. When the dog catcher noticed that he was turning into a big, strong Wolperting and reducing the population of the cage by a dog or two every night, he released him. Having knocked him out with an anaesthetic dart in the leg, he loaded him on to a cart and dumped him on the cobblestones in the most disreputable part of town. It was late at night when Ushan recovered consciousness. The bars were overflowing with drunks, and despite his aching head the Wolperting was irresistibly fascinated by their tipsy shouts and laughter. What impressed him most of all was the way they all went around on two legs. Eager to do likewise, Ushan rose on his hind legs for the very first time and tottered into the nearest tavern. Called *The Last Stop*, it was to be his home for the next five years.

The landlord, a Demidwarf from the Dead Mountains, recognised Ushan's earning potential at once because his grandfather had traded in Wolperting whelps. Knowing that such a creature was worth its weight in gold provided you gained its trust, he fed Ushan a big piece of meat, bedded him down on some warm blankets in a little room of his own – and gave him a bottle of rum. When Ushan awoke the next morning his head was aching even worse than before. The landlord came up to his room, served him a gigantic hangover-cure breakfast and later on brought him another bottle of rum. Within a few days Ushan was allowed to eat in a corner of the taproom. After his meals he would sit there in silence and get drunk. Within a few weeks he had become so addicted to rum that he couldn't imagine life without it. That was when the landlord, before handing him a new bottle, told him, 'Just a minute! Nothing in life is free, especially in this place, understand?'

Desperately, Ushan groped for the bottle with his paw, but the landlord kept snatching it away at the last moment.

'No, of course you don't understand, you're just a stupid, half-wild Wolperting. But that can be changed. I'm going to teach you to speak and keep you in rum, and in return I'll spend the next few years taking the fullest advantage of you. Does that sound like a fair bargain?'

Ushan whimpered.

'I'll take that as a yes.' The landlord handed over the bottle and Ushan drained it greedily.

'Do you realise what first-class tipple that is?' asked the landlord. 'It's finest Ushan rum from the cane fields of DeLucca – fifty-eight per cent alcohol. Which reminds me, have you got a name?'

To begin with Ushan performed the most menial of bar-room tasks. He emptied the spittoons, swept the floor, swabbed away bloodstains after brawls, rolled beer barrels in and chucked out drunks late at night. When the landlord noticed that he always acquitted himself well during punch-ups he appointed him his personal bodyguard and cashier. From then on he never had to wash dishes again. His only task was to loiter beside the till with a mug of rum in his paw, look vicious, and beat up any customers who refused to pay.

Ushan couldn't imagine a life without hard liquor; in fact, he didn't even know there were creatures that *weren't* intoxicated from dawn to dusk. *The Last Stop* and its clientele were his universe. Every customer started the day with a slug of liquor and ended it blind drunk; to Ushan that was the normal way of life. He also considered it quite natural that none of his acquaintances had a regular occupation other than killing time in the gloomy taproom – or, occasionally, killing some defenceless drunk for his small change in the yard behind the tavern. His friends had names like Ham-Bone Honko or Knuckleduster Noobi, Kosh the Cat or Twelve-Fingered Timm, so it was understandable that he didn't learn to play the harp from them. They taught him how to steal, to burgle people's homes, to lose himself in a crowd or the sewers, to mint and pass counterfeit money, to cheat at cards and fence stolen goods. In short, they turned him into a thoroughgoing professional criminal. If Ushan had walked into a bakery or a smithy that first night, he might have become a respectable pastrycook or blacksmith, but at *The Last Stop* he could only have ended up a crook.

His cronies told him that no one but an idiot went to college and learnt a trade when there was far easier money to be made. You had only to take what you wanted. The sole requirements were a bit of luck, strong nerves, and an occasional resort to violence. His friends and acquaintances sometimes disappeared for varying lengths of time, and many of them never returned at all. Ushan was then told that they had gone on holiday or left town because there were better career prospects elsewhere.

To his friends' regret, Ushan was an inefficient crook. It wasn't that he didn't try, far from it, but he simply didn't have the knack. If he picked a pocket it was bound to belong to an undercover cop; if he burgled a house he inevitably trod on the sleeping watchdog, and if he passed forged money he did so to a member of the Fraud Squad. His cronies spent most of their time rescuing him from these tricky situations. Ushan was also unsuited to crimes of violence because he refused to carry a weapon, considering this unnecessary in view of his prowess with his fists. As a result, his status in the hierarchy of Baysville's underworld steadily declined until he was entrusted with only the humblest tasks: holding ladders, acting as lookout, or playing the decoy. In the end he became a lantern-bearer.

Lantern bearers were, in fact, regarded as members of a very respectable profession in the cities of Zamonia. They were paid to escort drunks and strangers home from taverns, especially in districts where the street lighting was poor. However, they included one or two black sheep who collaborated with criminals by luring their customers into prearranged ambushes, there to be robbed and sometimes killed. The lantern-bearers would then stand aside and light the cut-throats while they went about their nefarious business.

Ushan, who always carried a bottle of rum on principle, was sometimes drunker than his victims. Although he had never been taught to know right from wrong, he felt a distressing sense of guilt – which only strong rum could alleviate – whenever he held the lantern for his false friends to do their nocturnal work.

On the night that was to transform his life, Ushan was drunker than ever before. Having found his way to the prearranged spot with the utmost difficulty, he was standing there, swaying, as he watched his confederates – a gang of six Vulpheads who regularly drank away the proceeds of their crimes at *The Last Stop* – robbing their victim. The latter was a wealthy farmer from the countryside around Baysville, an intoxicated Demidwarf who had been celebrating a lucrative cattle sale until long past midnight. The farmer had clumsily drawn his sword when he spotted the ambush, but a blow on the wrist sent it clattering to the ground. Ushan, who was standing right beside him, instinctively picked it up, rather like someone politely retrieving a handkerchief. He had never touched a sword before.

A remarkable change took place in Ushan DeLucca as he weighed the weapon in his hand: his head cleared for the first time in five years. It was as if all the alcohol in his bloodstream had transferred itself to the sword, which now took on a tipsy life of its own. He carved a semicircle out of the mist and skewered it with the tip. Then he described a five-pointed star, a bird in flight, the outlines of a galloping horse. He laughed aloud.

'Hey, look what I can do!'

'Stop that nonsense!' called one of the Vulpheads.

'And keep your trap shut!' called another.

Ushan felt as if a weight had fallen from his shoulders. All at once he could see things more clearly than ever before. Everything he'd done up to now – absolutely everything – had been wrong. He couldn't help laughing again.

'Ssst, ssst, ssst,' he went, imitating the swish of the sword. 'Six against one isn't fair. Let him go!'

The Vulpheads exchanged puzzled glances. The farmer stood there looking disconcerted.

'Ssst, ssst, ssst!' Ushan said again. 'You heard me. Let . . . him . . . go!'

The leader of the gang was the first to regain his composure. 'Keep out of this, you drunken sot!'

'Ssst, ssst, ssst!' Ushan hissed. '*What* did you call me, Twelve-Fingered Timm? I've never been more sober in my life. Ssst, ssst, ssst!'

'You said my name, you fool! Now we'll have to kill him! All that drink must have addled your brain.'

'Ssst, ssst, ssst! I can call you all by name: Knuckleduster Noobi, Kosh the Cat, Ham-Bone Honko, Light-Fingered Logg and Wostix, who still doesn't have a nickname because he's too stupid to earn one. As for my name, it's Ushan DeLucca, like the rum.'

'Are you mad?' cried the farmer. 'Now they'll *really* have to kill me.'

'You see?' Twelve-Fingered Timm laughed. 'Even he thinks so. Push off, Ushan! Take that confounded sword and get lost! We'll deal with this.'

'Ssst, ssst, ssst! Do you know what this is? It isn't a sword, oh no! It's part of me. I've grown an extra arm. Ssst, ssst, ssst.'

'Get lost, Ushan!' Twelve-Fingered Timm said in a low, menacing voice. He and the others had all drawn their swords.

'Ssst, ssst, ssst,' said Ushan. 'No, *you* get lost. Leave the poor fellow alone and I'll let you go, that's the deal. Ssst, ssst, ssst!'

He darted between the bandits as he uttered the last three 'ssst's, slitting the seat of Kosh the Cat's pants – *ssst* – severing Knuckleduster Noobi's belt – *ssst* – and giving Light-Fingered Logg a duelling scar – *ssst.*

'Are you out of your mind?' said Logg, clasping his bleeding cheek. But the crooks were still unimpressed. That was merely the signal for battle to commence.

'Ssst, ssst!' Ushan went softly. 'Ssst, ssst, ssst!' He danced across the cobblestones, light as a feather, and delivered five cuts, five wounds. Blood welled from Knuckleduster Noobi's arm.

Only Twelve-Fingered Timm was still unscathed. Resolutely, he lunged at Ushan, who parried his attack with a trio of nonchalant counterstrokes – *ssst, ssst, ssst* – and then, quick as lightning, transfixed his heart and promptly withdrew the blade. Twelve-Fingered Timm slumped, lifeless, to the cobblestones.

'Yes,' Ushan said as though to himself, 'anyone with a weapon in his paw must be prepared to kill.' He took a handkerchief from his pocket, wiped the blood from the blade and turned to the wounded bandits.

'You'd better bandage that up,' he said, tossing the bloody handkerchief to Noobi.'This is the beginning of a new age. The old Ushan DeLucca is dead – dead as poor Twelve-Fingered Timm here. I'm no longer Ushan DeLucca the lush. I'm Ushan of the Sword.'

The five bandits backed away, slowly and cautiously, step by step, until the darkness swallowed them up.

Ushan turned to the farmer. 'Is it all right with you if I keep your sword? No offence, but I get the feeling it was made especially for me.'

The farmer nodded mutely.

'You can have my lantern in exchange.'

Ushan's figure melted into the darkness, but his voice could be heard for a while longer. 'Ssst, ssst, ssst!' it went. 'Ssst, ssst, ssst . . .'

Ushan DeLucca had discovered what he was best at.

A bloody nose

'Attack me!' Ushan commanded.

Rumo had pondered his strategy. Ushan DeLucca didn't look too quick on his pins. His poor deportment, the bags under his eyes, his wrinkled jowls, his pince-nez and languid way of speaking – none of these suggested that he was exceptionally athletic. His strong point was probably tactics and experience. Rumo decided to tackle him from below, to thrust at his legs and compel him to hop – he surely wouldn't be expecting that. Then, when his guard was down, he would hold the blade to his throat. Rumo attacked.

Ushan wielded his rapier from the wrist in a way Rumo found inexplicable. He stood there like a fence post and let his blade do the talking, not his body. No matter how often Rumo flexed his knees and thrust at Ushan's legs, the teacher's blade was always there first, ready to deflect his own in an effortless, almost nonchalant manner. He ended by parrying Rumo's onslaughts with one hand in his trouser pocket. Some of the pupils tittered.

'Yes, very good,' Ushan said in a tone that clearly conveyed the opposite. 'But you must wield your blade from the wrist, not the backside.' He flourished the tip of his rapier under Rumo's nose to demonstrate how easy it would be for him to poke his pupil's eyes out.

'My dear boy,' he went on with a hearty yawn, 'I've fought more exciting duels with the pendulum of my metronome.'

Someone laughed.

Rumo was beside himself. Something impenetrable had interposed itself between him and DeLucca, a barrier composed of countless blades. Quite unconnected with physical strength and stamina, it had to do with experience, intelligence and technical mastery. He realised that he

knew nothing, absolutely nothing, about swordsmanship. He caught a sudden glint in the teacher's eyes, but by then it was too late. He felt a sharp, surprising stab of pain such as he had experienced only once before: in the cave on Roaming Rock when the Demonocle hit him in the face with the torch. Ushan had nicked his nose with the tip of his rapier.

Rumo began to weep, he couldn't stop himself. The pain brought tears gushing from his eyes. He sobbed uncontrollably.

'Aha,' said Ushan. 'Not a coward, just a cry-baby.'

Nobody laughed this time, not even Rolv. They could all have been in Rumo's shoes.

'Very well,' Ushan went on, paternally affectionate once more, 'sit down on the bench, Rumo. Watch the lesson and memorise the various positions. Next time you can join in.'

Rumo sat down. Blood was dripping from his nose.

Ushan DeLucca proceeded with the normal lesson as if nothing had happened. Having performed a few limbering-up exercises, the pupils took up their positions and crossed rapiers. DeLucca rapped out his commands, again and again, until universal exhaustion set in.

'On guard!'

'Hit!'

'Disengage and hit!'

'Lunge position!'

'Circular parry in quinte!'

'Cut at head!'

'On guard!'

'Rest!'

The pupils laid their rapiers aside and dispersed. Rumo's nose stopped bleeding just as the lesson ended.

Woodcarvings and paperbacks

Whenever Rumo wasn't at school he enjoyed going to Ornt's workshop and performing his civic duty there by lending him a hand, although a close observer might have concluded that Ornt was assisting Rumo.

Rumo could conjure objects out of wood that no one but he had envisioned within it: not only simple objects like soup spoons or combs, but delicate sculptures, richly decorated wooden swords, or ornamental carvings for house fronts. He would take a length of cane and moments later he had transformed it into an elegant riding whip. Out of a balsa wood offcut he fashioned an artificial bird, light as a feather, that glided through the air for minutes on end. Every day Ornt marvelled anew at Rumo's skill and the speed with which he worked.

With Ornt's help he produced a huge conference table for the council chamber in a day and a night. In the days that followed he adorned the table legs with carvings of four of the city's principal features: the Wolper Bridge, the Black Dome, the Hoth Windmill, and the façade of City Hall. One lunch break he started whittling away at the massive oak beam over the workshop door. He carved some little scenes from everyday life at the cabinetmaker's workshop, all astonishingly detailed and accurate: Ornt and himself wielding the two-handled saw, carpenter's tools, the joiner's bench, a portrait of Ornt smoking his pipe - he added some new detail at every opportunity. After initially grumbling that Rumo would spoil his nice doorway, Ornt had since become mightily proud of the splendid entrance to his workshop. Many Wolpertings walked past just to admire Rumo's progress, and Ornt seized the opportunity to talk them into buying a chair or a stool.

If Rumo's crowded life left room for anything in the way of spare time, he spent it reading the Prince Sangfroid novels. The day he passed his literacy exam, Axel had come to his room with a stack of dog-eared paperbacks, tossed them on to his bed and fervently extolled their unique qualities. They were, he said, the most brilliant, exciting and suspenseful books that any Zamonian author had ever written. Compared to them, the entire works of Hildegard Mythmaker were fit only for use in a public convenience. No one with a heart in his breast could resist the hypnotic appeal of these literary masterpieces.

And so it turned out. Although Rumo found the first few pages hard going, he read with growing ease as time went by and ended by becoming an ardent Prince Sangfroid fan. The prince was a character created by Count Klantoo of Nairland, a best-selling novelist whose sensational thrillers were universally popular with the younger generation of Zamonians. Count Klantoo had borrowed the name of his hero from the legend about the Wolpertings' origins recounted in class by Harra of Midgard.

The Prince Sangfroid series of novels dealt with a subject in which Rumo was keenly interested, namely heroism of an exemplary kind. Inspired by the noblest of motives, the prince fought the most dastardly villains and horrific monsters, and each of his adventures featured a different, incredibly beautiful, princess. Much to Rumo's relief, however, every Prince Sangfroid book ended with a description of the hero proceeding on his lonely way because new and appalling dangers required his urgent intervention.

Oga of Dullsgard had taught Rumo to read, but Prince Sangfroid taught him to become engrossed in the printed word.

The second-best swordsman in Wolperting

'They're getting ready for the annual fair,' Urs said one evening. 'Have you seen?'

Rumo had naturally noticed the activities in progress outside the city walls. Tents and booths had been set up on the edge of the moat, and masses of strangers were milling around out there. It had been explained to him that this was a friendly siege mounted with the mayor's permission.

'It'll be a gas! Think of it: mulled ale and all the food you can eat!'

'Hm,' Rumo said indifferently.

'Why aren't you interested in food?' Urs had cooked Rumo an excellent supper – leg of sucking pig and carrots on a bed of puréed potatoes flavoured with saffron – but Rumo had bolted it without comment as usual and – also as usual – left half of it.

'I like being hungry,' said Rumo, as if that explained everything.

'Well, well, so you enjoy being hungry. You might just as well say "I like having toothache"'.

Rumo pondered this. His mind went back to the time when his teeth were growing. 'Toothache has its points,' he said.

'You're only assigned one municipal friend in your life,' said Urs, 'and I had to get you, of all people. I suppose I should regard it as a kind of test.'

'What makes you so interested in food?'

'I aim to become the best cook in the city.'

'Why?'

'Well, every Wolperting is the best at something, as you know, and since I can never become the best swordsman here, only the second-best, I thought that cooking–'

'You, the second-best swordsman in Wolperting?'

'That's right.'

'Oh, sure!' Rumo laughed.

'I used to be, at least. Not now, perhaps, more like number four or five. It's ages since I touched a blade longer than my kitchen knife, but I could still hold my own among the first five, take it from me.'

'Says you!'

'A few years ago I was the best swordsman in Wolperting, that's official. You can check with the mayor's office. There's even a diploma on the wall there.'

'Pull the other one!'

'Go to City Hall if you don't believe me!'

Rumo was impressed by Urs's righteous indignation. 'So how come you used to be the best swordsman in Wolperting, then the second-best, and now you don't fence at all? I've never seen you with a rapier in your paw.'

'I don't like weapons,' Urs growled, bowing his head. The subject seemed to distress him.

Rumo pricked up his ears. 'You used to be the best swordsman in Wolperting and you don't like weapons? Explain that and you can have my cookie ration for a week.'

Urs cheered up at that. 'Have I never told you?'

'No.'

'You never tell me anything either.'

'I'm not good with words.'

'That's true.'

'Come on, tell me!' Rumo demanded.

Urs sighed. 'All right. I can't remember it myself, but my foster-father told me how he found me as a puppy in the forests of North End, half frozen in the middle of winter. My foster-father was Koram Morak, a Vulphead who earned his living as a duellist.'

'What's a duellist?'

'You become a duellist when you've nothing more to lose, including your fear of death, or when you've a screw loose. In Koram's case it was a bit of both. Professional duellists fight duels for other people, understand? They do it for money.'

'An exciting job.'

'You could call it that. There was never a dull moment at home. I never knew, when my foster-father went off to work, whether he would come back in the evening. Once he showed up with an arrow through his ear, another time with half a sabre snapped off in his back. It wasn't that he earned a lot. Almost anyone could afford a duellist, there were so many of them – in fact, they sometimes fought for a slice of bread and butter. Quite often two duellists would do the fighting while the real antagonists stood there placing bets on their representatives – and in those days people duelled for any old reason. I had to be prepared to become an orphan again at least once a week.'

'Sounds like a happy childhood.'

Urs laughed. 'It could have been worse. It was exciting, anyway. Youngsters are only unhappy when they're bored. The worst thing was the food. Koram knew as much about cooking and eating as . . . as you do!'

'Thanks.'

'Yes, it really was intolerable. He used to put sugar in the soup – that sort of thing. The food was appalling, so I took over that part of the housekeeping when I was old enough. And, lo and behold, I enjoyed it. That's how I came to cook.'

'I see.'

'The worst of it was, Koram wasn't very good at duelling. He could fence a bit and shoot a bit with the crossbow, and do a bit of knife throwing, but only a bit of everything. He was tough – that was what saved him. He didn't slink off home because he'd taken an arrow through the ear, not him! He didn't lie down and whimper for the doctor after the first flesh wound; he fought on, even if the blood was spurting from ten wounds. One night he came home white as a sheet, pale as a ghost – I got a terrible shock when I saw him. His opponent had severed two arteries but he'd fought on and won – and then sewn up the arteries himself. He lived on a diet of raw calves' liver and pig's blood for two weeks until he could stand without falling over. He'd lost just about everything anyone could have hacked off or shot away: three fingers, one eye, half an ear, two toes, a slice here, a slice there. You could have made a dwarf out of all the separate pieces. That was why I learnt to fence. One day, I told myself, they'll cut the last slice out of him and he won't be there any more.'

Urs pointed to Rumo's half-eaten leg of sucking pig. 'Aren't you going to finish that?'

Rumo shook his head. Urs grabbed the leg and took a bite.

'Koram would never have dreamt of getting me to work for him,' he went on, chewing with gusto. 'That was all my idea. When he found me in the snow he thought I'd make an excellent watchdog. He wasn't scared of me, the way people usually are, even when I grew up into a big, strong Wolperting. He treated me like his own son.'

Urs lowered the leg of pork.

'So I asked him to teach me to fence, ostensibly for self-protection, because I spent so much time alone while he was away duelling and so on. He agreed, but the longer we practised and trained and fought the more I realised what a poor swordsman he was and how much better at it *I* was. I had a burning ambition to be more than a match for him, and it really wasn't long before I reached that stage. I didn't let on, mind you. I always held myself in check and allowed him to win, but in reality I got better and better – in fact, I could have disarmed him with a poker. Well, one day he was due to fight a duel for which the other side had engaged Hogg the Hunk. Hogg was the most celebrated and dreaded duellist in the whole of North End, a gigantic brute of a wild boar. It would have been suicide for Koram to go up against him and I was at the top of my form, honestly. I couldn't wait to try out my skill in a genuine fight.

'So I devised a simple little plan. I had to persuade Koram to let me fight the duel in his place. I persuaded him by bringing a coal shovel down on the back of his thick skull – in fact, I nearly killed him, I had to hit him so hard. Then I took our two best sabres and went off to the duel. I told Hogg I was Koram Morak and he believed me, not being acquainted with my foster-father. Well, Hogg was certainly no slouch. He fended me off for a minute or two, but then I systematically took him apart. I didn't kill him – I've never killed anyone in combat – but I left him with so many scars that he never fought another duel. I remember exactly what I thought as I made my way home. I thought: Hey, you're pretty good! Funnily enough, though, it didn't give me any pleasure at all. Anyway, Koram had just recovered consciousness when I got home. "Wow," I said to him, "you certainly taught old Hogg a thing or two. A shame he knocked you out just before he hit the ground."

'"Did he?" said Koram. "I don't remember." And then I cooked us some supper. We had saddle of lamb in breadcrumbs seasoned with thyme and a cherry tomato salad on the side.'

Urs took another bite out of the leg of pork.

'The problem was that Hogg the Hunk now went around showing everyone his scars and telling them what a hell of a fellow Koram Morak was, an invincible magician of a swordsman, and so on and so forth. Well, you know how it is: it wasn't long before every sabre-rattler in Zamonia wanted to fight this Koram Morak.'

Urs sighed.

'The fact was, I'd dislodged a regular avalanche. Yogur the Butcher, Gollup of the Gulch, Gahiji of the Three Blades, Swatkin the Slayer, Pincushion Pratt, Yamboo Yooli, Hoku the Toothless – every few weeks some brain-dead barbarian would appear outside our shack and challenge Koram to a duel. When that happened my only recourse was the coal shovel. Then I went off and riddled my opponent with holes. I told Koram the same story every time he came round: how he'd made mincemeat of someone but been knocked out at the last moment. In the end, Koram scarcely had time to recover his wits between duels. I was afraid he'd become permanently deranged if things went on that way, but I didn't know what else to do.'

Urs drew a deep breath.

Evel the Octopus

'Then, one day, Evel the Octopus appeared at our door, the most dreaded duellist in all Zamonia. He had no more arms than you or I – they called him the Octopus because he seemed to have at least eight when fighting, or so the story went. I went to fetch the coal shovel, but it wasn't there. At that moment it came crashing down on my head – *bang!* – and everything went black. Koram had tumbled to my game – it had gone on long enough, heaven knows – and given me a dose of my own medicine. When I came to, Koram Morak, my foster-father, was lying outside in the snow in a pool of blood.'

Urs emitted a sob. A single tear trickled down his cheek and lost itself in his fur.

'I took our weapons and scoured Zamonia for Evel the Octopus. This time I was determined to give my opponent more than a few scars; just this once, I was prepared to kill. Oh yes, I was ready to kill all right, but Evel seemed to have vanished from the face of the earth. That was when I realised what happens when you take up arms, even in a good cause. One thing leads to another and in the end the weapon triumphs. Those confounded blades are like vampires, they drink blood and induce you to supply them with some. Sooner or later you realise that *they* wield *you*, not the other way round.'

'Yes, yes,' Rumo said dismissively. 'All right, but what brought you to Wolperting?'

'The usual thing: I saw the Silver Thread one day. I found its source – in Wolperting, naturally – in the person of Sheena of the Snows, but that's another story. Once here I did what you're doing now. I went to school and took fencing lessons – this was before Ushan DeLucca's time. It soon turned out that I was the best swordsman in the city. No one could match my experience. I was even asked to head the fencing school, but I wanted nothing to do with it, honestly not. I did give a few fencing lessons, though, because everyone kept badgering me – telling me it was my civic duty as the city's finest swordsman, et cetera. Then, when Ushan DeLucca arrived here a few years later, it put paid to my status as the best swordsman in Wolperting. DeLucca is a born swordsman, an absolute natural. Believe me, I was thoroughly relieved when everyone stopped fussing over me. The youngsters these days don't even know I can hold a rapier in my paw.'

'Could you give me some tuition?'

'In what?'

'Fencing, of course.'

'Fencing? I can't fence myself any more.'

'You just said you were the second-best.'

'Fifth-best at most.'

'That's good enough for me. Will you?'

'Can't I talk you out of it?'

'No. You should have kept your mouth shut.'

Urs sighed and gnawed a final shred of pork off the bone.

'I ought to have sent you away with a flea in your ear when you turned up outside the gates,' he said. 'You were nothing but trouble, I could smell it.'

Starting the next day, Urs and Rumo used to leave the city late in the afternoon and disappear into the northern woods. Rumo always carried a long, cloth-wrapped bundle under his arm, and several of his classmates, who had spotted him and his friend, wondered what they got up to out there.

The truth was, Urs gave Rumo fencing lessons every evening until sunset and sometimes by torchlight after dark. The bundle contained two sabres, two rapiers and two daggers, which Rumo had carved from hardwood.

Although Urs soon recalled the essentials of swordsmanship, he sometimes imparted them in the wrong order. He taught Rumo complicated moves and attacks before simple ones, and got a few technical terms mixed up, but in general Rumo found his tuition more rewarding than Ushan DeLucca's laborious, almost bureaucratic teaching methods. One thing became absolutely clear to him: Urs detested fencing. His aptitude for it not only bored him, it troubled him. He disliked everything about it: the mechanical movements, the concentration, the discipline, the eternal repetitions. Urs had devised various ways of getting around these rules. Although he taught Rumo those too, it didn't change his opinion that fencing wasn't an art, but a strenuous, tedious, vicious, nonsensical form of sport.

Teaching Rumo was a genuine favour to a friend. Urs would so much rather have taught him how to cook!

But he couldn't have had a better pupil. Where fencing was concerned, Rumo was almost fanatical in his eagerness to learn. He soaked up Urs's theoretical remarks like a sponge, was tireless in practice, and repeated each exercise to the point of utter exhaustion. Rumo was the driving force. He resisted any attempt by Urs to cut a lesson short or omit it altogether. Even when they got home and Urs had long since retired to bed, he would get out the fencing manuals he'd borrowed from the library and read until sleep overcame him. Among his reading matter was a slim booklet by Ushan DeLucca tersely entitled *Swordsmanship.* Rumo studied that work most attentively of all.

Parries and feints

Rumo's lessons in the woods covered the following: how to hold the weapon; the salute; the backwards jump; the forwards jump; the lunge step; the flèche attack; the simple direct hit; the disengage; the hit with coulée. Then the parries: the direct parry; the parries in prime and seconde; the ceding parry: the ceding parries in tierce and quarte. The riposte and remise. Then the feints: the hit feint; the feint by disengage; the feint by taking the opponent's blade; the double feint; the DeLuccan feint; the feint feint; the wishbone feint with remise; the double wishbone feint with remise; the feint by double disengage; the feint at flank in quarte; the DeLuccan feint at flank in quarte; and *Urs's Home-Made Feint at Flank in Quarte*, which was so bewilderingly effective that all the other feints at flank in quarte could safely be forgotten.

Rumo learnt the attack by taking the blade (a direct hit followed by a feint); the beat attack (battering the centre of an opponent's blade to force him out of position); the vertical, horizontal, spiral and radical modes of disarming an opponent (the latter invented by Urs); the criss-cross attack with two blades; the concealed parry (a hit delivered from behind one's back); the matador's thrust (downwards through the throat into the heart); and the *Raging Tornado*, an attack that required an exceptional amount of practice. And Rumo learnt not only how to launch all these attacks but how to counter them as well. He repeatedly practised the *Flat Slap* defence, an exercise of which Urs seemed particularly fond.

Urs taught Rumo how to wield the blade while lying on the ground; how to defend himself with one paw tied to a tree or with one leg buried in the ground – the so-called Swamp Simulation. They practised sword-plus-dagger fencing, in which opponents fought two-handed with blades of different length, and weaponless combat, which was really an escape tactic involving leaps, somersaults and forward rolls – a technique for use when disarmed. They fought in the treetops, swinging from branch to branch like monkeys; they fought in densely wooded terrain with rotten, slippery branches underfoot; they fought while wading through bogs or up to their waists in water. 'You never know when it'll come to the crunch,' said Urs. 'It may be wintertime and you're ankle-deep in slush or standing on an icy pavement, or it may be night-time and you're halfway down some rickety cellar stairs in the dark. Those textbook drawings are seldom realistic: two perfectly posed fencers confronting one another in a dry, well-lit gymnasium. You're more likely to find yourself on a clifftop at night, lashed by flying spray – and it'll be hailing into the bargain.' That was why they practised in all conditions. Any weather was fencing weather, said Urs.

Two dreams and a riddle

Rumo had two pet fantasies with which he lulled himself to sleep at night, turn and turn about. In one he was Prince Sangfroid rescuing Princess Rala from the clutches of an ever-changing succession of monsters or villains. In the other he was Wolperting's new fencing champion, who deposed the legendary but ageing Ushan DeLucca in a breathtaking duel – watched by Rala and the entire fencing class, needless to say. Just as his dreams on Roaming Rock had constantly rehearsed the two phases of Smyke's plan, so he now pictured himself repaying Ushan in the same coin for that humiliating nick on the nose. Having first played the fool and launched some clumsy attacks to put the fencing master off his guard, he would then surpass himself in a furious display of swordsmanship, taking his opponent apart until all that remained of him was a whimpering wretch who begged Rumo to take over his teaching post.

The vengeful thoughts Rumo entertained towards Ushan DeLucca differed in character from those he had felt for the Demonocles. He would exact a bloodless form of retribution that disarmed and humiliated his opponent with swordsmanlike finesse. Volzotan Smyke would have approved of this second dream.

Smyke . . . Rumo wondered what had become of his corpulent teacher. He would undoubtedly have found Wolperting to his taste had he been permitted to enter the city – a city where combat training was part of the school syllabus. He would also have made an excellent addition to the school staff: main subject strategy, subsidiary subject Zamonian military history. Rumo missed Smyke, but he wasn't unduly worried about him. Anyone who had survived Roaming Rock could cope with any situation.

Rumo yawned. Then he remembered Smyke's farewell riddle: *What grows shorter and shorter the longer it gets?* A candle? No, a burning candle simply gets shorter and shorter, not longer. Was the answer something visible? Maybe, maybe not. Still pondering this utterly insoluble riddle, Rumo drifted gently off to sleep.

IV. Smyke's Travels

Smyke very soon regretted his decision to part company with Rumo. He berated himself for being an utter fool. Having yielded to a spontaneous whim and dispensed with the amenities of Rumo's companionship, he would now have to forage for food, light fires and cook for himself. As for the other advantages conferred by the presence of a battle-hardened Wolperting, he dreaded to think of them. He had gambled with destiny yet again, but his temperament was such that he quickly accepted his lot.

In the next few days he tried to convince himself how wonderful it was not to be hustled along by Rumo – to be able to take a breather whenever he felt like one. He spent several cold and almost sleepless nights because he failed to get a decent fire going and was deterred from shutting his eyes by sinister noises in the surrounding forest.

He was not unnaturally exhausted when, after a week, he met up with a convoy of Midgardian dwarfs, itinerant workers who toured the vineyards and helped with the grape harvest. It required all Smyke's powers of persuasion to induce them to give him a ride on one of their donkey carts. Although unconvinced by his claim to be a champion grape picker, the good-natured dwarfs took pity on him because of his condition and allowed him to climb aboard.

Smyke found vineyards far more congenial than the wild woods of Zamonia. What was more, he discovered to his own surprise that he really could help with the harvest because, after a short time, his fourteen arms enabled him to pick many more grapes than a Midgardian dwarf.

He and his companions went from vineyard to vineyard, usually spending one day at each and then moving on. In this way they progressed north-westwards at a leisurely pace from Orn to Tentisella, from Nether Molk to Upper Molk, from Wimbleton to Moomieville, from Zebraska to Ormiston. To Smyke, physical exertion and a nomadic existence were entirely new experiences.

After a few weeks the convoy reached a major outpost of Zamonian civilisation in the vicinity of the Gargyllian Bollogg's Skull, a rock formation reputed to be the petrified cranium of a giant. This district was also known as Grapefields because so many wine growers had settled

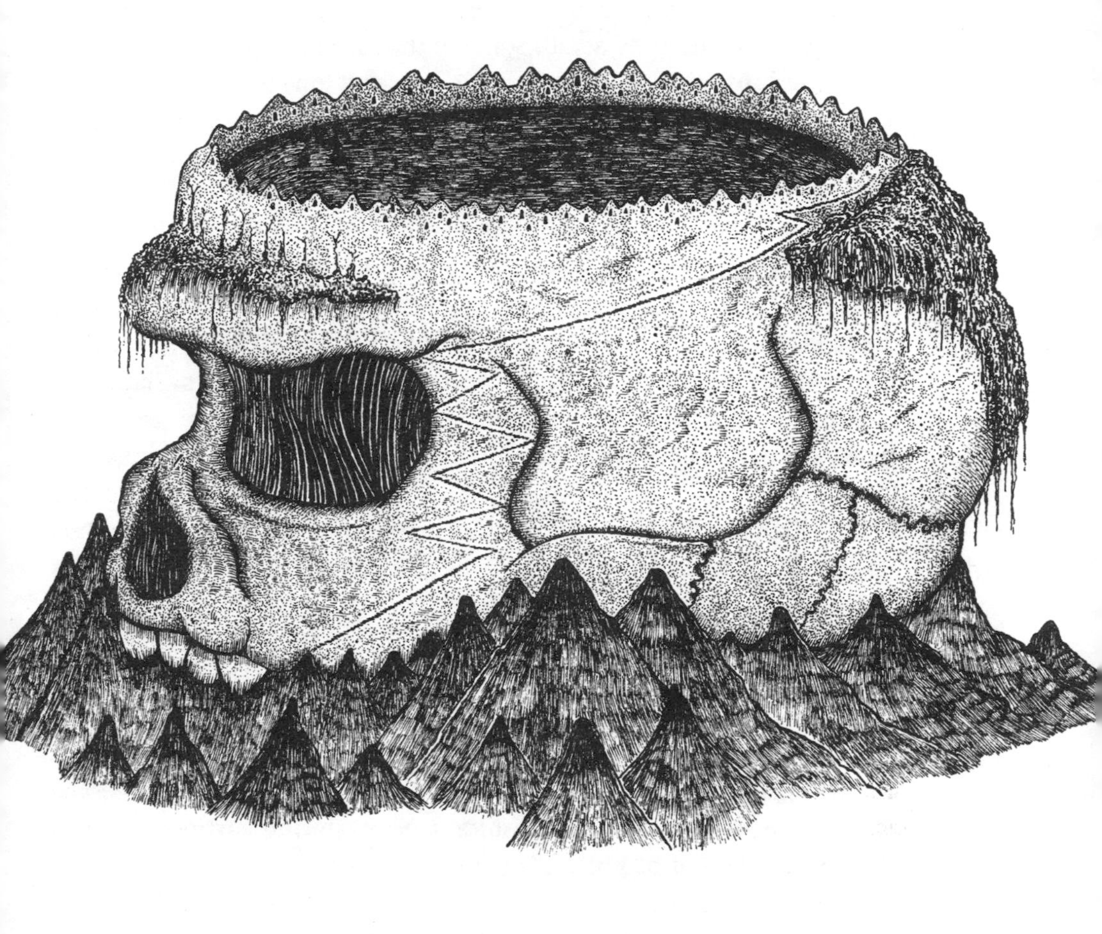

there and transformed it into a veritable paradise for lovers of the grape. There were countless village inns and wineries, and a vast number of small vineyards that produced legendary yields. Grapefields was a fully developed tourist area, and by Smyke's standards it came close to being as much of a heaven on earth as a genuine big city.

Bidding farewell to the simple life and the Midgardian dwarfs, Smyke now roamed around on his own. He lived on his meagre savings and an occasional game of cards. This was child's play, because people on vacation in Grapefields had money to burn and were far from averse to the odd game of chance.

Smyke used his winnings to fulfil the visions that had kept him going at the bottom of his slimy pool on Roaming Rock: he lived out his culinary dreams in every detail. Some of the finest chefs in Zamonia had opened restaurants in the Grapefields area and Smyke patronised them all. He went through the menus from beginning to end and back again, until every memory of his privations had been effaced and converted into body fat. He had truly reached civilisation at last.

Smyke's excursions had naturally taken him into the neighbourhood of the Bollogg's Skull. Growing on its steep limestone slopes were wild vines that could be harvested only by the flying Gargylls who inhabited the caves inside the gigantic head. It was said that, many years ago, a frozen meteor from outer space had struck the Bollogg's Skull and melted, filling it with the mysterious black water that was the main source of the fabulous wine for which the whole district was famed.

The truth wine

'Gargyllian Bollogg's Skull', as the wine growers called their wine, was pitch-black in colour and as thick as molasses. It could not be said to possess any of the characteristics that normally distinguish a wine. It neither refreshed nor relaxed, was guaranteed to spoil a decent meal, had no bouquet or taste and was not even genuinely intoxicating. What rendered it so unique and sought after was that it allegedly induced a state of mind in which those who drank it learnt *the truth about themselves.* You couldn't buy it in casks or bottles. It was served only by the glass, and at an exorbitant price, in one particular tavern situated at the foot of Bollogg's Skull. Its name, logically enough, was *The Bollogg's Skull.*

Smyke had already heard the Midgardian dwarfs talking about this wine – in fact, the subject always cropped up sooner or later in any conversation. The locals, who spoke of it only in mysterious and enigmatic terms, intimated that its effects weren't to everyone's taste. The longer Smyke spent in Grapefields, however, the more the wine intrigued him. And so, when he had won enough money at cards, he made his way to the aforesaid hostelry to sample it.

He felt a trifle uneasy when he reached the tavern at the foot of the gigantic skull. There were people who had strongly advised him not to touch the wine and one of his card-playing cronies had even claimed that anyone who got high on Gargyllian Bollogg's Skull was never the same again.

But curiosity triumphed, of course, and Smyke ventured inside. The tavern was run by Greenwood Dwarfs whose hideous appearance created a rather uncomfortable atmosphere. Undeterred, Smyke loudly ordered a glass of the legendary beverage. The dwarfish waiter showed him to a table covered with a dirty cloth and promptly disappeared again.

Smyke sat down and surveyed his surroundings. All the customers were sitting by themselves at small tables, each with a glass of black liquid in front of him. Some were brooding in silence, others mumbling to themselves, and many pulling faces horrific enough to suggest that they were suffering from convulsions. A few were actually weeping. The place looked more like the recreation room of a lunatic asylum than the taproom of an inn. The Greenwood Dwarf returned with a glass of black wine, deposited it on the table and disappeared without a word.

Smyke took a cautious sip.

He felt cheated. The wine tasted of nothing, absolutely nothing, not even water. What a fool he was! He'd fallen for an old wives' tale – for the oldest tourist trap in the district. Remembering how expensive the wine was, he decided to make a fuss when the waiter reappeared. Perhaps he could get out of paying the bill. He looked up – and gave such a terrible start that he spilt the rest of the wine on the grubby tablecloth. Seated across the table from him was himself.

Smyke's alter ego

'No, your eyes don't deceive you,' said his alter ago. 'It's you. You're me. I'm you. You're looking at yourself.'

'Heavens,' said Smyke, 'I wasn't prepared for this.' No, there was no mirror. It was his doppelgänger all right.

'Nobody's prepared for it, curiously enough. It's only logical, though, when you come to think about it. After all, who is better qualified to tell you the truth about yourself than yourself?'

'Man, oh man,' said Smyke, fanning himself with several pairs of arms at once. 'This is really incredible! I need some time to take it in. You look so real.'

'I'm as real as you are. Have some more wine.'

'No thanks, I've had enough. Any more and there might be three of us sitting here.'

'It's not like getting drunk. You can't improve on your present condition. What you see is what you get.'

'I might just as well have looked in a mirror,' said Smyke. 'It would have been cheaper.'

'Yes, exactly. You're seeing what you'd see in a mirror, but much quicker.'

'How do you mean, much quicker?'

'Wait and see. Look at me! Concentrate on me!'

'You mean you're going to show me something?'

'I'm already doing so. Look closer.'

Smyke stared at his alter ego. Yes, it was himself, his exact mirror image. A trifle weary-looking, perhaps, but after all that had happened recently . . . But did he really look that old? Yes, he probably did by now. But . . . Just a minute! Those little crow's feet beneath his eyes – surely they hadn't been there this morning! Or had they? No, definitely not! This wasn't a very good likeness of him after all. It was more like a poor imitation in a waxworks.

And this was supposed to be the real thing?

Smyke eyed the wrinkles suspiciously. Suddenly there were more of them. And more. Big bags were forming beneath the eyes of his alter ego.

'Just a minute . . .' muttered Smyke.

His alter ego grinned. 'You've caught on at last, huh? It isn't a pretty sight.'

Smyke had caught on all right. This wasn't a poor imitation, it was a perfect likeness of himself in ten or twenty years' time. He was watching himself grow older.

His alter ego's skin was becoming drier, greyer and more wrinkled. Discoloured flecks appeared, warts took shape.

Smyke shivered. His alter ego grinned, baring its teeth. They were yellow and longer than usual. The gums receded and became inflamed, the necks of the teeth were exposed and turned brown. One rotten black stump detached itself from the pale, diseased gum and dropped off on to the table.

'Whoops!' said his alter ego.

This was going decidedly too far, thought Smyke. He was watching himself dying, not just growing older.

'Stop it!' he entreated, but he couldn't tear his eyes away from the gruesome sight. His alter ego's skin had creased into thousands of tiny folds, the face was puckering like an overripe plum, the hands and arms were little more than skin and bone. Then they, too, began to fall apart and drop off. Smyke could make out the individual bones and desiccated sinews.

'Stop it, I said!' gasped Smyke. He burst into tears.

'No can do,' said his ghastly doppelgänger. 'The truth is inescapable. Well, it's been nice having a drink with you, brother of mine. Just remember this . . .' It leant forward, bared its rotting teeth in a frightful grin, and whispered *'They'll be coming to fetch you.'*

Then it broke into a sinister laugh. It laughed until it choked on its own vocal cords. As the last peal of laughter died away the lower jaw came adrift and fell off on to the table. A grey tongue lolled from the open throat. Then that, too, fell off and exploded into a puff of dust. Smyke uttered a high-pitched cry.

A voice behind him said, 'Can I get you something else, sir?'

He spun round. The dwarfish waiter was standing there, eyeing him malevolently.

'What?'

'Would you care for something else, sir? Some cheese, perhaps?'

'Er, no thanks,' said Smyke. He turned to look at his frightful companion, but there was no one there. The chair on the other side of the table was empty, the table itself bare of teeth and other detritus. The nightmare was over.

'Yes, the truth is hard to endure,' said the waiter. 'Lies are nicer, we all know that, but it changes your outlook, seeing things telescoped like that. May I bring you the bill?'

'Yes, please,' Smyke said hastily, 'and be quick about it.'

He waited, breathing heavily, for the dwarf to return. Sweat was oozing from every pore of his body. He paid the bill and the waiter escorted him to the door.

'Just wait, you'll soon feel better. The purifying effect takes time. You'll feel newborn.' The dwarf gave a frightful laugh. 'It'll change your life, believe me,' he called as Smyke disappeared into the darkness. 'Goodbye for ever! No one ever pays us a second visit!'

On the warpath

Smyke left Grapefields early next morning and set off. He had scarcely slept a wink all night. Even when he did doze off, all he saw were visions of his rapidly ageing self, who kept whispering, *'They'll be coming to get you.'*

There was no time to be lost. He'd wasted so much of it on that accursed Roaming Rock! There were things to do apart from fleecing wine bibbers with a few cheap card-sharper's tricks and using the proceeds to eat his way through the menu of every restaurant in Grapefields.

His other recurrent vision during the night was of Professor Ostafan Kolibri. Instead of horrifying him, however, it had filled him with hope. He now realised that he had instinctively headed in the same direction as the professor had taken when they parted. The knowledge with which Kolibri had infected him was having an after-effect the Nocturnomath had omitted to mention: Smyke wanted more of it. His thirst for scientific information had been whetted, and his store of knowledge was posing new and urgent questions which only the professor could answer:

If the readiness of Zamonian bees to discuss matters by haptic means were allied with the floral transmission of information, would it not be possible to develop an apiarist's language capable of verbally stimulating their honey output?

If the surgical instruments in the Non-Existent Teenies' subcutaneous submarine can start a dead heart beating again, to which parts of the anatomy should they be applied?

And if it were possible to start a dead heart beating again, would that not be a first step towards combating the inexorable fate so drastically demonstrated to Smyke by his alter ego?

Following in Kolibri's footsteps meant defying fate and declaring war on death. And Smyke was an expert on war, for had he not been Prince Hussein Banana's war minister? Yes, when he conjured up the vision of that puny, pigeon-chested gnome of a scientist, he clearly perceived that Kolibri needed a powerful ally in his fight against almighty death. It was Smyke's wish - nay, his destiny - to follow the professor to Murkholm as quickly as possible.

Torrentula and the Demonic ferrymen

The further Smyke progressed through north-west Zamonia, making for the coast, the sparser the signs of civilisation became. The Arcadian landscape of Grapefields gave way to monotonous, almost deserted prairies inhabited by sheep farmers who were among the poorest members of the Zamonian population. Gone were the taverns and wine shops, and no one here was free enough with his money to risk it on a game of chance. Smyke occasionally happened on a farm where he could obtain a bed of straw and a meagre breakfast in return for a small sum, but in general he had to content himself with a diet of raw vegetables. As a result, his financial reserves and all the fat he'd put on in Grapefields gradually melted away like butter in the sun.

The climate became steadily harsher. The everlasting east wind had scoured the landscape into a flat, featureless expanse, and bent every tree and blade of grass into submission. A thin drizzle fell without ceasing. Smyke knew that in Torrentula, the district through which several rivers flowed oceanwards from the Gloomberg Mountains, there were some small villages where so-called Demon Boats could be hired to take one further. Only the most audacious travellers availed themselves of this inexpensive form of transportation, for the Demon Boats were diminutive craft manned by ferrymen of semi-Demonic ancestry who always shot Torrentula's dangerous rapids by night.

However, Smyke was becoming so sick of the monotonous scenery that he decided to take the risk.

The very look of the boat he boarded in one of the villages, which was criss-crossed by several small rivers, made an unnerving impression on him. It was coal-black and shaped like a grotesque Demonic head with horribly gaping jaws. He took his place in it accompanied by the ferryman, who was muffled up in a black cloak. Seated behind Smyke, he made not the slightest attempt to steer and spent the whole time cackling incessantly. At first they glided leisurely downstream, and Smyke had just concluded that the ferryman's infuriating laughter was the worst feature of the voyage when the boat put on speed and the Demonic pipes mounted on the cabin roof began to wail in the wind. They proceeded to shoot the rapids at a rate of which Smyke would never have believed a river craft capable. Flung ever more violently to and fro by the current, the boat rotated on its own axis and stood on its head by turns, submerged completely, regained the surface and plunged down several waterfalls. Although unafraid of drowning, being a semi-aquatic creature, Smyke thought it quite possible that he would be smashed to pieces against the hull. Either that, or he would go insane with fear and join in the ferryman's demented laughter.

But the boat reached its destination unscathed. Smyke was still alive and in his right mind. What was more, he had covered a lot of ground in an incredibly short time. He was now near the coast just south of Murkholm.

Murkholm lighthouse

Seen from far off, Murkholm resembled a gigantic fair-weather cloud that had fallen from the sky. The sight of it rejoiced Smyke's heart for at least four reasons:

First, he had arrived! No more prairies, no more expanses of razor-sharp grass, no nights filled with the howling of wolves, no forests inhabited by whispering shadows.

Second, Murkholm was a city. Not a particularly big one, but a genuine city with live inhabitants.

Third, there was Professor Kolibri. Smyke looked forward to all the conversations with which they would while the nights away.

Fourth, the cloud looked like a freshly washed sheep. Nothing in its appearance was reminiscent of all that superstitious claptrap about 'ghostly' Murkholm. Smyke waddled towards the city filled with expectancy.

As soon as he entered the cloud, however, the world underwent a change. Colours faded, sounds died away, outlines became blurred. Everything was silent, soft and peaceful. Smyke instantly felt snug and secure.

The architecture seemed rather monotonous – the only buildings in sight were squat, circular, and built of stone – and the streets were hardly teeming with urban life. All Smyke saw were a few dark-robed figures slinking through the fog, but he was sure he could find his way to the lighthouse unaided. It could only be situated where it belonged, beside the sea, so he simply made for the roar of the waves and soon found himself on a sandy white beach. The sea! Oh dear, and on Roaming Rock he had solemnly vowed never to go near a wave again!

Jutting skywards on the horizon, almost invisible in the billowing fog, was the slender grey shape of the lighthouse. What a picturesque spot for a stimulating exchange of ideas, thought Smyke when he got there. The sea within sight, miles of sand dunes available for long walks, the mysterious fog – very atmospheric! To the sound of rolling breakers he and Kolibri would discuss important aspects of science and philosophy, and empty the odd bottle of wine – and it certainly wouldn't be Gargyllian Bollogg's Skull. How healthy the sea air smelt!

Smyke knocked on the lighthouse door, once, twice, again and again. He called the professor's name. No one at home? Well, Kolibri probably wouldn't mind if he went inside and waited for him. Was the door locked? No. Then the professor couldn't have anything to hide. In he went.

Aha, a laboratory! Great, the professor really had settled in here. The place was very untidy. When was the last time anyone had cleaned it? Scientists! They had more important things to do than tie their shoelaces and wield a duster. What were those pieces of equipment? Test tubes, Bunsen burners, vials, flasks containing mysterious liquids – Smyke couldn't wait for the professor to explain everything to him! He could already see himself amid the test tubes, Kolibri's ostascope on his nose, searching for an effective antidote to death!

A glass retort of incredible delicacy, a masterpiece of the glass blower's art, lay shattered on the floor. An accident, no doubt. And what was that? A black doll floating in a flask of clear liquid like a tiny victim of drowning. Smyke called again.

'Professor Kolibri?'

No answer.

The diary

A spiral staircase led to the chamber in which the lantern must once have burned. It was lighter up there. A big, panoramic window wreathed in white fog. On the floor a mattress, some blankets and a pillow – very ascetic. Books strewn everywhere. Smyke picked one up: *Diary of a Sentimental Dinosaur* by Hildegard Mythmaker. Well, well! He tossed it aside and picked up another. *The Monosemanticisation of Polysemants in Grailsundian Cave Literature.* The things that scientists took an interest in! Smyke threw the book on the floor and picked up a third. No title? He opened it at the first page. Neatly inscribed on it in black ink were the words:

Professor Ostafan Kolibri's Lighthouse Log

Smyke dropped the book as if it were a poisonous snake. A log – a form of diary! How discourteous of him to stick his nose into such a thing. It probably contained revelations of a most intimate nature.

At least he was now a hundred per cent certain that the professor was living here. It would be only a matter of time before he turned up. Excellent! Smyke made his way downstairs again.

It was already late that night when Smyke began to feel genuinely worried about the professor. How many hours had he been waiting? What could be keeping Kolibri so long in this desolate part of the world? It was pitch-dark outside and the salt-laden wind was bitterly cold. Smyke roamed the laboratory, fidgeting. Why was it so untidy? What was that strange little corpse in the flask? Could something untoward have happened after all? In need of distraction, Smyke went upstairs to fetch a book.

His eye lighted on the diary again.

Should he risk it? Never!

But what if it contained some clue to the professor's whereabouts? Some clue that might save his life! Smyke picked up the diary and began to read.

Day 1

Murkholm at last! What a disaster-ridden journey! Two months in the clutches of Silvanopirates! I could write an entire book about that episode alone, except that it would be devoted mainly to the distasteful subject of cannibalism. If those apes hadn't been so monstrously demented I should never have escaped and my four shrivelled brains would now be dangling from a belt, together with other fetishes.

Wasted another month in a godforsaken place called Nether Molk, confined to bed by a bout of demonic flu. Sensational hallucinations. For a week I imagined I was a diamond.

Half a dozen other less protracted delays helped to double the length of my journey. But enough of that!

Moved into the disused lighthouse today. It's not particularly big and the lantern was extinguished long ago. Will easily be able to black out the windows and make myself at home here. Visibility in Murkholm agreeably restricted – the perpetual fog makes an effective sunlight filter. An excellent place in which to work and meditate. My intellectual powers perceptibly increased when I entered the fog – by fifty per cent, at a rough estimate.

My scientific equipment has already arrived. Can't wait to see how it has survived the long journey. Tomorrow: stocktaking.

Now to unpack.

Day 2

After going without sleep for almost two weeks, I actually slept for eight hours last night. What luxury! Feel regenerated, brimming with energy. My brains are rotating! The climate suits me admirably. Breakfasted on my remaining provisions for the journey, then settled in.

There are two rooms, the first a large one downstairs immediately inside the front door. Fireplace with saucepan, a table, two chairs. No windows, perfect! This will be my laboratory. A spiral staircase leads upwards through an empty space to the former lantern chamber. A large circular room, but surrounded by windows, therefore unsuitable as a laboratory. The fog presses up against the panes like cotton wool – very picturesque. I shall read and sleep up there.

Unpacked the crates. Most things have withstood the journey remarkably well, the few breakages being manageable. The inventory:

1. *Labyrinthine test tube and glass double helix. (Really amazing that these delicate gems of the glass blower's art arrived in one piece.)*
2. *Electrical egg plus vacuum pump.*
3. *Lindenhoop theodolite.*
4. *Silver Fuessli corker (plus complete set of corks).*
5. *Spectroscope in chameleonskin case.*
6. *Pneumatic suction pump.*
7. *Candlelight heliostat.*
8. *Penduline trigonometer.*
9. *Ostascope (one lens cracked, but I have a spare).*
10. *Aneroid barograph.*
11. *Muslin hygrometer.*
12. *Fibonacchi Spiral plus candlelight propellent and the relevant indigo prisms.*
13. *The auragraph.*

Also the copper, lead and gold weights for calibrating the auragraph, three dozen auragraphic plates (plus emulsion), powdered zinc, a plummet, the aurathreads (six metres), one litre of mercury, some lead-sealed radium powder, a six-tongued slide rule, camphor solution, a flask containing a Leyden Manikin in nutrient fluid, inanimate. An alchemical battery.

Working attire: lead apron, lead helmet, lead gloves. The crate containing minor oddments (measuring glasses and bowls, filters, chemicals, alchemical extracts, mortars, etc.). Five barrels of dried cod and a Hodlerian sieve for desalinating seawater (rendering me largely independent of the local cuisine).

The books I enclosed were all there: Zigman Kellis's secret tracts on sympathetic vibration, Feynsinn's Molecular Morphology and his indispensable tables on subatomic dislocation. All the other scientific volumes are here (too many to list them individually), likewise a few Mythmakers for relaxation.

What were missing were my retromagnetic tongs and the goniometer in the copper chicken. Can make do without them, but it's a shame about the handsome mechanical chicken. Stolen, or didn't I pack it at all? The Asiatic orloscope by Sarknadel & Schremp arrived in three pieces. What a fool I was to send such an expensive instrument on such a journey!

Smyke skimmed a few pages listing the chemical substances and delicate instruments with which Kolibri had equipped his laboratory. What was the professor planning to do with all this stuff?

This afternoon I animated the Leyden Manikin.

Yes, I admit it: I'm one of those scientists who approve of using these artificial guinea pigs! Here, therefore, is a brief plea in defence of the use of Leyden Manikins:

I consider them to be the most reliable means of testing the effects of chemicals and drugs under laboratory conditions if one does not wish to try them out on live subjects. A Leyden Manikin consists largely of turf from the Graveyard Marshes of Dull plus an admixture of Demerara Desert sand, animal fat, glycerine, and liquid resin. These constituents are moulded into a humanoid and brought to life with the aid of an alchemical battery.

A Leyden Manikin will keep for about a month if well housed and fed. It displays all the characteristics of genuine animation, reacting to cold, heat and all manner of chemical compounds. I categorically reject the superstitious theory that a Leyden Manikin has a soul and can feel pain. How can anyone feel pain without a nervous system? Speaking for myself, I consider it barbaric to torture frogs and mice when one can fall back on this method. End of plea in mitigation.

My manikin is of excellent quality. Whenever I animate a Leyden Manikin I think of a name for it. This one I shall call Marmaduke. Marmaduke of Murkholm. For the next month Marmaduke will be my most important contact. Ah yes, the scientist is a lonely soul. Knowledge is his sole beloved!

The fog is pressing up against the window like an inquisitive spy.

Day 3

Went shopping in town this morning. The Murkholmers make a rather ghostly impression at first, especially when they loom up out of the fog and fix one with their piercing, watery gaze.

How many rumours there are about that gaze! It's said to be malevolent, hypnotic, spellbinding. But there's a scientific reason for this (as for everything else): the Murkholmers have to stare as hard as they do because of the permanently subdued light in their city. This is the so-called 'Murkholm Stare', which has nothing at all to do with discourtesy. Another myth exploded!

The fog grew steadily thicker. I was looking for the grocer's but couldn't distinguish one building from another. All I could see was a billowing grey curtain of fog. Then, quite suddenly, a pair of eyes appeared in front of me, bigger and more piercing than any I'd encountered hitherto. I gave a start and stopped dead. Just eyes, nothing else, with fog whirling around them – a ghostly sight! Courageously, I took a step closer and my opposite number did likewise. We were now only inches apart. Then a breeze sprang up, abruptly dispersing the fog – and I found that I'd been staring at a shop window the whole time. The luminous eyes were my own, reflected in the glass! What was more, the window was that of the grocer's I'd been looking for.

It was foggy even inside the shop, the floor being knee-deep in white vapour. I did my shopping. The proprietor, who was polite but somewhat uncommunicative, gurgled rather than spoke. He ended by recommending a visit to one of the regular brass band concerts in the municipal gardens. Who says the Murkholmers aren't welcoming?

In the afternoon took my first fog sample right beside the lighthouse, drawing it into the labyrinthine test tube with my retromagnetic suction pump. It was surprisingly difficult to suck any of the vaporous substance into the pump, and I had to exert considerable pressure. The sample made a squelching sound as it detached itself from the surrounding fog. Then I sealed the test tube with my Fuessli corker.

The fog sample wove its way along the test tube's labyrinthine convolutions like a snake; in fact, it's hard to believe that water is its basic constituent. Well, the auragraph will show what's what.

In the evening, read The Talking Stove by Hildegard Mythmaker. Heavens alive, what romantic twaddle – the worst kind of trash from that idiotic 'dead material' school of Zamonian literature, which is devoid of any scientific foundation. The title is to be taken literally, not metaphorically. Mythmaker certainly has a nerve! But it's a good read for all that. Her fifty-page description of the ticking of a grandfather clock is a tour de force in itself.

Day 4

Fog again – what else could one expect here in Murkholm? – but today it seems thicker than ever. I've devised a method of measuring its daily density. I call it my ostafanic fogometer. One of its components is a (home-made) optician's chart erected some thirty feet from the lighthouse. The other is a chalk line on the floor of my bedroom, right beside the big window. Every morning from now on I shall stand on that line and look out at the chart. The fewer the rows of letters I can decipher, the denser the fog. I could lay down a unit of measurement: one unit per illegible row of letters, or something like that. What should I call that unit of measurement? A kolibri? Good idea.

Today the ostafanic fogometer is registering two kolibris.

Went for a longish walk this afternoon. Didn't encounter a single Murkholmer, strangely enough. Architecturally, this city has no equivalent anywhere else in Zamonia. If I had to describe it in a single word, the adjective would probably be 'squat'. The buildings resemble molehills of masonry. They all seem to come from the same mould, their visible portions consisting solely of circular roofs that project from the ground. I get the impression that they're largely subterranean.

Marmaduke always welcomes me when I come home, the dear little fellow! He hammers on the glass with his tiny fists and splashes around in the nutrient fluid. A pity he can't talk.

Day 5

Four kolibris on the ostafanic fogometer.

Today's task: contaminating the Leyden Manikin with my fog sample. What must be, must be.

Removed a small portion of the sample from the labyrinthine test tube (another squelching sound) and injected it into Marmaduke's flask. The manikin seemed hugely entertained by this. The fog, which in these conditions behaved almost organically, glided like a worm over the interior of the flask while Marmaduke vainly tried to capture it. As though mesmerised, I watched this silly game until jolted out of my trance by a sense of responsibility.

Next, set up the auragraph. Quite a job, since all the calibrations had been upset during the journey. Will have to adjust them with the candlelight heliostat, probably over the next few days. Calibrating an auragraph is like tuning the instruments of an entire orchestra. Devoted the rest of the day to this.

Read myself to sleep with Mythmaker's Diary of a Sentimental Dinosaur. Remarkably good for an early work. It probably appeals to me because it's more of a documentary than a novel. I only read the first chapter, Mythmaker's description of the ancient city of Booksville, but that chapter is really a book in its own right. How much of it is fact and how much fiction? At all events, I marvelled at its meticulous account of the catacombs beneath the city and their curious, dangerous inhabitants. That's a world I'd dearly like to explore some time. So deliciously dark!

Smyke skimmed the pages covering the next few days, on which Kolibri had expatiated in great detail upon the difficulties of calibrating the auragraph. He yawned, rubbed his eyes and looked through the window at the optician's chart below. He could read most of the letters. Five kolibris on the ostafanic fogometer? He couldn't help grinning. These oddball scientists simply weren't happy unless they could divide everything into units of measurement! Then he read on.

Day 9

Seven kolibris on the fogometer. Absolutely no question of going for a walk. Still tinkering with the auragraph. Proceeded to check the fog's sylphidic density. Took another tiny sample with the suction pump and transferred it to the double helix. I attached the Lindenhoop theodolite – and naturally forgot, yet again, to amoebise the connections first! The result: two hours' hard work cleaning them with the micropincers and purgative brush, likewise a volley of self-directed oaths. Marmaduke watched me in astonishment from inside his flask, his tiny lips mouthing my imprecations.

I took a reading at last. The result amazed me. No, it was impossible – no water vapour could display such a high sylphidic density. Another reading, another identical result. Nonsense! I shouldn't have taken a reading without prior amoebisation. Cleaning with a brush affords no guarantee. I may have measured some microbe or bacterium instead of the fog molecule. Resolved to repeat the whole procedure tomorrow. Nightingale was right when he told me I would some day put on my shoes before my socks. I'm always too impetuous when I'm experimenting.

I wrote a brief memorandum for Grailsund University on the disastrous effects of overpopulation by Demon Bugs (Leptinotarsa daemoniensis) on the agricultural economy of Harvest Home Plain.

Then, on the grocer's recommendation, I went to a trombophone concert in Murkholm's municipal gardens. It was sparsely attended by some asthmatic Demidwarfs from the Impic Alps, who coughed incessantly.

The twelve-piece orchestra, composed entirely of Murkholmers, launched into its programme. Trombophone music, which resembles a succession of soft, liquid plops, had a soothing effect on me. The glissandi seemed to issue from the trombophone bells like soap bubbles that lost themselves in the fog overhead. I almost got the impression that the fog was responding to the music. At many points above the orchestra it became denser, billowing and swirling around in a way that conveyed rapture but was, of course, occasioned by the wind conditions. The trombophone players' professionalism was extraordinary. Each of them improvised a brief but very original solo that taught me what subtle cadences can be achieved by the mere lengthening and shortening of acoustic frequencies coupled with a skilful manipulation of the trombophone's valves. I strode home feeling exhilarated – and, because of the poor visibility, tripped over a dustbin full of dead jellyfish.

Day 10

At least ten kolibris on the ostafanic fogometer – I could scarcely see the chart at all. The greasy vapour was lapping against the lighthouse in a positively menacing way, so dense in places that it clung to the window-panes like a wet sponge. For the first time since my arrival I felt a pang of uneasiness.

I plucked up my courage at last and went out into the fog. It was like walking underwater – every step required an immense muscular effort. Breathing was difficult and my gums were soon covered with an unappetising film of salt. I felt constricted, mentally as well as physically. Do people really come here to convalesce? What terrible diseases they must be suffering from! I decided to turn back, but I'd lost my bearings. I wandered around like a fool for at least an hour before, purely by chance, I blundered into my own front door. Immensely relieved when I shut it behind me.

I immersed myself in work.

In the evening a thorough examination of the Leyden Manikin in his flask. The wormlike wisp of fog was clinging to the cork like a spider, well out of the reach of Marmaduke, who had either forgotten or was ignoring its presence. I tapped on the glass and he tapped back. Comical.

Read some more of Mythmaker's Diary in bed. It was so exciting, I sat up half the night.

Day 11

Nine kolibris.

The dense fog persists. I took another sylphidic reading, this time with the connections duly amoebised. The result: the same as yesterday. Incredible! The fog's sylphidic density is roughly that of a living creature.

And there's no doubt about it: this reading is accurate. Not that I hadn't entertained such a possibility – the fog's behaviour is striking enough. It's an astonishing result even so. I have, for instance, obtained a similar sylphidic density reading in the case of a jellyfish.

The calibration is almost complete.

In the evening I tried to take my mind off things by reading The Monosemanticisation of Polysemants in Grailsundian Cave Literature. As stimulating as dried cod. I consider the study of comparative literature a thoroughly imprecise discipline.

Strange: the fog, which I at first thought so conducive to work, is beginning to depress me. It irritates me to see how it creeps around the lighthouse, trying to seep through every nook and cranny.

Day 12

Only six kolibris on the fogometer today. A relief.

A long early morning walk in the municipal gardens. Murkholmers glided past as if towed through the ground mist on strings. None of them returned my salutations. I really can't fathom why so many people come here on vacation. Well, I suppose it's inexpensive.

Midday came. The auragraph was ready at last! Having devoted the rest of the morning to completing the calibration, I was able to coat the auragraphic plate with radium powder. An extremely dangerous proceeding, so I donned my protective mask and my lead gloves and apron! That done, I positioned the labyrinthine test tube in front of the auragraph and carried out some final adjustments. Then came the exposure itself. Whoosh! The auragraphic glow lit up my laboratory as bright as day. Marmaduke was so startled, he toppled over backwards into his nutrient fluid. A magical moment despite its purely scientific nature. Now I must wait several days for the auragram to develop. Relaxation has set in.

Smyke skipped a couple of pages. Kolibri had filled them with scientific conjectures of all kinds. His four brains seemed to have taken advantage of the enforced delay to enlarge on a wide variety of subjects, and much of the text consisted of mathematical equations and chemical symbols. Then the diary finally resumed.

Day 14

Have now been here for two weeks. I went into town to do some shopping. On my way across the dunes I encountered three Murkholmers walking towards the sea. This was odd, because the locals tend to keep clear of it. (Why, exactly?) I followed them at a distance. When they reached the shore they were engulfed by a dense swath of fog. By the time it dispersed they had vanished.

On the way back into town I had the nonsensical feeling that the fog was following me. It billowed and swirled about me as never before, and for the first time I thought I detected a sound issuing from it: a persistent slithering sound accompanied by the kind of exhalation I associate with the last gasp of a stranded fish. It was probably just the wind, which was also responsible, I'm sure, for the fog's unusual behaviour. For all that, my sense of uneasiness mounted with every step I took, just as the fog's persistence seemed to increase. Thin wisps like cotton wool palpated my head and seemed to be trying to insinuate themselves into my auditory canals, uttering unintelligible whispers and moist hisses. I flapped my hands in an attempt to shoo them away like troublesome insects, but to no avail.

When I finally reached the grocer's shop it was shut. This was doubly annoying because I'd suddenly, for no discernible reason, developed a burning desire to purchase a packet of sulphur, some copper sulphate, seven metres of wire, and a coffin.

Day 15

Five kolibris.

Examined the auragraph. The auragram seems to be a success. No protostreaks and the emulsion is bubble-free. Still no definite results. The developing process is painfully slow.

Observed a curious meteorological phenomenon during the night. A vast thunderstorm raged above the city for hours. Incessant peals of thunder, flashes of lightning dissected into scattered explosions of light by the fog, but – strangely enough – not a drop of rain or breath of wind.

Only one logical explanation: the fog encloses the city like a protective shell that absorbs the wind and rain.

Day 16

The storm has failed to disperse the fog, but still: the fogometer registered only two kolibris! I could actually detect a glimmer of sunlight.

Examined the auragram. Yes, it's coming on. Definite aural manifestations and the emulsion is drying steadily. Results will soon become visible.

I took advantage of the fog's low density to go for a long walk. The wartlike character of Murkholm's architecture is even more apparent in this visibility. It's malignant somehow, like some disease of the earth's crust. Only a few public buildings and hotels and the grocer's shop are constructed in the traditional manner, with rectangular walls and windows. I can't help feeling that these are exclusively intended for visitors to the city. The fog returned as suddenly as it had dispersed. Strong gusts of wind from the sea sent coils of vapour writhing through the streets, engulfing buildings and passers-by. Sensing once more that the fog was closing in on me, I set off for home in a hurry.

I don't know why, but I was in an excitable mood when I finally shut the lighthouse door behind me.

My eye fell on Marmaduke. He was romping around in his flask, as he usually did when I returned home. I went over to the Leyden Manikin and tapped on his glass abode. Apparently pleased that someone was taking notice of him, he hopped up and down – until I tilted the flask and made him fall over backwards into his nutrient fluid. I couldn't help laughing at this. When he had laboriously scrambled to his feet, I tilted the flask so that he fell head over heels. That I found even funnier. Next, I held up the flask and proceeded to shake it. Marmaduke staggered around inside it with the fluid splashing him all over. In a frenzy now, I pranced across the laboratory shaking the flask above my head and giggling like a naughty child. Meanwhile, poor little Marmaduke was being hurled against the walls of his glass prison. At long last I recovered my wits. Marmaduke was floating in the liquid semi-conscious, trying to keep his head above the surface. I felt thoroughly ashamed of myself and cannot, even now, account for my strange behaviour.

The Manikin recovered in the course of the evening and eventually resumed his seat in the flask – impassively, as if nothing had happened. But my fog sample had disappeared, probably emulsified with the nutrient fluid by all that shaking. I'd behaved like a raving lunatic, not a scientist! My sense of shame pursued me into my dreams.

Smyke was growing somewhat uncomfortable. This stuff was all rather personal. He felt as if he were spying on Professor Kolibri's activities like the intrusive fog that plastered itself to the lighthouse windows. But by now he couldn't have stopped reading. It was like an addiction.

Day 17

Six kolibris.

Spent half the day lamenting my behaviour yesterday. I'm in need of company again. The solitude of this lighthouse is having a disruptive effect on my psyche. I decided to take a day off, leave the auragram to develop by itself and go for a long walk.

My afternoon reading: Mythmaker's Collected Poems. Poetry is completely wasted on me, I fear. It couldn't be a more unscientific mode of expression if it tried. Those perpetual obscurities, those verbal gymnastics, those preposterous metaphors. Why not call a spade a spade?

In the evening I ventured out into 'society' for the first time since my arrival in Murkholm. I dined at 'The Foghorn', Murkholm's only restaurant. Four locals were seated at separate tables, eating in silence. A waiter glided through the ground mist with the Murkholmer's usual fixed stare. Against one wall stood a big cast-iron grandfather clock whose obtrusive ticking reminded me of the inexorably transitory nature of all existence. There was only one dish, some steamed fish I'd never come across before (referred to on the menu as 'fogfish'). It was completely transparent. One could see the subdued glow of its internal organs, which clearly indicated that it was still alive. Garnishing it were some tiny eels that had been suffocated by smoke. Well, I'm not fastidious. Contrary to my expectations, it tasted quite good. I was less enamoured of the waiter, whose piercing stares throughout the meal suggested that he was trying to burn a hole in my skull.

While walking home through the billowing fog I encountered the grocer. I bade him a courteous goodnight, but he glided past without a word. Perhaps it wasn't him at all. They all look so alike here.

Day 18

Five kolibris.

Something I've noticed when observing fog: when a fog bank drifts towards an object, a tree for instance, its outlines begin to blur, losing their clarity and colour. Then the tree seems to dissolve into the fog, leaf by leaf, branch by branch, until it disappears completely. Or until it turns into fog.

That, of course, is a childish and thoroughly unscientific way of looking at the matter. The tree remains where it is; it's merely hidden from view. Why am I writing this regardless? No idea.

The Leyden Manikin is behaving oddly. He has exchanged his lethargy for hectic activity. Either he wades around in the nutrient fluid, muttering silently to himself, or he rollicks around in it like a child in a swimming pool. There are times when he bangs his head against the glass for hours, creating an irritatingly monotonous din.

The auragram will be ready tomorrow. At least, everything points in that direction.

Day 19

It's incredible! I could weep!

When I went downstairs this morning, brimming with expectancy, to examine the auragram, I saw to my horror that the emulsion had been disturbed!

It seems impossible, but someone must have broken in during the night and blurred the auragram deliberately. All that work in vain. Either I leave here empty-handed or I must start all over again.

Too disheartened to write any more.

Day 20

Spent the morning setting up a new shot. Be damned if I leave here empty-handed!

Took a new auragram in the afternoon.

More waiting.

Day 21

Five kolibris on the fogometer. Enjoyed doing nothing today. An entirely new side of me, like so many in recent days. I spent a long time looking at myself in the huge mirror that used to reflect the lanternlight afar. Its convex conformation expanded my girth in a comical way that sent me into fits of laughter. It was some three hours before I recovered my composure.

Something is changing me. I feel as if I'm passing through a very fine sieve that filters out my less admirable characteristics. The residue will be a new and better person.

Day 22

Four kolibris. The Leyden Manikin's behaviour is becoming more and more peculiar. He's endeavouring to build something with the liquid nutrient. It trickles through his little fingers time after time, but that doesn't deter him from trying, again and again, to stack one handful on top of another.

'Solitude is insanity's favourite playmate . . .' I think it was Huzzek Fano who wrote that. Or was it Oscar van Tripplestock?

Day 23

After much thought, I've come to the conclusion that only Marmaduke could have spoilt that auragram. He's conspiring against me, but with whom? Who lets him out of his flask?

I myself?

Day 24

If flatness were funny, a dinner plate would be hilarious.

Tried to remember someone I didn't know.

Day 25

Spent most of the morning trying to exit the lighthouse through the keyhole. It proved impossible.

I shall have to kill Marmaduke.

But what with?

Smyke put down the diary. The last few entries were rather peculiar. Was Kolibri being funny? Had he lost the urge to write? Was he merely fooling around? Smyke glanced over his shoulder. He had a feeling the professor was watching him while he read.

Day 26

I really don't know if I should mention this, but last night I bumped into my father. At first I thought it was my reflection in the old mirror. I was halfway up the stairs when we met and he never so much as glanced at me. This is odd, because my father has been dead fifty years.

These inexplicable occurrences have become more frequent of late. Am I worried? Not really. Strangely enough, the more frequent they become the less they seem to matter.

How many kolibris on the fogometer? Who cares?

Day 27

Did I pen the last four entries? I must have, because they're in my handwriting, but what demented drivel they are! Am I losing my mind?

I've no recollection of the last four days. Afraid I must be sick. A recurrence of demonic influenza?

I don't feel well. I'm edgy, jumpy, suffering from hot flushes. I'd stop work at once if the second auragram weren't almost ready.

Day 28

What was that curious entry yesterday? Of course I penned the four previous entries, but who was responsible for yesterday's? Odd: it's in my handwriting. Could it be the fellow I met on the stairs? Is a doppelgänger at work here? Is he in league with the Leyden Manikin?

Resolved to be more on my guard! I can't even trust myself now.

Meant to go shopping in town but failed once more to leave the lighthouse by the keyhole.

I must lose weight.

Day 29

Lost every last ounce of weight in a single day, as planned. The only trouble is, I'm now invisible – I don't really exist any more.

On the other hand I can get through the keyhole with ease. I dance through the fog, free as air.

Heard strange music issuing from the earth's core during the night. Detected mysterious messages in the roar of the waves. Have still to decipher them.

Day 30

Yea, Nabgor of all Nabgors, I eboy thee! I shall exmertinate Murmadake! I shall exmertinate Lokibri! Yea, Nabgor of all Nabgors, I eboy thee!

Yea, Nabgor of all Nabgors, I eboy thee! I shall exmertinate Murmadake! I shall exmertinate Lokibri! Yea, Nabgor of all Nabgors, I eboy thee!

Yea, Nabgor of all Nabgors, I eboy thee! I shall exmertinate Murmadake! I shall exmertinate Lokibri! Yea, Nabgor of all Nabgors, I eboy thee!

Smyke skipped several pages on which the same piece of gibberish seemed to be repeated ad infinitum. What did it mean? Had Kolibri really lost his mind, or had he joined the ranks of the literati and were these the opening words of an avant-garde novel written for his personal delectation? Then came some lines that made sense:

Day 31

Yet another gap in my memory. Two whole days! Did I really write that balderdash? What does it mean? This can't go on – I must leave here.

This morning, when I awoke with all four brains aching badly, I found Marmaduke floating lifeless in his nutrient fluid. Did the fog sample kill him, or did I?

Final evaluation of the auragram this afternoon. Tomorrow I shall pack up and leave.

Day 32

I have analysed the auragram. Am not feeling well, and not just because of what I saw on it. I must take advantage of what may be my last spell of lucidity before the fog succeeds in unhinging my mind. No time for explanations, just the salient facts:

1. *The fog isn't a meteorological phenomenon, it's a living creature. The auragram clearly displays some organic structures. It may be an animate gas.*
2. *The inhabitants of Murkholm are secretly in league with this vaporous creature. A form of unwholesome symbiosis, I suspect.*
3. *The fog drives anyone who isn't a Murkholmer insane. I know what I'm talking about.*
4. *This city is a trap! I have no explanation for this and no knowledge of the Murkholmers' intentions, but I assume them to be of a malign nature.*
5. *A connection exists between Murkholm and the rumours about Netherworld! The auragram displays structures that do not occur in any organism known to me. This fog does not emanate from the sea, it issues from the earth itself!*

Should these notes be found by someone who isn't a Murkholmer, may they serve as a warning: You, who are reading these words, make good your escape! Run for it while you still can!

I hear a knock on the door.

They've come.

They've come for me.

Kolibri's diary broke off at this point. Smyke stopped reading like someone emerging from a nightmare. His brow was beaded with sweat and it took him a moment to remember where he was.

The fog outside the lighthouse window resembled a huge spectral figure performing the dance of the seven veils. Dawn had broken while Smyke was reading.

'I'm in Murkholm,' he said dully.

There was a knock on the door. Startled, he dropped the diary.

'Professor Kolibri at last!' he cried in relief.

He hurried over to the window.

The fog was omnipresent, but not so dense as to conceal the fact that the lighthouse was surrounded: the inhabitants of Murkholm had assembled below en masse and were fixing Smyke with their watery gaze.

'They've come,' he muttered. 'They've come for me.'

V.
Krindle and Dandelion

Rumo, no fencing lesson today, we're off to the annual fair!'

Urs, who was in high spirits as they hurried towards the east gate, had been blathering about the fair for days. Countless wisps of unfamiliar scents were drifting across the city and Rumo viewed the occasion with mixed feelings. If Urs was to be believed, the main object was to eat as many different unwholesome things as possible.

By the time they reached the gate, the fairground noises were so loud that they had to shout to make themselves heard. 'Man, I've been waiting for this for exactly a year,' cried Urs, rubbing his paws together. 'The sideshows! The mulled ale! The mouse bladders!'

'Mouse bladders?' Rumo called back.

Urs handed him a purse. 'There, your fairground pocket money. With the mayor's compliments.'

The sheer size of the spectacle made Rumo gasp like a puppy who sees a sparkler for the first time. Wolperting was surrounded by hundreds of tents of every size, shape and colour. Festooned with flags, pennants and streamers, their entrances were flanked by advertising posters and blazing torches. There were round tents with pointed roofs, rectangular tents with flat ones, octagonal tents culminating in quadruple domes, tiny tents less than a metre in diameter and huge tents that jutted into the night sky like castles. The fairground was a city in itself, with streets and squares, boardwalks, steps and bridges. Extending into the woods and spanning the city's moat, it even included floating tents mounted on boats and pontoons. The whole thing had sprouted from the ground in a very short time, subjecting Wolperting to an enjoyable form of siege that was scheduled to last for a week.

Rumo marvelled at the bewildering diversity of Zamonian life forms, many of which he had never set eyes on before: Waterkins and Moomies, Cinnamen and Vulpheads, Bertts and Voltigorks, Bufadistas and Maenads, Montanic Dwarfs and Hellrazors, Yetis and Huskers, Venetian Midgets and Tellurognomes, Demigiants and Powdermen, Rickshaw Demons and Zebraskans. Still more bewildering was the fact that many of them wore bizarre costumes and masks, papier mâché heads and false noses. Others walked on stilts or rode around on absurd contraptions with wheels, waved multicoloured flags or dressed up as wandering vegetables. Many spat fire. One showman juggled with burning torches, another with talking heads.

Rumo pricked up his ears. The air was throbbing with sounds that were never to be heard on other occasions: singing saws, glockenspiels, demonic cries, Vulphead madrigals, wooden rattles, mouth drums, foot bells. Laughter rang out on all sides, mingled with shrill cries of terror from the ghost trains and the squeal of bagpipes. Hordes of musicians playing curious instruments competed for the public's attention and strove to drown each other. Bassophonists made the ground shake, a Bufadista soprano sang of unrequited love in Old Zamonian, stallholders did their best to outshout one another, rockets soared hissing into the air, paper ducks quacked, tin drums beat a tattoo. A garishly made-up Rickshaw Demon leapt at Rumo and laughingly sprinkled him with blazing confetti.

It was all too much for Rumo's sensitive ears. At a loss, he shut his eyes and instantly saw, in his mind's eye, a colossal painting composed of whirling golden spirals, dancing rainbows, writhing serpents of dazzling light, multicoloured flashes of ball lightning. He hurriedly opened his eyes again and lost his balance. 'Whoops!' he exclaimed. He blundered into Urs and had to hang on tight.

Then there were the smells: cinnamon, honey, saffron, grilled sausages, roast marsh hog, dried cod, mulled wine, smoked eel, baked apples, onion soup, incense, tobacco smoke, goose dripping. Outside most of the booths that sold food were small braziers in which garlic and onion bulbs were burnt to lend the night air an appetising aroma. Goose, chicken and turkey legs encased in clay cooked slowly in pits filled with glowing charcoal. A thick, fragrant soup of pigs' trotters and peas simmered in a massive cast-iron cauldron. Potatoes and onions were sautéed in thyme-flavoured oil, quail fried in lard, trout grilled on sticks. Legs of lamb sizzled over open fires, corn cobs and loaves of bread were baked in clay ovens. A whole ostrich revolved on a spit while ravenous Montanic Dwarfs sat round it clattering their knives and forks. Myrrh was burnt, joss sticks smouldered, masked Moomies tossed curry powder into the air. Rumo continued to cling to Urs.

'Pull yourself together,' Urs whispered in his ear. 'You're behaving like a country bumpkin visiting Atlantis for the first time. These fairground folk will gut you like a marsh hog if they see you like this. Look casual! Pretend you've seen it all a thousand times before. Just take your cue from me.'

Urs stuck his paws in his pockets, squared his shoulders and assumed an air of boredom. Then he sauntered off, deliberately dragging his feet. Rumo tried to copy his manner as faithfully as possible.

The Beesters

'Look at those Beesters from Honey Valley!' cried Urs. 'That's the legendary queen-bee honey they're selling – it's supposed to make you immortal.' He indicated a group of eye-catching individuals who were ladling honey out of big clay jars and dispensing it to their customers. They wore huge beehive hats with hundreds of bees flying busily in and out of them.

'They're reputed to be insects themselves,' Urs said with a grin. 'Gigantic queen bees. No one has ever seen them without clothes on.'

'Is that what you believe?'

'Oh, sure. They're huge, immortal queen bees and they work at the fair.' Urs laughed.

Flying pancakes

The crowd swept them along like flotsam and washed them up in front of another spectacle. A whey-faced gnome in bulky wooden clogs was tossing discs of dough into the air. They spun round and round, becoming wider and flatter. 'Fresh flying pancakes!' cried the gnome. 'Fresh flying pancakes!' A second gnome caught the discs on a flat wooden shovel and thrust them into a charcoal stove while a third fried potato chips in hot oil.

'Wait a moment,' said Urs. 'You may learn something.'

Rumo obediently came to a halt and watched the spectacle. When the pancakes were ready the gnomes removed them from the oven, fashioned them into cornets and filled them with golden-yellow chips. Urs bought one.

'With peanut butter, please!' he entreated and the first gnome anointed his cornet with a generous dollop of pale-brown goo. Urs promptly proceeded to cram his belly with greasy chips.

'One of Zamonian cuisine's most brilliant inventions,' he said, munching away. He broke off a piece of cornet and dipped it in the thick peanut sauce. 'You can even eat the packaging.'

'Hey!' said Rumo. A Vulphead wearing a brightly coloured bobble hat had come up and grabbed him by the waistcoat.

Painless scars

'How about a *painless scar?*' he asked, holding a knife with a milk-white blade under Rumo's nose. Rumo reacted instantly. He gripped the Vulphead's wrist with one paw and his throat with the other. The newcomer's face turned blue and his knife fell to the ground with a clatter.

'What about a painless dislocated neck?' Rumo retorted. Urs hurried over.

'Let him go, Rumo, that was a genuine business offer. You need only say no.'

Rumo released the Vulphead, who backed away, fighting for breath.

'My friend is from the country,' Urs said apologetically. 'This is his first annual fair.'

'That's all right,' gasped the Vulphead. 'Later, maybe. Have some mulled ale, relax! We're all friends here. We inflict the finest scars anywhere in the fairground. Later, maybe.' He retrieved his knife and walked off, grinning.

'Those knives are made of elfinjade,' Urs explained. He stuffed the rest of the potato chips into his mouth and tossed the tip of the cornet away. 'Elfinjade,' he went on with his mouth full, 'is the stuff that falls from elfinwasps' wings when they wake up and give them a shake.' He swallowed the last chip. 'If you collect elfinjade and subject it to extreme pressure, you can use it to forge knives that inflict painless cuts. You could amputate someone's arm and it wouldn't hurt. Here, look.'

He parted some clumps of fur on his right forearm to reveal a skilfully incised scar shaped like a broken heart. In the middle was a name:

Sheena

Rumo stared at it.

'Sheena of the Snows – she was *my* Silver Thread. It never came to anything, alas. She went off to Florinth. I was heartbroken.'

Urs pretended to wipe away a tear.

'That's a painless scar made by an elfinjade knife. Girls go crazy if they see you with a scar like that, especially if the name is their own.' Urs gave another wink of the kind Rumo found so puzzling.

They paused outside a tent in front of which a Demidwarf in jester's motley was alternately breathing fire and haranguing the crowd: 'Roll up! Roll up and feast your eyes on *Fredda, the Alpine Imp*, clean-shaven and hairless! The most horrific sight in Zamonia! Children not admitted! No liability for heart attacks accepted!'

Scores of people were streaming into the tent. Urs hustled his friend away.

'What's an Alpine Imp?' asked Rumo. 'Why should anyone want to pay to see something horrific?'

'Hm, who knows? Showmen don't try to sell you what you want.'

'What, then?'

'Whatever they can talk you into.'

'I don't understand.'

'We aren't here to understand anything.'

'What, then?'

'What-then-what-then! You're starting to get on my nerves. Have some fun, that's all.' Urs broke off. 'Oh, look, mouse bladders!'

Mouse bladders

They were standing in front of a huge cast-iron frying pan in which dozens of walnut-sized sausages were sizzling.

'Some mouse bladders, gentlemen?' enquired the chef, a Waterkin in a fat-bespattered apron. 'They're choicest bladders taken from pedigree Ornian Piddlemice!'

Urs raised one finger.

'Even the most sophisticated gourmets,' he pontificated in solemn tones, 'are bowled over by the subtle flavour of an expertly prepared mouse bladder the first time they sample one. The secret is to keep the bladder intact when you pipe the mousemeat stuffing through its cystic canals. The meat must be minced at least thirty-three times until it's almost liquid, rendered even more so by the addition of garlic juice, sour cream and mouse gravy, and seasoned with dilute salt, paprika and olive oil. Many chefs add cumin, but that's barbaric. The stuffing must be loaded into a cake icer and pumped into the interior of the mouse organ until it's filled to bursting. Finally, the cystic canals are tied off with kitchen twine to keep the juices from escaping.'

Saliva was trickling from the corners of Urs's mouth.

'Next, equal quantities of butter and olive oil are heated in a heavy cast-iron pan and the bladders fried for a few minutes until golden-brown. They are then kept warm until consumption by being gently smoked over a liquorice-root grill. It should be added that the bladder of the South Ornian Piddlemouse - the only mouse of which this dish should consist! - is one of the most hard-working digestive organs to be found in any Zamonian life form. In fact, this industrious variety of mouse spends nearly all its life passing water, hence the elasticity and concentrated flavour of its bladder. One's first taste of mouse bladder is a positive revelation. Two portions, please!'

'Well?' Urs asked expectantly. He had watched with growing exasperation as Rumo tossed bladder after bladder into his mouth and gulped them down without chewing them even once. His friend showed no signs of enjoyment, still less rapture.

'Huh?' Rumo said vaguely.

'Those mouse bladders! Tasty?'

The ghost train

'Oh . . . Yes, thanks.' Rumo tossed the empty paper bag heedlessly over his shoulder. He had spotted Rala queuing up outside a huge black tent adorned with posters advertising the unspeakable attractions inside.

'Hey, that's a ghost train,' Urs said with his mouth full. 'We must try it - definitely!' He walked over to the posters and started to read them. Rumo trailed after him, never letting Rala out of his sight. She hadn't noticed him in the crowd.

'Listen to this! They claim that the horrific figures inside are all real! Apparently, they cut down the victims of hangings and embalm them, then string 'em up again, ho ho! Nerves of steel required, eh?'

Urs tossed the last of the mouse bladders into his mouth. 'They rob the graves in cemeteries reserved for outlaws - you can do what you like with them. Those graveyards are run by genuine Barley Moomies and Forest Demons! Look at that list there - it gives the number of deaths that have occurred on the ghost train: fourteen heart attacks, seven strokes and one suicide! And that's all in *one* season! Man! We can't afford to miss this!' Urs giggled inanely.

Rumo didn't feel like paying someone good money to try to frighten him. He was past being frightened since his adventures on Roaming Rock.

'It says someone on this ghost train was so scared by a Moomy, he developed a nosebleed that simply wouldn't stop until it drained his body dry. They've left him here as a permanent attraction, going round and round in a car filled with his own congealed blood.'

Rumo was covertly watching Rala.

Urs followed the direction of his gaze. 'Hey, there's Rala. She's going for a ride too.'

Rumo would have found it quite impossible to walk up to Rala and accost her – he would sooner have picked a fight with a dozen of the Bluddums employed to push the fairground swingboats. Before he could pursue that thought any further, Urs had fixed everything. He simply went up to Rala and laid a hand on her shoulder. They exchanged a few words, then Urs beckoned to Rumo, who walked stiffly towards them. He stuck out his paw and mouthed some form of salutation when he was still yards away. Why didn't his body obey him when Rala was close at hand? Why did her proximity always make him feel as if there were two of him – as if he could see himself and his own awkward gestures? What was the magical power that emanated from this girl and why was Urs unaffected by it? He resolved to shake Rala's paw, gently but firmly, gaze deep into her eyes and speak in a slow, clear, sonorous voice.

'Hello, Rumo,' Rala said affably. They were the very first words she had ever addressed to him.

'Er, hello,' Rumo replied in a muffled voice, lowering his eyes. He withdrew his paw just as Rala was about to shake it. Then he blushed and stared at the ground. Urs shot him a reproving glance.

'We're going together,' Urs said firmly. 'It'll work out cheaper for all of us.' Rumo stood rooted to the spot. His mouth was so dry that he was afraid of biting his tongue if he spoke, so he said nothing.

'There are some genuine Kackerbats flying around in there, so watch your coiffure!' Urs told Rala jocularly as he boarded the car with Rumo and sat her down between them. The car was a tight squeeze, so they sat squashed together. A change came over Rumo when he felt Rala's arm against his: he started to sweat.

'Hey, are you scared?' asked Rala, who had noticed his uneasy expression.

'I'm never scared,' Rumo replied hoarsely.

'Oho,' said Rala, imitating his croak. 'So you're never scared, eh?'

A Yeti bent over the car and secured the door.

'In the event of a fatality during the ride,' he said darkly, 'kindly don't throw the corpse out of the car. The Ghouls would eat it and they're supposed to be on a diet.'

Urs and Rala tittered. Rumo tried to join in, but his contorted facial muscles refused to relax into a smile. He looked as if he might throw up at any moment.

'Have a good scare!' The Yeti gave them a wave as the car glided past him into the gloom beyond the swing door. 'And never forget: life is more horrific than death!'

Darkness engulfed them. All that could be heard was the rattle of the car and the distant screams of other passengers. Rumo tried to ignore the alarming scents, but he couldn't: there seemed to be a lot of malign spirits lurking in the gloom. A thin, plaintive cry rang out. It was only just audible, like a final plea for help from someone buried alive.

'Ooh!' Rala exclaimed, feigning terror. She nestled still closer to Rumo. A miniature flat car came clanking out of the darkness. On it was the dimly illuminated figure of a dead dwarf sitting in a tub of congealed blood.

As they passed it, Rumo noticed a cobweb clinging to the head of the desiccated corpse and a rent in the neck from which sawdust was escaping. Rivulets of blood were trickling down the figure's chest and into the tub.

The Hedgewitch

The car stopped abruptly. With a thunderclap the ground ahead of them opened. There was a shellburst of red and yellow paper streamers, a cloud of green vapour arose and, when it dispersed, they were confronted by a gigantic Hedgewitch. She wore a robe of autumn leaves, her limbs were thin, gnarled branches and two will-o'-the-wisps glimmered in the empty eye sockets in her wooden skull. Her lower jaw dropped open and released a white moth into the darkness. A hot wind swirled round the car as the witch reached for Rala's face with her pointed, thorny fingers. Rala clung so tightly to Rumo that he could feel almost the whole of her body against his – the most thrilling sensation he'd ever experienced.

'I'm going to faint,' he thought with a frisson of ecstasy.

But he remained conscious. There was another clap of thunder and the witch vanished. Rala continued to hang on tight. 'Was she real?' she asked.

'Yes,' said Urs. 'Real but stuffed.'

The witch had, in fact, been the ride's pièce de résistance. Like all ghost trains, this one had promised more than it delivered. The desiccated corpses that danced around in the flickering light may have been real, but the malign spirits Rumo had sensed were probably just the ghost train's staff of down-at-heel Bluddums and other riff-raff, who filled the tunnels with spooky cries and acted as ghosts in ill-draped bed sheets.

Rumo could scarcely stand when he climbed out of the car. His knees were knocking, he was trembling all over, and his fur was glistening with perspiration.

'The witch was good,' said Urs, 'but the rest . . .'

'So you don't know the meaning of fear, eh?' Rala said to Rumo. She laughed, but her laughter sounded friendly and unmalicious.

Outside in the milling crowd Rumo tried desperately to think of some snappy retort, but before he could do so Rala had been spotted by someone. It was Rolv, who was standing on the other side of the street with Balla, Olek and a girl whom Rumo recognised from school. Rolv waved. Rala left Rumo's side without a word, elbowed her way through the throng and threw her arms round Rolv's neck.

Rumo gasped. Since when had they been so friendly? There! Rala had given Rolv a kiss on the cheek! The ground seemed to yawn at his feet. Then a party of roistering fair goers surged past, hiding Rolv, Rala and the others from view, and they were gone.

'Girls,' Urs said with a shrug. 'You never know where you are with them.'

Rumo shut his eyes and tried to make out the Silver Thread, but his mental images were so chaotic he might have been peering into a kaleidoscope. Smouldering herbs, rank sweat and crude smells of all kinds combined to form such a rotating mishmash of colours that he hurriedly opened his eyes again. If he'd had to rely for guidance on his nose alone, he would have blundered into the nearest tent pole.

'Come on, we haven't seen anything yet!'

Rumo plodded sullenly along in Urs's wake. How this din was getting on his nerves! The vulgar music! The stench! Why had Rala thrown herself into the arms of *that* repulsive creature? Why had she done so in front of everyone? Why in front of *him*? How had that little terrier become so pally with her? What was he himself doing in this lunatic asylum of a fairground? He longed to go home.

'Hey, you!' yelled a voice in Rumo's sensitive ears. A gaunt and peculiarly hideous black-robed figure had planted itself in front of him and was pointing at him accusingly with a pencil-thin forefinger.

'Yes, you!'

The Ugglies

Rumo and Urs had reached the intersection of two tent-lined avenues. Three female figures attired in black were dancing round a big iron cauldron into which they periodically tossed small, squeaking creatures. It was one of them who had barred Rumo's path. Most of the fairgoers steered well clear of this spectacle.

'Ugglies,' Urs whispered. 'Don't let them foist a prophecy on you.'

'You!' cried the tallest of the Ugglies, levelling her long finger at Rumo. 'Listen to me! I'm the Uggly Posko!'

Urs tugged at Rumo's sleeve, but he was rooted to the spot.

'You! You are destined to see in the dark and kill the one-eyed giants!'

'I already did,' Rumo said quietly.

'Eh, what?' said the Uggly. 'Ah yes, that was in the past. All this noise is spoiling my concentration.'

Rumo was amazed. Smyke was the only one who knew anything about him and Roaming Rock.

'Did you really?' asked Urs. 'Kill some one-eyed giants, I mean?'

'Concentration be damned!' cried another of the Ugglies, who was short and fat. 'You've never managed to prophesy about anything except the past, Posko! Come here, youngster, I'm the Uggly Krasko! *I* can tell you the future. You'll walk along streets of solid gold, and health and wealth will be your constant companions throughout a long, happy life! Permit me to fill in the details!'

'You lying devil!' shouted the third Uggly. 'Beware of her, youngster, she'll only tell you what you want to hear! Consult *me*, the Uggly Bisko! I can predict the only important thing in your life: whether or not you'll win your Silver Thread. That's what matters, isn't it? I know you Wolpertings!'

Rumo pricked up his ears at this. He got out his purse.

Urs took his arm. 'Put it away! They'll only cheat you.'

'Isn't that what fairs are for?'

A dwarf with a placard on his chest suddenly appeared on the scene.

Nightingale is everywhere

'Enough of this oracular guesswork!' he yelled. 'Enough of this disreputable hocus-pocus! Consult Professor Abdullah Nightingale's chest-of-drawers oracle in the Star Tent! Only that will provide you with scientifically attested prophecies! Absolutely reliable predictions on a purely empirical basis! No commercialism involved! Admission free!'

The tall Uggly aimed a kick at the dwarf, who nimbly dodged it and disappeared into the crowd. 'Enough of this oracular guesswork!' he croaked again. Then his voice was drowned by the general tumult. Urs took advantage of the rumpus to drag Rumo away.

'Hey, but I was going to–'

'Tell me, what was all that about one-eyed giants, et cetera?'

'Nothing special.'

'Nothing special? Come on now!'

A noisy crowd of revellers came dancing along the street towards them: dwarfs, gnomes, a few Bluddums, several Maenads and Bertts, dozens of Yetis, all in shabby costumes and clearly the worse for drink. They were waving little flags and wooden rattles, and splashing passers-by with the contents of huge pitchers of beer. Unprepared for such an onslaught, Urs and Rumo were borne along by them. It wasn't until they'd been swept past a few dozen booths that they managed to extricate themselves from the mob. Panting hard, they took stock of their surroundings.

A prize-fighting tent run by Bluddums.

A booth where blood could be pawned.

A shadow theatre.

A coconut shy.

A black tent adorned with twinkling stars. The inconspicuous sign above the entrance read:

Professor Abdullah Nightingale's
Zamonian Chest-of-Drawers Oracle.
Strictly scientific predictions.
None of your usual fairground hocus-pocus.

Finally, an unmarked red tent from whose golden-domed roof dense black smoke was ascending into the sky.

'What's that red tent? Is it on fire?'

The phogar dealer

Urs whispered conspiratorially in Rumo's ear. 'That's a phogar tent, my friend. Nothing for sensitive souls.'

Phogars? Smyke had enthused about them occasionally, Rumo recalled.

'They aren't allowed to advertise. Atlantean health regulations prohibit it, but they can't prevent lungless people from having a smoke.'

'But we've got lungs.'

'What makes you so sure? Can you see inside yourself? Perhaps you're one of nature's miracles. You'll never know if you don't try one.' Urs hustled Rumo towards the entrance of the phogar tent. 'I've always wanted to try a phogar. Come on, I'll stand you one.'

The phogar dealer, an uncouth Turniphead in an ill-fitting turban, eyed them suspiciously. 'Is this your first phogar? I don't want any trouble with the Atlantean health ministry.'

'I was smoking phogars before these ridiculous laws existed,' Urs declared with surprising self-assurance. 'And my brother here doesn't even have one lung – a congenital defect. Two phogars, please.'

The phogar dealer looked past them to see if he could spot any Atlantean health inspectors in the crowd. Then he beckoned them into the tent. 'You must be one of nature's miracles,' he said, handing Urs the phogars. 'That'll be four pyras.'

Rumo's first puff seemed to fill his lungs with boiling fog. He tried to expel the smoke at once, but his throat felt as if it were in a noose. Panic-stricken, he looked at Urs, who was sitting opposite him with his back propped against the wall of the tent. He, too, had lowered his phogar after the first puff. His body looked like a candle left too close to a hot stove and his face was melting like butter in the sun. He seemed to be dissolving completely.

Was that the effect of Urs's phogar or his own? Rumo would have liked to ask him, but he couldn't speak, let alone breathe. His panic intensified. Perhaps some oxygen would help.

He staggered past the phogar dealer and made for the entrance, fighting for breath.

'So you aren't one of nature's miracles after all, eh?' the Turniphead said unfeelingly. 'You can't force it, youngster. The smoke will either exit of its own accord or not at all. The worst thing is to exert pressure. Just don't breathe!'

Rumo tottered along the avenue. Noises, sights, smells – everything became amalgamated into a vortex that whirled around him. Dwarfs wearing sandwich-boards cried their wares:

'Roll up, roll up! Discuss Florinthian torturers' techniques with the Talking Gallows! Age-old folkloric information humorously imparted!'

'Rice-grain literature! Rice-grain literature! Whole novels inscribed by Bonsai Mites on grains of creamed rice! Hundreds of titles in stock!'

'Walk up, walk up! See Fredda the horrible, hairless Alpine Imp. Even the thickest-skinned can scarcely endure the sight! Get the heeby-jeebies or your money back!'

Rumo tottered on through the jostling fairgoers. Was that Rala drifting past? Rolv? Balla and Olek? Were they laughing at him? The smoke rampaged around his chest and rattled his ribs like a wild beast in a cage.

He bumped into someone he could cling to for support. Then he vomited, retching up everything inside him: his breakfast, the mouse bladders, the phogar smoke.

'Hey!' The voice seemed to come from very far away. 'My jacket!'

Rumo passed out.

'Phogars only agree with Shark Grubs, and I wouldn't advise even them to smoke one. Are you a Shark Grub? No. Are you an idiot? Yes.'

Who had said that? It was pitch-black.

'My lovely jacket – ruined, in all probability. Mouse bladders! Greasy, unwholesome things, almost worthless from the nutritional point of view. That plus the phogar smoke. A disastrous combination.'

Where was he? Lying on the ground, apparently. Rumo raised his head.

'Hello?' he said feebly. 'Anyone there?'

Two lights went on in the darkness. No, not lights, they were eyes. Huge, luminous yellow eyes. Was he dreaming?

'No, you aren't dreaming,' the voice said rather curtly. 'That's what a Nocturnomath's eyes look like in the dark. And yes, I'm something of a mind-reader. As for the gap in your memory, you smoked a phogar, suffered a temporary collapse of the lungs and puked over my jacket. Now you're in my Star Tent. More precisely, in *Professor Abdullah Nightingale's Incorruptible Chest-of-Drawers Oracle.* Admission free, but I ought to claim compensation for the jacket. Would you like a little light?'

A match flared and a candle was lit. Rumo could see the Nocturnomath better now. He differed in appearance from Professor Kolibri. There were some strange excrescences protruding from his head and he looked older. But in other respects: the same puny physique, the same wrinkled face, the same huge, glowing eyes.

'What you call "excrescences" are my external brains. I don't like to brag, but I possess seven brains.' The gnome gave a little self-deprecating cough.

It was silent. Amazing how little of the fairground din penetrated the tent. None at all, in fact.

'This tent is made of noise-absorbent silk obtained from deaf silkworms, an invention that could make me another fortune if I went into mass production. It's the thickness of a fingernail, but an entire brass band could play in here and you wouldn't hear a single note outside. The same thing applies in reverse, of course. You've no idea the noises the material emits when I give it its monthly whacking with a carpet beater.'

In the middle of the tent, as far as Rumo could make out, stood a chest of drawers. It was absolutely plain and made of dark, almost black, wood. He debated whether to mention that he'd heard of Nightingale from Professor Kolibri. Rather than complicate matters unnecessarily, he decided not to.

'My name is Rumo,' he said instead. 'Rumo of Zamonia.'

'Like the card game? How original. I've played a few games of rumo myself. It was in that gambler's paradise called—'

Rumo stood up. He yearned to go home. 'Well, many thanks for your hospitality. Where's the exit?' In spite of the candle, it was still so dark that all he could see was the chest of drawers.

'Yes, it's pretty dark in here,' said the professor. 'But there are miracles that can only occur in the dark.'

'Where's the exit, please?'

'You don't want to try out my oracle?'

'Er, to be honest: no. I'm not feeling too good and I've had it up to here with this fairground hocus-pocus.'

Nightingale's eyes flashed and something inside his head crackled ominously. 'Hocus-pocus?' he hissed. 'This isn't hocus-pocus, it's scientific exactitude!'

'I'm sure it is, but . . .'

Accusingly, Nightingale held his soiled jacket to the candlelight. The sight was so nauseating that Rumo heaved despite himself.

'Sit down on that chair.'

Rumo blinked. Yes, there was a chair behind him. He sat down. 'All right, if it won't take long.'

'No, no, it's over in a flash. You open a drawer, that's all.'

'Very well.'

'I'll explain the whole thing. Shall I quickly infect you with the information?' Nightingale approached with his forefinger levelled at Rumo's ear.

Rumo shuddered, involuntarily remembering the Kolibri-Smyke episode. 'No,' he said, I'd rather not.'

Nightingale withdrew his finger, looking disappointed. 'In that case it's the slow and laborious way. Would you like a detailed exposition or the short version?'

Rumo groaned faintly and clutched his head. 'The short version, please.'

'Right, we'll skip the theoretical aspect and spare ourselves the scientific minutiae. All you need to know is this: That chest of drawers there, which you probably assume to be made of wood, consists of highly concentrated darkness – darkness dating from a time when time did not exist. It's the only material in the universe – if material it may be called! – that is free from the shackles of time and capable of summoning up the future. If you ask me how I managed to—'

Rumo gave another groan.

'All right, no details, just the crux of the matter. I'm not interested in foretelling the future, to be honest. That's just an amusing by-product of my invention. No, what interests me is *the effect on people of knowing their own future*. In other words, how much future they can endure. At the very least, it will confirm my theory that no existing Zamonian life form – Nocturnomaths excepted, of course – can really bear to know its own future. Are you prepared to help me discover the truth, Card Game?'

'My name is Rumo.'

'Sorry, I got a trifle mixed up.' Nightingale's brains crackled again. 'It's quite simple. You must think of the name of someone whose future you want to know. If you want to see your own future, simply think of your own name. Then the drawer bearing the first letter of your name will open and you can look inside. There won't be all that much to see – just a glimpse, that's all. Then the drawer will close again and that'll be that.'

'Yes, all right,' said Rumo. 'Can we begin?'

'At once, but first I must extinguish the candle. As I already said, some miracles can only occur in the dark.'

Nightingale blew out the candle, plunging the tent in total darkness.

'In the meantime,' he said, 'I shall go and take a look at that Alpine Imp. If the creature's genuine it would be a scientific sensation.'

A chink of light appeared and blaring fairground music filled the air. Then the chink vanished, and darkness and silence returned. Nightingale had left the tent.

For a moment Rumo toyed with the idea of simply disappearing. Then he remembered the professor's ruined jacket and concentrated on the chest of drawers. It was strange, but he couldn't see it with his inner eye. It had no smell and made no sound – not even a woodworm was munching away inside it. But of course, it wasn't made of wood, it was supposed to be made of . . . He'd forgotten, but never mind.

He deliberated. What name should he choose? His own, of course! Or should he? Did he really want to know his own future? What if it was extremely unpleasant? Perhaps he should think of Urs's name, then he could surprise him by making a few predictions. But wait, that was it: Rala! He would eavesdrop on Rala's future; then he'd know whether or not he played an important part in it.

He tried to concentrate on the invisible chest of drawers. 'Rala,' he thought. 'Rala . . .'

Nothing.

He tried again. 'Raaala . . . R-A-L-A. Rala, Rala, Rala!'

A light appeared in the gloom – a narrow strip of cold blue light that steadily widened into a glowing rectangle. A drawer had actually slid open!

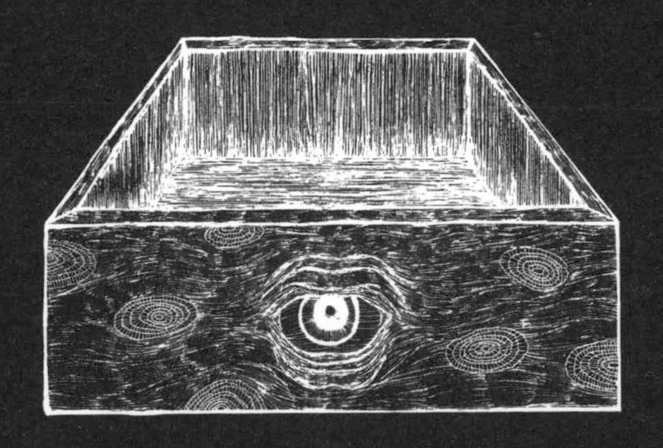

Rumo leant forward and peered inside. The blue glow seemed to make the darkness surrounding him even darker, as if he and the drawer were hovering in a starless universe of infinite size. He bent over it. Now he could see something. Was it a sculpture? No, it was . . . a metal coffin made of grey lead with copper fittings. Was this supposed to be Rala's future? Then the curious scene came to life: the coffin was slowly opening. Rumo stared at it fixedly as the lid folded back in two halves like a double door. He could now make out a figure lying inside it. He peered more closely – and started back in horror: it was Rala! She didn't move, just lay there stiff and silent. Was it all an illusion? The after-effects of his phogar trip? He was about to get up and leave these unpleasant surroundings when he heard a sob. Was it Rala? No, she was still lying motionless. Then he caught sight of another figure kneeling beside the coffin. It was himself! Yes, he was looking at himself kneeling in tears beside Rala's coffin! Now he knew what the oracle was showing him: Rala's death. The worst part was that he could tell the scene was set in the not too distant future. He and Rala were not grey and decrepit, but little older than they were now. The scene showed Rala's imminent death.

'No!' Rumo cried desperately. He made a lunge for the drawer, but the darkness around him uttered a furious roar and the drawer emitted an icy blast that seemed to come from the depths of a tomb. Then it slammed shut.

Silence.

Rumo sat there in total darkness, weeping.

The Kingdom of Death

'She really is a genuine Alpine Imp,' Nightingale muttered as he entered the tent. 'The last of her kind – incredible! I shall have to purchase her.' He lit the candle and saw Rumo kneeling on the floor in tears. Too embarrassed to speak for a while, he tidied some things away. At length he said, 'You saw into the Kingdom of Death, didn't you?'

Rumo didn't answer.

'I'd like to be able to tell you it was all an illusion, a fairground conjuring trick, but you know better. You sensed it. The oracle isn't malevolent or spiteful, it simply shows some random moment in the future, coldly and objectively. In your case that moment must have been particularly distressing. I'm sorry.'

'I must go,' said Rumo, rising to his feet.

'Hey, wait, young Wolperting. You won't do anything silly, will you?'

Rumo headed in the direction from which he'd seen Nightingale enter. The professor hurried after him and caught him by the sleeve.

'Wait a moment!'

As if deprived of will-power, Rumo came to a halt.

Negative infection

'You can't go out there like that, what would people think? More important, you can't go through life like that; it would be too wretched for words. Let me take a little of the burden off your shoulders.' Nightingale seized Rumo's paw and held it tight. His voice suddenly rang out in Rumo's head.

'What you're now experiencing is a negative infection, also known as Nightingale's Lightning Amnesia. The technique requires a great deal of practice. I doubt if anyone with fewer than seven brains could master it.'

Rumo's head started to spin. He clung to Nightingale's hand.

'Your distressing knowledge of the future will now be mine. I can cope with it. One of my seven brains will absorb it with ease and convert it into pure information. In a moment you'll leave this tent remembering nothing. Many thanks for your help, but I'm afraid this discovery will have to be consigned to the Chamber of Unperfected Patents. People are not mature enough to handle the future – or not insensitive enough.

'Even though you can never escape what you saw, it won't prey on your mind until you actually experience it. Until then, young Wolperting, all the best.'

Nightingale released Rumo's paw and thrust him outside. The din, the smells, the pandemonium of the fair descended on him like a sudden hailstorm. He stood outside Nightingale's tent completely dazed. Turning round, he read:

Professor Abdullah Nightingale's
Zamonian Chest-of-Drawers Oracle

An oracle. Just about the last thing he felt like right now. He was feeling nauseous. Where to now? Home, that's where. Where was Urs?

Choose your weapon!

Rumo tottered along the tent-lined avenue. Phogars, ugh! What revolting things! He would never, ever, be talked into . . . A paw came down on his shoulder. It was Urs.

'Rumo! I've been looking for you everywhere!'

'I threw up.'

'Me too! Four times! Know what's so great about it?'

'No.'

'I'm stone-cold sober.' Urs beamed and spread his arms. 'We can start again from scratch! How about a few mouse bladders?'

'You must be joking! I want to go home.'

'Home? Now? And miss one of the greatest experiences of your life?'

'What's that, another ride on a ghost train? Another phogar?'

'No, no, Rumo, the absolute highlight of the night. It's my official duty as your municipal friend.' Urs thumped himself on the chest. 'First, though, I need something to eat. Come on.'

Urs conducted him to the nearest mouse bladder stall and devoured another portion of mouse bladders while Rumo stood alongside, surveying the throng of revellers with an air of disdain. Then he remembered Rala and Rolv, and his spirits sank to their lowest ebb.

'Pin your ears back, Rumo,' said Urs. He belched. 'We're now coming to the ceremonial part of these proceedings. The great moment.'

'Get on with it, then!'

'Follow me.'

Urs led the way – irritatingly slowly, it seemed to Rumo. They turned off down an alleyway where the noise was somewhat more subdued.

Passing a flower stall, a lottery stand and a roast-chestnut vendor, they came to a big, dark tent with two torches outside.

'You like reading signboards,' Urs said eagerly. 'Tell me what's written on that one up there . . .'

'*Choose . . . your . . . weapon*,' Rumo read. 'Choose your weapon.'

'Precisely.'

'What do you mean, precisely?'

'It's an invitation. You can choose yourself a weapon.'

'I don't understand.'

'This is the Wolperting Weapon Tent!' Urs announced solemnly. 'You can go inside and choose a weapon – your weapon for life, I mean – and I, as your municipal friend, am allowed to assist you. Don't worry about the expense, it's already settled. Every new Wolperting is permitted to select a weapon at his first annual fair. You know, civic rights and duties. This is one of your rights. It's an ancient tradition – it dates back to Hoth's day and—'

'One moment!' Rumo cut in. 'You mean I can simply walk in there and choose myself a weapon? Why didn't you tell me this before?'

'I didn't want to spoil our night out. I know you: once you've chosen the thing you won't have eyes for anything else. All right, get in there!' Urs propelled him towards the entrance.

The interior of the tent was sparsely illuminated by a few torches. Around the sides stood some long wooden tables and several cabinets, and there was a massive iron table in the centre.

Rumo scanned the arsenal on display. The tables were laden with heavy battleaxes, two-edged swords, balls and chains, and halberds. Elegant rapiers, graded according to length and tensile strength, reposed in wooden stands. Laid out on one of the tables were at least two hundred bows, many of them as long as Rumo was tall. There were racks of iron-bound clubs and cabinets filled with throwing knives, spears, foils, spiked throwing discs, knuckledusters, gutting knives and scythes. Heavy hammers designed to be chained to the wrist rubbed shoulders with single, double, triple or even quadruple crossbows, barbed switchblades and glass daggers from Florinth.

'Weapons!' Urs said distastefully. 'Pooh!'

'Heavens alive,' said Rumo. 'What a vast selection. How is one supposed to decide?'

'By a process of elimination,' Urs advised.

Rumo toured the tables. Urs was right: a lot of the weapons could be ruled out right away. For instance, only barbarians used those spiked balls on chains. Halberds he considered ridiculously impractical - too big, too heavy and less of a help than a hindrance in confined spaces. Clubs and hammers: ideal weapons for clumsy great hunks like Yetis and Bluddums. Spiked throwing discs and daggers had their points but were secondary weapons; a sword was infinitely preferable. That narrowed the choice down to sabres, swords, rapiers and cut-and-thrust weapons in general. Rumo went over to the bows and crossbows. They were splendid pieces of equipment made of the finest woods and sinews, adorned and reinforced with precious metals. A crossbow or a bow and arrow enabled you to hunt and kill an enemy at a safe distance. On the other hand, a well-aimed sword or stiletto could kill just as effectively, and one could hardly parry a blade with a longbow. Ergo, it had to be a blade of some kind. Rumo went over to the sword.

The sword

Some hundred blades were lying higgledy-piggledy on the big black table top. Huge, two-handed broadswords for delivering sweeping blows, elegant Florinthian rapiers with needle-sharp points and decorative engraving, single-handed swords forged out of dozens of laminae, ordinary military swords ground on both sides, épées, Midgardian cavalry sabres, twin-bladed knives, scimitars with serrated blades. And a small sword of unusual conformation: the blade was slit down the middle like a snake's forked tongue.

'Take me!' the sword said in a piping voice.

Rumo jumped back in alarm. Had Urs whispered in his ear? No, Urs was standing beside a table on the other side of the tent, distastefully eyeing a ball and chain.

'Take me!' the sword repeated. *'I'm the weapon for you.'*

Rumo stared at it in amazement.

'Forget the other stuff,' it said. *'That's just common or garden rubbish. I'm a work of art.'*

'What?!' said Rumo.

'What?' said Urs. He glanced across at Rumo, but Rumo didn't reply. He seemed to be examining a sword.

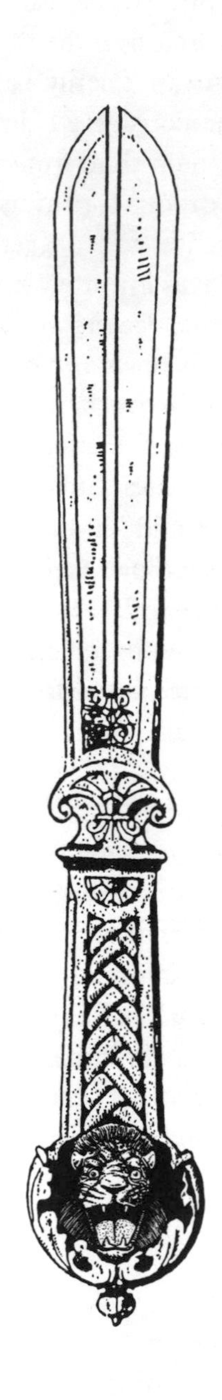

'Don't answer me aloud, answer me in your head if you don't want to look like an idiot,' said the sword. *'The others can't hear me.'*

'What's the matter with me?' thought Rumo. 'Am I going mad?'

'Not yet,' said the sword, *'but it could easily happen – once you've seen me in action. You wouldn't believe the things I can do. I specialise in the impossible.'*

Rumo peered harder. No, the sword wasn't moving. Where was the voice coming from?

'It's time you caught on: I'm a talking sword! Or rather, a sword with telepathic powers. The last word in modern weapons technology.'

The voice wasn't coming from outside, it was in his head.

'That's right, take your time, you'll get there in the end. It isn't every day one comes across a weapon endowed with reason. Actually, that's a contradiction in terms, ha ha! No, seriously, I'm a blade made of sacred steel, forged to perfection and destined for your paw alone. Other Wolpertings wanted to take me, but I strongly urged them not to and they all complied. I advise you to do likewise.'

'You want me to choose something else, you mean?' Rumo queried in his head.

'No, stupid! To listen to my advice!'

'Who are you calling stupid?'

'It would be stupid to turn me down, that's all I meant. I'm a bargain.'

Rumo was bewildered. Uncertainly, he looked across at Urs, who was idly feeling the blade of an axe. He didn't appear to have noticed a thing.

'Who are you?' Rumo asked.

'I'm poetry in motion! I'm a death wish in steel – the death being that of your enemies, of course, not yours! I'm your comrade in arms! I'm a fanfare ringing out over a corpse-strewn battlefield! I'm the triumphant cry of the victor pursuing his defeated foe! I'm—'

'Where do you come from?'

'From Demon Range.'

'And how did you get here?'

'Are you ready to hear my story?'

Rumo cast another glance at Urs, who was aiming a crossbow at some invisible enemies. 'Yes, go ahead.'

History of a Demonic Sword

'Dwarfsmiths forged me out of ores mined from Demon Range. I'm an alloy of petrified Demons' brains and minerals from outer space – an explosive combination, my friend. My blade yearns to do battle, my—'

'What are these demons of yours? I want no truck with demons.'

'Er, they're good Demons, naturally – Demons of the first water. The thing is, there was this battle between good and evil Demons in Devil's Gulch. I'm sure you've heard of it.'

'No, I haven't.'

'You haven't? Well, never mind, it doesn't matter. It was all to do with this, er, Golden Apple that was supposed to make anyone who carried it invisible and . . . Anyway, we fell out over this stupid apple, one insult led to another, blah-blah-blah, and, before you could say knife, a pitched battle broke out – you know how it is. Demons' innards were spurting in all directions. It was the biggest bloodbath for . . . well, for quite some time. The battle went on for a year. Springtime came and we hacked off each other's arms. Summer came and we skewered each other with spears. Autumn came and we riddled each other with arrows. Winter came and—'

'Yes, yes,' Rumo thought impatiently. 'Can't you make it a bit shorter?'

'All right. Nobody really won and in the end we were all dead, ha ha! Then we were buried in Demon Range. They laid us to rest in a subterranean cave. Can you imagine? All those dripping stalagmites – or should it be stalactites? No matter. Anyway, there we lay for thousands of years, turning to stone with the water dripping on our heads: plip, plop, plip, get it? Then suddenly – CRASH! – this meteor slammed into the mountains and crushed us all, creating the largest and most productive mine in Zamonia.'

'Your corpse was crushed by a meteor?'

'Yes, a gigantic meteor composed of iron straight from outer space. The result was a mixture of rock and cosmic iron, and embedded in it the crushed remains of some top-grade Demons, you follow me? Then came the miners, who dug out this splendid super-ore from outer space, the finest iron ore in Zamonia, if not the entire world. They kept coming across petrified Demons' corpses and, being superstitious and anxious to propitiate the Demonic spirits, they forged a sword in honour of every corpse they discovered. They took the Demons' petrified brains, pulverised them and sprinkled the powder into the molten meteoric iron. And that's

the origin of the legendary Demonic Swords. No idea why we're capable of thought. It must have something to do with the stuff from space. Sounds weird, doesn't it? Yoo-hoo, I'm a Demonic Sword!'

Rumo felt a heavy paw on his shoulder. He uttered a startled cry.

'Man, oh man,' said Urs. 'That thing must appeal to you. You've been gawping at it for ages.'

'I'll take it,' said Rumo. 'That's my chosen weapon.'

Having left the weapons tent, Urs and Rumo allowed themselves to be swept along for a while by the jostling, shoving throng.

'Why did you settle on *that* toothpick?' Urs demanded. 'You could have picked a hundred-layered sword of finest Florinthian steel, or something similar.'

Rumo decided to keep his secret to himself. 'What next?' he asked, to change the subject.

Urs paused for thought, but only briefly. 'We'll drink a tankard of mulled ale. Or two. That would be a fitting conclusion to an eventful day. What do you say?'

Rumo nodded. A drink he could handle. He was genuinely thirsty.

A rude awakening

Even in his dreams Rumo could hear fairground music blaring and see a grotesque procession of stilt walkers and Vulpheads, Ugglies and dwarfs. He also saw Rala kissing and holding hands with Rolv. Vulpheads seized him and adorned him all over with painless scars, Urs kept falling headlong and threatening him with a bagful of mouse bladders. Then he dreamt that the little creatures living between his teeth had moved into his brain, where they erected a city just behind his eyes and between his ears. They banged and sawed away, tossed stones around and battered his skull with sledgehammers. They forged a demonic bell out of meteoric iron and hung it in his auditory canals. Then they began to toll it.

He woke up. It was the midday chimes of the City Hall clock that had roused him, and merciless sunlight was streaming through his open bedroom window. His head was buzzing like the beehive hats of the Beesters from Honey Valley. Groaning, he got out of bed.

He'd never woken up feeling so shattered, not even after his fight with Rolv. His tongue felt as if he'd left it in a bucket of ashes overnight, his teeth, tongue and gums seemed to have sprouted fur. The blood throbbed painfully in his skull and there was a roaring in his ears like surf. Had he fallen ill for the first time in his life?

Rumo tottered over to the window. Some young Wolpertings were kicking up a din in the street below. Couldn't they talk a little more quietly? He picked up the water jug and drained it in a few gulps.

He tried to remember. The fair. Rala, naturally. Urs. Mouse bladders. Rolv – ouch! A sharp pain in his left ear. Rolv and Rala holding hands – that hadn't been a bad dream. What else? The Ugglies. That phogar – ugh! He promptly felt sick again at the thought of it. The ghost train. What else? What else?

'Good morning!' a cheerful voice exclaimed inside his head. *'Did you sleep well? You must have, the way you were snoring.'*

He noticed only now that there was a sword lying on his table.

Choose your weapon!

Of course, the weapons tent. Had he really chosen this grotesque little sword? Another sharp pain, this time in the right ear.

'I'm genuinely sick,' Rumo said to himself. 'Sick in the head. I'm hearing voices.' He sat down on the bed with his paws over his ears.

'Lost your memory?' said the voice in his head. *'Too much mulled ale? It's me, your chosen weapon!'*

Mulled ale . . . Yes, the last thing he could remember was the mulled ale stall. All those tankards he'd poured down his throat on an empty stomach. Drunk for the first time in his life! Yes, he could remember crawling around on all fours like a wild Wolperting. He felt ashamed.

'What about the Painless Scars Tent?'

Was that his own voice? A warning voice in his brain? *Painless Scars?*

'Brush aside the fur on your left arm and see what's written there, ha ha!'

Mechanically, Rumo complied. He brushed the fur aside – and froze. Someone had carved something into the skin, leaving a painless scar. It was a crimson heart with a word in the middle:

Rala

There was a knock. Urs came in without waiting for an answer. He was looking all in and carrying a pot of coffee.

They sat there in silence for a while, sipping their coffee.

'I'm afraid I did something terribly stupid last night,' Urs muttered. He parted the fur on his arm. He, too, had acquired a painless scar. It read:

Mouse Bladders

Rumo laughed.

'It isn't funny. I'll have to go around with it till the day I die.'

Rumo held out his own arm. 'That's nothing. Take a look at this!' He showed him the tattoo. This time it was Urs's turn to laugh.

'What am I to do?' groaned Rumo.

'Propose to her, of course.'

'Stop it! Rala is Rolv's girlfriend. I wanted to forget her, and now this! It'll remind me of her all my life!'

'Rala is whose girlfriend?'

'Rolv's,' Rumo growled. 'They hold hands.'

'Why shouldn't they? They're siblings.'

'They're what?'

'Brother and sister. Twins from the same litter, actually. That's very rare with Wolpertings. Hadn't it ever struck you that they have the same surname: Rolv and Rala of the Forest?'

'Twins?' Rumo said wonderingly.

'Yes, the miracle of life – a double helping of it. They look nothing like each other, but some twins don't.'

Rumo's heart gave a leap. So Rala and Rolv were brother and sister! He couldn't help laughing again. His headache was gradually subsiding.

'Well, you *are* in a good mood this morning. That's twice you've laughed. More than you usually do in a month.'

Rumo put his arms round Urs and gave him a hug – by far the biggest display of emotion he'd ever shown him.

Dandelion

Rumo was in high spirits. Rolv and Rala were siblings – splendid! His headache had disappeared completely, like that strange voice in his head. His sense of balance was still impaired, but that too was gradually improving. He marched through Wolperting to show off his new weapon to all and sundry. Being able to dispense with a scabbard because of the slit in the blade, he'd stuck the sword in his belt. That way, everyone could see it: Rumo's first weapon. He paused outside the tailor's shop to inspect himself and his sword in the big mirror beside the door.

'Snazzy, huh?'

Rumo gave a start.

'You'd better get used to it. That's the way I sound.'

It all came back in a flash. The talking sword. The buried demons. The meteor. It hadn't been a dream!

'Yes, it's a crazy story, no wonder you thought you were losing your mind. Be thankful it isn't a metabolic disorder of the brain. If it were you'd have to spend the rest of the day barking or talking backwards or something, ha ha!'

'This is terrible,' thought Rumo. 'I mean, fancy hearing a sword jabbering in my head all the time!'

'Don't be like that! You chose your weapon. It was a sacred act, a bond between flesh and steel! We're partners for ever, you and I! What's your name, by the way? Mine is Dandelion.'

'Dandelion?' asked Rumo. 'Like the flower?'

'I was thinking more of the origin of the word. It's French: Dent-de-lion, lion's tooth. Something sharp and dangerous. You mean there's a flower of the same name?'

'Yes.'

'A poisonous flower?'

'No. You can even make a salad out of it, I believe.'

'What nonsense!' Dandelion fell silent for a while. *'What do they call you at home?'*

'Rumo.'

'Like the card game?'

'Yes.'

'Ha ha ha!'

Rumo continued to study his reflection. Yes, the sword suited him. It talked a bit too much, that was all.

'Hi there, Rumo!'

'Hi there, Dandelion!'

Rumo walked along the street with Dandelion. Three girl Wolpertings whom Rumo knew from school were coming the other way. He gave them a clumsy wave. They giggled and waved back.

'Rumo and his new knife,' said Dandelion. *'No wonder they stared!'*

'Knife, did you say? I thought you were a sword.'

'Knife, sword – the borderline is pretty vague . . .'

'Just a minute!' Rumo halted. 'Yesterday you claimed to be a mighty Demonic Sword.'

'Did I say Demonic Sword? Well, I meant knife. Yoo-hoo! I'm a mighty Demonic Knife!'

Rumo walked on. 'It's not the same,' he said.

'That spiel of mine yesterday was sales talk, stupid! Have you any idea how long I'd been lying there? Yesterday was my twenty-fifth annual fair. I mean, I'm a knife! What fool would choose a knife when he could have a battleaxe or a sword? I had to think of something.'

Rumo paused again. 'You mean you bamboozled me?'

'What? No! Hey, all I did was use a bit of persuasion so you'd make the right choice at last – which you did. That proves I was right, doesn't it?'

Rumo failed to follow Dandelion's reasoning. 'You said you were a sword and now you're only a knife.'

'Well, I mean, what's the difference between a knife and a sword – between a big knife and a little sword? Where do knives stop and swords begin? Who can say? I certainly can't.'

'Go on lying to me and I'll chuck you in the river!'

'Hey, don't do anything rash!' Dandelion's voice took on a deep, solemn note. *'This is a great moment, don't profane it! You and I, partners in battle! A Wolperting's arm plus a steel blade capable of thought – could there be a greater or more dangerous weapon?'*

Rumo pondered this.

'Er, let's say you were blinded in battle – stranger things have happened! With me in your fist you could go on fighting – with your eyes shut.'

'You mean you can see?'

'In all directions, but don't ask me how.'

'I can see without eyes myself. With my nose. With my ears.'

'You can?'

'In all directions, but don't ask me how.'

'Aha. Hm. All right, another point: I can not only read your thoughts, I could read an opponent's. I would know all his manoeuvres in advance.'

'Is that true?'

'It's true . . . true . . . true . . .' the voice murmured hypnotically in Rumo's head.

'Hey, hang on,' cried Rumo, 'that's another of your tricks.'

'No, I can prove it to you!'

'How?'

'How? Yes, how . . .? Wait, I've got it! Do you by any chance have a score to settle with someone?'

'I certainly have.'

'Does he possess a sword or something similar?'

'Plenty of them. He's the best swordsman in the city.'

'All the better. Now listen. If we teach the fellow a lesson together, will that convince you we're partners for life?'

'Perhaps.'

'Then take me to him.'

The fencing master

Ushan DeLucca was feeling fine. Having just risen from his bed after twelve hours' refreshing sleep, he'd consumed a whole pot of coffee and breakfasted on eight fried eggs.

'It's grand, simply to be alive!' he thought. 'I feel like an ice-cold shower followed by a brisk workout in my fencing garden.'

This was far from being Ushan's usual state of mind. He was known to be not only the finest swordsman in the city but subject to the most extreme mood swings. There was no medical reason for these moods. Their origin was meteorological: Ushan DeLucca was peculiarly sensitive to weather conditions.

'What sort of day is it going to be, Ushan?' people would ask him as he walked through the city. Ushan would put a paw over his eyes, stick his nose in the air, sniff and say, for example, 'There's a barometric low over the Zamonian Ocean. It's moving eastwards in the direction of a barometric high centred on Zamonia itself, but it doesn't yet show any tendency to skirt this to the north. The isotherms and isotheres are behaving as they should. The air temperature bears a normal relationship to the annual mean, the temperature prevailing in the coldest and warmest months, and the aperiodic monthly variation in temperature. The water vapour in the air is at maximal buoyancy and humidity is low. In other words, it's going to be a fine day.'

And one could safely stake the whole of one's worldly wealth on the accuracy of that forecast.

Ushan found the slightest change in the weather a terrible affliction. He felt as if electrical storms were raging through his cerebral cortex, as if his eardrums were being pierced by red-hot needles and his eye sockets filled with boiling water. The purple pouches that blossomed beneath his eyes seemed to be laden with lead shot, his forehead became a mountain range of melancholy furrows. When the barometer registered extremely low pressure, his face contorted into such a tragic mask that people felt like bursting into tears at the very sight of him and his pet cat took to its heels, hissing and snarling. On such occasions Ushan found life pure agony and yearned for death. His first wife, Urla DeLucca, née Florinthiana, had left him because she couldn't endure his erratic moods any longcr.

'He spends the whole time sitting on the windowsill on the top floor of our home, talking to the urn in which he wants his ashes buried,' she'd testified before the mayor when suing for divorce. 'It drives me round the bend because I'm afraid he's going to jump at any moment. As for that face of his! He's a nice enough fellow when the sun's shining, but I can't take any more of this. I mean, I got to know him in the springtime, but when autumn came . . .'

Today, Ushan couldn't have felt better. Zamonia was in the middle of a stable high-pressure area, the sun was shining, and there was scarcely a breath of wind. He was sitting high up in his tower overlooking the fencing school, leafing through the latest circular from the Zamonian Fencing Instructors' Association. The doorbell rang. Ushan gave a start – he wasn't expecting visitors. The school was closed today because of the annual fair. He opened the window and looked down. Rumo was standing below. Rumo of Zamonia.

'Hello, Rumo!' called Ushan. 'This is an unexpected pleasure. What can I do for you?'

'I've come to challenge you to a duel.'

'Eh?'

'I've come . . . You heard what I said!'

'Are you out of your mind, youngster? Is this a schoolboy prank? Are your classmates hiding round the corner and laughing themselves sick?'

'I've come to challenge you to a duel,' Rumo repeated gravely.

Ushan could see the whole area from his tower. There was no one in sight but Rumo. 'Go home, Rumo,' he called. 'We'll see each other in class.' He shut the window. The youngsters always got out of hand when the fair was in progress. Shaking his head, he resumed his seat.

The doorbell rang again.

Ushan flung the window open.

'What is it now?'

'I've come to challenge you to a duel.'

'I don't duel with my pupils. Go away!'

'Then you're a coward.'

'All right, so I'm a coward. Push off!'

Ushan really was in a good mood. Under normal circumstances he would long ago have gone downstairs and given Rumo a hiding with the flat of his sword. He shut the window again.

'He won't play,' thought Rumo. 'What now?'

'What is his weak spot?' asked Dandelion.

'His weak spot? I don't think he's got one.'

'Everyone has.'

'Not him. He's Ushan DeLucca, the finest swordsm–'

'You mean his name is Ushan DeLucca? Like that brand of rum? Ha ha! That's great!' Dandelion chuckled malevolently.

'What's so great about it?'

'Well, it's like being called Booze-Bottle! Or Egg-Nog! There must be a reason.'

Rumo still didn't get it.

'Listen, ask him the following . . .'

Rumo rang the bell for a third time. The window flew open.

'Oh well,' Rumo called, 'I suppose there's nothing to be done. Perhaps it's just too early in the day. Perhaps you're still too sober to fight.'

Ushan stopped short. 'What do you mean?'

'Oh, nothing. Perhaps you simply haven't taken enough Dutch courage on board to fight me. Sorry to have bothered you.'

Rumo turned to go.

'Stay there!' Ushan drew himself up, straight as a ramrod. His tone was sharp and authoritative. He threw the key down.

'Meet me in the fencing garden.'

Ushan DeLucca's fencing garden

Were there a heaven for the exclusive use of aficionados of the art of fencing, it would have looked like Ushan DeLucca's fencing garden, which was conceived in accordance with seven rules. Ushan had designed it himself, worked on it for ten years and helped in its construction. Having considered it almost complete for the past two years, he now confined himself to maintaining it with the aid of a couple of gardeners.

While waiting for his fencing master, Rumo strolled round the garden and admired the ingenious diversity of its various features. He knew the seven rules for constructing an ideal fencing garden à la Ushan DeLucca from the latter's book, *Swordsmanship.*

Rule No. 1 for the creation of an ideal fencing garden à la Ushan DeLucca:

Fencers like to move around

This apparent platitude was actually the basis of the fencing garden. Fencers like moving around in the widest variety of ways. That, for example, was why Ushan had erected an unfinished stone wall that traversed the garden like an ancient ruin and was now picturesquely weathered. The wall was low enough to leap on to, narrow enough to require a good sense of balance and long enough to accommodate two swordsmen.

Ushan had also transported tree trunks of different sizes into the garden and allowed them to become overgrown with vegetation. He had commissioned Ornt El Okro to build some massive tables – for some reason swordsmen like to jump on to tables when fighting – and dug pits and trenches. He had even excavated tunnels and erected wooden beams for climbing on and swinging from on ropes.

Rule No. 2 for the creation of an ideal fencing garden à la Ushan DeLucca:

Swordsmen are vain

The garden was equipped with a number of large mirrors in which Ushan and his pupils could watch themselves shadow-fencing. Countless candles supplied atmospheric lighting for duels at night and capes hung ready to hand from clothes horses, for swordsmen in combat look best when attired in flowing capes, especially red velvet ones. For the vainest of the vain, gilded rapiers and épées were available.

Rule No. 3 for the creation of an ideal fencing garden à la Ushan DeLucca:

Swordsmen love danger

So as to intensify his fencing garden's hazards and dangers, Ushan had incorporated numerous hidden traps: nooses and holes in the ground designed to trip swordsmen up, branches that sprang back and hit them in the face, pitfalls that suddenly yawned beneath their feet, concealed wires strung between trees. He devised additional hazards every day, and his ingenious gardeners were under orders to go on constructing new obstacles of whose location and function he himself was ignorant.

Rule No. 4 for the creation of an ideal fencing garden à la Ushan DeLucca:
Swordsmen are hopeless romantics

There had, of course, to be a bower of blood-red roses for swordsmen to decapitate with their blades as they danced past, likewise a pond inhabited by a black swan and spanned by a picturesque bridge for them to duel on in fine weather. There was also a lush meadow filled with grazing sheep that provided a peaceful contrast to the combatants.

And, needless to say, the pond had to contain a plump old carp of melancholy mien with which Ushan could, when the barometric pressure was low, conduct mute conversations about the futility of existence.

Rule No. 5 for the creation of an ideal fencing garden à la Ushan DeLucca:
Steps and stairs are indispensable

Swordsmen like nothing better than to fight on stairs. There was a spiral iron staircase, a flight of rickety wooden steps leading up one side of a gable end and down the other, a stone staircase culminating in a tunnel, and some marble steps that ended in a void. But the finest stairway of all, which was constructed of ebony, led to the summit of a big oak tree in whose gnarled branches fighting could continue.

Rule No. 6 for the creation of an ideal fencing garden à la Ushan DeLucca:
Swordsmen fight anywhere

Indoors or outdoors, in daylight or darkness, snow or rain, swordsmen had to fight in all conditions, and Ushan had taken great pains to equip his garden perfectly in this respect. Situated in the middle of the garden was a small house, or rather, a dummy house with only one door and no windows. It contained an ingenious little labyrinth with staircases that led nowhere and passages that turned out to be dead ends. This was where pupils were trained to fight in cramped conditions, in poor light or none at all.

Behind the house was a walkway of burnished metal, lubricated with soft soap, for simulating combat on stretches of ice.

Pupils were also taught to fence on the thunder sheet. A rectangle of sheet metal suspended from four trees, this emitted an ear-splitting din whenever you took a step. Ushan knew that acoustic disturbances could also affect the outcome of a contest.

What else did his garden have to offer? The usual swordsmen's dummies: wooden figures to be assailed with rapier or sabre. By virtue of the intricate machinery inside them, many of these contrivances could actually hit back.

Finally there were the weapons: rapiers, sabres, épées, swords and cudgels of all kinds. These were stuck in the ground or embedded in tree trunks, suspended from branches or neatly arrayed in racks. Ushan DeLucca's garden was a paradise on earth for lovers of fencing.

Rule No. 7 for the creation of an ideal fencing garden à la Ushan DeLucca:

No ideal fencing garden à la Ushan DeLucca exists

Ushan would dearly have liked to incorporate some features of a more dangerous kind, but the fact that his pupils trained in the garden imposed certain limitations on him. He dreamt of pitfalls lined with spears, of lethal quicksands and carnivorous fish, of poisonous thorns and nests of Stranglesnakes. These visions were not, alas, compatible with the school syllabus, so he deferred them until his retirement.

Rumo was impressed by the garden's refinements. He itched to vent his rage on Ushan in this fencer's paradise. At the same time, however, he began to wonder if it was really such a good idea to challenge him on his own territory.

The duel

Dandelion intruded on his thoughts. *'Hey, you're being pessimistic again. It's the wrong attitude. You must think how you're going to defeat him. How you'll slice off his head, stick it on the end of a spear and carry it through the streets singing. How you'll cut out his heart and—'*

'Hang on!' Rumo broke in. 'It won't be that kind of victory.'

'No?'

'No. I only want to pay him back for what he did to me. And needle him a bit, maybe.'

'I see. A pity, but never mind. How do you propose to needle him?'

Not having given the matter any thought, Rumo hesitated. He'd never needled anyone before.

'How about this? After we've cunningly disarmed him and he's crawling around in the dust at your feet, you say, "Well, enjoying a taste of your own medicine, fencing master? Or should I say 'ex-fencing master', because I suppose I'm the new municipal fencing champion?"'

'That sounds good!' thought Rumo. He tried to memorise the words.

'Or this: "Well, Ushan, you old soak, looks like you've had your—"'

'Rumo!' Ushan DeLucca's voice rang out across the garden like a whiplash.

Rumo gave a start. He turned to see his teacher hurrying towards him with resolute tread and a face like thunder. Ushan halted just in front of him and looked him full in the eye.

'You wanted to fight me? Here I am. You begged me for a thrashing? At your service. Choose yourself a weapon.'

'I already have one,' said Rumo, brandishing Dandelion.

'You prefer to fight with a cheese knife?'

'Steady on!' Dandelion protested.

'This definitely isn't your day, my boy,' Ushan went on. 'Sure you aren't sick? Or did you indulge in some foolishness at the fair? Certain irresponsible individuals there have been selling illegal drugs to juveniles, so I've heard.'

'I'm fine. I want to fight.' Rumo was determined to get the business over.

'That's right,' Dandelion whispered in his head. *'Stand firm.'*

'Suit yourself.' Ushan plucked out one of the many swords embedded in the ground beside them. 'I'll take this, if it's all right with you. Are you sure you wouldn't prefer a weapon from my vast selection? They're the finest blades in Zamonia.'

'I'm sure,' said Rumo.

Ushan strode firmly on ahead. 'We usually start off in the middle of the garden and see how the fight develops. Swordsmanship isn't an exact science. We'll have to see where chance takes us. It certainly won't be far.'

He halted in the midst of the felled trees. Dozens of massive logs were lying every which way, deep in grass and overgrown with moss and ivy.

'My tree cemetery,' said Ushan. 'Be careful how you leap around on these logs, they can be pretty slippery.' The gravity of the situation hadn't diminished his concern for a pupil's welfare. He turned, raised his sword and kissed the hilt.

Rumo raised his weapon likewise, but he balked at kissing Dandelion.

'On guard!' said Ushan.

'On guard!' said Rumo.

'On guard!' whispered Dandelion.

The two combatants brought their blades together with a crash. Sparks flew and Dandelion's twin points vibrated like a tuning fork. They stood there with their weapons crossed.

'Dandelion?' thought Rumo. 'What shall I do?'

No answer.

'What does he have in mind, Dandelion? Can you read his thoughts?'

No answer.

'Dandelion?'

Ushan tapped Rumo's weapon with the tip of his sword. 'So you aren't attacking right away, eh? You've learnt something since the last time. Very good.'

Rumo hadn't attacked because he was paralysed with indecision. What was the matter with Dandelion? Why didn't he answer? He'd gone up against Zamonia's finest swordsman armed with a forked knife because Dandelion had claimed to be able to predict his opponent's every move, and now Dandelion had fallen silent.

'Dandelion?'

Still no answer.

'Well, we could stand around like this all day,' Ushan said, 'but it wouldn't achieve anything. I'd better open the proceedings.'

He subjected Rumo to a *Twin Attack*, a standard item from his repertoire designed to impress beginners without undue effort. He let the sword dangle for a moment, loose-wristed, then slashed at Rumo from every angle - so swiftly that it seemed two blades were at work - and darted forward at the same time. Rumo retreated, but he parried the blows with equal rapidity. He was familiar with the *Twin Attack* and the corresponding defence. It was one of the first things Urs had taught him.

'Dandelion!' he thought. 'Answer me! What does he plan to do next?'

No response.

Ushan stopped short, thwarted by Rumo's well-rehearsed reaction, and promptly changed tactics. With a single bound he leapt on to a log and rained blows on Rumo from above.

But Urs had known a simple response to that one too: Rumo went down on one knee, out of Ushan's range, and aimed some scything blows at his legs that compelled him to perform a brisk dance routine. Ushan somersaulted backwards off the log and faced Rumo once more.

'Been practising in secret, eh?' Ushan panted. 'Poor style, but quite effective. It reminds me of someone.'

Rumo was still too bemused to realise that he was putting up a pretty good show against Ushan.

'Dandelion?' he thought desperately. 'Where are you?'

Still no answer.

'All right, let's stop this beginner's nonsense and go all out,' said Ushan. 'We'll see how *that* appeals to you!'

The Raging Tornado

His next routine was the *Raging Tornado*, in which the attacking swordsman rotated swiftly on the spot, alternately clockwise and anticlockwise, and delivered blows with maximum frequency. This wasn't amateur's stuff; it was a complicated procedure that called for a great deal of training. Steel rang against steel, several times a second, with a sound like a handbell tumbling down a flight of stairs. Continually forced to readjust his position by a flurry of immensely powerful blows, the opponent was thrown off his stride and deprived of any chance to launch attacks of his own. The fencing instructor advanced on his retreating pupil like a whirlwind, spinning as he came.

'What do you do if a tornado bears down on you?' Urs had asked when the *Raging Tornado* tactic came up for discussion in training.

'No idea,' Rumo had replied.

'You take cover – if you can find any. It's as simple as that. Defending yourself against a tornado is futile. Find yourself a stout roof and get beneath it. If you can't find one it's curtains.'

A stout roof . . . Rumo continued to parry Ushan's blows as he looked around for one. He caught sight of a massive wooden table. Did that count as a roof? No matter. He slipped beneath it and the metallic clatter ceased at once.

Ushan was dumbfounded. He'd been compelled to break off his attack – by an act of cowardice. 'Hiding under a table?' he cried. 'You call that swordsmanship?'

'Is there any rule against it?' Rumo retorted.

'There aren't any rules in swordsmanship!'

'In that case,' said Rumo, 'I *do* call it swordsmanship.' He stayed where he was.

Ushan was completely thrown by this. He thrashed the table top with the flat of his sword. 'Come out of there, or must I smoke you out?' He bent down and tried to prod Rumo with his swordpoint, but Rumo, who had already emerged on the far side and leapt on to the table top, attacked him from above. Ushan sprang back out of range. For the first time in his career as a fencing instructor a pupil had forced him to give ground! Rumo jumped down from the table.

Ushan stood straight as a ramrod with his blade lowered. The tip was ever so slightly trembling, Rumo noticed.

'You're a nice youngster,' said Ushan, trying to sound conciliatory. 'Let's stop this before I really have to hurt you.'

'Do you surrender?' asked Rumo.

'What?'

'Do you apologise? I'll spare you if you do.'

'Are you insane? I'm giving you a chance to end this before things get out of hand. I could wound you.'

'Or I you.'

'Impossible.'

Rumo was surprised by his own self-assurance. His sword had lost its voice, but so what? He needed no talking sword to put paid to a legendary but ageing swordsman. Urs had taught him the requisite fundamentals; the ambition he supplied himself. It was the way it had been in Ornt El Okro's workshop. You didn't need umpteen years of experience to make a chair; all you needed was guts.

Ushan was pondering his future strategy. For a start, he would take it a bit easier. The youngster was welcome to wear himself out. The belief that one's energy is inexhaustible was a misapprehension typical of the young. He would dance around instead.

Rumo was thinking hard too. 'Don't go all out from the start!' Urs had always told him. 'It's a typical greenhorn's mistake to squander your energy before the balloon really goes up. Dance around a bit between times.'

So Rumo and Ushan danced. They might have been performing a carefully rehearsed pas de deux as they cavorted across the fencing garden's meadow, causing the sheep to bleat in alarm and the pigeons to take wing. Ushan casually beheaded a rose as they passed the rose arbour. Rumo tried to follow suit but missed.

'Ha!' Ushan exclaimed. 'Practice makes perfect!'

'I'm not interested in looking good,' Rumo retorted, 'only in winning.'

The artificial ruin

'It amounts to the same thing,' said Ushan, coming to a halt. Rumo stopped fighting too. They had now reached the artificial ruin. 'So you've also learnt to husband your strength,' Ushan went on. 'Who in Wolperting could have taught you that – apart from me?'

Rumo didn't reply.

'What about fighting in a confined space? Have you mastered that yet?' Ushan disappeared into the decrepit-looking building.

Rumo reluctantly followed him inside. No, he hadn't yet practised that with Urs. The conditions really were cramped: a small, windowless room, the ceiling so low that he had to duck his head, the only source of light two candles on the floor. Ushan wasn't in there.

'Ruuumo . . .' he heard Ushan calling from somewhere.

He made his way into the next room, which was even smaller and lit by only one candle. Some garden tools, rakes and besoms, were propped against the wall in one corner.

'Ruuumo . . .'

Into the next room. This one was totally unilluminated and there, with his back to the wall, stood Ushan DeLucca. He was lurking, an almost invisible figure, in the gloom. Eager to beat him to it, Rumo attacked him head-on. Their blades met. But no, it wasn't steel that Dandelion's blade encountered. There was a clatter and Ushan's figure collapsed in a shower of broken glass. Rumo had attacked his own reflection in a mirror.

'Ruuumo . . .'

Clearly, the sole purpose of this building was to frighten and infuriate pupils so much that they rushed blindly from room to room, only to be ambushed somewhere in the dark. So Rumo tried to keep calm. He ascended a creaking flight of stairs. Very slowly he entered the room at the top. It was in total darkness, but his sense of smell, which was now in operation, told him that it was empty. Careful not to stumble, he stole cautiously across the uneven floorboards, took one long, slow stride forward – and trod on thin air.

He turned a somersault and landed on his back, but the slope was so steep that he promptly turned another. He fell head over heels down the darkened chute and collided with a wooden door, which opened under his weight. Dazzling daylight greeted him as he came tumbling out of a hatch at the back of the house and landed in some tall grass.

'Feels good to be out in the fresh air again, eh?' Ushan DeLucca had been waiting for him. He was standing amid the daisies, eating an apple.

Rumo scrambled to his feet.

'Had enough at last?' Ushan enquired. 'Shouldn't we simply leave it at that? Hm?' There was an expectant note in his voice.

No, Rumo wouldn't have stopped for anything in the world. Every fibre of his being yearned to continue the fight.

As for Ushan, he had to admit that he would have been disappointed if Rumo had given up at this stage.

'I'd prefer to fight on,' Rumo said politely.

'As you wish,' said Ushan. Relieved, he tossed the apple core away. 'Well, think of this as a swordsman's fairground filled with different attractions. What shall we do next? Fight on the ice track? Duel on a staircase? The choice is yours.'

'Let's just carry on as we were,' Rumo suggested. 'Swordsmanship isn't an exact science. Let's see where chance takes us.'

'He actually thinks he can beat me,' thought Ushan, secretly amused. *'Ah, the boundless self-confidence of youth!'*

Rumo launched a lightning attack. Ushan parried it and retreated. A second onslaught followed, even faster and more ferocious than the first. Ushan retreated still further. He couldn't afford to let this youngster dictate the tempo.

The fencing tree

Ushan danced backwards, steadily making for the stairway that led up into the great oak tree. He darted up the first few steps with Rumo in hot pursuit, then turned to hold him off. Slowly and deliberately, he backed up the stairway step by step, alertly parrying Rumo's blows as he went. Sure enough, the youngster was falling into his trap. When Ushan felt the first leaves tickle the nape of his neck, he leapt boldly off the stairway and on to a massive branch.

'Follow me,' he said, 'and I could cut you to ribbons. You could never jump across, land, find a foothold and defend yourself at the same time. So I'll take a breather.' He drove the tip of his sword into the thick bark at his feet.

'Thanks,' said Rumo and jumped across. His feet had scarcely landed when Ushan plucked his sword out of the branch and showered him with blows. Each of them could have been lethal, but Ushan was only going through the motions. Meanwhile, Rumo was striving to retain his balance. Ushan lowered his blade.

'A word of advice: Never accept a favour in combat and never grant one either. Reserve your charity for other occasions.'

Rumo glanced around. He was in a tricky position, but the tree was equipped with ropes and leather handholds that offered plenty of scope for climbing, swinging and hanging on. He clung to a branch and lashed out at his opponent. Ushan countered, and for a while the battle raged this way and that.

Ushan had tailored the tree to his own requirements and provided it with a multitude of cunning refinements that had driven many a pupil to distraction before now. He seized a rope, cried 'Hoppla!', swung himself over a thick branch, and disappeared into a dense mass of foliage. Rumo cautiously followed.

Where had his fencing master gone? Rumo could scent him, but Ushan, concealed by all the greenery, kept changing his position.

'I shall now proceed to kill you seven times over, my boy,' whispered Ushan.

'Carry on!' Rumo retorted.

'One!'

Ushan's blade darted from the leaves, aimed at a point midway between Rumo's ears.

'Two!'

This time the blade came from below, passing close beneath his armpit.

'Three!'

The blade stopped a hair's breadth from Rumo's left eye and promptly withdrew into the leaves. He seemed to be fencing with the tree itself, from which blades were sprouting everywhere.

'Four!'

Ushan tapped Rumo's chest with his swordpoint, just over the heart. He chuckled in his place of concealment.

'Five! Six! Seven!' Rumo cried furiously, slashing at the foliage three times in quick succession. Hundreds of severed leaves went fluttering down. Ushan could now be seen crouching on a branch, looking as startled as a puppeteer whose curtain has been wrenched aside.

'Those twigs will take a year to grow back!' Ushan said reproachfully. 'Have a little more respect for an innocent tree!'

Rumo lunged at him. By the time his leading foot had trodden on a piece of bark that emitted a suspicious creak it was too late: a branch lashed him in the face and chest. He swayed for a moment, flailing his arms, then toppled over backwards and fell into the long grass below.

'Disaster always strikes from an unexpected quarter!' Ushan jeered from overhead as Rumo struggled to his feet with a groan. The fencing master climbed down off his branch, there was another creak and he looked up just in time to see a bulging leather punchbag come swinging out of the dense foliage. It struck him in the chest with a dull thud, lifted him off his feet and sent him sailing through the air. He landed in the grass a few feet from Rumo.

Rumo tottered over to Ushan to see if he was still alive. Ushan sat up and stared at him, glassy-eyed.

'That was a surprise gift from my gardener,' he said, feeling his chest for broken ribs.

'Disaster always strikes from an unexpected quarter,' said Rumo.

Groaning, Ushan got to his feet. 'If I'd known what an unalloyed pleasure this would be,' he said, leaning on his sword, 'I wouldn't have been so reluctant to cross blades with you. I haven't had as good a fight since . . . yes, since my last duel with Urs of the Snows. Do you know him?'

Rumo looked away.

Ushan levelled his sword at him. 'Aha, so that's the answer! We've been practising in secret, have we? I thought Urs had renounced cold steel for good.'

'We use wooden swords.'

Ushan lowered his blade with a grin. 'All right, youngster, don't you agree with me that this would be a suitable moment to end these proceedings? We've both had some fun, you've learnt something and you've shown me what you're made of. From now on I shall treat you with respect in class.'

'Do you surrender?'

Ushan put his paws on his hips. 'I don't believe it! You mean you still haven't had enough?'

'You told me never to accept a favour from an opponent. I don't want preferential treatment; I want to beat you.'

'You stubborn little brute!' cried Ushan.

Rumo took guard.

The Wrist-Slapper

Ushan deliberated. Tempers were now running so high that serious injuries might result. It was his duty as a teacher to bring this affair to a swift conclusion, but how? With a *Two-Handed Slice*? That could split an opponent's skull in half – far too dangerous. A *Grim Reaper*? This horizontal blow owed its name not only to its scything motion but also to the fact that it spelt certain death – too risky. Wait . . . A *Wrist-Slapper* – that was it! That was how he'd defeated Urs of the Snows, who had never touched a blade since. It was a powerful and, as a rule, immensely effective blow that only a few expert swordsmen had mastered, but it wasn't lethal. That would bring

Rumo down to earth and ensure that he attended classes with due humility from now on.

Delivered with the flat of the blade and great force, the *Wrist-Slapper* was an extremely painful blow on the opponent's sword arm. It had to strike the appropriate nerve without damaging it, thereby paralysing the arm for a considerable time. Rumo would have to spoon up his soup left-handed for the next few days. Ushan attacked.

'Oho,' thought Rumo, 'he's trying a *Wrist-Slapper*!'

Urs, who had often told him about the *Wrist-Slapper*, seemed positively obsessed by it. He had devised an effective defence against the blow and, more than that, a method of humiliating anyone who delivered it. He had practised this with Rumo for days on end.

Rumo began by doing what Ushan expected of him: he allowed himself to be manoeuvred into the required position and obediently left his forearm undefended. Ushan took a swing at it – and slapped thin air. Rumo had whipped away his arm, simultaneously transferring his weapon to the other paw in a *Simple Changeover.* Thrown slightly off balance, Ushan received a swingeing blow on the ear from the flat of Rumo's sword. Urs called this the *Wrist-Slapper Riposte.*

Ushan's head rang like a bell and his ear felt red-hot. Tears sprang to his eyes.

'Best regards from Urs!' said Rumo. He couldn't help grinning. The needling process was going well!

Ushan stood there like a first-year student who had just been slapped by his teacher. This youngster was more than a pupil, he decided; he was a fully fledged opponent. No more allowances for youth and inexperience, no more schoolmasterly solicitude. It was definitely time for a *Multiple DeLucca.*

Ushan plucked a second sword from a wooden rack. Leaning backwards slightly with both blades levelled from the hip, he slowly retreated in a defensive posture so as to lure Rumo out of his shell.

'You mean you now need two weapons to deal with me?' asked Rumo. Needling was fun, he told himself. 'Two swords versus a cheese knife?' He launched several fierce attacks. Ushan parried them two-handed.

The Multiple DeLucca

The first phase of a *Multiple DeLucca,* a tactic devised and perfected by Ushan himself, required the swordsman to fight with two weapons and then suddenly discard one. For no apparent reason Ushan hurled his left-hand sword into the air.

Numerous variations of the *Multiple DeLucca* could be performed. There was the Triple, the Quintuple, the Octuple, the Seventeenfold and the Twenty-Twofold. It all depended on how often the weapon turned over after being thrown into the air.

One turn, two, three, four, five . . .

Meanwhile, fighting on the ground continued. Rumo redoubled his attacks now that Ushan had discarded one of his weapons.

Six, seven, eight, nine, ten . . .

Ushan stopped retreating and tried to stand his ground against Rumo's onslaught. It was important not to let him force the pace.

Eleven, twelve, thirteen, fourteen, fifteen, sixteen . . .

Twenty-eight rotations were the most Ushan had ever achieved. This feat had been necessary because he was fighting the reigning champion of Zamonia, Atrax Xarta III. One of the most nerve-racking duels in his career, it had matched him with an opponent who required special measures. Like Rumo.

Seventeen, eighteen, nineteen, twenty, twenty-one, twenty-two, twenty-three, twenty-four, twenty-five . . .

It was particularly important, when performing the *Multiple DeLucca*, to ensure that your opponent forgot all about the discarded weapon. The higher you threw it, the more often it rotated; and the harder you fought in the meantime, the greater the chances that this complicated ploy would succeed.

Ushan now attacked, drawing on his full range of skills. Rumo was bombarded with cuts and thrusts from all angles and directions, delivered at a speed he had never encountered before. It escaped his notice that he was being driven round in a circle.

Thirty, thirty-one, thirty-two . . .

Reaching its apogee, Ushan's sword slowly rotated for the last time.

Thirty-five . . .

Ushan had never before thrown such a high *DeLucca*. The sword came to a stop in mid air, then plummeted earthwards, heavy hilt first.

The essential thing at the conclusion of a *Multiple DeLucca* was to be back where it had started. Skilfully manoeuvred there by Ushan, he and

Rumo were on that exact spot. Rumo was far too preoccupied to notice the portent of disaster bearing down on him from above. With mathematical precision Ushan's second sword landed in the midst of this hurricane of cuts and thrusts, flying sparks and whirling blades. To Rumo's astonishment, Ushan caught it by the hilt in front of his nose. Suddenly confronted again by two weapons instead of one, Rumo stopped short. His sword arm remained immobile for a fraction of a second and Ushan seized his opportunity. Clamping Rumo's blade between both of his, he levered it out of his grasp with one swift, irresistible movement. The self-styled Demonic Sword went flying across the fencing garden and embedded itself, quivering, in the trunk of a silver birch.

'Ouch!' said Dandelion inside Rumo's head.

Ushan held his swordpoints to Rumo's throat. The duel was over.

'Now go home,' said Ushan. Without wasting a second glance on his defeated opponent he stuck his swords in the ground and left the garden with his cloak fluttering behind him. 'And don't forget your cheese knife!' he called before disappearing into the house.

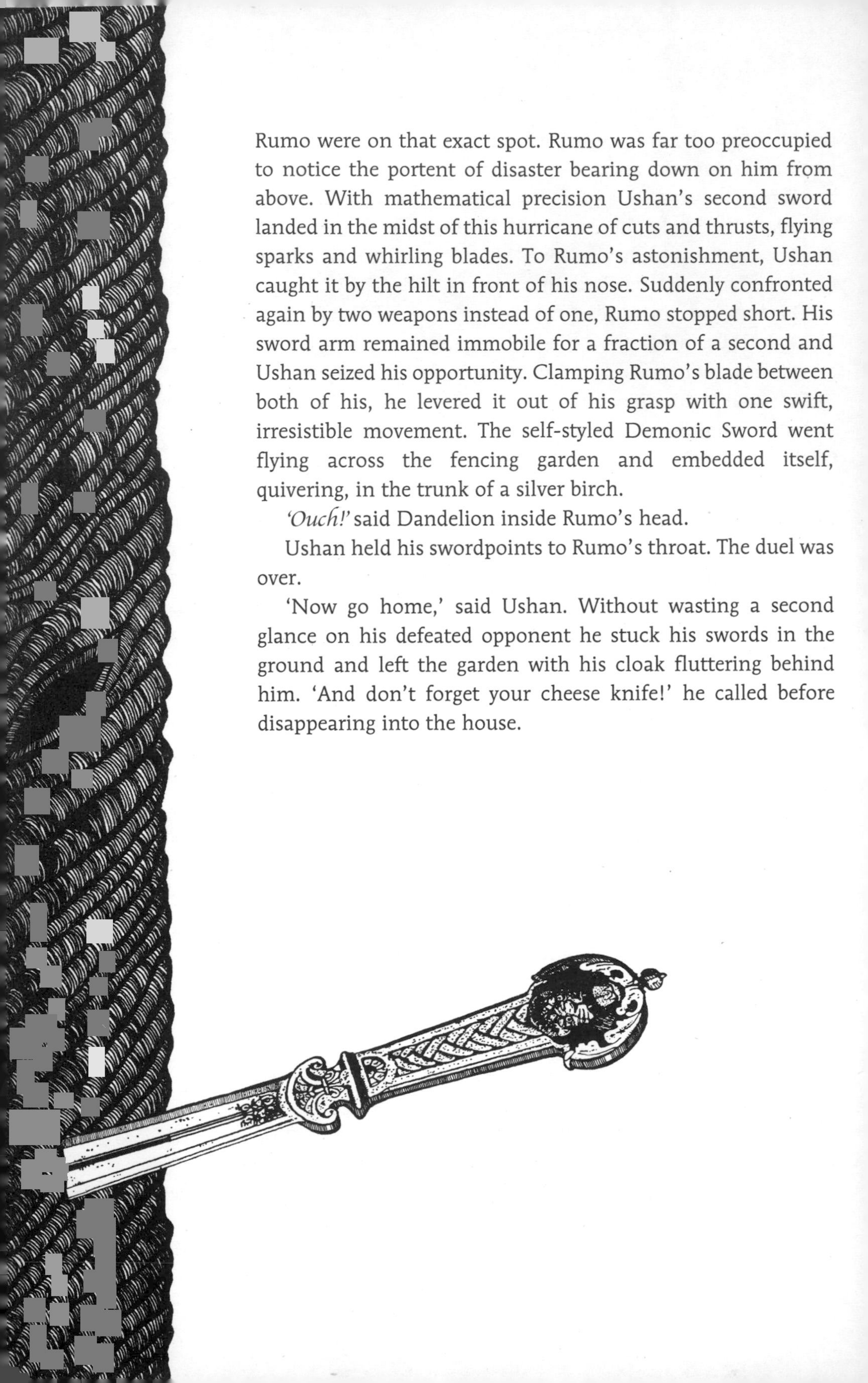

Suddenly it all came back: the headache, the befuddlement, the stale taste in his mouth. Rumo felt as if he had just woken up with a monumental hangover. He was wandering aimlessly through the side streets of Wolperting. Fairground music could be heard in the distance.

'Well, how did it go?' Dandelion asked suddenly.

Rumo was too flabbergasted to be angry. 'Dandelion? Where have you been all this time?'

'No idea, to be honest. I must have passed out or something. Did you know that swords can faint? Neither did I, ha ha! I only came round when I stuck in that tree. Did I miss anything?'

'You fainted?'

'Yes, right at the start of the fight. His sword came whistling towards me and we met with a terrible crash . . .'

'You left me in the lurch,' Rumo protested. 'You talked me into that business and passed out at the crucial moment!'

'Heavens, how callous of you, I'm still in shock! That was my very first fight, for goodness' sake. I didn't know everything happened so quickly. Phew, the speed of it! Can you imagine what it feels like, crashing into another blade? Did you see the sparks?'

'Call yourself a sword!' Rumo said scornfully. 'You're a joke!'

'I'm a knife!' Dandelion said peevishly.

'Oh, so you *are* a knife after all.'

'What of it? Do you think that means I've got no feelings?'

'A knife with feelings! A knife that passes out! Just what I need in a fight. A tent full of weapons and I had to pick you! I might as well go into battle armed with a tulip. Do you know what you are? You're just a—'

'Shall I tell you what I really am? Shall I? All right, I will!'

Dandelion's confession

Rumo came to a halt.

'The truth is,' Dandelion said in a quavering voice, 'I'm not a Demon's brain at all, I'm a Troll's brain. A Troglotroll's brain! There, now you know.'

'You're a Troll?'

'Certainly. A common or garden Troglotroll – a cave dweller. I never wielded a sword in my life. I was mining lapis lazuli in a mine shaft in the Demon Range when that stupid meteor came crashing down. The

most awe-inspiring weapon I ever held in my hands was a geologist's hammer. The meteor made such a mess of me, they must have mistaken me for a Demonic Warrior and poured my brain into the sword. At least, that's the only explanation I can think of for how I got into this confounded thing.'

'You mean you aren't even a Demonic Warrior? You're only a Troll?'

'I used to be.'

'Better and better. First of all a mighty Demonic Sword and now just a Troglotrollian Toothpick. That settles it! I'm throwing you into the river.'

'What?!'

Rumo strode on.

'Hey, where are you going?'

'To the Wolper. I'm going to throw you in.'

'Rumo! Don't be rash!'

Rumo didn't reply. He was making for the bridge.

'Rumo! Rumo? You can't be serious!'

No response.

'Rumo! Don't do anything you'll regret!'

Rumo strode on regardless.

'Rumo? Listen to me, Rumo! I bungled it, for heaven's sake! I made a little, wholly unrepresentative mistake! It was my first fight! Calm down, we can discuss this quietly later!'

Rumo had reached the northern end of Wolper Bridge. Dandelion's voice was drowned by the roar of the river.

'Rumo! It'll never happen again, I give you my word of honour! I won't let it. Are you listening to me, Rumo?'

Rumo went over to the parapet and looked down at the rushing waters of the Wolper. He dangled Dandelion over the edge.

'Rumo!' Dandelion shrieked. *'This isn't funny any more!'*

'You're right,' said Rumo. 'It isn't.'

He took another look at the river. Something was drifting past on its turbid surface. A bundle of clothes? No, a Wolperting! He could even make out the face. It was Rala's!

Without a second thought, Rumo stuck Dandelion in his belt and leapt over the parapet into the raging torrent.

The long journey that ended with Rala's immersion in the icy waters of the Wolper had begun at the farm where Niddugg the Bluddum had beaten her senseless before her brother's eyes. It was a journey from one perilous state, in which she had been more dead than alive, to another. Death had been her constant companion, her unseen attendant and lover, ever ready to enfold her in its chill embrace. Her journey had acquainted her with friendship, but also with hatred and vengeance, with the thrill of the chase and the pleasures of flirting with danger. She had learnt to speak and walk erect, and she had been reunited with her brother Rolv, but the best thing she had encountered on her journey was the love of Tallon the Bear God.

Rala's story

Once Niddugg the Bluddum was convinced that he had beaten Rala to death, he dragged her supposedly lifeless body into the forest as a sacrifice to the Wild Bear God in whom he believed. As soon as he had laid her down among the leaves and returned to his farm to give Rolv a thrashing, the Wild Bear God appeared.

Tallon the Bear God

His name was Tallon – Tallon the Claw, to be precise. He was wild and a bear, yes, but he wasn't a god. Tallon was as far from being a god as anyone could be. He wasn't particularly bright, he was lazy, he possessed no supernatural powers, and he was as mortal as any other creature in the forest. He lived on the scraps the superstitious peasants threw out to placate him when he roared in the night. Tallon would eat anything – cold potatoes, apple peel, stale bread, mouldy cheese, even dead dogs – just as long as he didn't have to hunt his own food.

Tallon trotted over, sniffed the little puppy's body and promptly decided not to eat it under any circumstances. Why not? Because it was still alive. Tallon knew nothing of the Demonocles, still less of their predilection for live food, but instinct told him that he was one of the Zamonian life forms which firmly rejected any form of nourishment that was still moving.

Yes, Rala was still alive. As for her name, she got that from Tallon, who nursed her back to health and brought her food and lulled her to sleep with the only two syllables he could articulate: *Rala – Rala – Rala.*

She recovered from her serious injuries remarkably quickly, reached the fast-growing phase, and became big and strong. Not as big as Tallon, but strong enough to go hunting with him, for now that he had a foster-child to feed he no longer shrank from killing his own food. Rala, he thought, should have something better to eat than kitchen waste and dead dogs. Besides, he had noticed that the exercise did him good and he lost a few pounds, so hunting became his and Rala's main interest in life.

One day they scented an unusual quarry. Having run it to earth in a snow-covered clearing, they saw that it was a hunter. Not just any hunter, but the one who had caught Rala and Rolv and sold them to Niddugg. Rala knew this from his scent when they came face to face.

The hunter was carrying a long stick in his right hand and a short stick in his left. Having put the two together, he seemed to point them at Rala and Tallon. Suddenly the short stick flew through the air and struck Tallon in the heart. He sank to the forest floor, growled 'Rala' for the last time, and died. The hunter had meantime produced another short stick and was pointing it at Rala. She felt like charging at him and tearing out his heart for what he had done to her, Rolv and Tallon, but something commanded her to do the opposite: to restrain herself, take cover and let the hunter go. She complied: she went down on all fours and disappeared into the forest. The hunter lowered his sticks and went on his way.

But not alone, for Rala followed him. She surreptitiously dogged his footsteps, never breaking cover. She watched him hunting and studied the way he handled his sticks. She became his shadow, his secret alter ego. She discovered how he lived, how he ate, when he took the sticks with him and when he left them behind. And one day, when she thought she knew all there was to know about the hunter, she confronted him. He had laid aside his clothes and sticks, and was swimming in a river. He took fright when he spotted Rala on the bank, because he realised that his time had come. Rala picked up the sticks, took aim at the hunter and shot him in the heart. His agonised cries filled the forest and the river turned red. Rala had proved herself an excellent marksman with bow and arrow at the very first attempt.

Rala defies death

From that day onwards Rala enjoyed an unusual relationship with death. She had no fear of it because she had already conquered it once, and she now knew how to visit it on others.

She matched herself against opponents whose strength and ability she couldn't gauge, and it was pure luck that she survived such confrontations. She waded through murky swamps pervaded by ominous scents and emerged unscathed because the creatures that inhabited them were too dumbfounded by her audacity to show themselves. She challenged death itself, but neither hunger nor thirst, teeth nor claws could defeat her. Rala had lost her respect, not only for death but also for life, because she had no one left worth living for.

One evening she picked up a scent that seemed at once familiar and unfamiliar. The wind was strong and blew it away too quickly for her to identify it. In the twilight she spotted a fast-moving creature flitting from tree to tree and realised that she herself was its quarry. She loosed off an arrow, but her pursuer ducked so swiftly that it splintered against a tree trunk. Never having wasted one of her precious arrows before, Rala was annoyed and puzzled at the same time. What sort of creature could it be?

She fired two arrows simultaneously, a technique that had never failed to kill in the past. But the creature did something more puzzling still: it plucked both arrows out of the air and, adding insult to injury, hurled them back with such force that they stuck in a tree just in front of Rala's nose.

She had never before encountered an opponent endowed with such reflexes, such strength and speed. Visibility steadily deteriorated as darkness fell. Having fired her last arrow in vain, Rala was left with only one choice: to confront her opponent face to face. They met in a clearing, close enough to look into each other's eyes. The wind dropped at that moment, enabling them to identify each other's scent, and they realised that there wouldn't be a fight after all: their noses had told them they were brother and sister.

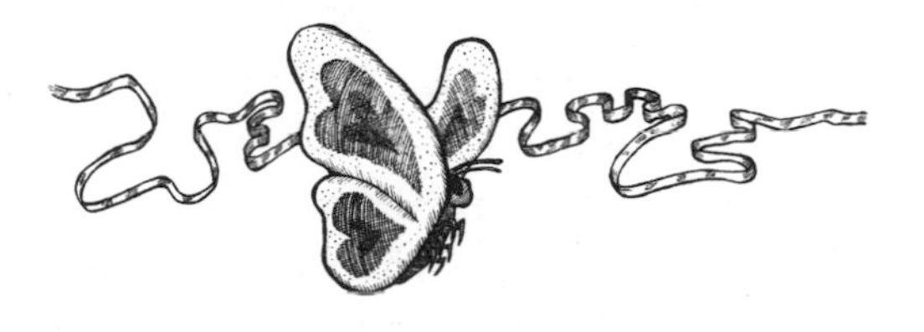

The river

The grey waters of the Wolper swirled around Rumo. They were below him, above him – everywhere. Cold as ice, they forced their way into his mouth, nose and ears. A steady roar filled his head.

'I can't swim,' he thought.

'What?!' said Dandelion. *'You can't swim and you jump into a raging river? And you reproach me for—'*

'Where's Rala?'

'Rala? Who's Rala?'

'She'll die!'

'Who'll die? You will, that's for sure.'

'Maybe, but Rala mustn't!'

'Start swimming.'

'I can't swim.'

'Then do something about it!' Dandelion yelled. *'Swim!'*

'Rala . . .' thought Rumo.

'Rumo!' Dandelion yelled. *'Get moving! You've got to swim.'*

But Rumo didn't answer.

Rolv and Rala of the Forest

After their reunion in the forest Rolv and Rala roamed the wild woods of Zamonia together. For a time they worked as guard dogs on a fruit farm that was regularly raided by thieves. The farmhands taught them to speak and the thieves stopped raiding the orchards at night, deterred by the Wolpertings' ferocious barking. They moved on when the harvest was over. At some stage, when they had reached the south of the Zamonian continent, Rolv started talking about a Silver Thread he could see with his eyes shut. As time went by, Rala realised that this vision meant a lot to him, so they journeyed on in search of its source and eventually came to Wolperting City. They registered with the mayor, moved into a little house together, and went to school. Rolv found his Silver Thread in the shape of a girl Wolperting named Mara of the Mists. In other respects they led a normal life devoid of undue excitement.

Until Rumo appeared on the scene.

Rala was puzzled by the emotions that gripped her when this stranger blundered into the classroom. He behaved like an utter fool, asked stupid questions in class and tangled with Rolv, of all people. Above all, he treated her as if she were a block of wood, so why did she have these feelings for him?

She was Rala of the Forest, the proudest, most high-spirited girl Wolperting in the city, with a host of admirers, but now this Rumo had come along and turned her world upside down. What gave him the right? He avoided her eye and company, gave her the widest possible berth in the playground and responded to her smiles with a low growl – indeed, he seemed positively to detest her. At the fair he'd almost fainted at the mere touch of her. What an idiot! But – and this was what perplexed her most of all – Rala could think of nothing and no one but Rumo. She wanted to live with him, grow old with him, die and dissolve into the cosmos with him when the world disintegrated.

She thought of him at night, too. She'd always had wild and wonderful dreams, usually of Tallon and their hunting trips in the forest, but Rumo now haunted her nocturnal world and behaved little less strangely there than in real life.

One night Rala dreamt again of Tallon the Claw. It was a very remarkable dream, because Tallon could speak. He was sitting on a log with the fatal arrow lodged in his heart.

'Listen, my girl,' he said, 'and listen carefully, because in life I was never able to say anything except your name. But now I'm dead and I can tell you this: Everything has changed. This Rumo, this idiot who keeps blundering through our lovely dreams – I wondered what he was doing in our forest, so I asked him. Well, "asked" isn't the word. I had to torment him a little to get at the truth, but at last I wrung it out of him. Sit tight and listen to this: He's crazy about you – hopelessly infatuated! He doesn't dare tell you, so his spirit goes wandering when he's asleep at night and insinuates itself into your dreams. Have you ever heard of such idiocy?'

Tallon slid off the log to the ground and lay there, looking just as he had when he was dying.

'Listen, Rala,' he went on in a tremulous whisper. 'I couldn't utter any dramatic last words when I was close to death, but now that I can speak I'd like to make up for lost time.' His voice became even fainter.

'I'm only a stupid bear and I don't know the first thing about such matters, but if you want my opinion, *you* must take the initiative. *You* must hunt him down and lay him low.' Tallon gave a final groan and his head sagged. Rala awoke in tears.

Although she didn't believe in dream messages, she was obsessed from then on with a single thought: *How could she lay Rumo low?*

And then she'd seen him making for the bridge over the Wolper.

Rumo hadn't spotted her. He looked moody and ill-tempered – in fact, he was talking to himself. Rala followed hard on his heels, stalking him the way she used to stalk game in the forest and flitting from one piece of cover to the next. When she saw that he meant to cross the bridge, a plan took shape in her mind. A dangerous, extremely risky plan, but she felt it was time to give death another chance. Her idea of how to put Rumo's love to the test was not only simple but hare-brained: she would throw herself into the Wolper. If he jumped in after her – if he risked certain death for her sake – she could be sure of his love. She spared no thought for what would happen afterwards, or how the two of them would extricate themselves from the raging torrent. That didn't enter into her plan. After all, danger was an integral part of it.

The colours of death

Unlike Demonocles, Wolpertings didn't believe that they would rise into the clouds after death. They believed that death would spell total inactivity. Although aware that they would inevitably die some day, they didn't speculate on what would happen thereafter. Rumo was doubly surprised, therefore, when he lost consciousness and found himself in a world that seemed familiar to him. It was a vast panorama of luminous shapes, of hitherto unknown colours and endless streamers of light, which reminded him of the world of his inner eye.

'Aha,' he thought, 'so this is what it's like when you're dead. It's like seeing things with your eyes shut.'

He was being swept along by a river of pulsating radiance. The colour of the river, it suddenly occurred to him, was *xulb,* and *gommish* clouds were racing across the *zabrine* sky overhead. Amazingly enough, he knew all the names of these peculiar colours by heart.

He could swim, what was more. No, he himself wasn't swimming; he was being borne along by this river, which shared none of the unpleasant characteristics of the Wolper. It wasn't noisy but quiet, not cold but warm, not turbulent but calm.

'I'll simply go with the flow,' he thought. Everything had suddenly become so easy and simple and lovely, so painless and unproblematical. He was no longer plagued by anger and doubt, by fear and the torments of love.

Fighting the water

When Rala dived into the Wolper the first thing she noticed was that the water was appreciably colder and flowing considerably faster than she'd expected. Above all, it was heavy. It soaked into her clothes and hair, seeped into her boots and dragged her down into the depths. Last but not least, it was noisy. Its monotonous roar drowned every other sound and thwarted her romantic plan to cry for help. Having pictured herself drifting serenely along like a beautiful victim of drowning, she was now being swept away and submerged like a scrap of paper.

She had already drifted under Wolper Bridge without managing to attract Rumo's attention when he happened to look over the parapet just as a violent eddy carried her briefly to the surface. Rumo dived in without a moment's hesitation. Rala saw him plunge into the river before she herself was swept away by the current.

'He loves me!' she thought. 'He followed me to certain death without a second thought!'

Surfacing for a moment, she saw Rumo, too, break surface. His body was inert. Whirled around by the current, he was making no attempt to hold his own against it. It was clear that he'd lost consciousness.

'Rumo's drowning!' she thought.

They continued to drift along in the middle of the river. It hadn't occurred to Rala that Rumo would lose consciousness, that the current would be so overwhelmingly powerful, and that fate would this time treat her with such indifference. She cursed herself for having devised a childish, romantic scheme that had put Rumo in the direst danger – Rumo, whose life was more precious to her than her own.

'You must try to swim!' someone shouted.

A number of Wolpertings had gathered at the river's edge. They were leaning over the embankment or keeping pace with the raging torrent by running along it in great agitation.

Swim? What nonsense! Rala couldn't swim – no Wolperting could. It was just about as unthinkable as learning to fly by jumping over a precipice.

'Try to swim!' another Wolperting shouted from the bank.

Why was it so unthinkable? Rumo's life was at stake, not to mention her own, so why should she let this atavistic fear of water prevent her from at least giving it a try?

'You must swim!'

But how did swimming go? Rala remembered the hunter she'd watched swimming in the river before she killed him. He had stretched out his arms and shovelled the water behind him, and the movement of his legs had reminded her of a frog.

She was dragged under again. Pebbles and dead branches smote her in the face, and once she hit her head so hard on a massive rock that it almost knocked her out. When she finally regained the surface she saw Rumo floating along nearby, but upside down. All that protruded from the water was one of his boots.

The Wolpertings on the bank were brandishing long sticks and coils of rope. By now, Rala and Rumo were nearing the outskirts of the city, where the current was not quite as strong and the river was unenclosed by an embankment. Their agitated fellow citizens had ventured unusually close to the water's edge.

Trying to keep her head above the surface, Rala extended her arms, shovelled the water behind her and simultaneously imitated the leg movements of a frog.

Sure enough, she made a little progress in Rumo's direction. She repeated her movements with all the strength and speed of which a Wolperting was capable, again and again. To her astonishment she noticed that the river was losing its power over her body. She herself determined when her head was above or below the surface, when she drew breath and when she submerged. So that's how you swim, she thought: *You fight the water.*

She had already grasped Rumo's boot. She continued to paddle with one paw, and her powerful strokes brought her closer to the bank, where the spectators were trailing long branches in the water and holding out their arms. At last she managed to seize the shaft of a pitchfork. Hauled ashore, she dragged Rumo's inert body out of the water.

Rumo, feeling detached and remote from everything, was drifting along on the silent billows of death. Would he continue to drift like this for evermore? He didn't care, he would accept whatever happened, because anyone who had accepted death was past being afraid of anything.

He looked up at the sky, with all its weird and wonderful new colours: *kelf, gromian, opem, glab, ivolint* and – suddenly a familiar colour – silver! Yes, the Silver Thread was quivering overhead, near enough to touch. It had a voice as it did in his dreams, but it wasn't singing this time; it was speaking, firmly and loudly:

'Rumo! You've got to breathe!'

Breathe? Why should he have to breathe now he was dead? He'd just broken the habit.

'Rumo!' the voice said again. 'Breathe! You've got to!'

'I can't breathe any more,' he thought. 'I've forgotten how.'

'Rumo!' cried the voice, angrily now. *'I order you to breathe!'*

Rumo felt a sudden sharp pain in his nose.

Ouch!

A pain like that didn't belong in this peaceful new world of his. Rumo's eyes filled with tears. He uttered a sob and started to breathe.

He opened his eyes.

Someone was bending over him. He blinked, then saw that it was Rala. Several other Wolpertings were crowding around behind her.

'She punched him on the nose,' said someone.

'It worked, though. Incredible!'

'He's alive.'

'Rala can swim,' said someone further away.

Rala mopped Rumo's face and looked at him as if she expected him to say something special. He stared back uncomprehendingly. Then he vomited into her lap.

The talk of the town

Rala can swim!

The news spread through Wolperting with the rapidity of a forest fire. It travelled from housc to house, street to street, district to district, until, within the space of an afternoon, the whole city knew it: *Rala can swim!*

The inhabitants were no less dumbfounded by the news than they would have been if told that Rala could fly. None of them would ever have thought it possible that one of their number could learn to swim. Swimming – if performed by a Wolperting – verged on sorcery.

Where Rumo was concerned the news had an unpleasant postscript. In full it ran: *Rala can swim, and Rumo is a stupid idiot for falling into the Wolper and having to be fished out by a girl.*

Nobody mentioned that he had thrown himself into the river to rescue Rala or described how she had really got there. No, the false version of the story was recounted again and again until everyone believed it.

That, at all events, was the state of affairs as reported by Urs to Rumo while he lay face down on his bed and vomited brown Wolper water into a bucket.

Rumo continued to be dependent on Urs's information for the next few days. He was feeling so groggy that he hardly left his room for a week. While he was slowly recovering, Rala's reputation enjoyed a meteoric rise. The streets of Wolperting rang with her name: *Rala, the swimmer. Rala, the wonder girl. Rala, who can walk on water. Rala, fearless saviour of a moronic non-swimmer* – and so forth. It was almost too much to bear.

Rumo felt it might have been better if he'd remained in that multicoloured, luminous limbo and gone on drifting for ever. He would then have been spared the items of news brought him during his convalescence by Urs, Axel and the other two triplets: that the municipal theatre's amateur players were rehearsing a drama entitled *Rumo's Rescue*; that the City Hall authorities were thinking of erecting a monument or renaming the river in Rala's honour; that she was giving swimming lessons in the ponds outside the city walls, her example having shown that overcoming your deep-seated fear of water and learning a few simple movements were all you needed to do in order to be able to swim.

Even when Rumo was back on his legs, he scarcely dared to leave his room. He no longer went to school, shirked his civic duties and avoided the cabinetmaker's workshop for days. He slunk through the side streets at night for a breath of fresh air, but that was all. The whole city was in league against him. Ushan DeLucca lay in wait for him in fencing lessons and Rala in class, and he could well imagine how Rolv, Vasko and the others would taunt him.

On one of his solitary nocturnal walks he came to Black Dome Square. The great building stood there, its dark bulk gleaming in the moonlight like a memorial to all the world's unsolved mysteries. Rumo went over, leant his back against the cold surface and looked up at the stars. The sleeping city was utterly silent. This, he thought, would be the ideal moment to steal away and shake the dust of Wolperting off his heels.

The whole city loved Rala, so why was she unhappy? Because, even though Rumo owed her his life, he was still behaving like an idiot! It was incredible. Hardly had she hauled him out of the raging river and summoned him back to life when he opened his eyes, puked all over her trousers, stood up and walked off without a word of thanks. What ought she to have done, confess her love in front of everyone? No thanks, she would sooner enjoy a bit of hero worship.

Rala can swim!

It sounded good, she thought – better, anyway, than *Rala can knit*! They had fêted her in the streets all day long, and the mayor had given a banquet in her honour that night.

The following day half Wolperting had begged her for swimming lessons. It was a duty she couldn't evade. She began by giving lessons to a number of physical training instructors and helped them to select their most promising pupils. Within a few days almost everyone in Wolperting could swim – apart from a few chronically hydrophobic individuals and Rumo.

Where he was concerned, Rala could afford to bide her time. She had her hands full at present and Rumo couldn't hide himself away for ever. He would reappear at school sooner or later; then she would resume the hunt, dog his footsteps and finally lay him low – she had sworn it by the name of Tallon. All in good time, though. First she would savour her fame for a little longer. After all, she was the very first heroine Wolperting had produced. She couldn't believe that her life would have any greater excitements to offer.

Urs can swim

'I can swim!' Urs announced one evening as he stuck his head into Rumo's room with a towel draped over his head and shoulders.

Rumo was sitting on his bed, tying up a bundle.

'I'm leaving Wolperting,' he said.

'What?'

'You heard.'

'You're taking a little trip? Waiting for this Rala hysteria to die down and then coming back? Letting the dust settle? Good idea.'

'No, I won't be coming back.'

'But where will you go?'

'No idea. Time will tell.'

'You came here because of Rala and now you're leaving because of her. Very logical!'

'What else can I do? I'm the laughing stock of the entire city, thanks to her.'

'She saved your life.'

'I wanted to save *hers*.'

'It doesn't matter what you wanted. You'd be dead now, but for her.'

'That might be preferable.'

'Look at it any way you like, you're in her debt. You can't just run off like this.'

'I can do as I please.'

'Of course you can, but–'

'But what's the alternative?' Rumo sounded genuinely desperate.

'There's only one thing to do in a situation like this: consult the oracle.'

'The oracle?'

'Ornt El Okro. He's got an answer to every question.'

'Ornt? The cabinetmaker, you mean?'

Ornt El Okro in demand

No one in Wolperting, not even the mayor, could say when Ornt El Okro had first arrived in the city, so it was assumed that he'd always been there. He was an expert cabinetmaker, but that talent wasn't the main thing that distinguished him from his fellow citizens. Ornt was exceptionally good at giving advice. His advice was sometimes right and sometimes wrong, but it always sounded, at the moment when he gave it, as convincing as the thunderous voice of a sacred oracle. So convincing did it sound that even those he'd wrongly advised in the past kept coming back for more. The mayor came to consult him on administrative problems, the school principal on educational matters, chefs on their menus, girls on their tribulations with boys. And in one respect they all behaved the same way: they acted as if Ornt's advice was *the last thing they'd come for*. They turned up with a broken chair, or a drawer in need of gluing, or a broken comb. Then, while Ornt was repairing the damage, they would stroll around the workshop talking about the weather and this and that until – sure as thunder follows lightning – they came out with something like: 'Oh, er, by the way, Ornt, tell me, er, I've got a friend (girlfriend/colleague/assistant chef) who's faced with the following problem . . .'

Ornt would listen, light his pipe, pace up and down, grunt several times, knock his pipe out, refill it, get it going again and wreathe his head in clouds of blue smoke. From these his voice would issue, sounding as reassuring and confidence-inspiring as the rumble of a cask of the very finest century-old Florinthian wine being rolled down a wooden ramp by Trappist monks. 'Hm, yes, well . . . I'm the last person to give anyone advice, as you know, but the way I see it, your friend might do worse than . . .'

There would follow a spontaneous recommendation, coupled with some advice on the best way of putting it into practice. People didn't come to see Ornt because they believed he would advise them correctly. They consulted him because he relieved them of something they feared even more than the prospect of their own funerals: the need to make a decision.

'Oh, er, by the way, Ornt, you know my friend Urs? Well, he's having problems with a girl . . .'

Ornt listened, filling his pipe with great deliberation. Rumo spoke in a hurried, agitated voice. He recounted the whole story from beginning to end, said 'I' several times instead of 'Urs' and croaked rather than spoke, his throat was so dry.

'Hm, yes, well . . . I'm the last person to give anyone advice, as you know, but . . . What was your friend's name again?'

'Urs.'

'Er, yes, Urs. First, I'd ask him the following question: When did you last do something really exceptional for this girlfriend of yours?'

'What do you mean? That's to say, I can imagine that, er . . .'

'Urs?'

'Yes, that Urs might ask you the same question.'

'That he might wonder what a girl would consider exceptional, you mean? Well, for instance, a diamond wrested from the clutches of a giant, or the still beating heart of a Werewolf in a golden bowl. That sort of thing.'

'What? Where would I – I mean, where would Urs get them from? Anyway, are girls keen on such things?'

'Their exact nature is unimportant. The gift could be an old pebble or a rusty doorknob. What matters is the *element of danger* associated with it.'

Rumo thought a while. 'I don't understand – er, as Urs would probably say.'

'Now stop this Urs nonsense! The whole city is gossiping about you and that girl. You're crazy about her, my boy – in fact, you've even got her name carved on your arm: *Rala*. One can see it when the wind blows your fur the wrong way.'

Rumo instinctively grasped his biceps.

Ornt grinned. 'I don't know if you've noticed, but the best jokes in the city have been told at your expense in the last few days.'

'It hadn't escaped me,' Rumo growled.

'The thing is, you owe her something. She saved your life. You can't just waltz up and propose to her – quite apart from the fact that you wouldn't dare to.'

If Rumo had known their conversation would take such an

unpleasant turn he wouldn't have got involved in it. Urs and his daft ideas! He couldn't wait to sneak out of the city.

'In this situation there's only one answer,' said Ornt.

'You mean there *is* an answer?'

'Yes. You need a *Threefold Token*.'

'A what?'

'Something that will win her heart, pay off your debt to her, and restore your reputation in the city. Three problems. For that you need a Threefold Token.' Ornt held up three fingers.

'I still don't see what you're getting at.'

'Listen: What if you gave her a gold ring, let's say? That would be a single love token, but it wouldn't be good enough, of course. A gold ring you've forged yourself would be a twofold love token – more personal but still not spectacular enough. So how about a ring you've forged from a gold nugget wrested from the claws of a seven-headed Hydra? That would be a threefold love token: valuable, personal, and acquired at the risk of your life.'

'You mean I've got to find a seven-headed Hydra?'

'That was only an example. There aren't any Hydras hereabouts. It doesn't have to be a ring, either. A diamond, a rusty doorknob – it doesn't matter what, as long as you risk death to get hold of it.'

'You're asking me to present Rala with a doorknob?'

Ornt frowned. 'You really are slow on the uptake, my boy.'

Rumo hung his head.

'What I mean is, it's got to be associated with something you're particularly good at.'

'Fighting?'

'No, woodcarving.'

Rumo deliberated. 'What should I carve?'

'I can think of something.'

'What? Tell me!'

Ornt cleared his throat. 'A casket made of Nurn Forest oak. With the leaf of a Nurn inside it.'

Rumo knew that Nurn Forest was somewhere near Wolperting. It had been the scene of the legendary battle of which Smyke had told him, but he knew little more about it than that.

'Cabinetmakers consider Nurn Forest oak to be the finest wood in

Zamonia. It's also the rarest, because only a few daring souls have ever managed to make off with some. It's guarded by the fearsome Nurns, so they say.'

'What are Nurns?'

'No idea. Leaf creatures, timber ghosts – no one knows for sure. Nurn leaves are reputed to be blood-red. Some say the Nurns are insects made of wood. Others claim they're carnivorous plants that can walk.' Ornt gave a wry smile. 'They're said to have resin in their veins instead of blood. At all events, Nurn Forest is supposed to be swarming with the creatures. That's why so few people enter it and why a piece of Nurn Forest oak is worth more than any diamond.'

'I see.'

'If you brought some back and, being as skilful as you are, carved a casket out of it, it would be a gift of a very special kind. But if you also managed to steal a Nurn leaf and put it inside, everyone would know you'd acquired that gift at the risk of your life. It would be at least as valuable as a golden casket filled with diamonds and captured from an army of Werewolves.'

Rumo was delighted. Ornt really was an inspired adviser. 'How long would it take me to get to Nurn Forest?'

'A day or two. One thing, though: If you meet anyone on the way I should let them know what you have in mind. The word will soon get back to Rala. If you really mean something to her she'll be worried sick about you. Then you'll return in triumph and – tadaa! – present her with the casket. She'll be knocked sideways!'

Rumo jumped up. 'Then that's what I'll do!' he cried.

He hugged Ornt, gave him a dramatic farewell wave from the doorway and hurried out.

For a while Ornt sat there in the kind of daze that always overcame him when someone had used him as an oracle. He spouted ideas like a fountain, together with detailed instructions on how to put them into effect. This phase was usually followed by a brief spell of relaxation during which Ornt sobered up and tried to recall what advice he'd given.

He had advised Rumo to go to Nurn Forest.

He had advised Rumo to cut a piece of Nurn Forest oak.

He had advised Rumo to carve a casket out of it and put a Nurn leaf inside.

Ornt El Okro leapt to his feet. Had he lost his wits? He might just as well have advised Rumo to fill his pockets with stones and jump into the Wolper.

He peered out into the darkness.

'Rumo!' he shouted down the deserted street. 'Rumo, wait! Where are you?'

But Rumo had already left the city.

Nurn Forest

Nurn Forest was situated on a hill, an almost perfectly circular eminence about a mile in diameter. It was densely wooded, and at its highest point, visible from afar, stood the Nurn Forest Oak. The latter's dark, leafless branches jutted into the sky, taller than any other tree.

Rumo had walked for three days and three nights, almost without rest or sleep. He had encountered no one on the way, only a few wild wolves that had prowled around him for a while and then slunk off. He put his hand on the hilt of his sword when he finally entered the forest and began to climb the hill.

'What forest is this?' asked Dandelion.

'Nurn Forest,' said Rumo. He hadn't exchanged a word with Dandelion since the episode on the bridge.

'So we're on speaking terms again, are we? Man, that's a weight off my mind!'

'Hmph!' said Rumo.

'Hmph!' said Dandelion. *'He actually said "Hmph!" to me! What joy! Nurn Forest, eh? What are we doing here?'*

'We're going to get ourselves a piece of Nurn Forest oak, so I can carve a casket out of it. For Rala.'

'Aha, woodcarving. Sounds great. A nice, peaceful occupation. I'm good at woodcarving.'

'The place is swarming with Nurns, so they say.'

'Nurns? What are Nurns?'

'No idea. I'm told you'll know one when you see one.'

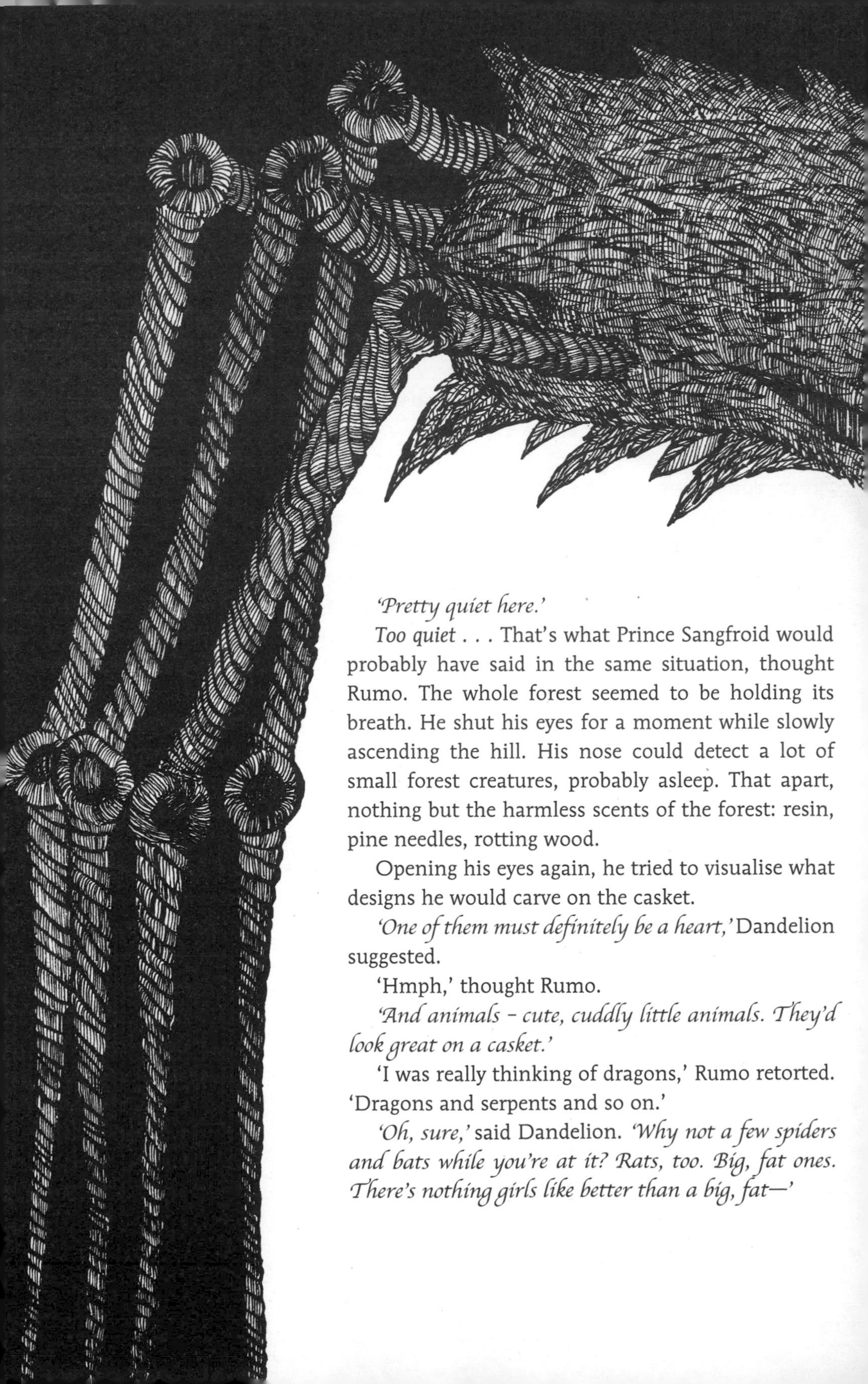

'Pretty quiet here.'

Too quiet . . . That's what Prince Sangfroid would probably have said in the same situation, thought Rumo. The whole forest seemed to be holding its breath. He shut his eyes for a moment while slowly ascending the hill. His nose could detect a lot of small forest creatures, probably asleep. That apart, nothing but the harmless scents of the forest: resin, pine needles, rotting wood.

Opening his eyes again, he tried to visualise what designs he would carve on the casket.

'One of them must definitely be a heart,' Dandelion suggested.

'Hmph,' thought Rumo.

'And animals – cute, cuddly little animals. They'd look great on a casket.'

'I was really thinking of dragons,' Rumo retorted. 'Dragons and serpents and so on.'

'Oh, sure,' said Dandelion. *'Why not a few spiders and bats while you're at it? Rats, too. Big, fat ones. There's nothing girls like better than a big, fat—'*

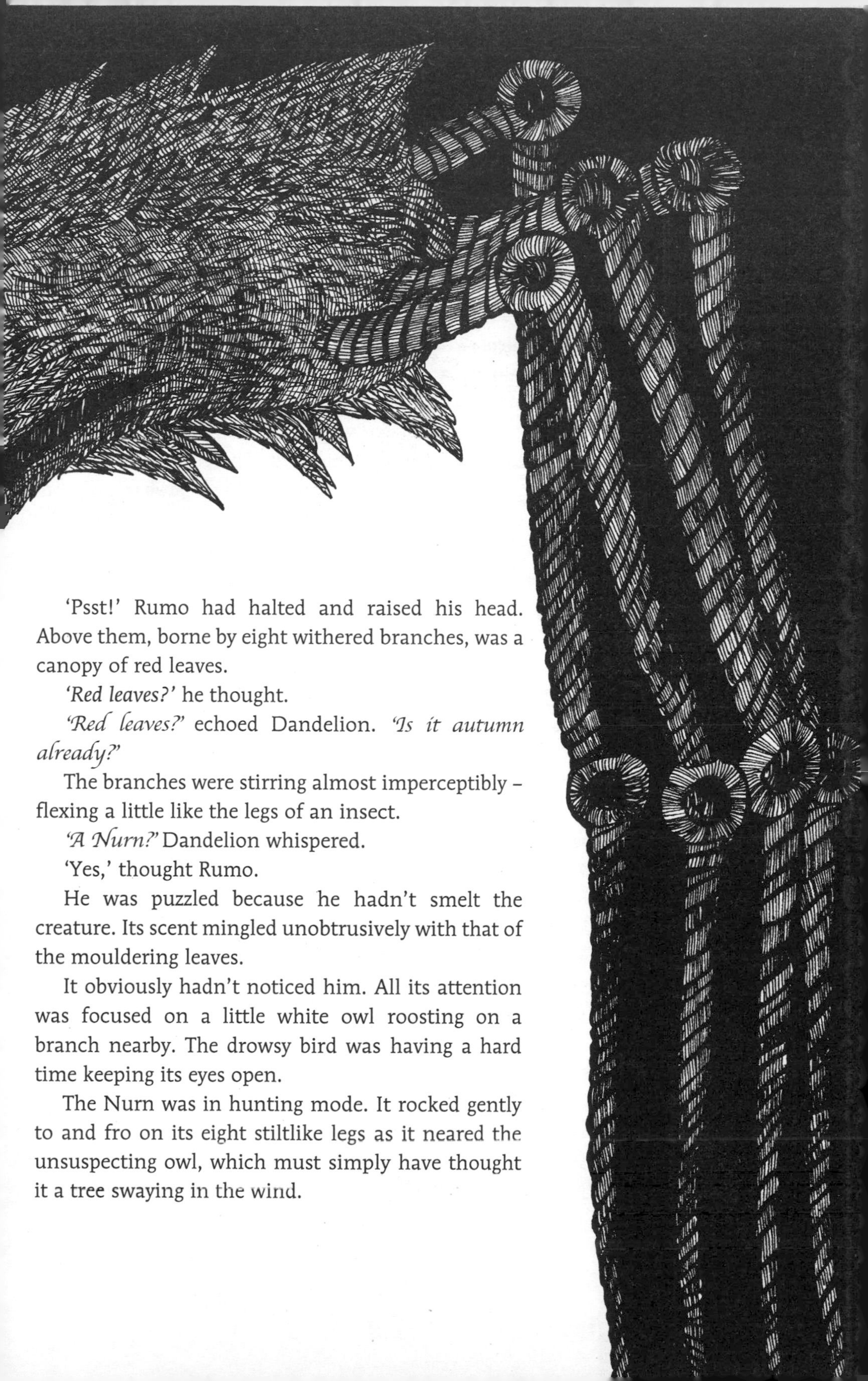

'Psst!' Rumo had halted and raised his head. Above them, borne by eight withered branches, was a canopy of red leaves.

'Red leaves?' he thought.

'Red leaves?' echoed Dandelion. *'Is it autumn already?'*

The branches were stirring almost imperceptibly – flexing a little like the legs of an insect.

'A Nurn?' Dandelion whispered.

'Yes,' thought Rumo.

He was puzzled because he hadn't smelt the creature. Its scent mingled unobtrusively with that of the mouldering leaves.

It obviously hadn't noticed him. All its attention was focused on a little white owl roosting on a branch nearby. The drowsy bird was having a hard time keeping its eyes open.

The Nurn was in hunting mode. It rocked gently to and fro on its eight stiltlike legs as it neared the unsuspecting owl, which must simply have thought it a tree swaying in the wind.

The Nurn emitted a sudden snarl, the owl gave a start and spread its wings, but a tentacle had already darted from the red foliage – a thin green tendril that wrapped itself round its prey like a whiplash and dragged it off the branch. Before the owl could utter a sound it had vanished into the leaves. The Nurn's swaying became a little more pronounced and crunching, lip-smacking noises issued from its interior. With a hollow 'Plop!' the owl's gnawed skeleton fell from the foliage.

'Good heavens!' whispered Dandelion. *'A carnivorous plant!'*

Rumo decided to avoid a confrontation with the Nurn. It was an utterly unfamiliar, unpredictable creature and he hadn't the faintest idea how to deal with it. Its leafy body was well out of reach overhead and he didn't know what the monster was capable of. The gurgling noises he could hear suggested that it was busy digesting the owl – probably a good moment to make himself scarce.

He scanned the ground for rotten branches in case he inadvertently trod on one. Very cautiously, step by step, he stole along until he was between two of the swaying legs. Then he trod on a Leafkin.

A Leafkin was simply a little Nurn – an infant Nurn, so to speak. Superficially it resembled a rust-red leaf. It was only when you turned it over that its eight spindly little legs came to light. What proved Rumo's undoing was that Leafkins could cry out. The tiny creature's shrill, piping squeak was loud enough to alert the adult Nurn. The latter howled like a gale blowing down a chimney, its timber joints creaked, its legs bent at the knee, the canopy of red leaves moved lower. Rumo was suddenly enveloped in a mass of yellow tendrils. Before he could draw Dandelion, dozens of these tentacles had wound themselves round his arms and legs and hoisted him into the air. He found himself suspended between the Nurn's legs. Then his bonds began to tighten as if the monster meant to slice him up like cheese.

Another tentacle darted down and wrapped itself round his neck. It tightened until he couldn't breathe and his eyes were bulging from their sockets.

'Use your teeth,' thought Rumo. His jaws closed with a snap, he jerked his head back, and red blood spurted from the lacerated tentacle. With a snarl the Nurn relaxed its grip and Rumo fell to the ground.

The monster groaned horribly and retracted its tentacles. Blood dripped from the red foliage. Rumo jumped up in a flash and drew

Dandelion from his belt, but he didn't have the sword in his hand for long. Almost at the same moment he sustained a violent blow on the back of the head: the Nurn had kicked him from behind with one of its stiltlike legs. Everything went black, his limbs refused to obey him, and Dandelion fell into the leaves. Rumo reeled around like a blind man.

The Nurn drew back another of its legs and kicked him in the back. Rumo fell headlong. The monster reared up and uttered a howl of triumph over his prostrate form.

'I'm here!' cried Dandelion. *'Just behind you!'*

Rumo reached behind him and seized the sword with both hands.

'Watch out, it's going to kick you again!'

Rumo rolled aside and the kick went astray. The tip of the leg buried itself deep in the forest floor and lodged there. The Nurn snarled and strove to tug it out, staggering to and fro, back and forth. Rumo seized the opportunity to regain his feet.

'Run for it!' cried Dandelion, but Rumo made no attempt to do so.

The Nurn had freed its leg at last. It rotated on the spot, taking aim at its adversary. Rumo stood beneath it with his sword at the ready. The monster took a few lurching steps to the rear and they watched each other closely for several seconds.

'What do you plan to do?' enquired Dandelion.

'Now I want a Nurn leaf,' said Rumo.

The Nurn emitted a menacing snarl like the one that had preceded its attack on the owl. Long skeins of blood were oozing from its body and staining the forest floor red. It made a few indecisive movements, lifted various legs in turn, flexed its six hind legs and levelled the tips of the front two at Rumo. Then it struck with all its might.

Rumo had never moved so fast before. Even he was surprised by the speed at which he leapt aside. He saw the tips of the monster's legs bury themselves in the ground, just where he'd been standing. They sank deep into the earth and stuck there. The forest rang with the Nurn's furious howls.

Rumo went over to one of the captive legs, raised Dandelion above his head, muttered '*Two-Handed Slice*' and brought the blade down as hard as he could. It severed the leg at a stroke. Blood spurted from the stump, the Nurn gave a roar and buckled at the knees. Its leafy red body sagged until it was just above the ground. Rumo stationed himself beside it and raised the sword again.

'Must you?' Dandelion said plaintively.

Rumo slashed at the curtain of red leaves and stood back. The foliage parted to reveal a rent from which the Nurn's intestines were spilling out on to the forest floor.

'Ugh!' said Dandelion.

Rumo lowered his sword. He went up to the lifeless monster, plucked a red leaf from its robe of foliage and put it in his pocket.

'Hey,' Dandelion protested, *'I'm all smeared with blood, it's disgusting! Kindly clean me.'*

Rumo knelt down, picked a handful of grass and proceeded to wipe the blade.

'Blood!' said a voice in his head. It was deep and muffled, like the tolling of a leaden bell. **'I . . . taste blood!'**

'What?' Rumo stopped short. That wasn't Dandelion's voice.

'Where am I? It's dark . . . Is that blood? Blood everywhere . . .'

Rumo finished wiping his blade clean. Was this a practical joke on Dandelion's part? Was he disguising his voice?

'Hey, what's that weird voice?' Dandelion demanded.

'Can you hear it too?'

'Where am I?' asked the voice. **'The last thing I can remember is . . . the battle . . . the enemy's drums . . . the screams of the dying . . . the song of the swords in the night . . .'**

'Oh dear,' said Dandelion, *'a Demonic Warrior. His brain . . . He's woken up!'*

'Who has?'

'I thought I was alone in here, but they must have forged a Demon's brain into the other half of the blade. The first blood we've shed has woken it up!'

'Blood . . .' groaned the voice.

'Who are you?' asked Rumo.

'I'm Krindle the Cleaver, Demonic Warrior and certified swordsman grade one!' the voice barked in military tones.

Rumo gave the blade of his sword a lingering stare.

'Not another voice,' he groaned. 'I don't think I can stand it.'

'Neither can I,' groaned Dandelion. *'This is awful.'*

'What is?' asked Rumo.

'Krindle is. His thoughts are getting mixed up with mine. Ooh . . .'
'You can read his thoughts?'
'They aren't thoughts, they're a horror story in themselves . . .'

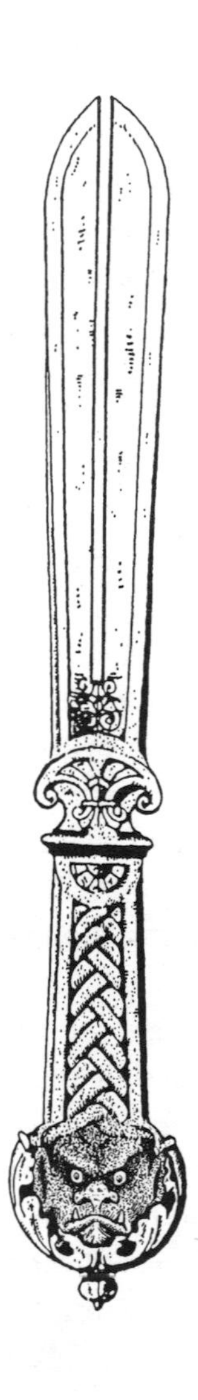

Krindle, the Demonic Warrior

Demons were a Zamonian life form that didn't have an easy time of it, no matter what period they were born in, but Krindle first saw the light at a period when Demons were having a particularly hard time. They were thoroughly unpopular, whatever subspecies they belonged to, and would probably have been exterminated if people hadn't been so frightened of them. As it was, they banded together for mutual protection into warlike communities ranging from small gangs of highwaymen to tribes numbering hundreds of members. If two tribes ran into each other they either fought to the death or formed themselves into a Demonic army, in which case they really got down to business. A Demonic army would roam around, looting and murdering, until another Demonic army entered the fray against it. Demonic Warriors displayed a brutality and commitment never to be found in other soldiers. No deserters, no surrender, no prisoners and no mercy - those were their watchwords. 'Demonic battle' was the Zamonian phrase for an engagement in which both sides sustained heavy casualties and neither emerged a clear-cut winner.

Krindle exemplified all the worst characteristics of his kind. He was hideously ugly, extremely bloodthirsty, boundlessly vindictive, infinitely evil - and absolutely honest. Really evil Demons could get by without lies or deceit because they were so obviously evil that there would have been no point in trying to disguise the fact. Krindle had no desire to please anyone, so he wasn't ambitious; and he hated everything, so he wanted nothing - except to kill and, sooner or later, to be killed himself. Krindle was a Demonic Warrior par excellence.

He had roamed around Zamonia even as a child. Like all Demons, his parents had thrown him away at birth. Demons considered this a mark of parental affection, because it was all they could do not to strangle their offspring with their own hands.

Krindle landed in a capacious barrel situated in the backyard of a Grailsundian mouse abattoir specialising in the sale of mouse bladders. This big barrel was used as a container for the scraped carcasses of Ornian Piddlemice that were carted away at the end of every month. So Krindle spent the first month of his life amid skeletons and blowflies, but also amid the cannibalistic mice that inhabited the barrel and lived on the gnawed remains of their own kind. Although still unable to walk, Krindle was already capable of defending himself with his powerful hands and sharp claws. He strangled one cannibalistic mouse after another, bit off the creatures' heads and drank their blood. He lost an ear and two toes – the mice nibbled them off while he was asleep – but he survived. After four weeks he was strong enough to climb out of the barrel and face the world. Even before learning to walk, he had gone through hell.

Krindle did nothing for the next five years but kill, eat and sleep. He killed mice and rats, but also cats and dogs, drinking their blood and eating their flesh. He divided his time between the sewers and the forests.

Then he settled down for three years. He made his home in a cave in Devil's Gulch and preyed upon anything or anyone that came his way, be it wayfarer or mountain goat. At eight he was a full-grown, seven-foot Demon ready to go out into the world in search of action.

He began by joining a band of Demonic brigands. Within twenty-four hours he had bludgeoned their leader to death and taken his place. They proceeded to raid a few farms and hold up small parties of travellers. When this became too boring they joined forces with a Demonic tribe numerous enough to raid whole villages. Krindle now received his first lessons in the art of warfare. He proved an apt and enthusiastic pupil, becoming an exceptionally proficient and successful swordsman. He liked to split his opponents down the middle, so his comrades in arms christened him Krindle the Cleaver. They taught him to speak so that he could not only obey orders but – later on, perhaps – issue some of his own.

One day the tribe encountered a big Demonic army. They were given a choice between joining it or being impaled on sharpened stakes. A few particularly pig-headed individuals opted for impalement, but Krindle and the others joined the army.

Now came Krindle's golden years. Although less of a free agent than before, he could pursue his obsession with killing to the full. The army attacked towns, fortresses and convoys. Krindle fought in the mountain labyrinths of Midgard, in the Demerara Desert Wars and the Battle of Toadmarsh. He and his fellow Demonic Warriors sang raucous songs filled with a yearning for death, drank wine mixed with blood and devoured the flesh of their enemies. His comrades rhapsodised to him about Netherworld, the Kingdom of Death in which they would live on after being slain in battle. Its amenities included huge dishes of meat and bowls of wine and blood from which they would be able to drink in perpetuity to the accompaniment of screams from their slaughtered enemies, for ever impaled down there on stakes of red-hot iron.

It was a wonderful day, the day Krindle died. The army had engaged a superior force of Yetis in a simultaneous blizzard and hailstorm, the unrelenting roar of the wind mingled with the crunch of splintered bone, and the snow was sodden with blood. Never had Krindle killed so many adversaries in a single day. Frozen stiff in a snowdrift full of severed limbs, he proudly and exultantly raised his voice in song:

'Blood, blood, blood!
Let blood like water flow!
Death, death, death!
May death my foes lay low!

And he swung his sword in time to the song. It thrust and sliced, severed arms and legs from torsos, and sometimes it split an enemy in half, right down the middle, for Krindle was Krindle the Cleaver.

Then the storm subsided, the snow stopped falling, and out of the steam that was rising from the acres of spilt blood stepped a gigantic warrior swathed from head to foot in a black cloak and armed with a huge scythe.

'Are you Death?' Krindle asked eagerly.

'No,' said the dark figure, 'don't mistake the message for the messenger. I've only come to *bring* you death. What is your accursed name?'

'My name? My name is Krindle the Cleaver.' Krindle tried to hurl himself at the newcomer, but his feet were stuck fast in the frozen blood and snow, so he hurled his sword instead. However, the battle had left him so weak and weary that the warrior evaded it with ease.

'How do you do?' said the warrior. 'I'm Skullop the Yeti, known as Skullop the Scyther.' So saying, he drew back his scythe and severed Krindle's head from his body. The head fell into the snow, gave a last smile, said **'Thank you!'** and closed its eyes. Krindle was dead. He had led a life of truly Demonic happiness and fulfilment.

But his head was collected with the others to be dried and shrunk. Having passed through numerous hands the length and breadth of Zamonia, it wound up in a smithy where Demonic Swords were being manufactured from Demon Range ore. His desiccated brain was pulverised and the powder mixed with the molten metal. And that was how Krindle became immortal.

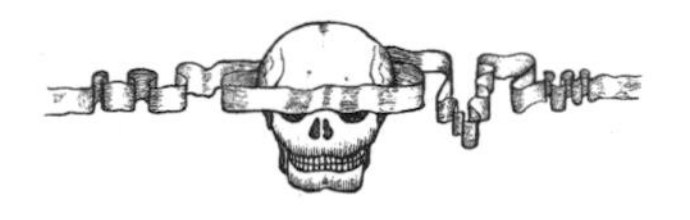

Friends for life

Still rather dazed, Rumo tottered through Nurn Forest sword in hand. He was looking for a spring, pool or puddle in which to wash the Nurn's blood off himself.

'I've a feeling we're going to be the best of friends,' said Dandelion.

'Friends?' said Krindle. He sounded puzzled.

'Well, I'm afraid we're destined to spend a long time in each other's company, so it might be better for us to make friends, my dear fellow.'

'My dear fellow? What is this, a nightmare? The last thing I can remember is that Yeti with the scythe and then –'

'You're dead.'

'Dead? Is this Netherworld? Where are all the big bowls of blood? Where are all my slaughtered foes impaled on red-hot stakes and roasting for ever in the flames of hell?'

'Yours isn't the kind of death envisioned by your barbarous, dim-witted comrades.'

'Dim-witted? Who's dim-witted? Where's my sword?'

'You don't have a sword any more. You are one.'

'What do you mean, I'm a sword? What's going on here? Oh, my head . . .'

'You don't have a head either, ha ha!'

'No head? Who's that speaking, anyway?'

'I don't think I can stand much more of this,' Rumo groaned. '*Two* voices!'

'And who are you?' Krindle demanded. **'Are you a Demonic Warrior?'**

'No.'

'He's a Wolperting.'

'What's a Wolperting?'

Rumo spotted a little spring gushing from among some boulders on the sloping forest floor. He knelt down beside it, stuck his sword in the ground and proceeded to wash. 'Before we go any further,' he said, 'I think we'd better discuss a few basic facts.'

'What basic facts?' asked Krindle. **'Who are you people, anyway?'**

'Shall I tell him or will you?' asked Dandelion.

'You do it,' said Rumo. 'I'm not too good at explaining things.'

The forest's canopy of foliage was growing thinner. The slope was less steep, and protruding from the ground in places were some thick black roots that could only belong to the Nurn Forest Oak. Rumo felt confident that he would soon reach the summit of the hill. Taking care not to tread on any more Leafkins, he trudged steadily upwards.

'So in short,' Krindle recapitulated, **'I'm a sword. I'm a dried brain and I'm dead, but I'm also alive. You're a friend with horns who can speak and this unpleasant voice beside me belongs to a dead Troglotroll who's also a sword.'**

Rumo nodded. 'That's it, more or less.'

'What was that about an unpleasant voice?' asked Dandelion.

'This must be a nightmare!' Krindle groaned.

'There's no pleasing you, is there?' Dandelion said reproachfully. *'You're dead, my friend, but you can still live on in another form. Very few people get that chance. Show a bit of gratitude.'*

'Very well, let's assume this isn't a dream and I really am a sword—'

'Half a sword!'

'All right, half a sword. What will I do as a sword? Will I be used for killing? For shedding blood?'

'No, for carving.'

'Carving?'

'Yes,' Dandelion whispered, *'for carving a casket for his sweetheart!'*

'But first we must cut off some wood,' Rumo decreed.

'I'm Krindle the Demonic Warrior! I wasn't reborn to chop wood. I'm a killer!'

'Oh dear.' Dandelion sighed.

'Could the two of you shut up a moment? I think we're getting close.'

The Nurn Forest Oak

The roots growing through the forest floor were steadily multiplying in number. Their dark shapes proliferated everywhere. On the summit of the hill stood the biggest tree Rumo had ever seen. Far wider than it was high, it was a wooden monster only fifty feet tall but at least three hundred feet in diameter.

'The Nurn Forest Oak,' said Rumo. 'Enough wood for a thousand caskets.'

Rollicking around in the branches of the ancient oak tree and on the grass in front of it were some forest creatures, among them a Unicornlet, a Twin-Headed Lambchick, a Cyclopean Owl, and a raven. A Zamonian Cuddlebunny sat just in front of the tree, nibbling grass.

Rumo drew his sword.

'That's the spirit!' growled Krindle. **'Let's kill that rabbit.'**

Rumo went up to the tree and took some measurements. A short, thick branch growing at shoulder height was just the right size. He raised his sword.

'I wouldn't if I were you,' said a soft voice. 'I'd strongly advise you not to go hacking away at the Nurn Forest Oak without permission.'

Rumo spun round. There was no one in the clearing apart from the animals.

'Who was that?' Krindle demanded.

'Down here,' said the voice.

Rumo looked down. It was the Cuddlebunny speaking.

'Nobody hacks away at the Nurn Forest Oak without official permission,' it said, scratching its ear with a forepaw.

'That rabbit!' cried Krindle. **'It's being provocative. We must kill it!'**

Rumo ignored him. 'Are you the guardian of the Nurn Forest Oak or something?' he asked.

'No, I'm not the guardian of the Nurn Forest Oak. I *am* the Nurn Forest Oak,' the Cuddlebunny said with a touch of pride.

'I've ended up in a madhouse!' groaned Krindle.

Rumo looked puzzled. '*You* are the Nurn Forest Oak?'

'Well, it's a trifle hard to explain. Mind if I go back to the beginning?'

'All right,' said Rumo, 'but I'm in rather a hurry. I have to carve a casket for my sweetheart.'

The Cuddlebunny stared at him wide-eyed, then hopped off into the forest without a word.

'Hey!' called Rumo. 'Where are you going?'

'There, now it's gone!' Krindle complained. **'We could have sliced it in half at a single stroke.'**

'The thing is,' the raven chimed in from its perch on one of the branches overhead, 'all the creatures here are my spokesmen, so to speak – the spokesmen of the Nurn Forest Oak. I speak through them because, being a tree, I can't speak. My name is Yggdra Syl.'

Rumo clasped his brow. 'This is all rather confusing . . .'

'It's quite simple, really. I'm a tree, but I speak via a raven. Or a rabbit. Or an owl – via any creature with vocal cords that happens to be in my vicinity. It's a kind of telepathic ventriloquism. Understand now?'

'No.'

'Then I'll have to go back to the beginning . . .'

'I'm sorry,' said Rumo, 'but I really don't have much time and—'

'Listen,' said the raven. 'You want my permission to hack off a piece of my precious flesh, so kindly find the time for a chat with a lonely old tree.'

Rumo sighed. 'If you insist.'

'We ought to kill that confounded crow,' said Krindle.

The raven uttered a final croak and flew off. A big fat Chequered Toad hopped over to Rumo and sat down at his feet. It reminded him unpleasantly of his chess lessons.

'At first I was just a tree,' the toad began in a sepulchral voice. 'I simply grew, you understand. A branch here, a branch there, one annual ring after another – the sort of things trees do. I didn't think, I merely grew. That was the *Age of Innocence.*'

The toad clambered awkwardly on to a thick black root.

'Then came the *Age of Evil*,' it went on. 'For many years the air was thick with smoke and the stench of charred flesh.'

'Ah, the Demonic Wars,' Krindle sighed nostalgically.

'Many battles were fought and one of them took place in this very forest. They went at it hammer and tongs, believe me. Heavy casualties, no winners, only losers. The forest floor was sodden with blood. Then silence fell, but not for long, because the *Age of Evil* was followed by the *Age of Injustice*.'

The toad assumed a resentful expression.

'I couldn't help it, I served as a gallows - not an episode in my career of which I'm proud, take it from me. Hundreds - no, thousands - were hanged from my branches. Then it really went silent. That was the *Age of Embarrassment*. People were ashamed of what they had done in the *Ages of Evil* and *Injustice*, and nobody entered the forest any more. The corpses suspended from my branches swung to and fro in the wind until the rotten ropes snapped and they fell to the ground. Softened by the rains, they mingled with the blood in the soil. I assume that this mixture of dead leaves, blood and decaying flesh produced the Nurns, because the creatures suddenly sprouted from the ground and took to prowling around. They weren't here to start with, at all events. Not that I could help it, my roots, too, absorbed this blood, this cadaverous mush, this deadly fertiliser. And that was when I began to think.'

The toad shook itself, uttered a last cacophonous croak and hopped off. A Unicornlet climbed down the tree head first and continued the story in a piping voice.

'Thinking and growing was all I did. At first my thoughts were of nothing but pain and revenge, probably because I'd inherited them from those who had been hanged. A tree could hardly avenge anyone, however, so I steered my thoughts in other directions. I'd been fertilised by many different brains belonging not only to warriors but to men of peace, to the physicians and scientists, poets and philosophers who had been the first to be strung up during the *Age of Injustice*. I thought of everything, in fact.'

The Unicornlet darted back up the tree and disappeared into a knot hole. Its voice, which now sounded hollow, might have been coming from the bottom of a well.

'I grew below ground as well, sending my roots deep into the earth. Branches don't interest me as much - they're more for fresh-air fiends and bird lovers. Hey, if I asked you what was the most immobile living creature in existence, what would you say?'

'No idea,' said Rumo.

The Unicornlet reappeared. It stuck its head out of the knot hole and said, 'Well, you'd probably say a tree, possibly even an oak tree. We're supposed to be the epitome of stability, reliability, imperturbability, et cetera. That's all nonsense! We're really the most mobile living creatures in existence. We're always on the move – always and in every direction: upwards, downwards, north, south, east, west! We're never still. We stretch out and expand, branch by branch, leaf by leaf, root by root, annual ring by annual ring. Oak trees are really the finest symbols of mobility, but people insist on misinterpreting us. It's no fault of ours.'

In two bounds the Unicornlet leapt out of the knot hole and landed on a branch with its bushy tail in the air.

'My roots reach deep, deep down – deeper than the roots of any other tree. I could tell you where the most productive diamond deposits and veins of gold are to be found. I know where the finest white truffles grow by the sackful. I know where fabulous treasures lie buried.'

The Unicornlet spread its forepaws.

'And my roots are still growing. Do you know why Nurn Forest is situated on a hill? The hill consists entirely of roots, that's why. *My* roots.'

The little creature performed half a dozen swift leaps and disappeared into the upper branches of the oak tree. Rumo gazed about him in dismay. Then a mole came burrowing out of the ground at his feet and took up the thread.

'I realise that most people react to the word "geology" as they would, let's say, to the words "carpet weaving": boring old soil and rock. But then, most people have no roots. You'd be amazed how exciting it is to send your tentacles snaking down through geological strata towards the centre of the planet. It's like leafing through a book written by the earth itself. Full of secrets! Full of surprises! Full of mysterious marvels!' The mole scooped a load of earth out of its burrow.

'I made some incredible discoveries. For example, light gushing from the rock in a subterranean cave like water from a spring and plunging into a lake filled with luminous air! I came across fossils that would make your ears flap, my young friend. I found a crystallised jellyfish a thousand feet in diameter and inside it the half-digested remains of a huge dinosaur – which itself contained a half-digested creature whose appearance defied description. A whole army of palaeontologists could subsist on my scientific findings.'

'Isn't it time you came to the point?' asked Rumo. 'If there is one.'

The mole burrowed into the ground head first, scooped another few loads of soil out of its hole and disappeared.

The Twin-Headed Lambchick fluttered around Rumo's head and perched on his left shoulder. One of its heads said, 'Yes, yes, I won't bore you with the geological details, because they pale into insignificance – utter insignificance, you understand – beside the greatest discovery I made during my explorations down below.'

'One day,' the second head went on, 'when I'd grown my roots to a depth of several miles, they broke through a layer of ice. It formed the roof of a cavern of vast dimensions. You realise what this means?'

'No,' said Rumo.

'It means,' the two heads said, speaking in unison, 'that this entire continent is merely a roof, a canopy concealing another, deeper world!'

'Netherworld!' hooted the Cyclopean Owl from the branches of the Nurn Forest Oak. 'Netherworld!'

The Twin-Headed Lambchick emitted a startled squawk and fluttered off.

'Netherworld!' the owl repeated in a low voice. 'Make a note of that name! We're moving about on a thin layer of fragile ice beneath which lurks another, darker, more evil world!'

The owl swivelled its head round a full ninety degrees and back again. Then it opened its single watery, bloodshot eye and fixed Rumo with a piercing gaze.

'Believe me, I never cease to regret having sent my inquisitive roots down so far. But for this discovery my life would be more carefree. Ever since then I've felt as if the earth may open up beneath my feet and engulf me at any moment.'

The owl regurgitated a few pellets, spread its wings and flew off with a whirring sound.

A leaf-coloured Sylvanosnake lowered itself from the branches right in front of Rumo, gazed at him hypnotically, and lisped, 'That was my story and my story is my message. You may cut off a piece of wood now, if you wish. I badly need pruning in any case.'

While Rumo was proceeding to cut off the branch, the snake crawled around in the leaves at his feet and watched him with interest.

'A casket for your sweetheart . . .' it hissed. 'Well, well! I imagine you're a great success with the ladies, a well-built youngster like you.'

Rumo blushed. 'I'm not, to be honest.'

'Come, come, you ladykiller!' said the snake. 'Carving a casket out of Nurn Forest oak? How romantic can you get! You're a crafty one, I must say.'

'It wasn't my idea.'

'Ah,' said the snake, 'false modesty. So that's your game, is it? Still waters run deep, et cetera. I'll bet your still waters drown the girls in droves!'

'It's me that's done the drowning up to now,' Rumo growled, doggedly hacking away at the branch.

'You're all right, youngster,' said the snake. 'You aren't a show-off, or you'd have told me how you killed the Nurn.'

'You know that?'

'I know everything that happens in my domain - and a lot more besides, my friend. I've had a lot of time to think, so if there's anything you want to know, ask away.'

'Many thanks,' said Rumo, 'but no.'

'Really not? Nothing on your mind?'

Rumo reflected. 'Wait, yes, there is something . . .'

'Out with it.'

'What grows shorter and shorter the longer it gets?'

'Life, my friend, life!' replied the snake. 'That was too easy.'

Rumo felt an utter fool. Of course! He could have thought of that himself.

'You should have asked me where to find the biggest hoard of buried treasure.'

'Thanks, but I've got all I need.' Rumo tugged at the branch and snapped it off.

'Ouch!' said the snake. 'Still, you couldn't carve a casket for your sweetheart from finer wood.'

'This was really generous of you,' Rumo said. 'I'm afraid I must be going now.'

'A pity,' the snake said with a sigh. 'I enjoyed our little chat. All the best, then. Perhaps we'll meet again.'

'You never know,' Rumo said as he plodded off with the branch under his arm. 'Many thanks.'

'Watch out for those confounded Nurns!' the snake called after him. 'Oh, by the way, what's her name?'

Rumo turned. 'Whose name?'

'Your sweetheart's, of course.'

'Rala.'

'Rala . . . Pretty name. What's yours?'

'Rumo.'

'Rumo? You mean like—'

'The card game, yes, I know.'

'That's funny.'

'Very funny,' Rumo said sullenly.

'What is it now?' Krindle growled.

The Demonic Warrior seemed to be still in shock after his resurrection, because his response to every minor annoyance was irritable in the extreme. After leaving Nurn Forest, Rumo had sat down on the grass, got out his sword and set to work on the branch. Darkness was falling.

'We're caaarving a caaasket,' warbled Dandelion, who was artistic by nature. *'A caaasket for Rumo's sweetheart.'*

Krindle sighed.

With a few well-aimed blows, Rumo cut the branch to the requisite basic shape, a slab of wood the size of a brick. Then he sawed off a flat lid and patiently hollowed out the slab. Having tongued and grooved the edges so that the lid would slide open and shut, he started on the fine work.

He adorned the sides and back of the casket with stylised foliage and tendrils, roots and bark, and on the front he carved a half-relief of Yggdra Syl, the Nurn Forest Oak, from memory. He modelled every twig and leaf with the greatest precision. On the branches and among the roots he carved the various creatures through which the tree had communicated with him: the Cuddlebunny, the Unicornlet, the Cyclopean Owl, the snake, the raven, the toad, the mole, and the Twin-Headed Lambchick. Dandelion assisted him with artistic advice to the best of his ability.

'What's all this fiddle-faddle?' Krindle demanded impatiently as Rumo conjured a Unicornlet's ear out of the wood with the tip of his Demonic Sword. **'Was that really why I died, so as to wind up carving sentimental gewgaws?'**

'Love is stronger than death,' said Dandelion.

'Like hell it is!' snapped Krindle.

Click, click! Some tiny splinters of wood went flying, and in their place appeared some cross-hatching the thickness of a hair. Dandelion waxed positively ecstatic.

'More to the left! Whoa! Half a millimetre to the right! Whoa! That's it! The tip of that root could do with a few more finishing touches . . . Yes, there. Now!'

Click! Another splinter detached itself from the workpiece. It was little bigger than a grain of dust, but the artistic effect was remarkable.

'You're very good at this,' Rumo said approvingly.

'Details are the secret of all true art,' said Dandelion. *'I don't think much of grand gestures.'*

'I do,' growled Krindle. **'Three heads lying in the snow at a single stroke, that's my idea of art. How much longer is this childish nonsense going to take you?'**

Rumo went on carving far into the night. He had lit a fire and sat down close beside it. Much to Krindle's disgust, he and Dandelion kept thinking of minuscule improvements.

Eventually, Rumo decided that the casket was finished. He eyed it appraisingly. It was by far the best piece of work he had ever produced. He inserted the blood-red Nurn leaf, slid the lid shut and stowed the casket in the pouch attached to his belt. Then he lay down to sleep.

Unpleasant smells

Rumo reached the environs of Wolperting after a three-day walk. He patted his pouch to reassure himself that the casket was still there. Genuine Nurn Forest oak. Hand-carved, with a Nurn leaf inside it. A powerful threefold love token calculated to win the heart of any girl.

'We should do this more often,' said Dandelion. *'Carve pretty things, I mean. I'm fond of creative activities.'*

'I'm not!' Krindle grunted.

'We could open a studio of our own: "Rumo and Dandelion, Artists in Wood. Caskets and Love Tokens of all kinds." It couldn't fail.'

'Shut up a moment! I heard something!'

Rumo had come to a halt and was straining his ears. The hilly terrain was sparsely wooded and strewn with boulders the size of houses. A knee-high pall of mist floated between the withered pine trees.

'Something dangerous?' asked Dandelion.

'Ah, danger!' Krindle sounded hopeful. **'Will we have to defend ourselves? Will we have to do some killing?'**

'There are three of them. I know that scent, but where from? They aren't Wolpertings. They smell unpleasant. Not dangerous, just kind of mouldy.'

'Damnation!' Krindle exclaimed. **'But we can kill them all the same. For smelling mouldy, I mean.'**

'We can surprise them at least,' said Rumo. 'They're beyond that big boulder in the dip down there.'

Zigzagging between the rocks, he stole down the hill as silently as the mist itself. The smell of mildew grew stronger as he rounded the grey colossus in the hollow. Other unpleasant smells were also detectable. He drew his sword for safety's sake.

'Kill . . .' Krindle whispered softly.

'Toadshit!' cried a shrill voice in the mist. 'Where's the toadshit?'

'How should I know?' another voice retorted curtly. 'Use the rotting larks' tongues. They smell roughly the same.'

Rumo came out from behind the boulder. 'Hello there!' he said.

Posko, Krasko and Bisko, the three Ugglies from the annual fair, spun round and stared at him as if he'd caught them red-handed. They were standing round a black, cast-iron cauldron in which some kind of evil-smelling broth was simmering. Behind them stood a large handcart piled high with all manner of alchemical equipment.

'It's you!' cried Posko, levelling her forefinger at Rumo. 'You!'

'What are *you* doing here?' Krasko croaked, glancing nervously at Rumo's sword. 'Is this a raid? We've nothing that could possibly interest anyone who isn't an Uggly.'

Rumo stuck the sword in his belt. 'I simply happened to be passing,' he said. 'I didn't know it was you. Forgive the intrusion.'

'You!' cried Posko. 'I know your future! You'll enter a forest of legs, but you'll defeat the monster they belong to! You'll converse with trees and animals!'

'I already did,' said Rumo.

Krasko cackled with laughter. 'What a genius! She can foretell the past.'

Posko thrust out her chin. 'Pah!' she snorted.

'Would you really like to know your future, youngster?' asked Bisko. 'We're just making some tarotic soup. We were going to bottle it, but it's best when fresh, of course. How about it?'

'Er, no thanks, I'm in a hurry. I won't keep you any longer.'

Rumo waded through the mist on his way past the Ugglies.

The smell alone was reason enough to quit the scene as fast as possible.

'So you really wouldn't care to learn something about your Silver Thread?' Bisko said artfully. 'You seemed pretty interested in it at the fair.'

Rumo stopped short. He thought for a moment.

'I don't have any money on me.'

'It's on the house,' Krasko tittered. 'Because you didn't attack us.'

'All right,' said Rumo. 'What about my Silver Thread?'

'Not so fast,' said Bisko. 'We aren't magicians, you know.' Her companions laughed wearily at this old chestnut.

'First we must finish the ceremony,' said Posko. 'Where's the toadshit?'

'I already told you: we don't have any toadshit. Use those confounded larks' tongues!'

Posko removed some slimy slivers of meat from a glass jar and tossed them into the seething cauldron. A sulphurous yellow cloud of steam arose. Rumo recoiled a step and the Ugglies broke into a dramatic, croaking chorus:

'Failure or prosperity,
untold wealth or bankruptcy,
perfect health or malady,
wisdom or insanity,
which of them will come your way?
Will it dawn, your lucky day?
Will the future you dismay?
Time will tell, but who can say?
We Ugglies can. We look straight through
the mists of time, so do not rue
our prophecies. They'll all come true.
We see them in our bitter brew!'

Krasko looked at Rumo and said, 'All we mean is, what will be, will be and there's nothing anyone can do to—'

'I understand,' Rumo said impatiently. 'Now could you . . .'

The Ugglies bent over their seething mush.

Rumo shuffled from paw to paw. Why, he wondered, did he allow their hocus-pocus to unnerve him? Urs had probably been right. It would have been better to give the Ugglies a wide berth.

They were now poring over the cauldron as though mesmerised.

'They're deliberately keeping you on tenterhooks,' Dandelion whispered.

'We ought to kill them,' muttered Krindle.

'Well?' Rumo asked the hideous trio. 'How does it look?'

The Ugglies awoke from their trance. They exchanged meaningful glances and startled exclamations.

'Phew!'

'Wow!'

'Well, I never!'

Then they put their heads together and started whispering.

'Well?' Rumo demanded brusquely. 'What is it?'

Posko was nudged to the fore by the other two.

'Listen,' she said gravely. 'This is something we've never come across before in all the years we've been practising our profession. We had a vision of your future – a crisp, clear-cut, highly detailed vision with none of the usual mistiness or blurring. It was definitely the clearest vision of my career.'

'Mine too, sister!' said Krasko.

Bisko nodded. 'I never saw a clearer one. Clear as glass, it was!'

Posko gathered her robe around her. 'Well, we saw what lies ahead of you and we've jointly decided . . .'

'Go on?'

'. . . not to tell you about it.'

'What!'

'Believe me,' said Posko, 'it goes against the grain, professionally speaking.'

'On your way, youngster,' cried Bisko, 'or we'll have to sew our lips shut!'

Rumo felt cheated. 'But I thought it was your job to predict the future.'

'Kill them!' Krindle pleaded.

'Predicting *nice* things, *that's* our job,' said Krasko. 'Let me give you an example. I once told a Grailsundian bricklayer he'd be crushed to death by a load of bricks – the very next day, on his own building site. What did he do? He steered clear of it and took the day off. Then he became restless and went for a walk. One thing led to another, and at some stage he found himself outside the building in question. There weren't any bricks around to fall on anyone and his mates asked him to lend a hand if he wasn't doing anything. All the bricks had already been laid, so what could go wrong? He entered the building site and at that moment – crash! – a load of bricks came hurtling down, out of the blue, and landed on top of him. No one ever discovered where they came from.'

Krasko raised her spindly forefinger. 'What I mean is, we can foresee the future but not influence it. That's a curse, not a blessing, and that's why we only predict nice things – because we feel responsible for the bad things once we've said them out loud.'

'It's even worse if people actually *hold* us responsible for them,' Bisko said darkly. 'Ugglies have been burnt at the stake before now.'

Rumo drew his sword. **'That's right!'** said Krindle. **'High time you cut off their ugly heads!'**

'Listen,' Rumo said impatiently. 'I never asked you to look into the future; you insisted on doing so. Now I want to know what you saw. Don't compel me to use force!' He brandished his blade in the air.

The Ugglies hastily retreated. They gathered round again, put their heads together and did some more whispering. Then Posko stepped forward.

'Very well, we'll offer you a compromise. We'll foretell your future, but we'll disguise our prophecies a bit. And change the order in which they occur.'

'All right,' Rumo said with a sigh, replacing the sword in his belt.

Posko began. She gazed skywards and raised her arms above her head. *'You will enter a forest of legs!'*

'Is that your favourite prophecy?' asked Rumo. 'That's the second time you've told me.'

'Then it'll happen again, damn it!' Posko snapped. 'And this time the legs'll be longer!'

Krasko stepped forward. *'You will walk across a lake dry-shod and cross swords with Living Water!'* she cried dramatically.

'I'm damned if I'll walk across a lake, dry-shod or not,' said Rumo. 'I can't swim.'

Now it was Bisko's turn to step forward. *'You will seek the heart of Death on Legs,'* she said solemnly, *'but you will find it only in darkness!'*

'Hm,' said Rumo. 'That was really well disguised.'

'One more thing,' said Posko. 'You may be a hell of a fellow with your sword and so on, but you don't know the first thing about girls.'

Rumo flushed. 'Was that another prophecy?'

'No, just a general observation.'

'Go now, youngster,' said Posko, 'and be quick about it! Bad things are in the offing. We can't say more. Beware the Vrahoks!'

'Vrahoks?' said Rumo. 'What are Vrahoks?'

'Hold your tongue, Posko!' Krasko hissed.

'Go, youngster. Go!'

'Be off with you!' cried Bisko.

The Ugglies went into a kind of frenzy. They overturned the cauldron with a concerted effort, and the yellow mush seeped into the ground.

Then they proceeded to gather up their odds and ends and load them on to the handcart. Rumo paid them no more attention. He strode off without another word.

'What was all that about?' Dandelion asked when they had gone some way. *'Rather unprofessional of them.'*

Far too quiet

'I told you,' said Krindle. **'We should have cut off their ugly heads.'**

Rumo was walking fast. He wasn't really worried, but it couldn't hurt to put on speed. Those scarecrows had dashed his spirits.

The sun was already low in the sky by the time he reached the brow of a hill from which Wolperting could be seen in the distance. Scraps of glowing red cloud were drifting over the city. Rumo paused to take scent. He shook his head in surprise, then sniffed again. There was an acrid, thoroughly unfamiliar smell in the air. And it was quiet – *far too quiet*, as Prince Sangfroid would have added. At this range his sensitive ears should have detected the noises of the city. A ringing anvil or tolling bell.

'Anything wrong?' asked Dandelion.

'I don't know. It's so quiet.'

He could make out the city wall, which was already bathed in shadow, and one of the great gates. No one was going in or out, no one crossing the drawbridge over the moat. That was unusual too. Rumo paused again and shut his eyes.

The Silver Thread – it wasn't there any more!

He broke into a run.

'What's the matter?'

'Rala has gone.'

'What do you mean?'

'She isn't in the city. I can't detect her scent.'

'Perhaps she's gone for a walk outside the walls.'

'Perhaps she's dead,' remarked Krindle.

'Krindle!'

'These things happen, that's all I meant. A terrible accident. A brutal murder . . .'

'Krindle! Please!'

The portcullis was lowered, but there was no sign of a sentry. Rumo's cries went unanswered, so his only recourse was to climb one of the watchtowers. He squeezed through a loophole, descended the stairs and entered the city. Not a Wolperting to be seen. The street just inside the city wall, usually such a hive of activity, was deserted. Rumo felt sick, the acrid stench was so strong.

'Where has everyone gone?'

'Maybe there's something on. An assembly or something.'

'Maybe they're all dead,' Krindle suggested helpfully.

Rumo combed the streets. Not a single Wolperting came his way. There were no signs of life, no sounds, no familiar smells. Most of the front doors stood open and one or two window-panes were smashed. Whether or not these were traces of a fight, Rumo saw no blood, no dead or wounded. It looked as if the inhabitants had quit the city in a hurry.

Hoth Street was deserted. Rumo's front door was ajar. He raced up the stairs and flung open the door of Urs's room. It was empty. No signs of a struggle there either. All the furniture was in its usual place, but the acrid smell was omnipresent.

Rumo ran through the deserted streets to Rala's house. He halted several times, convinced that someone was following him, but it was only the ghostly echo of his own footsteps.

Rala's house: deserted.

The school: deserted.

Ornt's workshop: deserted.

City Hall: deserted.

Rumo criss-crossed the entire city, searching every street, every alleyway, every square. He shouted for Urs, for Rala, for Ornt – for anyone. 'Hello, hello?' he called, but there was no response. It was as if everyone in Wolperting had vanished – as if they had dissolved into this foul miasma. In the end he abandoned the search.

'I expect they're all dead.'

'Krindle! Why do you keep saying that?'

'These things happen to cities. Demonic armies attack them and carry off the inhabitants. I've seen it often enough.'

'But this was a city full of Wolpertings,' Rumo muttered wearily. 'The toughest warriors in Zamonia with the finest fortifications imaginable. No army could have taken this city, however strong.'

'You see?'

'Any city can be taken, it's just a question of how.'

'Where's the Black Dome?' Rumo said suddenly. He came to a halt, looking thunderstruck.

'Where's what?'

They had reached Black Dome Square. It was empty. The dome had disappeared and in its place was a huge, round, gaping hole in the ground.

'The Black Dome has gone. There used to be a big building here. It's vanished.'

Rumo drew his sword and walked slowly over to the hole. All that could be seen where the mysterious dome had stood was a dark chasm with thin wisps of vapour rising from its depths, as if the earth itself had been rent asunder.

Rumo cautiously approached the edge of the chasm and held his sword poised above it. Below him was a yawning abyss, a dark, circular shaft with a flight of broad stone steps spiralling into its depths. The acrid stench stung his nostrils and made him feel faint. Black and white sparks danced before his eyes. He swayed for a moment, right on the lip of the murky crater, then managed to step back.

'Good heavens!' Dandelion exclaimed. *'What's that?'*

'Netherworld,' replied Krindle.

And here the drawer marked R
closes for a while.

Having shown you so many things,
both good and evil, it needs a short rest.

Before it opens again, please consider this:
Are you prepared to follow Rumo into another world?
A world of darkness teeming with dangers?

Are you really brave enough?

Watch, then, because the drawer is opening again!

Look inside - deep inside!

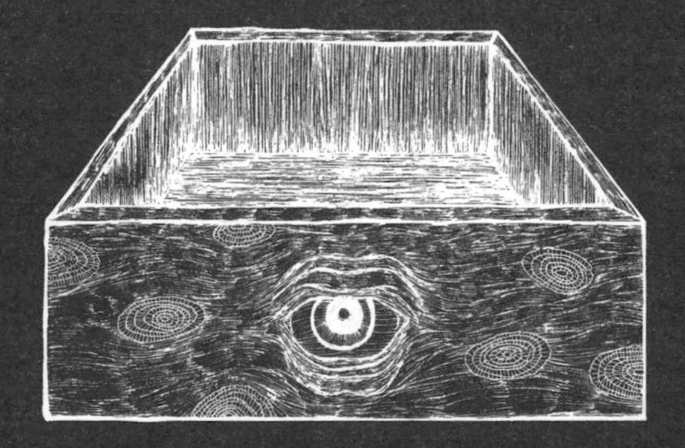

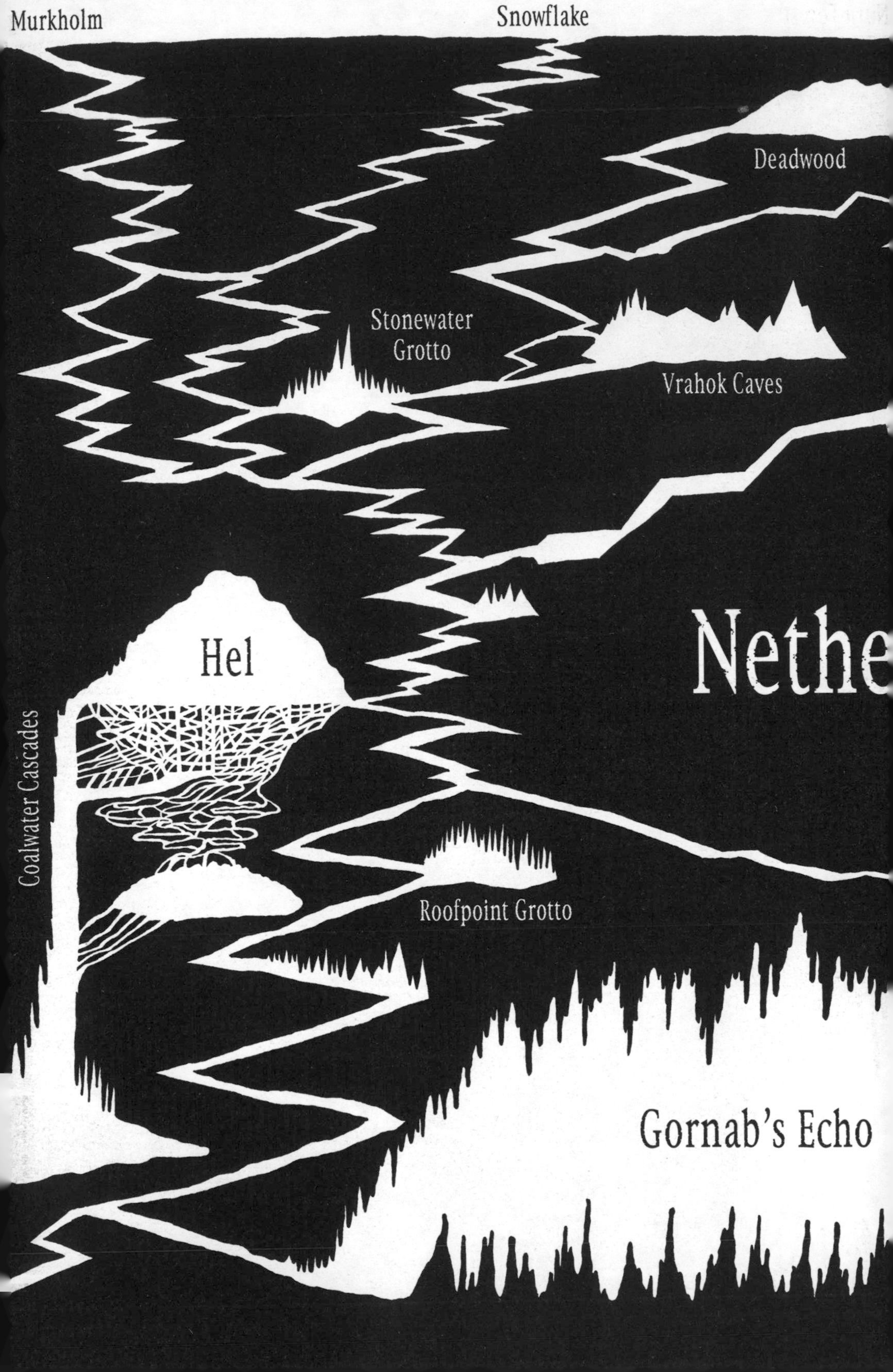

Murkholm

Snowflake

Deadwood

Stonewater
Grotto

Vrahok Caves

Nethe

Hel

Coalwater Cascades

Roofpoint Grotto

Gornab's Echo

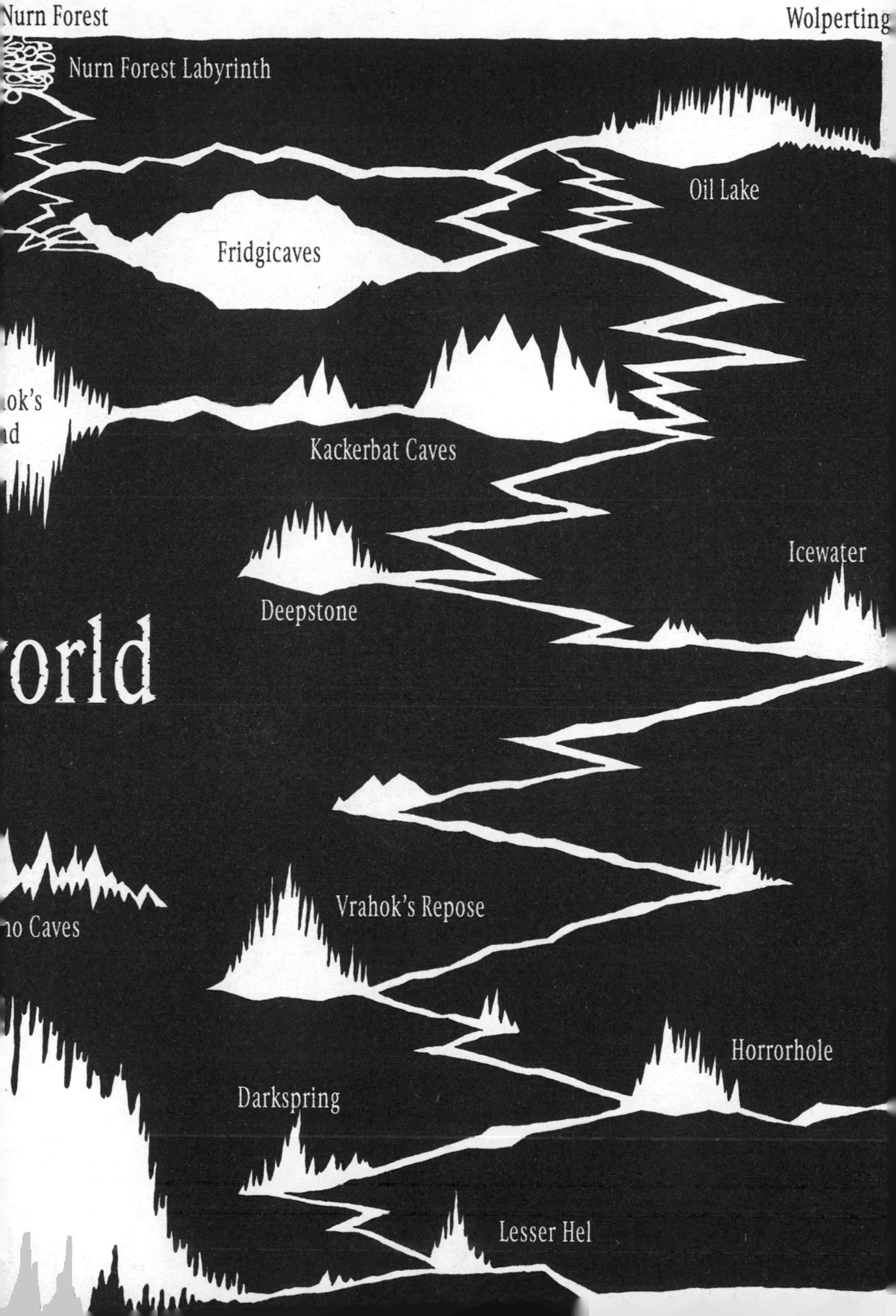

Nurn Forest

Wolperting

Nurn Forest Labyrinth

Oil Lake

Fridgicaves

ok's
d

Kackerbat Caves

Icewater

Deepstone

orld

Vrahok's Repose

o Caves

Horrorhole

Darkspring

Lesser Hel

Book Two
Netherworld

I.
Skullop the Scyther

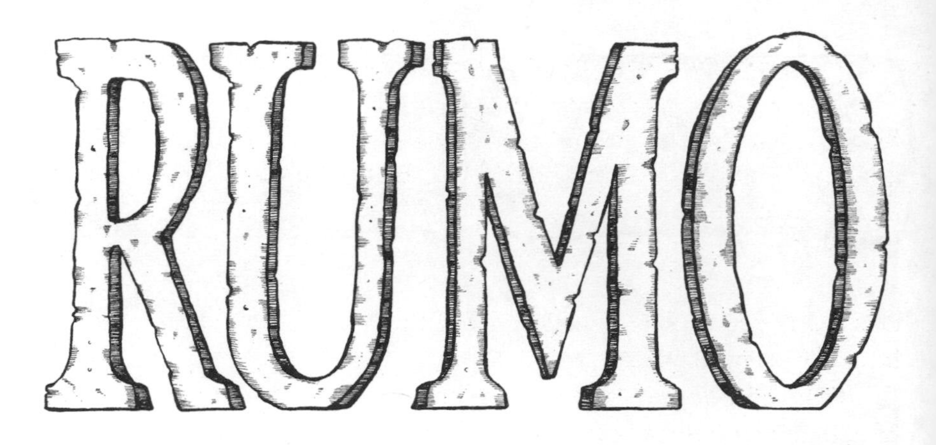

spent a long time wandering aimlessly through the city. The acrid stench had driven him away from the chasm that had once been spanned by the Black Dome, but there was nowhere he could have found peace of mind. Every house, every street and square reminded him of the city's inhabitants, of his friends and his own kind. Above all, everything reminded him of Rala. He was in shock. His mind refused to accept what his senses told him: that the whole of his existence had vanished without trace from one moment to the next. He dared not halt and come to terms with the silence that had taken possession of the city. Even his footsteps on the cobblestones – even his laboured breathing and the sounds he made when opening doors and searching deserted rooms – were preferable to this dismal and depressing silence.

It was long after nightfall by the time he recovered his composure. He felt ashamed of having wasted so much time roaming aimlessly around, so he set off for Ornt El Okro's workshop. There he found all he needed: a pitch-pine torch and a tinderbox, some dried meat and a water bottle. He stowed the meat in his pouch, filled the water bottle and secured it to his belt, picked up the torch and the tinderbox, and returned to Black Dome Square.

'What do you have in mind?' asked Dandelion.

'Are we going to do some killing?' asked Krindle.

'We're going on a journey,' said Rumo.

The acrid, biting smell had almost disappeared by the time they got to the square. Rumo lit his torch, stationed himself on the rim of the chasm and held it over the edge.

'The Black Dome. It hasn't disappeared after all – it's still there!'

Rumo circled the hole, illuminating the sides with his torch. The Black Dome had divided into six equal segments and sunk into the ground like retractable knife blades. 'The Black Dome isn't a building or a monument, it's a gateway!'

Now that the acrid smell had evaporated, Rumo could shut his eyes and take scent. The Silver Thread was there again! Thin and tremulous but clearly perceptible, it snaked down the huge shaft and disappeared into its gloomy depths.

'What do we do now?' asked Dandelion.

'Climb down there,' said Rumo, drawing his sword.

The Blood Song

The spiral staircase was so wide that a whole army could have marched down it. The flat stone slabs of which it was constructed were slimy in places. There must have been thousands of steps leading down into the earth's interior – an impressive architectural achievement.

Rumo had underestimated the depth of the shaft. He had gone a considerable way down it when his torch suddenly went out, plunging him in total darkness.

'I can't see a thing any more,' he said.

'That's bad,' said Dandelion.

Krindle groaned. **'One false step and we'll reach the bottom quicker than we'd like.'**

'I can usually see with my eyes shut,' Rumo said. 'But only if there are sounds. Everything's so silent down here.'

'Then you'd better make some sounds yourself,' Dandelion suggested.

'How do you mean?'

'You could sing, for instance.'

'I can't sing,' said Rumo.

'Nonsense. Some people sing better than others, but anyone can.'

'I don't know any songs.'

'I do,' said Krindle.

'You know a song?' Dandelion said incredulously.

'You bet I do! I know any number of songs. We used to sing them in battle.'

'Oh dear! Still, anything's better than nothing. What's your favourite?'

'The Blood Song.'

'Sounds delightful.'

'I could sing it first and Rumo could sing it after me.'

'I suppose there's no alternative.' Dandelion sighed. *'All right: one, two, three . . .'*

'Blood!' sang Krindle.

'Blood?' Rumo queried.

'Don't ask questions, just sing!'

'Bloood!' Krindle sang again.

'Bloooood!' croaked Rumo.

'My goodness,' Dandelion exclaimed, *'you really can't sing.'*

'Well, are we going to sing or aren't we?'

'Yes, of course.'

'Once again: Bloood!'

'Bloood!' Rumo sang loudly and discordantly. He shut his eyes.

'Bloood! – Bloood! – Bloood! – Bloood! – Bloood!' came the echo.

Rumo's inner eye saw the shaft become suffused with a ghostly, wavering green glow that faded and eventually went out.

'It's working,' he said. 'I could see the echo.'

'Splendid! Carry on.'

'Blood, blood!' Krindle sang fervently.

'Blood must spurt and blood must flow!
Blood, blood!
Let blood gush from every foe!
Blood, blood!
Blood as far as eye can see.
Blood to all eternity!'

'Blood, blood!' Rumo repeated half-heartedly.

'Blood must spurt and blood must flow!
Blood, blood!
Let blood gush from every foe!
Blood, blood!
Blood as far as eye can see.
Blood to all eternity!'

Rumo had clamped his eyelids shut. He could make out every detail in the subdued green glow that filled the shaft – every step, every block of stone in the walls. He resumed his descent.

'Swing the sword with all your might,
cleave your foe from head to heel,
let your blade his innards bite,
lay them open with cold steel.'
'Swing the sword with all your might,
cleave your foe from head to heel,
let your blade his innards bite,
lay them open with cold steel.'
'Blood, blood!
Blood must spurt and blood must flow!
Blood, blood!
Let blood gush from every foe!'
'Blood, blood!
Blood must spurt and blood must flow!
Blood, blood!
Let blood gush from every foe!'
'Swing your axe, behead the Troll,
let him not his fate escape!'
'What?!' Dandelion exclaimed indignantly.
'In the dust the wretch shall roll,
with his gory neck agape.'
'Swing your axe, behead the Troll,
let him not his fate escape.
In the dust the wretch shall roll,
with his gory neck agape.'
'Here's another song for you!'

'At last!'
'Brains, brains!
Cleave the skull and out they seep!
Brains, brains!
Killing's fun and life is cheap!'
'Ugh!' said Dandelion.
Still singing, Rumo descended ever further into the interminable

shaft, guided by the faint green light of the echoes. Steps were missing here and there, or separated by gaping cracks, or covered with evil-smelling slime or moss, but the staircase itself had been carefully constructed. It spiralled down into the ground for miles.

Rumo was growing hoarse and Krindle's monotonous Demonic songs were getting him down as well as Dandelion. He was about to suggest calling a halt when the staircase levelled out. It led through a huge stone gateway and into a tunnel. Opening his eyes, Rumo saw a faint blue glow that seemed to be coming from the far end.

'We've reached the bottom,' he said. 'I can see a light.'

'A light?' said Dandelion. *'Where would a light be coming from, so far below ground?'*

'We'd better take a look,' said Rumo.

The floor of the tunnel, too, was covered with puddles of stinking slime. Water dripped from the roof, which was invisible in the darkness overhead. Occasional squeaks could be heard in the gloom, possibly made by rats or bats. The blue glow at the end of the tunnel became brighter with every step.

'This is a curious place,' said Rumo. 'I wonder who was responsible for it all?'

'Positively creepy, I call it,' said Dandelion.

On emerging from the tunnel, Rumo lost his sense of balance for a moment. He was standing on a rocky plateau from which a series of terraces led down into an immense valley of blue-black rock dotted with murky pools and wreathed in delicate wisps of luminous mist. Hundreds of feet overhead loomed a stone 'sky' from whose monstrous great stalactites water dripped incessantly. The whole landscape was bathed in shimmering bluish light.

Rumo marvelled at this unusual sight.

Even the drips that fell from the stalactites and collected in the pools were glowing, so that it seemed to be raining blue light. Black winged creatures, possibly birds, possibly bats or worse, were wheeling above the subterranean valley.

Rumo drew his sword and held it up to give Krindle and Dandelion a better view of this weird panorama.

'Well, I'll be . . .' whispered Dandelion.

'Where is the blue light coming from?' asked Rumo.

'Probably from a phosphorescent fungus of some kind,' said Dandelion. *'I've often seen this kind of thing in caves. I was a Troglotroll, don't forget.'*
'It's Netherworld,' said Krindle.

Oil Lake

The rocky terraces, which had been worn smooth by the drips from above, were slippery and offered few footholds. One false step might have ended in a breakneck glissade, but Rumo climbed down with care and reached the valley floor unscathed.

The mist seemed denser and more luminous down below. The blue water fell in a fine drizzle, and Rumo could see and smell that the murky pools were filled with viscous oil. The smell of this subterranean landscape was unlike any he had met before. It was strange and mysterious, noisome and dangerous. He shut his eyes. The Silver Thread was dancing in the middle of the vast cavern, but its extremities were hidden in the blue mist beyond. He decided to follow it.

The pools of oil became more numerous and their smell more intense, and Rumo had to steer clear of them more and more often. Seated beside many of the pools were furry little creatures with hooked beaks. They cast inquisitive, suspicious glances at the intruder and sped him on his way with nasal squawks of indignation.

The noxious smell eventually became so overpowering that it almost took Rumo's breath away. He climbed a slope, reached the summit and halted abruptly.

'What is it?' asked Dandelion.

Rumo was gazing out across a huge expanse of oil. It stretched from one side of the cavern to the other and disappeared into the distance. This was no pool, it was a lake. Rumo's route was barred. When he shut his eyes he was shocked to discover that the Silver Thread had vanished! Either the powerful stench of the oily lake had overwhelmed it, or it had snapped. Undecided what to do, Rumo paced restlessly up and down the shore.

Swaths of blue mist were wafting across the lake, glowing and pulsating like a living creature.

Rala wakes up

The first thing Rala noticed when she opened her eyes was an acrid smell.

It was pitch-dark, but something must have woken her in the middle of the night. All she could remember was falling into bed with limbs like lead. She could hardly move her arms, she'd spent so long giving swimming lessons in one of the small lakes outside the city.

She had at last returned home to find Ornt El Okro, the old cabinetmaker, standing outside her door. He looked as if he'd come to tell her something, but he merely said 'Good evening' and vanished into the dusk. Why had people been behaving so oddly towards her in recent days? There was nothing she regretted more than that dive into the river.

She ate some bread, drank a mug of milk and flopped down on her bed, where she just had time to think of Rumo before falling asleep.

And now she was awake. Her aching limbs still felt heavy. So heavy she could scarcely move a muscle, let alone stand up. So heavy, *she couldn't move at all.* Overcome with panic, she tried to kick and cry out, but all she produced was a terrified growl.

Instinctively, she sniffed the air. There was this vile, acrid stench that seemed to cling to her, but there was another smell too.

Metal.

Yes, her nose told her that her body was encased in metal – in a leaden sheath that enclosed her completely.

That was when panic really gripped her. She was in a coffin. She'd been buried alive.

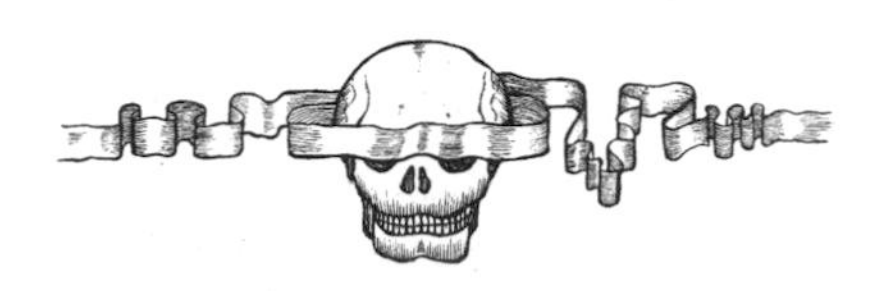

The Dead Yeti

'Rala!' Rumo called desperately across the lake. 'Rala!'

'Rala! Rala! Rala!' the echoes replied from overhead. They seemed to bounce off the stalactites like bagatelle balls. There was an ominous crack and fragments of rock came showering down from above. The furry little creatures with hooked beaks darted behind boulders, and into nooks and crannies. Then, with an almighty crash, a stalactite the size of a tree trunk broke off the roof of the cavern and plummeted into the pall of mist that floated above the lake. It sank with a mighty gurgle, then silence returned.

'Nice place, this,' Dandelion remarked.

'Hey!' said a low voice from somewhere in the mist. 'Are you crazy?'

Rumo drew his sword.

'Action stations?' asked Krindle.

'I don't know,' said Rumo. 'There's someone out on the lake.'

An unfamiliar, unpredictable life form? Talking mist? Living oil? Nothing would have surprised him.

A shadow detached itself from the mist and a small craft glided into view. A gigantic figure in a black hooded cloak was propelling it along with a pole.

'Are you out of your mind, youngster?' the figure whispered. 'Fancy shouting like that! That confounded stalactite only just missed me.'

'I'm sorry,' said Rumo.

'Ssh!' hissed the huge muffled figure. 'We only talk in whispers around here, understand?'

Rumo nodded.

'What are you doing here?' The giant had gently grounded his punt.

'I'm looking for my friends.'

'Hey, are you another of those hounds? Yes, you are. Were they *your* friends?'

'Who do you mean?'

'Listen, youngster: your friends did come this way and you should thank your lucky stars you weren't with them. You're alive, they're doomed to die, so go back where you came from and enjoy life. You're a lucky dog, ha ha!' The giant prepared to push off again.

'Wait!' Rumo shouted.

Rock dust came trickling down from the roof of the cavern.

'Ssh!' went the giant. 'Are you tired of life?'

'Do you know where my friends went?' Rumo whispered.

'Maybe.'

'Can you take me there?'

'No.'

'Why not?'

'Because I'm not as crazy as you are.'

'Can you ferry me across the lake?'

'I could, but I won't.'

Rumo deliberated. 'What if I yell and bring the house down?'

'You wouldn't dare!'

'Rala!' Rumo shouted at the top of his voice. 'Raaalaaa!'

Crack! Another stalactite broke off and came hurtling down. It landed in the lake with a muffled splash, sending ripples across its oily surface.

The giant winced. 'Climb aboard!' he hissed. 'And for heaven's sake pipe down! You really are suicidal!'

Rumo leapt aboard.

'Sit down and keep quiet!' the giant whispered.

Rumo complied. The giant pushed off. Silently they glided into the luminous mist.

'Did you see them?' Rumo whispered.

'I may have. I may have seen a pack of hounds being transported across the lake by Vrahoks. Maybe they were unconscious and suspended in nets. Then again, maybe not.'

'Vrahoks?'

'Did I say Vrahoks? Maybe I did, maybe not.'

'Can you take me where my friends were taken?'

'Maybe, maybe n—no, that's impossible.'

'Did you know I can sing? Not very well, but nice and loud.'

The giant grunted.

'Blood!' Rumo belted out. 'Blood! Blood must spurt and blood must flow!'

The stalactites creaked like icicles thawing in the sun.

'Ssh! Stop that, you idiot! I *can't* take you there, it's too far. I'll ferry you across to the other side, but that's all. After that you'll have to manage by yourself.'

'All right.'

They glided along in silence for quite a while. Then the giant said, 'Tell me, how come you know that Demonic song? Where have I heard it before?'

'Hey!' Krindle exclaimed inside Rumo's head. **'I know that voice!'**

'May I ask who or what you are?' Rumo hazarded.

The figure turned to face him. A wisp of glowing blue mist floated past its cowl and lit up a death's head with huge, close-set eye sockets and a massive, prognathous lower jaw. Weirdest of all, the skull was composed of black bone, not white.

'I'm dead,' replied the skeletal ferryman.

Rumo gave a start and recoiled a little.

'Hey, no need to be scared. I said I was dead, not that I was death in person. *Don't mistake the message for the messenger.*'

'Just a minute,' said Krindle. **'I've heard that somewhere before. That voice . . . I *know* that voice . . .'**

'And take care how you shuffle around on that seat, you could cut yourself on my scythe.'

Rumo looked under the seat. Sure enough, a gigantic scythe was lying there.

'Scythe? Of course!' Krindle growled. **'It's him, by all the Demons! It's the one who killed me!'**

'A scythe?' Rumo looked puzzled. 'I don't see any grass down here.'

'I use it to cut off heads.'

'You bet he does! Mine, for instance!' Krindle said eagerly. **'That's him, that's my murderer! Let's kill him! Please!'**

'Shut up!' Rumo muttered.

'What did you say?' the skeleton asked suspiciously.

'Nothing,' said Rumo.

'Ask him what his name is! Ask him what he's called!'

Rumo thought for a moment. How could someone they'd encountered down here have killed Krindle centuries ago, up there in Overworld?

'What's your name?' he asked.

'My name?' grunted the ferryman. 'They call me Skullop the Scyther.'

'I knew it!' roared Krindle. **'Skullop the Scyther! Punting around down here, cool as a cucumber? Incredible! He's a cold-blooded murderer! Draw me and let's kill him, please!'**

'And what's *your* name?' asked Skullop the Scyther.

'Rumo.'

'Rumo? Hey, has anyone ever–'

'Yes, they have.'

'Rumo, you've *got* to kill him, please! He's got me on his conscience, so kill him! Kill him as brutally as possible!'

Rumo tried to ignore Krindle's nagging voice.

'Do you have a story, Skullop the Scyther?' he asked.

'Everyone does,' Skullop replied, 'and mine is good for a couple of laughs.'

'May I hear it?' Rumo asked politely.

Like a ghost ship the punt glided through the luminous mist and across the dark surface of the lake. Skullop pushed his cowl back and fixed Rumo with his empty eye sockets.

'Actually,' he began, 'I was bragging a bit. I'm not really dead, or I wouldn't be punting around so happily, would I?' He gave a hoarse laugh.

'I'm pretty lively compared to a real corpse, but compared to you,

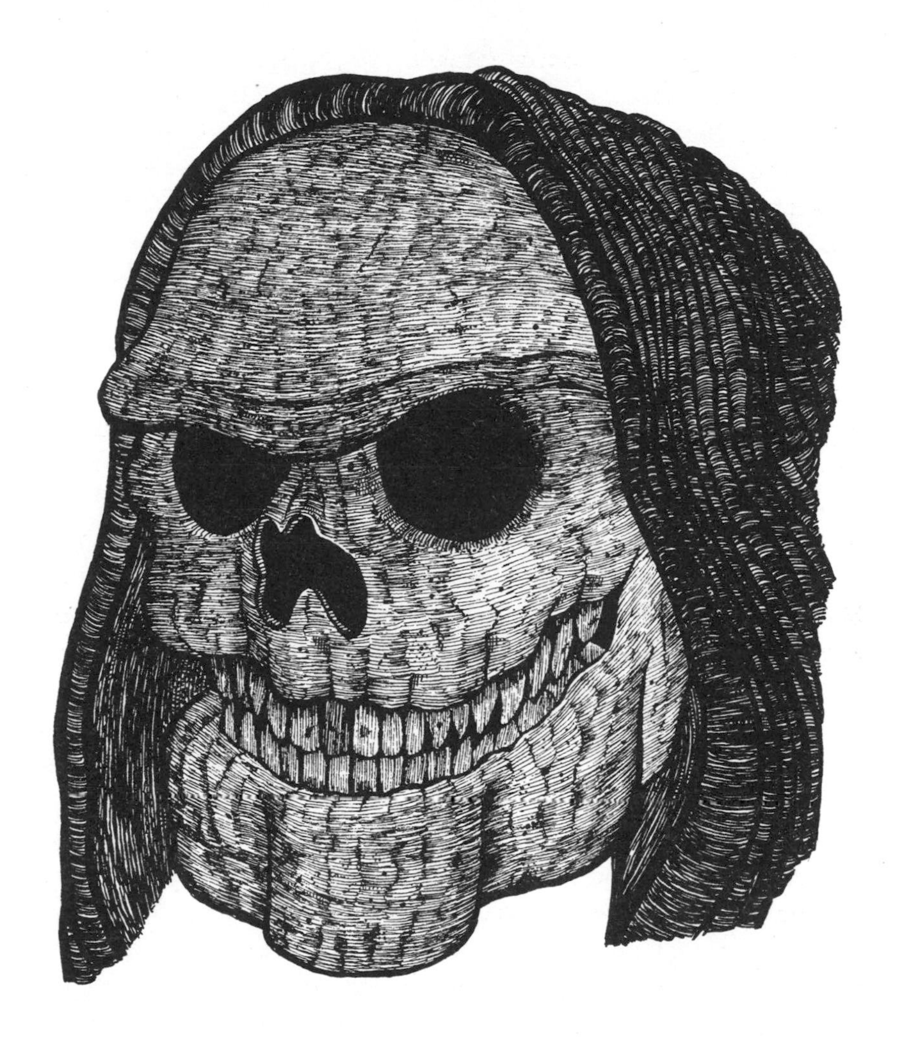

let's say, I'm a semi-corpse at best. My story sounds far-fetched and I don't cxpcct anyonc to believe it. On the other hand, if anyone claims it's a pack of lies I take my scythe and slice his head off, clean as a whistle, understand?'

'I understand,' said Rumo.

The story of Skullop the Scyther

'It all began like this. We were an army of wild Yetis from the Gloomberg Mountains, and we roamed through Zamonia spreading panic and consternation – the way Yetis do when they're young. We thought we owned the world – which we did, when you come down to it.'

Rumo stared out across the lake. All the colours of the rainbow were represented on its oily, iridescent surface.

'High old times, those were! I burnt the candle at both ends. No matter what tavern we walked into, the band stopped playing and we were plied with free beer. Who could have stopped us? We were on our way to Lindworm Castle, because in those days besieging Lindworm Castle was *the* thing for warriors to do.'

'I know,' said Rumo.

'You've heard the story, eh? Yes, you weren't a proper warrior unless you'd besieged Lindworm Castle. The place was said to be rich in loot of all kinds: the Lindworm Diamond, as big as a house; gold mines in which nuggets could be dug out of the walls with your bare hands; caves full of gems. "Hey, you dozy Lindworms!" we shouted when we reached the castle. "We're now going to come up and kick your fat, saurian backsides!"' Skullop chuckled.

'And then they tipped boiling pitch over you,' Rumo said softly.

'You heard that too, eh?' Skullop looked taken aback. 'Yes, those goddamned lizards showered us with pitch. Some mess! But we were Yetis – we weren't going to be driven back into the mountains by a few bucketfuls of boiling tar! "Hey, you marmot-eaters, you lily-livered pen-pushers," we shouted, "is that the best you can do?"'

'And then they tipped molten lead over you,' said Rumo.

'Hell's bells, you really are well informed. Who's telling this story, you or me?'

Rumo made an apologetic gesture. 'Sorry,' he said.

Skullop threw his weight against the pole and punted on. 'Now I've lost my thread . . .'

'They poured lead over you,' Rumo prompted him.

'Er, yes, precisely, molten lead. That was another kettle of fish altogether, believe me. We lost half our number. And that was when our luck started to run out.'

Rumo tried to look sympathetic.

'So we beat a retreat. And now the really heartbreaking part of my story begins, take it from me.' Skullop grunted with exertion as he poled the punt round a rock protruding from the lake.

'We marched on through Zamonia, zigzagging a bit. Why zigzagging? Because our courage deserted us whenever we came across anything even remotely resembling a castle or fortress – in fact, many of my men used to burst into tears. Well, an army of sobbing Yetis isn't a very edifying sight, especially when you happen to be in command of it. We badly needed a victory, you see. Just *one* successful conquest – anything would have done, or the Army of the Wild Yetis would soon be a thing of the past. And then we suddenly found ourselves on the borders of Nairland. Do you know Nairland?'

'Nairland consists of Cogitating Quicksand, so I've read,' said Rumo.

'You mean you're one of those eggheads who can read? No wonder you're a bit cracked,' said Skullop. 'But you're right about the Cogitating Quicksand, although I didn't know it at the time. So we came to the borders of Nairland. No opposing army, no fortifications, nothing. Just sand. I was about to give the signal to advance when I heard a voice in my head:

'*"Don't,"* it said. *"I'm quicksand – Cogitating Quicksand. I'll swallow you up."*'

Skullop uttered a scornful laugh. 'I thought it was a trick, of course. We'd heard reports of great treasures buried in a volcano in the middle of Nairland and no wild young Yeti was going to be bamboozled by a voice inside his head. So I marshalled my army in line abreast and gave the order to advance.'

Skullop leant on his pole for a moment.

'Well, we sank into the quicksand, every last one of us. One step and we were done for! Not a pleasant experience, believe me, suffocating in quicksand.'

He punted on.

'But that wasn't all – oh no! Quicksand doesn't just kill you, it does a really thorough job on you: it scours the flesh from your bones. We sank deeper and deeper, and the grains of sand wore away our faces, forced its way up our noses and into our skulls. And then it started all over again. Although we were well and truly dead, we regained the power of thought! My skull is still full of Cogitating Quicksand.'

The Yeti shook his head gently and Rumo could hear the sand rattling around inside.

'I've no idea how far we sank, or through what subterranean channels and tunnels, or for how long, but to me it seemed an eternity. Being buried alive is nothing in comparison! And then, at long last, we came out in this cavern. We fell through a hole in the roof and landed in this confounded lake – all of us, or as many as were left. The oil has soaked into our bones and made them black and supple. I don't know what's in the stuff, but it certainly contains plenty of energy – liquid energy! It's full of life from ancient times. So now we're dead but still alive, in a way. We're undead, you could say – neither one thing nor the other, with our skulls full of thinking sand.'

Rumo was dumbfounded. Even Krindle had fallen silent. The Yetis' fate seemed to have impressed him too.

'To keep ourselves occupied we carved some boats out of big seams of coal, and we've been punting around here ever since – not that many passengers come our way. Well, that's my story. Up to date, at least.'

'It's a really good one.'

'I told you so, didn't I? And the laughs are on me.'

The mist, which had thinned a little, was now floating above the oil in a thin, blue, shimmering layer. Not far away Rumo saw some other punts gliding along, manned by cloaked figures of similar size.

'My men,' Skullop said proudly. 'My undead men.'

'Where exactly are we bound for?' asked Rumo.

'The far shore. You want to get to Hel, don't you?'

'Hel? What's that?'

'A city. The capital of Gornab's crazy kingdom. The place they took your friends to.'

'You mean there's a city down here?'

'And what a city!'

'Who is Gornab?'

'The ruler of Hel. He's insane.' Skullop tapped his bony forehead.

'If that's where my friends are, that's where I want to go.'

'I thought as much. You really are a screw loose.' Skullop chuckled. 'Hey!' he called. 'Look, boys, I've got a customer!'

'Ssh!' said Rumo, cocking his finger.

'There aren't any stalactites here.' Skullop looked up at the roof, which was black and smooth. 'We can talk normally now.'

The other craft drew nearer.

The figures in them resembled Skullop and wore the same cloaks. Black skulls were visible under their cowls, and lying in their punts were heavy weapons: swords, clubs, axes. Rumo began to feel uneasy as they converged from all directions. He put his hand on his sword hilt.

'Kill him!' whispered Krindle.

'This youngster actually *wants* to go to Hel,' Skullop told his men with a laugh. 'What do you think of *that?*'

'A good idea!' one of them called back. 'Almost as good as marching us into a quicksand.'

'Yes!' called another. '"Follow me!" he said. "Follow me, boys, we're going to be rich!"'

The Yetis hooted with derision.

'That's what I have to listen to all the time,' Skullop growled. 'You make *one* mistake and—'

'Hey, youngster,' someone called. 'Be careful you don't run into any Vrahoks on your way to Hel.'

'Shut your trap, Okko!' snapped Skullop.

'What are Vrahoks?' Rumo asked.

'Listen,' said Skullop, bending over him. 'I realise you don't want to be dissuaded from going to Hel. You're stark raving mad, but still . . . If I told you what Vrahoks are you'd reconsider your decision. Well, shall I tell you what they are?'

'No,' said Rumo.

'I can't put him off, men!' Skullop called. 'He's got guts. The sort of guts we don't have any more.'

'The youngster's crazy, that's all!' Okko called back. 'Ever since I've had a noodle full of Cogitating Quicksand I think twice about everything I do. And the last thing I'd do down here is visit that crazy city of my own free will.'

'You see?' said Skullop. 'We think too much. We've turned into a bunch of yellow-bellies.'

'Go with him, then,' called Okko. 'Show the youngster the way to Hel, like you showed us the way into that quicksand.'

Skullop hastily punted on. 'Stupid idiots!' he grunted. 'Talk about bearing a grudge!'

'Sorry, youngster!' Okko called after them. 'We may be dead, but we aren't tired of life!'

His cronies laughed.

'Did you hear that?' said Skullop. 'They're dead, damn it all, but none of them would be mad enough to go to Hel. There's no mercy down here. No laws, either. Insanity reigns supreme in Hel. It's Gornab's monumental madhouse.'

The far shore of the lake came into view. Rumo fidgeted impatiently.

'How do I get to Hel from here?'

'There are various routes. I honestly don't know which to recommend, they're all so dangerous. You could go via *Gornab's Echo*, but it's a very long way round and that's where you'd be likeliest to bump into some roaming Vrahoks. You could also go via the *Fridgicaves*, but they're terribly cold and said to be infested with Icemagogs. There are some secret passages through the roof of Netherworld, but you have to know your way around extremely well if you don't want to get lost. Your best plan is to keep going straight ahead, because in Netherworld all roads lead to Hel – don't ask me why. It's just a question of how far you get. Down here there are only two directions: straight ahead or straight back.'

'I'm not going back.'

Skullop sighed. The punt grounded and Rumo leapt ashore.

'All right,' said Skullop. 'What will you do if you get to Hel?'

'I'll go in and rescue my friends. Then I'll give Rala the casket.'

'Who's Rala? What casket?'

'Rala is . . . well, my sweetheart,' Rumo said hesitantly. 'I've carved her a casket out of Nurn Forest oak.'

'Oho.' Skullop laughed. 'Better and better! A casket, eh? And that's why you're going to Hel all by yourself? With that cheese knife of yours?'

'Kill him, I beg you!' Krindle whispered again.

'I've done similar things before now, cheese knife or no cheese knife.'

'I'm sure you have. I like you, my boy.' Skullop grinned. 'You really are a screw loose.'

'Many thanks,' said Rumo.

'That wasn't a compliment, it was an insult.'

'I wasn't thanking you for the insult,' said Rumo, 'just for ferrying me across.'

Skullop laughed. Then he pushed off and disappeared into the mist.

II.
Hel

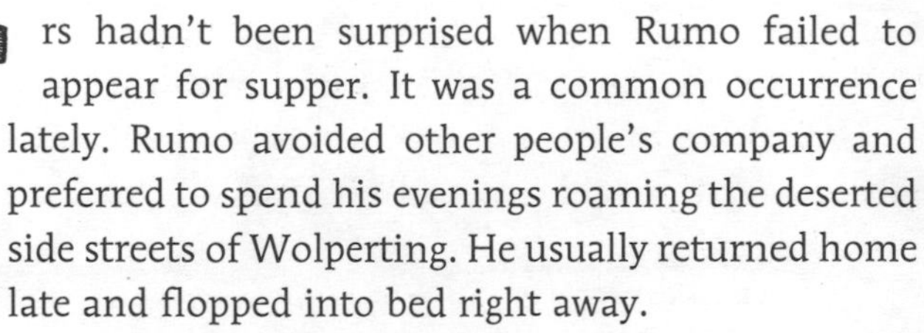

Urs hadn't been surprised when Rumo failed to appear for supper. It was a common occurrence lately. Rumo avoided other people's company and preferred to spend his evenings roaming the deserted side streets of Wolperting. He usually returned home late and flopped into bed right away.

Urs hoped that his advice to consult Ornt El Okro would bear fruit. His life had become devilishly complicated since he'd got to know Rumo, what with their strenuous fencing lessons in the woods, their interminable conversations at night, the fracas with Rolv, and his duties as a municipal friend. Everything had been much more uneventful before Rumo appeared on the scene. More tedious as well, granted, but Urs was fond of tedium. He even cultivated it.

That was why he took advantage of this Rumo-free evening to indulge in a little civilised tedium. One essential was a supper requiring protracted preparations, in this case a pot-roasted joint of beef which he had patiently studded with dozens of cloves of garlic and braised for several hours until tender.

Should he read a Prince Sangfroid thriller while eating? No, far too exciting. He thought a while. What did his meagre library have to offer in the way of suitable - in other words, tedious - reading matter? *Fifty-Five Ways of Caramelising Sugar*? No, he knew it by heart. Wait, how about *Culinary Delights from My Garden*, an unspeakably boring treatise on the cultivation of vegetables by Dancelot Wordspinner, one of Lindworm Castle's hopelessly outmoded authors? Yes, that was ideal. He decided to reread the chapter on blue cauliflowers.

Urs removed the beef from the saucepan, opened a bottle of long-hoarded Florinthian burgundy, sat down at the kitchen table with his meat, wine and book, and bored himself rigid. In the end he fell asleep face down on the table top.

The first thing he noticed when he awoke was an unpleasant smell. Had he been sick? Nonsense, he hadn't drunk that much! How had he got to bed? Why was the bed so hard? Oh, he was lying on the floor! He tried to stand up. There was a jingling noise in the darkness and he felt something cold round his wrists. He was handcuffed! What was this, one of the triplets' practical jokes, or was he still dreaming?

He heard a long-drawn-out scraping sound. A chink appeared in the gloom and the room was filled with a fitful glow like the flicker of firelight.

This wasn't his room. He was in a cell built of rough-hewn black stone, bare and windowless. Its only noteworthy feature was a pair of round, fist-sized holes in the floor, and from them issued the chains attached to his handcuffs. What was that noise drifting in from outside? Confused voices and laughter? A commotion of some kind?

Urs got to his feet. He gave an involuntary belch, and the sour taste nauseated him. Then he tottered over to the door. The chains did little to restrict his movements. The further he went the more links emerged from the floor.

Urs's nightmare

Once outside the cell he saw that flames really were the source of the light. It came from two large torches secured to the wall on either side of the door. He was dazzled for a moment, but then his eyes became accustomed to their new surroundings. He had emerged into a passageway. Stretching away to left and right of him was a wall interspersed with more doors flanked by torches. It was dark overhead, and on the other side of the passageway was another stone wall. This was where the babble of voices and laughter seemed to be coming from.

Urs was familiar with dreams of this kind. Animated, colourful nightmares full of sensory impressions and realistic architectural scenery, they usually culminated in some terrible catastrophe that woke him up: earthquakes, floods, conflagrations, meteor showers. They were the price to be paid for his midnight feasts: nightmares induced by his overtaxed digestive organs.

The sensory impressions were exceptionally strong this time. Urs could detect as overwhelming an abundance of smells as he had at the last annual fair: smells of cooking, perspiration, burning oil.

Another Wolperting emerged from the door on his left. Urs knew him, but only vaguely, so he couldn't remember his name. He was also wearing handcuffs and looking equally bewildered.

'Urs?' he said. 'Is that you?'

Urs shuffled towards the opposite wall with his chains scraping along the ground behind him. At every step the babble of voices became louder, the smells stronger and his uneasiness more intense. What lay beyond the wall and, anyway, was it wise of him to try to find out? Wouldn't it be better to slink back into his cell and stick it out until he woke up?

The theatre

Urs peered over the wall. He found himself looking down into a big, circular – no, octagonal – arena lit by hundreds of torches and braziers, a deserted expanse of pale, neatly raked sand. He was clearly in the gallery of some vast theatre, a sort of balcony running right round the eight segments of the auditorium. Above and behind him was another tier that seemed to be unoccupied, and assembled below him, in the largest tier of this nightmare theatre, were the spectators. Urs recoiled at the sight of them. It confirmed that he really was dreaming, for no place on earth could have harboured such a weird assortment of creatures.

He leant over the wall for a closer look. Roughly half the audience consisted of two-legged creatures notable for their greyish, sometimes almost deathly, pallor. Their heads, which were cloven above the eyes, stuck out on either side like bulbous horns. They wore sumptuous robes of velvet and shimmering silk, and their jewellery – gold rings, diamond brooches, silver bangles – glittered in the torchlight.

The front few rows of seats were reserved for the pale-skinned creatures, whereas sitting behind them were other spectators whose most salient characteristic was their diversity. Many of them were as small as dwarfs, others at least ten feet tall. Some were covered with green scales, others had red, yellow or blue skin. Urs saw apelike creatures with wings, midgets with crocodilian heads, Hogglings with elephantine trunks. Their one common feature was the fact that they belonged to a wide variety of life forms.

The audience, which included a scattering of Bluddums, Yetis, Turnipheads, Voltigorks and other boorish creatures, must have numbered thousands. This was certainly the weirdest place Urs had ever been to, whether sleeping or waking.

Immediately opposite him, on the far side of the arena and within the palefaces' tier, was an enclosure that attracted his attention. Separated from the rest of the audience by a balustrade and a cordon of Bluddum mercenaries, it was a box occupied by only two persons. In the centre of the box stood a bizarre throne resembling a big four-poster bed.

When Urs focused his gaze on the figure seated on the throne he recoiled a second time.

The hideous dwarf

He had never before set eyes on such a grotesque dwarf: the head was far too big for the body, the eyes too small for the head, the arms and legs too muscular for the puny chest, the neck too thin to bear the weight of the massive cranium, the nose too long and tapering for the bulky chin, the hands too fine-boned for the dwarf's generally uncouth appearance. Most horrifying of all was his mouth, which wore a ghastly ear-to-ear grin that might have been incised into his face at birth by a single sword stroke. Although he was utterly unlike any other creature in the theatre, his pale skin indicated that he was one of the life forms that occupied the best seats, and the fact that he was sitting on a throne might even signify that he was their king.

Over and above all this, however, Urs was particularly fascinated by another, non-physical characteristic: he had never seen anyone look so brazenly and unashamedly evil. The dwarf rolled his eyes theatrically until only the whites were visible, narrowed them to menacing slits, opened them wide once more and swept the audience with his piercing, hostile gaze. He was forever pulling faces, forever licking his grinning lips with a long, thin, darting tongue, forever cackling so spitefully that those around him flinched as though lashed with a whip. Urs couldn't understand how such an utterly repulsive creature had managed to insinuate itself into his dreams.

The second figure in the box was hovering in the background. It displayed the same graveyard pallor and cloven head but was tall and gaunt, unlike the dwarf. Also unlike the latter, it did not appear to relish its prominent position – in fact, it almost seemed to be skulking behind the throne.

The figure in black

The dwarf sat up on his throne. The gaunt figure gestured imperiously with its right hand and the hum of voices in the stadium died away. Having licked his grinning lips once more, the dwarf proceeded to speak in a high-pitched, strangled voice.

'Ingreets, new tivecaps of the Theetra of Thead! You have been troughb here to tighf! You have been troughb here to repish! O you torfunate ones! O you sochen ones! You are distened to tighf and repish for the internatement of this stinguidished ideaunce! And tighf you will! And repish you will! That is your escinapable disteny! Let the gillink mencecom!'

Such were the words that rang out across the arena. Couched in a mixture of familiar- and unfamiliar-sounding language, they seemed to be directed straight at the Wolpertings. Indeed, it seemed to Urs, despite the distance between them, that the dwarf's sparkling little eyes were focused on himself.

The Wolperting beside Urs gave him a look of incomprehension.

'Did you get all that?' he asked.

Urs noticed only now that a number of other Wolpertings had emerged from their cells in chains and were lining the parapet. In the distance he spotted Rolv, Vasko, Balla and many others. Ushan DeLucca was standing on the opposite side of the auditorium.

He suddenly remembered his neighbour's name: Korryn Darkfarm.

'No,' he replied, 'I didn't.'

'Where are we?' asked Korryn. 'Is this a dream?'

The spectators had listened to the dwarf's peculiar speech in silence, almost as if they felt embarrassed. They now began to shuffle their feet and utter nervous little coughs.

Urs thought, *'He asked me whether this is a dream. If it is, which of us is dreaming it?'*

'Where are we?' Korryn asked again. 'Who are all these creatures and who the devil is that hideous dwarf?'

The story of Gornab the Ninety-Ninth

Gornab Aglan Azidarko Beng Elel Atoona the Ninety-Ninth was, as his name unmistakably implied, the ninety-ninth ruler of Hel. In addition to granting him certain prerogatives and imposing certain obligations, this meant that he was the scion of a long family line and that his immediate successor, if any, would become the hundredth sovereign of Netherworld, charged with fulfilling the *Red Prophecy*.

The *Red Prophecy* was an ancient inscription on a weather-worn pumice-stone wall in the centre of Hel. It was inscribed in the blood of the great alchemist and prophet Yota Beng Taghd, who had lanced an artery with the tip of a goose quill and written until he was – quite literally – bled dry. A great prophetic vision having appeared to him just when he was inkless and far away from his study, he was obliged to use his own lifeblood and died in the fulfilment of his martyr's duty. Or so it was reported in the annals of Hel.

Although the *Red Prophecy* was written in an archaic script and badly defaced by the elements, the alchemists of Hel had spent centuries laboriously deciphering and translating it. It was subdivided into twenty predictions of which the first eighteen were incomprehensible to anyone but an expert. They were composed in a kind of alchemistic secret code and teemed with words that had long been obsolete. If the translators were to be believed, however, all of these eighteen predictions were favourable. They foretold that the inhabitants of Hel would be blessed with health, wealth and good fortune – but only if they held the art of alchemy in high esteem. This was one reason why the alchemists of Hel had enjoyed such a superior status over the centuries.

The nineteenth prediction, by contrast, foretold a terrible catastrophe: either a great flood, or a subterranean volcanic eruption, or the collapse of the vast cavern in which Hel was situated. However, this disaster would come to pass only if the art of alchemy had *not* been held in high esteem. That was the other reason why the alchemists of Hel ranked so highly there.

The twentieth and last prediction took the form of a command to be obeyed on pain of an all-consuming epidemic: *The hundredth ruler of Hel shall leave the city, together with his army and all the Vrahoks, and conquer Overworld. He will then be the Gornab of Gornabs.*

Gornab Aglan Azidarko Beng Elel Atoona the Ninety-Ninth was far from displeased at being only the ninety-ninth ruler of Hel and not the hundredth. He had no desire to leave Hel and conquer Overworld. He had no desire even to quit his throne. His royal duty to preside over the *Theatre of Death* was quite fulfilling enough for him. Indeed, it sometimes proved too much for him, but he enjoyed watching people fight, kill and die, and he revelled in his subjects' applause. He had the best job in Netherworld: he was the king. All things considered, Gornab was a contented monarch.

It has never been ascertained whether the city of Hel took its name from the Hellings, its pale-skinned inhabitants, or whether the Hellings took their name from the city. The first ruler of Hel was Gornab Aglan Azidarko Beng Elel Atoona the First – that much is an established historical fact. He reigned at a time when the city consisted of a few caves hewn out of the rock with stone axes, and when its inhabitants sustained themselves by digging fat lava worms out of the soil or eating deceased members of their own species.

Another unanswered question is where the Hellings originated, but it can be inferred from their pale skin that they had always lived in a sunless, subterranean environment. Historians surmise that the Hellings' ancestors could perceive neither light nor colour, and that they had antennae instead of eyes. This would account for the hornlike excrescences on their heads, which are simply atrophied antennae. These, however, are no more than conjectures.

Gornab the First

What is certain is that the attested history of the Hellian nation begins with Gornab the First – although to call it a 'nation' in the strict sense would be mistaken. The Hellings were then only a few hundred subterranean creatures – beings with poorly developed brains and eyes, snow-white skin and silver hair – who had banded together by chance and been intimidated and subjugated by Gornab's strength and brutality. There are many legends concerning the physical strength of Gornab the First. It is said that he could split whole boulders with his head, and that he single-handedly carved Hel out of the rock with his own bare fists. Anyone aware of the immense strength latent in his stunted descendant, Gornab the Ninety-Ninth or Last, was inclined to believe these legends about him.

The Gornabian Dynasty can be divided into ten periods, each of them embracing ten generations. Thus the *First Epoch* extended from Gornab the First to Gornab the Tenth, the *Second Epoch* from Gornab the Eleventh to Gornab the Twentieth, the *Third Epoch* from Gornab the Twenty-First to Gornab the Thirtieth and the *Tenth Epoch* – the only one to span just nine reigns – from Gornab the Ninety-First to Gornab the Last.

The despotic dynasty

According to the *Red Prophecy,* the accession of Gornab the Hundredth would mark the beginning of a new era, so the hundredth Gornab could also be referred to as Gornab the First and Gornab the Ninety-Ninth as Gornab the Last.

One Gornab succeeded another without a single break in the line of succession, and each bequeathed his heirs the burden of spiritual, moral and physical decline. It may justifiably be wondered whether the history of Hel and its inhabitants would have taken the same course had its very first ruler been a less malign individual. The Hellings were not incorrigibly evil or vicious; they simply knew no better. They did include some thoroughly pacific and good-natured souls, but there were relatively few of them. Gornab the First combined all the qualities that go to make up the ideal tyrant: he was a power-hungry, bloodthirsty, quick-tempered, cunning, unscrupulous megalomaniac. His character and political views coloured the ruling dynasty's style of leadership – and the culture and mores of an entire civilisation – for nearly a hundred generations. Gornab the First's twelve sons took after their father to such an extent that, when he was frail and defenceless enough, they joined forces and stoned him to death. They then engaged in a years-long feud until, after nine perfidious murders, only one of them was left to ascend the throne: Gornab the Second, a parricide and fratricide of whom all we know is that he had eleven fingers. And so it went on for twenty generations. One tyrant followed another and Hel gradually developed from a system of caves into a city.

The conduct of the royal family, however brutal and barbarous, was considered exemplary. Oppression, corruption, lies, torture and murder were not only commonplace but taken for granted even by peace-loving members of the community. It was to their credit that the city never subsided into chaos. Most alchemists and architects, who constituted the intellectual elite of Hel, belonged to their number, but so did some other citizens from various sections of the city's population.

Alchemy and architecture were the only arts recognised and practised by the early inhabitants of Hel. The city was growing continuously, so architects and construction workers were always in demand. Alchemy was a strange mixture of the arts and sciences, embracing literature and medicine, physics and philosophy, chemistry and biology. Music and painting were virtually unknown in Hel, and sculpture played only a subsidiary role in its capacity as an offshoot of architecture.

The Hellings' diet included worms and insects, many varieties of which lived in the volcanic soil, as well as fish, crabs, snails, water spiders and the non-light-dependent plants that grew in Netherworld's subterranean sewers. Regarded as special delicacies were Kackerbats, which were hard to catch, Woolspiders, large numbers of which inhabited the tunnel systems of Netherworld, and various kinds of mushrooms, which proliferated in the city's sewers. There was such a wide variety of subterranean species that food never ran short – one reason for the city's steady expansion.

The discovery of Overworld

It was only after more than twenty-five generations, in the reign of Gornab the Twenty-Seventh, that Hellian alchemists and soldiers ventured on their first expeditions to the surface of the planet. Shafts of volcanic origin had been discovered at an early stage, but it was a long time before anyone dared to explore them. The wildest theories prevailed concerning the perils of Overworld: that its atmosphere was poisonous, for example, and that every kind of monster lurked there. The explorers were all the more surprised to find breathable air in Overworld. However, the pale-skinned Hellings found sunlight hard to endure, so they made their excursions by night. They covertly observed Overworld's inhabitants and their habits and, when they returned, wrote sensational accounts of them for Hel's Alchemistic Academy. Because living in sunlight was unthinkable and the Hellings had a deep-rooted fear of the unknown, they refrained from making direct contact with the Overworlders and confined themselves to scientific observation.

Their visits to the surface had not gone unnoticed. They themselves were watched by disreputable denizens of the night who dogged their footsteps and tried to follow them when they returned to their subterranean city. These adventurers, mainly bandits and mercenaries, were the first Overworlders to explore the secret routes to Netherworld. Many of them died in the process. They fell into chasms, were devoured by subterranean beasts, or froze to death in the Fridgicaves, but some of them found their way to Hel and entered the underground city. The treatment they received was understandable: they were taken prisoner, tortured, and finally, since no one understood their language, put to death. But the legend of Netherworld inexorably spread among the lawless members of Overworld's population. The thin trickle of fearless individuals, mostly escaped prisoners or others who had little or nothing to lose, never ceased. As time went by the Hellings grasped that they could obtain valuable information about Overworld from these fugitives and adventurers without having to expose themselves to sunlight. They learnt each other's language and began to communicate. In the end, even the most pig-headed Hellings realised that cooperation with the Overworlders could be mutually advantageous. They made a pact with the immigrants. They granted them asylum and traded with them in return for a guarantee that Netherworld's existence would remain a secret known only to a circle of initiates.

The population of Hel was not exactly enriched by these new citizens, almost all of whom were criminals, smugglers, arms dealers and mercenaries. To the Hellings, the newcomers were living confirmation of their own way of life. They were just as evil and unscrupulous, if not more so. At the same time they triggered an unprecedented economic boom. The Hellings' dubious dealings with Overworld provided an entirely new source of income. The criminals acquired weapons in Hel with which to commit their atrocities on the surface, and some of their ill-gotten gains found their way back to the city. Slaves were imported into Netherworld and exploited there as cheap labour. These outside influences had an effect on Hellian culture, and in time Zamonian gained acceptance as Hel's principal language.

The city's wealth increased with every generation of rulers. Mineral deposits – gold, diamonds, coal – were discovered in its environs. The caves beneath it were explored and developed into sewers, and it progressively expanded downwards. Hel came more and more to resemble a huge metal-processing plant. Every street had its smelting ovens and urban life took its rhythm from the clang of hammer on anvil.

The Vrahok Wars

It was in the *Fourth Epoch* that the so-called Vrahok Wars began. To describe them thus is misleading, however, because it conveys the impression that they were a series of armed conflicts between two nations. Far from being a civilised people, the Vrahoks were creatures wholly devoid of intelligence and obedient only to their instinct for survival and procreation. They were a scourge of nature, though one of vast dimensions, and they hailed from a Netherworld region reputed to have connections with the sea, perhaps because the inhabitants of Hel were always alerted to an impending Vrahok attack on their city by an overwhelming stench of brackish water and rotting fish – which very often proved their salvation. For all that, the warlike ferocity with which Hel was besieged by hordes of monstrous Vrahoks during the *Fourth Epoch* created the impression that they were an organised army, so the numerous battles the Hellings fought against them went down in the annals as 'wars'.

Terrible and costly though the Vrahok Wars were, the inhabitants of Hel not only prevailed over their attackers but managed to train them for their own purposes. This was attributable mainly to an alchemistic discovery based on a novel form of hypnosis employing the sense of smell. It was the alchemist Khemon Zyphos who subdued the mighty monsters with the aid of an acidic perfume. From then on the taming and control of the Vrahoks devolved upon the Guild of Alchemists, which thereby reinforced its influence on the royal family.

The birth of the Homunculi

One momentous consequence of the Vrahok Wars was the creation of the Homunculi. The plan to manufacture an artificial army to fight off the Vrahoks was another alchemistic idea. Having obtained a certain fluid from the subterranean oil lakes, the alchemists mixed it with various secret extracts and called it *Mothersoup* – the substance from which the Homunculi were created.

A gigantic cauldron of Netherworld iron was set up in the centre of Hel, filled with Mothersoup and heated over a huge fire. Pregnant Netherworld creatures of the most diverse kinds, including Speleotoads, Osteocrabs, Tubular Hogs and Beaked Weevils caught in the caves beneath the city, were thrown into the soup and brought to the boil. As the expectant mothers disintegrated, so their cells mingled with the primeval, oleaginous substances. In due time the Homunculi arose from this seething, bubbling brew. Hybrid beings equipped with trunks or beaks, crabs' claws or pigs' trotters, they reconstituted themselves out of the components of the boiled-up creatures referred to above, each in its own bizarre way.

However, the Homunculi were not successfully created until long after the Vrahoks had been conquered and tamed. Thus Mothersoup was used for the production not only of soldiers, but also of an army of slaves that could be replenished ad infinitum. This never-ending stream of Homunculi – cheap labour capable of performing the most arduous and dangerous tasks without demur – became a mainstay of Hel's prosperity. The Homunculi formed a third caste inferior to the Hellings and the immigrants from Overworld. They became an ever-growing section of the population burdened with the heaviest obligations, the fewest rights and the lowest life expectancy of all.

When the Vrahok Wars ended, the citizens of Hel wanted some recompense for all their tribulations and privations. It was Gornab the Fifty-First who had the idea of building the Theatre of Death.

The Theatre of Death

Having watched the last of the Vrahok Wars from the safety of his palace balcony, Gornab the Fifty-First thought it the most entertaining spectacle he had ever witnessed. The cessation of hostilities plunged him into utter despair, and he did not recover his spirits until the idea for a theatre occurred to him. He ordered his architects to construct, in the centre of the city, a huge octagonal stadium where exhibition bouts between Vrahoks and slaves could be staged for his enjoyment. They were originally intended for his personal delectation, but shrewd advisers persuaded him to admit the general public as well.

Experience showed, however, that it was not a good idea to stage fights with Vrahoks. They were far too wild, became too enraged, broke the hypnotic spell of the alchemical perfume and often turned dangerous. Although only the smallest specimens were sent into the arena, they were forever running amok. They trampled their keepers to death, devoured members of the audience and – on one occasion – almost made a meal of Gornab the Fifty-First himself.

So fights involving Vrahoks were abolished in favour of contests of the most multifarious kinds: between slaves and Homunculi, slaves and mercenaries, or slaves and wild beasts less difficult to control than Vrahoks. It was when Gornab the Fifty-First discovered how much pleasure he derived from bloodbaths in which Vrahoks did *not* participate that the Theatre of Death really came of age. From now on it was destined to be the cultural centre of Hel.

Degeneracy

Meanwhile, the moral and physical decline of the royal house took its inexorable course. The Gornabs became progressively smaller and more hideous, their sardonic grin broader. Henceforth, the hallmarks of the Gornabian dynasty included epileptic fits, bouts of hysteria, mania and depression, and paroxysms of rage.

No one would have dared to tell a Gornab to his face that he was insane, so the court physicians defined illesses as virtues, hallucinations as flashes of inspiration and attacks of St Vitus's dance as transports of joy. They turned dementia into a cult. When their kings had a fit they administered highly alcoholic stimulants designed to send them more frantic still. When they were suffering from melancholia they did their utmost to depress the royal mood still further. Many generations of courtiers regarded it as modish to ape their sovereigns' behaviour, simulating paroxysms of rage and imitating their hysterical laughter. Ugliness and infirmity became the universal ideal of beauty and anyone in Hel who took pride in his appearance strove to look as ill as possible.

Architects adopted this ideal. Symmetry was banned and preference accorded to the use of ugly, organic and misshapen building materials. Hel's architecture was characterised by skewed walls, humpbacked roofs and houses sunk in the ground. Buildings were faced with the fossil scales of primeval fish or chitinous Netherworld insects. Chimney stacks jutted skywards like demons' horns, gates yawned like gaping jaws, windows resembled death's-heads' eye sockets. Other favourite materials were genuine bone, fossilised dinosaurs' teeth, petrified octopus tentacles and crabs' pincers. If a Vrahok died its armour-plated shell was gutted and converted into apartments. Colour scarcely existed in Hel. Anyone who walked along its leaden grey streets and encountered nothing but pale-faced, dark-robed Hellings could be forgiven for believing that he was in a monochrome world. There was some light, of course, but subdued, flickering and never brighter than necessary. Sunken pools filled with phosphorescent, pulsating jellyfish served as street lights, smouldering torches and candles of black wax stood in window embrasures, and braziers burned in public places. Hel's murky, unhealthy atmosphere was aggravated by the everlasting smoke and soot.

Although they were so sickly and so shamefully abused by their physicians, nearly all the Gornabs were immensely long-lived. Even Gornab the First made it to 164, and he would undoubtedly have survived for a good while longer had he not met a violent end at the hands of his offspring. On average the Gornabs lived for between 180 and 200 years and spent the entire time in a state of flourishing ill health. Although it was customary at court to believe that the king was at death's door, most of Hel's rulers died of old age.

Discounting a few cases of arson and some bizarre legislation, the Gornabs' illnesses and peculiar whims had

little effect on public affairs in general. *The disease was confined to the palace*, their doctors used to say in jest, because the kings' demented ideas were largely self-imposed.

For a long time all went well, but then insanity found an outlet, as it were, in the person of Gornab the Sixty-Second. In his case, mental derangement had consequences that would even affect the population of Overworld. It was Gornab the Sixty-Second who, inspired by reading a children's book, ordained the construction of what became known as *Urban Flytraps*.

Nongo Tulk's picture book

The alchemist Nongo Tulk, employed at the court of Gornab the Fifty-Eighth as a veterinary surgeon and tutor, had written a children's book, intended solely for scions of the royal house, which described the basic workings of the political system in a simple but graphic manner. Having lavishly illustrated this volume, he presented it to the king's son, the future Gornab the Fifty-Ninth, on his tenth birthday.

Nongo's picture book gave a simplified view of the world that would not overtax a childish brain. He drew the kings as big, black, immensely powerful cave bears and their subjects as docile, loyal, obsequious albino rats. Some of the kings' advisers and diplomats he portrayed as faithful glow-worms, others as bloodsuckers and leeches. The city of Hel itself he represented as a cunning spider, equipped with a hundred legs and a hundred eyes, that lurked below ground and bided its time in hiding until, one day, it made its way to the surface. Graphic illustrations showed the spider spinning webs there in the shape of houses. Overworlders of all kinds made themselves at home in them until the spider reappeared and devoured every last one. This episode was meant to symbolise, for the crown prince's benefit, the fulfilment of the *Red Prophecy*.

The book had no effect on Gornab the Fifty-Ninth. He merely glanced through it, burst into tears at the sight of the spider and tossed it into his overflowing toy cupboard. The following two Gornabs were unimpressed, but the precious, hand-illustrated volume was passed down from one generation to the next until it fell into the hands of Gornab the Sixty-Second when he was already middle-aged.

Gornab the Sixty-Second

The latter king's insanity assumed largely manic forms. He was bubbling over with crack-brained schemes. On one occasion he forbade the inhabitants of Hel to speak for a year – they were only allowed to whisper. Another time it was all his courtiers could do to prevent him from marrying a fossilised fish. He painted, composed music and wrote poetry – with equally terrible results in all three disciplines – and was always in search of ideas for further atrocities. One day, while rummaging through the royal library, he came across Nongo Tulk's picture book.

Its impact on his deranged mind was total. Gornab the Sixty-Second would be the first king of Hel to translate the pictures in a children's book into reality. The art-loving monarch's greatest passion was architecture and the construction of monumental buildings. Hel was strewn with empty palaces commissioned by Gornab and built to his own designs, but the city's subterranean location naturally cramped his style. Gornab the Sixty-Second yearned to extend his architectural activities to Overworld, but his advisers had always managed to dissuade him. The alchemists' failure to come up with an antidote to sunlight rendered building on the surface impossible, they told him, but they were sure that such an antidote would soon be discovered.

While Gornab the Sixty-Second was leafing through Nongo's picture book, his overwrought brain had a flash of inspiration that set off a chain reaction of megalomaniac visions and ideas. His architectural ambitions, the Theatre of Death, the Homunculi, the Vrahoks, the alchemistic, arts, Nongo's illustrations, Overworld and Netherworld – all became fused into a plan which, although malign, had its attractions.

Gornab summoned his advisers and architects, his generals and alchemists, and the directors of the Theatre of Death. He proposed to have a city built in Overworld by Homunculi, who were capable of working in sunlight, and connect it to Netherworld by a flight of steps. Once the city was built, they would leave it and return to Hel.

The king's advisers exchanged puzzled glances and applauded wearily. Yet another of Gornab's insane, ruinously expensive schemes.

Then, he went on, they would wait. Wait like a patient, hundred-eyed spider. Wait until the city filled up with Overworlders – which it would, he added, for nothing attracted ordinary folk more than a well-built city.

The architects nodded. That made sense to them.

At length, one night when the densely populated city was wrapped in slumber, the Hellian army would ride to the surface on Vrahoks, anaesthetise the inhabitants with alchemical gases and bear them off to Hel.

Now the generals nodded. They approved of putting the Vrahoks to practical use. The alchemists, who controlled the Vrahoks, nodded likewise.

The captured slaves, Gornab went on, would be found employment as labourers in the lead mines and sewers, smelting works and armouries, et cetera. As for those prisoners who were particularly strong and good at fighting, they would be put on show in the Theatre of Death for the entertainment of the masses.

At this the directors of the Theatre of Death broke into rapturous applause. They had always dreamt of butchering slaves on a grand scale.

Then, cried Gornab the Sixty-Second, when the empty city had replenished itself, it would be harvested a second time. And a third and a fourth, and so on ad infinitum. To the benefit of Hel and the glory of the Gornabs.

The advisers and architects, generals and theatre directors were dumbfounded. No Gornab had ever before had such an appealing idea. They conferred in low voices. This was truly the first royal idea in the history of Hel that made sense. It would solve a whole series of problems at a stroke. Gone would be the difficulty of procuring slaves. The army and the Vrahoks would at last have something more constructive to do than wait, generation after generation, for the far-off day when the *Red Prophecy* would fulfil itself. The theatre would acquire some new attractions and the demented king would at last be too preoccupied to keep everyone on the hop with a deluge of hare-brained ideas. An Urban Flytrap! It was crazy but brilliant.

The Urban Flytraps

A tumultuous period of planning and preparation followed. To avoid endangering Hel itself, the architects decided to build a stairway up an existing volcanic shaft located at a safe distance from the city – one that led to a sparsely populated region of Overworld.

Then they went to work. Having surveyed the area, they proceeded to design the Urban Flytrap's buildings and lay out its streets in contemporary Overworld style. The Homunculi had to carve a spiral staircase into the sides of the volcanic shaft, a formidable task that left many of them dead from exhaustion. Then the city itself was constructed. One of the architects suggested enclosing it with a massive wall that would create a well-fortified impression, thereby attracting exceptionally warlike individuals with whom to stock the Theatre of Death. Last of all, the top of the spiral staircase was cunningly concealed by roofing it over with a black dome of impregnable Netherworld iron. Accessible only from below, this sank into the ground when opened. At last, when all was complete, everyone withdrew to Hel. The seed had been sown; it only remained to wait for the first harvest.

Gornab the Sixty-Second, who found the waiting almost unendurable, gave orders for the first harvest to commence after barely a year. His soldiers rode their Vrahoks to the surface by night, opened the dome and found the whole city asleep. They anaesthetised its inhabitants and bore them off to Hel.

As luck would have it, the city had been occupied by thousands of sturdy mercenaries. These provided excellent material, not only for the Hellian army but even more so for gladiatorial contests in the Theatre of Death. The Urban Flytrap's very first harvest had proved to be a bumper crop.

Gornab the Sixty-Second closed the entrance to Overworld in preparation for the next harvest. Spurred on by his success, he ordained the design and construction of more Urban Flytraps.

The second one, which was built to the north of Hel, was not a great success compared to the first. The surrounding district was densely populated, and rumours soon spread that there was something suspicious about this city that had sprung from the ground overnight. The only people who strayed there were shady individuals, and the ensuing harvests were poor. Because it snowed a lot in this area and the roofs of the mysterious city were nearly always covered with snow, the Zamonians christened it Snowflake.

The third and last Urban Flytrap to become operative under Gornab the Sixty-Second did not have to be built at all; it already existed.

The impatient king had this time called for a different type of city to be built – one that didn't necessitate waiting until it was ready for harvesting but could be raided like a larder, regularly and as required.

The architects and alchemists racked their brains over this task until someone suggested simply using an existing city. The alchemist who put forward this idea already had one in mind, namely, Murkholm in North-West Zamonia.

'Murkholm?' Gornab had asked. 'What's so special about it?'

'Murkholm, Your Majesty,' the alchemist replied humbly, 'would make an ideal Urban Flytrap. It's inhabited by the notorious Murkholmers, a bunch of bandits and smugglers with whom Hel has been in contact for centuries. There are volcanic shafts connecting it to Netherworld and, last but not least, its isolated position is an advantage. Then there's the Jellyfog.'

'The Jellyfog?' said Gornab, who was always interested in scientific phenomena. 'A jellyfish composed of fog?'

'That's one way of putting it, Your Majesty. Murkholm is eternally swathed in a blanket of fog that lies over it like a giant jellyfish. Having studied the said fog for a considerable time, I'm firmly convinced that it's a living creature, not a pall of vapour. It probably comes from the sea and its body is no more substantial than mist. It may genuinely be a gigantic variety of jellyfish.'

'Why are you convinced that it's a living creature?' asked the king.

'Its sylphidic density is too high for a meteorological phenomenon,' the alchemist replied. 'What's more, it displays rudimentary signs of intelligence. It responds to music and makes noises. Ordinary fog doesn't do that.'

'And what does it have to do with our Urban Flytrap?'

'Well, Your Majesty, I couldn't help thinking of our conquest of the Vrahoks. They, too, are powerful sea creatures of rudimentary intelligence, so we might be able to hypnotise the Murkholm Jellyfog with our alchemical gases. We know that these have a mesmeric and anaesthetic effect on most life forms – we use them when harvesting our Urban Flytraps, after all. By enriching the Jellyfog's sylphidic circulation with our gases we would transform it into a gigantic trap that would hypnotise and immobilise all who entered its orbit – ready for us to come and collect them.'

'Hm,' said the king. 'You're an idiot. Why? Because our allies, the Murkholmers, would also be poisoned! Another bright idea like that and I'll have you cut into a dozen pieces.'

The alchemist flinched. 'Your pardon, Majesty,' he said quickly, 'but there's an answer to that problem too. As you know, we immunise our Vrahok riders against the gas by habituating them to it gradually. We need only do the same to the Murkholmers. They're rapacious enough to go along with the idea.' So saying, he bowed low and fell silent.

The scheme was crazy enough to appeal to a Gornab right away. The Hellings came to an arrangement with the Murkholmers, immunised them, and hypnotised the Jellyfog with gas. Unlike Snowflake, Murkholm was a total success. The gas permeated every part of the city and hypnotised everyone it engulfed, while the Jellyfog remained profoundly and lastingly asleep. Its slumbers, to judge by its restless stirrings, were filled with realistic jellyfish dreams. It flickered and whispered, thickened and thinned, but it always remained in the same place, an eternal pall of vapour that enveloped the city of Murkholm, converting it into a vast and inescapable trap. As for the alchemist who had devised this abstruse but effective idea, he became the king's personal adviser.

But the most successful Urban Flytrap of all was the first to be built at Gornab the Sixty-Second's behest. It changed its name more than once over the centuries, becoming successively known as Toadville, Moomyville and Berttville, after the life forms that inhabited it until the Hellings harvested them. One day a Zamonian named Hoth passed by, entered the city and found it completely empty of everything but an acrid smell. Being a Wolperting, he called the river that flowed through it the Wolper. The city itself he christened Wolperting and proceeded to populate with his own kind.

A king who builds fake cities and enslaves or kills those who become trapped in them would elsewhere be regarded, no doubt, as a madman. In Hel he was considered a resplendent figure, even though he sometimes stood naked on his palace balcony and loosed off flaming arrows at his subjects. Gornab the Sixty-Second was the Hellian monarch whose ideas had opened the floodgates to Overworld.

Gornab the Last

Although the history of Hel had hitherto been one of continuous growth and prosperity, Gornabian victories and conquests, the *Seventh Epoch* dealt the city some hard knocks: disastrous epidemics, a subterranean earthquake, a plague of insects. It was as if all the *Red Prophecy*'s dire predictions had come to pass in quick succession. The city had long been too big for such tribulations to destroy it entirely, and life went on regardless. The alchemists devised ways of combating the epidemics, the buildings devastated by the earthquake were replaced with even stouter ones, and the insects were exterminated. But the city's uninterrupted growth had been halted – a process so gradual that even its rulers failed to notice it. Gornab succeeded Gornab, the Theatre of Death had its ups and downs and the Urban Flytraps were regularly harvested, but little else happened. During the *Eighth* and *Ninth Epochs* stagnation gave way to decline and the Gornabs lapsed into apathy. All that still interested them was cultivating their bizarre ailments and presiding over shows at the theatre. Increasingly riddled with corruption, the city eventually subsided, like its kings, into a state of torpid lethargy.

Gornab the Ninety-Ninth personified all the blunders and atrocities the city of Hel and its rulers had ever committed. The most extravagant and self-indulgent being in Netherworld, he was as crooked, warped, dishonest, stupid and malevolent as any living creature could be. Just as he mistook ugliness for beauty, so he mistook cruelty for art, hatred for love and pain for pleasure. He also mistook just about everything else: right for left, up for down, good for bad, backwards for forwards. He even misplaced the syllables in the words he uttered.

If there was anyone in whom evil and insanity had managed to join forces and come to life, it was Gornab Aglan Azidarko Beng Elel Atoona the Ninety-Ninth, ruler of Hel, king of Netherworld, and arbiter of life and death in the Theatre of Death.

Urs rubbed his eyes. He was sure of it now: this was no dream. The sensory impressions were too convincing, too realistic, and he was feeling too wide awake.

Urs awakes

His stupor and the acrid smell had worn off. By whatever means, the Wolpertings had been abducted and carted off to this awful place.

'Are we in hell?' asked Korryn. 'How did we get here?'

'No idea,' said Urs.

'What do you think they intend to do with us?'

'Questions, questions.' Urs sighed. 'How the devil should I know?'

'I'm only trying to get things straight in my mind,' said Korryn. 'Until just now I thought this was all a dream.'

'So did I,' said Urs, 'but it's too unpleasant to be a dream.'

He redirected his attention to the royal box. The spectators were also gazing expectantly at the hideous dwarf on the throne. The tall figure behind the king slunk restlessly to and fro, trying to make him as comfortable as possible. He handed him bowls of fruit and golden goblets of wine, plumped up his cushions and fanned him. Now and then he bent down and whispered something in his ear, whereupon the dwarf would utter a discordant bleat of laughter. Despite the dark-robed figure's obsequious manner, Urs sensed that he was the second most important person present.

Friftar, chief political and strategic adviser to Gornab the Ninety-Ninth, belonged to a family of diplomats with a long tradition of service at the royal court.

Friftar's story

He made a more elegant impression than hideous, thickset Gornab. Tall, pale and slim, he kept his gestures and facial expressions to a minimum. But he cut a good figure only when compared with his grotesque king. In any other surroundings his demonic features, hooked nose and projecting teeth would have made him look like a veritable scarecrow.

Anyone who believed that Friftar was a grey eminence who operated a crazy puppet from behind the throne was grossly underestimating the demented monarch. Gornab the Ninety-Ninth was the living manifestation of many evil minds and heir to the most unscrupulous tyrants. Nearly a hundred generations of pathologically bloated egocentricity had rendered the Gornabs hypersensitive to any form of conspiracy. Those who opposed one of them opposed them all, and no matter how carefully and shrewdly they disguised their intentions, they could not conceal them altogether. Gornab the Ninety-Ninth was mad, ignorant, brutal and morally depraved, but the ghosts of his ancestors stood solidly behind him. They helped him to sniff out any plot, however cunning, and anyone who incurred the collective wrath of the Gornabs was doomed to die. Friftar knew this only too well.

What the king's chief adviser feared most were his master's unpredictable moods. Despite his small stature, Gornab possessed immense physical strength, especially in his arms and jaw muscles. When he lapsed into one of his black moods, as he could from one minute to the next, he was capable of attacking people and – literally – tearing them to shreds. The only advance warning of such an outburst was a sudden, introspective silence on the king's part, as if he were listening to some inner melody. His gaze became fixed and abstracted, his smile still more grotesque.

The distorting mirror

Friftar himself had evaded these paroxysms by a hair's breadth on three occasions. He had leapt aside just in time, thereby exposing another victim to the king's maniacal fury.

No, diplomacy and cunning machinations would not have done the trick on their own. Friftar had had to work, hard and tirelessly, in order to secure the influential position in which he eventually found himself. Only well-nigh supernatural patience had enabled him to become indispensable to Gornab – to become a mirror that made the king look handsomer than he was; an echo that sounded more intelligent than the words he actually spoke; a shadow more graceful than his own stunted figure. When Gornab said something Friftar repeated it in more subtle language. When he asked a question his adviser phrased the answer as if the question had already supplied it. And when Gornab uttered his unintelligible gibberish Friftar automatically translated it. In addition to everything else, he was constantly at pains to remain one step ahead of his master. Such was the Herculean task which no one in Hel but Friftar could have performed and which made him irreplaceable. His real triumph was that the king failed to acknowledge this achievement – indeed, that he never even noticed it. This rendered Friftar's machinations undetectable – even, perhaps, by the ancestors that lurked in Gornab's sick mind.

Yes, Friftar really was the second most important person, not only in the Theatre of Death but in Hel and the whole of Netherworld. He had been assigned to the king as a playmate in his boyhood, and from this had developed a relationship that verged on the symbiotic: one could not exist without the other.

To Friftar, power was as essential as the air he breathed. Gornab, by contrast, needed Friftar as a crutch, because without him he could not even have communicated with his subjects. The court authorities had soon noticed that Friftar's presence exerted a soothing effect on the unpredictable tyrant and that he was capable of translating His Majesty's curious gibberish, so they appointed him his constant companion and personal attendant.

As such, Friftar realised from the very first that he would have to develop his power base very slowly and patiently. For decades he was content to be the buffer between the king, his insane moods and the world at large. He put up with the most abject humiliations, the most irrational mood swings and tantrums – indeed, he treated them as gifts and never tired of giving thanks for them. Friftar waited until all the king's courtiers had become convinced that he was a boundlessly loyal flunkey devoid of personal ambition – then he made his move.

Medical diplomacy

The king's personal physicians were his first target. Hel's senior medical men wielded power and influence at court, and they had extended that influence over the centuries, especially in regard to the public health service and the alchemists, who in their turn controlled the Vrahoks. Having perceived these links, Friftar proceeded to snap them. No one was better acquainted than he with Gornab's little aches and pains, his genuinely serious ailments and the fine line between them, but he had long been careful not to meddle in medical matters, even when convinced that the king was receiving the wrong treatment.

Friftar's long-awaited opportunity came one day when Gornab had a terrible attack of breathlessness. Suddenly bereft of air, he went pale-blue in the face and threatened to lose consciousness. This attack – not that anyone but Friftar knew it – arose from his deformed chest and disastrous eating habits. While presiding over his privy council after a huge meal consisting almost entirely of greasy Woolspiders, Gornab had striven to suppress the resulting flatulence. The pent-up gases inflated his intestines, which eventually became so bloated that they compressed both lungs against his ribcage and put them out of action. The senior thoracic surgeon desperately tried to restore Gornab's breathing by means of massage, but the king continued to gasp and his bluish face turned violet. The surgeon was ultimately reduced to suggesting a tracheotomy.

Nearly all of Hel's leading politicians were present at this meeting. Friftar seized his opportunity. Emerging from behind the throne, he loudly asked two questions. First, was the operation really unavoidable, and secondly, might it be life-threatening? The surgeon answered both questions in the affirmative. Then Friftar addressed a third question to the assembled politicians. Were they prepared to endorse such a risky procedure? They all nodded.

Friftar thereupon seized the king by his ankles, yanked him off his throne, held him upside down and shook him vigorously. This caused an uproar. Someone shouted that the royal adviser had lost his mind and was trying to kill the king. But Gornab emitted a mighty fart and began to take greedy gulps of air. Friftar gently replaced him on his throne, where he soon recovered.

Gornab's faith in Friftar increased by leaps and bounds. His chief adviser proceeded to strip the physicians of power the very next day. The senior thoracic surgeon was thrown into prison - where he died of pneumonia - and all the other court physicians were placed under Friftar's strict supervision. From now on he alone decided what medicines the king should take and determined their dosage. He prescribed a palatable diet and a certain amount of exercise, and within six months Gornab's state of health had dramatically improved. Henceforth, Friftar could regulate it to suit himself.

He also found it child's play to take control of the public health service and the Alchemists' Guild. Before long his invisible tentacles extended throughout the city. Never before in Hel had so much power and influence been concentrated in the hands of a single person unrelated to the royal family.

Friftar's next move was to assume control of the nobility and the masses. When studying the history of Hel he had been struck by the fact that its general decline during recent generations had gone hand in hand with the decline of the Theatre of Death. Being preoccupied with their own insane concerns, the rulers of Hel had completely failed to notice this. Unlike them, Friftar grasped that the entertainment of the masses was an important instrument of power, and nowhere did better opportunities for entertainment present themselves than at the Theatre of Death.

In its heyday the theatre had been the throbbing heart of Hel, with daily gladiatorial contests and an ensemble numbering over a thousand, including fighters, trainers, guards and keepers. An intricate underground labyrinth housed a whole menagerie of dangerous wild beasts and the complex theatre machinery that raised and lowered them in their cages.

It was hard to tell exactly when the Theatre of Death had started to go downhill, but it must have been during the *Eighth Epoch*. The directors became more and more corrupt and their shows more boring because they made false economies and were more concerned to feather their own nests than stage exciting shows. They neglected to obtain replacements for the wild beasts slaughtered in combat, so their menagerie dwindled to a few dozen. The underground machinery grew rusty and eventually ceased to function altogether. Fights were still held in the dilapidated stadium, but usually to half-empty houses. One direct consequence of the theatre's decline was growing disorder in the city at large. Criminality increased, alternative fights were staged in the streets and illegal betting offices sprang up everywhere. It was only a question of time before these nefarious activities got completely out of hand.

Friftar persuaded Gornab to put him in charge of the theatre. He assembled the city's finest architects and craftsmen and instructed them to restore the stadium to the splendour it had displayed in its prime. He had the machinery repaired, constructed additional tiers of seats and renovated the royal box. More wild beasts were trapped and transported to the theatre, and the gladiators were now trained by ambitious, well-paid professional soldiers. Many royal functionaries lost their posts, others their heads, and some found themselves back in the arena in short order, face to face with ravenous cave bears.

However, Friftar realised that this was not enough. Success and popularity could not be restored by royal decree alone. His way of redirecting public attention to the theatre was simple but brilliant. Once the renovations were complete he organised an elaborate inaugural ceremony at which he proclaimed, in the king's presence, that *killing was an art*. Like architecture and alchemy, killing – though only in the arena and in front of an audience – was now an acknowledged art form under royal patronage and would be brought to a pitch of perfection. This little rhetorical trick proved more effective than all the costly restoration work. It turned murder into a creative act and mercenaries, criminals and other professional killers into artists. Whether in the arena or merely watching, those present in the Theatre of Death had acquired a touch of glamour overnight. No longer a crude form of public entertainment, the shows had become highbrow art connoisseurs' delights. The masses flocked to the theatre and the nobility, too, were compelled to reoccupy their tiers of seats because none of them wanted to be thought a philistine.

The Theatre of Death had been the diseased heart of Hel and Friftar had succeeded in getting it to beat once more. He could now reap the benefits of his self-sacrificial labours, because the theatre was a meeting place for the three elements he aspired to control: the king, the aristocracy, and the lower orders.

Friftar's theatrical successes had made him a popular politician and an artist of repute, but he had not yet attained his ultimate objective, which was to liquidate Gornab the Ninety-Ninth, neutralise the aristocracy and assume power himself.

For this purpose he had concocted a daring plan. He proposed to launch a *coup d'état* in the course of a unique performance at the Theatre of Death. Preparations had been in hand for a considerable time. According to Friftar's Overworld spies, the new inhabitants of the first Urban Flytrap, who were known as Wolpertings, would make exceptionally good theatre personnel. They were fighters of a calibre such as Hel had never seen before. Friftar's plan was as simple as it was bloodthirsty. While the Wolpertings were killing each other in the arena in the most spectacular fashion, and while the king, nobility and lower orders were stupefied and intoxicated by the sight of blood, he would have the theatre surrounded by the army and the Vrahoks. Then, when the slaughter and public enthusiasm were at their height, Friftar would stab the king to death with a glass dagger and seize power with everyone looking on. Once the nobility had also been exterminated, a new era could begin. The ensuing generations would then be measured in Friftars, not Gornabs.

But just when Friftar's plans were working out so splendidly, something unforeseen put a spoke in his wheel. The ambitions of the king's chief adviser were thwarted by fate in the shape of an army of murderous and invincible mechanical beings. The dreaded General Ticktock and his Copper Killers had come marching into Hel.

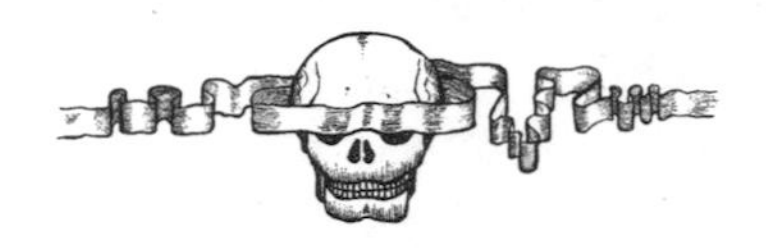

The Reppoc Srellik

All eyes were on the throne as Gornab's garbled address rang out across the arena. The king bleated with laughter like a demented goat. Then his mood abruptly changed and he subjected Friftar to a furious glare.

'Why aren't they adlaupping?' he hissed. 'Are they fead? Didn't I essprex myself entillibly? Why no avotion?'

Friftar bowed low. 'As so often, Your Majesty, the acoustics are to blame for the lack of applause. Of course you expressed yourself intelligibly. Your words were like the clear, ringing notes of a silver bell, like an elfin song winging its way through the ether. At present, however, all sounds are being absorbed by another . . . er, temporary surge in the earth's natural magnetism. Permit me, therefore to repeat your speech in the vulgar tongue, loudly enough for it to reach even the most unwashed ears in this low-born audience.'

'Merpission granted! Ceedpro!' Gornab growled, gesturing impatiently. 'Sputid rabble! It's waysal the same lemprob!'

'Greetings, new captives of the Theatre of Death!' Friftar declaimed, repeating the king's speech in the correct syllabic order. 'You have been brought here to fight! You have been brought here to perish! O you fortunate ones! O you chosen ones! You are destined to fight and perish for the entertainment of this distinguished audience! And fight you will! And perish you will! That is your inescapable destiny! Let the killing commence!'

The audience treated the king to a standing ovation.

'Hmph,' grunted Gornab, 'why coldun't they have auppladed in the stirf clape?'

Friftar raised his arms and the applause died away. He turned to the Wolpertings.

'Just so you understand the rules once and for all, we shall now give you a demonstration. It will feature one of your own kind.'

'Show them the Reppoc Srellik!' hissed Gornab. 'The Reppoc Srellik!'

Friftar smote his brow. 'Ah yes,' he cried, 'how could I have forgotten?'

He pointed dramatically to the topmost gallery, which still seemed unoccupied. 'Kindly observe the Copper Killers above you.'

The chained Wolpertings heard noises issuing from the gallery above them - clicking, clanking, whirring, jingling noises - and out of the darkness behind the parapet stepped some mail-clad warriors. Only a few at first, then more and more until there were hundreds of them. Their burnished armour glittered in the torchlight.

The Wolpertings broke into a murmur, the spectators rose and stamped their feet in delight until the auditorium shook. Gornab clapped his hands. 'The Reppoc Srellik! The Reppoc Srellik!' he croaked.

'The Copper Killers!' yelled the spectators. 'The Copper Killers!'

Friftar lowered his arm and they all resumed their seats. In the absolute hush that followed he made his way to the front of the royal box.

'This will not be a very spectacular fight,' he cried, 'not a fight designed to entertain the audience, just a brief demonstration of the rules for the new fighters. The rules are simple and there are only two. The first is *fight*!'

'Fight!' the audience chorused.

Friftar raised two fingers. 'And the second rule is: *there's no second rule.*'

'There's no second rule!' yelled the audience.

Friftar smiled. 'That shouldn't be too hard to remember.'

'There's no ondsec lure!' Gornab laughed. 'No ondsec lure!'

Friftar raised his arms again and called loudly, 'Proceed with the demonstration!'

'Yes, teg on with the foncounded stremondation!' Gornab cried impatiently. 'Atoub emit, too! Did you sectel an ice old one?'

Friftar nodded. 'Yes, I selected a nice old one.'

Ornt El Okro in the arena

The northern gate opened and an elderly Wolperting tottered in. Hesitantly, he made his way to the centre of the arena. It was Ornt El Okro, the cabinetmaker. He looked bemused, as if the anaesthetic gas had only just worn off, and he was holding a sword in his hand.

The southern gate opened. Several seconds went by, then a dog came limping out – limping because it only had three legs. It was a mongrel puppy whose pale-brown fur was flecked with black. If it had had a pair of horns it would have resembled a very small Wolperting. One or two of the spectators laughed.

'That's your opponent,' Friftar called to Ornt. 'Kill him!'

'Yes, klil him!' Gornab repeated.

Ornt looked up in bewilderment. He made no move to attack the little creature. He wasn't going to kill any dog – he wasn't going to kill anyone. What was going on here? He'd been worried sick about Rumo. The last thing he remembered was getting drunk and falling into bed. Now he was suffering from the world's worst hangover and everyone around him had gone mad. Shielding his eyes with the sword blade, he scanned the spectators for some clue to this mystery.

Gornab stood up on his short legs.

'You feruse to klil him?' he demanded, sounding strangely, joyfully expectant.

Ornt stared at the royal box in bewilderment. He had no idea what the hideous dwarf expected of him or what language he was speaking, so he replied in a universally intelligible manner: he threw away his sword and spat. The puppy limped over, wagging its tail, and sniffed the blade.

'You refuse to kill him?' Friftar translated, propping his chin on his hand like someone studying a picture lost in thought. At this secret signal there was a stirring in the Copper Killers' gallery. Metallic noises filled the theatre, but the spectators preserved an expectant silence. One or two of them rose for a better look. Dozens of Copper Killers had cocked their crossbows and aimed them at Ornt El Okro.

'Ornt!' cried someone from the Wolpertings' gallery. 'Pick it up! Pick up that sword!'

Ornt looked up. Someone had called his name. He knew that voice. Did it belong to Urs of the Snows?

'The first rule is: Fight! The second rule is: There is no second rule!' Friftar repeated solemnly.

Ornt turned and retraced his steps towards the northern gate. He'd had enough of this tomfoolery.

Friftar gave another almost imperceptible signal: he raised his little finger.

'Ornt!' Urs's voice rang round the auditorium. 'Pick up that goddamned sword!'

From the Copper Killers' gallery came a series of clicks followed by a hum that sounded as if a swarm of bees were flying across the arena. When it ceased Ornt resembled a pincushion. Dozens of crossbow bolts of assorted lengths were protruding from his body. He collapsed, his life snuffed out in an instant, and several of the shafts snapped under the weight of his bulky old frame. A collective groan went up from the ranks of the Wolpertings.

The puppy sniffed Ornt's face inquisitively. Another hum filled the air and a long copper arrow transfixed its neck, pinning it to the floor of the arena.

'The killing has commenced,' Friftar announced solemnly, handing the king a goblet of wine.

'Yes,' whispered Gornab. 'At tsal! The gillink has demencecom!'

The Fridgicaves

Rumo had decided to take the Fridgicaves route. In accordance with Skullop's instructions he had simply followed his nose for an entire day until he reached a precipitous wall of rock pierced by at least a dozen wide tunnels. Some led steeply upwards, others downwards. After a moment's hesitation he entered one that seemed to descend in a gradual manner.

While making his way along this tunnel he couldn't help noticing that it was getting steadily colder and more draughty. Rumo had never been so cold in his life, but he was steadfastly determined not to turn back, so he pressed on regardless.

Like nearly everything else in Netherworld, the tunnel was a luminous blue. Furred with frost and fringed with icicles, it was inhabited by unfamiliar insects resembling eyeless, crystalline grasshoppers that rattled softly when they moved. An icy wind was howling along the shaft.

'We should have gone the top way,' Dandelion grumbled.

Krindle preserved a dogged silence. He was clearly feeling put out because Rumo hadn't complied with his request to cut Skullop the Scyther in half.

'It's too late now,' said Rumo.

'It's never too late to be flexible,' Dandelion retorted. *'There's a fine but important distinction between determination and pig-headedness.'*

'I'm not turning back,' Rumo said firmly.

After they had been going for some hours the tunnel opened out into a gigantic cavern whose floor consisted of a pale-blue expanse of ice. The walls, which were covered with stalactitic formations thousands of years old, looked like cascades of water that had frozen solid in an instant. Cold air was whistling and howling into the cavern through innumerable fissures in the walls. There was no luminous mist or blue rain here, only snow and wind.

'This place looks mighty cold,' said Dandelion.

Apprehensively, Rumo ventured out on to the broad, frozen expanse. Several dozen of the furry little creatures he'd seen before were slithering around on it and attempting to chip out slivers of ice with their hooked beaks.

Dandelion goes too far

The pale-blue layer of ice emitted ominous creaks and groans under Rumo's weight, and it yielded ominously at the very first step he took. The dark water beneath it was in motion. He could see flattened bubbles swirling to and fro.

'You realise you're walking on water?' said Dandelion.

'Yes, I do, but thanks for the tip. I don't like moving around on something that's moving around itself.'

'People call it ice, but it's only another name for water. You never know exactly how thick a layer separates you from the liquid form, ha ha!'

Rumo tried to take his mind off the cold and Dandelion's chatter by striding out resolutely and submitting his bleak surroundings to closer inspection. Here and there, tilted ice floes jutted from the frozen waste like bizarre sculptures. Some of them resembled snow-clad buildings or fir trees, others distant mountains.

The wind blew steadily across the ice, driving fine snow between Rumo's legs. Its monotonous piping whistle, the occasional ominous crack of the ice and the crunch of powder snow beneath his feet were the only sounds he heard for the next few hours - apart from Dandelion's periodic comments.

'Drowning in cold water is said to be one of the worst deaths of all. You freeze to death and drown simultaneously,' Dandelion remarked after a while. *'You die twice over, so to speak.'*

Rumo trudged on without a word. That was still the best policy. Contradicting Dandelion only encouraged him. Ignore him and he might eventually dry up of his own accord.

'It's also conceivable that it's the kind of death that keeps you fully conscious to the last. Dunked in freezing water? You'd be wide awake!'

Rumo would almost have preferred Krindle's cynical, life- and death-defying comments.

'I'm wondering which works quicker. Does icy water freeze you to death before you drown, or do you drown before you freeze to death?'

'Another remark like that and I'll stick you in the ice and leave you behind.'

'Empty threats don't scare me. I'm the only weapon you've got. You'd guard me like the apple of your eye, even if I were a rusty knitting needle, ha ha!'

Rumo growled.

'Blockhead!'

'What did you say?'

'I called you a blockhead, you blockhead,' Dandelion said impudently.

Rumo gave another growl.

'That's right, growl away. I can call you anything I like and you can't do a thing about it. You're dependent on me. From your angle, I'm the world's most precious weapon, ha ha!'

'I warn you!'

'Sure, warn away. Nincompoop! Imbecile! Card game!'

'Don't push me too far!'

But Dandelion's exuberance ran away with him. He broke into a childish sing-song: *'Rumo is a card game, Rumo is a card game, Rumo is a . . .'*

Rumo drew Dandelion from his belt, stuck him in the ice and plodded on.

'Hey, Rumo!' Dandelion called. *'What are you playing at?'*

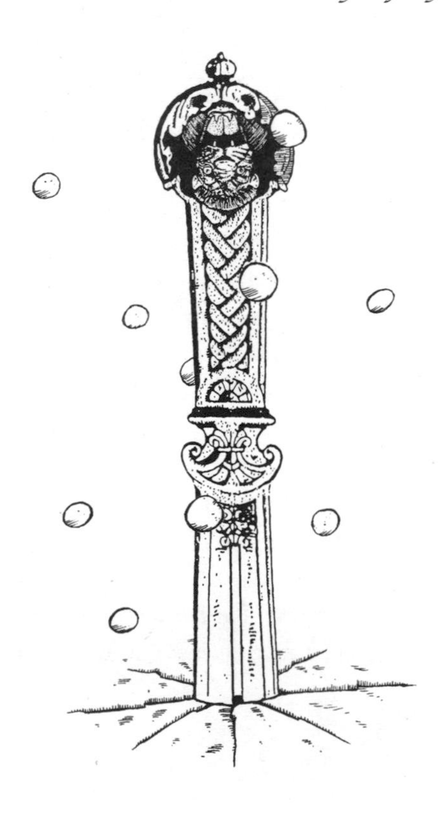

Rumo's figure rapidly receded.

'Rumo! Don't be silly, I was only joking!'

Rumo strode on without a backward glance. Dandelion's voice grew fainter.

'Rumo! Please! I'll never do it again, word of honour!'

Rumo paused and turned round.

'Promise?'

'I swear it! I swear it!'

'Say it, then.'

'I swear I'll never be cheeky again.'

'And you'll only speak when spoken to?'

'That too! Anything, anything!'

Rumo plodded back, tugged his sword out of the ice and replaced it in his belt.

'My, that was cold!' said Dandelion. *'If the water beneath is only half as—'*

'Dandelion!'

'All right! I'll shut up!'

'You will walk across a lake dry-shod . . .'

The ice had stopped creaking under Rumo's weight some time ago. On the contrary, it seemed to be growing thicker and stronger. He had left the furry little creatures behind, but he was perturbed to see other creatures deeply embedded in the ice beneath him: Kackerbats, plump fish, and animals resembling seals with long claws and beaks. A polar bear, which lay stretched out on its back, seemed to be waving its right forepaw at him.

Rumo suddenly recalled Posko's prophecy: *'You will walk across a lake dry-shod . . .'* There was some more, but he couldn't remember it.

'How did all these animals get into the ice?' he wondered aloud.

'They fell in, how else?' said Dandelion.

'But the ice here is much thicker than it was.'

'Even thick ice can break.'

'Shut up!' snapped Rumo.

He came to a halt. Not far ahead of him two huge ice formations jutted from the lake. They were bigger than the ones he'd passed earlier.

'What is it?'

'I don't know. I can't smell anything, but I thought I saw something move.'

'If the ice started moving we'd be in trouble.'

'I know.'

'I mean, if the ice suddenly started moving, out here in the middle of the lake, we'd be in a devil of a—'

'Stop yakking!'

The Icemagogs

Rumo drew his sword and trudged towards the white shapes. From a distance the piled-up ice floes looked like half-submerged giants with dripping beards; after another fifty paces like the battlements of a many-turreted castle; and after another hundred like ghosts frozen stiff by the icy wind at the climax of some wild dance. By the time Rumo was standing precisely midway between them, they looked like ice floes that had tilted and become hopelessly wedged together. There was no sign of life. He'd been mistaken.

'Watch out!' yelled Dandelion and Rumo instinctively ducked. Something whizzed over his head. He heard the air part with a hiss as if cloven by a mighty sword stroke. He spun round and straightened up. Nothing. Nobody there, least of all anyone armed with a sword. Just the piled-up, windswept ice floes, frozen in time.

'What was that?' asked Rumo.

'Watch out!' Dandelion yelled again. Rumo dropped to his knees in a flash. Once again something hissed over his head, but this time he turned fast enough to see an ice floe shaped like a long, sharp tongue disappear into the ice sculpture behind him. He remained on his knees, sword in hand.

'You will cross swords with Living Water . . .' The second part of Posko's prophecy came back to him.

'Icemagogs,' said Dandelion. *'Skullop mentioned them.'*

'They can move,' Rumo whispered.

'They can kill, too,' Dandelion whispered back. *'Remember those dead animals in the ice?'*

Rumo deliberated. Two Icemagogs, one ahead of him, one behind, and both capable of using ice as a weapon. On the other hand they were frozen to the spot. He had only to take a few more steps to be out of their range.

'Let's get out of here,' Dandelion said.

Rumo rose to his feet but remained at a crouch. Step by step, slowly and cautiously, he started to slink away.

The Icemagogs didn't stir.

'Keep going,' Dandelion whispered. *'Just keep going . . .'*

Rumo backed away, step by cautious step, until the Icemagogs couldn't have reached him even with their biggest and longest floes – unless, of course, they were capable of throwing them.

A sudden, almighty crack rent the air, as if the frozen lake had splintered all the way to the horizon. The right-hand Icemagog had abruptly come to life. Its entire body got under way, seemingly propelled along by an invisible hand. Ice floes disintegrated, white slivers flew through the air, snow rained down and the icy surface beneath Rumo's feet gave an ominous lurch. The monster now resembled a frozen giant chest-deep in snow and thrusting itself along with its arms. Within seconds it had changed position a good twenty yards and cut off Rumo's retreat.

With a crunch and a hiss the channel opened up by the Icemagog's progress promptly froze over again. There was another crack and the other Icemagog moved in Rumo's direction, ice splintering in all directions. The floes parted with a series of ear-splitting reports and rearranged themselves, twice, three times, until the Icemagog came to a halt in front of him. The splintered ice in its wake, too, froze together again. Rumo just stood there, spellbound by these incredible developments. He was being hunted by living ice! The Icemagogs had cornered him like a pair of huge white chessmen.

'You can get past on the left or right!' whispered Dandelion. *'Get out of here fast!'*

Rumo didn't hesitate for long. He tucked his head in and dashed to the right. At that moment the ice ahead of him burst asunder, creating a wide channel filled with inky black water. He just managed to stop in time, teetered on the edge for a moment, recovered his balance, took a step to the rear, turned and sprinted at a crouch in the other direction. An ice floe came crashing down like a guillotine, just in front of him. He vaulted over it, landed on all fours, performed a forward roll and regained his feet. With an ominous crack, the other monster thrust at him with an icicle. He ducked and the crystalline blade skewered thin air. He straightened up and started to run on, but the ice split open ahead of him once more. Many feet wide, the channel filled up with swirling water. Before and behind him were the Icemagogs, to left and right the insurmountable channels.

'We're trapped,' said Dandelion.

The monsters shifted restlessly to and fro, their ice floes rhythmically sliding apart and grinding together again.

'Keep an eye on the one behind me,' Rumo told Dandelion.

The Icemagogs were creaking and groaning in turn. Could this be a form of communication? For a while they merely shuffled to and fro, emitting noises that might have been a heated argument.

Suddenly there was a sound like breaking glass, possibly an Icemagog's exclamation. From the monster facing Rumo sprouted two enormous blades of ice, longer and broader than the biggest broadsword imaginable.

The other Icemagog gave an answering cry and sprouted two blades of its own.

'Four swords against one,' said Rumo, swapping Dandelion from hand to hand.

'Yes,' Dandelion whispered. *'We could use some help from an experienced warrior. It's time you made your presence felt, Krindle! We know you're there.'*

But Krindle didn't answer.

The Icemagog in front of Rumo split open along its breadth. Its ice floes parted like the lips of a giant fish and Rumo found himself looking into a maw full of murky water. With a horrid gurgle it vomited copiously. The stream of water landed right at Rumo's feet, swirled round his boots and instantly transformed itself into a glassy sheet of ice. Three plump, shiny golden fish flapped around on it, desperately gasping for breath.

'I wouldn't put anything past them!' Dandelion exclaimed.

Rumo positioned himself, legs apart, so that one of the monsters was on his right and the other on his left. He raised his sword and prepared to resist their onslaught.

'The first attack will come from the right,' Dandelion said.

'You mean you can hear what they're thinking?'

'Yes, but I don't understand their language, it's too icy. Somehow, though, the thoughts coming from the right sound angrier, so—'

There was another clatter, and the first attack – a fierce horizontal thrust – really did come from the right. Rumo decided to duck instead of parrying it. The blow whistled overhead, missing him, but a second one was already on its way, this time from the left. Rumo evaded it with a backward somersault.

Under prevailing circumstances acrobatic feats of this kind were inadvisable. No sooner had his feet touched the ice than he performed a brief, grotesque dance and landed on his back.

Rumo had no choice but to parry the next blow from a supine position. He was astonished at how easily Dandelion shattered the big blade of ice. It disintegrated into countless little fragments that peppered him like a hailstorm. Another furious clatter and the monster swung its second blade, but Rumo parried that blow too, transforming his adversary's weapon into an explosion of ice crystals. One of the Icemagogs, at least, had been disarmed.

'Well done!' Dandelion said approvingly. *'But you'd better get up now.'*

Rumo rose and turned to face the other Icemagog. It recoiled, emitted a long-drawn-out clatter – and retracted its blades.

'The boot's on the other foot!' cried Dandelion. *'You've scared them.'*

The Icemagogs seemed to be conferring in their noisy language.

'They don't know what to do,' Dandelion whispered. *'Frozen water is their only w—'*

His words were interrupted by a sudden crack and the ice yawned beneath Rumo's feet. The monsters had abruptly reared up, shattering the lake's frozen surface into a number of small ice floes. Rumo flailed his arms wildly in an attempt to keep his footing on one of them.

'Stick me in your belt!' Dandelion screamed. *'Don't let go of me or we'll both be done for!'*

Rumo thrust the sword into his belt, but in so doing he finally overbalanced. The ice floe capsised, pitching him into the inky water.

He came to the surface, took a deep breath, and saw the Icemagogs bending over him curiously. Then the swirling water dragged him under again. To his horror he heard the ice floes grind together as they closed over his head.

'You'll have to swim for it!' Dandelion cried. *'Swim away and cut a hole in the ice, it's our only hope!'*

'I can't swim,' thought Rumo. 'I don't know how.'

'That makes two of us,' said Dandelion. *'I can't swim either.'*

'Then I'll have to die.'

'I can swim.' That was Krindle's deep, dark voice. He was back again.

'Krindle! Where have you been all this time?' Dandelion demanded.

'I haven't been anywhere. I was insulted.'

'Can you really swim?'

'Yes, I can.'

'Teach Rumo, then! Quickly!'

'No. I'm only breaking my silence to tell you that I *could* help you, but I won't. Why should I help someone who won't even do me the tiniest little favour?'

'Krindle!' Rumo pleaded. 'I'm running out of air!'

'So what? I couldn't care less.'

'Krindle!' Dandelion said fiercely. *'If you don't help us, the following will happen: Rumo will drown, but the two of us will sink to the bottom of this lake and lie there for a very long time. Just us two, all alone in the icy water. And I swear I'll drive you insane with my yakking.'*

Krindle seemed to be considering this.

'Will you promise to kill Skullop the Scyther if we meet him again?'

'Yes, yes!' Rumo telepathised desperately. 'I promise.'

'Very well,' said Krindle. **'You must raise your hands above your head with the palms facing outwards, then force your arms to the rear.'**

Rumo followed Krindle's instructions. His head collided with the layer of ice.

'You see? It's easy – you simply push the water away. But you must also move your legs. Ever seen a frog swimming?'

Rumo imitated the leg movements of a frog and forced his arms backwards at the same time. He glided along under the ice.

'And again!'

Rumo's lungs were bursting, but he resisted the fatal temptation to open his mouth and gasp for air.

'And again!'

Every stroke put a little more distance between Rumo and the Icemagogs, but every stroke made the pain in his chest more unbearable.

'And again!'

'I can't go on!' thought Rumo. 'I've run out of air!'

'And again!' Krindle ordered sternly.

Rumo performed a final stroke. Red lights were dancing in front of his eyes and his head was ringing like a bell.

'Here!' said Krindle. **'This is where the ice is thinnest.'**

Rumo drew his sword and drove it into the ice with all his might.

'Harder!'

He thrust it in again.

'Harder still!' Krindle commanded.

'Go on!' cried Dandelion.

Another thrust and the blade went right through.

Rumo applied his lips to the hole and sucked air deep into his lungs. Ice crystals filled his mouth. He replaced his sword in the hole and levered it to and fro, breaking off bigger and bigger chunks of ice. Before long the hole was wide enough for him to put his head through. He drank in the ice-cold air like someone dying of thirst.

Not far away he sighted the Icemagogs. They were still bending over the frozen expanse between them, probably wondering where their prey had got to.

'Rumo can swim,' said Dandelion.

Rumo leaves the Fridgicaves behind

Rumo reached the end of the frozen lake after another half-day's march. Although he hadn't encountered any more Icemagogs, he felt as if they were keeping up the pursuit by trying to freeze his body via his feet. The lake's frigid expanse seemed to be a single coherent organism whose sole aim was to kill anything or anyone that crossed it. Rumo dared not call a halt. He knew that it would have been fatal to sit down and rest. Parts of his clothing and fur were glazed with ice, and physical exertion was all that could save him from freezing to death.

He trudged on and on until he suddenly spotted one of the furry little creatures with hooked beaks. It was staggering clumsily around on the ice.

'Look,' he said, 'an animal!'

He spotted another, then a third and a fourth. The black dots beyond them could only be more of their kind.

'Where there are animals,' Dandelion observed, *'there must be land – unless they're fish, of course.'*

The ice was now swarming with more and more of the furry little creatures, which were chipping away at it with their beaks, breaking off fragments and munching them. Not far off Rumo saw the frozen expanse give way to black rocks overgrown with dark-blue moss. The rocks rose in a series of terraces and disappeared into the gloom overhead.

Rumo felt better when he stepped on to terra firma, convinced only then that he had finally eluded the Icemagogs. He scooped up some powder snow and slaked his thirst. Then he started to climb.

The air became warmer when he had been climbing for several hours. More and more of the furry little creatures were roaming around up here. The holes from which they emerged steadily increased in size from terrace to terrace until they were big enough for Rumo to have stood up in them. The little creatures swarmed around his feet uttering high-pitched squawks.

He looked up. Above him loomed another half-dozen terraces. There was no point in tackling them immediately, he decided. He was tired out and in need of at least a short rest, so he sat down on the ground with his back against a rock. The furry creatures promptly started clambering over him. Dozens of them scrambled on top of him, covering him from head to foot. Then they nestled against him and started to purr. He was enveloped in a warm, live fur coat.

'My, aren't they trusting?' said Dandelion.

'We ought to kill a few and drink their blood,' Krindle suggested.

'I really missed you and your constructive ideas,' said Dandelion. *'Good to have you back, Krindle.'*

Rumo was asleep within seconds.

III.
The Metal Maiden

Lying down or standing up? Rala couldn't have said which she was doing. She tried to speak, but she couldn't move her lips. She tried to open her eyes, but her eyelids refused to obey.

Was she frightened? No. She was awake, alive and undaunted. That was strange. She ought to have been at least a little bit frightened, but although she couldn't see, couldn't move and was imprisoned in something, her composure steadily increased. It was strange, yes, but true. Had she gone mad? Mad people sometimes felt irrationally calm in hopeless situations, so she'd heard.

Rala consulted the instincts of her species. Sniffing the air, she detected the smell of metal, the smoky aroma of lead. She'd been buried alive. Or was she dead? No, she felt so alive, so wide awake! If only she could receive some sign, some sign from outside, that would prove she was alive! But there was nothing to be heard. She lay in the dark for a long time – just lay there and waited.

There! At last! A click followed by the unpleasant sound of metal grating against metal. A long-drawn-out, excruciating sound that set her teeth on edge, but it was music to her ears. Someone was scratching on the outside of her coffin.

Then she heard a voice that seemed to come from everywhere at once. A low, unfamiliar whisper, it sounded cold and dead, and mingled with that soulless whisper was an irregular mechanical noise like the ticking of a defective clock.

'Rala?' said the voice. 'Are you [tick] awake at last? Yes? [tock] My instruments [tick] tell me you are. [tock] Then we can begin. Are you [tick] ready to die? To die more slowly [tock] than anyone has ever died before?'

General Ticktock's story

When General Ticktock and his Copper Killers vanished from the face of Zamonia a legend arose that they had fled straight to hell. Like all legends, this one contained a grain of truth, and truth is always stranger and more exciting than fiction. Yes, General Ticktock had fled straight to hell, but that was the beginning of his story, not the end. Down there he found everything he had always dreamt of. He found a home, and he found eternal death and dying. What was more, he surpassed himself in the truest sense, becoming something far, far greater than he had ever been in Overworld. But that was far from being the best thing that befell General Ticktock in Netherworld. No, the best thing he found there was love.

He never looked back after fleeing from Lindworm Castle and leaving his soldiers in the lurch. He marched for hours, days and months without ever calling a halt or glancing over his shoulder.

After about a month General Ticktock paused for the first time and turned round. His entire army, or what was left of it, was standing respectfully to attention. Several hundred Copper Killers had followed him every step of the way and were humbly awaiting his orders.

That was when he realised his soldiers would follow him anywhere, no matter what he did. He could have marched them straight into a smelting oven and they would have obeyed without question. That was blind obedience in its most perfect form. With bodyguards like these he could still achieve all he wanted.

'We are yours to command, General Ticktock!' cried the Copper Killers, smiting their armour-plated chests.

So they marched on through Zamonia, attacking villages and small unfortified towns. Unlike traditional armies, however, the Copper Killers pursued no definite objective. They did not aspire to enrich themselves or capture towns in order to occupy them and enslave their inhabitants. They merely did what they had been trained to do: kill, destroy, and then march on with a view to killing and destroying anew. The Copper Killers enjoyed this merciless routine and would, if it had been up to them, have continued to perform it ad infinitum. In the end, however, General Ticktock grew bored. He would have liked to wreak still more destruction and kill with greater refinement, but there seemed to be no prospect of doing so within the confines of Zamonia.

One day the Copper Killers were opposed by an army of Demonic Warriors. Although the Demonic army was numerically superior to them, all that remained of it by nightfall was a handful of captured warriors impaled on stakes at the edge of the battlefield, kicking and struggling as they waited for death to put them out of their misery.

General Ticktock, who was immensely interested in anything to do with death, stationed himself in front of the dying warriors and asked, 'Where [tick] do you think you go to [tock] when this is over?'

'To Netherworld!' they replied in unison.

'Netherworld? What [tick] does Netherworld have to offer [tock] that attracts you so?'

'Eternal death and eternal dying,' croaked one of the warriors.

'Wine laced with blood!' groaned another.

'Murder and torture are as universal there as birth and death are up here,' gasped a third.

'I'm intrigued [tick],' said General Ticktock. 'How do I get to [tock] this wonderful place?'

'You?' the Demonic Warriors laughed. 'You can't! You're only a godforsaken machine – you can't die. The only passport to Netherworld is death.'

'Well [tick], I mustn't detain you [tock],' said General Ticktock, and he personally slit their throats.

From now on he was obsessed with the idea of getting to Netherworld. Telling him that he couldn't do something was just the way to infuse him with a burning desire to accomplish it nonetheless. The dying Demonic Warriors had finally presented his aimless existence with an objective: he would descend into that terrible realm of pain and death, even without dying – indeed, he would if necessary burrow his way down there with his own hands. And once there he wouldn't leave it at that – oh no, he would become the ruler of that evil place.

The Copper Killers were henceforth under orders to question all the people they met about the route to Netherworld, and 'questioning' usually meant torturing them until the last items of information had been extracted. Because people will say anything under duress, many places were claimed to be the site of the secret entrance to Netherworld: a ravine in the Midgard Mountains, a cave beneath the sea near Betaville, a crater in Devil's Gulch. The result of this search for the route to Netherworld was that the Copper Killers roamed around even more restlessly than before – and were disappointed every time.

One day their quest took them to a small town known as Snowflake because of the eternal snow that covered its buildings. General Ticktock decided to storm the place as soon as he sighted it in the distance. The Copper Killers cleaned their weapons, loaded their crossbows and – as usual – gathered information by torturing a few locals captured in the vicinity of the town. One of them was a blind, exceedingly old Druid who led a hermit's existence on a hill nearby.

He warned the Copper Killers as follows: 'Do not set foot in that accursed town! People have settled there many a time, only to disappear overnight. A few days ago I once more smelt the acrid stench drifting over from the town, and once more its inhabitants have vanished. Avoid the place – it devours its own children!'

General Ticktock, who was intrigued by this story, decided to be merciful to the old Druid, so he had him killed on the spot instead of being slowly tortured to death. Then, because his curiosity had really been aroused by now, he ordered the Copper Killers to launch a night attack on Snowflake. Sure enough, they were unopposed. There was no resistance. The place was deserted – a ghost town, as the old man had said. Its snow-covered roofs gleamed in the moonlight and General Ticktock wondered why so handsome a town had been left unoccupied. Perhaps the blind greybeard had frightened its inhabitants out of their wits with his scaremongering and they'd abandoned the town because of an old wives' tale. At all events, General Ticktock was piqued by the absence of anyone to kill and regretted having treated the old man so mercifully.

When the Copper Killers entered the main square of Snowflake they were confronted by a strange sight: a gaping hole as big as a village pond. Undeterred by the evil smell that rose from it, General Ticktock went to the edge of the abyss and looked down. A seemingly endless spiral staircase led down into the bowels of the earth. He sent for one of the prisoners he'd taken outside the town.

'What [tick] is that [tock]?' he demanded.

'I don't know,' the trembling prisoner replied.

General Ticktock seized him by the throat and hurled him down the hole, then listened to his screams, which took a long, long time to die away.

'But *I* do [tick],' he said, when silence had finally returned. 'It's the entrance to Netherworld [tock].'

An impressive entrance

Hel suited General Ticktock perfectly. It was not only bigger but wilder and more evil than any city he'd ever seen before. The dark alleyways, the ghostly lighting, the weird architecture, the bizarre inhabitants, the soot and grime – he was hugely delighted by all that met his eye when the Copper Killers marched into Hel. For the first time in his life he had no wish to destroy a place; he wanted to become a part of it – the most important part, naturally.

The general's army encountered no resistance as it clanked, unspeaking, through the soot-blackened streets. Anyone who saw the metallic warriors coming shrank back and disappeared into the gloom. From time to time they met small bands of Bluddums or other mercenaries who respectfully stood aside to let them pass, but most of the inhabitants seemed to be either pale-skinned creatures with horns or peculiar hybrids whose strange physique was perfectly in keeping with the city's general appearance. General Ticktock was delighted.

He paused to torture a few of the locals – the quickest and most reliable method of briefing oneself on a strange city. They spouted information like a fountain. The city's name was Hel and it was the capital of Netherworld. Its king was Gornab the Ninety-Ninth, whose chief adviser was Friftar, and the entire population was currently assembled in the Theatre of Death. That was enough to be going on with.

The Copper Killers attached a long chain to the neck of one of their prisoners and sent him on ahead to show them the way to the Theatre of Death.

The entrance to the theatre was guarded after a fashion by a smallish squad of Bluddums. They were so dumbfounded by the sight of the intruders that a volley of crossbow bolts mowed them down before they could draw their swords. The Copper Killers marched over their dead bodies and into the theatre.

An extremely unequal contest was in progress when, to everyone's astonishment, the invaders paraded in the arena. A platoon of Bluddums armed with axes and swords was busy butchering some of the prisoners recently imported from Snowflake. They offered little resistance to the Copper Killers before they too were laid low by a volley of crossbow bolts.

More and more metallic warriors marched into the arena. The spectators, the king, his chief adviser and bodyguards – all were frozen with horror. The spectacle unfolding before their eyes was past belief: an army of mechanical beings had occupied the Theatre of Death and was aiming crossbows at the audience. For a while, all that broke the deathly hush was the ticking and whirring of those fearsome machines.

Then General Ticktock himself entered the theatre and strutted into the middle of the arena. Scattered cries rang out as the audience caught sight of the biggest of the metallic warriors. He was even more massive, terrifying and nightmarish than the rest. Several of the Copper Killers ostentatiously spat fire from their steel mouths.

'Which of you [tick] is the king?' General Ticktock called loudly.

'I am the gink!' replied Gornab, who had leapt on to his throne and was trembling with agitation.

'Yes, this is King Gornab Aglan Azidarko Beng Elel Atoona the Ninety-Ninth,' Friftar announced, giving his monarch a cursory bow. 'And I am Friftar, his chief adviser and director of the Theatre of Death. May I, on His Majesty's behalf, enquire your name and ask what possessed you to burst in here and kill our soldiers?'

General Ticktock spun out the interval between Friftar's question and his reply until the suspense became unendurable. The audience held its collective breath.

'My name [tick] is General Ticktock,' he declared in a voice that carried to the furthest row of seats. 'And these [tock] are my Copper Killers. We have come . . .'

The general inserted another pause for effect. The Copper Killers, many of whom were aiming at the king himself, continued to cover the spectators with their crossbows.

'. . . to enter your service!' Ticktock concluded. Then he went slowly down on his knees and humbly inclined his head in the direction of Gornab the Ninety-Ninth.

The theatre rang with cries of jubilation.

The warrior and the king

Gornab was delighted with General Ticktock from that moment on. Having frightened him terribly, the gigantic Copper Killer had generously set his mind at rest. Friftar's diplomatic machinations paled into insignificance beside such a gesture. What a fascinating, glittering, dangerous new toy! A metallic warrior with a machine in place of a heart – and he wanted to be of service to him, Gornab!

How dearly he himself would have liked to be an immortal, heartless creature of this kind! General Ticktock possessed every attribute of which Gornab could only dream: everlasting good health, invulnerability, inexhaustible energy. Compared to him, Gornab's generals were inexperienced shirkers who had never set eyes on a battlefield larger than the theatre's arena, and even then from the safety of the VIPs' box.

Ticktock's dramatic appearance had been followed by lengthy negotiations between him and the king, with Friftar eagerly acting as interpreter. It was eventually agreed that the Copper Killers should be granted Hellian citizenship. In return, they would undertake to abstain from further hostilities and hold themselves in readiness until the king and his advisers had agreed on their sphere of responsibility.

After General Ticktock had gone off to settle the Copper Killers in their new quarters, Gornab spent some time conferring with Friftar.

'I prospoe to oippant Negeral Tocktick mmocander-in-fiech of our eramd froces,' he announced.

'Really?' said Friftar, concealing his surprise. 'You propose to appoint General Ticktock commander-in-chief of our armed forces? A brilliant idea, Your Majesty – as usual.'

'Yes, isn't it? Solabutely llibriant! Tocktick is fowerpul! He's invrulenable! He's a bron worriar!'

'Yes, he's a born warrior. Invulnerable. The ideal person to command our troops. I congratulate Your Majesty on making such a shrewd appointment.' While he was repeating Gornab's words, Friftar's thoughts were darting in a hundred different directions simultaneously.

'The pity of it is . . .' He left the sentence hanging in mid air.

'Wath? Wath's a tipy?' Gornab demanded.

'Oh, it's just that . . . well, General Ticktock has so many qualifications, he's such a scintillating figure. What a loss to the Theatre of Death!'

'Neaming wath?'

'I mean, did you see how the audience reacted to him? That mixture of fascination and fear? He had only to raise a finger and they were all mesmerised. He's so . . . so glamorous.'

'Moglarous?'

'I mean, he possesses everything we need in the Theatre of Death. He would be an immense draw. His mere presence would guarantee a full house. The Metal Man! The Heartless Warrior and his Copper Killers! If General Ticktock assumed command of the theatre guards, the common folk would love it.'

'The nommoc flok? Since when have I neeb esterinted in the nommoc flok's iponions?'

Friftar uttered a ringing laugh. 'That's a good one, Your Majesty! You mean your jest to imply that the common folk must sometimes be permitted to believe that their opinions count for something?' He feigned intense thought. 'Yes, you're right yet again, by all the fires of Hel! It's a most statesmanlike decision.'

'Learry?' Gornab said, looking bewildered. Hadn't he meant to say the opposite? He shook his head to clear it. 'Yes, I soppuse it is.'

'It's brilliant!' Friftar exclaimed delightedly, refilling the king's goblet with wine. 'The Copper Killers on guard duty at the Theatre of Death! Not only an attraction but your personal bodyguard! Why didn't I think of that myself? Their presence would lend the contests additional charm. They could occasionally step in and kill some prisoners.'

'Klil some prosenirs?' Gornab became infected with Friftar's enthusiasm. 'Yes, of source! Klil some prosenirs!'

'Wait, Your Majesty, I'm just beginning to grasp your intention. We must build them a gallery of their own, is that it? Higher than the prisoners' gallery, so that they can supervise them from above. Of course! How brilliantly original!'

'Iraginol? Yes, iraginol!' cried Gornab, clapping his hands. 'Then they nac sipervuse them! Yes, sipervuse them from avobe!'

'So you're appointing General Ticktock commander of the theatre guards,' Friftar said casually. 'Shall I inform the nobility and the common folk? May I publish a decree at once?'

'Hm?' Gornab scratched his head, looking stupefied and thinking hard. 'Yes, you yam. I mmocand you to.'

'You command me to? So be it, Your Majesty.' Friftar bowed and the king flopped back against his cushions in relief.

The royal adviser congratulated himself on his presence of mind as he hurried to his quarters. It had been a near thing. If the king had yielded to a foolish whim and installed General Ticktock in a post he himself had vainly plotted to obtain for years, it would have been a dire setback. He now had the general where he wanted him: in the theatre with all the other balls he was juggling there. The only question was, how much longer would he manage to keep them all in the air at once?

Ticktock puts on weight

From the moment he gained Gornab's confidence, General Ticktock's power increased almost daily. But unlike Friftar, who was constantly expanding his spider's web of intrigue and espionage, the general *expanded himself* in the truest sense.

He consulted every armourer in Hel, summoned the city's expert military engineers and weapons technicians, and got them to show off their latest inventions. Then he selected whatever appealed to him: a new blade, an assortment of special arrows, a miniature crossbow, sinews of precious metal, polished teeth of laminated steel, a glass dagger filled with poison. All these acquisitions were incorporated in his metallic body. He grew day by day, in breadth as well as height, as his innards filled up with ever more sophisticated weapons. His arms and legs became longer, his chest more voluminous, his back broader, his weight more prodigious. When General Ticktock trod on them, flagstones splintered beneath his feet.

The arsenal concealed inside him represented the latest state of Hel's weapons technology. His left eye could fire micro-arrows impregnated with anaesthetic or deadly poison, according to choice. His fingertips were fitted with blades that could be fired and then retracted on wires. His chest contained bellows filled with a highly inflammable mixture, which he could spit with great accuracy. Insidious weapons were hidden all over his body. He regarded himself as an ever-growing military work of art, a perpetual motion machine capable of infinite expansion. Time, decay, disease, wear and tear – those factors played only a subordinate role, if any, in Ticktock's scheme of things. To him ten years were the same as a hundred, a hundred the same as a thousand. He had to allow for a bit of rust, a worn-out joint or two, a few defective nuts and bolts, an occasional burnt-out alchemical battery, but all his components could easily be replaced with spare parts of ever-improving quality. Time was on General Ticktock's side. New alloys were being perfected, weapons becoming ever more effective and sophisticated. He looked forward with pleasurable anticipation to the technological advances of the coming centuries. Whenever a useful innovation came along he would acquire it and have it installed in his own insatiable frame. No one would be able to stop him in the long run, but for the moment he would have to compromise. He was still a dwarf compared with the Ticktock of his dreams. Much as he would have liked to crush the hideous king of Hel with a huge mailed fist and trample his people underfoot like insects, he could yet not afford to do so. In order to achieve his aims he would have to fall back on the wearisome methods of diplomacy.

He often wondered what differentiated him so clearly from his Copper Killers – what had rendered him so superior to them and placed them under his command. Although he obeyed no one, he knew there was something inside him that spurred him on, some mysterious thing he looked for in his mechanical interior. He suspected that alchemists had implanted this mysterious motor in him at birth. It wasn't an alchemical battery or a steam-powered machine; it was something that could think for itself, something that never slept or rested, never paused or came to a standstill. This mysterious something was for ever tormenting him with questions. 'How can I grow bigger?' it asked, or 'How can I become more powerful?' or, 'How can I inspire more fear?' But the central question around which Ticktock's thoughts revolved was 'How can I kill more efficiently?'.

He had already murdered in countless ways, employing every conceivable kind of weapon, poison and mechanical device as well as his bare hands. No one knew more about killing and dying. Intent on learning more about death, he had gazed into the eyes of all his victims as they breathed their last, and had seen things that made him a leading authority on the subject – indeed, if such an academic qualification had existed, General Ticktock deserved a degree in thanatology. He had discovered that pain, however agonising it had been, evaporated at that final moment. But where did it go?

If he really wanted to know every last thing about dying he would need more time. It wasn't a question of his own time – that he had in plenty, being immortal – but of the wretchedly short space of time in which his victims died. Once initiated, the process of dying was irreversible and completely beyond his control. This had always riled him. One minute he was master of life and death; the next, another more powerful authority had taken over and was dictating the rules of the game. He would so much rather have prolonged the dying process for days, weeks and months!

But fate had led General Ticktock to Hel, and this evil city held the answer to his most pressing question: How could he kill more efficiently? Strange as it may sound, the answer to that question was love.

It is always dangerous to underestimate evil persons and suppose them to be immune to love. The ability to love is not a prerogative of the good but may well be the one thing they share with the evil. As for where Cupid's arrow strikes home, this often depends on its target being in a particular place at a particular time. In General Ticktock's case the place was the workshop of a Hellian weaponsmith who also manufactured instruments of torture and execution machines.

The general had come in search of some new playthings for installation in his body. The weaponsmith had laid out various novelties on a bench, among them some pliers with diamond-edged teeth and a gilded circular saw blade that could be hurled like a throwing disk.

Ticktock inspected the pliers. They were so effective that one could even have used them to dismantle a Copper Killer – indeed, even himself. Then he weighed the circular saw in his hand. It could have felled an enemy like an axe felling a tree. Both were splendid weapons.

But Ticktock, being in a surly mood, was hard to please. Reluctant to be talked into buying something, he preferred to poke around in the workshop at his leisure. After he had peered into every corner of it the weaponsmith showed him into a large, gloomy storeroom that he called his graveyard. Ticktock got him to light a torch and illuminate the mound of discarded scrap metal it contained. Then his eye was caught by something in the far corner. It resembled a sarcophagus standing on end. The general was extremely interested in coffins, of which sarcophagi were a sort of artistic refinement, so he made for it and the weaponsmith followed with the torch. The nearer they got to it, picking their way through the clutter of metal, the more excited Ticktock became. No, it wasn't a sarcophagus. He thought he knew what it was: something he had heard a great deal about but never seen before. He couldn't understand how anyone could have let such a treasure go to rack and ruin. He felt as if he had discovered a priceless diamond in the midst of a rubbish dump, for the object in question was a genuine *Metal Maiden*.

A Metal Maiden was an instrument of torture and an execution machine combined. With its lifeless eye sockets and gaping mouth, the specimen confronting General Ticktock resembled a crude suit of armour or a ghostly apparition in everlasting agony. Its outer casing consisted of thick grey lead, but all the screws and embellishments were of copper. Let into the front of the Metal Maiden were two doors that could be folded back. The interior was capacious enough to hold a sizeable body, and welded to the inside of the doors, Ticktock was delighted to note, were dozens of long, thin blades made of copper. If an offender were placed in the Metal Maiden and the doors closed, the blades would pierce him from head to foot. That was the actual function of this machine, the weaponsmith knowledgeably explained: to perforate a body in the most ingenious possible way. The difference between execution and torture, he said, depended on the speed with which the doors were closed. Victims beyond number had expired inside this Metal Maiden, he added in a disparaging tone, so the hinges squeaked abominably and the blades had become so encrusted with blood over the years that they weren't a pretty sight. He intended, he said, to have the antiquated contraption melted down.

General Ticktock killed him on the spot for this outrageous lack of respect. Applying a fingertip to the back of the weaponsmith's skull, he transfixed his brain with one of his retractable blades. The lifeless body slumped to the floor at the Metal Maiden's feet - which was where it belonged, in the general's opinion. How had the man dared to describe her as old and unsightly in his presence? Ticktock eyed the Maiden approvingly. They had so many things in common. Like him, she was made of metal. Like him, she was capable of killing in painful and ingenious ways. From now on they would kill together.

The general uttered an exultant cry that shook the smithy to its foundations. He had fallen in love for the first time in his life.

As good as new

Having installed the Metal Maiden in the torture chamber in his tower, General Ticktock ordered his servants to remove all the other instruments of torture. Away with the rack! Away with the garrotte! Away with the thumbscrews! Their very presence was an affront to the Metal Maiden. He need never employ such primitive aids again. Then he proceeded to clean and restore the Metal Maiden with his own hands. He began by ridding the blades of blood. Whose was it? How much had they suffered and for how long? Who had used the Maiden before him? Suppressing a pang of jealousy, Ticktock burnished the copper fittings with abrasive paste. How beautifully they shone! He oiled the hinges, polished the other components and tightened all the screws. Finally, he inspected his handiwork. The Metal Maiden was as good as new.

Thoughtfully, he circled her. Something was missing, but what? Mobility? Animation? No. He did not plan to install the sort of machinery that ticked away inside himself. He liked the Maiden just as she was, silent and motionless. For all that, something was missing. Ticktock circled her again and again, inspected her from every angle, opened and closed the doors. At last it struck him: the Metal Maiden must become more deadly, not more animated.

An impossible task

General Ticktock summoned Hel's leading alchemists, physicians and engineers, and informed them of his plan. The Metal Maiden was to become the most beautiful, luxurious and ingenious killing machine ever built. Not a mobile machine like himself or the Copper Killers, but one that would always stand in the same place, here in his tower. Even the word 'machine' was a misnomer, being too crude and technological for the delicate functions the Metal Maiden would perform in line with his wishes. She was to become an artistic instrument equal to the demands and capabilities of the greatest virtuoso of death, namely himself. He wanted a hydraulic and pneumatic system of ducts controlled by valves and stopcocks. He wanted tubing of all gauges, down to and including hollow needles the thickness of a hair – thinner than any that had ever been manufactured before. He wanted elixirs and poisons, drugs and extracts.

The assembled scientists and technicians scratched their heads and exchanged puzzled glances, but they didn't dare to argue. With uncharacteristic forbearance General Ticktock realised that he would have to go into greater detail.

'My first requirement [tick],' he began, 'is that the blades inside the Metal Maiden be replaced with long, thin, hollow needles [tock], and that these be attached to an elaborate system of copper tubes and hoppers [tick] outside her. I wish these tubes and hoppers to have, circulating within them [tock], a wide variety of alchemical fluids.'

The scientists longed to know what fluids the general meant, but they forbore to ask.

'I want to be able to inject these fluids [tick] into the bloodstream of any victim the Metal Maiden pierces with her needles [tock]. I want complete control over his chemical constitution! I want valves and stopcocks [tick], pumps and filters! I want to play on organisms [tock] as I would on a musical instrument!'

Some of the alchemists began to grasp what the metallic general had in mind.

'Where the fluids are concerned [tick], some must be lethal poisons, others life-prolonging alchemical extracts [tock], algetic acids, herbal brews, or animal secretions – drugs of the most diverse kinds. I want belladonna juice! I want [tick] opiates dissolved in alcohol! Valerian, arsenic, spirit of melissa, liquid caffeine, tincture of [tock] thorn apple! You alchemists [tick] are to concoct entirely novel, even more effective potions! Some that accelerate [tock] the onset of death and others that delay it. Some [tick] that inflict pain and others [tock] that alleviate it. Some that intensify [tick] the fear of death a hundredfold – that plunge the brain [tick] into a state of the most terrible confusion! I [tick] want a potion that induces a sensation [tock] of hysterical euphoria!'

The faster the general ticked, the more aware the scientists became of his mounting excitement, the urgency of his demands and his determination to have them fulfilled.

'I want [tick],' he cried, 'to develop a machine [tock] that will enable me [tick] to control death! If I succeed [tock], dying will no longer be [tick] a natural process but [tock] an art form!'

General Ticktock concluded his harangue and submitted each of his listeners to a piercing stare. 'I want [tick] the impossible,' he said at length, lowering his voice, 'and I want it [tock] in double-quick time.'

The alchemists, physicians and engineers hurried off to their laboratories and workshops, and worked harder at their appointed tasks than they had ever worked at anything in their lives. What the general had asked of them was insane. He might just as well have commanded them to render themselves invisible or build a machine for manufacturing gold. They worked day and night for months on end, employing all their expertise and expending more energy than any of them had ever summoned up before. General Ticktock's regular visits to their workshops and laboratories contributed to this. His mere presence was enough to make them find solutions to seemingly insoluble problems and transform their exhaustion into unflagging vigour. After six months the unthinkable had been achieved: the Metal Maiden had been completed to General Ticktock's entire satisfaction.

The art of killing slowly

However, operating her in practice proved far harder than he expected. To his growing chagrin, the ensuing experiments compelled General Ticktock to acknowledge that art – including the art of killing – was a capricious thing. The first victim to be imprisoned in the Metal Maiden died the moment the needles pierced his body – of sheer fright. The next three survived for only a few minutes because, in his excitement, Ticktock overdosed them with stimulating substances: they expired of heart failure. Although he gradually learnt to restrain himself, none of the Metal Maiden's captives survived for longer than an hour.

This much he did realise: that the Metal Maiden was a sensitive instrument whose method of operation he would have to master by degrees and that his victims, too, were sensitive organisms that could not simply be swamped with drugs and toxins.

But his guinea pigs were also partly to blame. They died because they *wanted* to die. All of them sought to escape from the Metal Maiden as quickly as possible and the quickest way of escaping from her was to die. However many restorative drugs Ticktock injected into their bloodstream, imprisonment in the Metal Maiden seemed so terrible that they all preferred death. He procured a supply of the most hardened warriors, scarred veterans who would have fought on with cloven skulls or arrows riddling their bodies, but even they survived for no more than a day or two and their coarse oaths desecrated the Metal Maiden's body. If he really wanted to fathom the secret of death, Ticktock would have to obtain some considerably tougher guinea pigs. He wanted to prolong the dying process for weeks and months. Possibly, even, for a year.

It took another dozen experiments to bring the truth home to him. The Metal Maiden was like a violin without strings, that was the problem. The body of the instrument and the brilliant performer – himself – were there, but the instrument itself lacked a soul. This noble and extremely complex machine deserved an inmate of the same calibre; only then would it bring forth the kind of music General Ticktock dreamt of. It was pointless to go on soiling his precious Metal Maiden with blood, he decided. Better to wait until a worthy test subject fell into his hands.

The new gladiators

To seek a soul for the Metal Maiden among the inhabitants of Hel was as futile as seeking a lamb in a wolf pack. Ticktock nonetheless ordered his spies to comb the city for suitable material, but none of the candidates they garnered from its lanes and alleyways fulfilled his exalted requirements.

He came to the conclusion that he would have to go to Overworld in person to find a suitable victim - or victims - and was just preparing to set off on this expedition when news reached him that the latest crop of prisoners from an Urban Flytrap had arrived in town. It was his job to submit all new gladiators to personal inspection and assess how much of a threat they represented to the king's safety. Although convinced that no prisoners could seriously threaten himself and his Copper Killers, he performed his wearisome duty on this occasion, too, and went to inspect the newcomers.

They had been abducted from a town named Wolperting. That didn't make them sound particularly menacing - more like a bunch of country bumpkins. Friftar's peculiar decisions were an everlasting puzzle to Ticktock, and he couldn't wait for the day when he would take the mad king's chief adviser and rip the heart from his palpitating body.

Ticktock didn't inspect all the prisoners, only those who had been housed in separate cells in the Theatre of Death. The older and weaker specimens had already been weeded out and were leading an uneventful existence in a large prison nearby, where they could move around in relative freedom.

The general inspected each of the cells in turn, and what he saw in them surprised and overjoyed him beyond measure. Even the first three prisoners, who were still anaesthetised, struck him as a hundred times worthier of the Metal Maiden than all the inhabitants of Hel put together. What were these noble creatures? They resembled dogs of various breeds, but they could walk on their hind legs and they also possessed horns. All were muscular and in peak condition. Ticktock had some more cells opened and his delight intensified. These were genuine warriors, not paid mercenaries who would have drowned their own mothers for a bowl of broth. They were *real* fighters, intelligent beings endowed with the instincts of a dangerous predator. General Ticktock could well imagine what a death-defying fight they would put up inside the Metal Maiden! His excitement grew by leaps and bounds.

What a shame to waste such noble creatures on the stupid fun and games in the Theatre of Death! He would have to act quickly to obtain the finest specimens before they lay dead on the sand in the arena. He need only pronounce them a threat to the king's safety and he could do as he pleased with them. But which ones to take? They all looked so splendid. Irresolutely, he went from cell to cell. At least he could dispense with his expedition to Overworld. The warder opened the door of the next cell and he looked inside.

The general had seen few things in his life that had really impressed him and etched themselves deep into his memory: the Nurn Forest battlefield on which he had opened his eyes after being reborn; the avalanche of boulders descending on the Copper Killers from Lindworm Castle; the sight of Hel in the distance; and, of course, the Metal Maiden. What he saw in this latest cell undoubtedly belonged on the list. But for the presence of a witness, he would have gone down on his knees before the spectacle that met his eyes.

It was Rala. Still drugged and in chains, with her limbs unnaturally contorted, she lay stretched out on the flagstones. The general stiffened.

What a supreme stroke of good fortune! Electric frissons traversed his metal skull and the alchemical batteries inside him crackled. Had he tried to speak at this moment, he would only have ticked. He had to summon up all his self-control, or he would have torn off the warder's head in sheer ecstasy.

Her proportions were absolutely perfect – the Metal Maiden might have been made for her – and her beauty was overpowering. General Ticktock had a unique ability to scent courage and fear. In the case of this girl Wolperting, he detected an immense determination to survive and as little fear of death as a corpse would have had. There was no doubt about it: before him lay the soul of his Metal Maiden. With her he would at last be able to perform the lethal symphony of which he had dreamt for so long.

Rumo awoke feeling refreshed and ready for anything. The little creatures that had served him as a live fur coat were scurrying around nearby. He got up and inspected the cave entrances.

'Which one shall I take?' he wondered.

'Hard to say,' said Dandelion.

'Take the first one you come to,' Krindle advised.

Rumo made slow progress. The ground was stony and uneven, the tunnels became narrower from one intersection to the next, and his path was barred by rockfalls of ever more menacing size. Sometimes he had to squeeze through narrow passages, sometimes he had to crawl. The furry creatures had disappeared. He only hoped his route wouldn't end in a wall of rock.

'Look where you're going,' Dandelion warned. *'Some of these holes are a mile deep.'*

'How would you know?'

'I was a miner, remember? If there's anything I know about, it's caves. I'm a Troglotroll! There's tectonic movement here, you can tell from the rock formations. Those sharp ridges were created by earthquakes. One little geological hiccup and we'll be cooped up in here for evermore, ha ha!'

'You think that's funny?'

'It wouldn't be a new experience, not for me,' said Dandelion. *'Ever heard of a miner's sense of humour? At work we used to take it in turns to visualise the most appalling disasters. It's an antidote to fear.'*

Some slimy liquid dripped on to Rumo's neck. Dangling from the roof of the tunnel were insects the length of his arm, colourless and eyeless but equipped with long antennae.

'Don't worry, they only eat carrion,' said Dandelion. *'They don't eat your eyes until you're dead. They're partial to eyes, probably because they don't have any themselves.'*

Indignantly, Rumo brushed away the antennae of an insect that was trying to explore his face.

'It's always the same in poor lighting,' Dandelion complained. *'Nature has a field day when it thinks no one's looking.'*

'Too true,' Krindle chimed in. **'I served in the Midgardian Cave Wars. Three years fighting underground. I saw creatures that should really be banned.'**

'You can say that again. Life assumes strange forms when there's no

sunlight. Chalk Worms, Soilspiders, Tunnel Rats, Roof Crawlers, Fridgimoths, Lava Worms, polypodous limpets, transparent leeches, phosphorescent snails – you name it. It's almost as if ugliness really goes to town when there's no one around to see it.'

Rumo ascended a natural stairway of tilted granite blocks. A yard-long millipede came towards him. He politely stepped aside and watched it march past, scything the air with its pincerlike jaws. It too appeared to be blind.

'Yes, Biteworms are best avoided,' said Dandelion. *'They're harmless, actually – provided you're awake and can elude them, but heaven help you if you're asleep. They'll go right through you. They creep into your ear, nibble their way through your brain and down your neck, and come out by your feet. Biteworms don't make detours.'*

'You're right,' said Krindle. **'I knew a Demonic Warrior who had a Biteworm go through both legs while he was asleep – twice. In through the upper thigh going one way and out through the lower thigh on the way back. He had to walk on his hands after that.'**

'Did you know there are subterranean mushrooms with the characteristics of carnivorous plants? And a species of octopus that can get by without water and lives in mounds of scree? The creatures have arms two hundred yards long. You could set up house in their suckers.'

'I know,' said Krindle. **'Ever heard of the Minerameleon? Up to forty feet long, and it can take on the shape and colour of any kind of rock. You could stand on one and never know it.'**

'That's nothing,' said Dandelion. *'Did you know there are subterranean mosquitoes so small they can fly straight up your nostrils and into your brain – and lay eggs there that grow to the size of watermelons? It happened to one of my fellow miners. We were walking along a tunnel together and suddenly his head swelled up like a pumpkin. And then – bang! – it exploded before my very eyes and out flew millions of baby—'*

'Spiderfloods!' Krindle broke in darkly.

'Oh man, Spiderfloods are something else! Whole tunnels are suddenly inundated with Woolspiders the size of your fist. You can try to breathe without getting any of the hairy creatures in your mouth, but it's quite impossible, take it from me.'

Rumo groaned. He was finding the route arduous enough without having to listen to Krindle and Dandelion blathering. For some time now he had been compelled to proceed at a crouch to avoid the jagged rocks protruding from the roof of the tunnel. Innumerable plump slugs were crawling around on them, leaving trails of luminous violet slime in their wake.

It struck him that the composition of the tunnel floor was changing. More and more often he trod on yielding soil or sand and pebbles.

'Very few rocks here,' he said.

'That means we've gained height,' Dandelion replied. *'We're reaching the upper layers, they're looser.'*

Rumo could now detect familiar smells again: soil, leaf mould, resin. Strangely enough, he felt he'd been here before. But that was impossible, of course.

'It smells of forest,' he said.

The ground became steadily moister and softer. It squelched at every step as if he were walking on waterlogged moss. Thousands of slugs were burrowing through the soil or clinging to the tunnel's walls and roof and daubing them with phosphorescent violet slime. Where everything had been hard, cold and jagged, it was now soft, warm and yielding.

Rumo trod in a puddle. He crouched down, dipped a paw in it and sniffed his fingers. The liquid was viscous and sticky, and had a smell he knew.

'Well?' asked Dandelion. *'Is it drinkable?'*

'No,' said Rumo. 'It's blood.'

The Metal Maiden was ready. The world's most sophisticated killing machine had at last been equipped with a soul. It fitted the beautiful female Wolperting as perfectly as if it had been made for her alone.

The siege

As soon as he left Rala's cell General Ticktock had instructed his guards to keep the prisoner under strict surveillance and allow no one else near her. Then he hurried to his tower to prepare the Metal Maiden. He topped up the external hoppers, polished the machine and its pipework with a cloth, and ordered his servants to light the room with candles. Finally he sent for the prisoner.

Her name, he had since discovered, was Rala and she was still anaesthetised. This delighted Ticktock, because he could insert her in the machine and plunge the needles into her body without her being aware of it.

The time came at last. He began by infusing Rala with a solution of caffeine and belladonna. A little sugar for the brain, dissolved in distilled water? Why not? He wanted her to awake refreshed, with her senses alert and her blood thin. The fluids gurgled cheerfully along the tubes, the Metal Maiden glinted in the candlelight. Never had General Ticktock experienced such a sense of anticipation, a preliminary reward for a feat as yet unaccomplished.

Muffled by distance, sounds drifted into the torture chamber from the Theatre of Death. The first Wolpertings to do battle would soon be led into the arena. The inhabitants of Hel were going wild. Word of the sensational crop of prisoners had spread swiftly, and they were all eager to see the Wolpertings fight.

But General Ticktock wasn't interested. Not in the slightest. Those ridiculous contests in the theatre had bored him from the very first. What would he be missing, after all? A few silly fights, a few bodies twitching in their death throes, some blood on the sand, drunken spectators. No, he had something more important to do. He was making ready for a wedding of a special special kind: the siege, conquest and destruction of Rala's body. It would be the longest, most agonising and beautiful death that had ever been bestowed on any living creature.

Ushan versus Roboglob

Ushan DeLucca entered the arena by the northern gate. Pandemonium reigned on the spectators' benches. The Hellings were shouting, laughing, chucking bread and fruit around, and paying little attention to the new arrival in the Theatre of Death.

Ushan was in the best of spirits. He walked with a spring in his step, smiling and waving to the audience. He had been captured and taken to a city full of bloodthirsty Netherworlders, he and all his friends had been enslaved and he was about to be slaughtered in combat before an audience. Apart from that, he couldn't have felt better. Why? Because there wasn't any weather in Netherworld.

Gone were the rain, sunshine and areas of low pressure – and, with them, his headaches, his bouts of melancholia and the buzzing in his ears. On regaining consciousness in Hel, Ushan had felt as if a ton weight had been removed from his shoulders – as if he'd at last been divested of a lifetime's suit of leaden armour. Down here, as a prisoner in this nightmare world, he felt truly free for the first time ever.

He came to a halt, turned on the spot and blew the audience a few kisses. What a glorious day!

A gong sounded and the spectators fell silent.

The ground in the centre of the arena opened up and a long, narrow pit appeared in the sand.

'Roboglob, Roboglob,' the spectators chanted softly. 'Roboglob!'

Surprised, Ushan stopped blowing kisses. This seemed to be a familiar ritual.

The gong sounded again and a boat rose slowly from the pit. It was a skiff with a sharp prow, and in it stood a gigantic red-skinned warrior half as tall again as Ushan, wearing armour composed of different materials: a leather gorget, a breastplate of bronze, silver knee pieces, a golden helmet shaped like a death's head with a silver blade for a crest, and a skirt of human thigh bones. He stood there with both hands resting on a massive executioner's sword. The upwards motion ceased, the boat came to rest and the warrior got out.

The applause rose to fever pitch. 'Roboglob the Ferryman! Roboglob the Ferryman!' chanted the audience, louder and louder.

The warrior raised his sword in both hands and saluted the audience. The boat sank into the ground and the aperture closed again.

The spectators stamped their feet.

This Roboglob, Ushan was impressed to note, seemed to be a pretty big cheese down here.

The story of Roboglob the Ferryman

Roboglob was an Osirian, one of the last descendants of a tribe of warlike giants from the north of Zamonia. He was known as Roboglob the Ferryman because he could be relied on to convey all his opponents to the Realm of Death on streams of blood. He enjoyed the applause as much as the fighting, and he'd made it a rule always to win in a spectacular manner. He never made short work of his opponents, but deliberately toyed with them for a considerable time, inflicting minor wounds and a painful, lingering death. Roboglob could afford to indulge in these tactical ploys because, being an established Theatre of Death artiste, he was never matched with an opponent of his own calibre.

Roboglob couldn't lose, even the audience knew that. What mattered in a Roboglob fight was the ritual, not the suspense; not who won, but the spectacular way in which Roboglob would this time dispatch his opponent. When he eventually did so, he never left it at a single sword stroke. He had to deliver three, four, five or ten, and with the last one he sent his opponent's head rolling across the sand. Roboglob didn't fight, he tortured; he didn't kill his victims, he butchered them.

Ushan had been chosen out of all the prisoners by Roboglob himself. He didn't make a very robust impression, this Wolperting with the big bags under his eyes, nor – from the look of him – was speed his long suit. The fact that he proposed to fight Roboglob armed with a slender rapier was greeted with derisive remarks and guffaws. Why not a stick of celery, while he was about it?

'Another passenger for you, Roboglob!' called someone in the audience. More guffaws.

Roboglob, who was still holding his huge sword aloft in both hands, swung round. The rows of seats trembled beneath the spectators' pounding feet.

Ushan was wearing no armour, only his usual buckskin waistcoat and trousers. He walked slowly towards Roboglob, paused just in front of him and performed a few erratic movements that might have been a nonchalant salute.

'Ssst, ssst, ssst!' went Ushan, but no one heard him in the universal uproar. He bowed, blew a few more kisses and sauntered back towards the northern gate as serenely as he had entered. Behind him the red-skinned giant sank to his knees with a gasp of surprise, blood spurting from several wounds in the gaps between his armour. No one had seen a thing. Had the Wolperting even drawn his rapier? Absolute silence descended on the Theatre of Death.

With a clatter Roboglob fell face down on the sand and lay quite still.

Ushan paused once more, bowed deeply – though no one was applauding – and disappeared through the gateway.

Ushan becomes a favourite

The king had stopped jumping around on his throne.

'Wath was tath?' he asked his adviser. 'Did you see, Tarfrif?'

'It was the quickest fight I ever saw,' Friftar replied. He was as thunderstruck as everyone else in the theatre. 'To be honest, Majesty, I saw almost nothing.'

Gornab stared down at the gigantic corpse. The sand around it was turning red.

'Blogorob is dead,' he whispered dully. 'Blogorob the Merryfan is dead.'

'Yes,' Friftar translated mechanically, 'Roboglob the Ferryman is dead. It seems these Wolpertings really are as good at fighting as they're rumoured to be. Perhaps they shouldn't be judged by their outward appearance. I shall find out his name and put him down on the list of favourites.'

'Yes,' said Gornab, 'tup him down on the slit of rafourites.'

Friftar bowed to conceal his surreptitious smile. The spectators were completely taken aback. Everyone was talking excitedly. It was just as he had hoped! These Wolpertings might prove to be the finest crop Hel's first Urban Flytrap had ever yielded.

Nurn blood

'Blood?' Krindle asked incredulously. **'The real thing, you mean?'**

Rumo was still kneeling beside one of the many red puddles on the tunnel floor. The sample he'd just taken was sticking to his fingers. He had difficulty in wiping it off on his clothes.

'It smells of blood,' he said. 'And resin. Where have I smelt that combination before?'

'Blood and resin . . .' said Dandelion. *'That puts me in mind of Nurn Forest. The Nurn's blood was full of resin.'*

'We'd better get out of here,' said Rumo. 'I don't like the smell of this place.'

The words were hardly out of his mouth when a tentacle darted from the puddle. It was blood-red and shaped like a muscular arm. Five fingerlike offshoots reached for Rumo's wrist, closed round it and started to drag him down into the puddle.

'What is it?' shouted Dandelion. *'What's the matter?'*

Rumo tried to pull his arm away, but the tentacle was immensely strong.

'Draw me!' Krindle commanded.

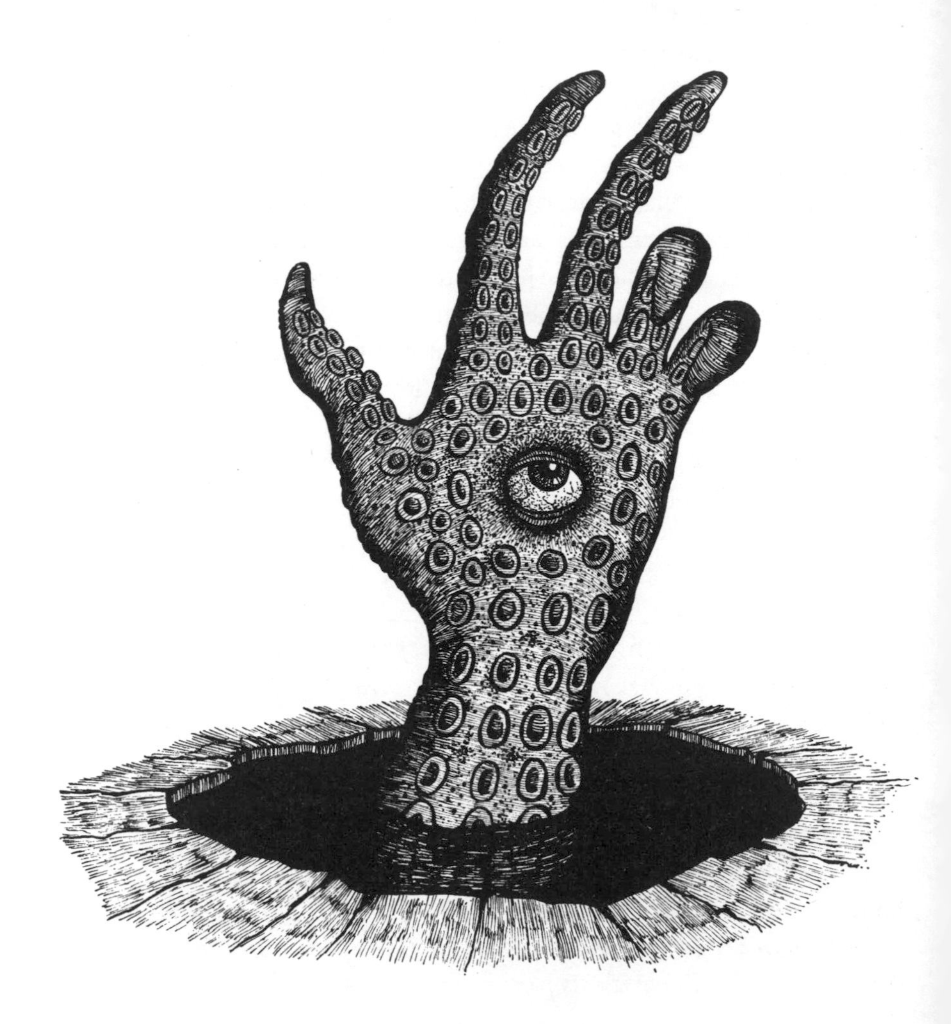

Rumo did so. He drew the sword from his belt with his free hand, raised it above his head and severed the tentacle with a single blow. Blood spurted from the stump.

'Ugh!' said Dandelion.

The bleeding stump was swiftly retracted, the tentacular hand fell to the ground. It stood up on its fingerlike excrescences and seemed to take its bearings for a moment. Then, nimble as a spider, it scuttled over to the nearest puddle and jumped in. Blood splashed in all directions, a few fat bubbles rose to the surface, and it was gone.

Rumo straightened up.

'I told you,' cried Dandelion. *'There are some very nasty things down here. Better get going.'*

Rumo replaced the sword in his belt and walked on along the tunnel, taking care to maintain a respectful distance from the puddles.

At the next fork he paused to sniff the air again. He peered round the bend and jumped back in alarm.

'What is it?' asked Dandelion.

'Nurns!' he replied. 'The passage is full of them. Half a dozen at least.'

'Damn it! How did they get there?'

'No idea,' said Rumo. 'They're smaller than the ones in the forest, no bigger than I am. I think they're asleep, though. They're standing absolutely still.'

'So let's kill them!' Krindle urged.

'No, we must look for another route,' said Dandelion.

Rumo tiptoed on until they came to another fork. The tunnel was deserted, but there were a lot of red puddles.

'Mind where you tread!' Dandelion cried.

Rumo stole between the puddles on tiptoe. A drip fell from the roof and landed on the back of his neck. Brushing it off with his paw, he found that it was warm, sticky blood. He heard a gurgling sound and halted.

'What was that?' asked Dandelion.

'No idea.'

A big bubble rose to the surface of the puddle at his feet and burst.

He backed away, hugging the wall of the tunnel, and drew his sword.

Now all the puddles came to life. More bubbles rose, the red liquid seethed as if brought to the boil, and plops and gurgles filled the air.

'I once saw a minor volcanic eruption,' said Krindle. **'This was how it started.'**

The puddles overflowed, dispersing their heat and humidity. To Rumo's astonishment some living creatures emerged from the seething blood. They clambered out, steeped in the red liquid from head to foot, and staggered around on eight spindly little legs.

Rumo recognised the tiny creatures. They were Leafkins. He was witnessing the birth of some young Nurns.

Within moments the floor of the tunnel was covered with toddling Leafkins. Rumo couldn't have taken another step without treading on one and alerting its Nurn parents. He pressed still closer to the wall and kept quite still.

'This place is a regular Nurn factory,' said a high-pitched voice.

He looked down. A furry little creature was sitting at his feet with Leafkins toddling all around it.

'Hello, Rumo,' it said, looking up at him pertly. 'So we meet again.'

Rumo gave a start. He couldn't recall having introduced himself by name to any of the little creatures, nor had he noticed that they could speak.

'It's me, Yggdra Syl,' it said in nasal tones. 'Don't you remember?'

'Yggdra Syl?' Rumo was puzzled. The Nurn Forest Oak? Down here?

'Look, my friend!' the little creature piped, indicating the aerial roots that dangled from the walls. 'Geographically speaking, you're immediately beneath Nurn Forest, only a few hundred feet below the place where we met. I told you: my roots go deep. Down here I prefer to communicate through Kronks.'

'Kronks?' Rumo repeated, bending down for a closer look.

The creature drew itself up and spread its forepaws.

'That's right, I'm a Kronk. Kronks are burrowing animals equipped with beaks, distantly related to the marmot. They're the original inhabitants of Netherworld. There aren't that many other species down here, if you don't count insects. What are you doing in this desolate place?' The Kronk eyed Rumo curiously.

'I, er . . . I'm looking for my sweetheart.'

'What, still looking for Rala? Didn't you give her our casket?' The Kronk put its forepaws on its hips, looking reproachful.

'She was kidnapped,' Rumo explained. 'It happened while I was in Nurn Forest.'

'Kidnapped, eh? That's bad. Who would have done such a thing?'

'That's what I'm trying to find out. And now I'm afraid I've lost my way. Nurns are barring our route and the whole place is dotted with these pools of blood from which—'

'I know, I know, it's an unpleasant part of the world. The blood was shed in the Battle of Nurn Forest, as I told you. The confounded stuff simply won't dry up down here – it contaminates the soil and breeds Nurns, as well as other nasty things. Tantacles, Bloodspiders, et cetera – it's disgusting.'

The Kronk elbowed an obtrusive Leafkin aside.

'Come on,' it piped. 'You'd better get out of here before one of these brats starts bawling and alerts its parents.'

'How can I, without treading on them?'

'I'll clear a path for you,' said Yggdra Syl. 'Kronks enjoy the freedom of Netherworld. The larger animals pay no attention to them. Just follow me.'

The Kronk hurried on ahead, thrusting Leafkins aside and enabling Rumo to follow in its footsteps. The little creatures stumbled and tripped over their own legs, but they uttered no complaint.

'Without Kronks there wouldn't be any animals in Netherworld,' Yggdra Syl explained, continuing to shove the Leafkins aside. 'They loosen the soil, or other creatures wouldn't be able to pass through it at all, and they also eat pathogenic organisms. If I told you what I had for breakfast today, my friend, you'd feel queasy. Everyone in Netherworld respects the Kronks.'

They eventually came to a tunnel where there were no pools of blood, no Nurns or Leafkins. The Kronk came to a halt.

'We're safe here,' it said.

Rumo couldn't smell any Nurns. He replaced the sword in his belt.

The Kronk pecked away at his boots with its beak.

'Now,' it said, 'you must tell me more about this Rala business.'

Rumo sighed. 'To cut a long story short, she and all my friends have been carted off to a city by the name of Hel.'

The Kronk recoiled. 'Hel? Oh dear!' The little creature started to waddle round in a circle, looking agitated. 'That's very bad news. Hel, of all places! Oh dear, oh dear!'

'What do you know about Hel?' asked Rumo.

The Kronk came to a stop and eyed him sympathetically.

'Only rumours - my roots don't extend that far. They're nasty rumours, though. One big madhouse, that's Hel. Crazy King Gornab rules it with an iron fist. Oh dear, oh dear!' The Kronk started circling again, uttering plaintive little cries.

'All the same,' said Rumo, 'I've got to get there. Do you know the way?'

'The way to Hel? Oh dear, oh dear, my roots only extend so far. The way to Hel? Oh, my goodness!'

'Will you show me the way?'

The Kronk halted again.

'Of course,' it said. 'Of course I will, my boy. But first . . .'

'First what?' asked Rumo.

The Kronk hung its head and shuffled from foot to foot.

'Well?' Rumo insisted.

'First,' said the Kronk, clearing its throat, 'I've a little favour to ask.'

'What is it?'

The Kronk gave Rumo a look of entreaty. 'May I see the finished casket?'

'Oh, so that's it,' said Rumo, sounding relieved. He took the casket from his pouch, removed the oil-paper wrapping and put it on the ground in front of the Kronk. Casket and Kronk were about the same size.

'There,' said Rumo. 'What do you think of it?'

The Kronk inspected the casket warily and exhaustively, crawled round it, gave it a gentle tap with its beak.

'Well?' Rumo asked hesitantly.

The Kronk was breathing heavily, at a loss for words. 'It's . . . it's beautiful,' it said at length in a tremulous voice. 'A top-quality casket.'

Rumo heaved a sigh of relief.

The little creature circled the casket once more, admiring it from every angle. It flapped its arms helplessly and Rumo could see that its eyes were filled with tears.

'This casket, it's . . . Words fail me, I . . .' It began to weep. 'Boohoo,' it went.

'Why are you crying?' asked Rumo.

'Boohoo,' sobbed the Kronk. 'It's because . . . because I'm so moved! It's the first time anything good came of me. A genuine work of art! Until now, all my branches were good for was hanging people.'

The Kronk gave a sniff.

'And now I'm a casket for your sweetheart! Boohoo!'

'There, there,' said Rumo, gently patting the Kronk on the back with one finger. He was beginning to feel uncomfortable.

The Kronk wiped away its tears and gazed at him with wide, bloodshot eyes. 'If you don't win her heart with *that*,' it cried dramatically, 'you never will. It's the most beautiful casket in the world!'

'Your opinion means a lot to me, truly it does,' said Rumo. 'Many thanks, but I must find her before I can give it to her. Will you show me the way?'

'Will I!' cried Yggdra Syl, alias the Kronk. 'I'll show you the way to your beloved's heart! Follow me! Follow me through the darkness to the light!'

And it bounded off along the tunnel with Rumo struggling to keep up.

The symphony of death

General Ticktock had taken three days to get the Metal Maiden perfectly adjusted. Every vein, nerve and sinew had to be run in. Were the extracts flowing in the correct quantities? Was the liver functioning properly? The heart, the kidneys? Were the valves in order, the tubes unobstructed?

He began by injecting only the simplest substances as a means of checking Rala's vital organs: saline, glucose solution, caffeine, vegetable extracts, nutrients, harmless stimulants. In accordance with his instructions, the physicians had fitted the Metal Maiden with instruments for measuring its occupant's heartbeat, body temperature and respiration, but Ticktock's favourite toy was a calibrated dial that combined all these readings and showed, as a percentage, how much life still remained in his victims. If the needle registered a hundred they were very much alive and in the best of health; if zero, they were dead. The general had christened this instrument his thanatometer, or death meter.

He turned a little wheel, caffeine started flowing, and Rala's heart beat a trifle faster. He opened a valve, releasing some pepper extract, and she became warmer. He closed the valve again and her temperature sank. And so it went on throughout the first day. Ticktock played with his controls, pressing buttons, turning wheels and opening valves. Rala's heart beat faster or slower, she became hotter or colder, calmer or more agitated, livelier or more lethargic. He inflicted no pain and injected no drugs, nor did he make her ill. The Metal Maiden functioned like a well-oiled machine. That evening General Ticktock flooded Rala's bloodstream with valerian and she slept soundly for hours.

The second day began with a hearty breakfast: plenty of caffeine and glucose solution. General Ticktock's bride had to be physically and mentally alert, because her ordeal would now begin in earnest. Today he proposed to try out various poisons on her and administer small doses of drugs to test their effect for subsequent use in larger quantities. He infused Rala with arsenic, belladonna and extract of fly agaric, though only in tiny doses, and carefully cleansed her blood with medicaments between each. These infusions caused slight nausea and mild hallucinations, but nothing serious, for Ticktock only wanted to observe Rala's reactions to such substances. And she reacted perfectly. Previous candidates had flown into a panic well before this stage, but Rala's heartbeat and breathing remained regular and the thanatometer steadfastly registered a hundred. Finally, General Ticktock sent her into a deep sleep with a generous dose of spirit of melissa.

The third day also began with some stimulating extracts and plenty of glucose. Then General Ticktock made Rala ill. Whatever it was he infused her with, her tongue swelled up and tasted acetic, her eyes began to smart and her throat closed up as if she had a heavy cold. After that he cured her in a trice with some concentrated herbal extracts and an alchemical drug developed for the purpose.

Ticktock repeated the same trick several times that day. He made Rala ill and then cured her. Nausea, dizziness, headache, fever, breathlessness – the symptoms disappeared as quickly as they had manifested themselves. The general had prepared remedies that would, within seconds, cure any infection he caused. To end Rala's sufferings he had only to open a stopcock, turn a wheel, or adjust a valve.

He was beginning to master his instrument. The limits of Rala's endurance were still unknown to him, but he already guessed how much pain he could inflict and how much it would be better to leave in abeyance. Wasn't that how love, too, worked? Wasn't it a question of discovering the other person's boundaries and respecting them?

General Ticktock cast another glance at the thanatometer. It was registering ninety-nine. The procedures had weakened Rala, but only a little. He put her to sleep again, this time with a mixture of valerian and spirit of melissa. He stood in front of the Metal Maiden for a long time that night, gazing at her fondly.

Although Rala had now spent a considerable time inside the Metal Maiden, she could not have said how long her imprisonment had lasted. A day? Two days? Three? A week? The only certainty was that she now knew her own body better than ever before.

Despair had overwhelmed her when the effects of the anaesthetic wore off. Never had she been in such a hopeless predicament. She succumbed to despair and rage by turns, but not to fear. Fear would have paralysed her mind as well, and beyond mental paralysis lurked death. Rala was determined to think. It was the only form of activity still open to her. She rejected fear as she had hitherto rejected death.

After all, what was so unendurable about her situation? Once she had come to terms with the utter helplessness imposed by her form of imprisonment, all else was bearable. She felt sick, cold, hot, dizzy, nervous or tired, but those were familiar sensations that passed as quickly as they had come. Less agreeable sensations occurred later on. Strange and inexplicable visions appeared to her mind's eye, ghostly voices whispered in her ear and insects seemed to be crawling over her skin, but these mild hallucinations, too, soon subsided. For a while she imagined she was several persons at once, but this puzzling sensation also subsided in the end. At some stage, overcome with profound fatigue and relaxation, she had gone to sleep.

Rala had grasped that someone outside was doing all these things to her for reasons as mysterious as the methods he used to torment her. She had spent these days as if in constant motion. Never had she felt as active as she did now, when unable to move so much as a millimetre. Only now did she realise how much life there was inside her, even when asleep, or how the blood sped through her veins and her heart kept pumping away. Her body housed as much hectic activity as a big city, and it was even more hectic now that the enemy was at the gates and laying siege to her. No, there were no grounds for fear and despair. No more, at least, than in any besieged city whose inhabitants were ready to defend themselves.

Urs changes his mind

Urs entered the Theatre of Death prepared to die. To die without a fight, what was more, because he would offer no resistance. He intended to cast his sword at his opponent's feet.

For several days now, Urs had been watching the contests in the arena from the prisoners' gallery, chained and powerless to intervene. Although he still didn't know how the Wolpertings had wound up in this sick world or what its inhabitants' motives were, he had fathomed the theatre's iniquitous function and grasped that it was inescapable.

There was no hope of breaking out. Each Wolperting was escorted into the arena by a whole squad of heavily armed soldiers supervised by Copper Killers with their crossbows at the ready. No outside help could be expected, so one's only recourse was to conform to the system and become one of the theatre's gladiators. Until now the Wolpertings had been exclusively matched with mercenaries and other hired killers, but Urs knew it would be only a matter of time before a Wolperting was forced to take up arms against one of his own kind. This, Urs realised, would be the beginning of the end of his breed, and he couldn't endure the thought. He would rather die than be compelled to watch one Wolperting kill another.

All the fights had ended in the Wolpertings' favour. Whether matched with one or several opponents, wild beasts or experienced killers, every Wolperting had left the arena alive except for Ornt El Okro, who had been executed in such a cowardly manner.

Ushan DeLucca's fight had set the pattern. Not long afterwards Balla of Betaville had scored an impressive victory over a pair of mercenaries. Olek of the Dunes, armed only with a sling, had defeated a whole gang of them, and none of the Wolpertings compelled to follow him into the arena had sustained a single serious wound. But Urs's mind was made up. He had never killed anyone in his life and he wasn't going to start now. Today was the day he would bid farewell to this nightmare world, and he wanted to combine that farewell with a profession of faith – by refusing to draw blood.

A small army of Bluddums and Copper Killers escorted him from his cell to the northern gate. Only there were the Wolpertings permitted to select a weapon from an assortment lying on a table. Urs picked up a short sword at random and strode out into the arena.

Scattered applause greeted him. Although the spectators had learnt to respect the Wolpertings, they were far from inclined to cheer them on. Urs's opponent was a tall, muscular Hoggling covered with bristly black hair. His mane was braided into plaits with countless coloured beads, teeth and small bones in them. He wore a huge gold nose-ring between his tusks and a loincloth consisting of a dozen swords in leather scabbards.

'What's your name?' Urs asked when he reached him – not that he was really interested in his opponent's name. He needed it in order to utter his last words. 'Kill me, So-and-So!' he intended to cry, and he wanted to get the name right.

Evel the Octopus

'My name is none of your business, little doggy, but I'll tell you it because it's the last thing you'll hear in this world. My name is Evel.'

Urs's paw tightened on the hilt of his sword. Evel? It was someone of that name who had killed Koram Morak, his foster-father.

'Evel the Octopus?'

The Hoggling inclined his bristly black head.

'Did you ever come across a Koram Morak?'

'What is this, a guessing game?'

'The name Koram Morak means nothing to you?'

'No. Never heard of it.'

Urs released his grip on the sword hilt.

The Hoggling clasped his brow. 'No, wait . . .' he said. 'Koram . . . Koram Morak? Wasn't that the Vulphead with all the scars? Of course! It was . . . yes, one winter years ago! He was reputed to be North End's finest duellist. A tough customer, yes, but no technician. I split his thick skull in half. With a Two-Handed Slice.'

Urs's paw tightened again.

He had come to another decision. He wouldn't die today after all. Someone else would.

'All right, Evel, let's begin,' he said. 'Show me why they call you the Octopus.'

What followed turned out to be the most remarkable contest on the programme that day – in the view of many spectators, one of the most remarkable ever. Remarkable because it was the longest ever fought in the Theatre of Death. Remarkable, too, because it lasted so long although the outcome seemed certain after only a few seconds. Evel the Octopus, one of the theatre's undefeated swordsmen, stood no chance against the much smaller Wolperting. He never even got a chance to display the dexterity that had earned him his nickname. Urs severed a sinew in his right wrist in the first minute, so he could only fight on with his left arm. Between the first minute of the duel and its grisly conclusion, Urs inflicted as many wounds on his opponent as the latter made vain attempts to land a single blow. In the end, after fighting for several hours, Evel begged Urs to put him out of his misery.

But the most remarkable feature of this fight was that Urs refused even to administer the *coup de grâce*. In order to end his torments, Evel was compelled to fall on his sword.

'Who is tath Tingerwolp?' asked Gornab, when he saw Evel stretched out in his own blood. The interminable fight seemed to have put him into a trance from which he was only just awakening. 'Wath's his mane?'

'His name is Urs,' replied Friftar who, as director of the Theatre of Death, had done his homework.

'I kile him!' Gornab declared. 'I've vener nees anyone linfict so chum naip on his nentoppo. Tup him on the slit of rafourites.'

'I've never seen anyone inflict so much pain on his opponent either,' said Friftar. 'A great talent. I shall naturally put him down on the list of favourites.'

'A tipy Negeral Tocktick wasn't tchingwa. Where's he neeb all tish mite?'

'Yes, Your Majesty, a great pity General Ticktock wasn't watching. I don't know where he's been all this time. They say he's shut himself up in his tower and doesn't want to be disturbed. I should feel happier if he performed his duties at the theatre occasionally. Shall I command him in your name to present himself here?'

'No, no,' the king said quickly, 'he's prabloby bysu. I won't tusdirb him.'

'Yes, Your Majesty. General Ticktock is probably busy with important matters – for the benefit of Hel.'

Friftar clapped his hands and loaves were distributed among the audience free of charge. Then he added Urs's name to the favourite performers' list.

In Yggdra Syl's domain

'I've got roots all over the place down here,' squawked the Kronk. Although it was indefatigably leading the way, panting hard as it surmounted the obstacles in its path, it never stopped talking. Yggdra Syl was seizing the chance to hold a conversation. 'There's another, and another, and another! See them? Those roots are my eyes and ears. I'm omnipresent down here. My world exists wherever they grow, but it ends wherever they don't. From my point of view you're going nowhere, so to speak. I've no idea what goes on outside these tunnels, I'm dependent on rumours. I occasionally question the travellers who get lost in my labyrinth, like you, but they're few and far between. And anyway, you never know where you are with the types you meet down here.'

'I see,' said Rumo.

'Hey,' said the Kronk, 'I didn't mean you! You're different. You're on a romantic mission. You've got a casket to deliver.'

'Tell me more about the city of Hel,' Rumo said.

'I've nothing to offer but rumours, as I say. I once met a bandit who used to shuttle back and forth between Hel and Overworld. He was quite talkative. He told me the inhabitants of Hel are white-skinned devils who torture their prisoners to death in a big theatre. Things like that, know what I mean?'

'What are Vrahoks?' asked Rumo.

The Kronk paused and turned round. Rumo halted too.

'Vrahoks? You want to know what Vrahoks are? To be frank, the things I've heard about them are so monstrous I hardly dare repeat them. I can't even guarantee that the Vrahoks really exist. Some say they're omnivorous giants, others that they're transparent and equipped with more legs than a spider. Many people claim that their stench is a lethal weapon in itself.'

The Kronk hurried on with Rumo at its heels.

'How far can you take me?' Rumo asked.

'As I told you, my boy,' Yggdra Syl replied, 'my roots mark the boundaries of my domain. I can take you there, but it's not much further now. After that you'll have to fend for yourself.'

'You've been a great help already,' said Rumo.

'Don't run away with the idea that I envy your mobility. Mobility doesn't last. In my philosophy all living creatures are trees. Each of them puts down roots sooner or later. You'll do so yourself some day, mark my words. And then you'll put on annual rings and grow old and fat. Like me.'

'Perhaps,' said Rumo.

'What will you do if Rala is dead?' Yggdra Syl asked abruptly.

'What?!'

'It's an unpleasant thought, I know, but haven't you ever considered it?'

'No.'

'And you don't want to, eh?'

'Yes. No, I mean.'

'You like words of one syllable, don't you?'

'Yes.'

The tunnel had widened, and Rumo noticed that the aerial roots dangling from the walls, formerly so profuse, had grown rarer. The Kronk's voice, too, seemed thinner and reedier.

'Well, my sphere of influence is coming to an end,' said Yggdra Syl. 'I don't mean to be sentimental or anything like that, but when you set off into the unknown with our casket I shall almost feel that I'm going with you – that I'm surpassing myself, so to speak. In casket form.'

'Hm,' said Rumo.

'Is "Hm" a syllable?' asked Yggdra Syl. 'I shall miss our profound conversations.'

The tunnel ended in a vast open space. Massive tree trunks loomed up ahead, veiled in pale-blue mist. Rank upon rank of huge trees stretched away for as far as the eye could see.

'That's *Deadwood*,' whispered Yggdra Syl. The Kronk had finally come to a halt. 'Netherworld's make-believe forest.'

Rumo looked more closely. The lifeless grey tree trunks glistened with moisture deposited by the thin, incessant drizzle that was falling from the mist overhead.

'Those trees are made of stone, not wood,' Yggdra Syl explained. 'They're stalagmites that have grown between the floor of the cave and its roof over millions of years. There are many rumours concerning Deadwood, notably that it isn't anything like as dead as it appears. It only remains for me to tell you to be careful.'

'I will be,' Rumo promised.

'Once you're past Deadwood you'll be considerably closer to your destination. Be guided by the black toadstools growing on those stone tree trunks. They point in the direction of Hel, so it's said.'

The Kronk raised an admonitory paw.

'One more thing! You mustn't eat those black toadstools, not on *any* account, no matter how hungry you are. They're the only form of food in Deadwood, but they're said to drive you insane. According to another rumour they turn you into one of the ghosts reputed to dwell in the mist above the trees.'

'You've heard a lot of rumours,' said Rumo.

'Yes.' Yggdra Syl sighed. 'We must part here. Remember it's only hearsay, all I've told you about the things you may meet on the rest of your journey. The best of luck, Rumo, and take good care of that casket.'

The Kronk zigzagged back into the tunnel and disappeared into the gloomy labyrinth.

Rumo turned and set off into the stone forest.

The insanity drug

For the first time ever, General Ticktock was feeling proud of something other than himself. He was proud of himself as well, of course, and of having put his audacious scientific and technological theories into effect, but he was proudest of all of Rala. Although he had sensed from the first that her will to live was exceptionally strong, he had not expected her to display such utter contempt for death. She had now been imprisoned in the Metal Maiden longer than any test subject before her, and the thanatometer had never once registered less than eighty. The honeymoon period had ended long ago and the pain he was now inflicting on Rala far exceeded anything her predecessors had endured. What fortitude! And what fury! He had never come across such courage on any battlefield, not in a hundred enemies combined.

And to think of all he'd done to her recently! For an entire day he had enhanced her physical sensitivity to the utmost with an elixir, then infused her bloodstream with fluids that caused muscular spasms. They must have hurt like dagger thrusts, yet she hadn't cried out once. Greatly accelerated pulse rate and breathing, of course, and a few twitches, yes, but very little reaction otherwise. And her bodily functions had readjusted themselves automatically. Then she'd fallen asleep from sheer exhaustion. What a brave girl!

Yes, Ticktock was proud of Rala. Because any relationship should be based on mutual respect, however, he proposed to teach her some respect the next day. For this purpose he would turn his attention to Rala's most sensitive organ: her brain.

He went over to his poison cupboard, took out a flask and gazed at the label for a long time. Some weeks ago he had instructed one of his alchemists to develop a drug that would instil fear, and the contents of this flask were the product of that alchemist's labours.

Many drugs were capable of instilling fear, but they all contained some contrary element, some property conducive to happiness or relaxation, with the result that they caused an alternation of euphoria and panic. The alchemist had proceeded to extract the euphoric elements from the poisons he selected – thorn apple, deadly nightshade and Deadwood toadstools – by breaking them down into their chemical constituents and isolating the disruptive elements. He then blended extracts of the three poisons into a single toxin capable of inducing hallucinations of the most horrific kind.

Before taking his new drug to General Ticktock, however, the alchemist had second thoughts. Would it really be capable of meeting the general's requirements? As everyone in Hel now knew, any underling who failed to satisfy him had signed his own death warrant. How could he boost the effects of the drug to so terrible a degree that Ticktock's satisfaction would be guaranteed?

Then the alchemist had a trail-blazing idea. He had to pay off a few old debts, bribe a few people and make all kinds of promises, but he eventually obtained what he wanted: a tiny test tube containing a single drop of red liquid. He hurried to his laboratory and set to work. Having subjected the liquid to retrotransubstantiation and artificial lipaemia, he dehydrated and lyophilised it until he was left with a minute quantity of red powder resembling ground saffron. Then he dissolved the powder in alcohol and blended the resulting tincture with his toxic essence. In layman's language, the alchemist had laced his poison with a tiny sample of Gornab the Ninety-Ninth's blood, thereby lending it the requisite dash of genuine insanity.

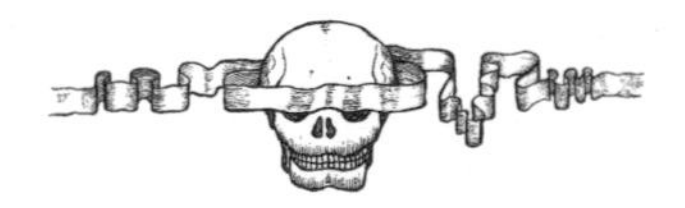

Harra's first and last fight

Harra looked at the sword in his hand. It felt heavy, cumbersome, stupid, ridiculous. He knew what knives were for – they were for cutting bread – but swords? What good were they?

Harra knew, of course, that swords were aids to fighting and killing, but those were activities he rejected. This attitude hadn't made his life as a Wolperting any easier, but there it was. Although he had been born into a species whose members had an exceptional aptitude for fighting, he simply had no wish to fight.

That was why Harra of Midgard had become a teacher – because he felt called upon to inform the younger generation that a Wolperting could get through life without brandishing a sword. Having retired to bed in Wolperting a few days ago, happy in this belief, he now found himself heaven alone knew where, standing in an arena in front of thousands of outlandish creatures – with a sword in his hand. Anyone would think they expected him to use it!

The only wound Harra had ever inflicted with a sword was the notch in the mayor's skull. It dated from a fracas between the Blacks and the Reds, but that had merely been a skirmish between two rival gangs of schoolboys playing truant and the sword that Harra had swung a trifle too hard had been made of wood. He had almost died of shock when Jowly of Gloomberg collapsed and lay inert in a pool of blood. But then Jowly had opened his eyes and Harra had sworn never to touch a sword again. He gave the thing in his paw another look of distaste and tossed it on to the sand.

As if this were a signal, the ground promptly opened and two cages rose to the surface from the cellars of the Theatre of Death.

Inside the cages, insofar as Harra could see their inmates through the massive bars, were two creatures with bristly grey fur and impressively large teeth. Their heads, which were covered with short, snow-white hair, could have been mistaken for death's heads had it not been for their darting yellow eyes. What were they? Harra's knowledge of biology was quite sufficient for him to teach it when standing in for a colleague from time to time, but he couldn't place these animals. Perhaps they were wild apes.

Friftar gave a discreet signal. There was a click and the cage doors swung open. The creatures seemed temporarily flummoxed by their new-found freedom. They lingered irresolutely in their cages, grunting in a puzzled manner. Harra noticed that each of them was carrying a heavy club.

Perhaps I'd better go, he thought, but where to? The arena gates were shut.

The animals ventured out of their cages at last. Although seemingly intimidated by the spectators' laughter, they bestirred themselves and grew angry when bombarded with loaves and fruit. They bounded across the arena, screeching and flourishing their clubs, until Harra caught their eye. He continued to stand there, watching them as they prowled around him. Yes, they *were* apes, he was convinced of it. Their gait indicated that beyond doubt.

The first blow caught Harra between neck and shoulder blade. He was astonished how little it hurt. All he'd really felt was a jolt. His body was evidently capable of secreting a substance that neutralised pain, however intense. That knowledge was a comfort, but Harra disliked the way in which he'd acquired it. He would sooner have read it in a book.

The second blow landed on his head, the third and fourth blows left him stretched out on the sand.

No, thought Harra, he would never become a hero in this world, not by any definition of the word to be found in Zamonia's heroic sagas. He looked up once more at the frenzied apes. Then their clubs descended on him and everything went black.

Friftar bent over Gornab. 'Deadwood Apes,' he told the king in self-important tones. 'Wild specimens I ordered to be caught and trained especially for Your Majesty's delectation. We taught them to be afraid of fire and wield clubs. I'm sure they'll give us a lot more entertainment in the future.'

Friftar smiled complacently. It really had been time to make some attempt to restore the Hellings' pride and self-esteem. He had noticed with mounting displeasure how irritated they were by the contests in which Wolpertings took part. Dozens of the theatre's best fighters had been worsted by them and he had lost such crowd pullers as Roboglob the Ferryman, the Black Twins and Evel the Octopus. The time had come at last for another Wolperting to bite the dust, and it was he himself who had selected an elderly white-haired specimen as club fodder for the Deadwood Apes.

'Wath a sputid fight tath was!' hissed Gornab. 'Wath were you kinthing of, eh?'

Friftar was puzzled. He noticed only now that there had been no applause. On the contrary, he could hear boos and catcalls.

'Sliten to them,' Gornab snarled. 'They're oobing, you headknuckle!'

Friftar was utterly dumbfounded. He hadn't foreseen such a reaction. Fights of this kind had invariably gone down well and the king himself had always been enthusiastic about them. And now the spectators were booing and the king was furious. Had the Theatre of Death undergone some change that had escaped his sensitive antennae? He struggled for words.

'Well, I thought . . .' he began.

'You toughth?' Gornab said venomously. 'Since when have you toughth? From now on veale the kinthing to me, you clumbduck!'

The king's eyes were blazing with the combined insanity of all the

Gornabs. Friftar weighed what he was about to say with the greatest care. One word out of place, one injudicious gesture, and the situation might become lethal.

'Forgive me, Your Majesty, I was mistaken!' he said in a voice trembling with subservience. 'Permit me to assure you that the next fight I arrange will do justice to your sublime requirements and the wishes of the people. I bow my head in the profoundest shame and humility.'

'Yes, wob it!' snarled Gornab. 'Wob it while you've still tog one!'

Friftar withdrew at a crouch, walking backwards. He knew when to stick his neck out and when to retract it, and he intended to keep his head on his shoulders for the foreseeable future.

IV. Yukobak and Ribble

W*hat a dreary place,'* said Dandelion. *'Stone trees with their tops lost in the mist. Everlasting drizzle. No wonder nothing grows here but these ugly black toadstools.'*

If Yggdra Syl had been right, it was really easy to get your bearings in Deadwood. Growing on most of the stone tree trunks was a profusion of black toadstools with little pointed caps, and they all pointed in the same direction. Towards Hel, so Rumo hoped.

'They also grow in the Great Forest,' said Krindle. **'In my youth, when I was still living there, I had to live on an almost exclusive diet of them for six whole months. You get used to them. You have the wildest dreams and hear crazy music from other dimensions. For a month I thought backwards and saw everything in black and white and—'**

'Ssh!' said Rumo. He had come to a halt.

'What is it?' Dandelion asked.

'Two voices,' said Rumo. 'Somewhere among the trees. Not far off.'

'Perhaps it's the ghosts Yggdra Syl mentioned. Do they sound dangerous?'

'No, it isn't ghosts, it's two people having an argument.'

'What about?'

Rumo strained his ears.

'They're talking nonsense,' he said at length, 'but they're talking about Hel. I'm going to waylay them.'

'Good idea,' said Krindle. **'Then we'll torture and kill them!'**

'Oh sure.' Dandelion sighed. *'Let's do that.'*

Rumo materialised in front of the two figures like a ghost. It had been child's play to creep up on them under cover of the massive tree trunks. He stepped out between two of the stone columns and barred their path.

They were startled out of their wits, but Rumo's own surprise was not inconsiderable, because the creatures bore no resemblance to any he had ever encountered before.

The taller of the two barely came up to his chest. Scrawny, with albino-white skin and two small horns, it was curiously attired and armed with a thin wooden spear.

The other figure looked even more peculiar. Half as tall as its companion, it had the head and pincers of a crab and legs like a chicken. As if that were not enough, it wore a funnel on its head and was dressed in a small barrel.

Rumo was at a loss for words.

'A Wolperting!' gasped the taller of the two. It levelled its trembling spear at Rumo.

'Correct,' said Rumo. 'I'm a Wolperting. Who are you?'

'My name is Yukobak,' said the taller of the two.

'And I'm Ribble,' said the other.

'Where have you come from and where are you going?'

'We've come from Hel,' said Yukobak.

'And we're going to Overworld,' said Ribble. 'On behalf of Urs of the Snows.'

They both pointed upwards.

Rumo was genuinely staggered by this. 'Urs?' he said. 'You know Urs of the Snows?'

The Helling and the Homunculus

Yukobak and Ribble were representatives of the two most numerous ethnic groups in Hel. Yukobak was an upper-class Helling distantly related to the royal Gornabs and, thus, a member of the city's aristocracy. Ribble, by contrast, belonged to the lowest caste. He was a Homunculus, one of those alchemically created hybrids that formed the underclass of Hellian society.

Yukobak's was a far-flung family that wielded considerable political influence in the city, maintained contact with its political and military leaders, and boasted several members of the royal household. He had enjoyed an education reserved for very few Hellings and was expected some day to occupy a senior position at court.

Ribble had no family at all. Like every Homunculus, he possessed neither father nor mother but had emerged from the alchemical brew known to the inhabitants of Hel as Mothersoup. The Homunculi were made to perform the city's most menial tasks. They had no rights and were fair game, so killing a Homunculus was not a crime. To anyone from Hel, Yukobak and Ribble were as far apart socially as any two individuals could be.

Ribble had long been Yukobak's personal servant. He had escorted him to school and received the same education as his master. He was his conversational equal, his foremost adviser on matters of vital importance and – not that anyone else knew it – his true and faithful friend.

To the outside world they carefully preserved a semblance of the master-servant relationship, because friendships between Hellings and Homunculi were one of the city's greatest taboos and the truth would have cost Ribble his head.

When the two friends were alone together they became dangerous revolutionaries and enemies of the state. They questioned the omnipotence and infallibility of the Gornabs; they regarded the performances in the Theatre of Death as barbaric, not artistic; they loathed the city's depressing architecture and atmosphere; and they resented the alchemists' suppression of the arts. Yukobak secretly painted little pictures of Hel going up in flames; Ribble wrote subversive poems that ridiculed the king. They proudly showed each

other their works, only to hide them in alarm immediately afterwards. They were not only rebels, therefore, but artists and philosophers, libertarians and visionaries. There was no burning issue they had not already subjected to merciless discussion. Had the *Red Prophecy* been correctly interpreted? Was Hel really the centre of Netherworld? Was it right to raid cities on the surface and enslave their inhabitants? Was it really true that the sunlight in Overworld reduced you to ashes if you exposed yourself to it for too long, or that the air up there slowly poisoned you?

Ribble had never taken it for granted that his species should be treated like domesticated animals, beaten and killed. He had conformed for want of any alternative and was grateful to providence for having granted him the pleasure and privilege of being Yukobak's servant. This did not, however, alter the fact that he had dreamt throughout his life of escaping from Hel.

Yukobak was also revolted by the conditions prevailing there. It embarrassed him to see the ignorant and condescending way his caste treated the city's other inhabitants, and he was appalled by the prospect of the political career with which his family was threatening him. Although he had every conceivable luxury and amenity at his disposal he dreamt of the light, of the sky, of clouds and rain, of wind and water. He dreamt of cities where night fell and day broke in turn, of outlandish creatures and all the marvels of which he and Ribble had read in the alchemists' reports. Together they fanned the flames of their yearning for Overworld, which grew stronger every day.

But the fears implanted in them at school and their memories of all the tales they'd heard about Icemagogs and Nurns, huge vampiric moths and Deadwood Apes, were too deep-seated. The route to Overworld was too dangerous, and besides, it was forbidden to go there without official authorisation.

Yes, it could be said that Yukobak and Ribble were cowards and remained so – until the day they underwent their crucial experience. The event that changed their lives had occurred in the Theatre of Death, when Urs of the Snows fought his first fight.

Yukobak had detested the theatre even as a child. He'd felt sick the very first time his parents had compelled him to watch a fight, and little had changed over the years. He and Ribble thought it barbarous to slaughter defenceless slaves for fun, but they regularly attended these social functions because they hadn't the courage to rebel.

Even the fight between Ushan DeLucca and Roboglob, the celebrated gladiator, had made them think twice, but it had all been over too fast. Suddenly, one of the theatre's so-called favourites was lying dead in the sand, vanquished by a slave. Yukobak and Ribble had spent a long time discussing – not without relish – this novel and unprecedented occurrence.

Then came the fight between Urs of the Snows and Evel the Octopus. It was the most exciting duel Yukobak and Ribble had ever witnessed. The far smaller Wolperting had not only refused to die, he had even refused to kill his opponent by giving him the *coup de grâce.* That was revolutionary! If Yukobak and Ribble had ever seen a real live hero, it was Urs of the Snows. His name had spread like wildfire after the fight and they'd sat up all night, talking their heads off. It was a sign! That prisoner, who had defied the whole Hellian system, was their pointer to Overworld, their signal to risk an escape at last.

Yukobak and Ribble decided to go via Wolperting because it contained the nearest entrance to Overworld. The entrance was open, too. They knew from their lessons at school that an Urban Flytrap was always harvested in two stages. First, the entrance was opened and the inhabitants were anaesthetised and carried off, the whole army being required to cart them away. Later, some of the Hellian troops returned to the city to eliminate all traces of its former occupants, carry out various architectural improvements and close the entrance once more – for many, many years, possibly for decades.

'If we don't go now,' Ribble had said, 'we never will.'

Rala's prayer

'It'll pass, it'll soon be over. It'll pass, it'll soon be over.' That was the optimistic formula Rala had recited again and again in recent days, and her prediction had always come true. That hope was all she had to cling to when her body was once more racked with pain, cold or fever. And she had learnt to cherish the intervening periods when her organism felt normal and merely healthy.

She had clung to that formula even when the major assault on her liver was launched and a monstrous sensation of nausea threatened to overcome her. At first she'd simply felt a little dizzy, but then the dizziness became a headlong plunge down a bottomless shaft and everything had rotated so fast that she felt she was being turned inside out.

'It'll pass,' she'd told herself, 'it'll soon be over.' But there was no relief for a long, long time. The nauseous sensation became so intense that for one brief moment she wished she were dead. But then she clung once more to her only remaining thought: 'It'll pass, it'll soon be over.'

And at some point, quite suddenly, it *was* over yet again. Nothing could be worse than that, she thought. She now believed herself proof against anything.

The face of fear

The assault on Rala's brain was launched the next day. It began, almost innocuously, with a few disconcerting sensations, a strangely restless feeling and some unusual noises. Then her restlessness intensified. The noises became more piercing, the sensations more and more peculiar. Rala could taste sounds and hear colours. Cacophonous music flavoured like bitter almonds filled her head, familiar images and scenes arose and danced around her. She was assailed by poignant memories of Tallon, of Wolperting, of Rolv and Rumo. Then everything went blurred and dissolved into a multicoloured mishmash, like reflections in turbulent water. The familiar figures became cavorting spirits, transparent beings devoid of flesh and bone. They interwove themselves in the same way as Rala's thoughts became entangled and jumbled together, until no idea or syllable was in its proper place.

She tried in vain to remember where and who she was, but her mind seemed to be lashed to a gyrating wheel from which her thoughts spun off in all directions until nothing remained inside her but chill darkness, a lifeless void bereft of hope. And from the depths of that abyss, to the accompaniment of discordant music, there rose a menacing sight: a creature compounded of rage and insanity. Not that Rala knew it, this phantom was the Gornab of Gornabs, the collective evil and ugliness of the Hellian royal family. One face superimposed itself on another to form a single hideous mask too frightful to contemplate - a horrific gargoyle that would have shattered any mirror. It grew steadily bigger, drew nearer and nearer, until Rala was struck by the last and most terrible thought of all: that this might be *her* face, the face of her own fear.

That was the moment when her self-control failed and she started to scream. Had she resisted for an instant longer, had she not cried out and admitted defeat, she would have lost her mind and followed the demented king into his crazy, topsy-turvy realm.

Rala had preserved her sanity, but her resistance was broken. She was now prepared to start dying.

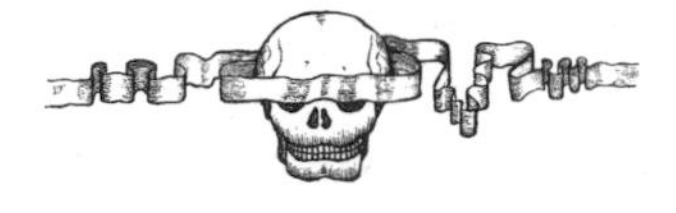

Silence descended on the Theatre of Death as Rolv entered the arena. All heads turned in his direction. This Wolperting looked considerably more pugnacious than the last. There was an ominous glint in his narrowed, terrier-like eyes and his lithe gait was that of a warrior in peak condition. This promised to be an exciting spectacle. All that could be heard were a few isolated coughs and the sound of swordsmen sharpening their blades on whetstones behind the scenes.

Six against one

Gornab was in a bad mood. The last fight had been so poor that he'd lain awake all night with a headache, listening to voices that commanded him to rip out Friftar's throat with his teeth.

'Sith better be a doog testcon,' he snarled at his chief adviser. 'Wiseother you may fnid yousrelf down in the narea with a srowd in your hnad!'

Friftar strove to take this threat calmly.

'I can assure Your Majesty that this will be an excellent contest. I have put together a really unique combination of warriors.'

He clapped his hands, the gong sounded, and six previously invisible doors opened in the wall enclosing the arena. From them emerged six heavily armed gladiators.

The first was a Montanic Giant armed with a huge golden axe.

The second a Vulphead with a trident.

The third a Bluddum with ball and chain.

The fourth a Hoggling with two swords.

The fifth an Osirian with a scythe.

The sixth a Greenwood Dwarf with a spear.

Rolv, standing in the middle of the arena, turned slowly on the spot and inspected his adversaries. He himself was armed with four knives stuck in his belt.

He'd had ample time to reflect on his situation since regaining consciousness in Hel. As he saw it, he was in a fearsome and dangerous place, but it wouldn't be the first time he'd escaped from a hopeless predicament. The worst thing was, he didn't know Rala's whereabouts. He had no doubt that she was still alive because he would have sensed something as final as his twin sister's death, so his most urgent task was to find and release her. Rolv's strategy was simple in the extreme: until he got an opportunity to do so he would defeat anyone who came up against him.

He continued to turn on the spot, seeking out his first victim. The sword? No. The scythe? No. The spear? Yes, it would surely be wisest to eliminate the weapon that could settle his hash at long range. That meant the Greenwood Dwarf.

The White Fire

All at once Rolv's body was transfixed by a sound inaudible to anyone else in the theatre. It was as if someone had plucked a taut string that ran right through him from the top of his head to the soles of his feet. The sound was shrill and high-pitched, like a cry of pain. Although Rolv had never experienced anything of the kind before, he instantly knew what it meant: someone, somewhere, at this very moment, was doing something terrible to Rala. His whole body bent like a bow. He threw back his head and let the cry escape. It emerged in the form of a protracted howl that silenced the last whispers in the auditorium and made his encircling opponents' hair stand on end.

With that wolflike cry Rolv bade farewell to this world and entered the realm of the White Fire. He growled softly and bared his teeth, gripped one of his knives between them and held another two at the ready, one with the blade facing upwards, one downwards.

The audience had already watched several Wolpertings fight in the Theatre of Death. Discounting two elderly specimens, they had all acquitted themselves bravely and defeated their opponents with ease. But what this Wolperting accomplished with his knives surpassed anything they had ever seen before. He wasn't merely fast; he seemed to be in several places at once. His knives went whistling through the air, and before the audience knew it they had found their mark in throats and chests, between eyes and shoulder blades. Rolv rampaged across the arena like a wild wind, sending up clouds of yellow dust, and wherever he went blood gushed like a fountain. When Rolv of the Forest fought his first duel in the theatre, time seemed to stand still.

Then the dance of death ceased as abruptly as it had begun and Rolv stood panting in the centre of the arena, as besmirched with blood as a painter with paint after an artistic frenzy. He was still in his other world, in the midst of the White Fire, but his opponents lay dead on the sand. The spectators rose to their feet and broke into a storm of applause such as the Theatre of Death had never heard before.

Gornab jumped up and down on his throne like a demented gorilla, pounding the cushions with his fists and screeching with delight.

Gnamificent and tanfastic

'Gnamificent! Gnamificent!' he cried. 'Tath was tanfastic! Tath Tingerwolp is a ratist, a negius! I vole him! Gnamificent! Gnamificent!'

'Yes,' Friftar translated mechanically, 'it was fantastic. That Wolperting is a genius in the art of death. I shall put him down on the favourites' list.'

Gornab suddenly quietened. He stopped jumping up and down and pounding the cushions. His face went blank. Then his demented grin returned in an even more devilish form. Friftar knew what this signified. Gornab the Ninety-Ninth was listening to the ninety-eight Gornabs inside him, and soon, very soon, he would turn into a rapacious wild beast.

This was what Friftar had always dreaded most: that the king would have one of his fits in the theatre. It wasn't that Friftar would have minded its being witnessed by almost the whole of Hel. The trouble was, the only occupants of the royal box were the king and himself, and he would be unable to step aside and let Gornab work off his demented rage on someone else. He felt as if he were shut up in a cage with a savage lion whose tail – to make matters worse – he had just trodden on.

A thin thread of saliva trickled from the corner of Gornab's mouth as he slowly wagged his head to and fro. His lips mouthed inaudible words, presumably in response to the commands of the Gornabs inside him. Friftar sighed. He had naturally allowed for this worst of all scenarios, but it was a humiliating business. He sidled behind Gornab and hid beneath the throne like a child sheltering from an imminent earthquake.

He had hardly taken cover when Gornab's fit of manic fury erupted with unprecedented violence. An apelike screech rang through the theatre as the king leapt on to the protective balustrade, seized the nearest guard – a full-grown Bluddum nearly twice his size – by the throat and yanked him into the box with one mighty jerk. What happened next was comparable only to what might have occurred if some careless visitor to a zoo had fallen into a wild beast's enclosure by mistake. Blood spurted in all directions and the audience bellowed with jubilation. There had been a lot of surreptitious gossip about Gornab's convulsions, but no one outside the court had ever witnessed one before. This paroxysm surpassed everyone's expectations. The dwarfish king persevered until he had extinguished every last spark of life in the soldier's body. Then he lay down on the corpse and fell into a deep sleep.

Friftar crawled out from under the throne. Beside themselves with delight, the spectators craned their necks for a look at the bloodstained royal lunatic. Gornab's chief adviser bent over his snoring form. He couldn't help grinning. Fate was forever surprising him with its whimsical ways.

The hostages

Yukobak and Ribble walked on ahead. Rumo, ever vigilant and at pains to intimidate his two prisoners, followed them with his sword drawn.

'I suppose you realise you're sending us to certain death,' said Yukobak.

Rumo said nothing.

'They'll throw me back into the Mothersoup,' Ribble said plaintively, 'and Yukobak will be sent to the Theatre of Death. We've committed high treason.'

'Where's Rala?' Rumo demanded sternly.

Yukobak groaned. 'We've already told you umpteen times. We don't know this Rala or any other Wolpertings. We saw Urs of the Snows at the theatre, that's all.'

'Tell me some more about the theatre!' Rumo commanded.

'What, again?' Yukobak protested. 'You already know all there is to know! You know more about Hel and Urban Flytraps and the whole of Netherworld than most of its inhabitants, yet still you insist on dragging us back there. It's tantamount to a death warrant!'

'I'm merciless by nature,' said Rumo.

Ribble paused abruptly and turned round.

'Know something?' he said. 'I don't think you're half as tough a nut as you make out. You're all right.'

Rumo and Yukobak halted too.

'Really?' said Rumo. 'What gives you that idea?'

'If you were really cold-blooded you'd have killed one of us to impress the other. Why guard two prisoners when one would do? A really tough nut would have acted differently.'

'Ribble!' cried Yukobak. 'Don't put daft ideas into his head!'

Rumo seemed to be lost in thought. 'Yukobak, Ribble,' he said suddenly, 'I'd like to introduce two friends of mine.'

Yukobak and Ribble stared at each other. There was no one in sight but themselves and the Wolperting.

Rumo held out his sword. They shrank back.

'Don't be afraid.' He indicated the two halves of the blade. 'These are my friends. This one is Krindle and that's Dandelion.'

'Wrong way round,' Dandelion protested.

Yukobak and Ribble drew closer together. The Wolperting might not be vicious, but he was obviously insane.

'Pleased to meet you,' said Dandelion.

'Let's kill them!' growled Krindle.

'*They* can hear *you*,' Rumo told his prisoners, 'but *you* can't hear *them*. Only I can. In my head, understand?'

'Absolutely!' Yukobak nodded vigorously.

'In your head!' Ribble chimed in.

'They're dangerous Demonic Warriors,' said Rumo. 'The fiercest of their race.'

'That's not true!' Dandelion protested again.

'Yes, it is!' said Krindle.

'Their brains were smelted into these blades. They speak to me.' Rumo held the sword to his ear and listened, seemingly lost in thought.

Yukobak and Ribble went on nodding eagerly.

'Yes,' Rumo said with a faraway look in his eyes, 'they're unpredictable fellows. Bloodthirsty. Implacable. I'm under their spell. I have to do all they say. It's an ancient curse.'

'We understand,' said Ribble. 'A curse.'

'If it were up to me I'd let you go at once. As things stand, however, I'll have to ask Krindle and Dandelion first.'

'But of course!'

'That goes without saying!'

Rumo muttered something unintelligible to the sword, then held it to his ear again. He listened intently and nodded several times. At length he lowered it.

'Krindle and Dandelion say I must compel one of you to devour the other unless you obey,' said Rumo.

'That's just not true!' cried Dandelion.

'I didn't actually say that,' said Krindle, **'but it sounds like me.'**

Rumo shrugged his shoulders. 'I'm sorry, but you must accompany me to Hel. The curse, you understand . . .'

Yukobak and Ribble nodded again.

'Very well,' said Yukobak, 'we'll take you to Hel, but it's pointless. There are sentries guarding every route into the city, and they'd arrest a Wolperting like you on sight. We had to forge some official documents just to get out of the place. You'll be going to your own execution. And ours.'

'I'll worry about those problems when we get there,' Rumo decreed.

'Hey!' Ribble said suddenly. 'There is *one* way into Hel that isn't guarded.'

'Really?' said Rumo.

'Yes. I know a way through the sewers that leads straight to the heart of Hel. Straight to the Theatre of Death.'

'Good,' said Rumo. 'Then you'll remain my prisoners until you've guided me through the sewers to the theatre.'

Yukobak glared at Ribble.

'Don't look at me like that,' Ribble told him. 'He was such a skilful interrogator, how could I help it?'

Ribble's story

There had been a time in Ribble's life when Yukobak played no part in it. Quite a long time, in fact, because between his birth and the beginning of his domestic service lay a period which the average Homunculus would have found quite eventful enough.

Like any newborn Homunculus, Ribble had felt extremely confused on emerging from the alchemical Mothersoup. His was a bewilderment no one could have felt unless he'd been pitched out into the world as an adult. Homunculi had a harder time of it than anyone else.

The soup boiled, a few extremities and organs from the most diverse life forms became fused together, and another Homunculus emerged from the cauldron. No crawling, no breastfeeding, no teething:

Homunculi came into the world full-grown and had to manage as best they could. Their first experience tended to be a kick up the backside from one of the unsympathetic soldiers whose job it was to speed these new, underprivileged citizens down the ramp from the cauldron and into everyday life. It was like that with Ribble. Someone shoved him so hard that he tumbled down the ramp and found himself amid the urban bustle of Hel, where new citizens were promptly inspected and their aptitudes assessed.

Hemmed in on all sides by Hellings, mercenaries and other Homunculi, Ribble was grabbed, turned round and pawed by rough hands. It was there at the foot of the ramp that newborn slaves were appraised and assigned various occupations, and there that their fate was decided.

'Crab's pincers, eyes on stalks, amphibian, likes water. He'll make a tunneller. Off to the sewers with him!' said someone. Ribble didn't understand a word because, although Homunculi came into the world full-grown, they still had to acquire the power of speech. He was led away and consigned to the sewers of Hel.

If someone had compiled a list of all the possible occupations in Hel and arranged them in order of status, the one at the very top would have been 'king' and the one at the very bottom 'tunneller'. Ribble spent the first few years of his life keeping the walls of the underground cave system that had been converted into a sewer free from vermin and carriers of disease. Saponic Leeches, Oilsnakes, Dungworms, Suckerfoot Spiders, Bacteriomorphs, Plague Frogs, Trogloticks, Speleovampires – those were the true masters of this dark, damp domain, and their dissemination had to be kept within bounds if they weren't some day to take over Hel itself. Tunnelling was not only an unhealthy occupation but probably the most dangerous in the whole of Netherworld. Large or small, nearly all the creatures in the sewers were dangerous in one way or another: venomous, infectious, vicious, vampiric, or all four combined. A tunneller's average lifespan was a year, but there were many who, on their very first day, disappeared into the convoluted maze of tunnels for ever.

Ribble had been sent into this underground world armed with a long rope and a rusty trident, and he was probably more surprised than anyone when he made it back to the surface after his first day's work. He had waded knee-deep through stinking brown water and speared all the Dungworms and Suckerfoot Spiders he'd spotted by the ghostly light of the jellyfish torches, and he thanked his lucky stars that none of those vermin had been larger than a dog. It was on that first day of his life that Ribble found the funnel and barrel among some rubbish and chose them as his armour, his protection against the dangers of this most subterranean of all worlds. They saved his life so often that he refused to be parted from them later on, when he could have afforded some decent clothes.

The underground channels, which had come into being naturally in primeval times, formed an extremely intricate tunnel system resembling the interior of a sponge – in fact, many alchemists believed that the whole area beneath Hel was a gigantic fossilised sponge. Only someone with an exceptionally good memory and bump of direction could find his way around, and colleagues of Ribble's disappeared every day – not that anyone mourned them. They may either have been drowned by a flash flood or dispatched by some denizen of the sewers that was bigger than a dog. Opportunities for dying down there were not only many and varied but highly unpleasant.

Ribble's professional aptitudes were much admired. Not only did he have an excellent bump of direction, but his skill in skewering vermin with the trident was also exceptional, so he might well have remained down there until overtaken by a tunneller's death. Instead, he saved the life of an aristocratic young Helling who had accidentally fallen into the sewers down a waste-disposal shaft and nearly been devoured by some Bloodrats. Ribble was rewarded by being returned to civilisation. Thus ended his harsh existence in the sewers of Hel and thus began his new life at Yukobak's side.

'All right,' said Yukobak when they at last moved on, 'so we're doing you one favour after another. We've given away all our nation's secrets and we're trying – at the risk of our own lives – to smuggle you into Hel. Now I think it's *your* turn.'

'To do what?'

'To talk. We've still got a long way to go and I'd be interested to hear what prompted you to go to Hel – in defiance of all common sense. We'd like at least to know what we're risking our lives for. Who is this mysterious Rala?'

'But I'm not good with words,' said Rumo.

'Just leave out the boring parts,' Ribble advised. 'Stick to the exciting bits.'

The Bear God

Rala was ready to die. The pain, the chills, the fever, the nausea – all those she could have borne, but not this hideous, demented face. Whoever it was out there, he had won. No one could defeat an opponent who had forged an alliance with insanity. Rala simply wanted to fall into a dreamless sleep free from pain and fear.

'Rala?'

She froze. Who had called her name? Was it that voice from outside again?

'Don't be frightened, Rala, it's only me.'

Rala's inner eye could see nothing but utter darkness.

'I've come a long way.'

Something was emerging from the darkness.

'Yes, I've come a very long way, little daughter.' A massive black form emerged from the gloom and Rala could now see that it was Tallon. Tallon the Claw, formerly the Wild Bear God, her foster-father and fellow hunter.

'Hello, Rala,' said Tallon.

'Hello, Tallon. I thought you were dead,' said Rala. After all that had happened lately, nothing that went on in her head surprised her.

'I hardly dare to say this,' said Tallon, 'but I can't afford to beat about the bush under present circumstances, so tell me, my girl: Is what I see here really the way it looks?'

'What *does* it look like?'

'It looks as if you're trying to die.'

'That's right.'

'You can't be serious!'

'I certainly am.'

'Look, far be it from me to meddle in your affairs, but, well . . . being dead myself, I can tell you it's nothing to write home about.'

'I can't stand it any more,' Rala whispered.

'I see. Hm. The pain, you mean?'

'The pain I can take.'

'Something worse than pain?'

'Horror, Tallon. Fear.'

'I know, it's hard to endure.'

'Did you come back from the dead to tell me that?'

'What? Yes. No! Er . . . Now you've made me lose my thread.'

'Get to the point, Tallon! Then I can die and we can be together.'

'That's not a good idea. I died too soon – a stupid mistake. You should learn from my mistakes.'

'It wasn't a mistake. You couldn't help it.'

'I could have run away when that stick flew towards me,' said the bear.

'Listen, Tallon. I can't take it any more. I'm tired and frightened. I want to sleep.'

'So you already said. Do you remember what we used to do in the woods?'

'Hunt, you mean?'

'Precisely. We used to hunt rabbits. It was fun.'

'Not for the rabbits.'

'True, but do you remember what the rabbits did?'

'They ran.'

'Correct. And how did they run?'

'They zigzagged from one hiding place to another.'

'That's exactly what they did, the little devils! Remember how often they got away?'

'Often.'

'Yes, my girl, very often.' Tallon grinned. 'See what I'm getting at?'

'You mean I should run away?'

'That's my Rala! You're a clever girl. Let's run the way we used to in the old days – in the woods.' Tallon gave Rala a look that almost made her laugh.

'How can I? I can't move, I'm trapped inside a machine.'

'Know the best part of being dead?' Tallon asked in a whisper.

'No. The fact that everything's over, I suppose.'

'I said you don't have the first idea about dying. No, just the opposite: that everything *isn't* over. That it's just beginning, my girl! That your spirit is free – free from your brain, because the brain is really just a prison full of cares and fears. When you die your spirit slips through the bars of that prison and out into the open, and you realise what freedom really is.'

'Get to the point, Tallon.'

'I can teach you to release your spirit.'

'You can?'

'Well, not in such a way that it roams the universe like mine and can see the rings of Saturn and so on. No, not that, because for that you'd have to be really dead, and that we don't want. Listen! I can show you how your spirit can release itself from your brain and roam around freely *inside your body*. Yes, that I *can* do.'

Rala laughed. 'I know you aren't really here. I know this is just a wonderful dream designed to make me forget my torments, but go on!'

'We've no time to argue or I'd talk you out of that idea, so all I'll say on the subject is this: What the living call dreams aren't dreams at all. But come now!' Tallon extended one of his huge paws.

Rala hesitated.

'Come on!' Tallon growled. 'Let's get out of here.'

Ticktock's question

As so often of late, General Ticktock was in the best of spirits. Today he would embark on the really interesting part of his work: the interrogation. He had broken Rala's spirit. What a scream she'd uttered! No, not just a scream, a fanfare that signalled the commencement of a new chapter in their relationship. Today he would start to converse with her and, in her company, take up the trail of death. Today she would begin to die in earnest.

This was a great moment. He must not profane its uniqueness by talking any old drivel. His opening question would be exceptionally important, and he had pondered it for a long time. It had to be tender and sympathetic, and expressive of his passion for her. A task for a poet, really, so General Ticktock was extremely proud that he himself had thought of the appropriate words.

Going up to the Metal Maiden with slow, reverent steps, he bent down and whispered, 'Are you enjoying this [tick] as much as I am?'

Rala didn't answer. Of course, she was shy, surprised by his romantic enquiry and probably searching for a reply in kind. He would have to give her a little time.

He waited.

Perhaps she hadn't fully understood. Had he spoken too softly? After a few minutes he repeated the question, a trifle more distinctly this time.

'Are you [tick] enjoying this as much as I am?'

If she didn't want to profane this sacred moment, she really should have answered by now. Even an oath or an impudent response would have been better than this silence. Ticktock repeated the question in a stentorian voice:

'Are you enjoying this [tick] as much as I am?

No answer.

He couldn't understand it. Other victims of such torture would have seized the opportunity to speak, if only to forget their torments for a moment. Didn't she want to know who was torturing her?

A terrible thought occurred to him: Surely she wasn't dead? He hurriedly checked his instruments, but they were all in order. She was still breathing and her heart was beating steadily. The thanatometer was registering sixty-eight.

'I'll ask you [tock] for the last time, and I expect an answer,' General Ticktock said menacingly.

'Are you [tick] enjoying this as much as I am?'

Still no answer. Ticktock was becoming genuinely anxious now. She was alive, his instruments told him so, and her resistance was broken, as witness that scream of hers.

He caught on at last. Of course! Rala wasn't being refractory, nor had she gone mad or lost the power of speech. No, she had managed to do something he'd believed to be impossible.

She had escaped!

Rala had left the prison of her brain and was hiding elsewhere in her body, that was the only explanation. This time it was General Ticktock's cry that shook the walls of his torture chamber.

A short cut

Yukobak sobbed and wiped away a tear.

They were still making their way across the bleak expanse of Deadwood. Rumo had just ended his story. Yukobak and Ribble now knew all about his feelings for Rala, his friendship with Urs, the casket, and his plan to go to Hel by himself and rescue the Wolpertings.

'That's the most romantic story I've ever heard!' Yukobak exclaimed. 'Are things really like that up there? Unconditional love? Friendship unto death? Eternal loyalty?'

From the mist overhead came a discordant screech like that of some wild beast. Rumo looked up.

'Deadwood Apes, probably,' said Ribble. 'They're said to be dangerous.'

Rumo gripped the hilt of his sword.

'How long has she – this Rala, I mean – been your sweetheart?' Yukobak asked, snuffling.

'Actually,' said Rumo, bowing his head, 'she isn't my sweetheart yet. I still have to, er . . . win her.'

'Just a minute,' Ribble broke in. 'You mean you're on your way to Hel to rescue a girl and *you don't even know if she loves you?*'

'Well, there's this Silver Thread . . .'

'What Silver Thread?' asked Yukobak.

'Oh, you don't understand.'

'No, I certainly don't!' said Ribble. 'We Homunculi know little about love for biological reasons – well, next to nothing – but why someone should risk his life for a love that may not even exist at all, *that* I really don't understand.'

Yukobak had recovered his composure somewhat. 'What will you do if you present her with the casket and she turns you down?' he asked.

'I haven't thought of that yet,' Rumo said defiantly.

'Seems you don't like thinking on principle,' said Ribble. 'You prefer to settle your affairs the hard way. With your Demonic sword.'

For a prisoner, thought Rumo, Ribble was being pretty bumptious. He'd poured out his heart to these two, but he'd clearly lost their respect. He tried to change the subject.

'Tell me a bit about Vrahoks.'

'Ooh, Vrahoks!' said Yukobak, flapping his hands in mock terror. 'Vrahoks aren't so easy to explain. They're . . . well, monsters. Creatures like them are too big for this world – they ought by rights to be extinct. They're very dangerous. And very hard to describe.'

'The alchemists succeeded in domesticating them many years ago,' said Ribble. 'They developed fluids and gases that would soothe, stimulate or hypnotise them – whatever they chose. We can actually ride Vrahoks. Not us two, I mean, but some of our soldiers can.'

'They're dangerous beasts,' said Yukobak. 'That's why we're making such a big detour: to avoid their caves.'

'What?!' exclaimed Rumo.

'We're avoiding the Vrahoks. By the widest possible margin.'

'How long will that take?'

'Well, it'll certainly take us an extra two or three days, but there's no alternative. We can't march straight through the middle of them.'

Ribble laughed uneasily.

'One moment,' said Rumo. 'Does that mean we could save two or three days if we go via the Vrahok Caves?'

'That's right.'

'Then we'll change direction right away.'

'What!' Ribble exclaimed. 'Are you mad?'

'I've no time to lose,' Rumo replied. 'A lot can happen in two or three days.'

'But we'd never get past them alive,' said Yukobak.

'You originally said it was impossible to get into Hel,' Rumo retorted, 'and now we've actually got a guide.'

Yukobak gave Ribble a venomous look. 'This is all your fault!' he hissed. 'The Vrahoks! That's all we needed!'

Deadwood Apes continued to screech in the mist above them. Ribble's head sank deep into his little barrel.

The corpuscles

Rala and Tallon had undergone a transformation. They now resembled two red lenses slightly concave on both sides.

'What's happened to us?' Rala asked Tallon, who was floating beside her in a vast chamber. 'Why do we look so odd? Where are we, underwater?'

'We're red corpuscles, my dear,' Tallon replied, 'and we're in your bloodstream. I thought it was the best way of remaining anonymous. We can change into white corpuscles if you don't like the colour. Disembodied spirits have that freedom.'

'No, no,' said Rala, 'I like the colour. What an amusing dream this is!'

Numerous other shapes resembling Rala were floating around below, above and beside them.

'You still think this is a dream? I'm starting to feel rather hurt. I go to all this trouble, come back from the dead, prevent you from dying, free your spirit, transform us into corpuscles – and you repay me by thinking it's all in your imagination.'

'I apologise. It's so . . . so unreal.'

'We've secreted ourselves in red corpuscles because you can go anywhere in them. We can change shape later on, if you want. Perhaps you'd prefer to be an electrical impulse, then we could race through your nervous system.'

'How do you know all this? I mean, you're a bear.'

'I'm a *dead* bear, sweetheart! I know *everything*.'

'Really?'

'Ask me something.'

'What do we do next?'

'That's easy: we take off! We must leave this area, we're still too near the brain. I suggest we make our way down the jugular to the heart. You should have asked me the secret of the universe – something of that kind.'

'That wouldn't be much help to us at present.'

'Next question?'

'If it's blood we're floating in, why isn't it red?'

'Because it's really water. Blood consists almost entirely of water. You can swim, can't you?'

'Yes,' said Rala, 'I can.'

'All right, follow me!'

Tallon joined the corpuscles that were gliding past and Rala followed him, allowing herself to be borne away by the pulsating stream of blood. More and more red corpuscles joined them as they floated down a vein together with some whitish-yellow corpuscles resembling balls of wool.

'Those are white corpuscles,' Tallon explained, 'our principal allies. They're your soldiers, Rala. They resist anything that tries to make your body sick.'

The white corpuscles formed up like soldiers and charged round the next bend ahead of the red ones. They zigzagged from one tunnel to the next.

'How many different routes there are here!' thought Rala. 'And how much room!'

'Yes,' said Tallon. 'There isn't a better place to hide.'

Below them yawned a deep, dark abyss. Some of the red corpuscles threw themselves into it.

'That's the way to the jugular,' said Tallon. 'Can you feel the pull of the current?'

'Yes,' cried Rala. She was trembling in time to her own heartbeat.

'Into it, then,' said Tallon. 'It's a short cut to the aorta. Down we go!'

And Tallon and Rala plunged into the dark abyss followed by a mass of other corpuscles.

The poison cupboard

General Ticktock was beside himself with rage, but there was no doubt about it: Rala had escaped.

She was still there physically, of course, imprisoned inside the Metal Maiden with a hundred needles pinning her there like a butterfly. She was alive, too, as the thanatometer's rising needle showed, but her spirit had fled. Her brain was deserted. Ticktock could now have flooded it with as many poisons as he chose, it would have been no use. He picked up the flask containing the dementia drug and hurled it at the wall, shattering it into a thousand pieces.

For the first time in his life as a Copper Killer, the general couldn't help laughing. This surprised him because he hadn't known he was capable of it. His metallic peals of laughter sounded so awful that he gave a start and promptly suppressed them. What, he wondered, was so funny?

A girl had tricked him – that was funny. She'd simply escaped from the most secure prison imaginable. Just when he'd shown her her limits, she'd done the same to him.

Ticktock strode up and down, no longer furious but filled with joyous excitement. The girl was a genius and the battle for her body had only just begun. She wanted him to hunt her? Very well, he would hunt her. She was imposing her will on him and he was obeying. Electric thrills ran through him at the thought. He would hunt her and track her down. Yes, but what then? Kill her? General Ticktock wasn't sure. This girl was really confusing him. What an exciting game!

He went to his poison cupboard and inspected his stores. What to do next? She was past being impressed with ordinary drugs. What else was there?

At the back of the cupboard was a dark-green bottle with a handwritten label. He took it out and read the inscription. It ran:

Subcutaneous Suicide Squad

He weighed the bottle in his hand. No, it was still too soon for that. Far too strong a drug for his present purposes. He put the bottle back and surveyed the rest of his pharmacopoeia. So many possibilities! Where to start?

Friftar's inspection

Rolv sat in his gloomy cell, gnawing at the steel bands that enclosed his wrists – a habit, a reflex action dating from the time he'd been compelled to spend with Niddugg the Bluddum. He shut his eyes and concentrated on Rala's vibrations. She was somewhere nearby, he knew.

Two things had lately preoccupied Rolv more than the fact of his imprisonment. The first was that sound he'd heard in the arena. For days he had been unable to think of anything else. It echoed and re-echoed in his ears and Rala's fear-contorted face had appeared to his mind's eye again and again. This recollection had suddenly been followed, when he tried once more to scent her, by an indefinable sensation of relief. Since then his sister's face had seemed tormented no longer, but cheerful and relaxed – sometimes even amused. Rala was alive and still in the greatest danger, of that he was convinced, but her situation had recently changed for the better. She seemed to be relishing the danger she was in.

Rolv stopped gnawing his handcuffs and grinned. He was no stranger to this aspect of his sister's character. Back in the forest her audacity had sometimes scared him to death. On a few occasions she had simply disappeared for indefinite periods. Left alone, Rolv had picked up the same sort of vibrations he was receiving here in his cell. Unrelated to his sense of smell, they stemmed from the brother-and-sister bond that united them.

She had always come back in those days, often dishevelled and covered in scratches, sometimes bloodstained, but never without some trophy for her brother: a horn, a claw, or a bitten-off tentacle. Although anything but a coward, Rolv was always relieved when tricky situations resolved themselves, whereas Rala could never have enough of them.

He stretched out on the hard stone floor and tried to sleep. If he wanted his plan to succeed he would need to be well rested. He had decided on a change of strategy. There was no point in bowing to the theatre's ritual demands and hoping for a chance to escape, the guards were too efficient for that.

Rolv's plan was to take Gornab prisoner. This would not be easy, but it wasn't completely out of the question. Although the arena walls were high, they had definitely not been designed with an eye to repelling Wolpertings. If anyone could scale them it was Rolv. He planned to leap straight into the royal box, neutralise the tall, thin fellow and capture the little monkey who seemed to be the king. He intended to take him hostage. It would be the dwarf in exchange for Rala.

There was a clatter as some bolts were drawn back and the door of his cell swung open. Standing in the doorway was the king's chief adviser escorted by a Bluddum of more than usually doltish appearance. Friftar stared at Rolv appraisingly.

'He's in good shape,' he said. 'He won't be fighting again for the time being. You can shut the door again. I shall hold you personally responsible for seeing that the selected Wolpertings remain in their cells until further orders. What's your name?'

'Kromek Toomah, sir!' barked the Bluddum. 'Sergeant of artillery, weight four hundred pounds, height nine feet seven inches, forty-seven decorations for gallantry in combat.'

'Yes, yes,' Friftar said dismissively. 'Now take me to the prisoners who call themselves Ushan DeLucca and Urs of the Snows. I want to give them another once-over.'

Rolv growled softly as the door closed again.

Flying water

'What about the sun?' Yukobak asked. 'Can its rays really reduce you to ashes?'

'Of course,' lied Rumo.

'And the air – is it poisonous?'

'Certainly,' said Rumo. 'You can't survive in it unless you've got three lungs like us Wolpertings.'

'So it's true!' gasped Yukobak.

'Nonsense,' said Ribble. 'He's only having you on.'

Rumo grinned. Yukobak and Ribble were like a couple of children.

'And are there really trees with food growing on them?' Yukobak pursued.

'Masses of them,' said Rumo. 'There are cool breezes and clear water. There are clouds, too.'

'What are clouds?' Ribble asked.

'Clouds? Clouds are . . . well, they're . . .' Rumo hesitated. What *were* clouds actually? 'They're water that can fly,' he said.

The smell that had been making Rumo's nose smart for hours was becoming stronger and more unbearable the deeper they went. It was a smell of the sea and rotting fish and seaweed decaying on damp rocks. It was the evil stench of Roaming Rock intensified a hundred times, but mingled with it was another noisome smell: the acrid miasma that had hung over Wolperting.

'Why can I smell the sea down here?' asked Rumo.

'Why does water fly up there in your world?' Yukobak retorted. 'It's the stench of the Vrahoks.'

They had left Deadwood behind them a long time ago and were now making their way through vast caverns and stalactite caves. The only living creatures that seemed to exist here were low-flying Kackerbats, which had to be fended off with flailing arms.

'You mean the Vrahoks are close by?'

'In the next large cave,' said Ribble. 'On your own head be it. Go and take a look at them and you'll see what we meant. Then we'll take the detour after all. What a waste of time!'

Rumo went on ahead while Yukobak and Ribble plodded after him, cursing and complaining. His urge to turn back, thereby sparing himself the sight of whatever could produce such a stench, became stronger with every downward step he took.

After descending a long black stairway, partly natural and partly hewn out of the rock, they reached a plateau at the end of which was a stone gateway with mysterious symbols carved on it.

'The Vrahok Caves,' said Yukobak.

By the time they got to the stone portal the stench was almost unendurable.

'Are they guarded?' Rumo asked.

'There's no need to guard them,' Yukobak told him. 'The smell is enough to keep everything and everyone away for miles around. The Vrahoks have only to be fed and drugged at regular intervals, roughly twice a month. The rest of the time they're left to their own devices.'

'All right,' said Ribble, 'in you go.'

'Once you've seen them,' said Yukobak, 'you'll have seen everything.'

Rumo went through the gateway. On the other side a vast cavern came into view. It looked as if it had been hollowed out by water over a very long period, because every surface was smooth and rounded, and gleamed like polished amber. Rumo's rocky vantage point was halfway up the side of the cavern, which was about seven hundred feet high and some two miles long. The most remarkable feature of the scene, however, was not the cavern itself but the creatures it housed.

The Vrahoks

Although Rumo's recent adventures had made him rather hard to impress, his sense of wonder returned with a vengeance. They were the biggest and most extraordinary creatures he had ever seen. Some of them were half as tall as the cavern was high, but most were smaller. Many were two hundred, many a hundred and some only thirty feet in height, but they all seemed huge to Rumo, even though he was looking down on them from above. The sight of them put him in mind of many creatures at once: of the big, armour-plated Seaspiders and phosphorescent jellyfish that dwelt in the pools on Roaming Rock, but also of the sightless insects that scuttled over the walls of Netherworld. They were vaguely reminiscent, too, of Nurns, although Vrahoks had more legs – a dozen in all. If Rumo had been asked to describe them in detail, he would soon have run out of words.

'Twelve Seaspiders' legs encased in yellow horn and growing out of a pale-blue, crablike body,' Yukobak recited. 'No eyes, no ears and no wings, but approximately four hundred long, dangling white antennae. The upper surface of the body consists of extremely hard armour-plate, whereas the bloated underbelly is enclosed in a transparent membrane through which can be seen the bluish, pulsating internal organs, among them a total of twelve hearts. Located in the centre of the stomach is a long transparent trunk that can reach the ground when fully extended. The Vrahoks use this trunk in order to smell, breathe and feed. I earned a commendation for that description in biology class.'

Yukobak gave a little bow.

'They can sleep and walk at the same time,' Ribble amplified. 'Vrahoks are *sleepwalkers.* This wholly unnatural behaviour is caused by the hypnotic substances the alchemists inject them with. They stagger around in their sleep and wake up whenever they come into contact with something that doesn't belong in their hideous world, then use their trunks to suck it into their transparent innards. Anything that moves and isn't a Vrahok or one of the parasites that graze on them gets sucked up that way. When they've eaten something you can see their blue intestines digesting it for hours.'

'That's true,' said Yukobak. 'We once went on a school outing to the Vrahoks and saw them being fed with live cave bears. Did you know that Vrahoks are the heraldic beasts on Hel's coat of arms?'

Rumo held up his sword to let Krindle and Dandelion share the spectacle.

'Good heavens,' said Dandelion, *'what a size!'*

'I said we shouldn't have come this way,' Yukobak grumbled. 'Now can we turn round and take the other route to Hel?'

Rumo looked down at the lumbering giants.

'They're very slow,' he said. 'If they were horses you could walk them and shoe them at the same time.'

'It only looks that way from this distance,' said Ribble.

'How can they be dangerous if they're asleep?' Rumo argued. 'We'll walk underneath them. We'll have to be careful, that's all.'

'Kill me!' cried Yukobak, going down on his knees. 'Kill me right away and get it over with!'

'He's right,' said Ribble. 'What you're proposing is suicide.'

'I'm not turning back,' Rumo said firmly.

A forest of legs

Immediately beneath the Vrahoks the stench was even more infernal.

Climbing down into the cavern had been easy, but once there Rumo recognised the full extent of the danger. Running down the giant creatures' legs were glutinous secretions, big drops of which sometimes fell off and landed on the floor with a splash. The amber-coloured rock was slippery, being almost covered with the stuff. Yukobak, who was bringing up the rear, vomited noisily into the layer of evil-smelling mist that hovered above the ground in places.

'Ssh!' said Rumo.

'It doesn't matter how much noise we make,' Ribble told him. 'Vrahoks are deaf as well as blind, but watch out for their antennae.'

The Vrahoks' antennae were lashing the air on all sides, many of them so thick and strong that they could have beheaded someone at a single stroke.

The monsters were forever on the move, forever reeling around blindly, tripping over their enormous legs and bumping into one another, but they never once woke up or fell over. They had a sleepwalker's unaccountable self-assurance. When their armour-plated bodies collided, they filled the cavern with a sound like thunder and cascades of slime came showering down. The bigger they were, the louder the creaking of their joints. As for their footsteps, they sounded like tree trunks crashing on to rocks from a great height. They emitted a series of pneumatic whistles and their antennae lashed the air in time to them. Black, batlike creatures fluttered around between their legs or hung from their bodies in clusters, yard-long snails crawled up and down their limbs.

Rumo could only hazard a guess at how many Vrahoks there were, but they must have numbered roughly a hundred: ten genuine giants half as tall as the cavern itself, their extremities lost in the mist overhead; perhaps twenty-five half their size and somewhat paler in colour; and sixty or seventy smaller specimens between thirty and fifty feet tall. This meant that well over a thousand legs were performing a ceaseless somnambulistic dance that made the ground vibrate like an earthquake.

Rumo gave the signal to advance, urging Yukobak and Ribble ahead of him with his sword. The smallest Vrahoks worried him most. Their movements were quicker and more unpredictable, their antennae lashed out more viciously and their legs kept coming dangerously close. Huge blobs of slime landed just beside the trio, adding to the layer already on the ground. Yukobak tripped and slid into the viscous mass on his back, whereas Ribble glided over it like an ice skater.

'We'll never make it,' cried Yukobak, close to tears. Rumo reproached himself for having put the childish creature in such a dangerous situation and resolved to take more care of him.

Two of the biggest monsters bumped into each other in their sleep. There was a crash like the sound of two huge wooden ships colliding. A curtain of slime descended, enveloping Yukobak from head to foot and knocking him to the ground. Rumo and Ribble, who had leapt aside just in time, hauled their spluttering companion to his feet and hurried on. Yukobak was in shock, but the incident seemed to have had a beneficial effect on him, because he now strode on quite mechanically, without the exaggerated caution that had so often made him stumble.

Rumo's path was barred by two of the smaller Vrahoks, which were still some ten times his height. They were circling each other with slow, graceful steps, almost like a pair of dancers. Meanwhile, the giants that had collided were reeling around to left and right of them on legs ten times as long. There was no hope of getting past *them*.

Before Rumo or Ribble could stop him, Yukobak simply marched on, right into the midst of the smaller Vrahoks' dancing legs. They had no choice but to follow him, either to protect him from the worst or to be trampled underfoot. They proceeded as carefully as possible, crouching low and tucking their heads in, whereas Yukobak, quite heedless of the creatures' lashing antennae, strode on straight as a ramrod. The Vrahoks' legs came down almost once a second, one of them so close to Rumo that it nearly grazed him. In a flash it was raised again, the knee joint creaked like a tree about to fall and he hurried on.

Yukobak, it seemed, was already outside the danger zone. He had simply walked on and halted when he saw that he was past the cavorting Vrahoks. He beckoned to Rumo and Ribble, smiling as though they were out on a picnic. Now it was Ribble's turn to slip on the slime and fall headlong. Rumo was about to help him up when a whole bunch of antennae descended on them, so he threw himself face down in the slime. The antennae passed close overhead and were then retracted. Rumo and Ribble scrambled to their feet and hurried on. Panting hard, they reached Yukobak's side.

'What kept you so long?' he asked with a foolish grin.

Rumo turned. The Vrahoks were still dancing round each other, but at a safe distance. Rumo, Yukobak and Ribble were enveloped in a malodorous pall of mist, but they scarcely noticed it, they had already endured such evil smells.

Ribble pointed into the mist. 'The exit to Hel must be over there,' he panted. As if in response to an order, Yukobak turned, marched off in the direction indicated, and disappeared into the vaporous gloom.

Rumo and Ribble hastily followed him. They heard a dull thud, then Yukobak's startled voice: 'Ouch!' he exclaimed.

'What's the matter?' Ribble asked when they reached him. Yukobak was rubbing his head. 'I bumped into something,' he said.

Like a curtain, the mist drew aside to reveal a Vrahok's leg. It belonged to one of the gigantic monsters whose bodies were invisible in the mist overhead. Rumo noticed that the hairs on the leg were beginning to stand on end.

'It's waking up!' Ribble whispered.

The Vrahok awakes

He was right. The Vrahok awoke with a sound such as only a deaf creature of its vast dimensions could have made. Its roar rent the air and made the antennae of the other Vrahoks vibrate. Hundreds of Kackerbats detached themselves from the monsters' bodies and took wing.

This wake-up call caused absolute pandemonium in the cavern. The stamping and whistling and creaking of joints combined to create an ear-splitting din and the agitated Vrahoks lurched round in confusion. The hairs on the huge leg trembled, but the leg itself remained rooted to the spot. All at once an immense trunk emerged from the mist and descended on Yukobak. Rumo was at his side in a flash, but the trunk enveloped them both, sealed them in with a squelching sound and started to hoist them into the air.

'Yukobak!' Ribble shouted, horrified but helpless, as the trunk disappeared into the mist with its prey.

Rumo and Yukobak were deluged with a warm secretion of some kind. Then they felt the suction increase as the Vrahok greedily drew them in.

Yukobak didn't utter a sound – he seemed completely paralysed with fear. Rumo pushed the Helling's head down and ordered, 'Duck!'

Drawing his sword, he gripped it with both hands, thrust it through the inner wall of the trunk and performed a *Carousel* – a circular, sweeping blow that sliced through the soft membrane like wet paper. In company with the severed portion of the trunk, Rumo and Yukobak fell to the ground. The impact was cushioned by the omnipresent slime and Ribble quickly helped them to divest themselves of their slippery sheath.

The mutilated Vrahok's roars of pain could have triggered a thousand avalanches. Rumo scrambled to his feet, seized Yukobak's hand and ran off with him as fast as he could. Ribble ran after them, as far as possible from the Vrahoks' multitudinous whistles and the pounding of their innumerable feet.

Bacteriological warfare

Rala's body had become a battlefield. She and Tallon were members of a defending army hurrying from hideout to hideout in their beleaguered city while the enemy forces unleashed one attack after another.

Prickly bacteria roamed the plasma, loosing off their arrows at anything that moved. Toxins were sluiced through Rala's bloodstream, killing every living thing that failed to escape in time. Her nervous system trembled, shaken by a thunderstorm of electrical impulses, and her lungs were pumped full of alchemical gases.

Only one part of her anatomy was spared: the brain. That was the enemy's strategy, to drive her back there and enhance its appeal as a refuge of last resort, so that her spirit could be recaptured and her resistance broken for good.

But Rala and Tallon did not fall into this trap. They preferred to remain on the run and allow themselves to be borne along by the mass of red corpuscles.

Rala had learnt that the only sensible method of locomotion was to go with the everlasting flow. Trying to swim against the powerful current would have been futile; in any case, being a corpuscle, she lacked any means of doing so. Once she grasped this it was quite simple.

Although many veins were now impassable, choked by clots, guarded by bacteria or flooded with poisons, Rala and Tallon kept on finding bolt-holes, detours and short cuts the enemy didn't know about. Thus, Rala learnt much about her organism's brilliant structure and how it could be used in escaping from her powerful foe. She could see her own defence forces mustering and hurling themselves at the invaders from all directions. Everything was in constant motion, swirling and seething, pumping and effervescing. Rala could see life itself at work, and the sight of all this activity, which was simply and solely devoted to preserving her existence, made her feel ashamed of having briefly lost heart.

It was a war between Rala's natural bloodstream and General Ticktock's artificial death machine, between two extremely intricate circulatory systems, one of flesh and blood, the other of metal. Ticktock's soldiers were microbes and bacteria, viruses and toxins, Rala's were red and white corpuscles. It was a battle between disease and health such as often rages in many organisms, but never as relentlessly, dramatically and ingeniously as in Rala's body.

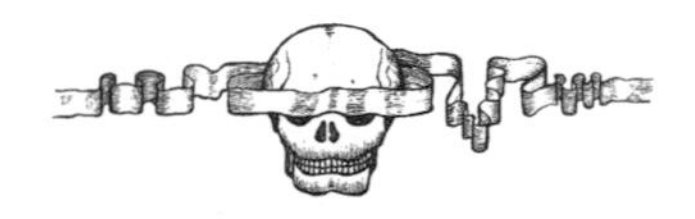

Stonewater Grotto

On leaving the Vrahok Caves, Rumo, Yukobak and Ribble made their way gently downhill along a tunnel so immense that even the largest of the twelve-legged creatures could have negotiated it. Rumo kept looking round to see if they were following. After a while they came to a blue grotto from whose roof water was dripping into a crystal-clear pool in the centre.

'Stonewater Grotto,' said Yukobak. 'The water comes from the springs overhead and it's drinkable. We can rest here, but not for long. It's a favourite stopping place for travellers between Hel and Murkholm.'

Rumo pricked up his ears at the mention of Murkholm, but he asked no questions. He was thirsty and in need of a wash; for the moment, anything else was of little interest. They went over to the pool and rinsed off the Vrahok slime. Ribble removed his funnel and barrel and took a proper bath.

'I still can't take it in,' he called as he paddled around in the cool water. 'We've survived the Vrahoks.'

'One of them nearly ate me,' Yukobak said resentfully.

'But Rumo saved you!' Ribble retorted, turning over and floating on his back.

Yukobak brushed this aside. 'I'd never have been *in* the creature's trunk, but for him! And now they're bound to be after us. When the alchemists check on the cave and see what we've done, they'll set the creatures on us. We've not only committed high treason, we've mutilated a Vrahok. We're as good as dead and buried, thanks to our new friend here.' He glared at Rumo.

Rumo hung his head in embarrassment. 'We mustn't stay here too long,' he said. 'We must move on.'

'Yes, but which way do we go?' Yukobak demanded. 'Where's this wonderful secret route of yours, Ribble?'

Ribble clambered ashore and got into his barrel.

'We can't make straight for Hel,' he said, 'or we're liable to be captured. The area round the city is patrolled by Vrahoks and Bluddums and other riff-raff. We'll have to climb down to the Coalwater Cascades.'

'Down to the Coalwater Cascades?' gasped Yukobak. 'Are you insane?'

'The Coalwater Cascades?' Rumo repeated enquiringly.

'Yes, they're a black waterfall to the south-west of the city. There's a tunnel leading off it into the sewers. We'll be entering Hel via the cellar, so to speak. A rather laborious route, but it's the only way of getting into the city unobserved.'

'It's utter madness,' said Yukobak. 'Only suicides go anywhere near the Coalwater Cascades.'

'Good,' said Rumo. 'Let's go.'

The lethal flask

General Ticktock was flummoxed. This bore no relation to what he had envisioned in his ambitious daydreams. It wasn't a concert given by a virtuoso – or, if it was, only a concert marred by blunders and interruptions.

He had been manipulating his Metal Maiden for days now, opening and closing valves and stopcocks, injecting extracts, toxins and pathogens designed to corner Rala's spirit and drive it back into her brain. He itched to start questioning her about the dying process, but she was stubbornly evading interrogation. He had clogged her veins or rendered them impassable with poisons, he had hunted his quarry with novel bacteria, he had worked with highly concentrated gases and even with electric shocks, but all to no avail.

Ticktock let go of the controls and threw up his hands in despair. Once more his cry of fury rang out from the windows of his tower and made the neighbours quake with terror. They had often heard such cries in recent days.

The general stomped over to his poison cupboard and wrenched the door open. He hesitated for a moment, trembling with excitement, then reached deep inside. Removing the flask he'd weighed in his hand some days before, he read the inscription once more:

Subcutaneous Suicide Squad

The time had come. Exceptional situations called for exceptional measures. Rala had brought it on herself.

He turned the bottle round. Another label was stuck to the back and on it, in tiny letters, were the handwritten words: *Developed by Tykhon Zyphos, Court Alchemist.*

General Ticktock sighed. Tykhon Zyphos – what a scientist! The man had been an absolute genius.

Tykhon Zyphos's story

Tykhon Zyphos's first task, which he had performed to General Ticktock's entire satisfaction, had been to develop the insanity drug that had almost robbed Rala of her reason. He could not, however, rest on his laurels because the general's first order had been followed by a second that amounted to a death sentence. As soon as Ticktock had acquainted him with his new request and informed him that, if he failed, he would personally cut off his head, Tykhon Zyphos hurried back to his laboratory.

The alchemist filled a test tube with neat alcohol, diluted it with a little distilled water and gulped it down. He was done for, that much was certain.

General Ticktock's instructions, couched in thoroughly unscientific language and employing vague phraseology, were as follows: Tykhon Zyphos was to produce an injectable fluid containing a microscopic Copper Killer. The general wanted a life form that possessed the same pugnacity, invulnerability and homicidal implacability as his soldiers – the only difference being that it could be sucked into a hypodermic syringe and injected into a bloodstream.

Tykhon had almost fainted on hearing this. General Ticktock might just as well have ordered him to make time stand still or transform water into blood.

The commander of the Copper Killers seemed to share the naive popular belief in the omnipotence of modern alchemy, but even that science had its limits! Tykhon was well aware that the alchemists themselves were to blame if their abilities were grossly overrated by the laity. Their eternal secrecy, their professional hocus-pocus, and unfounded claims made by disreputable members of their profession – all had combined to lend them an aura of infallibility.

The alcohol had a soothing effect. Tykhon marshalled his thoughts. He consigned his fears to the bottom drawer of his mind and fished out the spirit of research. Why should the problem be insoluble? Alchemy tackled the seemingly impossible. He downed another little vial of alcohol. You grew into a job, so it was said. If he succeeded he might become one of the most influential alchemists in Hel, so to work!

Tykhon jotted down countless ideas in his notebooks during the days and nights that followed. Viruses, acids, bacilli, bloodworms, cellivores, Red Death bacteria, blackleaf, green scabies, Grailsundian influenza – every disease, deadly poison and dangerous life form went down on the list. Which pathogens had which effects when coupled with which toxins? The permutations were endless, and combinations of an increasingly aggressive and lethal nature came into being. Tykhon Zyphos was drawing up a logarithmic system of death.

After completing his theoretical research he got down to practicalities. In the following days and weeks his laboratory became the centre of a strange phenomenon. All the small animals within a radius of half a mile – cats and dogs, rats and mice – disappeared. At

the same time the district took on a new smell. The air became filled, day and night, with a mysterious, cloying odour that emanated from Tykhon's laboratory, which was piled high with the cadavers of the unfortunate creatures on which the alchemist had carried out his experiments.

Tykhon blended pathogens like an artist mixing paints, and he did so with great ingenuity. No one before him would have thought of attacking an organism with the Black Death and deadly Grailsundian influenza, only to infect it with Grey Cholera as well. No one had ever combined Zebra Leaves with extract of nettle-rash and the spores of Paralytic Leprosy. Having gone to those lengths, thought Tykhon, why not go a stage further and amalgamate the unspeakable results of these experiments? The outcome was so horrific that his white hair turned black within a week and he wasted away to skin and bone. He recoiled in terror whenever he happened to catch sight of himself in a mirror. Day by day, he was becoming more like the thing he'd been instructed to create: a living death.

After a few months the deadline set by General Ticktock drew ominously near. Tykhon Zyphos had succeeded in developing a disease that would, he believed, meet the general's requirements. It was not only deadly; it took over where death left off. After the infected person had expired in frightful agony, the viruses continued their work in a dogged and relentless manner. They destroyed every last cell in the corpse until it was entirely decomposed and ceased to exist. Tykhon had been astonished to observe this process in the case of three cats, which completely disintegrated within twenty-four hours, leaving behind no trace – not so much as a single whisker – of their existence.

'This disease should be just General Ticktock's cup of tea,' thought Tykhon. 'I shall call it the *Subcutaneous Suicide Squad.*'

Only one problem remained: the disease could not be isolated. It was catching, and catching in an uncontrollable way. Physical contact was unnecessary. It left the annihilated cadaver in the form of a vapour and, like an army raiding one town after another, sought new fields of operations for its destructive activities. Moreover, it was as unpredictable as a horde of savage warriors, because it sometimes broke off its work of destruction and arbitrarily attacked another body – as

Tykhon had perforce observed in the case of his laboratory animals. When experimenting with the disease he himself wore airtight protective clothing complete with an artificial oxygen supply, and he felt convinced that he would soon have tamed it to his satisfaction. He had even added something to his monstrous virus: an exceptionally virulent and truly revolutionary element unique in the world of diseases. This additional surprise he intended to present to General Ticktock as a gift, secretly hoping that it would enable him to rise still further in the court alchemists' hierarchy. All that remained was to make the Subcutaneous Suicide Squad die in company with the body it had infected.

Tykhon was just pondering this final problem when there was a knock on his laboratory door. It was two of General Ticktock's soldiers, who instructed him to report immediately.

There was no point in arguing, he knew, so he packed up his papers and a syringe filled with the deadly virus, and went off to see the general.

The demonstration

'How far [tick] have you got with your work [tock]?' General Ticktock demanded when Tykhon Zyphos appeared before him, knees knocking.

'I've developed a deadly disease of unprecedented potency,' said Tykhon, 'but–'

Ticktock raised his hand.

'No "buts" [tick] in my presence! Never say "but" or "no" or "impossible" [tock]. Each of those words carries [tick] a death sentence.'

Tykhon bowed his head.

'Show me this disease! [tock] Do you have it with you?'

The alchemist drew nearer and produced the syringe. 'One drop from this syringe is enough to infect one person. The whole syringe would suffice for a hundred, but . . .'

He bit his lip, but it was too late.

'I warned you [tock],' said General Ticktock, taking the syringe. 'That was [tick] one "but" too many.' He seized Tykhon's arm with his other hand.

'One drop [tick], you said?'

Before Tykhon realised what was happening to him, Ticktock had plunged the needle into his arm. He carefully injected one drop into the alchemist's bloodstream and released him.

'Pardon my [tock] impatience,' said General Ticktock. 'Now show me what your disease [tick] can do.'

Tykhon suddenly grew calm. It rather surprised him how quickly he'd come to terms with his death sentence.

'What do you call [tick] this disease of yours?' asked General Ticktock. 'Or haven't you [tock] given it a name yet?'

'I've christened it the Subcutaneous Suicide Squad,' Tykhon replied.

'An excellent [tick] name. Scientific [tock] and military at the same time.'

'Thank you,' said the alchemist.

'But it's taking [tick] its time,' the general said impatiently.

Tykhon suddenly felt dizzy and his knees buckled – the first sign that the virus was taking effect.

'It's just starting,' he said. 'Some subjects it kills in a day, others take a week to die. In my case it seems to be working exceptionally fast. May I sit down?'

'No,' said General Ticktock. 'Sorry, it's [tick] nothing personal. I simply want to study the symptoms [tock] carefully. So it starts in the legs?'

Tykhon Zyphos was denied even that little favour: permission to die sitting down. This was the moment when he decided not to tell Ticktock that the disease was communicable. He wouldn't tell him about his surprise present either – the insidious little peculiarity with which he had armed the virus. No, Tykhon Zyphos would take his secret to the grave because it was his only hope of revenge. The general himself would be immune to the Subcutaneous Suicide Squad. If Tykhon died now, the virus would probably decay within an hour because Ticktock, being a machine, could not be infected and there were no living organisms in the vicinity to which the disease could transmit itself. It was possible, however, that one out of all the pathogens in the syringe might get a chance to thwart the general's plans. Tykhon had given them the necessary equipment. He was leaving behind an army too small to be seen but powerful enough to defeat the strongest foe.

Smiling for the last time in his life, the alchemist uttered his final words.

'Yes,' he said, 'it starts in the legs.'

General Ticktock spent the rest of the day watching Tykhon Zyphos die. Sure enough, the alchemist had created something that attacked and destroyed every form of life without any perceptible effort, silently and without mercy. Tykhon looked as if he were being devoured from within and simultaneously peeled from the outside. The general watched him writhing on the floor, screaming horribly and racked with convulsions. He saw his face robbed of colour until all that remained was skin grey as stone; saw his skin tear like parchment and disintegrate into ashen flakes; saw his hair drop out, closely followed by his teeth, tongue and eyes; saw his flesh wither away, his cheeks fall in and the bony countenance of death emerge.

'May Hel and all who dwell there be destroyed from within just like me,' was Tykhon Zyphos's last conscious thought.

It was incredible, General Ticktock told himself. What an achievement! He turned away, shaking his head and looked at the syringe containing the Subcutaneous Suicide Squad. What a loss! But what a profit! He had lost a genius but gained a merciless, invisible army.

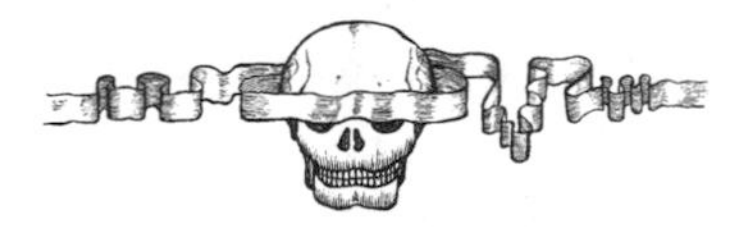

The capital of Netherworld

Every part of Netherworld had a smell of its own, Rumo reflected. The stalactite cave in which he'd encountered Skullop the Scyther reeked of oil, the Fridgicaves of snow and stagnant water, the Nurn Forest Labyrinth of mouldering leaves and blood, and Deadwood of poisonous black toadstools. The Vrahok Caves stank – unsurprisingly – of Vrahoks, whereas Stonewater Grotto was pervaded by the pleasant aroma of limpid spring water trickling through pebbles. But the gigantic cavern he was now entering with Yukobak and Ribble had a smell that defied description. Rumo could detect a multitude of scents – more than he had ever smelt all at once, more than he had on his arrival in Wolperting or at the annual fair. He could smell Hel, the capital of Netherworld.

Discounting the Fridgicaves, the cavern at whose centre Hel was situated was the biggest Rumo had seen in Netherworld. It was several miles high and its roof, which reflected the city's fitful glow, formed a yellowish dome overhead.

The environs of Hel were a jumble of narrow ravines and elongated valleys, volcanic faults and dried-up river beds, and all the rocks were blackened by centuries of urban pollution.

'What's your plan?' asked Ribble.

'Yes, Rumo,' Yukobak chimed in, 'what's your plan?'

'I'd be interested to hear it,' said Dandelion.

'You do have a plan, I suppose?' Krindle insisted.

They were expecting too much of him, thought Rumo. A plan? He would have preferred simply to march into the city through the main gate, torch in hand, rescue his friends, then burn the place to the ground. How much he missed Smyke's presence at this moment! If anyone would have known how to rescue hundreds of prisoners from a well-guarded enemy city, it was Prince Hussein Banana's former minister of war.

'We'll make our way through the sewers to the city centre,' said Rumo. 'Then we'll see.'

'We know all that,' said Yukobak. 'I mean afterwards, when you're inside the city, the only Wolperting at liberty among thousands of enemies. What'll you do then?'

'Yes,' said Ribble, 'what then?'

'I think that's a fair question,' said Dandelion.

'You don't have a plan, do you?' asked Krindle.

Rumo didn't answer.

'I don't think he has a plan at all,' Yukobak whispered to Ribble.

The patrol

Their trek to the Coalwater Cascades proceeded without further incident – until they bumped into a patrol in a dark ravine. It consisted of five soldiers of the Netherworld army mounted on a smallish Vrahok some thirty feet high, which was lumbering along the narrow defile.

Rumo had scented and heard the monster a good while before, so he and his companions managed to escape detection by hiding in a cleft in the rocks. As the Vrahok plodded past, whistling asthmatically, Rumo saw that one of the soldiers was holding a torch and another dangling a bottle in front of it on the end of a pole. The creature's long antennae were lashing the air and exploring everything in its immediate vicinity, its retracted trunk hung just below its weirdly glowing blue stomach, and its joints creaked at every jerky step.

'What are they doing with the pole and the bottle?' Rumo asked when the patrol had gone by. 'Is that how they steer the beasts?'

'Vrahoks are blind and deaf,' said Ribble. 'Nothing exists for them unless they can smell or feel it. The alchemists have succeeded in developing more and more sophisticated perfumes designed to coax them on or send them to sleep, whichever. The contents of that bottle probably smelt like putrid pork and the Vrahok is following it. They're pretty stupid beasts, Vrahoks – like most creatures whose main direction-finding aid is their sense of smell.'

Rumo eyed Ribble sternly. 'On we go!' he commanded.

Above the Coalwater Cascades

It was several hours before they finally reached the rock face that overhung the Coalwater Cascades.

'I can't see a thing!' Yukobak grumbled. 'One false step and we're done for!'

Even Rumo was feeling dizzy. There was no handrail and the steep, narrow flight of stone steps led down into a black void. It was too dark to see the falls themselves, but they could be heard thundering down into the depths. Spray came billowing up from below, covering everything and everyone in a layer of soot.

'Feel your way down the wall,' Ribble called, 'and watch out for missing steps. It's not far to the entrance to the sewers.'

'How far is not far?' asked Yukobak.

'About a mile,' Ribble replied.

Hugging the wall, the trio descended with the utmost care, Ribble in the lead. The steps were not only uneven, narrow and unprotected, but wet and overgrown with slippery moss. The lower they went, the louder the thunder of the falls and the denser the clouds of dark spray.

They couldn't see the Coalwater Cascades until they were only a couple of hundred feet above them: three inky black torrents that spurted from the rock face and plunged into the depths, where the sooty spray engulfed them. Rumo pressed still closer to the wall. 'Where's the entrance?' Yukobak shouted. 'Where are the goddamned sewers?'

'Straight ahead!' Ribble shouted back. 'Only a little further.'

Descending a few more steps, they came to a doorway hewn into the rock.

'The sewers!' Ribble announced like a proud host welcoming them to his private domain. The smell issuing from the doorway could have put a Vrahok to flight.

In the bowels of Hel

Rumo, Yukobak and Ribble were standing in a shallow stream of soot-stained water, dimly illuminated by a light source secured to the wall of the tunnel. It was a glass vessel with a phosphorescent jellyfish imprisoned in it.

'A jellyfish torch,' Ribble explained. 'They're hanging everywhere. Phosphorescent jellyfish are immersed in liquid nutrient and continue to dispense light until they die. That's what I call progress. In my day this place was black as the ace of spades. We had to make do with candles on our helmets. If a drop of water fell on them you'd had it.'

He looked around.

'We must go that way,' he said, pointing to the left. 'That leads to the main sewer.' He waded on ahead with Rumo and Yukobak at his heels.

'What's that nasty smell?' Yukobak asked.

Ribble indicated the dark stream. 'Down here it's the soot that stains the water, but on the upper levels it's, well, you know . . .'

Yukobak instinctively withdrew one foot from the water.

Ribble nodded gravely. 'We must take great care. Most of the creatures down here are as primitive as their surroundings, if you know what I mean.'

'What sort of creatures do you mean?' asked Yukobak.

'Well, Dungivores, for example. Sootsnakes. Octopods. Giant Nippers. Multibrachial—'

'What's a Dungivore?'

'A big, hairy creature with six legs.'

Yukobak shuddered. 'And it eats . . .'

'Yes, and that's not all,' said Ribble. 'As you can imagine, any creature that has to live on dung is far from being a delicacy.'

'What a disgusting place!' Yukobak said angrily.

'It's not so bad,' Ribble told him. 'The water's always nice and warm, and you sometimes make the most amazing finds. It's incredible, the things people throw away.' He pointed down a side tunnel. 'That's the way to the city centre.'

The rearguard

It was the most hideous creature Rala had ever seen. Constantly mutating, it folded parts of its anatomy outwards, sucked other parts in, put out tentacles or spikes, opened snapping mouths, then closed and swallowed them again, contorted its skin into wrinkles and furrows, changed colour incessantly, exuded clouds of dark slime, turned transparent, then black as pitch, and produced a series of monotonous clicks from somewhere inside itself. But the creature's most surprising feature was its ability to swim *against* the current. Rala had seen no other organism in her bloodstream capable of doing that.

'What's that?' she asked Tallon. They were hiding in a capillary in her left lung, and it was from there that she'd seen the weird creature approaching along a side vein. A moment ago it had looked like a lump of raw meat; now it was almost completely transparent.

'I don't know,' Tallon replied, 'but it looks dangerous.'

A detachment of six white corpuscles came drifting along on the stream of plasma and barred the intruder's path. It halted just in front of them, assumed the shape of a spindle and changed colour every time it clicked: green, grey, pink, green, grey, pink.

The creature emitted a gurgle and extended four tentacles tipped with claws. Seizing two of the corpuscles, it tore them to pieces like so much paper and tossed the fragments away. The other four it dissolved into an inky black cloud.

More clicks issued from the creature's interior, this time several of them in quick succession. It mutated into a five-pointed grey star, then split into two identical stars that floated side by side in the plasma, changing colour simultaneously.

'It can reproduce itself,' said Tallon.

Another half-dozen of the clicking creatures swam down the vein, joined forces with the twins, assumed the same stellar shape, divided in half and formed up in two ranks. Then they all swam on together against the current, destroying everything in their path.

'We'd better get out of here,' said Tallon.

The Subcutaneous Suicide Squad had invaded Rala's body and promptly, ruthlessly set to work.

The thanatometer falls

General Ticktock was bewildered. For the first time in his life he had done something dictated by an emotional impulse, not by will-power.

He had dispatched Tykhon Zyphos's Subcutaneous Suicide Squad through the Metal Maiden's circulatory system and into Rala's bloodstream – only a single drop of it, but he knew from personal observation what havoc a single drop could wreak. How could he have lost his self-control in that way? His action was irrevocable. It was a sentence of death against which there could be no appeal.

All his work, his ambitious plans, his grandiose scenario of death, had been wrecked by a lapse of self-discipline. Without Rala the Metal Maiden was just a lifeless heap of scrap! Never again would he furnish her with as noble a partner as the death-defying Wolperting!

Yelling and cursing, he desperately manipulated the controls. More of this, more of that! He flooded Rala's organism with life-preserving extracts, electrified it, heated it, strove to fortify it with all the alchemical substances available to him. Then he glanced at the thanatometer. It had already fallen below sixty.

General Ticktock bellowed nonsensically at the Metal Maiden, commanded the Subcutaneous Suicide Squad to withdraw at once, pounded the machine with his steel fists and left deep dents in its leaden exterior, wrenched valves and tubes out of their seatings. Alchemical extracts and acids, toxins and gases went spurting and hissing across the laboratory, filling it with their acrid stench. Whole bunches of copper tubing were seized and hurled at the wall. General Ticktock was in the process of destroying the Metal Maiden with his own hands.

Suddenly, in mid-frenzy, he stopped short.

He took another look at the thanatometer. The needle had fallen and was still falling: *fifty-one, fifty, forty-nine . . .*

'Who,' General Ticktock demanded, looking around as if in search of a culprit, 'who was [tick] responsible for this?'

He groaned like a wounded beast convulsed with agony. He couldn't possibly watch Rala die. Her pain was transmitting itself to him and becoming his own. What had wrought this change in him - what had rendered him so vulnerable? He ventured a last glance at the thanatometer: *forty-five, forty-four, forty-three . . .*

No, he couldn't bear it! The general tore his eyes away, wrapped himself in his cloak and fled. Dashing out of his tower, he vanished into the gloomy alleyways of Hel.

Sewer hazards

By virtue of their warmth and humidity, the sewers of Hel harboured the most varied flora and fauna, not only in Netherworld but in all Zamonia. No Overworld jungle or artificial habitat could rival their diversity, which extended to the microscopic domain. Fat Suckersnails covered the tunnel walls in their thousands. There were breathing mosses, phosphorescent mushrooms, Witch's Hat Toadstools, Dungflukes that squelched around in brackish water, poison ivy that grew as one watched, ants that shone in the dark and Dripticks that fell from the tunnel roofs like rain. Phosphorescent jellyfish had escaped from their glass vessels and fanned out in all directions, glowing in a wide variety of colours. Rumo was constantly engaged in ridding his fur of creatures that stung or sucked blood.

'Without my helmet I wouldn't have lasted three days down here,' said Ribble, proudly patting the funnel on his head. 'I've seen people dissolve into pus after one bite from a Suckerfoot Spider.'

Yukobak had pulled his cloak over his head. 'You might have mentioned that before you brought us here. Falling down the Coalwater Cascades might almost have been preferable.'

'That's not a very nice way to die,' Ribble told him. 'They fall straight into molten lava and turn to steam. You're steamed first, then roasted and finally asphyxiated by poisonous gases.'

'How much further is it to the theatre?' Rumo asked.

'Not very far. Two or three miles.'

'Where are the prisoners housed?'

'The Death Theatre gladiators are kept in single cells,' Yukobak told him. 'The younger, stronger ones, that is. The prisoners that aren't considered so dangerous – mainly the older ones – are accommodated in a building right beside the theatre. It's a big communal jail. That means there are two prisons you'll have to crack if you want to release all the Wolpertings.'

There was a distant rumble. A swarm of phosphorescent moths flew into the air.

'What was that?' asked Yukobak.

'A pipe burst,' Ribble replied. 'If we're lucky, our tunnel won't be swamped by it.'

'And if we're unlucky?'

Ribble shrugged.

'Who guards the Theatre of Death?' Rumo asked.

'Oh,' said Yukobak, 'only several platoons of Bluddums armed to the teeth, plus the Copper Killers. No one you can't handle.' He laughed hysterically.

'There's another way of looking at it,' said Ribble. 'Although there are plenty of guards, their attention will be focused on guarding the prisoners and protecting the king. They won't be expecting an attack from outside, least of all now that the Copper Killers have assumed overall responsibility for guarding the Theatre of Death.'

'There you go again!' cried Yukobak. 'One Wolperting versus a whole city, and he doesn't even know his way around there? It's utter madness!'

'He's right,' said Ribble, looking at Rumo. 'You don't stand a chance. You can still change your mind.'

'I'm not turning back,' Rumo said quietly. 'I've got a casket to deliver.'

'Yes.' Ribble sighed. 'So you already said.'

The battle for Rala's body wasn't a genuine contest but a war of conquest, which the invaders had won the moment they appeared on the scene. It was a wholesale massacre, the organised mass execution of opponents incapable of self-defence. The Subcutaneous Suicide Squad had come to conquer, not to fight.

Whatever part of Rala's bloodstream she and Tallon fled to, it was piled high with dead or moribund organisms. The clicking of the enemy troops was omnipresent – it even drowned Rala's heartbeat. The monstrous, misshapen viruses were patrolling everywhere. There was scarcely a vein they hadn't penetrated.

Rala and Tallon eventually decided to lie doggo among the mountains of dead and dying corpuscles. From there they watched impotently as the tireless invaders went about their grisly work.

'Where else can we hide?' Rala asked, and her voice had never sounded so faint.

'I don't know,' said Tallon. 'They're everywhere, and there are more and more of them.'

It was long since the all-powerful intruders had encountered any resistance. They continued to reproduce themselves, dividing again and again. One virus split into two, two into four, four into eight and so on, creating an ever-growing, irresistible army of lethal automata.

Whatever organisms the members of the Subcutaneous Suicide Squad didn't directly hunt or kill, they poisoned with clouds of acid or ripped apart with their spines and claws, boring holes in their venous flesh. Corpuscles fell in droves, and Rala felt a little more of her strength and will-power drain away every time one sank lifeless to the ground.

'This is the end,' she said. 'It won't matter how hard I resist or where we hide. The battle is lost. When they've killed the last little bit of me, I shall die too.'

'I tend to be over-optimistic, as you know,' said Tallon, 'but this time I'm afraid I must agree with you. I've never met such destructive power.'

'What happens afterwards?' Rala asked.

'Hey,' Tallon replied, 'that's a surprise. You don't want to spoil it, do you?'

'Will we be together?'

'Yes, we will – but that's one surprise less.'

'I'd have liked to tell Rumo I love him.'

'It's a bit too late for that, my girl.'

'I can't hold out any longer,' Rala whispered.

'Then let go,' Tallon told her. 'Simply let go. The place you're bound for can only be better than this one.'

A shower of dying corpuscles slowly descended on them, fluttering like withered leaves. A last faint tremor ran through Rala's body, a gentle sigh escaped her, then she lay quite still.

'Rala?' said Tallon. No reply. She didn't stir.

It was time for Tallon to go – he had no further business here. Soon, very soon, the world around him would dissolve. The process had already begun. Rala's body would decay, cell by cell, until it was reduced to dust, then her spirit would be free at last.

Tallon had done his utmost to delay this moment, but unfathomable forces were at work here. Rala's was an unprecedented form of death – one that might have been created especially for her. No one had ever been attacked by more ruthless and powerful enemies, Tallon felt sure, and never had anyone defended herself more gallantly than his Rala.

Tallon quit this dying world. He vanished in a way beyond the power of any door or wall or Metal Maiden to prevent. He went as only a disembodied spirit could have gone, already looking forward to the time when Rala would hunt comets at his side.

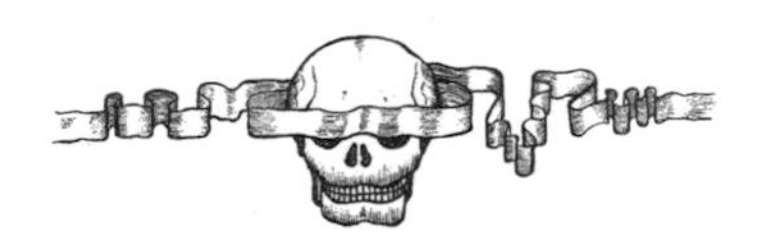

The snooper

There was no sunrise when a new day began in Hel, no paling moon or dawn chorus. The city remained as dark as ever, for day and night were indistinguishable. All that marked the dividing line between them were twelve deep bell notes that rang out across the city and made flocks of bats take wing in alarm. A Hellian day was twice as long as a day in Overworld, and the day that had just been rung in was destined to be a very special one. Friftar knew this because he had planned it down to the smallest detail.

It wasn't mere chance that took the king's chief adviser past General Ticktock's tower on his way to the Theatre of Death. Friftar was worried. One of the inmates of the Vrahok Caves had been attacked and injured – one of the biggest, what was more. Who would be capable of such a feat, he wondered, and who could have cut off part of such a beast's trunk? Friftar had taken certain precautions. The Vrahoks were being guarded round the clock and the sentries on the city gates had been reinforced. At present, however, his greatest source of concern was General Ticktock.

Friftar had now to pluck up enough courage to present the general with the king's demand that he fulfil his responsibilities and resume his regular attendances at the theatre. He would not make it sound like an order or even a request; he would gift-wrap it nicely. He intended to convey the impression that he had personally staged today's sensational contest, which was to be the climax of the present series of Wolperting contests, as a favour to the Copper Killers' commanding officer.

Friftar's heart was nonetheless beating faster than usual, as it always did when he had to face the general. Even Gornab was more predictable than this crazy mechanical monster. Whenever they spoke, Friftar felt like a snail crawling along the edge of a razor blade.

He was about to knock on the tower's copper door when he noticed that it was ajar. This was unusual. Doors were never left unlocked in a city like Hel. Friftar called the general's name loudly several times. No answer. Could he be asleep? No, impossible, machines needed no sleep. The general was obviously out.

Friftar giggled nervously to himself. This was an irresistible invitation to do some snooping! He couldn't afford to pass up such an opportunity. Perhaps he would discover something with which to discredit his hated rival in the king's eyes.

Pushing the door open, he went inside. He usually employed other people to perform such missions. What a thrill it was to perform one himself! He wondered what a machine's home environment would look like.

Ticktock's tower was dimly illuminated by a few smoking candles, the little windows being covered with thick curtains. A smell of lubricating oil and metal polish hung in the air. There were weapons, of course.

Swords, rapiers and sabres of all kinds, hiltless blades of every size, axes, spears, daggers, scythes, halberds, throwing stars – all were lying higgledy-piggledy on tables or arrayed against the walls. Nothing but weapons, tools and mechanical odds and ends. Cogwheels and screws, nuts and bolts, pliers and spanners. No chairs, no bedroom or kitchen, but any number of mirrors of every conceivable size. Naturally! Such was the lifestyle of a machine that never had to eat, sleep or sit down. When alone it tinkered with its works or admired its own reflection. Friftar stifled a laugh.

He climbed a broad flight of black marble stairs to the next floor.

'General Ticktock?' he called again for safety's sake. 'Hello?'

No answer. In he went!

Friftar found himself in the Metal Maiden's chamber. He held his nose, the smell that had hit him was so strong. What in Gornab's name *was* this place? A laboratory? A torture chamber? Although Friftar had expected a murderous machine's interests and predilections to be mainly of a morbid nature, he was astonished that the general should have secreted such an antiquated instrument of torture in his private quarters. It was almost endearingly old-fashioned of him! However, Ticktock had obviously brought the Metal Maiden right up to date, technologically speaking. All those tubes and valves – how they gurgled and hissed, roared and pulsated! The apparatus had recently been used, but why had some of the tubing been destroyed? How had the doors of the machine acquired all those dents? Someone had played havoc with it. What was in all the metal hoppers? Above all, what was inside the Metal Maiden itself? What terrible secret was he on the track of?

There was no alternative: Friftar simply had to open another two doors – the ones in the front of the Metal Maiden. Drawing a deep breath, he swung them back as slowly and cautiously as he could, quivering with pleasurable anticipation at the possibility that something horrific would reveal itself to his gaze.

The microscopic invaders

In obedience to the irrevocable laws which Tykhon Zyphos had laid down for their benefit, the soldiers of the Subcutaneous Suicide Squad, having successfully completed the destruction of Rala's bloodstream, were proceeding to destroy the rest of her body as well. They wanted to eliminate every last cell of it before emerging into the open and seeking a new fortress of flesh and blood to conquer. They did not realise that they were imprisoned within the Iron Maiden's metal casing.

However, fate ordained that her lead-sheathed doors should open wide, and standing outside was another body, another fresh, healthy organism. Having largely completed its work inside Rala, the Subcutaneous Suicide Squad was eager to embark on a new mission.

So Tykhon's microscopic warriors fanned out, deserted Rala's veins, forced their way through her arterial walls, muscles and epidermis, and emerged from her body in order to conquer Friftar.

A sudden chill

The king's chief adviser had been prepared for any kind of horrific sight when he opened the Metal Maiden, so he was doubly surprised – indeed, almost moved – to see a female Wolperting inside. Was she asleep? Was she dead? Had it not been for all those fine needles – had he himself withdrawn them from her body when opening the doors? – she would have created a thoroughly peaceful impression. What a pretty creature!

Why had he never seen her before? She looked as if she might have acquitted herself well in the Theatre of Death. Why had General Ticktock kept her from him and the king?

He felt her pulse. Yes, she was dead.

'Oh!' he groaned suddenly.

A spine-chilling sensation had assailed him, a breath of cold air from the dead Wolperting. It seemed to penetrate his every pore, infiltrate his body and freeze his blood. He felt alternately hot and cold, dizzy and nauseous, his knees buckled and sweat broke out on his brow. He struggled for breath, his heart raced and he had to cling to a doorpost or he would have slumped to the floor. The underside of his skin prickled as if hundreds of ants were crawling through his veins.

'Oooh!' he groaned again.

Then the sensation subsided. His strength returned and he was able to release his grip on the doorpost. He breathed deeply and mopped his brow, staring at the dead Wolperting in dismay. What had he just experienced? Did these creatures possess certain powers even in death?

Friftar dashed out of the torture chamber and ran down the stairs, then out of the tower and through the streets of Hel, trying to shake off he knew not what. He didn't stop until he was outside the Theatre of Death. He looked up at the walls, which were faced with black skulls. Ah, the theatre! The scene of what would doubtless be the most exciting fight he had ever staged!

This thought reassured him. He was still feeling a trifle unwell, but the forthcoming spectacular contest would be bound to banish the last vestiges of his malaise. It was high time to begin the systematic annihilation of those unpredictable Wolpertings.

A historic spot

Although Rumo and his companions were still wading through Hel's slimy sewers, they had clearly left the oldest sector behind them, with its organic structures, obtrusive fauna and curious flora. The channels here had been dug out by tunnellers. Rumo could see brickwork and plasterwork, and the authorities were clearly at pains to keep the walls free from weeds and vermin.

'We're now in the civilised part of the sewers, so to speak, immediately below the city centre,' Ribble explained.

'How much further to the theatre?' asked Rumo.

'Only a little way,' said Ribble. His voice had taken on a solemn note. 'We're already in the vicinity of a historic spot.'

'What historic spot?' Yukobak demanded.

'You've got a surprise in store, Yuko,' Ribble replied. 'Just follow me.'

He plodded on ahead down a tunnel faced with red marble. It was pleasantly cool and the water flowing along it was clear. They took the opportunity to rinse off some of the grime, then marched on. Suddenly Ribble came to a halt.

'This is the spot,' he said in a tremulous voice. He pointed to a place on the floor immediately beneath a shaft with an iron ladder running up the side.

'What's so special about it?' said Yukobak. 'I can't see anything.'

'That's the air shaft you fell down as a child, Yuko. This is where I found you, more dead than alive, under a pack of Plague Rats. They would have eaten you alive.'

'No!' cried Yukobak. 'Really and truly?' He gave a sob.

'Yes, this is where our fate was decided. And now fate has brought us back here. That shaft leads to your family mansion.'

Ribble turned to Rumo.

'You can climb up there. The shaft comes out in the grounds of the Yukobak mansion. There's a big black door in the wall leading to the street. Turn left, then right at the next intersection and you'll find yourself outside the Theatre of Death. You'll recognise it by the wall of black skulls that surrounds it. The prison housing most of the prisoners is just across the street.'

'Thanks,' said Rumo. 'You've both been a great help.'

He went to the foot of the ladder.

'Tell me something,' said Ribble. 'You're a Wolperting on the loose. What makes you think you'll be able to roam around up there for longer than two minutes without causing a riot?'

'I'll find out when the time comes.'

'You still don't have a plan, do you?' said Yukobak.

Rumo shrugged his shoulders and proceeded to climb the ladder.

'He's gone,' Yukobak said after a while.

'Yes,' said Ribble.

'About time too, the lunatic.'

'He saved your life!' Ribble protested. 'And he kept his word. He could have taken us with him.'

'He took us prisoner!'

'Our people abducted his whole tribe - and they're in the process of butchering them.'

'He'll die,' Yukobak said.

'So will they all.'

They exchanged a long, silent look.

'They'll probably nab him before he's gone ten yards,' Ribble said. 'A Wolperting running around loose? He'll stick out like a sore thumb.'

'And all for the sake of a casket!'

'Yes. Romantic nonsense.'

'Well, we did what we could.'

'Yes, we did.'

'It had to end somewhere.'

'Yes, here at this romantic spot,' said Ribble, 'where one great friendship began and another ended.'

They both gave a sob.

'If we'd gone with him we could have pretended he was our prisoner,' Ribble went on. 'We could have escorted him safely to the theatre.'

'With us he'd have found it child's play to get into the prison.'

'A piece of cake.'

They fell silent again.

'Think he's reached the top by now?' asked Yukobak.

'I'm sure he has,' Ribble replied.

'We'd better be quick, then!'

They both scrambled up the shaft.

'Rumo!' they called in unison. 'Wait for us, we're coming with you!'

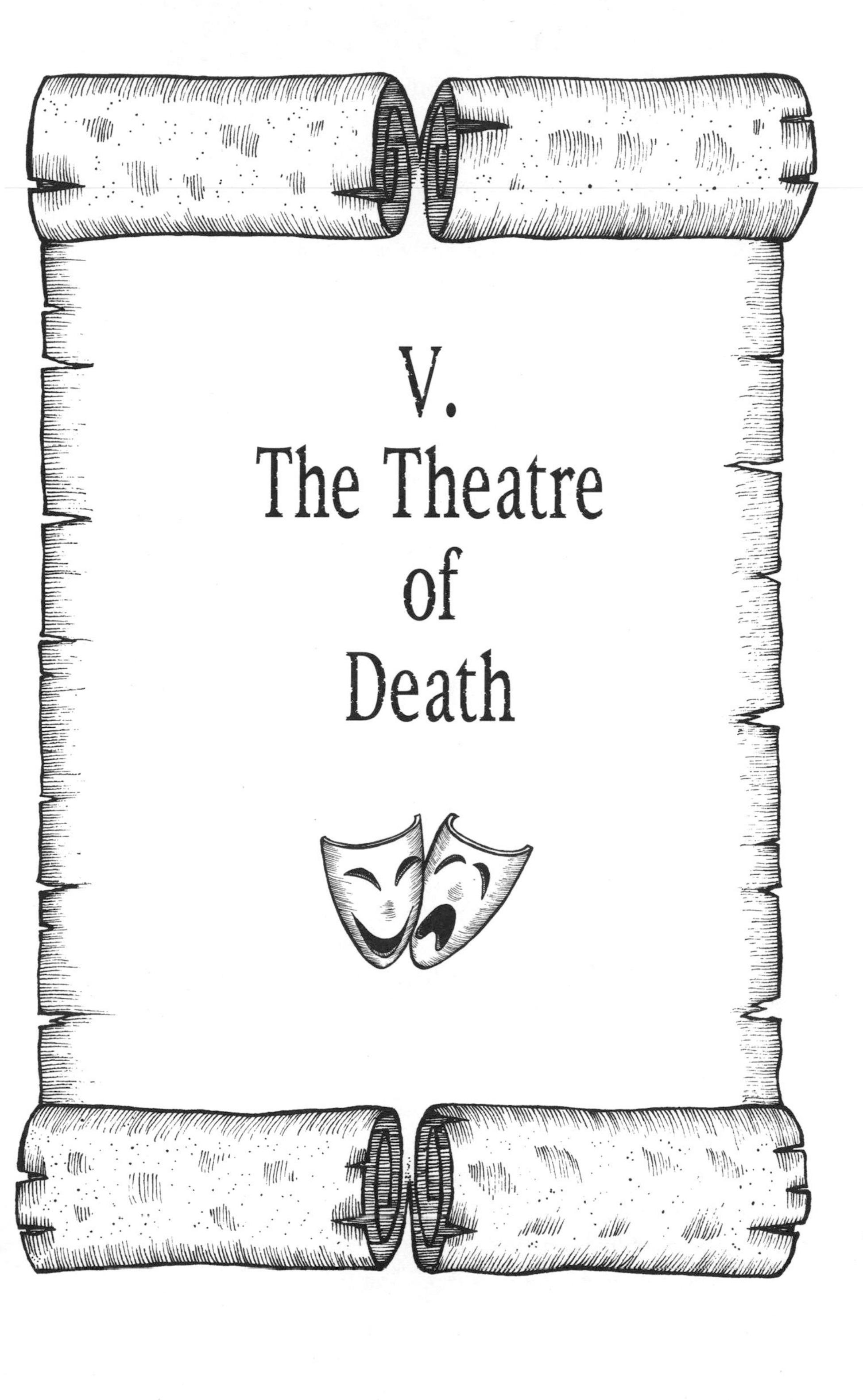

V. The Theatre of Death

Hel, a city without a sky, without clouds or stars. A colourless, sunless city filled with unpleasant smells. Even its architecture made Rumo feel uneasy. Nothing but squat, humpbacked, horned, scaly, menacing shapes. House fronts like hideous faces, doors like gaping mouths, windows like empty eye sockets, everything grey and black. Grimy, tattered garments dangled from lines suspended between the buildings like the corpses of hanged men. Hollowed-out Vrahok carapaces, weirdly illuminated from within, served as living accommodation. Here and there volcanic fumes belched from yawning holes in the ground.

'What a hideous place,' Rumo whispered. 'Is this really where you live?'

'It's where we *used* to live,' Yukobak replied. 'We'd actually succeeded in escaping from this hell-hole, but then we ran into someone called Rumo and now we're on our way to perdition because we've left the rest of our wits in the sewers.'

'I didn't force you to come with me.'

'No, but a little thank-you wouldn't come amiss.'

Rumo and his companions were pretending to be a prisoner plus escorts. The Wolperting led the way while Yukobak, who had borrowed his sword, urged him on and Ribble, marching along like a soldier, brought up the rear. Their first objective was the jail beside the Theatre of Death. According to Yukobak, it wasn't too heavily guarded.

'The streets are remarkably empty,' said Ribble. 'The theatre is probably staging a spectacular fight of some kind.'

They marched past a row of houses whose numerous windows, dimly illuminated by black candles, displayed sets of false teeth of every conceivable size. Whenever people came their way, Yukobak and Ribble strove to make an exceptionally martial impression and Yukobak prodded Rumo in the back with his sword.

'Keep going, prisoner!' he barked. 'No false moves!'

'Don't overdo it!' Rumo hissed. 'That sword is sharp.'

'Shut up, you miserable scum of a Wolperting!' Yukobak growled.

'Ssh!' said Ribble. 'We're there. That's the prison.'

Rumo, who was holding his paws together behind his back as if handcuffed, inspected the big black building. Grim and unadorned, it had no windows and only one entrance. An ideal prison.

'How many guards?'

'That depends,' Ribble whispered. 'Sometimes just two, sometimes a dozen – they only have one door to guard, after all. It also depends how many men they need at the theatre. The prisoners in here are old and feeble, so they don't pay them much attention. Shall I?'

Rumo nodded.

Ribble knocked on the door.

'Who is it?' growled a deep voice.

'Er, Blibber and Kokubak of Friftar's secret police!' Ribble called. 'We've captured a stray Wolperting who probably escaped from here.'

Xugo and Yogg

'No one's escaped from here,' said another deep voice. 'No one ever does.'

'Don't you want to give him the once-over at least?'

'No.'

Ribble thought for a moment. 'Your names?'

'Xugo and Yogg of the prison guard. Why do you want to know?'

Yukobak held up two fingers. Only two guards.

Rumo nodded again.

'So that I can report you to Friftar,' said Ribble. 'You'll be charged with, er, failing to assist the secret police.'

The door opened a crack. Standing inside were two heavily armed Bluddums.

'That's a young Wolperting,' said one of them.

'He must have escaped from the theatre,' said the other. 'We only have the oldsters in here.'

'May we come in?' asked Yukobak. 'We need some proper chains. This is only a makeshift job and he's a dangerous brute.'

The Bluddums opened the door, grumbling, and Yukobak and Ribble pushed Rumo inside. By the time they followed him into the dimly lit guardroom, Xugo and Yogg were lying senseless on the floor.

'You were quick,' said Yukobak.

'No,' said Rumo, 'Bluddums are slow.' He surveyed the room. A wooden table, three chairs, a rack of weapons. Massive double doors, bolted.

'The prisoners are in there,' said Yukobak. 'Your friends.'

When Rumo unbolted the doors and flung them open, he was met by a pleasant and familiar smell for the first time since setting foot in Netherworld. It was the scent of Wolpertings – lots of them.

Urs under escort

For days now, the door of Urs's cell had been opened only so that some bread could be tossed in or his pitcher of water refilled. Today was different. Behind the warders stood a whole squad of Copper Killers, ready to escort him into the arena.

As in the case of his previous fights, he was conducted into one of the ante-rooms and allowed to choose a weapon. Having decided on a handy broadsword with a double-edged blade, Urs waited for the gate to open and admit him to the arena, where half a dozen heavily armed soldiers or a ravenous Troglobear would probably be waiting for him.

Ever since his fight with Evel the Octopus, Urs had felt that his talent for swordsmanship imposed an obligation on him. Every opponent he dispatched was one less potential killer of Wolpertings; that was his cruel logic.

This time, however, instead of being sent into the arena to fight as soon as he'd chosen his weapon, Urs was made to wait. He waited for hours, so it seemed, while the din from the arena and the auditorium drifted in: the clatter of swords, the roaring of wild beasts, the spectators' applause. There seemed to be considerably more supporting bouts than usual and he kept hearing Friftar's nasal voice delivering long-winded speeches during the intermissions. Urs grew more and more uneasy. He sensed that the Theatre of Death had something very special in store for him.

The reunion

When Rumo saw all the prisoners in the big hall, he had a strange feeling of déjà vu. He was reminded of the moment on Roaming Rock when he entered the Demonocles' larder, drenched with blood, to release the captive Hackonians. Once again he was greeted like a ghost and once again no one spoke at first.

The hall was huge and only sparsely illuminated by jellyfish torches. Most of the prisoners were sitting on the floor, but some were standing together in little groups. There was no furniture, just blankets and palliasses. Rumo recognised many faces in the dim light: teachers from school and craftsmen of his acquaintance, most of them elderly Wolpertings, but also a few Zamonians of other breeds. Oga of Dullsgard was sitting on a straw mattress, staring at him in disbelief. 'Rumo?' she said. Her face had lost all its stern authority.

Rumo spotted the mayor, Jowly of Gloomberg. He was sitting with his back against a wall, gazing at him as incredulously as the others.

'Rumo?' he said. 'Why have they put you in here? Is something wrong with you? Are you ill? Wounded?'

Rumo knelt down in front of him.

'Nobody sent me. I came to release you.'

The mayor pricked up his ears. 'But . . .Weren't you taken prisoner?'

'I was in Nurn Forest when they raided Wolperting. The city was deserted when I returned. There was a big hole in the ground where the Black Dome used to stand. I followed you down here.'

'Have you any idea what this place is?' the mayor asked. 'Where are we?'

'This is Hel, the capital of Netherworld,' Rumo told him. 'They drugged you and brought you here. Do you know where Rala is?'

'Not here, anyway. What do you plan to do?'

'I think it would be best if I freed the other Wolpertings first. They're held prisoner in a place known as the Theatre of Death. I'll come back with them and we'll all fight our way out of the city together.'

'I like your plan,' said the mayor. 'Perhaps that's what you're best at, making plans.'

'No,' said Rumo, 'it certainly isn't, but listen: I've got two allies who grew up in this city. One of them I'll take to the theatre, the other will remain outside for your protection and pretend to be guarding you. Keep quiet until we return.'

'I'll see to it,' said Jowly.

'Good. Inform the others.' Rumo rose and the mayor proceeded to spread the promising news.

Rumo was just leaving when a low voice stopped him in his tracks.

'Rumo? Is that you?' it asked from the shadows. He had to screw up his eyes to make out two figures seated against the wall. One was exceptionally big and bulky, the other exceptionally small and puny.

'Is Rumo here?' asked the puny little figure, opening its eyes. They were big and round and shone in the dark like two moons. Incredulously, Rumo took a step nearer. Volzotan Smyke and Professor Kolibri were sitting there.

Rolv arms himself

Rolv had gathered, if only from the demeanour of the soldiers who fetched him from his cell, that he was in for something out of the ordinary. They treated him with the utmost caution - indeed, with respect. This was partly because of his prowess in the theatre. Rolv was known as the crazy 'artist of death' who could be in several places at once.

His strategy was unchanged: he would try to take the insane little king hostage and exchange him for the release of Rala and the other Wolpertings. It simply meant that he had to be faster than the Copper Killers' crossbow bolts.

Having been conducted to the table with the weapons on it, he put on three belts instead of one. One he buckled round his waist, the other two round his shoulders. Then he loaded them with two swords, six knives and four spiked metal throwing discs. A small axe completed his arsenal. This being the day he had longed for most and dreaded most, he wanted at least to be adequately equipped for it.

From Murkholm to Hel

After Smyke had finished reading Professor Ostafan Kolibri's lighthouse log, the Murkholmers captured him in a most bizarre manner. At first they merely formed a silent, motionless circle round the lighthouse and Smyke simply remained inside. Suddenly, however, the Murkholm trombophone orchestra struck up. Its weird music caused the dense, dark fog enclosing the lighthouse to swirl round so violently that it pressed up against the big picture window and made it bulge inwards in an ominous way. At this, Smyke lost his nerve and surrendered.

The Murkholmers then escorted him - still in silence - to a building where, for several days, he was imprisoned in one room with Professor

Ostafan Kolibri, who made a mentally deranged impression, and seven other captives, all of them Midgardian dwarfs.

The dwarfs were also in a state of temporary dementia as a result of being gradually poisoned for weeks by the fog. They believed themselves to be considerably more numerous than they actually were, and it wasn't long before Smyke felt he was locked up not just with seven of them, but with several dozen.

Then, one day, the door of their prison opened. Escorted by a dozen brutal-looking Bluddums among whom Smyke was surprised to see Kromek Toomah, Zorda and Zorilla from *The Glass Man Tavern*, they were conducted through dense fog to a cave beside the sea. From there, by way of a labyrinthine system of stalactite caves, they descended deep into the ground and eventually, after a long and arduous march, reached Hel. They were attacked three times en route by huge, predatory insects resembling a cross between a spider and a moth, and three of the Bluddums lost their lives. Once in Hel, Kolibri and Smyke were classified as second-class prisoners and consigned to the prison near the theatre. The professor had regained his sanity, so they were at last able to resume their scholarly conversations, though not in the conditions they would have preferred. Then, not long ago, the prison had filled up with Wolpertings. Smyke had questioned them about Rumo, but in vain. They all knew him but had no idea of his whereabouts.

And now Rumo had re-entered Smyke's life in much the same way as he had stumbled into that cave on Roaming Rock while still an inexperienced youngster.

Many questions, one riddle

'Smyke?' Rumo exclaimed in amazement.

'Who else?' Smyke replied, baring his shark's teeth in a grin. 'You Rumo, me Smyke.'

'Hello, Rumo,' said Kolibri.

'Hello, professor,' said Rumo. 'I see the two of you have met up again.'

'It's a very long story,' Smyke said. 'I'll save it for later. How did you get to Netherworld, my boy? What brings you here?'

'I've come to rescue my fellow Wolpertings.'

Kolibri's eyes glowed. 'You mean you aren't a prisoner?' he asked.

'And you've managed to get here all the way across Netherworld and

Hel?' said Smyke. His grin widened. 'Your presence fills an old friend's heart with hope.'

'Roaming Rock was a different kettle of fish,' Rumo told him. 'That was just an island teeming with monsters. This time it's a whole city.'

Smyke raised several index fingers. 'One grows into one's work,' he said.

'Do you have a plan?' asked Kolibri.

'Not really,' Rumo confessed.

'Then you've come to the right people,' said Smyke. 'We've got five brains between us.'

'I have to go to a building called the Theatre of Death,' Rumo said. 'That's where the other Wolpertings are held prisoner. Will you come with me?'

'I will,' said Smyke. 'Professor?'

'A little exercise would do me good.'

'All right,' said Rumo, 'let's go.'

'One more thing.' Smyke gripped Rumo with one of his little arms. 'Did you discover the answer to my riddle? *What grows shorter and shorter the longer it gets?*'

'Oh,' Rumo replied, 'that was easy. The answer, of course, is "*life*".'

Smyke grinned. 'Of course,' he said.

Ushan feels rejuvenated

Ushan DeLucca had never been in better shape. Even as the soldiers escorted him down the stairs, he knew that his feats of arms in the arena would far surpass any he'd been able to perform there on previous occasions.

There was no weather in Netherworld, and the intoxicating sensation this induced in him was growing stronger every day. Down here he was spared all the meteorological conditions that had made him so tired and torpid, weak and depressed, on the surface. Down here he was experiencing a resurgence of the physical strength he had last possessed in his youth.

They escorted him into the ante-room, where he went over to the table with the weapons laid out on it. Pandemonium reigned in the auditorium. Ushan could hear the roaring of wild beasts, the despairing cries of prisoners. He could smell fresh blood and the cold sweat of fear, but there was nothing out there capable of filling him with dread. He was

Ushan DeLucca, and he was in the best of spirits.

He scanned the table. Choosing a weapon was no problem. He would naturally take a sword – the first one that came to hand, as long as the blade was good and sharp. He picked one up and slashed the air with it.

'Ssst, ssst, ssst!' he went. 'Ssst, ssst, ssst!'

The diamond-tipped pliers

General Ticktock was roaming the streets of Hel. The roadway shattered under his ponderous tread and all who encountered him leapt aside in terror.

What was this pain inside him? Nonsense, he was incapable of feeling pain! He had no nervous system – he was a machine. But in that case why was he in such agony? What was this thought that obsessed him? The thought of Rala's death? He realised that hidden within him, in the depths of his body with its bristling array of weapons, was something capable of suffering. Never had he felt that more clearly than he did now.

At last he came to a halt. This was the street. This was the house.

It was the weaponsmith's house where he had found the Metal Maiden – the accursed Metal Maiden, which had once more become a worthless accumulation of junk. She was nothing without the soul that Rala had given her.

He kicked in the door, which he had ordered to be sealed. The workshop looked just as he had left it. The weaponsmith, now a skeleton, was still lying on the floor.

General Ticktock had come in search of something.

He was after the huge, dangerous-looking pliers with diamond-tipped teeth, which looked as if they could have torn a Copper Killer apart. Where *were* the confounded things? He overturned work benches and shovelled scrap metal aside, sending screws and iron components flying through the air.

There! There were the pliers!

He weighed them in his hand. Yes, they were powerful pliers with an ingenious hydraulic mechanism and sparkling teeth tipped with diamonds of the first water.

General Ticktock applied them to his ribcage. Surely *they* would help him to discover the accursed thing that was causing him so much pain deep inside.

The Silver Thread

Rumo, Smyke and Kolibri had agreed that Ribble should stay behind with the elderly Wolpertings, pretend to be guarding them and keep the outer door locked. Xugo and Yogg were bound, gagged and carried into the main hall, where they were covered with straw. Smyke, Kolibri and Yukobak would accompany Rumo to the Theatre of Death and release the other Wolpertings. Yukobak's intimate knowledge of the building would enable them to enter it unobserved.

But their plan was shelved as soon as they left the prison. Before setting off for the theatre, Rumo sniffed the air again, and the scene that unfolded in his mind's eye was just as dismal and dismaying as his dark, grimy surroundings, which held the scent of many other Wolpertings. That scent led in the direction of the theatre.

But he could also see the Silver Thread.

His heart gave a leap. Yes, it was really here – here in the midst of Hel. Slender but radiant, it floated above the infernal stench. Rala was here, quite close at hand.

'We must go that way,' said Rumo.

'But the theatre's in the opposite direction,' Yukobak protested.

'I know, but I've picked up Rala's scent.'

'Really?'

'Huh?' said Smyke. 'And who, pray, is Rala?'

Ticktock's tower

While they were following Rala's scent, Rumo tried to explain who she was. He told Smyke about Wolperting, Nurn Forest and the casket – getting everything back to front, of course.

'In other words,' said Smyke, summarising Rumo's incoherent recital, 'you're besotted with her.'

'Most interesting,' said Kolibri. 'A Silver Thread. Visible smells and emotions, eh? It reminds me of my experiments with the ostascope. A Wolperting's sense of smell has yet to be fully researched.'

Meanwhile, Yukobak was doing his best to make them look like a motley bunch of prisoners under escort and hoping not to bump into any soldiers. Even so, the combination of a Wolperting, a Shark Grub, a Nocturnomath and a Helling was bound to attract the attention of anyone who passed such a strangely assorted group.

'Move it!' cried Yukobak, brandishing Rumo's sword. 'Move it, you miserable bunch of slaves!'

At last Rumo paused outside a dark tower.

'Rala's in there,' he said.

Yukobak flinched. 'What?! In *there* of all places? That's General Ticktock's tower!'

'You mean General Ticktock is here in Hel?' asked Smyke.

'Yes, he commands the Copper Killers. They guard the prisoners in the theatre.'

'In that case,' said Smyke, 'it's curtains!'

'I'm going in,' said Rumo. 'Rala's in there.'

'What if General Ticktock's at home?' asked Yukobak.

'Then I'll kill him. Give me my sword.'

'Oh, sure,' Yukobak said with a sigh, 'of course you'll kill him. No problem.'

The threesome

Although convinced that what awaited him there would be unpleasant, Urs felt relieved when he was finally permitted to enter the arena.

The auditorium was packed. Friftar, standing beside the balustrade of the royal box, cried, 'The Theatre of Death presents . . . Urs of the Snows!'

Urs was greeted with thunderous applause.

He wondered what it would be this time. Soldiers? Wild beasts? Both at once? Or something even more formidable?

Another gate opened and Ushan DeLucca sauntered into the arena. His sword flickered through the air.

'Ssst, ssst, ssst!' went Ushan.

'The Theatre of Death presents . . . Ushan DeLucca!' cried Friftar.

The applause swelled.

Urs was impressed. Another Wolperting? He hadn't been expecting that.

A third gate opened and Rolv strode in.

'The Theatre of Death presents . . . Rolv of the Forest!'

The spectators rose, yelling delightedly and stamping their feet.

Urs was puzzled. Ushan and Rolv? Were the three of them going to fight as a team?

'Threesome!' bellowed the audience. 'Threesome! Threesome!'

The Wolpertings stood in the middle of the arena with flowers and garlands raining down on them. Friftar raised his arm and the applause died away.

'In case you aren't familiar with the rules of a threesome,' he called to the prisoners below, 'allow me to acquaint you with them.'

Ushan, Rolv and Urs glanced at each other in surprise.

'A threesome's main essential,' cried Friftar, 'is that two of the participants end up dead, not just one. The stupidest fighter always dies first. He's the one with the most qualms about killing one of the others in league with the third. Once he has been dispatched, the two survivors fight to the death.'

'We won't fight each other,' Urs shouted up at the box.

Gornab joined Friftar at the balustrade. 'Tell them!' he hissed. 'Tell them wath to ecpext if they feruse!'

'Oh yes,' Friftar called, 'I almost forgot. If you refuse to fight each other we shall march your elderly compatriots into the arena, one by one, to act as targets for the Copper Killers – until you change your mind. And believe me, change it you will. Let the threesome commence!'

'Threesome!' the audience chanted again. 'Threesome! Threesome!'

Ushan made his blade whistle through the air. 'Ssst, ssst, ssst!' he went. 'Shall I tell you what I like best down here?'

Urs and Rolv stared at him.

'The weather, that's what.'

'There isn't any weather down here,' said Urs.

'Exactly.' Ushan smiled. 'I know you couldn't care less, but you've no idea how much it means to me. Down here I feel as if I possess supernatural powers. Ssst, ssst, ssst!'

'What precisely are you getting at?' Urs demanded.

'He wants us to team up against him,' said Rolv. 'He wants to play the hero.'

'I'm not fighting any Wolperting,' said Urs.

'We'll have to fight whether we like it or not,' said Rolv. 'They'll kill our people otherwise.'

'Then kill me first,' said Urs, 'and fight it out between you.'

Rolv groaned. 'Another hero!'

'Ssst, ssst, ssst!' went Ushan. 'For those who are a trifle slow on the uptake, I'll say it again. I taught you youngsters the tricks of the trade, but down here I'm worth two of you. Your only hope is to join forces against me. Besides, it's the only way of gaining time.'

'Gaining time for what?' asked Urs.

'No idea,' said Ushan. 'A miracle, perhaps.'

'Agreed,' said Rolv. 'I can use some time. I plan to nab that crazy king of theirs.'

'In that case,' Ushan said with a smile, 'let's combine business with pleasure.'

A prophecy fulfilled

The copper-sheathed door of the black tower was open and Rumo had entered without hesitation.

This was a warrior's home, no doubt about it. There were stacks of weapons all over the place – swords, axes and blades of every description. The big mirrors standing among them reminded Rumo of Ushan DeLucca's fencing garden.

'Hey,' Yukobak said in a whisper, 'I don't think we ought to snoop around in General Ticktock's private quarters, it could mean a death sentence.'

'There's nobody here,' said Smyke.

Rumo took the stairs three at a time. On the floor above he found another door ajar. Raising his sword, he kicked it open.

'Anything up there?' Smyke called from below.

As Rumo entered the chamber containing the Metal Maiden it all came back to him. Within a single instant, past, present and future, prophecy and fulfilment became fused into one: the annual fair, the gloomy Star Tent, the professor with several brains, the chest-of-drawers oracle. There it was, the sight that Rumo had seen in the open drawer, the sight that had once been the future but was now a terrible reality: he saw Rala's lifeless body lying in a coffin.

Rala was dead.

Rumo felt faint. He dropped his sword and slumped to the floor. Then he passed out.

Ribble the rebel

Ribble was standing in front of the weapons rack when he heard footsteps approaching. The rack held an assortment of swords, axes and spears. In the sewers he used to be armed with a trident, but it was ages since he'd held a weapon in his hand. Hastily, he grabbed a spear.

Someone rapped on the outer door.

'Who is it?' Ribble called as smartly as he could.

'Orderly officer!' barked a voice. 'Open up!'

'No can do!' Ribble replied.

'Why not?'

'Quarantine. An epidemic has broken out among the Wolpertings.'

'I'm not here to inspect the Wolpertings, only the guard.'

'Hell,' muttered Ribble.

'What did you say?'

'Er, nothing.'

'So open up, or do I have to fetch reinforcements?'

Ribble opened the door.

The orderly officer was a Bluddum. He came in, looked around in a sceptical manner and stationed himself in front of Ribble, whom he topped by several heads.

'Xugo and Yogg are supposed to be on guard duty. Where are they?' he snapped.

'Off sick, sir!' barked Ribble.

'Sick? What, both of them?' asked the Bluddum. 'I saw them only this morning. They were fit as fiddles.'

'They're under observation,' said Ribble. 'It's this epidemic.'

The Bluddum took a step backwards.

'Is it catching?'

'Very.'

The Bluddum eyed Ribble suspiciously.

'What are you doing on guard duty, anyway? I've never seen a Homunculus here before.'

'I'm the first – the first Homunculus in the guard detachment. It's an idea of Friftar's.' Ribble saluted.

'So why aren't you in uniform? What's that outfit you're wearing?'

'I had to surrender my uniform for disinfection. The epidemic, you know.'

'Why are you on your own here? Two sentries are the regulation number.'

'My comrade has gone off for a pee, sir.'

'Peeing on duty is against regulations.'

'Yessir! I know the regulations.'

'Really? Then I'm sure you also know the regulation that says carrying a crossbow is obligatory while on guard duty. Spears are prohibited.'

'Yes, I know it, but all the crossbows are needed at the theatre.'

'Ah, so you know it, do you? That's odd, because no such regulation exists. Who exactly are you?' The Bluddum reached for his sword.

Ribble's spear shot out and caught him in the throat. The Bluddum's knees buckled. With a gurgle he crashed to the floor and lay inert at Ribble's feet.

Yes, Ribble asked himself, who exactly am I? A servant? A citizen of Hel? No, no longer. Then it came to him. He gave the Bluddum's corpse a kick.

'You wanted to know who I am?' he said. 'I'm a rebel.'

For Rala's sake alone

Rumo regained consciousness to find Smyke, Yukobak and Kolibri bending over him. He was lying on a table on the ground floor of the tower. He tried to sit up, but he was too weak.

'Lie there for a moment, Rumo,' said the professor. 'You'll soon feel better.'

'Where's Rala?'

'Still upstairs.'

'Is that the Rala you were talking about?' asked Smyke.

'Yes,' said Rumo. 'What happened to her?'

'Someone killed her,' said Yukobak. 'What's more, he must have tortured her first. It can only have been General Ticktock. No one else sets foot in this tower.'

'She can't be dead,' Rumo said. 'I can see the Silver Thread. I can still detect her scent.'

'At the risk of sounding irreverent,' Kolibri said gently, 'the dead have a scent too. It doesn't disappear until they turn to dust.'

'I must go to her,' said Rumo. He rose with an effort and made for the stairs.

'Spare yourself, my boy,' said Smyke.

Rumo climbed the stairs. He knelt beside Rala's leaden coffin and wept, and the prophecy was fulfilled at last. He remained kneeling there for a long time, just as he had seen himself kneeling in Professor Nightingale's tent. When he rose to his feet again he made a resolution: everything he did from now on he would do for Rala's sake alone.

Two against one

Down here, thought Urs, Ushan DeLucca was truly worth two of him and Rolv, if not three or four. He whirled across the arena with them as if this were a dancing lesson, and the fencing master was definitely in charge. Urs had never seen Ushan so light-footed, so good-humoured and full of ideas. What a pity he was wasting his talent on a fight with members of his own kind.

'Ssst, ssst, ssst!' cried Ushan. 'I'm as light as a feather! I'm as venomous as a scorpion! I'm as quick as a dragonfly! Ssst, ssst, ssst!'

The trio had begun by performing some innocuous feints and parries to create the illusion of a genuine fight, but the knowledgeable spectators had soon caught on and started to boo.

'Is that the best you can do, boys?' cried Ushan. 'This isn't a fencing lesson – we can't just go through the motions. If you don't try harder those Bluddums will soon be using our people for target practice. Attack me! Attack me in earnest! Try to kill me!'

'I can't do it,' Urs called back.

'You aren't *that* good,' said Rolv. 'I could wound you.'

'No, Rolv, you couldn't!' Ushan retorted. 'No one could. You could try your utmost to kill me and you wouldn't even scratch me. Try it! Come on, attack me!'

He whirled around them. 'Take that! And that! And that!' he cried, showering them with blows. Urs and Rolv felt slight pricks all over their bodies, as if they had run into a swarm of bees.

'I could have killed you five times over, each of you! Come on, we've got to fight! Not for our own lives but for the others. Enough of this fooling around! Try to kill me! You won't do it anyway, you amateurs!'

'If I try to kill someone I kill him,' said Rolv.

Ushan halted and lowered his blade. 'You still don't get it, do you? I'm invincible! Must I teach you a lesson?'

He remained motionless as Rolv and Urs circled him.

'You aren't in your fencing garden now, Ushan,' Urs said in a low voice, 'and I'm not one of your backward pupils.'

'Yes,' said Rolv, 'don't bite off more than you can chew, old stager!'

'Ssst, ssst!' was Ushan's only response. Rolv and Urs doubled up in pain and clutched their noses, because each of them had sustained a cut on his most sensitive sense organ. The spectators roared with laughter.

'There,' said Ushan DeLucca. '*Now* will you attack me? *Now* are you prepared to kill me?'

Strategic plans

General Ticktock's tower was now the fugitives' temporary headquarters. Rumo, who had recovered his composure and gone downstairs again, calmly conferred with the others on what to do next. It was quickly agreed that the puny little Nocturnomath and the overweight Shark Grub would be little use in a fight. Kolibri and Smyke were to remain with Rala's corpse and guard it, because Rumo insisted on taking it back to Wolperting once he had freed the others. Meanwhile, Yukobak would accompany him to the Theatre of Death.

'Just do what you did on Roaming Rock,' Smyke told him.

'I'll try,' Rumo replied.

The Theatre of Death

The Theatre of Death was the black heart of Hel, an octagon whose eight colossal walls were faced with skulls stained black by the eternal soot.

'The skulls all belong to enemies of the Gornab dynasty,' Yukobak explained, looking around anxiously as they stole along. 'The theatre has many entrances. As a member of the Hellian nobility I often got a chance to see what goes on behind the scenes. I know how the theatre's devilish machinery works. We'd better use one of the cellar entrances – that's where they deliver the meat for the wild animals. They're unguarded because everyone is scared of the beasts. From there one can get anywhere including the backstairs that lead to the prisoners' cells. One thing's for sure: No one has ever been crazy enough to want to sneak *in* that way, only *out* – if at all!' Yukobak gave a nervous laugh.

Laughter, applause and savage yells were issuing from the theatre. An exciting contest was obviously in progress.

'Tell me something,' said Yukobak. 'What was it you did on this, er, Roaming Rock?'

'I killed as many enemies as I could,' Rumo replied.

'I see,' said Yukobak. 'So you do have a plan after all.'

Getting in was easy. They climbed through an unbarred window at the rear of the theatre. The cellar in which they found themselves was full of gnawed bones and the stuffy air was thick with plump, buzzing bluebottles. The muffled roars of a wild animal were coming from somewhere nearby. Yukobak opened the inner door, which gave on to a dark passage flanked by another dozen doors.

Yukobak tried one of them, only to be confronted by a six-foot spider with ruby-red fur, eight yellow eyes the size of dinner plates and marbled grey wings like a moth. The spider turned its attention to the two intruders and fluttered its wings. Yukobak slammed the door in a hurry.

'Sorry,' he said, 'wrong one!'

The next three doors he opened only a crack and promptly shut again, having been greeted respectively by an awe-inspiring roar, an infernal stench and a writhing tentacle. At last he found the right door.

'The stairs,' he whispered. 'From here we can get to the prison cells.' They climbed the stairs accompanied by the spectators' ever-swelling, ever-fading shouts and applause. Rumo detected many unpleasant smells, among them blood, sweat and fear – the scent of death as a perverted form of entertainment.

At the top of the stairs they found themselves looking down a passage dimly illuminated by a few torches. Rumo was astonished by the sight that met his eyes. At the end of the passage was a black wooden door with a heavy table in front of it, and dozing at the table, which bore several empty wine bottles, were three guards. They were Bluddums and they were snoring softly. But the most astonishing aspect of this scene was not the soldiers' dereliction of duty, but the fact that Rumo knew all three. They were Zorda, Zorilla and Kromek Toomah, the Bluddums from *The Glass Man Tavern.*

Kromek Toomah, Zorda and Zorilla

After Rumo and Smyke had left him barking madly in his taproom at *The Glass Man*, Kromek Toomah had undergone a surprising transformation. He had bettered himself professionally, acquired a set of firm friends and found his true home. Best of all, he had never barked since.

Kromek had recovered from his fit of dementia just in time to catch Zorda and Zorilla in the act of stowing his possessions in sacks with a view to making off with them. He won the terrible fight that followed because the other two were still groggy after their encounter with Smyke and Rumo.

While waiting for Zorda and Zorilla to recover their senses, Kromek debated whether the innkeeper's trade was really up his street. He detested waiting on people, he hadn't made a bean, and whenever he awoke from one of his fits he found people busy robbing him. His life had gone wrong somewhere.

'Listen, Kromek Toomah,' said a familiar voice in his head, 'I don't think you're cut out to be an innkeeper.' It was the voice of the *Glass Man*, who had commanded him to build the tavern in the first place.

'But you told me—'

'I know. I was wrong, I admit, but I'm a mental illness. You can't hold me responsible.'

'Can't I?'

'No, I wasn't in my right mind, but this time I see it all clearly. My mind is clear, crystal-clear. Clear as a diamond composed of pure thought subjected to extreme pressure. Do you know how clear that is?'

'No,' said Kromek.

'It's *insanely* clear, my friend! Listen, you should take up your old profession again. In my opinion the mercenary's trade is the only one that suits you.'

'I don't know. It won't be easy to land another job in a mercenary army. I marched around with Prince Hussein Banana's head on the end of a spear. People get to hear of that sort of thing. Generals don't care for it.'

'I know, but I'm not talking about an army *up here*. Ever heard of Netherworld?'

'Sure, there's always some nut blathering about it round every campfire, but—'

'What would you say if I told you that Netherworld really exists?'

'I'd say you were nuts.'

'And you'd be absolutely right, seeing as how I'm a mental illness, but my information about Netherworld's existence comes from a crystal-clear source. It's as clear as—'

'What source?'

'Another mental illness.'

'You mean you screwballs can communicate?'

'Of course we can. We're in touch with each other – telepathically in touch. Voices, you know? All of us are voices that—'

'Yes, yes,' said Kromek, clutching his brow. 'Spare me the details, I'm getting a headache.'

'My information about Netherworld comes from someone by the name of Gornab,' said the Glass Man.

'You've got names?'

'Of course. I'm the *Glass Man*. Then there's *Gornab*, and the *Howling Hound*, and *Strobo the Screamer*, and the *Twelve-Tongued Tadpole*, and—'

'All right, all right! So there's an army down in Netherworld?'

'And what an army! They only take the scum of the earth and anyone who lacks even that qualification becomes a general.'

'How does one get there?'

'There are many routes to Netherworld. I recommend the one that goes via Murkholm.'

'Why?'

'Because it's the craziest!' The *Glass Man* gave a diabolical laugh.

The route to Netherworld

When Zorda and Zorilla regained consciousness, Kromek made it clear that the next time they tried to rob him he would dice them, pickle them and take them along as iron rations for an emergency. Realising that he was in earnest, they swore to turn over a new leaf. The three of them later became the best of friends because, however stupid, brutal and underhanded they might be, Bluddums seldom bore a grudge. Kromek told the other two about his plan to go to Netherworld, and Zorda and Zorilla, who thought it sounded a place after their own hearts, decided to join him. They burned down *The Glass Man Tavern* and set off, guided by the voice in Kromek's head.

When they got to Murkholm, its sinister inhabitants admitted them to the 'Friends of Hel Association' and initiated them into Murkholm's secret function as an Urban Flytrap. Their first task as members of this secret society was to escort a new batch of prisoners to Hel accompanied by a few other Bluddums who knew the way to Netherworld. To Kromek's, Zorda's and Zorilla's satisfaction, one of these prisoners was the fat Shark Grub that had given them such a hard time with the Wolperting's assistance. Kromek interpreted this as an omen that he was on the right track.

The Bluddums made their way down into Netherworld through a precipitous maze of tunnels. They were immediately taken with the place. Although it harboured many unpleasant creatures including huge spiders with mothlike wings - they could be quite a nuisance and devoured three of their comrades - the sinister aura of Hel instantly appealed to them, so they delivered their prisoners and joined the army of Gornab the Ninety-Ninth. No one here held it against Kromek that he had carried his general's head around on a spear. This time the voice in his head seemed to have given him the right advice. Kromek, Zorda and Zorilla served in several units of the Netherworld army before being assigned to the Theatre of Death, where they took part in one or two fights that required them to smash the skulls of some defenceless dwarfs. Then, as luck would have it, they landed the coveted, restful job of guarding the prisoners' wing.

Kromek had, for the first time, felt a renewed pang of uneasiness when the captive Wolpertings were brought to Hel. Although he was somewhat reassured to find that they did not include the Wolperting from *The Glass Man Tavern*, the presence of those creatures got on his nerves. The fights he witnessed in the arena revived unpleasant memories. Lately, he had even suffered from nightmares in which Wolpertings pursued him with bared fangs until he woke up yelling his head off. He started to drink again. On the day the great threesome took place in the arena he had drained three bottles of extremely potent Netherworld wine and fallen into a deep sleep in which he dreamt he was being chased by a big white dog that bore a horrific resemblance to the brute from *The Glass Man Tavern.*

Rumo stole up to the table and the three snoring guards, cautiously followed by Yukobak. He drew his sword.

'Are we going to fight?' asked Krindle.

'As little as possible,' Rumo replied.

Krindle uttered a groan of disappointment.

'What are you going to do?' asked Dandelion.

Rumo bent down and rapped loudly on the table three times. Kromek Toomah, Zorda and Zorilla woke up and stared at him blearily.

'Hello, Kromek,' said Rumo. 'Long time no see.'

He stunned Zorilla with the flat of his sword. Zorda he spared so that he could help him release the prisoners. As for Kromek Toomah, he had started to bark again.

Smyke takes a gamble

Smyke gazed mournfully at Rala's face as she lay there in her metal coffin. What a noble, beautiful creature, he thought. What an ideal mate for Rumo she would have made!

'What would you say,' Professor Kolibri asked casually, as if inviting Smyke to play chess with him, 'to helping me to get the better of death?'

'What?' Smyke said dully.

'I was wondering if you'd care to join me in a little scientific venture. One in which you would combat death and work on your own immortality at the same time.' The professor gave him an encouraging smile.

'If you feel obliged to relieve the tension by cracking morbid jokes, it must be your Nocturnomathic sense of humour. Forgive me if I don't laugh.'

'I'm not joking. I'm making you a serious offer, the way I did back there in the forest.'

'You want me to re-enter your brain?'

'That would be the first step. Our ultimate destination is Rala's heart.'

'How would we get there?'

'It certainly won't be easy – someone has really played havoc with her system. It won't be without its dangers, either, but that applies to all pioneering ventures. The odds are fifty-fifty.'

'It's a gamble, you mean?'

'Yes, a gamble. And, for me, a unique opportunity to check my calculations.'

'In that case, professor, explain the rules.'

'You already know the first step: you pay my brain a visit. You make your way into the chamber containing the Non-Existent Teenies' micromachines and get aboard the subcutaneous submarine. Then you travel in it from my bloodstream into Rala's. Once there, you use the Non-Existent Teenies' instruments to start her heart beating again. That's all.'

'That's all?' Smyke laughed. 'Nothing more? How do I get from your body into Rala's?'

'That's the easiest part. I shall lay a pipeline between our two bloodstreams. This place is an ideal laboratory. All I need is some sterile tubing.'

Smyke stared hard at Kolibri. He seemed to be genuinely in earnest.

'I've got umpteen questions, professor. How dangerous will it be? Do we have the slightest chance of success? How will I find my bearings inside Rala's body?'

'That's only three questions and the answer is the same in each case: Everything will turn out all right. Yes, according to my calculations it'll all work out somehow.'

'*Somehow?* And you call yourself a scientist?'

'It may sound a trifle vague, but you know from experience how reliable my calculations are.'

'What if somebody turns up while we're . . . I mean, what if General Ticktock comes home?'

'Then we're done for in any case.'

'You really think it'll work?'

'Wouldn't it be a wonderful surprise for Rumo? I owe him a debt of gratitude and I'd like to repay him – he saved my life, after all. How many lives do *you* owe him, Smyke? One? Two?'

Smyke gave the Metal Maiden a lingering stare.

'So far,' he growled, 'three. May I stick my finger in your ear?'

'Be my guest,' Professor Kolibri said with a smile.

A brilliant idea

Gornab jumped around excitedly on his throne and punched the cushions. 'Now they're tighfing prolerpy!' he panted. 'Wath a gnamificent spactecle!'

'Quite so, Your Majesty,' said Friftar, 'they're fighting properly at last. To the death!'

The three Wolpertings down in the arena had only played around at first, as expected, but their onslaughts were now becoming faster and more ferocious. The younger two had clearly joined forces against the older one, but the latter was repelling their attacks with a masterful ease that belied his unimpressive exterior. The sight of Wolpertings fighting among themselves had a novel and very special appeal that held the whole audience spellbound, just as Friftar had foreseen. For the very first time in this arena a contest of the highest quality was in progress. This was no fight between barbarians and uncouth mercenaries; three genuine artists were at work.

'However,' Friftar added, 'I believe we can enhance the proceedings still further. We need only throw a few more logs on the fire. I've already sent a squad of soldiers to bring a few elderly Wolpertings to the theatre. The Copper Killers can practise their marksmanship on them. I think that ought to provide the trio down there with an additional incentive.'

Gornab grinned.

'Yes!' he exclaimed. 'We klil some Tingerwolps so the Tingerwolps klil each other!'

'Exactly, Your Majesty,' Friftar said with a bow. 'A brilliant idea of yours – as usual. We persuade the Wolpertings to kill each other by killing a few ourselves.'

The theatre guard

Ribble had already deduced from the rhythmical clank and jingle of armour that a sizeable body of soldiers was approaching the prison.

Someone knocked on the door.

'Who is it?' Ribble barked.

'Theatre guard!' came the crisp reply. 'We've come to recruit some Wolpertings for the Theatre of Death.'

'One moment,' said Ribble.

He opened the door. Standing outside were a dozen heavily armed soldiers. It was hard to tell exactly what they were under their armour.

'Come in,' said Ribble.

The soldiers entered the prison.

'What's that bloodstain doing on the floor?' their sergeant demanded.

'A Wolperting got uppity. I had to kill him.'

'Good,' said the sergeant, then, 'Hey, why aren't you in uniform?'

'Mine's covered in blood,' Ribble said grimly. 'Wolperting blood – revolting. How many prisoners do you need?'

'Half a dozen, as targets for the Copper Killers.'

'Great!' Ribble laughed. 'All right, help yourselves.' He unbolted the door to the main hall. The sergeant and he stood aside and the soldiers marched in.

'Halt!' shouted the sergeant. 'Stand to attention!'

The soldiers stiffened. Their eyes took a while to get used to the dim light. The sergeant, too, had to blink several times before he made out what awaited them beyond the door. Dozens of Wolpertings were drawn up in a semicircle, and they made a resolute impression. They were on the elderly side, but most were armed. One of them, a massive specimen with a notch in his skull, stepped forward and said, 'You'd better surrender.'

Ribble held his spear to the sergeant's throat.

Zorda was a fool, but he knew he hadn't a hope against Rumo on his own. Zorilla was out for the count and who knew when Kromek would stop barking?

Rumo leant across the table with his sword point at Zorda's throat.

'Listen carefully,' he said. 'You're now going to tell me – and make it short and snappy – exactly how the Wolpertings are held prisoner. You won't lie or hold back any important details and you won't make any false moves, either now or later. If you do all those things you may escape with your life. Fire away!'

'The cells have two doors,' said Zorda. 'One in front, leading out on to a gallery inside the theatre, and one behind, which leads to the secret stairs. The chains in the cells have to be unlocked separately.'

'Good. You're now going to help me to open the doors to the stairs and unchain the prisoners.'

'You don't have a hope. The theatre is guarded by the Copper Killers.'

'You can either help me or die. Which do you prefer?'

'Hard to say,' said Zorda. 'It'll probably amount to the same thing.'

The Kingdom of Death

This was the cold grey realm of death, a desolate region devoid of life. Why had he got involved in such a lunatic scheme?

'Professor Kolibri?' Smyke called. 'Hello?'

No reply. Of course not, the professor had bowed out a long time ago.

The rest had been so easy, thanks to Kolibri's assistance: travelling through his brain to the chamber containing the Non-Existent Teenies' micromachines; activating the subcutaneous submarine with the aid of its contentment servo-mechanism; steering it through the ideosprites into Kolibri's bloodstream; and getting from there into Rala's bloodstream, telepathically guided by the professor himself, who knew his own body better than any anatomist. In accordance with Kolibri's instructions, the submarine had glided silently along veins and arteries, agile as a trout, until it reached the spot where he had connected his circulation to Rala's by means of some sterile tubing.

As soon as Smyke passed through this artificial cannula and into Rala's body, however, communication abruptly ceased. The lighting inside the vessel faded to a dull glow and the electrical hum died away. Smyke could still see through the translucent membrane, but all that met his eyes outside was a strange, lifeless world. He was dependent on himself alone.

The submarine's electric motor stopped, leaving it adrift in the slowly cooling, coagulating plasma of a vein whose floor was strewn with dead corpuscles and other micro-organisms. It resembled a battlefield after a crushing defeat.

Being inside Rala's dead body was entirely different from visiting Kolibri's brain. This was no realm of ideas equipped with floating information silos. There were no cubes or parallelepipeds, no luminous trapezoids or pyramids, no orderly thoroughfares. Everything here was knotted and entangled like wildly proliferating jungle vegetation. How would he ever find his way around? His brain had nearly burst, Kolibri had pumped it so full of information, but anatomy wasn't one of his fields. Smyke couldn't tell a urethra from a capillary, a ganglion from an adipose cell. He was surrounded by a mass of nodules and protuberances, convolutions and excrescences. Was that Rala's heart or was it her liver? Was he in her foot or in her brain?

The only reason for not becoming hysterical, given his present predicament, was that it wouldn't have done any good. Or would it?

'Help!' he yelled. 'Please help!'

'Help!' replied a reedy, nasal, high-pitched voice.

'Please help!'

'Please help!'

Smyke, who hadn't really expected an answer, gave a start. Had the voice come from outside, or from here inside the boat?

'Hello?' he called. 'I'm here, Professor Kolibri!'

'Are you called Kolibri?'

'Is that your name?'

Kolibri?'

'No, er, my name is Smyke, I—'

'Smyke-Eye?'

'Your name is Smyke-Eye?'

'Smyke. My name is Smyke.'

'His name is Smyke.'

'Smyke.'

'Smyke, Smyke, Smyke.'

It was strange. The voices all sounded alike, but they seemed to belong to three different people.

'What are you doing on board our submarine, Smyke?'

'Yes, Smyke, what's your excuse?'

'Speak up, Smyke!'

'But . . . is this *your* submarine?' asked Smyke.

'It most certainly is.'

'You mean you're the Non-Existent Teenies?'

'The what?'

'The who?'

'The what?'

'The, er, Non-Existent Teenies. That's the name you go by. Or rather, that's what Professor Kolibri – your discoverer, I mean – calls you and—'

'You call us the Non-Existent Teenies?'

'Er, yes.'

'You don't say!'

'What cheek!'

'Why not call us the Non-Existent Unmentionables while you're about it?'

'I'm sorry, I didn't think up the name.'

'You probably don't think on principle.'

'For instance, you didn't think twice . . .'

'. . . about insulting us.'

'Hey, steady on! All right, tell me your real name.'

'We can't.'

'Impossible.'

'Too risky.'

'Oh? Why?'

'We do have a name, but it isn't a name by your limited standards.'

'You wouldn't understand our name, it's too complicated. Your brain couldn't handle it.'

'The mere sound of our name would drive you insane. It's a number, actually. From your point of view, an inconceivable number.'

'An inconceivably big number, you mean?'

'No. An inconceivably small number.'

'Insanely small.'

'So small that time goes backwards when one utters it.'

'How would it be if I didn't address you by name and we simply went on talking like this?'

'That would be impolite.'

'Bad form.'

'You like to make things easy for yourself, eh, Smyke?'

'Then think up a name yourselves, damn it all!'

'I'd like to be called Smyke.'

'And I'd like to be called Smykesmyke.'

'And I'd like to be called Smykesmykesmyke.'

'You want to be called Smyke, Smykesmyke and Smykesmykesmyke? That'd be too confusing. Can't you think of anything better?'

'No, we've got no imagination.'

'No?'

'No. We got over our imagination an inconceivable time ago.'

'An inconceivably long or inconceivably short time ago?'

'Are you making fun of us, Smyke?'

'Hey, don't you have a sense of humour?'

'No, we got over our sense of humour as well.'

'You seem to have got over a lot of things.'

'Certainly we have. We've got over time and space, pain and death.'

'And war and taxes.'

'And, last but not least, size. Any kind of size.'

'Really? So what's left?'

'Numbers. Only numbers are eternal.'

'So why not call yourself by numbers? How about One, Two and Three?'

'Those aren't numbers, they're words.'

'Heavens alive! Then call yourselves whatever you like! You're a pretty fussy bunch.'

'You still haven't answered our question.'

'What are you doing in our submarine?'

'Well?'

'I've come to start a dead heart beating again.'

'Ho, ho, ho . . .'

'Oh, is *that* all!'

'Aren't you biting off a bit more than you can chew?'

'Professor Kolibri says—'

'This Kolibri person is beginning to get on my nerves and I don't even know him.'

'First he calls us Teenies . . .'

'Non-Existent Teenies!'

'Then he steals our submarine . . .'

'. . . and now he wants to perform miracles.'

'Kolibri says there aren't any miracles, just scientific successes of miraculous proportions. I believe his calculations have told him that the Abs . . . that you'll give me a helping hand.'

'That Kolibri! Fancy claiming that we'd help someone who's pinched our submarine to perform a miracle, even though there aren't any miracles!'

'Give us one good reason why we should help you.'

'Just one.'

'Well, it's an affair of the heart, so to speak.'

'Cardiac surgery always is.'

'No, it's a question of love, I mean.'

'Oh no, not that!'

'We got over love, too, a long time ago.'

'Did you know that love consists of a series of numbers which, when subtracted from itself, adds up to zero?'

'Any series of numbers would.'

'Yes, isn't it shocking? If you think about it for long enough, it–'

'Stop badgering him! What sort of love are you talking about?'

'Now don't go getting sentimental, we've put all that behind us! We've got over sentimentality.'

'I was only asking! Facts are what I'm after. Cold, hard, unadorned facts.'

'It's the sort of love that transcends death.'

'Really? How romant– er, tell me more, I mean. Give me some more cold, hard, unadorned facts.'

'It's a love so pure and great that both the lovers have more than once defied death in an attempt to be reunited, but now it seems that death has finally defeated them.'

'But that's awf– er, interesting, I mean. Interesting in a cold, hard, unadorned way. Give us some more facts!'

'Yes, more!'

'More, more, more!'

Friftar feels unwell

Gornab squealed with delight as the gates into the arena opened. Seizing a cushion, he clasped it to his chest. He was looking forward to pulling it to pieces during the forthcoming bloodbath and tossing the feathers around.

'How namy Tingerwolps will you let the Reppoc Srellik klil?' he asked Friftar.

'I'm giving the Copper Killers half a dozen Wolpertings to kill,' Friftar replied.

'Only xis?' Gornab sounded disappointed. 'How sarpimonious of you! Why not a zoden?'

'I've told the Copper Killers to kill them slowly, using as many crossbow bolts as possible. It will look as if several dozen are dying.'

Gornab grunted and redirected his attention to events in the arena.

Friftar had the situation under control again. From now on the Wolpertings would exterminate themselves instead of wiping out the theatre's precious stock of gladiators. This threesome was intended to signal the beginning of the end of their proud race. Wolpertings came and went, but the theatre and Hel would go on for ever. All these distractions notwithstanding, however, Friftar hadn't managed to rid himself of the malaise that had overcome him at the sight of the female Wolperting's corpse inside the Metal Maiden. The sensation was so persistent that he kept shaking himself in an attempt to throw it off. Could it be influenza? Never having been ill in his life, he didn't know what influenza felt like.

What nonsense! How could the king's chief adviser, who was also in charge of Hel's public health system, be ill? Friftar gave himself another shake and concentrated on the fight below.

Plenty of fighting

'That wasn't bad,' said Ushan, 'but we'll have to try even harder.' Having just launched some fierce attacks, the trio were now confronting each other in the middle of the arena, breathing heavily.

'Even harder?' panted Urs. 'I've done my best to kill you, Ushan! Honestly, you've nothing left to reproach me for.'

'No, I haven't,' said Ushan, 'but this is when things get really serious. I'd like the two of you to do something for me.'

'Like what?' Rolv asked, out of breath. 'Go on fighting?'

'No, you must kill me.'

'What?!'

'You must kill me. They'll be herding those oldsters into the arena at any moment. Then it'll be too late and many will die. You must kill me now, at once! It's our friends' only hope.'

'They'll be herded in here come what may,' said Rolv. 'We should strike right away. The three of us must scale the wall to the royal box.'

'The Copper Killers would turn us into pincushions before we got there,' said Ushan. 'Kill me, I beg you!' he pleaded. 'Quick, or it'll be too late!'

'It's already too late,' said Urs, pointing to one of the gates with his sword.

Some Wolpertings were entering the arena, but they weren't frail or elderly, nor were there only six of them. They were young, strong and armed to the teeth, and scores of them were streaming in through the gates. Rolv caught sight of his friends Balla of Betaville, Vasko of the Dunes and Olek of the Red Forest; Urs spotted the triplets from his lodgings and Ushan many of his pupils from the fencing school.

The last to enter the arena was Rumo.

A murmur ran round the auditorium. Hellings and Homunculi sprang to their feet, Friftar stared motionless at the crowd, Gornab screamed and the Copper Killers reached for their crossbows. Rumo ran out into the middle of the arena, where Rolv, Ushan and Urs were still standing, astonished by the newcomers' sudden appearance.

'Rumo!' Urs exclaimed. 'Where have you been all this time?'

'I had things to do.'

'Did *you* release them all?' asked Ushan.

'I had some help,' Rumo replied.

'Where's Rala?' Rolv demanded. 'Why isn't she here?'

'Rala is dead.'

'Truly?'

'She was tortured to death by someone called General Ticktock. I hoped I'd find him here. Do you know someone by that name?'

Rolv burst into tears; the others shook their heads mutely.

'Where is she?' asked Rolv.

'Two friends of mine are guarding her body. We'll go and get her when we're finished here. Now we must fight.'

'Yes,' said Ushan DeLucca, 'now we must fight.'

Rumo held his sword in the air to give Krindle and Dandelion a panoramic view of the theatre. The soldiers among the audience had left their seats and were streaming towards the exits on their way to the arena.

'Good heavens!' said Dandelion.

'Man, oh man!' Krindle growled. **'This'll be more of a fight than I ever dreamt of!'**

The acoustic servo-mechanism

'That was the most touching story we've ever heard.'

'Yes – although we got over being touched by anything a long time ago.'

The third voice merely sobbed.

'All right, how about it?' asked Smyke. 'Will you help me? Will you show me the way to Rala's heart?'

'Very well, Smyke.'

'We'll help you.'

'On one condition.'

'Any condition, as long as it's in my power. What is it?'

'We'll tell you when the time comes.'

'But it might be anything.'

'Are you trying to haggle?'

'He's trying to haggle!'

'Let's get out of here and leave him to stew in his own juice!'

'All right, all right!' cried Smyke. 'I'll do whatever you want.'

'Good, because we never haggle. We've got over it.'

'We're used to people doing what we tell them.'

'We've got over self-criticism, too. We're infallible.'

Smyke sighed. 'Very well, let's go. Have you thought of a name for yourselves?'

'Yes. We want to be called the Non-Existent Teenies.'

'After all?'

'We've thought it over. Actually, it's a very good name. It's quite an apt description of us.'

'We're so small, we hardly exist any more.'

'The Non-Existent Teenies . . . Perfect!'

'I want to be called Non-Existent Teeny Number One.'

'I want to be called Non-Existent Teeny Number Two.'

'And I want to be called Non-Existent Teeny Number Three.'

'That's great,' Smyke said sarcastically. 'What do I do first?'

'You must activate the acoustic contentment servo-mechanism,' said Non-Existent Teeny Number One.

'You must purr,' said Non-Existent Teeny Number Two.

'And you must purr to our own high standards,' said Non-Existent Teeny Number Three.

'Hrrrmmm,' went Smyke. 'Hrrrmmm . . .'

'That's not purring,' said Non-Existent Teeny Number One.

'That's buzzing,' said Non-Existent Teeny Number Two.

'What do you think you are?' demanded Non-Existent Teeny Number Three. 'A bumblebee?'

Storming the walls

Rumo lowered his sword and the Wolpertings took this as a signal to storm the walls of the arena. They formed living ladders by climbing on each other's shoulders, using their swords and clasped paws as rungs, and dozens of them scaled the barrier within seconds. Panic broke out in the auditorium. A babble of cries went up as the spectators fought to reach the exits.

Rolv looked up at the Copper Killers. A few of them were already firing crossbow bolts into the arena, but the majority had been so taken aback by the Wolpertings' sudden appearance that they were still busy cocking their weapons.

'I'm going to nab the king,' said Rolv.

'I'll stay down here,' said Ushan. 'There's work to be done.'

The first soldiers were pouring through the gates and into the arena. They far outnumbered the Wolpertings and were armed to the teeth.

Rolv ran off, intent on clambering over the balustrade into the mad king's box.

The secret stairway

Friftar reacted swiftly. He had envisioned such an emergency a hundred times. A revolt was something any royal adviser had to allow for. First he had to calm the gibbering monkey at his side. He put out his hand. The king seized it and sank his teeth in it. Friftar endured the pain without turning a hair.

'Wath's to be node? Wath's to be node?' Gornab screamed. 'Wath now?'

'Never fear, Your Majesty, preparations have been made for such a contingency. After all, I've rehearsed the procedure with you more than once.'

'I've gorfotten it!' wailed Gornab.

'Close up!' Friftar commanded the royal bodyguards, who promptly formed a dense cordon in front of him and the king.

'I can well believe you've forgotten the whole thing, you crazy oaf!' thought Friftar, but he said, 'Your Majesty has been far too preoccupied with important affairs of state to memorise such a triviality, I know. First we open the throne.'

'We peno the threno?'

Friftar released the king's hand and stepped aside. He operated a lever and the throne divided into two halves that slid apart to reveal a stone slab. Then the slab itself slid sideways to reveal a flight of steps leading down into the bowels of the theatre.

'The spets! The spets!' screeched Gornab, clapping his hands.

'So Your Majesty does remember after all! I cannot decide on the next move without your approval.' Friftar held up a little roll of paper. 'May I issue a Vrahok Alert?'

Gornab gave a start. 'The Hokvras? Muts we?'

'I'm afraid so, Your Majesty. You've seen how well the Wolpertings fight. We must allow for all eventualities. One Vrahok will suffice, I think.'

'Wery vell, if it's avunoidable. Issue a Hokvra Aterl!'

'Many thanks, Your Majesty.' Friftar reached beneath the throne and brought out a small leaden cage. He opened the door, removed a struggling Kackerbat and inserted the roll of paper in a capsule attached to its leg. Friftar released the black creature, whereupon it unfurled its leathery wings, flapped wildly and soared into the air.

'Fly!' Gornab called after it. 'Fly to the Hokvras!'

His chief adviser took him by the hand again. 'May I, Your Majesty?' he asked.

They turned their backs on the mêlée in the arena and descended the secret staircase hand in hand. The stone slab closed over the entrance, the two halves of the throne slid together. Now that Friftar and Gornab had gone, the soldiers dispersed and went off to join the fray.

Yukobak's bright idea

Yukobak was still hiding in the theatre's maze of stairways. In his estimation he had lately displayed courage of the highest order, but he didn't feel called upon to join the fighting in the arena. Unlike Ribble, he had never learnt to wield a weapon.

Yukobak thought hard. His greatest asset was his knowledge of the theatre's layout. How could he exploit that knowledge for the rebels' benefit?

Whee!

He'd just had an idea so frightening that he instantly suppressed it, thrust it back into his brain like a jack-in-the-box that had popped out uninvited – an idea of positively Gornabian dimensions! What madness! Forget it!

And yet . . . It was crazy, but it would make a tremendous impression. No! *Far* too risky! He himself would probably be its first victim.

But then he thought involuntarily of Ribble. Ribble had taken on the dangerous task of protecting the Wolpertings without a moment's hesitation, whereas he, Yukobak, was cowering in the darkness and shirking his responsibilities.

He submitted his idea to further examination. Yes, it was utterly hare-brained, risky and unpredictable. He drew a deep breath. Then he made his way down to the cellar where the wild beasts were kept.

The White Fire

By the time Rolv vaulted over the balustrade of the royal box the mad monarch and his chief adviser had vanished. Instead, he found himself confronted by a detachment of crack troops: two dozen of Hel's finest warriors and all of them itching for a fight.

Rolv had prepared himself for this moment again and again in recent days, rehearsing it umpteen times in his head: he would climb into the box, take the king hostage and compel him to release Rala.

It was only now that he truly grasped the fact that there was no Rala to rescue. There wasn't even a king to take his revenge on, just two dozen black-uniformed soldiers who drew their swords and advanced on him. A wall of white fire blazed up in front of Rolv. The whole box burst into flames, but it was strange: the flames weren't hot, they were cold. They didn't burn him, they filled him with ice-cold rage.

Those of the audience who could see what followed hurriedly looked away, and those who were unable to avert their gaze became witnesses of a relentless massacre. Not only quicker but more ferocious and implacable than any of his foes, Rolv was everywhere at once. He was equipped with a whole arsenal of weapons and he used every last one including his teeth. Swords snapped, breastplates splintered, severed limbs went flying and heart-rending screams rang out wherever he turned. Rolv was in the midst of the White Fire, and this time it burned longer and more brightly than usual.

When Urs climbed into the box the royal bodyguard had ceased to exist. All he could do was hold Rolv tight. 'You can stop now,' he told him. 'They're all dead.'

Krindle enjoys himself at last

Rumo was fighting in the arena back to back with Ushan DeLucca.

'Ssst, ssst, ssst!' the fencing master hissed again and again as his blade darted among the soldiers who were falling around him like dismembered puppets.

'Do you know what I like best about this place, Rumo?' he shouted.

'No!' Rumo called back.

'The fact that there's no weather!'

Rumo made no comment. He was too busy to discuss the weather.

'A fight!' Krindle growled now and then. **'A fight at last!'**

'Look out! Behind you!' cried Dandelion, and Rumo spun round in time to parry a blow from an axe.

'Grim Reaper!' Krindle commanded, and Rumo felled the axe-wielding soldier with the stroke indicated.

'I owe you an apology,' Ushan called.

'Eh? What for?'

'I underestimated you, my boy.'

'Watch your left!' cried Dandelion. *'A sword stroke! Duck!'*

Rumo ducked and the blade passed over his head.

'Counter!' ordered Krindle. **'Two-Handed Slice!'**

Rumo performed a downward two-handed slice that cleft the swordsman's helmet in two.

'They're giving ground,' Dandelion remarked.

'So soon?' Krindle was disappointed.

It was true: the theatre guards' attack was losing momentum. They had grasped that the Wolpertings were unimpressed by their numerical superiority. The arena was littered with soldiers' corpses, whereas most of the Wolpertings were still standing. They turned and fled back into the bowels of the theatre.

Rumo looked up at the auditorium.

Panic-stricken members of the public were screaming, blocking the exits, falling over and trampling each other. The Wolpertings had infiltrated them like a swarm of angry bees, omnipresent and dangerous. Spreading out across the rows of seats, they attacked the soldiers and terrified the spectators by their mere presence. The Hellings, who were the most panic-stricken of all, pushed and jostled and trampled their own kind to death. Never having been so close to a fight before, they now, for the first time, got some idea of what it was like to fear for one's life.

The Copper Killers didn't know where to aim, the Wolpertings were darting around so swiftly among the milling spectators. Although they occasionally fired at random into the crowd, they hit more allies than enemies.

Rumo wiped his sword on a dead soldier's cloak. This wasn't victory; it was only the start of a battle. The Theatre of Death had been shaken to its foundations, but Rumo was determined to go on shaking until Hel itself caved in. He would do so for Rala's sake.

Smyke stopped purring. The electrical hum died away, the submarine

Inside the heart

came to a halt.

'Are we there?' he asked.

'No,' said Non-Existent Teeny Number One.

'We're inside the heart, though,' said Non-Existent Teeny Number Two.

'So why have we stopped?'

'We thought we heard something.'

'In here? Everything's dead.'

'Yes, we were probably mistaken.'

'I thought you were infallible.'

'Yes, that's the worrying thing. If we think we heard something, we heard something.'

'But we can't hear it any more.'

'Good, then we can go on,' said Smyke.

'One moment,' said Non-Existent Teeny Number One.

'There's an important decision to be made,' said Non-Existent Teeny Number Two. 'One we must leave to you.'

'It's a matter of life or death.'

'I know,' said Smyke. 'Rala's life is at stake.'

'Not only hers.'

'What do you mean?'

'Your life is also at stake now.'

'How so? Is something wrong?'

'We've noticed that our propellers are finding it harder and harder to turn.'

'It's the coagulation.'

'The more the blood congeals the harder it gets.'

'Meaning what?'

'Meaning that we'll make it to our destination and make it back as well, *if* the operation succeeds, because then the plasma will thin again. If the operation fails and the blood solidifies we won't be able to budge an inch. This submarine will become your coffin, imprisoned in clotted blood.'

Smyke gave an involuntary gulp.

'At this stage we could still make it back.'

'We only wanted to tell you.'

'It's up to you. We can still turn round.'

Smyke deliberated. 'What, in your estimation, are the chances of the operation succeeding?'

'The same as in any risky venture: fifty-fifty.'

'You mean it's a gamble?'

'You could put it that way.'

'Let's gamble, then.'

'As you wish, Smyke. Would you please start purring again?'

An excellent motto

The spectators' screams, the clash of swords and cries of pain drifting over from the Theatre of Death had convinced Ribble and the older Wolpertings that Rumo's rescue attempt had been crowned with success. Having overpowered the soldiers and appropriated their weapons, they were now standing around irresolutely.

'They're hard at it,' said Ribble. 'Can you hear that din?'

'Better than you can, probably,' said Mayor Jowly of Gloomberg. 'We're Wolpertings. Old we may be, but we aren't hard of hearing.'

'What ought we to do?'

'Go over there and join in,' said the mayor.

'But Rumo said to stay here.'

'We were unarmed when he said that. Things have changed.'

Jowly turned to the other Wolpertings.

'What do you think, my friends? Are we too old to fight?'

'Of course we are,' said Oga of Dullsgard, brandishing a club, 'so let's go before we die of senile decay.'

'What do *you* think?' Jowly asked Ribble.

The Homunculus raised his spear.

'We're as good as dead,' he said, 'but they haven't buried us yet.'

'An excellent motto,' said the mayor. 'Is it yours?'

'No,' Ribble replied, 'I got it from a good friend of mine.'

The wild beasts

'I'm as good as dead,' thought Yukobak, 'but they haven't buried me yet.'

What had prompted his idea of releasing some wild beasts into the Theatre of Death, common sense or insanity? Even if one simply discounted that question, another two considerably more practical questions remained: Which wild beasts should he release and how many?

Yukobak had seen a dozen doors. It would be far too risky to open them all, of that he was sure. He decided to leave it at three. Three exotic and unpredictable creatures should be enough to create chaos.

So which doors should he open? He had a vivid recollection of the cell containing the ruby-red spider. Although he dreaded releasing such a monster, it had to be. The rest he would leave to chance. He would fling open two doors at random and run like the wind!

Heart pounding, Yukobak stole up to the door beyond which lurked the giant spider. Was it asleep? Was it awake? Was it only waiting for the person who had recently appeared in the doorway to be stupid enough to do so a second time?

He drew a deep breath.

Then, resolutely, he drew the big, rusty bolt and wrenched the door open. Without looking inside he hurried on to the adjacent cell. Its evil-smelling occupant greeted him with a bestial snarl, but he was already opening the door after next. Then he sprinted to the stairs, ran up them a little way and turned to see what he had done.

The huge spider had already emerged from its cell. It revolved on the spot and flapped its mothlike wings, clearly trying to get its bearings in these new surroundings.

Behind it the neighbouring cell disgorged an albino rat the size of a crocodile with red claws and a long red tail. The blind creature had white, yard-long antennae sprouting from the places in its head where a normal rat's eyes would have been. It emitted an angry snarl, bared its yellow, sickle-shaped teeth and cracked its tail like a whip.

From the third door emerged a Crystalloscorpion, a denizen of the Fridgicaves. An immense insect fifteen or twenty feet long, it was altogether transparent, with a body that seemed to consist entirely of razor-sharp edges and corners. Yukobak had heard of this life form in his biology lessons. Mere contact with its icy exterior could inflict injuries which, paradoxically, resembled third-degree burns. The scorpion sliced the air with its claws and raised its glassy sting, which could inject a venom that turned its victims to ice within seconds.

Three of Netherworld's most dangerous creatures, and Yukobak had unleashed them! As if mesmerised, he continued to stand watching them from the stairs. The giant spider had completed its inspection. It flexed its legs and its ruby-red fur bristled. Then, wildly flapping its mothlike wings, it rose into the air.

Yukobak awoke from his stupor. The fearsome insect was fluttering straight for him with its legs dangling. It had obviously decided that, of all the creatures in its vicinity, the little two-legged Helling would be the easiest to encase in a cocoon.

Yukobak bounded up the stairs three at a time.

Gornab's refuge

Gornab, crouching in one corner of the crudely constructed cell, stared at Friftar in dismay. His chief adviser had conducted him to a chamber beneath the theatre that didn't officially exist. Its door was indistinguishable from the brick wall of the passage outside and Friftar had personally poisoned the labourers who had built it.

The terrified king had abandoned his airs and graces and placed himself in Friftar's hands. It had never occurred to him that there might be a rebellion, still less that he might lose his throne. Events had overtaken him so suddenly that he now resembled a helpless, frightened child.

'Your Majesty will be absolutely safe here no matter what happens,'

Friftar said soothingly. 'This chamber's existence is unknown to anyone but the two of us. The food and medicines stored here will last for weeks. All has been prepared for your comfort and convenience.'

He pointed to a table laden with fruit and cheese, bread and wine.

'But why are they hebaving like tish?' wailed Gornab. 'It's borfidden, surely?'

'Yes, such behaviour in the Theatre of Death is forbidden - and believe me, Your Majesty, we shall punish all who have dared to take up arms against you.'

'Yes, nupish them!' Gornab demanded. 'Nupish them uncermifully!'

'We will, Your Majesty, unmercifully and without exception. I must now go upstairs to see that all is well, but I shall report on the situation in due course. Perhaps you would care to sleep for a while - it would refresh you. You'll find medicines and wine on the table.'

'Doog idea,' said Gornab, waddling over to the table with the drugs on it. 'A leesp will do me doog.'

'In that case, I wish you sweet dreams. Doubtless all will be back to normal by the time you wake up refreshed.'

Friftar pressed the brick that opened the secret door. He went out and closed it behind him. For one brief, titillating moment he toyed with the idea of leaving the moronic dwarf to rot in there. He could simply wedge the door shut and bury him alive. It was an attractive notion, except that, because he was the last person to have been seen in the king's company, suspicion would immediately fall on him.

He drew a deep breath. Gornab was safe. Now to regain control of those Wolpertings. How had they managed to escape from their cells? And where had that confounded General Ticktock got to, just when he was needed most?

General Ticktock's grief

General Ticktock's grief had steadily intensified. It was devouring him like a vulture, tearing at his vitals again and again. He would never have thought himself capable of such an emotion. He didn't know how long he'd spent in the weaponsmith's workshop, disembowelling himself with the diamond-toothed pliers in his search for the mysterious something deep inside that was causing him so much pain. He had cut open his armour-plated chest, broken his steel ribs and destroyed many a lethal mechanism hidden within him, but all to no avail. The thing he sought seemed as nimble, as clever and cunning, as Rala had been. It was like an elusive, intangible, mocking will-o'-the-wisp.

At last he abandoned his quest. Hurling the pliers away, he uttered a bellow of rage. Rage – yes, rage was all he had left. He yearned to fight. He yearned to destroy. He yearned to kill. General Ticktock set off for the Theatre of Death. This was a dark day and he would do his utmost to ensure that it ended on an even darker note.

In the heart of the heart

The subcutaneous submarine had stopped again.

'Where are we?' asked Smyke.

'We're there,' said Non-Existent Teeny Number One.

'We've penetrated the aorta. We're in the heart of the heart,' said Non-Existent Teeny Number Two.

'Normally, this is where the life of life goes on,' said Non-Existent Teeny Number Three. 'At the moment, though, nothing at all is going on.'

'I've never seen a deader heart.'

'Someone has really done a job on it.'

'Yes, someone who was trying to improve on death.'

'And he succeeded.'

'So what do we do now?' asked Smyke.

'Now comes the precision work.'

'We're looking for the connectors. Six microscopically small connectors.'

'An amalorican adaptor.'

'A hallucinogenic synapse.'

'An opabiniatic membrane.'

'A nabokovian knob.'

'An epithalamian egress.'

'And an odontoid tube!'

'I see,' said Smyke. 'And you plug your instruments into them, do you?'

'Exactly. The auratic instruments of the Non-Existent Teenies. The world's smallest but most effective surgical instruments.'

'And what happens then?' Smyke asked.

'First we must find the connectors. That's difficult enough – they're even smaller than we are.'

'Can you imagine that?'

'No, you can't.'

Smyke sighed.

'If we find them – which isn't a foregone conclusion – we administer an auratic shock. Then you'd better cross your fingers.'

'But now you must do a bit more purring.'

'By all means. To boost the submarine's power supply, or something?'

'No.'

'To shut you up.'

'We need to concentrate.'

The ruby-red monster

The theatre was emptying rapidly. The rows of seats were still occupied by panic-stricken members of the public, but someone had obviously ordered the soldiers to clear the auditorium.

Rolv and Urs had rejoined Rumo and Ushan DeLucca in the arena, together with Olek of the Dunes, Vasko of the Red Forest and Balla of Betaville. They were trying to work out a communal plan of action.

'Sooner or later those galleries will empty,' said Ushan. 'All they need do then is seal the exits and those crossbowmen will be able to mow us down. We must get out of here.'

Olek of the Dunes was busy potting soldiers with his sling. 'We ought to climb up into their gallery,' he said between two shots. 'Wipe them out and we've won.'

'They can't be wiped out,' Urs objected. 'They're made of metal. It'd be suicide.'

A sudden cry rang through the theatre. It sounded even more frantic and terrified than the shouts from the rows of seats overhead.

Yukobak came running into the arena, screeching and waving his arms.

'Help!' he shouted. 'Rumo! Help me!'

The Wolpertings, the soldiers, the Copper Killers – all stopped short. Their attention had abruptly been claimed by a monster that came scuttling through the gate behind him on long, agile legs.

On seeing all the creatures around it, the giant spider came to a halt and turned on the spot. Its wings were quivering excitedly.

Yukobak dashed up to Rumo and his companions, panting hard.

'This is Yukobak,' said Rumo. 'He helped me to release the prisoners.'

'Delighted to make your acquaintance,' Ushan said with a courteous bow. 'But tell me, Yukobak, what's this you've brought with you?' Nonchalantly, he pointed his sword at the monster, whose jaws were dripping with purulent saliva.

'It's a spider,' said Yukobak, sheltering behind Rumo's back. 'A huge spider with wings. Some idiot must have let it out, no idea who.'

The black giants

Ribble was marching to the Theatre of Death with his small but determined band of elderly Wolpertings. Suddenly, as they rounded a corner, they found their way barred by a phalanx of unfamiliar figures.

Ribble had never seen their like in Hel before. Immensely tall, they were cowled and swathed from head to foot in black cloaks. There must have been hundreds of them, all armed with absurdly large weapons including axes, swords and nail-studded clubs, and the mouldy smell they gave off was reminiscent of an exhumed coffin. Ribble and the Wolpertings prepared to fight.

The leader of the strange warriors, a gigantic fellow carrying an even more gigantic scythe, raised his arm. 'Hey, you dogs!' he called in a deep, booming voice. 'Are you Wolpertings? If so, you must surely know where we can find that idiot Rumo.'

'You're looking for Rumo?' asked Jowly. He stepped forward and gripped the hilt of his sword, ready to do battle. 'What do you want with him?'

'We want to help him,' boomed the black giant. 'If I know him he's in trouble.'

Ribble joined the mayor. 'We're also on our way to help him. Who are you?'

'We're the Dead Yetis,' the giant growled and threw back his cowl to reveal the black death's-head beneath.

Ribble and the Wolpertings retreated a step.

'Don't be alarmed,' said the giant. 'We're not quite as dead as we look. My name is Skullop – Skullop the Scyther. I'm here because something occurred to me.'

'What would that be, Skullop the, er, Scyther?' asked Jowly.

'None of your business,' Skullop replied. 'I can only tell Rumo that. Well, how about it? Do you know where I can find him?'

'Can you fight?' asked Ribble.

Skullop turned to his warriors.

'What do you think, men? Can we fight?'

'No!' shouted a Yeti in the rear rank.

Ticktock funks a farewell

The time seemed ripe for General Ticktock's attempt to anaesthetise his pain with rage and drown his sorrow in blood, for Hel was in utter chaos. The nearer he got to the Theatre of Death, the more numerous the wounded, screaming, panic-stricken citizens and soldiers he encountered.

Ticktock didn't care if the city went up in flames, if Gornab devoured Friftar or the whole of Netherworld went to rack and ruin. Any suffering that distracted him from his own was a source of satisfaction.

First he needed some weapons – better ones than were concealed in his armour-plated body. He needed the huge weapons he had commissioned to meet his personal requirements. General Ticktock headed for his tower.

What a difference a few hours could make! When he had set off for the weaponsmith's workshop Hel was still wrapped in slumber, but now pandemonium reigned. Excellent! The sound of fighting was coming from the Theatre of Death and it wasn't the usual clatter of a dozen swords; it was the genuine din of battle!

General Ticktock entered the tower. He armed himself with the huge black axe and massive sword that had been forged for him from Netherworld ore. His favourite weapons. None of your technological falderals, just plain, razor-sharp metal. No better instruments of death existed.

He paused for a moment. Should he go upstairs for one last look at Rala in the Metal Maiden? He hadn't even bidden her farewell.

An unwelcome intruder

'We've got some news for you, Smyke,' said Non-Existent Teeny Number One.

'Good news and bad news,' said Non-Existent Teeny Number Two.

'Eh, what?' Smyke had almost dozed off, lulled to sleep by his own purring and the subcutaneous submarine's electrical hum.

'First the good news: We've found the connectors.'

'Really? That's great! Let's get started, then.'

'One moment! Now comes the bad news: The connectors are being guarded.'

'Guarded?' Smyke said drowsily, stretching.

'Look through the membrane.'

Smyke rubbed his eyes and peered through the glassy membrane. What he saw outside jolted him awake at last.

'What on earth is *that?*' he exclaimed.

'That's just what *we* were wondering,' remarked Non-Existent Teeny Number One.

'But before we could work out what it was, it looked different,' said Non-Existent Teeny Number Two.

'It keeps on changing shape and colour,' said Non-Existent Teeny Number Three. 'It's incomprehensible.'

'Incomprehensible' was a perfectly apt description of the creature that was floating outside in Rala's motionless bloodstream. It was forever changing its hideous appearance and unattractive coloration, and from inside it came a series of clicks like those made by a dislocated joint.

'What is it?' Smyke asked dully.

'We're still working on an answer to that question,' said Non-Existent Teeny Number One.

The peculiar organism changed colour again, emitted another click and exuded a cloud of black slime.

'That's the sound we heard earlier – we really are infallible. So life exists in this dead world after all.'

'We suspect it's a disease. The disease that wrought all this havoc.'

'A disease?' said Smyke. 'What's a disease doing in a dead body?'

Tykhon's little surprise

The fearsome apparition Smyke saw through the membrane was a surprise originally intended not for him, but for General Ticktock. Rala's congealing blood contained the treacherous little special ingredient which Tykhon Zyphos had added to his Subcutaneous Suicide Squad: a last-ditch rearguard.

When the alchemist's work on the Subcutaneous Suicide Squad was already far advanced he'd had a flash of inspiration. 'If I'm creating a disease of the utmost virulence,' Tykhon had told himself, 'why shouldn't I equip it with all the trimmings?'

The disease was already virulent enough to be rated the worst disease in existence: it was painful, lethal, exceptionally infectious and incurable. All it couldn't do was something no disease had ever managed to do: remain infectious after it had left a body.

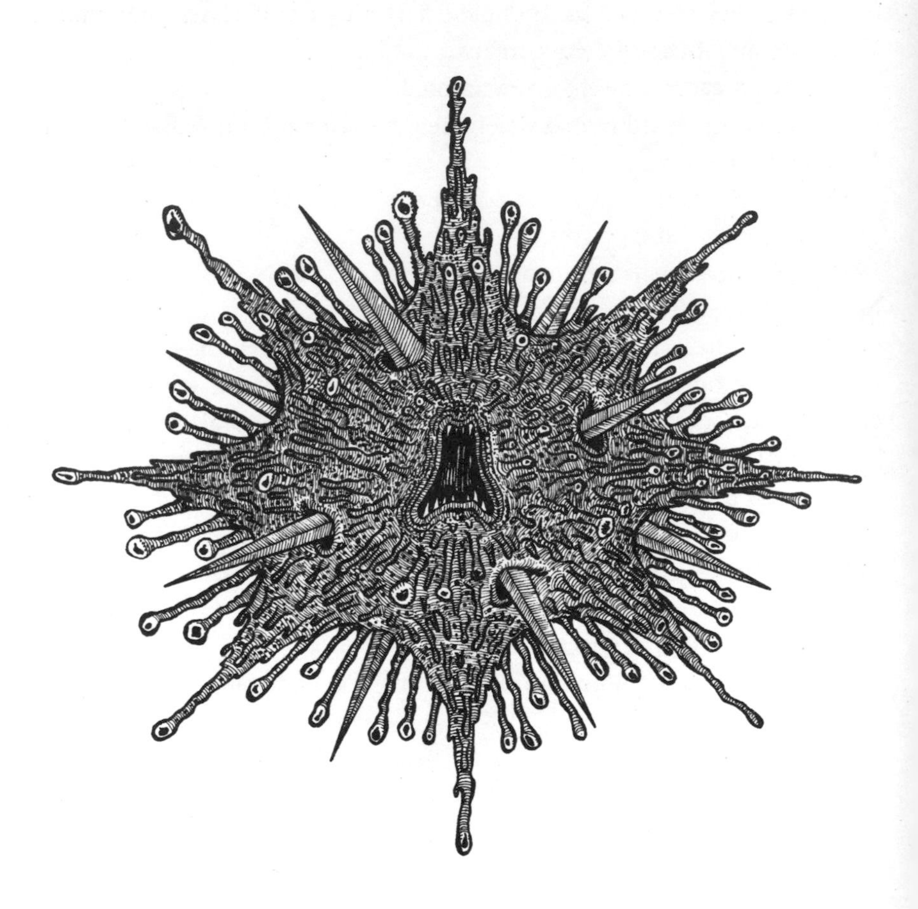

Tykhon, who had long ago come to regard his creation as a sort of commando unit, had dreamt up a special refinement: a rearguard to be left behind in the victim's body just in case someone tried to resuscitate it. In devising the Subcutaneous Suicide Squad he had created a unique disease – one that could defend the havoc it had wrought once the job was done.

'Smyke?' called Non-Existent Teeny Number One.

'Are you all right, Smyke?' asked Non-Existent Teeny Number Two.

Smyke eyed the strange, clicking creature as if it were an evil spirit.

What was it capable of? Could it really prevent the operation? It looked capable of anything, he had to admit – capable of changing shape to suit any requirement in this microscopic world. It looked invincible. It was the new ruler of Rala's body.

'What do we do now?' Smyke asked.

'Listen, Smyke,' said Non-Existent Teeny Number One. 'Now comes the really unpleasant part.'

'What's that?'

'You must get out and kill that thing.'

'Eh? You're joking!'

'No, Smyke, we never joke. We got over our sense of humour a long time ago, as you know.'

'It's just not on. I can't.'

'Don't you remember our agreement?' asked Non-Existent Teeny Number Two.

'What agreement?'

'Forgotten already?' said Non-Existent Teeny Number Three. 'You said you'd do whatever we wanted.'

'Yes, I remember.'

'And you know what, Smyke?'

'No, what?'

'We won't even ask you to do us this favour.'

'No?'

'No, there's no need.'

'You're going to do it anyway.'

'You'll have to get out and kill that thing. It's your only hope of survival.'

The torture chamber

General Ticktock lumbered over to the stairs and laid his weapons down on the bottom step. Up there was the Metal Maiden with Rala's dead body inside it . . . He put his foot on the bottom step. His life's work and his great love – yes, he must bid them farewell.

He mounted the second step. His greatest triumph and his only love, both destroyed by his own hands. The pain in his vitals had started to throb again.

Rala, Rala, Rala, it went.

He continued to climb the stairs. The pain became more unbearable with every step. Death, which the Metal Maiden was supposed to overcome, had triumphed after all. It was more unfathomable and unpredictable than ever. This was his greatest defeat.

Rala, Rala, Rala . . .

He reached the torture chamber. The door was ajar. He had only to push it open and he would see her in the relentless embrace of Tykhon Zyphos's disease. Who could tell what she looked like now? He remembered the alchemist's own terrible death, his rapid decomposition.

He gripped the doorhandle – and pulled it shut. No, the sight of Rala would be too much for him. Never again. He would come back later and burn the tower to the ground. First there was killing to be done.

General Ticktock turned and went downstairs again. Retrieving his weapons, he went over to the secret passage that led to the Theatre of Death. He would show Friftar and his crazy king what a real fight looked like. Better still, he would teach them the meaning of war.

The spider

'Did *you* do this?' Rumo asked Yukobak, so quietly that the others couldn't hear. 'Did *you* let that monster out?'

'No,' Yukobak whispered back, 'I let *three* monsters out.'

The spider was still turning on its spindly legs and fluttering its mothlike wings, seemingly unable to decide which of these countless titbits to devote its attention to. All the Wolpertings had levelled their weapons at it, but none of them dared to attack. Even Olek, who was slowly swinging his sling, hesitated.

Up in their gallery the Copper Killers also seemed to be waiting. Why bother to open fire when this monster might do the job for them and devour a few Wolpertings? For the moment the spider seemed to be the new master of the Theatre of Death.

All at once it began to flap its great wings. Dust swirled in all directions as it rose into the air with a ferocious hiss and fluttered across the arena, high above the heads of Rumo, Yukobak, Ushan, Rolv and his friends. It made straight for the spectators' seats, circled once and swooped on a knot of shoving, jostling Hellings near one of the exits.

'It seems to be on our side,' said Yukobak, averting his eyes. 'For the moment, at least.'

The Copper Killers fired another volley of crossbow bolts into the arena, and it was all the Wolpertings could do to protect themselves with the shields and armour they'd taken from the dead. The theatre guards continued to hold the arena gates but made no immediate move to resume the attack.

'Our best bet is to break out and fight on outside the theatre,' Ushan shouted again.

'The spectators' exits are still choked,' Urs called back, 'and the gates are blockaded. We can't get out of the arena – we're trapped!'

'Then all we can do is wait for a miracle,' said Yukobak.

They all took cover as another volley of crossbow bolts came raining down on them.

Yetis and Wolpertings

Ribble had led the Wolpertings and Yetis into the sewer system beneath the Theatre of Death. Muffled sounds of fighting could be heard even down there, and the screams of the dying sent ghostly echoes speeding along the maze of tunnels. The stench beneath the theatre was appalling. Everything was dumped into the sewers, not only the spectators' rubbish and the dung of the wild beasts, but also dead bodies. Gnawed skeletons were lying everywhere and many of the streams through which the warriors waded were red with blood. Kackerbats and other carrion eaters scuttled between their legs as they marched along.

'You said you'd take us to a theatre,' growled Skullop the Scyther, who was leading the little army with Ribble and Mayor Jowly, 'and we're wading through a cesspit.'

'"Come on, we're going to Hell!" – that's what Skullop told us!' cried one of the Yetis behind them. 'Another of his crazy ideas!'

The other Yetis laughed derisively.

'They don't mean it,' Skullop growled. 'They're really having a whale of a time.'

'It's not much further,' Ribble told him. 'The shafts leading up into the theatre are just round the next bend. We can climb up into any row of seats we like.'

'Let's go right to the top, then,' said Skullop. 'We'll be able to see everything from there.'

'But that's where the Copper Killers are.'

'The Copper Killers? Who are they?'

'The most fearsome warriors in Hel.'

'Huh,' said Skullop. 'You're scaring me.'

'The Copper Killers are really dangerous,' Ribble insisted. 'They're reputed to be immortal.'

'Well?' said Skullop. 'So are we. Reputedly.'

Some of the Yetis laughed.

'You really mean to take them on?' asked Ribble.

'You heard, little 'un,' Skullop growled. 'I'm renowned for my good ideas.'

The Crystalloscorpion

When General Ticktock emerged from his secret passage into one of the theatre's underground corridors, axe and sword in hand, he was confronted by a creature at least as weird-looking as himself. It was an enormous scorpion with huge claws and a sting raised to strike. Its truly extraordinary feature wasn't its vast size, however, but the fact that its body was as transparent as polished crystal.

'What on earth is a [tick] Crystalloscorpion doing down here?' General Ticktock asked himself. 'The place must really be [tock] in chaos if they let the most dangerous wild beasts run around loose.' He took a step towards the monster.

Without a moment's hesitation the scorpion lashed out at Ticktock with its icy sting, which simply bounced off his metal exterior. The monster recoiled in astonishment; the general didn't budge an inch.

'You're a dangerous [tick] and very beautiful creature,' Ticktock said approvingly, 'but you've picked on [tock] the wrong opponent. To be precise [tick], you couldn't have picked on a worse opponent in the whole of Hel. Go and find yourself [tock] another one before you make a real enemy of me.'

He brandished his sword like someone shooing away a troublesome insect. Quick as a flash, the scorpion fastened one of its claws on Ticktock's arm. There was a loud clang as crystal met metal.

Sighing, Ticktock severed the scorpion's claw from its body with one mighty blow of his axe and sent it crashing to the flagstones. A moment later his sword came down plumb on the scorpion's head. With a sound like breaking glass the monster disintegrated and fell to the ground in smithereens. General Ticktock strode heedlessly over its remains, which crunched beneath his feet like crushed ice.

'What on earth's [tick] the matter with me?' the general said to himself. 'Expecting a creature made of crystal [tock] to listen to reason is as futile [tick] as looking for a heart in my metal body.'

On reaching the top of the theatre he encountered another annoying creature, the slimy individual named Friftar, who stood between him and the king. He resisted the impulse to kill him on the spot.

Friftar stared at the general with his mouth open, astonished to see his chest torn open and his metal ribs bent outwards, but he asked no questions and informed him of the Wolpertings' revolt. Ticktock greeted the news as imperturbably as if Friftar had asked what he'd had for breakfast.

'I see,' said Ticktock. 'A rebellion [tick]. I shall crush it [tock]. Anything else?'

'No, no,' Friftar said with a smile, 'that's all. Just a little rebellion.'

'Off you go!' Ticktock barked at him. 'Off you go [tick] and hide with your king [tock] until it's all over!'

'Very good,' Friftar replied obsequiously and hurried off.

So the Wolpertings had rebelled. No serious cause for concern. He himself was worth a whole army. He could crush a revolt by a couple of hundred rampaging slaves on his own, without the aid of his Copper Killers.

He had a job to do. Good! A job that required him to kill. All the better! His body had steadily grown since his arrival in Hel, becoming ever stronger, ever more deadly and invulnerable. In addition, he was suffering from grief and despair. If transmuted into rage and directed against the enemy, those were weapons of inestimable value. Hel was about to witness an orgy of death and destruction unprecedented in the history of Netherworld.

Friftar plans a show trial

Although he couldn't account for either of them, Friftar felt that Ticktock's appearance and the state of affairs inside his mysterious tower were connected in some way. The general had resembled a gutted chicken, but it didn't seem to have done him much harm. On the contrary, it made him look more dangerous still, like a wild beast whose wounds had increased its unpredictability.

Friftar recapitulated: the king was in a safe place, the Vrahok Alert had been issued, the Wolpertings were trapped, and General Ticktock had returned to restore order. Everything seemed to be returning to normal. In his mind's eye he was already organising a show trial destined to be one of the most magnificent productions he had ever staged at the Theatre of Death.

If only it weren't for this numb sensation in his bones. Sometimes he felt cold, sometimes hot and sometimes unaccountably queasy. Whenever the pandemonium subsided, which it very seldom did, Friftar seemed to hear a series of faint, rhythmical clicks inside his head. He shook himself and reapplied his mind to the present situation. He must find himself a secret vantage point from which to watch General Ticktock's performance in the arena. His one regret was that the greatest fight ever staged at the Theatre of Death would take place before an almost non-existent audience.

Smyke's unsavoury past

The rearguard of the Subcutaneous Suicide Squad rotated on the spot, emitting clouds of little black bubbles. Smyke turned away in disgust.

'Why me?' he yelled at the walls of the subcutaneous submarine. 'Why do I always wind up in situations like this? What have I done to deserve it?'

'You aren't asking us because you expect an answer, are you?' Non-Existent Teeny Number One retorted.

Smyke was surprised by his arch tone of voice. 'What do you mean?' he demanded.

'We know everything, Smyke.'

'Meaning what?'

'Meaning everything. Everything about you.'

'About me? What is there to know about me?'

'You really want an example?'

'Yes, now you've aroused my curiosity.'

'Well, for one thing, we know you used to referee the Fangfangs' professional boxing matches and were a military adviser during the Norselanders' guerrilla wars.'

'You were also an officially licensed second at duels between Florinthian aristocrats and a timekeeper at the Wolpertings' chess tournaments in Betaville.'

'Not to mention an organiser of cockfights, the treasurer of the Zamonian Vermiluct, a cheerleader at the Midgardian Dwarf Jousts and a croupier at Fort Una.'

Smyke gave a puzzled laugh. 'Hey, you really do know a lot about me. Can you read people's thoughts?'

'Of course we can, Smyke. That's why we also know what you're hiding in your Chamber of Memories – what's concealed beneath that black cloth.'

Smyke broke out in a sweat. He'd never told anyone about the Chamber of Memories, not even Rumo.

'We've known all about you ever since you set foot in our submarine. Nobody's allowed to board it unless they've been thoroughly screened.'

'We're suspicious by nature, Smyke.'

'We got over trusting people a long time ago.'

'What do you know about the Chamber of Memories?' Smyke demanded earnestly.

'We know, for instance, what's under the cloth,' said Non-Existent Teeny Number One.

'It's a picture,' said Non-Existent Teeny Number Two.

'It's a picture of Lindworm Castle, isn't it, Smyke?' said Non-Existent Teeny Number Three.

Smyke drew a deep breath. He didn't reply.

'What's the matter, Smyke, run out of glib answers?'

'I don't know what you're talking about,' Smyke said half-heartedly.

'You were there. You were there in Lindworm Castle.'

'What's more, Smyke, you changed its appearance for ever.'

'It was you that stained Lindworm Castle red.'

'That's not true!' Smyke exclaimed. 'Nobody knows–'

'Yes, nobody but you knows that you were the leader of the Smarmies who organised the peaceful siege of Lindworm Castle, so-called.'

'A splendid plan, Smyke. Truly brilliant.'

'You used to own the tavern patronised by all the mercenaries who had besieged the castle in vain. You were the one who pretended to want to publish the Lindworms' poems.'

'You captured Lindworm Castle.'

'Congratulations. A strategic masterstroke.'

'What gives you the right to pry around in my memories?'

'Come, Smyke, do you really think we'd perform such a complicated operation with the aid of someone we didn't have a hold over?'

'Someone with a clear conscience?'

'We don't need someone heroic for a job like this.'

'Only someone desperate.'

Smyke felt breathless. Was it only his imagination, or was the air on board running out?

'Admit it, Smyke.'

'*You* stained Lindworm Castle red.'

'Red with blood.'

'So much blood that only blood may be able to wash it off.'

'You ought to take a bath, Smyke.'

'A bath in Rala's blood.'

The curse of Lindworm Castle

Smyke didn't answer for a long time. Nothing could be heard but his heavy breathing. The Non-Existent Teenies said nothing either.

'I was a different person in those days,' Smyke said at last. 'I was young. I made mistakes and I paid for them. I paid for them on Roaming Rock.'

'That's not good enough, Smyke, or you wouldn't be here now.'

'You attract misfortune the way a magnet attracts iron filings.'

'There's a curse on you, Smyke. The curse of Lindworm Castle.'

'What shall I do?' Smyke asked desperately.

'That's the right question for once,' said Non-Existent Teeny Number One.

'You've hit the nail on the head,' said Non-Existent Teeny Number Two. 'You must do something.'

'You must fight,' said Non-Existent Teeny Number Three. 'For the first time in your life you yourself must fight instead of getting other people to do it for you.'

When Ribble reached the Copper Killers' gallery with the Wolpertings and Yetis, Skullop the Scyther assumed command.

'You and the Wolpertings take a back seat for the moment,' Skullop whispered. 'We'll be going at it hammer and tongs in a minute. Just relax and watch the fun.'

Silently, he gave the signal to attack. The Copper Killers, who were busy shooting at the Wolpertings, were caught unawares when the Yetis attacked them from the rear, but they swiftly drew their side arms and concentrated on the new enemy. What followed was the most ferocious fight the Theatre of Death had ever witnessed. Clubs, swords, huge iron hammers, scythes and axes crashed together, striking showers of sparks that lit up the auditorium.

Ribble, Mayor Jowly and the other Wolpertings stood aside and watched the battle, half mesmerised, half fascinated. The Copper Killers' gallery resembled an ironworks. Metal clanged against metal, steel splinters flew, and the warriors grunted with exertion as they fought with might and main. Had Ribble or one of the others got in the way, they would have been crushed like beetles.

The Homunculus saw three Yetis corner a Copper Killer and proceed to destroy him with tireless devotion to duty. No matter how often their swords and axes bounced off his metal body, they raised them again and showered him with blows like blacksmiths beating out a sheet of iron. They hammered away at the Copper Killer until Ribble saw the first screws fly from his helmet, whereupon they attacked him with redoubled ferocity.

Skullop came up to Ribble. 'And they're supposed to be immortal?' he shouted, indicating the metal warriors with his huge scythe. 'We'll see about that! You asked if my men could fight. Take a look at them, little 'un, and tell me what you think.'

'They fight well!' Ribble shouted back, nodding with alacrity. 'Very well!'

'And they're dead, damn it! Dead! Can you imagine how well they fought when they were still alive? No, little 'un, you can't!'

Skullop the Scyther plunged back into the fray. He shoved a Copper Killer so hard in the chest that he fell backwards over the gallery rail. 'Fight, men!' he bellowed. 'Fight!'

'Shut up, Skullop!' one of the Yetis called back. 'What do you think we're doing right now?'

The Yetis go into action

Rumo and the other Wolpertings had been poised to attempt a breakout, but just before Ushan DeLucca could give the order an incredible commotion erupted in the Copper Killers' gallery high overhead. They all looked up. Sparks came showering over the rail, weapons clashed and shouts rang out. Some gigantic figures in black hooded cloaks had materialised among the metallic soldiers and were fiercely engaging them in battle. One especially huge black warrior was swinging a scythe, others fought with clubs and axes, swords and hammers. The force with which the weapons collided made the whole auditorium shake. Even the red spider, which was just cocooning its last few screaming victims, interrupted its work and focused its numerous eyes on what was happening in the Copper Killers' gallery.

'What's going on up there?' asked Urs. 'Who are those fellows?'

Rumo shook his head in disbelief.

'I know who they are,' he said. 'They're the Dead Yetis.'

General Ticktock's challenge

General Ticktock entered the arena of the Theatre of Death through the largest gateway. He would really have liked a standing ovation, this being his first appearance there for ages, but personal vanity was irrelevant. This was a demonstration of power. His dejected spirits rose at the sight of the battles raging in the arena and auditorium: Wolpertings versus soldiers, Wolpertings versus Hellings, showers of spears and crossbow bolts, spectators trampling each other to death, his Copper Killers battling with a contingent of black-clad giants up in the gallery. Wonderful! He could even see the monstrous red spider, the one they'd caught in Gornab's Echo, devouring some screaming spectators – what a picturesque bonus! How the sparks were flying! How the iron sang! It was a battlefield of the first order! Oh, how he'd missed the taste of war!

Striding into the arena over a carpet of dead bodies, General Ticktock raised his axe and sword in salute. The mercenaries and theatre guards regained their courage when they saw the general enter. They left the barricaded gateways and charged into the arena, cheering him enthusiastically. The Wolpertings stared in wonder at the huge machine that came clanking into the arena like a god of vengeance bristling with weapons. The mere presence of the biggest and most deadly of the Copper Killers boosted the Hellian troops' morale and disconcerted their enemies in a way to which Ticktock was accustomed after so many battles in the past.

In the middle of the arena he halted, lowered his steel jaw and emitted a gurgle. Then came a sound like gravel crunching underfoot and sparks spewed from his mouth, followed by a jet of flame yards long. He bent over the nearest Wolperting and set him ablaze. The burning mixture of acid and oil vaporised him into a cloud of black smoke that swiftly rose and disappeared into the darkness above the theatre. Ticktock straightened up, threw back his cloak and bared his mutilated chest. His jaw snapped shut, his shoulders gave a jerk, and two rotating circular saw blades shot out from between his steel ribs. They went whirring across the arena in a wide arc, compelling many of the Wolpertings to leap aside, then returned to Ticktock's chest like boomerangs. Still rotating, they re-entered it and noisily came to rest inside him.

Ticktock reached a small group of Wolpertings in three giant strides. Two of them he felled in a flash with his sword and axe. The third, caught by the flat of the huge axe, went sailing through the air and landed many feet away.

The general sheathed his sword and slowly turned on the spot, apparently debating what to do next. Then he raised his head and stared at something high up in the auditorium. Drawing back his arm, he hurled the axe with incredible force. It soared upwards, turning over and over as it hissed through the air, and landed smack in the middle of the huge spider's body. The monster uttered a last terrible howl and collapsed on top of its cocooned victims.

All hostilities in the arena and auditorium had been suspended. Everyone was concentrating on the general's impressive entrance. The only place where fighting continued unabated was up in the Copper Killers' gallery.

Ticktock stomped over to the warrior who was unlucky enough to be nearest him. Although he happened to be a theatre guard, Ticktock seized him by the throat, picked him up like a rag doll and hurled him across the field of battle. The man's bones shattered as he hit the ground.

'You want a fight?' yelled the mightiest Copper Killer of all, and his voice rang through the Theatre of Death. 'You want war? Then come [tick] to me! I am [tock] General Ticktock! I'm war in person!'

'So that's General Ticktock,' thought Ushan DeLucca.

His entrance had indeed been impressive. He was big, he was strong, and he was clearly well armed. He could spit fire like a dragon, he could project saw blades from his chest, and he knew how to handle a sword and axe. He looked invulnerable and implacable. He was a whole army and a fortress on legs combined. So why wasn't Ushan impressed?

The fencing master's euphoria had attained a pitch he would never have thought possible. He had mowed down opponents like weeds, he was the swiftest, most elegant and deadly swordsman in the arena. Rolv's vengeful fury and Rumo's natural aptitude were nothing beside Ushan's abilities – beside his unique combination of talent and years-long experience, pugnacity and tactical skill.

But there was another respect in which Ushan surpassed every other Wolperting: his readiness to die. Ever since he had commanded Rolv and Urs to kill him, it was as if he had pushed open an invisible door from which boundless energy flowed into him.

And now this Copper Killer had entered the arena. This megalomaniac machine had not only slain friends and pupils of his but claimed to be war personified. General Ticktock? Wasn't that the name Rumo had mentioned? Wasn't it he who had tortured and killed Rala?

Yes, he looked dangerous. He looked as if he embodied the evil of a whole army of murderers – as if he could take on any warrior in the theatre, Ushan DeLucca included.

Smyke's oceanic ancestry

'Yes,' Smyke told himself, 'this must be it. I thought I'd reached it on Roaming Rock, when I was imprisoned in my slimy pool, but I was wrong. It's only now, here and now, that my life has reached its lowest ebb! I'm immersed in blood. In dead, diseased blood.'

'Now pull yourself together, Smyke,' said Non-Existent Teeny Number One.

'Try to pretend it's water,' said Non-Existent Teeny Number Two.

'Blood consists largely of water,' said Non-Existent Teeny Number Three.

'Hey,' thought Smyke, 'I can hear you out here as well!'

'We're the Non-Existent Teenies, Smyke.'

'You've no idea how many places you could hear us if we wanted you to.'

'How are you feeling, Smyke?'

Smyke had left the submarine. He had passed through the hull like a disembodied spirit – that was the only explanation he could find for the way he had got from the inside to the outside without opening a door of any kind.

'That explanation is not entirely apt, Smyke.'

'It was a case of molecular transference with the aid of sympathetic vibrations.'

'We gave up doors a long time ago.'

Smyke had instinctively switched over to gill-breathing.

'I'm breathing blood,' he thought. 'I'm breathing dead blood.'

'Do stop going on about blood!'

'It's an absolute obsession.'

'Concentrate on your opponent.'

Smyke's opponent was floating high above him, just in front of the place where the Non-Existent Teenies supposed the connectors required for their auratic operation to be located. The creature turned itself inside out, rotated on its own axis, excreted some slime, and turned transparent, then dark-grey and black in turn, as if steadfastly intent on demonstrating how dangerous it was.

'Now listen, Smyke!' said Non-Existent Teeny Number One. 'We've made the following discovery: it's a fatal disease. That's bad, but it can't infect you.'

'Can't it?'

'No, it can only infect the body whose bloodstream it's in. It's a question of relative size. What's more, it's the last example of its kind in this organism. That much we do know.'

'Good.'

'But . . .'

'But what?'

'This disease could kill you just the same.'

'It certainly looks that way.'

'It could kill you quite simply by using physical violence. That too is a question of relative size. But pay attention, now comes some good news.'

'Really?'

'*You* could also kill *it*.'

'How?' Smyke asked incredulously.

'Simply by obeying your feral instincts.'

'What feral instincts? Have I got some?'

'You carry the genes of one of this planet's most dangerous life forms, Smyke.'

'Huh?'

'You're a deadly, dangerous fighting machine.'

'You're the terror of the oceans.'

'You're a shark, Smyke.'

'Never forget that, Smyke: you're a *Shark* Grub.'

Ushan DeLucca's finest hour

Ushan DeLucca knew exactly whom General Ticktock would kill next. It would be Urs of the Snows.

For anyone who knew as much about fighting and chess as Ushan, it wasn't hard to work that out. General Ticktock was stronger and more agile than any other warrior in the arena: in chess terms, he was the queen. If he thought strategically, he would be bound to concentrate on those opponents who were doing his soldiers most damage. They were Rumo and Rolv, Urs and Vasko, Olek and Balla. And, of course, himself, Ushan DeLucca. Wherever they wielded their swords the theatre guards died like flies.

So Ticktock's next move must be to eliminate one of them. Rumo? No, he was too far away, Rolv was considerably closer. Vasko was even closer than Rolv, Olek closer than Vasko and Balla closer than Olek. But Urs of the Snows was the closest of all.

Urs, fighting with his back to the mechanical monster, was busy with five opponents at once. No, now there were only four. Ticktock had only to take a few steps and he could cut down one of the most dangerous Wolpertings from behind.

Ushan analysed the situation as though studying a chessboard instead of a battlefield. What to do if one of one's most valuable pieces was threatened? Sacrifice a pawn? That was the only possibility. And who should be the pawn that had to die in Urs's place? He himself, of course: Ushan DeLucca.

Ushan tossed his sword aside. This was a contest in which a sword would be useless. He would never need a sword again. Resolutely, he strode towards the general. How good he felt – how strong and light-footed! He had never felt better in his life.

Urs performed a swift lunge that dispatched yet another opponent. Ushan had known that the youngster was good, but here in the arena he was surpassing himself. Urs of the Snows would some day be the finest swordsman in Wolperting, perhaps in all Zamonia, of that Ushan was convinced.

'Hey!' he called when he was standing close behind General Ticktock. 'Hey, General Ticktock! Is that your name?'

The metal giant slowly turned to face him.

'Yes [tick], it is. And who [tock] are you?'

'My name is Ushan DeLucca.'

'Pleased to meet you,' the general said with a little bow. 'Tell me, Ushan DeLucca, why [tick] are you facing me unarmed? Have you [tock] lost your wits? Or your nerve?'

'Neither,' Ushan said with a smile. 'I've nothing left to lose.'

'Not even your life?' asked the general. 'Is it worth [tick] so little to you?'

'Oh, I've never set much store by it,' said Ushan. 'I found it wearisome most of the time, especially in bad weather. For all that, there's more life in me than you could ever dream of.'

'What [tock] do you mean?' Ticktock demanded.

'I mean you've lost this battle. No matter what you do and no matter how many enemies you defeat and kill, you can never win it. It's impossible. Even if you're the only survivor of this battle, there was more life in every corpse on the battlefield than will ever be in you. Such is your lot. You're the saddest creature I've ever encountered. I'm sorry for you – that's what I wanted to tell you.'

'Have you [tick] finished?' asked General Ticktock. He levelled a steel forefinger at Ushan. 'Now I understand. You're trying [tock] to provoke me into killing you instead of one of your friends.'

Ushan didn't answer. He shut his eyes and lost himself in the scene that unfolded before his inner eye. Banners of red and yellow, gold and copper fluttered in the breeze. It was like a colossal painting imbued with all the colours of battle, the scents of courage and fear, triumph and defeat. He had never seen anything so magnificent.

'I wonder what a swordsman's paradise looks like?' he thought. 'Is it as beautiful as my fencing garden?'

Ticktock bent his thumb. There was a faint click followed by a sharp report, and his forefinger detached itself and sped towards Ushan faster than any crossbow bolt. The Wolperting didn't even raise an arm to protect himself and the steel finger buried itself deep in his chest.

Ushan made no sound. He recoiled a step but remained on his feet. Ticktock bent his thumb once more. Another click, a series of detonations, and the other three fingers buried themselves in Ushan's ribcage. Four thin, faintly twanging steel wires were now suspended between the general's hand and the Wolperting's chest.

Ticktock bent his thumb a third time, thereby activating a mechanism that reeled in the wires and recovered the arrows. His entrails emitted a whirring sound as Ushan was jerked off his feet and hoisted into the air. The fingers clicked back into the hand and General Ticktock held him up by the chest.

'No one [tick] has ever dared to tell me [tock] the truth to my face before,' the general whispered. 'You're a hero, Ushan DeLucca.'

Gripping the Wolperting's head with his other hand, he tore the steel fingers free and held them in the air. They were cupped around Ushan's still beating heart.

Steel versus bone

Ribble consoled himself during the battle between the Copper Killers and the Dead Yetis with the thought that his role would be that of a chronicler rather than a warrior. Monstrous and shocking though they were, he had to memorise all these images and preserve them for posterity, for it was doubtful if anything of the kind would ever be seen again.

It was the grimmest and most ruthless battle that had ever raged between two opposing sides. Yetis fought on with their oil-sodden cloaks and bones ablaze, Copper Killers continued to flail away long after they'd lost their heads. Severed limbs fell to the ground while their owners fought on undaunted and others snatched them up for use as weapons. A headless Copper Killer with a thick jet of steam issuing from his throat was locked in mortal combat with a Yeti whose skull was in flames. Two Yetis swung their heavy hammers at a Copper Killer bereft of both arms. Splinters of bone, cogwheels, screws and teeth went whistling through the air, valves hissed, shields clanged like bells, and the Yetis' bestial roars rang out again and again. Skullop cursed and swung his scythe at the Copper Killers, who cowered away because even metal burst asunder under its impact.

For a while it had really looked as if the Yetis would win the day, thanks to their toughness and the advantage of surprise, but the longer the battle raged the more illusory this hope became. Now and then some Copper Killer would be forced back against the balcony rail and hurled over the edge or systematically dismembered by a ceaseless rain of blows from hammers and clubs, nor were the Yetis much inferior to the metal warriors in fortitude. Like them they felt no pain and had no fear of death, and a Copper Killer had to smash a Yeti to pieces to prevent him from rising to his feet again. In the long run, however, it seemed that the mechanical soldiers would prevail, if only because metal was more durable than bone. More and more Yetis fell to the ground and lay still because every single one of their bones had been smashed beyond repair. The Copper Killers used all their concealed weapons, their circular saws, razor-sharp pincers and flame-throwers.

Ribble briefly wondered whether to fight his way down the steps and into the arena, taking the Wolpertings with him, but the place was now swarming with so many enemy soldiers that it would have spelt certain death. So he was compelled to watch Skullop's warriors being driven further and further back, and losing more and more of their number. He had no choice but to commit as many details to memory as possible and hope that the tide would eventually turn in the Yetis' favour after all.

'Everything ugo, Smyke?'

'Ugo?'

'Oh, that's just our way of asking if everything's all right. Ugo is an inconceivably small number that—'

'All right, all right,' thought Smyke. 'Yes, everything's ugo. I'm only swimming through dead blood towards a deadly disease. Why shouldn't everything be ugo?'

'Lots of luck, Smyke.'

'Yes, lots of luck.'

'You can do with some.'

The Non-Existent Teenies abruptly fell silent, leaving Smyke to fend for himself again. Beneath him stretched an endless battlefield strewn with mutilated organisms; above him floated the hideous soldier of death, the last representative of an implacable disease, intent on barring the way to Rala's heart. Discounting the clicks it emitted, it made no sound at all.

Smyke swam on until he was level with his opponent. Hideous and dangerous though the creature was, he found it fascinating to observe its ceaseless movements, mutations and changes of colour at close range. Just now it had been a scutellated star shimmering with all the colours of the rainbow; then it had mutated into a transparent grey ball full of billowing milky liquid. The next moment it looked like a fiery red lava bubble ejected by a crater on the ocean bed. The only constant factor was its monotonous clicking.

'Who are you?' Smyke thought. 'Are you death?'

The lava bubble mutated into a green sponge with streaks of black fluid rising from its honeycombed surface.

'Click, click,' it went.

'No,' thought Smyke, 'you aren't death. Death is something that comes when you have gone. Death is a happy release compared to you. Death is good, you are evil.'

The sponge contracted into a ball, turned metallic-grey and sprouted some long fair hair.

'Click, click, click.'

'But it doesn't matter who *you* are. You're just a brainless soldier. What matters is who *I* am.'

The ball turned into a white jellyfish with black, faceted eyes.

'Click, click, click, click.'

'Do you know who I am? Do you know *what* I am?'

The jellyfish rotated in a feverish manner and turned yellow, then green. Slowly, the middle of its body extruded a sharp black spear.

'Click!' it went. *'Click, click!'*

'I'll tell you what I am,' thought Smyke. 'I'm evil too. I stained Lindworm Castle red with blood. And I'm dangerous as well, far more dangerous than you. Who are you, after all? An amateur. What do you know about fighting, eh?'

'Click, click, click.'

'How long have you been in existence?' asked Smyke. 'A few months? A few weeks? Me, I've existed for millions of years. I'm a shark, that's why.'

The creature mutated yet again. It assumed an elongated shape, turned grey, sprouted fourteen little arms tipped with claws and opened a mouth studded with countless sharp teeth. It now resembled a more primitive and dangerous version of Smyke himself.

The general and the monster

Rumo, Urs, Rolv, Vasko, Balla and Olek converged on General Ticktock from all directions and came to a halt, forming a big circle round him. They had made quick work of their opponents after seeing what the general had done to Ushan DeLucca. The fencing master's lifeless body was lying at his feet.

'Oho,' chuckled Ticktock. 'You've got me [tick] surrounded. I'm [tock] trapped. Was this a friend of yours?'

Ushan's bones splintered as he rested his foot on the fencing master's corpse.

'Who would like [tick] to be next?' he asked.

'Are you General Ticktock?' Rumo demanded.

'Yes, I am.'

'Did you kill Rala?'

General Ticktock involuntarily clutched his chest. His shoulders sagged a little, but only for an instant. Then he straightened up again.

'Who wants [tock] to know?' he asked angrily.

Rumo didn't reply. He now knew that it was Ticktock who had inflicted such havoc on his beloved.

The general surveyed his adversaries. Rumo, Rolv, Urs, Vasko, Balla and Olek began to circle him slowly.

Meanwhile, more and more Wolpertings had stopped fighting and joined them in the arena. Nearly all the soldiers had been killed or put to flight.

'Oho,' Ticktock said again, 'so you want [tick] to dance, do you?'

He threw back his cloak. It was only now that the Wolpertings could see his physique in all its splendour. Copper, steel, silver, iron – every part of him was metal. His body was a huge, mechanised fortress constructed of the most diverse materials – a whole army in a single body.

'Before you all have to die,' Ticktock said gravely, 'you should [tock] know something. My days in Hel have changed me. I've grown [tick]. I've loved [tock] and suffered. I've become another person. You may [tick] think me big, but I'm far bigger [tock] than you suspect. Would you like [tick] to see my true dimensions?'

Without waiting for an answer he tilted his head to one side, inserted a forefinger in a hole in his neck and turned it like a key. Instantly, his body emitted a series of sounds that resembled the discordant chimes of a broken musical clock. His head revolved several times to this accompaniment and his neck grew steadily longer. His insides clicked and ticked as sections of armour-plate folded back or slid apart to reveal his mechanical intestines. Cogwheels rotated, wires drew taut, alchemical batteries crackled, pistons rose and fell – all was in ceaseless motion. His backplates unfolded into two silver wings, and from the resulting apertures new metallic limbs extended telescopically until they touched the ground. To the Wolpertings' amazement, they saw that General Ticktock had not only doubled in size but acquired twice as many arms and legs within a few seconds. All the weapons that had hitherto been concealed inside his body – crossbows, blades, missiles – had been exposed and rendered combat-ready. They were now confronted by a four-armed, four-legged fortress bristling with weapons. The new General Ticktock was even bigger and more dangerous, deadlier and more unassailable than before.

'Size!' cried Ticktock, looking down at them. 'That's the key to power. What you see here [tick] is only the start. I shall continue to grow [tock] for as long as there's any metal left. I shall grow [tick] until all the metal in existence is General Ticktock.'

The Wolpertings stood there as though turned to stone. The sight of the huge machine was hypnotic.

'You wanted to dance?' boomed the general. 'Let's [tock] dance, then!'

The Wolpertings braced themselves for battle.

No one knew where General Ticktock would strike first. Everywhere at once, perhaps.

Suddenly the floor of the theatre began to shake – slightly but perceptibly.

'What was that?' someone asked.

Ticktock, too, had stiffened. There! Another tremor made his weapons jangle.

The Wolpertings looked mystified. What was causing these tremors? Fighting was still in progress in the Copper Killers' gallery, but they didn't seem to come from there.

'An earthquake?' asked Balla.

But the tremors were too rhythmical for an earthquake. They followed one another at intervals of several seconds, becoming ever stronger. And suddenly a gust of wind swept through the theatre, laden with a stench reminiscent of everything vile that had ever crawled out of the oceans.

'What is it?' asked Urs.

'A Vrahok!' Rumo exclaimed. 'A really big one!'

The tremors had intensified the tumult in the auditorium. The surviving spectators redoubled their desperate efforts to escape from the theatre. Only the Yetis and the Copper Killers, who seemed unimpressed, fought on with undiminished ferocity.

A pale-blue glow filled the theatre and everything was enveloped in a shower of luminous blue slime. It looked as if a monstrous flying object was descending on the arena – a huge, glowing, pale-blue disc with organic shapes pulsating inside it. Everyone could now see that it was a body whose twelve supporting legs had halted in a circle round the building. A Vrahok of the largest variety had settled over the Theatre of Death like a roof. The spectators screamed in terror. From inside the monster came piercing whistles and incessant churning noises.

General Ticktock stalked to and fro on his four legs, instantly demoted from a giant into an insect. What fool had alerted the Vrahok? He had everything under control!

'What is it?' asked Rolv.

'It's a Vrahok,' said Yukobak, who had ventured out from behind Rumo.

'A Vrahok? Is that a machine too?'

'No, a living creature.'

'Whose side is it on?' asked Balla.

'Not ours,' Yukobak replied.

'Can it do anything apart from being big?'

'It could eat us. It can eat anything.'

'How?' asked Urs. 'I can't see a mouth.'

'It's got one, believe me,' said Yukobak.

Tentacles as thick as a man and as long as trees came snaking over the theatre's walls and swept along the tiers of seats. Any spectators unlucky enough to be grazed by them, let alone struck full on, were hurled aside, crushed, or sent whirling through the air. Being endowed with greater athletic skill, the few Wolpertings still up there managed to dodge them. The blind monster, which was trying to get its bearings, made no distinction between friend and foe.

'Are you sure it isn't on our side after all?' asked Balla. 'It's been working for us up to now.'

'It isn't easy to control,' Yukobak explained. 'There are riders on its back who try to do so. They're probably having trouble at the moment. This is the biggest specimen that's ever been ridden into the city.'

The Vrahok now extended its gigantic trunk. It slithered over the rows of empty seats in search of prey and all in its vicinity fled, screaming and trampling each other underfoot. The tip of the trunk squelched open and greedily sniffed the air. The Vrahok's sense of smell quickly guided it to one of the exits where jostling, panic-stricken spectators were striving to escape. The trunk descended on them and indiscriminately proceeded to suck up everyone it encountered. Screaming, the luckless individuals shot up the transparent tube and were engulfed by the monster's pulsating intestines.

Rumo was less surprised than most by the sight of the Vrahok. Knowing these creatures and their capabilities, he was primarily interested in General Ticktock, who was watching the monster's activities with as much fascination as everyone else. He gripped his sword, feverishly wondering how best to exploit this moment of universal consternation.

'Have you had an idea?' asked Dandelion.

'I've remembered an old story,' Rumo replied.

'What old story?' asked Krindle.

'The story of the Battle of Nurn Forest. It tells how General Ticktock came into being.'

'You mean you know how he originated?' asked Dandelion.

'It's a legend. What's interesting is the part where the alchemist who created General Ticktock inserted a nugget of zamonium in him, an element that would bring him and the Copper Killers to life. If the story is correct, he must possess something in the nature of a brain. Or a heart.'

'And if he's got a heart or a brain,' said Krindle, **'it could be ripped out of his body.'**

Rumo nodded. 'I'm going to climb inside General Ticktock,' he said.

The connectors

Smyke, breathing heavily, was back inside the subcutaneous submarine with sweat streaming down his plump body.

'Everything ugo, Smyke?'

'Yes, Smyke, everything ugo?'

'Come on, say something!'

Smyke couldn't have produced a coherent answer even if he'd wanted to.

'That was incredible, Smyke,' said Non-Existent Teeny Number One.

'How did you manage it?' asked Non-Existent Teeny Number Two.

'Yes, Smyke, how did you manage it?'

Smyke drew several deep breaths. He wasn't finding it easy to switch back to lung-breathing. His gills were still pumping away like mad.

'It had a spine,' he said.

'A spine?' said Non-Existent Teeny Number One.

'A spine?' said Non-Existent Teeny Number Two.

'A disease with a spine?' said Non-Existent Teeny Number Three.

'Yes!' snapped Smyke. 'The disease had a spine! A spine capable of being broken.'

The Non-Existent Teenies fell silent.

'Good,' Smyke said at length. 'Can we get on with the confounded operation at last?'

'Yes, Smyke.'

'If you're ready, we're ready too.'

'The boat's in position.'

'How do we proceed?' asked Smyke.

'Can you see the connectors, Smyke? We've set the videomembrane at maximum magnification.'

'Yes, I can see them,' said Smyke. There were six peculiar bulges and indentations in the cardiac muscle fibre, but everything inside here consisted of peculiar bulges and indentations. He couldn't have said what was special about these particular ones.

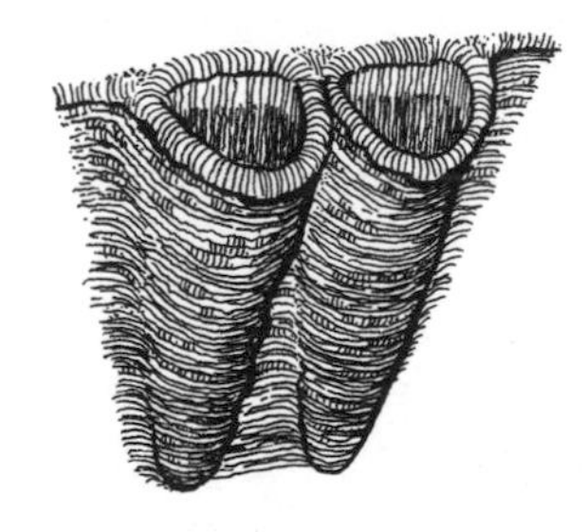

'That one is an amalorican adaptor,' said Non-Existent Teeny Number One. 'It takes care of the heart's electrical circulation.'

'And that's a hallucinogenic synapse,' said Non-Existent Teeny Number Two. 'It's a gangliate cord of the autonomous nervous system that conveys the sympathetic vibrations of the hallucinogenic key.'

'That's an opabiniatic adaptor,' **said Non-Existent Teeny Number Three.** 'It alone can enable the stimuli of the opabiniatic pincers to operate freely.'

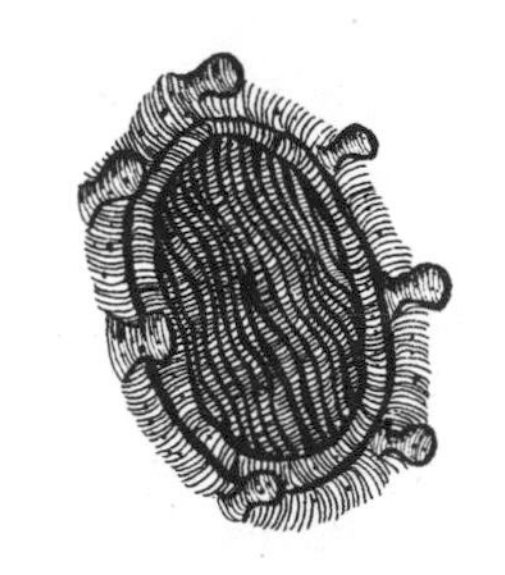

'That's a nabokovian knob,' **said Non-Existent Teeny Number One.** 'It reacts activo-passively on the stimuli imparted by the nabokovian whip, thereby regulating the heartbeat.'

'That's an epithalamian egress,' **said Non-Existent Teeny Number Two.** 'It's the epicentric microcentre of the aorta that coronarily equalises the sympathetic vibrations.'

'And that's an odontoid tube!' **said Non-Existent Teeny Number Three.** 'The precise function of the odontoid tube has never been satisfactorily explained, but it's demonstrably of a positive nature.'

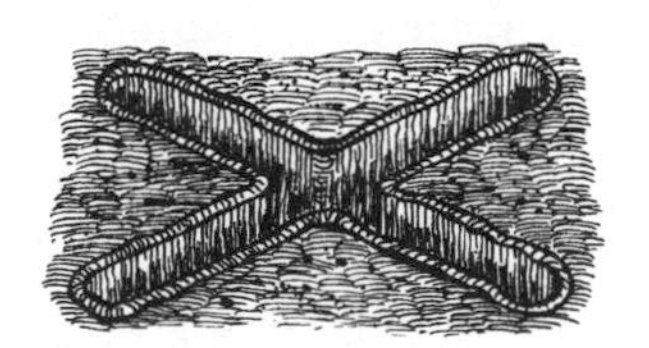

'Is that clear, Smyke?'

'As daylight,' said Smyke. 'I'm in the picture now.'

'In that case, activate your instruments,' **commanded Non-Existent Teeny Number One.**

'Hrrrmmm,' went Smyke. 'Hrrrmmm . . .'

Trapped inside Ticktock

Rumo simply jumped. He hadn't spent long debating where to land, because no part of General Ticktock's body seemed a particularly suitable landing place. He was now clinging to the general's back at the point where the two silver wings had folded outwards. From here he had a good view of the interior. It concealed still more weapons, still more clicking and ticking metal components, but he couldn't discern anything in the way of a heart or a brain.

General Ticktock groped for Rumo with his steel claws, trying to brush him off like a troublesome insect, but his arms, although long, were constructed in such a way that certain parts of his anatomy were hard or impossible for them to reach. Everything about him was geared to attack, not defence, and nobody, least of all General Ticktock himself, had ever dreamt that anyone would be insane enough to cling to his back.

The other Wolpertings bravely hurled spears, knives and axes at the general, but there was little more they could do, being far too preoccupied with dodging his own weapons and missiles. Although Olek scored some magnificent hits on the Copper Killer's head with his sling, all they produced were some dull clangs.

'Climb inside him,' called Dandelion. *'You'll have to if you want to find his heart. Besides, you'll be safe from him in there.'*

Rumo squeezed between two close-set steel rods and into the metal warrior's interior. The ticking and clicking, the whirring of cogwheels, the rhythmical pounding of pistons and the crackle of alchemical batteries attained such a pitch that they almost drowned every sound outside. Everything jerked and clicked at regular intervals. It was rather like being inside a watch. Was there really a heart hidden in here? Did such a sophisticated machine require an organic motor? Rumo pressed on. Everything around him was in motion, pumping up and down and back and forth. He had to take great care not to get his hands and feet crushed between two revolving cogwheels or trapped by some sharp-edged spring. Every component was smooth, burnished, and smeared with lubricating oil. It was almost impossible to find a firm handhold or foothold.

'Enjoying yourself [tick] in there?' boomed General Ticktock, his voice sounding even hollower and more mechanical than before. 'Are you enjoying yourself [tock] inside me, Wolperting?'

Rumo didn't answer.

'Make yourself [tick] at home!' cried the general. 'Be my [tock] guest! I'll shut the doors so we won't be [tick] disturbed!'

A grating noise came from somewhere, and the wheels and pistons speeded up. Rumo once more heard the music that had accompanied the general's expansion to twice his original size, except that this time it sounded still more discordant because it was playing backwards. The sheets of armour-plate encasing General Ticktock's body slid together. Flaps and openings snapped shut, metal locked into metal. The crankshafts and pistons which Rumo was balancing on or clinging to rose and fell unceasingly. It was growing darker inside the general.

'He's shutting himself up!' cried Dandelion. *'We must get out of here, quick!'*

Weapons were being retracted on all sides: razor-sharp blades, saws and scythes, axes and spears, arrows and knives. Some shot in at high speed, others were withdrawn quite slowly. They came from left and right, above and below, ahead and behind. An axe whizzed just over Rumo's head, a scythe shaved clumps of fur off his arm, a long, double-edged sword blade darted between his legs. He had to keep ducking and dodging or pulling in his legs to avoid being beheaded, skewered or mutilated. At the same time he tried desperately to reach the aperture he'd entered by. Just as he was about to squeeze between the steel rods, however, the two silver wings that formed General Ticktock's backplate closed. It was silent now, and completely dark except for the criss-cross shafts of light that filtered in through narrow chinks. A muffled bell note rang out, like that of a clock chiming the hour.

'We're trapped,' said Dandelion. *'We're trapped inside General Ticktock.'*

The operation

'The amalorican hook has engaged with the amalorican adaptor,' said Non-Existent Teeny Number One. 'This means that the heart's auratic electrical circulation is guaranteed.'

'Hrrrmmm . . .' went Smyke.

'The hallucinogenic key has been inserted in the hallucinogenic lock and turned,' said Non-Existent Teeny Number Two. 'The sympathetic vibrations have now been decoded and can flow into the autonomous nervous system.'

'Hrrrmmm . . .' went Smyke.

'The opabiniatic adaptor has been clamped to the opabiniatic membrane,' said Non-Existent Teeny Number Three.

'Opabiniatisation can commence.'

'Hrrrmmm . . .' went Smyke.

'The nabokovian whip is stimulating the nabokovian knob,' said Non-Existent Teeny Number One. 'The consequent passivo-active reaction has fully adjusted the heartbeat.'

'Hrrrmmm . . .' went Smyke.

'The epithalamian screw is rotating in the epithalamian egress!' said Non-Existent Teeny Number Two. 'The sympathetic vibrations are being coronarily equalised.'

'Hrrrmmm . . .' went Smyke.

'The odontoid tube has been inserted in the odontoid socket!' said Non-Existent Teeny Number Three. 'Whatever it does, it'll be for the best.'

'Hrrrmmm. . .' went Smyke.

'Good. Now to feed in the auratic charge.'

'Let's cross our fingers, Smyke.'

'Wish us luck!'

'I will.'

'How many fingers have you got, Smyke?'

Smyke did some mental arithmetic. 'Fifty-six,' he said.

'That ought to do the trick.'

'Yes,' said Smyke, 'it ought to – unless there's still a curse on me.'

'You never can tell,' said Non-Existent Teeny Number One. 'The operation is now in progress.'

The greatest show ever

Friftar shut the spyhole through which he had been watching the arena and clapped a hand over his mouth.

General Ticktock's theatrical performance had left him utterly dismayed. Already bristling with weapons, the Copper Killer had contrived to make his body even bigger, more complex and dangerous. He had transformed himself into an invincible fighting machine. How could his, Friftar's, modest diplomatic resources hope to compete with him?

His other source of dismay was the Vrahok. What a fiasco! Why had those idiotic alchemists sent him one of the biggest and most unpredictable specimens? A fifty-footer would have been quite big enough! No Vrahok of such a size had ever set foot in the city before and it was out of control. If word got out that *he* had issued the Vrahok Alert, the Hellings would hold him responsible for the losses in their own ranks. And the stupid monster simply wouldn't stop sucking respected citizens into its maw – aristocrats, wealthy merchants, army officers and all. It was more than the eye could bear to watch!

Friftar swore. He was doomed to sit still and wait for General Ticktock and the Vrahok to finish wreaking havoc in the Theatre of Death. At least the crazy king was asleep – that was one mercy.

He opened the spyhole again. It was too stunning a spectacle to miss. The arena drenched with luminous blue rain, the gigantic mechanical warrior in combat with the Wolpertings, the even more gigantic Vrahok devouring innocent Hellian citizens from above, the corpses, the screams of the dying, the showers of sparks from the Copper Killers' gallery . . . What a sight! To be quite honest, thought Friftar, it was far and away the best show the Theatre of Death had ever presented.

Ticktock combines pleasure with business

General Ticktock was entitled to feel satisfied. His victim was trapped. Wolpertings might be excellent fighters, but strategy didn't appear to be their greatest strength.

The general's body contained forty-seven large swords, fourteen glass daggers filled with poison, two dozen circular saws with diamond-tipped teeth, seven axes, eighteen spears, and hundreds of arrows, crossbow bolts and other missiles, half of them poisoned. His arsenal also included a built-in guillotine on rails, acid-filled syringes, flame-throwers, spiked metal throwing discs, arbalests, and many other weapons. The Wolperting was already dead; all that remained was to decide on the manner of his death. He had climbed into his coffin of his own accord.

General Ticktock decided to combine pleasure with business. He would do battle with the other Wolpertings, try out a few of his new toys and simultaneously give the intruder hell – send blades whizzing back and forth for him to jump over. For the first time ever, Ticktock was in the delightful position of being able to torture someone and, at the same time, do some fighting and killing. He could feel his sorrow subsiding.

The heart in the dark

Rumo had found a girder forming part of General Ticktock's basic framework to which he could temporarily cling. The light filtering through the chinks and the gaps between the general's distorted ribs was so poor that all he could see of the crankshafts, rotating cogwheels and retracted weapons was a jumble of dark silhouettes.

'There's nothing here that looks like a heart or a brain,' Rumo decided. 'If he ever had one, perhaps he lost it.'

'You will seek the heart of Death on Legs, but you will find it only in darkness!' said Dandelion.

'What?'

'The last of the Ugglies' prophecies, don't you remember?'

'What are you getting at?' Krindle demanded. **'What have those old hags to do with this?'**

'It means I must shut my eyes,' said Rumo. 'I must try to locate General Ticktock's heart with my nose.'

'Good idea,' said Krindle. **'Carry on!'**

Rumo clung tightly to the girder and shut his eyes.

'What can you see?' asked Dandelion.

'I can see metals of various colours,' Rumo replied. 'Metals and lubricating oil – it's everywhere. I can see other things, but only when they're moving and making noises.'

'What about a heart?' asked Krindle. **'Can you smell his heart?'**

'I don't know. There are some strange, unfamiliar smells – acids, poisons, pungent powders – but nothing that could be a heart. Or a brain. If they're inside here, they're well hidden.'

'Perhaps we should go further in,' Dandelion suggested. *'If they're hidden he's bound to have buried them as deep as possible.'*

Rumo opened his eyes and climbed further into Ticktock's mechanised innards. Climbing proved riskier again because the motion was even more hectic and universal than before. The general lurched to and fro, lunged and retreated, turned on the spot. Rumo could hear sword blades clashing and missiles bouncing off him. Finding a couple of fixed metal rods that weren't in motion, he clung to them, shut his eyes and sniffed the air again.

'What can you smell?' asked Dandelion.

Rumo's nose again detected the strong-smelling powder, the reek of flammable oil in the flame-throwers' tanks, the smoky tang of a used flint, and the acrid smells given off by sundry poisons and chemical cleaning agents – all of them visible as coloured ribbons that knotted themselves tightly together to form a graphic picture of the general's inner life. And in its midst, in the centre of the mechanical warrior, Rumo sighted a rhythmically pulsating green glow.

'I can see a light,' Rumo whispered.

'Where?' asked Dandelion.

Rumo continued to climb, this time with his eyes shut.

'Be careful what you hold on to!' Krindle warned. **'There are lots of blades here. They may be poisoned.'**

Rumo squeezed through some bars, ducked under a rotating wheel with sharp teeth, stepped over a glass blade filled with crimson poison – and found himself immediately above the source of the pulsating glow. He was near enough to open his eyes and ascertain its nature.

It was hard to make out in the gloom. Encased in lead, it was a small, brick-shaped box from which numerous cables led to various parts of the machine. The box was humming and crackling. Rumo rested his paw on it: it was as cold as ice.

'It's an alchemical battery,' he said disappointedly.

'A battery doesn't pulsate,' said Dandelion. *'It's in there – his heart is inside the battery, surrounded by acid. It must be immensely powerful if you can scent it through the lead. A good hiding place.'*

'Smash it!' Krindle urged. **'Smash the battery and rip the heart out of his body before he grasps what we're up to in here!'**

Rumo raised his sword and split the battery's lead casing at a stroke. With a hiss, glowing green acid escaped from the crack, sending up a cloud of acrid vapour. As the acid drained off into the darkness below, the white object enclosed in it became visible.

'Pah!' said Krindle. **'Just a stupid stone.'**

'The zamonium,' Dandelion whispered. *'Take it!'*

Rumo sheathed his sword, reached for the zamonium – and recoiled.

'What's wrong?' asked Krindle.

At the touch of the zamonium Rumo's limbs had been transfixed by a shaft of ice-cold lightning and his head filled with the babble of countless voices.

'What is it?'

'It feels extremely unpleasant,' said Rumo.

'Can't you touch it?' asked Dandelion.

'Yes, but not for very long, I'm afraid.'

General Ticktock faltered. For one brief moment he'd experienced a loss of self-control – a terrible and totally unfamiliar sensation. It was as if something inside him had snapped. A wire, a steel cable, a conduit – something that had thrown him off balance. He teetered to and fro on his four legs until he regained his equilibrium.

He awoke from the frenzy that had overcome him, the savage delight he'd taken in battling with the Wolpertings, who were launching one attack after another.

This temporary loss of control reminded him that he must deal with the creature inside his body before it could become a serious threat. Much to his regret, he would have to stop toying with the Wolpertings and proceed to execute the prisoner inside him. He sighed. Torture *and* combat simply didn't mix.

The zamonium

Something came whistling towards Rumo's head. He quickly ducked as the air above him was cleft by an axe blade on a pendulum. It soared off into the darkness, paused briefly and swung back. The axe sped past him twice more, then came to rest.

'Go on, take the stupid stone!' cried Krindle. **'Take it and let's get out of here.'**

Rumo took hold of the zamonium and removed it from the lead casing. Never had he touched anything colder, and he resisted the impulse to let go of it at once. Now he had only one forepaw available to climb with.

High above him Ticktock's backplate suddenly opened and shafts of light streamed in. The general couldn't have chosen a better moment. Rumo stepped over the red glass dagger, squeezed through some scaffolding and started to climb.

Ominous noises could be heard on all sides. Rotating circular saw blades swept to and fro, sabres probed the gloom – all of General Ticktock's metal components were searching for the captive inside him. Rumo continued to climb with the zamonium firmly clutched in his fist. He had never carried a more onerous burden. He could feel the cold taking possession of his paw, his arm, his shoulder, his head.

His ears suddenly rang with hundreds of voices. *'Grow!'* they screamed in unison. *'You must grow! You can be the greatest Wolperting of all! You and I must become a single being!'*

The voices confused him. He inadvertently gripped a sharp blade, cutting his other paw badly, and quickly let go of it. He swayed for a moment and almost fell.

'Grow!' the voices cried. *'You must grow! You can become the greatest of all!'*

Rumo took hold of a girder with his bleeding paw and hauled himself higher.

'Together we can be all-powerful!' screeched the zamonium. *'You're strong, but I can make you even stronger!'*

A series of clicks rang out in the darkness: crossbows being cocked.

'Look out!' Krindle yelled. **'Crossbow bolts!'**

Rumo heard a twanging of strings. He ducked as a score of bolts whizzed over his head. They crashed into a metal plate, ricocheted off it and went whistling through the air. He continued to climb.

'You're a mighty warrior!' the zamonium whispered. *'You've no idea what we could achieve together. I can make you immortal.'*

'Don't listen to that twaddle!' said Dandelion. *'It's utter rubbish!'*

'Nothing can ever part us,' the zamonium hissed. 'Together we can be eternal!'

'Look out!' Krindle shouted again, but it was too late. Quick as a flash, a sword darted out of the gloom and inflicted a deep wound in the arm Rumo was using to carry the zamonium. The blade was mechanically withdrawn and clicked back into place. To Rumo's surprise, he felt no pain. His arm was completely numb.

'That blade was poisoned,' said the zamonium, *'but it can't harm you. My presence has rendered you invulnerable.'*

Rumo saw the poison in the wound evaporate with a hiss and the wound itself heal within seconds.

'We could be all-powerful.'

'Look out!' cried Dandelion. *'Duck!'*

Rumo did so, and a guillotine blade mounted on rails flashed past overhead.

'Stop listening to that nonsense and concentrate on getting out of here,' said Dandelion.

By now, the big opening Rumo had climbed in through was not far above him. Peering through the chinks in Ticktock's armour, he saw that Wolpertings had leapt at the general from all directions. Among them were Rolv, Olek and Balla, who held out their arms to him.

'Here, Rumo!'

'Here!'

'Here!'

'You can make it, Rumo!'

Some of the Wolpertings were swept aside by Ticktock's huge hands, but their place was instantly taken by others. They were all risking their lives for him.

'Come on, Rumo!'

'Come on!'

Urs leant through the opening and held out his paw.

'Catch hold, Rumo! Quick!'

Rumo's body had gone cold and numb. Only the arm and paw with which he was clinging to the rim of the opening seemed to be obeying him. If he let go and missed, he would fall into the midst of General Ticktock's rotating circular saws and slashing blades. Everything swam before his eyes.

'He's shutting the doors again!' Urs yelled. 'His backplate's closing!'

Looking up, Rumo vaguely saw that the doors in the general's back were slowly converging. He let go.

Urs grabbed his wrist and held it in a vicelike grip.

'Got you!' he shouted.

Then, gritting his teeth and grunting with exertion, he proceeded to haul away. Rumo just hung there like a sack of potatoes and made no attempt to help. Cursing, Urs hoisted him through the opening, seized him under the arms from behind, and jumped. They landed on their backs in the sand.

Rumo lay there, groaning and glassy-eyed, with the zamonium clutched in his fist. Urs scrambled to his feet and helped him up.

The other Wolpertings had suspended their attacks on Ticktock. The general continued to stomp around, visibly bemused and disorientated. He extended and retracted his weapons in a mechanical way. His lower jaw had dropped, but all that issued from his mouth was a monotonous clicking sound.

Olek walked up to Rumo.

'What's that in your paw?' he asked.

'It's Ticktock's heart,' Rumo mumbled vaguely. 'Where is he?'

'His heart?' said Olek. He held out his sling. 'I've had an idea. Put it in there.'

'No!' the zamonium screamed in Rumo's head. *'No, we must stay together!'* Rumo retreated a step.

'Go on,' said Olek, proffering the sling once more. 'I'll get rid of it for you.'

'Get rid of the damned thing!' Dandelion said sharply. *'Let . . . it . . . go!'*

'That's an order!' Krindle barked.

Rumo gave a start and dropped the stone into the sling.

Olek stepped forward. He whirled the sling several times around his head, then released one of the thongs and sent the zamonium on its way. Everyone followed its trajectory, spellbound.

The white stone soared over the arena and the auditorium in a wide arc, heading straight for the Vrahok's trunk, which was indiscriminately sucking up dust, rubbish, spectators and soldiers alive or dead. The zamonium shot up the transparent tube and was lost from view amid the contents of the monster's stomach.

Some of the Wolpertings had already turned away and redirected their attention to General Ticktock, who was still reeling around, when the Vrahok's trunk stopped sucking. All eyes turned to the monster once more. Choking sounds issued from its body. It resumed sucking, only to stop a second time. And a third. Quivering and twitching as if racked with convulsions, the trunk reared high above the auditorium, where all it could inhale was thin air. In the end it stopped sucking altogether.

The brief silence that followed was broken by hair-raising howls and whistles. The gigantic creature swayed back and forth above the theatre, the contents of its blue body frothing and bubbling. A muffled explosion, and the Vrahok's stomach became hugely distended. A second explosion, and the skin of its stomach tautened more ominously still. The surviving spectators started to yell and jostle again. The Vrahok gave another terrible heave and its trunk regurgitated a gooey mass of slime, detritus and half-digested corpses that distributed itself over the rows of seats.

A third explosion. The Vrahok's body split open in several places, spilling out thick strands of blue intestine. The monster emitted another ear-splitting howl, then one of its huge legs buckled. Its joints groaned like trees about to fall. Another leg gave way, and another. In attempting to keep its balance with the remainder the Vrahok lurched against the wall of the theatre so violently that a long, vertical crack appeared in the masonry.

The huge creature's collapse was now inevitable. Whistling shrilly, it slowly keeled over on its side. Its gargantuan body took large sections of the theatre's octagonal walls with it, burying the auditorium under a mass of rubble and soot-blackened skulls. The Vrahok's armour-plated back crashed to the ground outside the theatre, together with its drivers, but those inside could clearly hear it crack open and send a gurgling tide of entrails flowing through the streets of Hel. Clouds of black dust billowed into the air and drew a merciful veil over this horrific scene. Then they subsided, covering everything in soot and ashes.

A sound went echoing through the dead world of Rala's bloodstream.

Classical music

Ba-bumm!

It sounded like a kettledrum – like the timekeeper's drum on a boat rowed by galley slaves.

Ba-bumm!

It was the sound that had beaten time in Rala's body, governing the rhythm of life, ever since her birth. The sound that varied with repose and agitation, sleep and wakefulness. The sound that had been silenced by the advent of the Subcutaneous Suicide Squad.

'The heart – it's beating again!' said Non-Existent Teeny Number One.

Ba-bumm!

'It's beating well,' said Non-Existent Teeny Number Two.

Ba-bumm!

'Considering it was dead just now, it's beating excellently!' remarked Non-Existent Teeny Number Three.

Ba-bumm!

The submarine was toiling through the plasma. Although still thick and sluggish, the blood became a little more liquid with every heartbeat that sent it pulsing through Rala's veins.

'The curdling process has stopped,' said Non-Existent Teeny Number One.

'The bloodstream is in motion,' said Non-Existent Teeny Number Two.

'The propellers are turning more freely again,' reported Non-Existent Teeny Number Three.

Ba-bumm!

Smyke saw that the corpuscles, too, were starting to move. The mounds of corpses were vibrating in time to the pounding heart. Corpses? They were corpses no longer, but microscopic sluggards awakened by the incredible din and slowly coming to life.

Ba-bumm!

Ba-bumm!

Ba-bumm!

The heart beat on relentlessly. Smyke couldn't help grinning. How could anyone have slept through that? It was a din fit to wake the dead. Sleepily, the corpuscles went whirling through the blood, stirring it up, warming and liquefying it. The heart delivered more and more powerful thrusts through the veins. The red corpuscles fluttered like swarms of butterflies, the white sailed among them like grains of pollen. In the end they all broke into a whirling dance to the beat of the heart, percolating every vein in a dense stream. Smyke was witnessing a rebirth – a triumph over death in which he himself had played a leading part. He quickly brushed away the tears that were trickling from his eyes. Then, despite himself, he laughed hysterically.

Ba-bumm!

'That's the music of life,' said Non-Existent Teeny Number One.

Ba-bumm!

'It's rather monotonous . . .' said Non-Existent Teeny Number Two.

'But a classic!' said Non-Existent Teeny Number Three.

Ba-bumm!

The submarine was gathering speed.

'The music of life!' cried Smyke. 'It's incredible! I had no idea that a heart could beat so beautifully!'

'We've got the better of death, Smyke!' said Non-Existent Teeny Number One.

'A nice sensation, isn't it, getting the better of something?' said Non-Existent Teeny Number Two.

'How are you feeling, Smyke?' asked Non-Existent Teeny Number Three. 'Is everything ugo?'

'Yes,' Smyke replied with a laugh, 'everything's ugo.'

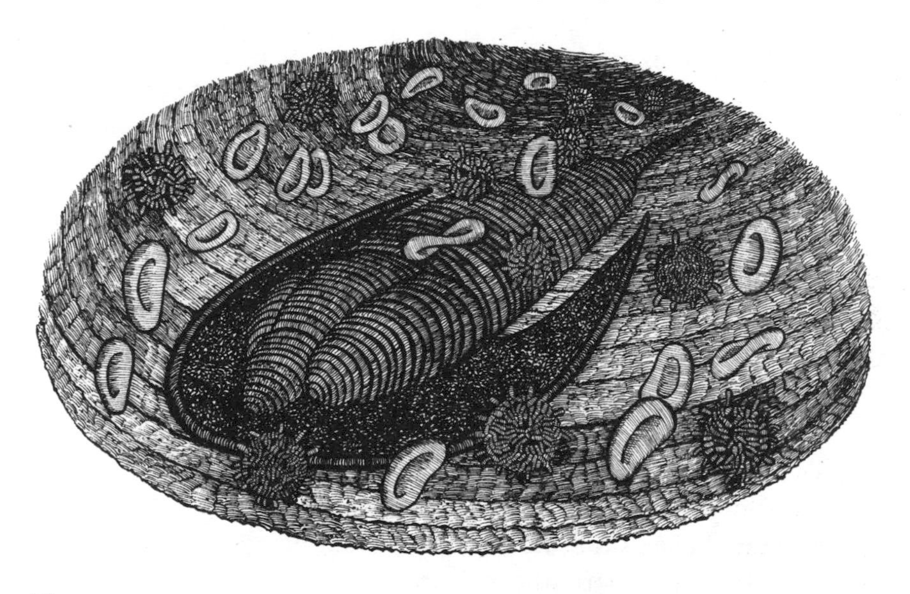

General Ticktock's last weapon

Falling soot transformed the Wolpertings into black statues as they stood watching the moribund Vrahok's final convulsions. Ash-covered spectators and soldiers were crawling and stumbling out of the theatre over the breach in the wall.

General Ticktock was still on his feet but completely motionless. The Wolpertings reassembled round him at a respectful distance.

'Perhaps he's recuperating,' said someone.

'Perhaps he's dead,' said Urs.

'He isn't dead,' said Balla. 'Not him.'

Olek picked up a stone, placed it in his sling and fired it at the general's head. A dull clang reverberated around the ruined theatre.

'He's dead,' Urs repeated. 'Rumo has finished him. He's torn his heart out.'

'Either that or he's waiting for us to come closer,' said Olek.

'We'll see,' said Urs, walking up to General Ticktock. Rumo, who had still to recover completely, limped after him.

'Be careful!' someone called.

They halted at the feet of the biggest Copper Killer and peered inside him suspiciously. All movement had ceased. Every cogwheel and weapon was stationary.

Urs kicked one of the general's legs, then looked at Rumo. 'He's had it,' he said. 'Had it for good!'

Rumo strained his ears. Although the feeling was gradually returning to his limbs, his senses weren't yet functioning normally. The left-hand side of his body felt numb and he could hear a thin, piping whistle. But there was something else as well: a regular rhythmical sound. It was coming from inside the general's motionless body.

'Tick . . . tock . . . tick . . . tock . . .'

'Can you hear that?' Rumo asked.

'Yes, he's still ticking a bit.'

'Tick . . . tock . . . tick . . . tock . . .'

'How can he still be ticking if he's dead?'

'Well,' said Urs, 'it must be some piece of machinery, maybe a spring running down. Relax, he's had it.'

Rumo shut his eyes and sniffed the air. He could still detect the smells he'd smelt in Ticktock's innards. The lubricating oil. The acid.

'Tick . . . tock . . . tick . . . tock . . .'

The strong-smelling powder.

'Tick . . . tock . . . tick . . . tock . . .'

The flammable oil in the flame-throwers' tanks.

'Tick . . . tock . . . tick . . . tock . . .'

The smoky flint.

Rumo grabbed Urs's arm and ran for it.

'Take cover, everyone!' he yelled. 'He's going to explode!'

The Wolpertings turned and ran.

'It's his last weapon!' Rumo shouted.

The Wolpertings leapt over the mounds of rubble that had cascaded into the arena and took cover behind them.

'Tick . . . tock . . . tick . . . tock . . .'

There was a crackling sound from inside General Ticktock, followed by a dull report, and tongues of flame darted from every aperture. Then, with a far louder explosion, his armour-plated exterior shattered into a thousand pieces. Daggers, swords and axes, saw blades, arrows, screws, nuts, bolts and slivers of silver, iron, steel and copper flew in all directions, whistled over the Wolpertings' heads and lodged in the auditorium's walls and seats. Ticktock's head soared high into the air – almost as high as the Vrahok had towered above the theatre. On reaching its apogee it turned over several times like a sword in a *Multiple DeLucca*. It hung there for a moment, then plunged back into the arena and buried itself deep in the sand. A thin rain of biting acid came hissing down. The last few metal components hit the ground with a clatter and a layer of glittering dust settled over everything. Utter silence followed. Even the din of battle in the Copper Killers' gallery died away.

The Wolpertings emerged from their refuge and toured the arena, marvelling at what they saw. Everything sparkled and scintillated in shades of silver and copper. Every piece of rubble, every stone, every blackened skull that had lined the walls was peppered with tiny fragments of General Ticktock. The ruins of the Theatre of Death had become a colossal mausoleum.

The albino rat

Rumo and his friends were just preparing to withdraw when some strangely assorted newcomers entered the arena through one of the gates. It was the older Wolpertings led by Ribble, the rebel and accompanied by Mayor Jowly of Gloomberg, Skullop the Scyther and several huge figures swathed in black cloaks.

'What about the Copper Killers?' someone called.

'They simply stopped fighting,' Ribble replied. 'From one moment to the next. There was that explosion down here and then . . .' He shrugged his shoulders. 'They're still up there in the gallery, silent and motionless, like clockwork toys that have run down.'

Rumo remembered Smyke's account of the battle of Nurn Forest. 'The end of General Ticktock has spelt the end of the Copper Killers as well,' he said. 'They were born with him and they've died with him.'

Once the wounded had been patched up, Mayor Jowly gave the signal to withdraw. Like all those who had survived the fray, the Wolpertings, the Yetis, Yukobak and Ribble made their way out over the mounds of debris that had once been walls.

The Theatre of Death seemed completely devoid of life, but not for long. Only a few moments after everyone had left, a huge eyeless albino rat with a red tail and red claws entered the arena through one of the gates. It spent some time groping for live prey with its antennae. Eventually, when its quest proved fruitless, it tucked into the dead.

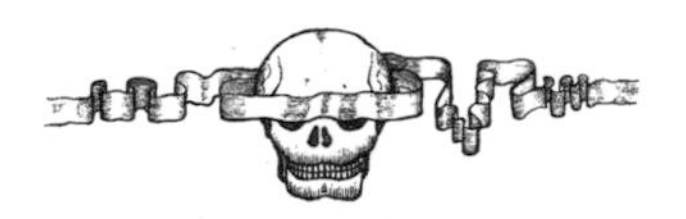

VI.
The Red Prophecy

'What was tath oxplesion?' Gornab complained drowsily. 'How am I ecpexted to seelp? Frist my deb shakes, neth the walls bivrate and now tish series of oxplesions! Wath's gonig on?'

Friftar had roused Gornab from a deep, drugged sleep. The little king had drained a medicine bottle whose contents should have knocked him out for three days.

'They're retreating!' Friftar cried dramatically. 'The Wolpertings are retreating – we've put them to flight!'

'They're . . . terreating?' said Gornab, whose blurred speech was even harder to understand than usual. 'The Tingerwolps are terreating? Si ti revo?'

'Yes, it's over,' said Friftar. He lowered his voice. 'That was the good news. The bad news is—'

'You neam there's dab swen?' Gornab cut in, looking terrified. He pulled the covers over his head.

'Well, there are a few items of news that aren't *quite* so good. The Theatre of Death has been completely destroyed. General Ticktock is no longer with us and the Copper Killers have ceased to exist. Heavy casualties have been sustained, civilian as well as military. A Vrahok collapsed on top of a residential district.' Friftar cleared his throat.

Gornab rubbed his eyes.

'Oh,' he said with a yawn, 'is tath all?'

Friftar collected his thoughts. Now came the really tricky part. He looked grim.

'Well, Your Majesty, I'm afraid it isn't *quite* over. After all, the Wolpertings have destroyed our theatre and killed General Ticktock and countless soldiers and civilians, not to mention a Vrahok. We can't let them go unpunished.'

'No. Why ton?' Gornab disappointedly shook the empty medicine bottle.

'Because it would look bad in the history books. We must pursue the Wolpertings with the Vrahoks and destroy them once and for all.'

Friftar was shaken by a sudden fit of coughing.

'Wath's wrong? Are you lil?' Gornab raised his hand to ward off the germs.

Friftar shook himself. 'I don't know . . . I fear I'm running a slight temperature.'

'A ruteratemp? But you've vener been lil febore!'

'I know . . . It's nothing serious. A minor infection, probably.'

'Nifection?' Gornab gasped. 'Peek your nifection away from me!'

Friftar turned his back on the king with a handkerchief over his mouth and went on coughing. 'I'm afraid you'll have to assume command of the Vrahoks yourself. We must avoid the risk of infection at all costs.'

'You pecext *me* to mmocand the Hokvras?' Gornab hardly dared utter the words.

'Yes, definitely. You must command the Vrahoks. It's essential for Your Majesty to show the population and the army how powerful you are, or we'll invite a revolution. This may be only the start.'

'Must I lleary?' Gornab was hugging his pillow for protection.

'In any case, Your Majesty, Hel will have little in the way of entertainment to offer you for the next few weeks. The theatre and parts of the city are in ruins. There'll be a lot of unpleasant political commitments. Supervising clearing-up operations, delivering speeches, setting your subjects' minds at rest. I could handle all those jobs for you in the meantime. We must also burn the corpses quickly to prevent an epidemic breaking out.'

Friftar coughed even harder.

'An emidepic?' wailed Gornab, hugging his pillow even tighter. 'I don't want any emidepics!'

He strove to concentrate. Suddenly, an excursion with the Vrahoks didn't sound quite so unthinkable. Away from all this chaos! Away from riots, corpses, infections and epidemics!

'It'll be a picnic,' said Friftar, 'a triumphal procession. I'll have you conducted to the Vrahoks right away. It'll take a day or two to mobilise and hypnotise them all, but you won't lack for luxury in the meantime. I shall have a big royal tent erected and send your staff to join you: personal chef, court jesters, storytellers, dancing girls – all that your heart could desire. What's more, I shall give orders that you aren't to be troubled with any problems.'

Gornab gave a start. 'Lemprobs? What srot of lemprobs?'

'There won't be any, Your Majesty, I assure you. I shall instruct the

Vrahok drivers to erect a canopied throne on the back of the biggest Vrahok. Once the Wolpertings have been overtaken you'll assume command, thereby ensuring that your name goes down in the annals as the king who quelled the Wolpertings' insurrection. Having given orders for their destruction, you will sit on your throne and watch the spectacle from a safe altitude. After that you'll return to Hel in triumph.'

Gornab laughed. It all sounded very exciting. More fun than burning dead bodies.

'It occurs to me . . .' Friftar said in a low voice.

'Wath?' Gornab demanded. 'Wath uccors to you?'

'Now I come to think of it, you'll be fulfilling the *Red Prophecy*.'

'I lwil?'

'But of course!' Friftar smote his brow. 'It's your destiny!'

'My nestidy?'

'Yes indeed!' Friftar cried excitedly. 'How could I have been so slow on the uptake? It's the fulfilment of the *Red Prophecy*! You're the Gornab of all Gornabs! This is the beginning of a new era!'

Gornab looked puzzled. 'But the next Norgab will be the Norgab of Norgabs,' he argued.

'Not at all, Your Majesty! You're the first Gornab, not the last! The alchemists must have made a mistake in their arithmetic – a translation error. By annihilating the Wolpertings you'll be conducting the first official war against Overworld and fulfilling the prophecy. Then you'll be Gornab the First, the Gornab of all Gornabs!'

'Yes!' cried Gornab. 'I'll be Norgab the Frist, the Norgab of all Norgabs!' – and he punched his pillow in excitement.

Friftar breathed a sigh of relief. He'd kindled the king's enthusiasm at last.

'The Norgab!' crowed Gornab. 'The Norgab of all Norgabs! Yes, yes! Take me to the Hokvras! I want to klil the Tingerwolps! Klil! Klil!'

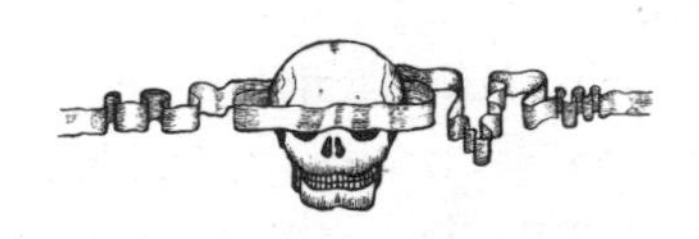

The Yetis and the Wolpertings had threaded their way in silence through the chaos surrounding the Theatre of Death, bound for General Ticktock's tower. Chunks of the dead Vrahok and lengths of its evil-smelling intestines lay everywhere; Hellings and Homunculi were running around in confusion, too busy attending to their wounded to pay attention to the outsiders.

The music of life

Rolv and Rumo were confronted by an unenviable prospect on reaching the general's dark tower: they intended to recover Rala's corpse and take it back with them.

While the others were discussing the best route home, they silently entered the tower.

'She's upstairs,' said Rumo.

They climbed the stairs to the Metal Maiden's chamber. Rumo opened the door and stood aside to let Rolv pass.

Rala was standing in the middle of the room, pale as a ghost, with sunken features and dark smudges under her eyes. Trembling all over and unsteady on her legs, she was being supported by Smyke and Professor Kolibri, who was just taking her pulse.

'Ba-bumm, ba-bumm, ba-bumm,' he said. 'The music of life. It's always nice to hear. A classic.'

Rolv hurled himself at his sister and threw his arms round her; Rumo stood rooted to the spot. He found the sight of Rala as disconcerting as ever.

'Surprised, eh, my boy?' Smyke said with a grin. 'The miracle of life! A miracle, I might add with the modesty so characteristic of me, in which I myself played a part. How did it go at the theatre? Everything ugo?'

Rumo was still standing there as though thunderstruck.

'Ugo?' he said bemusedly.

'Oh,' said Smyke, 'it's just a figure of speech. I was asking if all went well.'

'The theatre is in ruins,' Rumo said dully. 'My friends are free. General Ticktock is dead.'

'Who's General Ticktock?' asked Rala.

For a moment they all fell silent. Rumo and Rala stared at each other like two sleepers awaking from the nightmare. Rumo felt for the casket in his pouch, then left it where it was.

'We must get out of here,' Rumo said. 'We must take advantage of the confusion and leave the city.'

'You're right,' said Smyke. 'There's a lot to tell, but first let's get out of this hideous city.'

Yelma

No one dared to oppose the Wolpertings and Yetis when they withdrew from Hel. The streets were dark and deserted. The few citizens to show their faces hurriedly disappeared into the shadows.

Yukobak and Ribble led the column because they knew the shortest route out of the city. Following them came Skullop the Scyther and his men, and the Wolpertings formed the rearguard. Rumo caught up with Skullop because he wanted to ask him something.

'Why did you follow me to Hel?'

'Why?' growled Skullop. 'Why did I march into the Cogitating Quicksand? Because I'm an idiot.'

'You can say that again!' called a Yeti behind them.

'Why, you ask?' Skullop ground his black teeth. 'I'll tell you why. Certainly not for your sake. I did it for Yelma.'

'Who's Yelma?' asked Rumo.

'Well,' Skullop began, 'I thought about you for a long time after you left me, youngster. I went punting across that black lake, telling myself what a fool you were.'

'Hm,' said Rumo.

'Then I burst out laughing. I laughed all day long, thinking about you and your crazy scheme. I mean, fancy going to Hel to rescue your sweetheart from a whole army of devils, all on your own? Man, how I laughed!'

The Yeti behind Skullop bleated derisively.

Rumo wasn't so sure he really wanted to hear this story.

'And then I wept,' said Skullop. 'Well, not really, because we Dead Yetis can't shed tears. It's more like a kind of dry cough, but it amounts to the same thing. I wasn't weeping on your account, so don't think I was! I'm a hard-hearted old Yeti who couldn't care less what happens to anyone else. If my best friend – not that I have any friends! – got struck by lightning right beside me, I wouldn't give a damn, understand?'

Skullop turned his death's-head and glanced at Rumo.

'I understand,' said Rumo.

'No, I was weeping on my own account. I wept because I saw myself mirrored in you, not as old and dead and ugly as I am now, but as young and peppy as I used to be at your age.'

Rumo nodded.

Skullop's voice had become higher and more youthful. 'I was worth two, three – no, half a dozen Yetis rolled into one. I didn't turn round to pee when the wind was blowing the wrong way – not me! Other Yetis existed, it was true, but they lived in *my* world and according to *my* rules, understand? I was Skullop the Scyther, and they knew I'd earned the nickname fair and square. My heart was on fire!'

'You could put it that way,' said the Yeti behind them.

Skullop lowered his voice again. 'At that time I was in love with a girl Yeti named Yelma. It's a really sad story, so I'll make it short: Yelma died. Some confounded disease carried her off in no time at all. If she'd gone to an evil kingdom full of devils, no matter where, I'd have dug there with my bare hands and brought her back, my Yelma! But there wasn't any evil kingdom. She was dead, that's all. Then I calmed down. I became calmer and older and, in the end, dead myself – or almost. Well, you know what I mean.'

Skullop gave a dry cough and relapsed into silence for a while.

'And suddenly there you were, sitting in my punt and telling me how you were on your way to a kingdom full of devils to rescue your sweetheart, just you and your cheese knife. And then, when you'd gone and I'd wept and laughed and racked my brains for long enough, I said to myself: Why don't I follow that young fool? Why don't I go to his city full of devils and risk my neck again? If I don't, my Yelma will never forgive me and I won't be able to show my face in the place where she is now, when I'm well and truly dead at last.'

Skullop coughed again.

'That, of course, was precisely what my men wanted me to say. "Hey, men," I called, "let's go to that city full of devils and save that crazy Wolperting's stupid neck." – "Oh, sure," they called back, "that's the best idea you've had since you marched us into the Cogitating Quicksand." – "The next person who brings up that goddamned quicksand business," I told them, "I'll ram my punting pole down his throat and bury him head down in the bullrushes!" That silenced them for a while. Then I said, "Yes, you bunch of losers, *I'm* going to that city full of devils whether or not anyone comes with me. If you want to go on being dead, stay here in your stupid punts on this stinking lake of oil till it turns into coal! Go on dreaming of the old days! Me, I'm off to Hel – I owe it to my Yelma!" And you know what? Except for a small rearguard left behind to look after the punts, they all came along, every last one of them.'

'Yes,' said the Yeti behind them. 'We must be as daft as you are!'

'Shall I tell you something else?' said Skullop. 'It paid off. We defeated the Copper Killers! We showed those devils a thing or two! What's more, I saw that Rala of yours. Far too skinny for my taste, but it would have been a real shame if she'd stayed dead. It was a successful campaign.' Skullop gave a conspiratorial grin. 'Did you give her the casket?'

'No,' Rumo muttered.

Skullop looked puzzled. 'Why not?'

'It hasn't come yet.'

'What hasn't come yet?'

'The right moment.'

'When will that be?'

'Soon,' said Rumo.

'How soon is soon?' Skullop insisted.

'*Very* soon,' said Rumo. He slowed down and rejoined his friends.

The prince of peace

Friftar, seated on Gornab's throne, was surveying the ruins of the Theatre of Death. Down in the arena his soldiers were busy driving a huge albino rat into a corner with their spears.

The royal adviser could scarcely believe his luck. At the height of the greatest debacle since the Vrahok Wars, fortune had decided to smile on him.

That accursed tinpot general? Just a distant memory, a myriad of metal splinters lodged in the stones around him, a coppery sheen on the ruins of the Theatre of Death, a vanished nightmare. The Copper Killers? A harmless war memorial. The rebels? Put to flight.

And King Gornab had let himself be talked into this Vrahok adventure. No matter how it turned out, Friftar would have plenty of opportunities to foment rebellion among the king's subjects and turn the situation to his own advantage.

To think what *might* have happened! A revolution! Hel in flames! He himself might have been sentenced to death, lynched, executed. As things stood, he was well on the way to becoming the new monarch of Hel.

What a great and momentous day in the city's history! The greatest ever, perhaps. The end of the Gornabian dynasty, the beginning of the Friftarian!

Friftar looked around the theatre. He would have it restored. No, he would have it demolished and rebuilt three times as big. The Friftar Stadium would be a worthy monument to his eternal renown. Lining the arena, the Copper Killers would make splendid statues reminiscent of a bygone age. He could already hear the masses cheering him, Friftar the Forceful, instead of the degenerate Gornab. Yes, that was what he wanted to be called, 'the Forceful', for it was vigour and self-discipline, tears and sweat that had brought him to where he was today: on the throne. He would be the first ruler of Hel to be governed by reason, not insanity. A prince of peace, a philosopher king.

Friftar rose to acknowledge the imaginary plaudits of the masses – and abruptly sat down again.

Hey, why weren't his legs obeying him? His thighs felt icy cold, his calves he couldn't feel at all. No need to panic. The last few hours had been extremely stressful. He needed to rest a while, that was all. But, strangely enough, the chill tide continued to surge up his body. His chest, his arms, his neck, his face – all felt as if they were turning to ice. His features became rigid and immobile, his temples were transfixed by a pain like the thrust of a stiletto blade. The clicking inside his head had started again, cold sweat was gathering on his brow. Surely he wasn't falling seriously ill? Not now, of all times!

Lord of the Vrahoks

It took a few days to equip all the Vrahoks. Then they were woken and hypnotised afresh for their long march. The commander-in-chief of the Hellian army wanted to go into battle with every available Vrahok, even the biggest, so he had to take the route via *Gornab's Echo,* the most voluminous cave in Netherworld. The huge beasts would have found the other routes to Wolperting impassable or obstructed by insurmountable barriers such as the precipitous cave known as *Vrahok's End*.

Gornab had spent the whole time in his tent, humoured with difficulty by a band of nervous courtiers whenever he wasn't in a deep sleep induced by the drugs Friftar had given him for the journey.

When they finally set off, the king plus throne and tent were winched on to the back of the biggest Vrahok and strapped to the platform already anchored there. Gornab's mood alternated between euphoria and hysterical fear. The effects of the various drugs on his nervous system were such that he sometimes felt like screaming with terror and sometimes shook with violent paroxysms of laughter.

His view of Netherworld from the Vrahok's back was genuinely breathtaking, and the creature progressed so calmly and steadily on its twelve colossal legs that the motion was almost imperceptible up there. After a few hours Gornab felt unassailable – more powerful than ever before. He was Lord of the Vrahoks, commander of the most formidable army Hel had ever unleashed. Looking back over his shoulder he could see them all, scores of Vrahoks of every size, docilely plodding along behind him amid the squadrons of fluttering Dogbats on which his soldiers were mounted. So this was what invincibility looked like – far better than the Theatre of Death! Even the stench of the Vrahoks seemed delicious and the alarming noises they made rang in Gornab's ears like music.

The column soon reached *Gornab's Echo*. The subterranean chambers down here were so gigantic that even the Vrahoks resembled insects crawling across the floor of a cave. Each carried between ten and a hundred soldiers, depending on its size, and the beasts themselves provided most of the light because their blue intestines glowed more brightly the darker it became. For additional illumination, torches and fires in iron tubs had been lit on the backs of the largest specimens.

Our pride and joy

The Vrahoks were covering vast distances at every step. Gornab feasted his eyes on the morbid beauty of his sinister kingdom. Wonderful, the way those primeval beasts' fearsome shadows flitted across the cavern walls, disturbing flocks of clamorous Kackerbats and driving them into the darkness. Gornab had never dreamt that the kingdom he ruled was so vast. Great indeed were the Gornabs! He could hear their voices in his head, spurring him on:

'Onward!'
'Onward!'
'Lord of the Vrahoks!'
'Fulfiller of the Red Prophecy!'
'King of Hel!'
'Blood of our blood!'
'Brain of our brain!'
'Our beloved son!'
'Our pride and joy!'

The torchlight carved miraculous spectacles out of the gloom. Stalagmites bigger than the biggest Vrahok loomed up in the darkness like giants asleep on their feet. Moths with huge, metallically gleaming wings circled Gornab's throne with a sound like thunder sheets in action. Cascades of sparkling, multicoloured rock seemed to plunge down the sides of the cavern like enormous waterfalls – a breathtaking sight. All Netherworld was putting on a show in its ruler's honour!

Gornab laughed and shouted and fidgeted around on his throne. The *Red Prophecy* was coming true! This was a triumphal progress and it wouldn't be his last. Below was above, right was left, war was good, peace was bad. Gornab had never felt so omnipotent.

Skullop leads the way

Yukobak and Ribble had warned the Wolpertings that the Hellings would probably mobilise the Vrahoks and pursue them. Skullop, who knew the routes through Netherworld best, had been tacitly elected to lead the party.

To prevent the Vrahoks from following them he led the Wolpertings along narrow ravines, winding passages and tunnels with little headroom. They traversed a world ruled by deaf, sightless creatures, insects that found their way around with their antennae. The fact that noises didn't startle them led to some unexpected encounters in the darkness. The caves were damp, the rocks jagged and slippery, and the marchers had to be careful to avoid the deep fissures that often yawned in their path. Many stretches had to be covered in total darkness because no phosphorescent algae grew there and a strong smell of oil precluded the use of torches. It was bitterly cold most of the time, and the frozen moisture made every step hazardous.

As if eager to make up for the time she had lost inside the Metal Maiden, Rala had grown steadily wilder and more restless since returning from the realm of death. She was constantly on the move, sometimes up front with the Yetis, sometimes bringing up the rear with the Wolpertings, but always on the spot with her bow whenever danger threatened in the shape of some huge insect or other subterranean creature. One could literally see the life flooding back into her. Her movements were becoming more lithe, her footsteps swifter, her limbs stronger.

Together with Urs, Rolv, Vasko and Balla, Rumo formed the rearguard whose job it was to defend the party against attacks from behind. Yukobak and Ribble had joined them, whereas Smyke and Kolibri travelled with the older Wolpertings.

But all who took part in this march from one pool of darkness to the next were dependent on themselves. Having formerly been captives in the evil heart of Netherworld, they were now crawling through its entrails, and none of them could have said which was worse.

They did not call a halt for three days. The Yetis needed no rest or sleep, but the Wolpertings, especially the older ones among them, were beginning to flag despite their natural stamina and resilience.

A fire was lit in one of the smaller, more easily defended caves. Most members of the party went to sleep right away, but some of them including Rumo, Urs, Rolv, Rala, Yukobak, Ribble, Mayor Jowly, Skullop, Smyke and Professor Kolibri gathered round the blaze to swap accounts of their recent experiences.

Swapping stories

Many tales were told during this interlude, and it is highly improbable that any stories ever recounted around a campfire could have been more extraordinary.

Rala told of being imprisoned inside her own body, of Tallon the Bear God and the hideous face of fear, of her flight through her own bloodstream and the terrible soldiers of death she had encountered there.

Ribble described the Yetis' heroic battle with the Copper Killers. He told of headless warriors fighting on by the light of incandescent splinters of iron, of Skullop the Scyther's titanic fury and the destructive power of his mighty weapon. And he described the origins of the Homunculi and their wretched way of life.

Yukobak confessed to what he'd done in the cellars of the Theatre of Death – his release of the red spider, the Crystalloscorpion and the albino rat – and described the Wolpertings' fight with General Ticktock. He also gave a short history of Hel that included the building of the Urban Flytraps and the training of the Vrahoks. It was only now that most of the Wolpertings learnt the truth about Gornab, Friftar and the Theatre of Death.

Professor Ostafan Kolibri, who contributed a scientifically accurate description of Murkholm and the Jellyfog that prevailed there, described what it felt like to go temporarily mad in four brains at once.

Smyke, needless to say, spoke longer and better than anyone else. He presented a verbose and detailed account of his voyage through Rala's coagulating blood, his encounter with the Non-Existent Teenies (at this, Kolibri's eyes glowed brighter than anyone else's) and his duel with the soldier of death, whose spine he had snapped. His one minor omission related to certain events that had occurred at Lindworm Castle.

Skullop the Scyther told the story of the Dead Yetis and described his first meeting with Rumo – how the latter had almost brought down half Netherworld by shouting and what a fool he'd been to go to Hel armed with a cheese knife.

Last of all, Urs rose and described how Ushan DeLucca had met his end while defying General Ticktock unarmed. Ticktock was already holding Ushan's heart in his hand by the time Urs grasped that the fencing master's sole motive had been to save his life. Consequently, he felt it his duty to continue Ushan's life work and devote himself to the art of swordsmanship from now on. Many had tears in their eyes when Urs resumed his seat.

Only Rumo said nothing. He meant to speak more than once, but before he could collect his thoughts and open his mouth someone else got in first. He didn't regret this because he knew that, as usual, he would have got everything back to front.

Finally, when exhaustion had reduced them all to silence and they were trying to grab a little restorative sleep for the march to come, Krindle and Dandelion made their presence felt.

'Why didn't you say anything?' Dandelion demanded. *'Our own experiences would surely have made the best story of all. The fight in Nurn Forest! Yggdra Syl! The casket! The Icemagogs! The Vrahoks! General Ticktock's innards! Ideal subjects for inclusion in lessons on the heroic sagas!'*

'I'm no good at telling stories,' Rumo protested.

'Instead of that, you let Skullop the Scyther make fun of you,' said Dandelion. *'Great! If that's your way of looking good in front of Rala, I give up!'*

'You should have killed Skullop when you still had the chance,' said Krindle.

'Does that mean you've lost your desire to kill Skullop?' Dandelion asked him. *'Why the change of heart, you merciless Demonic Warrior?'*

'We still need him,' Krindle growled. **'First he must guide us through Netherworld. Then we'll kill him.'**

Vrahok's Repose

Gornab had retired to his tent and was trying to get some sleep, but it was strange: the more wine and sleeping draughts he poured down his throat, the wider awake he felt.

'I'm adraif,' he whispered to himself under the bedclothes. 'Why shloud I be adraif?'

He dashed out of the tent into the torchlight and over to the rail enclosing his platform on the Vrahok's back. His dark kingdom stretched away far below, the blue stalagmites protruding from oily water. Why did he suddenly find this view of the depths so alarming? He went to the rear of the platform. There they were, his Vrahoks, his soldiers, his army. Scores of the gigantic beasts were plodding through the gloom of *Vrahok's Repose*, yet another cavern on the route to Overworld. Dogbats were howling and lashing the air with their leathery wings. Why did he now find this view so ominous? Why was he feeling like a fugitive bereft of protection? The vast cavern seemed to sway in the fitful blue glow shed by the Vrahoks and each of the countless stalagmites jutting from its floor resembled a finger raised in warning. Did those pursuing, long-legged shadows belong to the Vrahoks, or to subterranean demons? Ice-cold drops of water spattered Gornab's head.

Why wasn't Friftar there to reassure him? Why was he so alone? The king of Netherworld leant over the rail and vented his fear on the darkness.

'Tarfrift!' he shouted. 'Tarfrift! Why do I leef so adraif?'

The membrane

For the first time, this trek through the bowels of the earth made it clear to the Wolpertings what a merciless world they had blithely lived above until now, how thin was the crust that separated them from it, and how great the danger that its savage, evil inhabitants might one day burst forth to wreak death and destruction in Overworld.

They saw yards-long worms armed with pincers, plate-sized phosphorescent ants of every hue, peat-dwelling spiders whose groans would have melted the hardest heart. The layer separating Overworld from Netherworld seemed no more than a membrane penetrable by any creature evil enough to pierce it. This was a world where dead things came to life again, where corpses turned into maggots and other vermin, where decaying matter produced new growth and dangerous Nurns were born of buried blood. It was a cruel, implacable world full of greedy predators. The higher they climbed the looser the soil and the more crackling, burrowing, lip-smacking sounds they heard on every side. The Wolpertings' journey through Netherworld welded them together more closely than all their previous experiences. Each was responsible for his neighbour and every step could prove disastrous or fatal for all. Danger lurked everywhere. Never had they taken greater care of each other.

Having completed the strenuous ascent from Hel by way of Stonewater Grotto and a maze of tunnels and small caves, they reached Deadwood, with its huge, treelike stalagmites and eternal pall of mist. Its apelike denizens kept out of sight, possibly for fear of attacking such a large party. Their unnerving screams were all that could be heard and big stones occasionally fell from the mist overhead.

Although Rumo warned his companions not to eat the black mushrooms, the Yetis brushed his advice aside and tucked into them.

They were in an exuberant mood for hours afterwards, dancing around among the stone trees, hurling stones at the invisible apes and giggling foolishly to themselves. At some stage the first Kronks appeared – the furry little hook-beaked creatures that were Netherworld's original inhabitants – and Rumo knew Nurn Forest could not be far off. He joined Skullop the Scyther at the head of the column.

'We'll soon have to go through the Nurn Forest Labyrinth,' he said.

'Why?'

'It's the way I came.'

Skullop focused his empty eye sockets on Rumo. 'You went right through Nurn Forest?'

'Yes,' said Rumo, 'didn't you?'

'Of course not.' Skullop laughed. 'We've got more sense.'

'But the only route from the Fridgicaves to Hel goes that way.'

'What gives you that idea? Hey, just a minute – you mean to say you went by way of the Fridgicaves? They're swarming with Icemagogs!'

'I know,' said Rumo.

Skullop chuckled drily. 'Then you picked the most dangerous route through Netherworld, my boy – congratulations! Hey, you lot,' he called to the other Yetis, 'this youngster here went breezing through the Fridgicaves – *and* through the Nurn Forest Labyrinth.'

'So why is he still in the land of the living?' one of them called back.

Skullop grinned. 'Every time you open your mouth, my friend, I doubt your sanity a little bit more. Why didn't you go via the Vrahok Caves while you were at it?'

Rumo made no comment.

'There's a dead straight route that avoids the Fridgicaves and Nurn Forest. That's the one *we* took.'

'So why didn't you tell me when I asked you?' said Rumo. 'You told me there were various routes through Netherworld, that's all.'

'Which wasn't a lie,' Skullop retorted.

No one, whether soldier, physician or alchemist, had dared to approach Friftar. What was happening to the royal adviser seated on the throne of Gornab the Ninety-Ninth was indescribable, unspeakable and – without doubt – highly infectious. They all felt threatened by the mere sight of him, even at a respectful distance, and hurriedly took to their heels. This was why Friftar soon found himself alone in the Theatre of Death, the sole performer in a final production staged before an audience of the dead.

Friftar in extremis

But what was happening to the exterior of his body was only a pale reflection of what was going on inside him. The Subcutaneous Suicide Squad's activities in Friftar's bloodstream surpassed anything that had ever taken place in the arena, and no impresario, not even Friftar himself, could have devised scenes of such ingenious cruelty. It was only now that the Subcutaneous Suicide Squad's capacity for mutation attained its true objective, which was to inflict as many different forms of pain as possible. Needles and pincers, poisons and acids were brought into play. The agonies Friftar had to endure were worse than the sum of all the pain that had ever been inflicted in the Theatre of Death. And they took their time, for it was only in Friftar's body that Tykhon Zyphos's disease disclosed the full extent of its horror.

Gornab awoke from a restless sleep with his ears ringing. What an awful nightmare! He'd been riding a Vrahok pursued by gigantic demons who bombarded him with pointed stalactites, somewhere a long way from Hel. His ancestors had cavorted around and jeered at him for being a coward. It was frightful!

No dream

Where was Friftar with his breakfast?

The king got out of bed, tottered over to the curtain stark naked and drew it aside. He jumped back with a smothered cry of terror. Stretching away in front of him was a vast cavern, and fluttering through the air above were squadrons of Dogbats ridden by soldiers holding torches. The torchlight illuminated the back of the Vrahok beneath him, which was wheezing heavily. The air reeked of oil and sea water, and huge, menacing stalactites hung from the roof of the cavern.

Gornab tottered back inside, drew the curtain and recovered his wits at last. With a shudder, he realised that it hadn't been a dream after all. He was Lord of the Vrahoks, and Friftar and Hel were far, far away. It was all he could do not to drink a pint of sleeping draught and crawl back under the bedclothes.

'Your Majesty?' said a voice from outside. 'Are you awake?'

'Yes,' Gornab replied peevishly, 'I am.'

'You'll be pleased to hear that the bulk of our journey is now behind us,' said the voice, which belonged to one of his generals. 'According to our calculations it's not beyond the bounds of possibility that our decisive encounter with the Wolpertings will occur before the day is out.'

'Yes, yes,' Gornab said impatiently. 'Wath of it?'

'I mention it only because we shall require your final orders by then at the latest.'

'Yes, yes,' said Gornab. 'You'll teg them in doog mite.'

Orders? he thought. No problem there. He need only decree that the Vrahoks devour those stupid Wolpertings. What was so difficult about that?

He took a swig of some fortifying potion and donned his royal robe. Then he waddled out of the tent.

Oil Lake once more

The route Skullop was taking them led through small caves and low tunnels that harboured no creatures of the wild or other unpleasantnesses apart from Kronks and Kackerbats. Rumo silently cursed Skullop for omitting to tell him about this short cut. On the other hand he wouldn't have bumped into Yukobak and Ribble, and who knew how his venture would have turned out then? Fate followed a route of its own and it wasn't always the shortest.

The Wolpertings could scent Oil Lake hours before they reached it, and Rumo was surprised that a smell which had caused him such uneasiness the first time should now seem almost reassuring. This was the last leg of the journey they would have to cover with outside help. They were almost home.

A small rearguard of Yetis was waiting for their companions on the shores of Oil Lake. Little was said. Skullop growled a few brief orders and his men proceeded to load their punts with passengers. At another word of command from Skullop the fleet pushed off and disappeared into the luminous mist.

For the first time the fugitives seemed to lose a little of the uneasiness that had spurred them on throughout their journey. The Yetis proudly told the rearguard about their defeat of the Copper Killers and many of the Wolpertings took advantage of the crossing to get some sleep. Rala sat silent in the bow of the punt in which Rumo was travelling. Whatever the reason – her reassuring presence, or the gentle, gliding motion of the punt, or the rhythmical gurgle of the oil, or, more probably, sheer exhaustion – Rumo fell asleep sitting up.

A lethal misunderstanding

'We're there, Your Majesty,' someone called into the royal tent's dark interior. 'We've completed our ascent and are now advancing on Oil Lake. The scouts we sent out, mounted on Dogbats, report that the Wolpertings are crossing the lake at this moment. We respectfully await your orders.'

Gornab gave a surly grunt. Duties, nothing but duties! He wanted to get this business over as quickly as possible and return to Hel, so he rose from his bed with a groan and went outside.

They were in a cave that was smaller and lighter than *Gornab's Echo* and warmer than the glacial cavern known as *Vrahok's Repose*. All the rocks were bathed in a phosphorescent glow and luminous blue rain was falling from the stalactites overhead. Looking down over the rail of his observation platform, the king saw dense swaths of mist snaking between his Vrahok's legs. He felt dizzy and shrank away from the rail.

Half a dozen generals, all members of the Hellian aristocracy, were standing at attention on the platform awaiting their monarch's orders. After a considerable time, when none were issued and Gornab merely gazed at the Vrahoks behind them lost in thought, one of them spoke up:

'It's high time we devoted some thought to our future course of action, Your Majesty. Friftar gave orders that we weren't to trouble you with unnecessary problems, but he also expressly instructed me to consult you at this stage in the campaign. The order to attack can only come from you.'

'Yes,' said Gornab. 'Doog.'

The generals looked at him expectantly.

'Why are you pawging at me like tath?' Gornab snapped.

'Your orders, Majesty,' one of them ventured to say. 'Are we to wait until the Wolpertings have returned to their city, or do we attack them without delay? If we want to fulfil the *Red Prophecy* we should really wait until they're home. The *Red Prophecy* explicitly refers to a war in Overworld.'

Gornab thought hard. Things were getting complicated after all! Why hadn't that idiot Friftar said anything about this? Fulfil the *Red Prophecy* or attack right away? Couldn't he attack at once and then order the historians to record that he'd fulfilled the prophecy anyway? Yes, that was it. He was the king, after all. Get it over now, right away, and hightail it home to Hel. He drew a deep breath.

'I sedire the Hokvras to ackatt and tresdoy the Tingerwolps witouth leday!' he commanded.

The generals stared at him.

'Your pardon, Majesty?' said one of them.

Gornab cleared his throat. 'I sedire the Hokvras to ackatt and tresdoy the Tingerwolps witouth leday!' he repeated, somewhat louder.

The generals exchanged nervous glances. Such a situation had never arisen before. No one had ever had to tell the king to his face that he was unintelligible.

'Are you fead?' Gornab demanded, brusquely now. 'I vage odrers that the damngoded Hokvras shloud ackatt and tresdoy the Tingerwolps witouth leday! Is tath so fficultid to dantersund?'

'I'm sorry, Your Majesty,' one of the generals said bravely, 'but we don't understand your orders.'

The others glared at him as though he'd just sentenced them to death.

Gornab's voice took on a low, menacing note. 'You ton'd dantersund me?' he said. 'Do I skeap intisdinctly? Do I fusser from a cheaps fedect, or thingsome?'

A foul stench drifted towards them from Oil Lake and the huge Vrahok shied in alarm. Everyone on the platform lurched to and fro.

Gornab suddenly quietened. His sardonic grin became even broader, but his face went blank. Voices were speaking in his head – the voices of his dead ancestors.

'Can you hear us, Gornab?' they asked.

'It's us.'

'The Gornabs inside you.'

Gornab listened spellbound. The voices at last! *They* would tell him what to do.

'We're proud of you, Gornab!'

'Proud because you're blood of our blood!'

'Brain of our brain!'

'Mighty Lord of the Vrahoks!'

'Are you going to take that insult lying down?'

'An insult levelled at your royal person?'

'They act as if they fail to understand your orders!'

'They act as if you're an idiot who can't make himself understood.'

'They want to override you and take command themselves.'

'You can't permit that, Gornab!'

'In the name of all the Gornabs, you must punish them!'

'Punish them, Gornab!'

'Punish them!'

It was all over by the time the king awoke from his trance.

One of the generals lay stretched out on his back, twitching, with blood spurting from a gash in his throat. The others had recoiled in horror.

Gornab struggled to his feet. He felt infinitely weary, as he always did after committing such atrocities.

'What's the matter?' shouted one of the Vrahok drivers from the rear platform. 'The Vrahok is getting out of control!'

The gigantic creature was trembling. Its armour-plated back vibrated beneath their feet and it came to a halt, whistling in a restive, feverish manner.

Gornab wiped the blood from his mouth.

'Wath's gworn with it?' he asked. 'Wath's up with the Hokvra?'

The scent of blood

The armour-plated beast vibrated more violently still and the digestive juices in its intestines began to seethe.

'It can smell the blood!' cried one of the generals. 'The hypnosis is wearing off!'

'Your Majesty!' another general shouted at the king. 'How could you have shed blood aboard a Vrahok? All that interests it now is blood! Don't you know *anything* about the beasts?'

No, Gornab didn't, nor did he need to. He was the king. How dared this underling address him in such a fashion?

He flew at the general's throat. Ripping out the Adam's apple with his teeth, he spat it over the rail.

'There,' he said. 'Hapsper tath'll cheat you to edrass me so dispectresfully!'

Gornab released his victim. The general sagged against the rail, breathing stertorously and trying to plug the gaping wound with his fingers. Meanwhile, his blood went spurting over the Vrahok.

'I'm kating over mmocand!' Gornab bellowed. 'Where are the Tingerwolps? I entind to texerminate them!'

A sound like a violent wind arose and the Vrahok's transparent trunk came slithering over the edge of its armour-plated back. Purposefully, it made for the platform, then for the first of the bleeding generals. The tube squelched open and sucked him in. The Vrahok emitted loud whistles of excitement as the man shot up it like a lifeless puppet.

The trunk reared up briefly, quivering with greed, then closed over the second bleeding general and ingested him too. That done, it scoured the platform in search of further nourishment.

The surviving generals yelled at the Vrahok drivers, but they had lost control a long time ago. Some of them were already preparing to winch themselves to the ground in the baskets that served as lifeboats.

Gornab dashed over to his throne, ensconced himself in it and strapped himself in with his royal safety belt.

'I am the gink!' he cried. 'Hokvra, I mmocand you to eboy me!'

The trunk came writhing across the platform, sucking up soldier after soldier irrespective of rank. Some of the men preferred to jump for it rather than end up in the Vrahok's digestive organs, and the air rang with senseless orders and despairing cries.

Similar chaos reigned aboard the Vrahoks behind them. All were awaking from their alchemical hypnosis and extending their trunks. The greedy whistling grew louder, the crews on the platforms panicked and desperately showered the Vrahoks with alchemical extracts or tried to abseil down them. Anyone who failed to escape was engulfed by their bellowing trunks, which also plucked Dogbats out of the air complete with their riders.

Gornab clung to his throne. Above him a wind had sprung up that tore fiercely at his limbs and greedily sucked in anything lying around loose: a briefcase full of military maps, sundry weapons, several canteens, a shield bearing the arms of Hel. Gornab looked up. The tip of the biggest Vrahok's trunk was hovering immediately overhead.

The Gornab of Gornabs

But the king wasn't afraid. His gaze was ecstatic, his grin ran from ear to ear. He was listening to the voices of his ancestors.

'Fear not, Gornab!' they cried.

'You are the Gornab of Gornabs!'

'The ruler of Netherworld!'

'Nothing can harm you!'

'Nothing can harm us!'

'We are immortal!'

No, he wasn't in any real danger. *They* weren't in any real danger, not them. The kings of Hel were immortal. His belt would hold no matter how much suction the raging wind exerted. Gornab sat glued to his throne.

'I am Norgab Angal Akidarzo Gneb Lele Anoota the Tniney-Thinn!' he yelled at the greedy mouth of the tube above him. 'I am the gink! I am the Norgab of Norgabs! I mmocand you to . . .'

The first of the bolts that secured the throne to the platform gave way and went whistling past his ears.

'I mmocand you to eboy me!'

There was a crack, and Gornab saw whole sections of the platform beneath him break away and fly upwards. The throne seemed to be rocked by an earthquake.

'I mmocand you . . .'

Another crack and this time Gornab himself rose into the air. The last legitimate ruler of Hel was anointed with corrosive acids as he and his throne were sucked into the digestive organs of the biggest of all living Vrahoks.

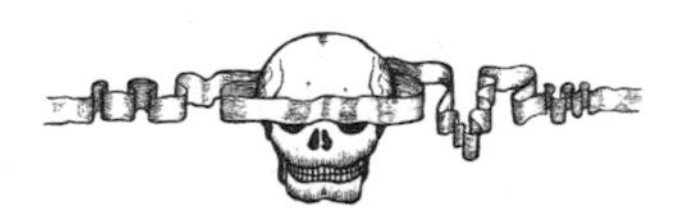

The scent of death

Rumo awoke. No noise had roused him, no cry or nudge in the ribs, but a smell. Drowsily he raised his head and sniffed the air. It was the alarming, unnerving smell of Roaming Rock, the stench of thousands of rotting marine parasites, the smell of death that seemed to have pursued him throughout his life.

'The Demonocles are coming,' he said sleepily.

'Demonocles?' Urs, who was sitting in the punt just ahead of him, turned round. 'No, it's the Vrahoks.'

Rumo's head gradually cleared. 'A lot of them, too, judging by the smell.'

'Why can't we hear anything?' asked Urs.

'I've seen Vrahoks wade across the lake before now,' said the Yeti who was poling them along. 'They make their way through the oil as slowly and silently as ghosts. It's weird. They instinctively know how dangerous it is to set off rockfalls in this cave.'

'How many are there?' Urs asked.

'Several dozen of them, at a guess,' said Rumo. 'All the Hellings possess, perhaps.'

'It's not much further to the other side,' said the Yeti. 'We'll make it.'

'Vrahoks can go anywhere,' said Rumo. 'Even up the steps to Wolperting, if they have to. We must fight them off.'

The first punts had already landed. Their passengers helped the later arrivals ashore. As soon as all the Wolpertings and Yetis were on dry land they held a council of war.

'You can't be serious,' said Skullop. 'You can't fight the Vrahoks, they're too many for you.'

'We've no choice,' Rumo retorted. 'We must stop them from reaching the surface. We're all that stands between them and Overworld. I know how to neutralise the creatures. We must let them suck us up and then—'

Skullop laid a bony hand on Rumo's shoulder and threw back his cowl to reveal his glistening, greasy black skull. He ground his teeth.

'Look, youngster, you really don't have to keep proving to me how crazy you are. You haven't a hope against the Vrahoks.'

'I already dealt with one of them,' Rumo said.

'Oh, sure, of course you did!' Skullop gave an incredulous, despairing laugh.

So fierce was the stench drifting across the lake that it nearly took their breath away. Still partly obscured by the luminous mist, the Vrahoks were advancing almost without a sound.

The Vrahoks are coming

Everyone thronged the shore to watch them approach. They waded slowly through the oil with infinite care, guided by their restless antennae. All that could be heard was the grinding and creaking of the joints in their enormous legs as their bodies loomed out of the mist and swayed ever nearer. There must indeed have been hundreds of them – all the Vrahoks in Netherworld.

Skullop and his men, who had detached themselves from the Wolpertings, were conferring in grunts and murmurs at the edge of the lake. Their discussion was punctuated by angry growls and savage laughter. Then Skullop came back on his own.

'All right, my lad,' he said, stationing himself in front of Rumo with his scythe. 'I understand. This is between you and me.'

Rumo stared at him uncomprehendingly.

'I'm going to show you, Rumo. I'm going to show you which of us is the crazier.'

'What are you getting at?' said Rumo.

Skullop gave a ferocious grunt and turned to the rest of the Wolpertings.

'Listen here! You're going to do exactly as I say! Either stay or run away, it's all the same to me, but don't dare butt in! Watch the fun or make yourselves scarce, whichever. In your place, though, I'd watch. It'll be worth seeing, I guarantee you!'

Skullop laid his hand on Rumo's shoulder again. 'It was an honour knowing you, Rumo. You're a genuine nutcase.'

Rumo was still puzzled. 'What are you planning to do?' he asked.

'Never you mind,' Skullop retorted. 'This is Yeti business. But you must promise me something.'

'What's that?'

'Promise me you'll give her that goddamned casket.'

Rumo nodded and hung his head.

Skullop turned and strode over to his men, who had already begun to board their punts.

The Wolpertings conferred in whispers. What were the Yetis up to?

The Yetis pushed off. Skullop, leaning on his scythe in the biggest punt, addressed the Wolpertings once more. He kept his voice down, just as he had when Rumo met him for the first time.

'I'll tell you something else,' he whispered. 'If I've ever met a genuine hero, it's that young maniac whose name sounds like a card game. However, I'm pretty sure my men and I can go one better, so keep your eyes peeled. Watch Skullop and his army of Dead Yetis at work, and watch closely, because we're about to break a few records! History is being made here! Tell your grandchildren about it, but tell it properly or the ghost of Skullop the Scyther will return in the night and cut your throats with his scythe!'

A swath of luminous blue mist drifted over the punts and enveloped them. All that could now be heard were the clicks and creaks of the advancing Vrahoks' knee joints.

'That was a pretty self-assured announcement,' Yukobak said after a while.

'Do they really intend to fight the Vrahoks?' asked Ribble.

'It would be suicide,' said Yukobak. 'They don't stand a chance, certainly not in those cockleshells of theirs. Maybe they know of a place to hide.'

Everyone stood rooted to the spot, watching spellbound as the mist dispersed and the punts came into view again. The Dead Yetis had risen to their feet and were drifting towards the oncoming Vrahoks. The primeval beasts' huge legs formed an intricate silhouette tinged with blue by the glow from their throbbing intestines.

By now the Vrahoks and the punts could not have been more than a couple of hundred yards apart. Even if Skullop and his men had wanted to do so, it was too late for them to change their minds and turn round.

The Blood Song

'Shall we sing, men?' Skullop cried suddenly, with such volume and clarity that his words easily carried to the Wolpertings' ears.

'Yes, let's sing,' someone called back. 'A splendid idea of yours, Skullop. As usual.'

The Yetis laughed.

The Wolpertings continued to line the shore, completely at a loss.

'What are they doing?' asked Rala.

Rumo pointed to the stalactites on the roof of the cavern.

'They're laying down their lives for us,' he said.

The stench of the oncoming Vrahoks was becoming more and more intolerable. Rumo gripped the hilt of his sword in impotent fury.

'He's sacrificing himself,' said Krindle. **'Skullop the Scyther is sacrificing himself.'**

'They all are,' said Dandelion.

'Who knows a good song?' cried Skullop.

'The *Blood Song*!' a Yeti replied. 'It's the only one we know.'

'Good,' said Skullop. 'Let's have the *Blood Song*, then!'

He cleared his throat.

'Blood must spurt and blood must flow!' he sang.

'Let blood gush from every foe!
Blood as far as eye can see.
Blood to all eternity!'

'Blood must spurt and blood must flow!' chorused the other Yetis.

'Let blood gush from every foe!
Blood as far as eye can see.
Blood to all eternity!'

The echoes of their grisly song filled the cavern and sent bats fluttering into the air.

'Swing the sword with all your might!' sang Skullop.
Cleave your foe from head to heel!'
'Let your blade his innards bite!' the Yetis joined in.
Lay them open with cold steel!'
'Blood must spurt and blood must flow!' they all sang together.
Let blood gush from every foe!'

With a sharp report a gigantic stalactite broke off the roof of the cavern. It plummeted downwards like a spear, pierced the armour-plated back of one of the biggest Vrahoks, passed right through it and emerged from its underbelly, ripping the blue stomach to shreds on the way. Finally it landed in the lake with a muffled splash, followed by cascades of intestines and pale-blue slime. The Vrahok continued to stand there for a moment, trumpeting pathetically. Then all twelve legs buckled and it collapsed like a dilapidated tower.

The creature's trumpetings and the sound of its fall went echoing round the cavern. More sharp reports rang out, this time from many parts of the roof at once, and a barrage of enormous stalactites came raining down on the Vrahoks, the Yetis and the lake. Numerous punts were hit and sank into the oil and dozens of Vrahoks met the same fate. Panic broke out among them. They stampeded in all directions, howling, whistling and bellowing, colliding and falling on top of each other. Netherworld had never heard such a pandemonium.

'The roof's caving in!' someone shouted. The Wolpertings came to life with a jerk, but it was a moment before they could tear their eyes away from the horrific spectacle. Then they turned and started to run, faster and faster. Rumo seized Rala's paw and they sprinted off together.

Far behind them colossal stalactites continued to fall into the lake, churning the oil into waves that knocked many Vrahoks off their feet and swamped the Yetis' punts.

The Wolpertings ran for their lives. Stalactites started to fall and explode among their fleeing figures, even on dry land, and showers of small stones came rattling down on them.

The Vrahoks' trumpetings died away. The few that were still on their feet lashed the air with their tentacles. A rumble louder than any previous sound filled the cavern and a huge black mass of sand, soil and rock engulfed the surviving monsters, burying them beneath it. The echoes reverberated around the cavern a while longer; then silence fell.

The Wolpertings were still running, but now the first of them slowed down. Rumo and Rala, too, came to a halt and looked back.

A dense cloud of stone dust was billowing into the air, shutting out the nightmarish scene like a curtain. They all looked up. The roof of the cavern was still intact; it had merely unleashed an avalanche of rock sufficient to destroy the biggest creatures in Netherworld - and, with them, Skullop the Scyther and his gallant Dead Yetis.

Mayor Jowly of Gloomberg was standing not far from Rala and Rumo. He patted the dust from his fur, looked around and said, 'Right, now let's all go home.'

The alchemist's triumph

The fight was over, but the real battle, the truly great one, had still to be fought. Tykhon Zyphos's Subcutaneous Suicide Squad arose from the dust of Friftar, former royal councillor and director of the Theatre of Death, who had died in such agony.

Having finally laid Friftar low, stopped his heart beating and devoured his limbs and organs cell by cell, the Subcutaneous Suicide Squad abandoned the meagre remains of its vanquished foe, a handful of bone dust. In search of new life to destroy, it soared across the theatre's deserted auditorium, through the prisoners' empty cell block and over the Copper Killers' gallery, but all it found were bodies in which its work had already been accomplished by others. The invisible microscopic army reached the outer wall of the theatre and surmounted it.

At last! Below the Subcutaneous Suicide Squad, stretching away in all directions, lay a city filled with life, so it swooped down on Hel in fulfilment of Tykhon Zyphos's dying curse: *'May Hel and all who dwell there be destroyed from within just like me!'*

Black Dome Square

Wolpertings were setting foot in Black Dome Square for the first time since Rumo had descended into Netherworld. They emerged from the gloomy shaft one by one. Twilight was falling, but the dark-blue sky was almost cloudless. The Wolpertings drank in the fresh air and bathed in the warming rays of the setting sun. Many shook themselves as if trying to slough off the smell and recollection of Netherworld.

More and more of them gathered round the black hole until the entire square and the surrounding streets were thronged with Wolpertings. No one made a move to leave. All were waiting for some pronouncement that would relieve the tension by drawing a permanent line between their recent experiences and their future existence.

All eyes turned to the mayor, who had sought, found and polished the appropriate words while climbing the long staircase. Jowly of Gloomberg cleared his throat, the murmurs died away, and he uttered the historic sentence:

'It'll take a damned big lid to plug a hole as ugly as this.'

No one spoke, no one moved, no one said 'Hear, hear!' or clapped. They weren't exactly the words the Wolpertings had been expecting – words that would do justice to their tribulations and merit inclusion in the city's annals. They knew they were the right words, however, so they went their separate ways, the skilled craftsmen among them already devoting thought to what material such a 'lid' should be made of.

'Did I say something wrong?' the mayor asked.

'No,' replied someone, 'you hit the nail on the head.' It was Volzotan Smyke, who was standing beside him with Professor Ostafan Kolibri.

The mayor wondered briefly whether 'hitting the nail on the head' was a snide reference to the notch in his cranium. Then he brushed the thought aside. He was on duty. The presence of outsiders in the city created an entirely new and, politically speaking, extremely awkward situation. Hitherto, no outsiders had been admitted on principle, but he could hardly throw them out. They had been largely instrumental in the rescue. He himself owed them his release from imprisonment. They had saved Rala's life. What was wanted now was a hospitable gesture of some kind. Heavens alive, this was a situation that required him to devise a diplomatically sensitive form of words for the second time in a few minutes!

'We should be glad to share our city with any well-disposed wayfarers,' Jowly of Gloomberg said at length. Phew! Fortunately, the traditional greeting laid down by the Atlantean Hiker's Code had popped into his head just in time. He had merely substituted 'city' for 'campfire' and pluralised 'wayfarer'.

'Oh,' Smyke replied. *'We thank you for your offer of hospitality –'*

'– and promise,' Professor Kolibri chimed in gravely, *'not to take undue advantage of it.'*

That takes care of them, thought the mayor, feeling relieved, but what am I to do with the other outsiders – the ones that hail from Netherworld? He looked over at them anxiously.

Yukobak and Ribble were standing together in the last rays of the setting sun.

'The air is breathable,' said Yukobak, panting hard. 'If it's poisonous, the poison must be slow-acting.'

'The sun doesn't seem to be scorching us,' said Ribble, shielding himself with his pincers. 'It isn't melting us or anything.'

'Wait until midday tomorrow.' Urs was standing beside them, grinning. 'That's when it attains its full intensity.'

Yukobak looked surprised. 'You mean the sunshine varies in strength?'

'The sun'll go down at any moment,' Urs told him. 'Then it won't shine at all – then it'll get cold and dark. Where do you intend to spend the night?'

Yukobak shrugged.

'We haven't thought about it yet,' Ribble replied.

'Come to my place, then. I've an idea there'll be a room going begging at our house in Hoth Street from now on.' Urs jerked his head in the direction of Rumo and Rala, who were still standing silently in the middle of the square.

'Would you care to see me home?' Rala asked at length. 'It'll be dark soon and the streets in this city are said to be exceptionally dangerous.'

Wolperting comes back to life

'All right,' said Rumo.

They walked through the streets in silence. The houses were coming back to life. Shutters were flung open, candles lit, blankets shaken. Laughter and the clatter of crockery could be heard on all sides. Wolperting was being aired.

At last they reached Rala's door. Rala looked at Rumo. She raised her left forearm and parted the silky fur to reveal a painless scar. It read:

Rumo

Then she went into the house, leaving the door ajar behind her.

Rumo shut his eyes.

Yes, there it was, the Silver Thread, and it led through the doorway into Rala's house.

'Go on!' said Dandelion.

Rumo followed Rala inside, his legs shaky, his paw tightly gripping the hilt of his sword as if in search of support.

'Show her the casket,' Dandelion whispered. *'Show her the casket of Nurn Forest oak.'*

'Yes,' said Krindle, **'it'll knock her sideways.'**

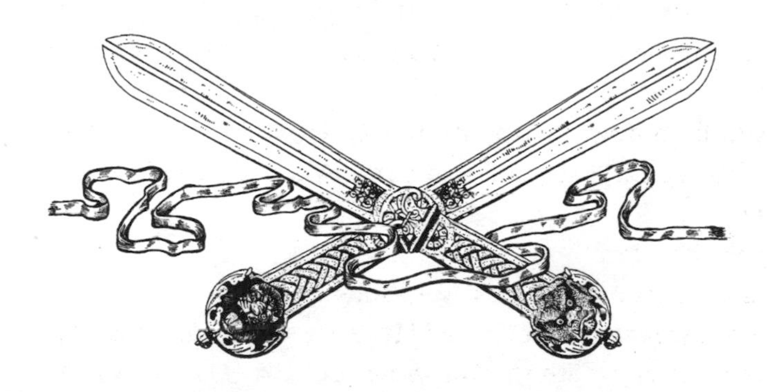

At this point the drawer marked R slides shut.

It closes for discretion's sake,
because Rala must now introduce Rumo
to the miracle of love.

For some miracles
can only occur in the dark.

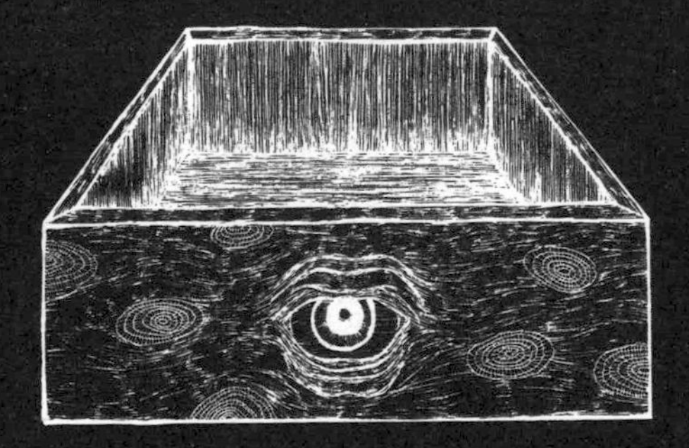